OF SERPENTS AND RUINS
FORGOTTEN KINGDOM

JESSICA M BUTLER

FORGOTTEN KINGDOMS

OF
SERPENTS
&
RUINS

USA TODAY BESTSELLING AUTHOR
JESSICA M. BUTLER

Copyright © 2024 by Jessica M. Butler.

All rights reserved.

No part of this book may be reproduced in any form or by any electronic or mechanical means, including information storage and retrieval systems, without written permission from the author, except for the use of brief quotations in a book review.

Jessica M. Butler/Enchanting Chimera Publishing

Publisher's Note: This is a work of fiction. Names, characters, places, and incidents are a product of the author's imagination. Locales and public names are sometimes used for atmospheric purposes. Any resemblance to actual people, living or dead, or to businesses, companies, events, institutions, or locales is completely coincidental.

Cover Art: Stef Saw of Seventh Star Art

Character Art by:

Lumie.Art (Stella and Brandt Couple Pose)

SamaiyaArt (Brandt Solo Image and Stella Solo Image; Ebook Title Page; Crown Headers)

Maps by Elle Madison

FORGOTTEN KINGDOM COLLECTION INTRODUCTION

Forgotten Kingdoms Collection

Eight women.

One sacrifice to save their kingdoms.

A chance to reclaim the love they lost.

Collection notes:

Forgotten Kingdoms is a collection of full-length stand-alone fantasy romance novels with fated mates and a guaranteed happily ever after. With vampires, fae, shifters, and everything in between, each book features a unique heroine and her epic love story that can be read in any order. All relationship dynamics are strictly M/F.

Authors and books in this set include:

Of Blood & Nightmares by Chandelle LaVaun

Of Dragons & Desire by G.K. DeRosa

Of Death & Darkness by Megan Montero

Of Shadows & Fae by Jen L. Grey

Of Elves & Embers by Robin D. Mahle & Elle Madison

Of Mischief & Mages by LJ Andrews

Of Serpents & Ruins by Jessica M. Butler

Of Claws & Chaos by M. Sinclair

Draconia

- Kingdom of Fuoco
- Kingdom of Terre
- Kingdom of Eyre
- Kingdom of Aquos

Aei...

- Court of Moon and Stars
- The Never Court
- Sacre...

Vargr

- Kingdom of Nightfall
- Kingdom of Eventide
- Isle of Wildcrest

Sepeazia

- Kingdom of Kropelki
- Kingdom of Ognisko

Isramaya

- Court of Blood
- Court of Nightmar...

TER

MAGIARIA

MYRKFELL

COURT OF
FIRE AND SUN

SANCTUARY
OF
SEERS

RIA

VONDELL

THE WILDLANDS

MOUNTAIN

ISRAMORTA

SWAMP CLAN

SUMMER COURT

SLATE CLAN

TEMPEST CLAN

WINTER COURT

CINDER CLAN

TALAMH

REA

SEP

Kingdom

Castle
Serpentfire

Auntie
Runa's

Shadow
Hall

Kingdom
of
Kropelki

AZIA

SERPENTS

EMBER LORD'S
CREST

SACRED
TEMPLE

KINGDOM
OF
OGNISKO

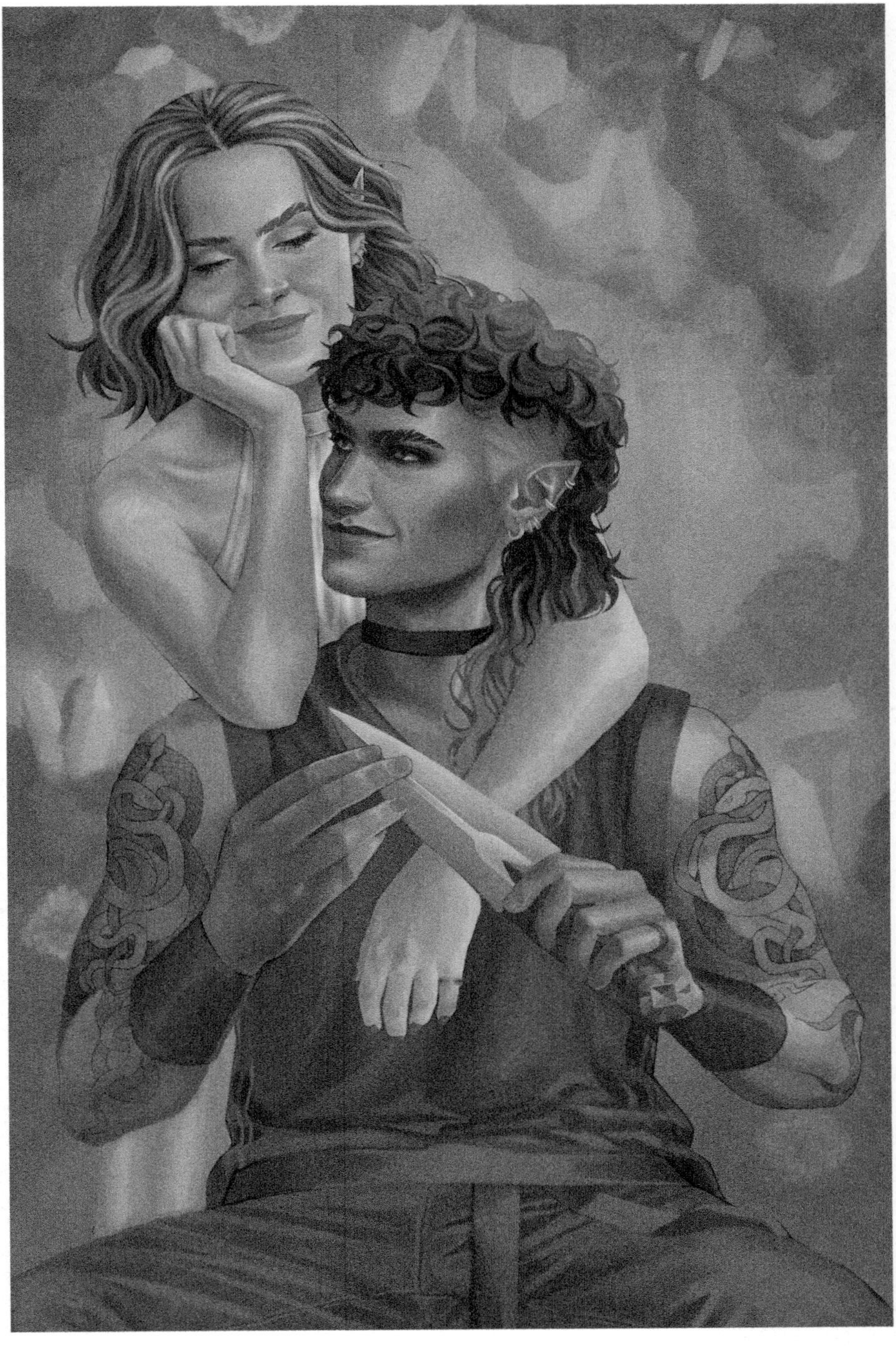

CONTENTS

1. Chapter One: Stella — 1
2. Chapter Two: Stella — 9
3. Chapter Three: Stella — 21
4. Chapter Four: Stella — 31
5. Chapter Five: Stella — 41
6. Chapter Six: Stella — 55
7. Chapter Seven: Stella — 65
8. Chapter Eight: Stella — 77
9. Chapter Nine: Stella — 89
10. Chapter Ten: Brandt — 99
11. Chapter Eleven: Brandt — 113
12. Chapter Twelve: Stella — 125
13. Chapter Thirteen: Stella — 135
14. Chapter Fourteen: Brandt — 145
15. Chapter Fifteen: Stella — 149
16. Chapter Sixteen: Stella — 157
17. Chapter Seventeen: Stella — 165
18. Chapter Eighteen: Stella — 175
19. Chapter Nineteen: Stella — 191
20. Chapter Twenty: Stella — 199
21. Chapter Twenty-One: Stella — 211
22. Chapter Twenty-Two: Stella — 223
23. Chapter Twenty-Three: Stella — 233
24. Chapter Twenty-Four: Stella — 245
25. Chapter Twenty-Five: Stella — 257
26. Chapter Twenty-Six: Stella — 267
27. Chapter Twenty-Seven: Stella — 279
28. Chapter Twenty-Eight: Stella — 289
29. Chapter Twenty-Nine: Stella — 297
30. Chapter Thirty: Stella — 305
31. Chapter Thirty-One: Stella — 319
32. Chapter Thirty-Two: Stella — 327
33. Chapter Thirty-Three: Stella — 335

34. Chapter Thirty-Four: Stella — 345
35. Chapter Thirty-Five: Stella — 355
36. Chapter Thirty-Six: Stella — 365
37. Chapter Thirty-Seven: Stella — 379
38. Chapter Thirty-Eight: Stella — 393
39. Chapter Thirty-Nine: Stella — 401
40. Chapter Forty: Stella — 415
41. Chapter Forty-One: Brandt — 427
42. Chapter Forty-Two: Stella — 439
43. Chapter Forty-Three: Stella — 453
44. Chapter Forty-Four: Stella — 465
45. Chapter Forty-Five: Stella — 473
46. Chapter Forty-Six: Stella — 483
47. Chapter Forty-Seven: Stella — 493
48. Chapter Forty-Eight: Stella — 499
49. Chapter Forty-Nine: Stella — 507
50. Chapter Fifty: Stella — 521
51. Chapter Fifty-One: Stella — 525
52. Chapter Fifty-Two: Stella — 533
53. Chapter Fifty-Three: Stella — 543
54. Chapter Fifty-Four: Stella — 551
55. Chapter Fifty-Five: Stella — 565
56. Chapter Fifty-Six: Stella — 577
57. Chapter Fifty-Seven: Stella — 585
58. Chapter Fifty-Eight: Stella — 591
59. Chapter Fifty-Nine: Brandt — 595
60. Chapter Sixty: Stella — 603

Glossary — 625
Of Claws and Chaos Chapter One: Evera — 627
Identity Revealed Chapter One: Amelia — 635
About the Author — 643
Also by Jessica M. Butler — 645

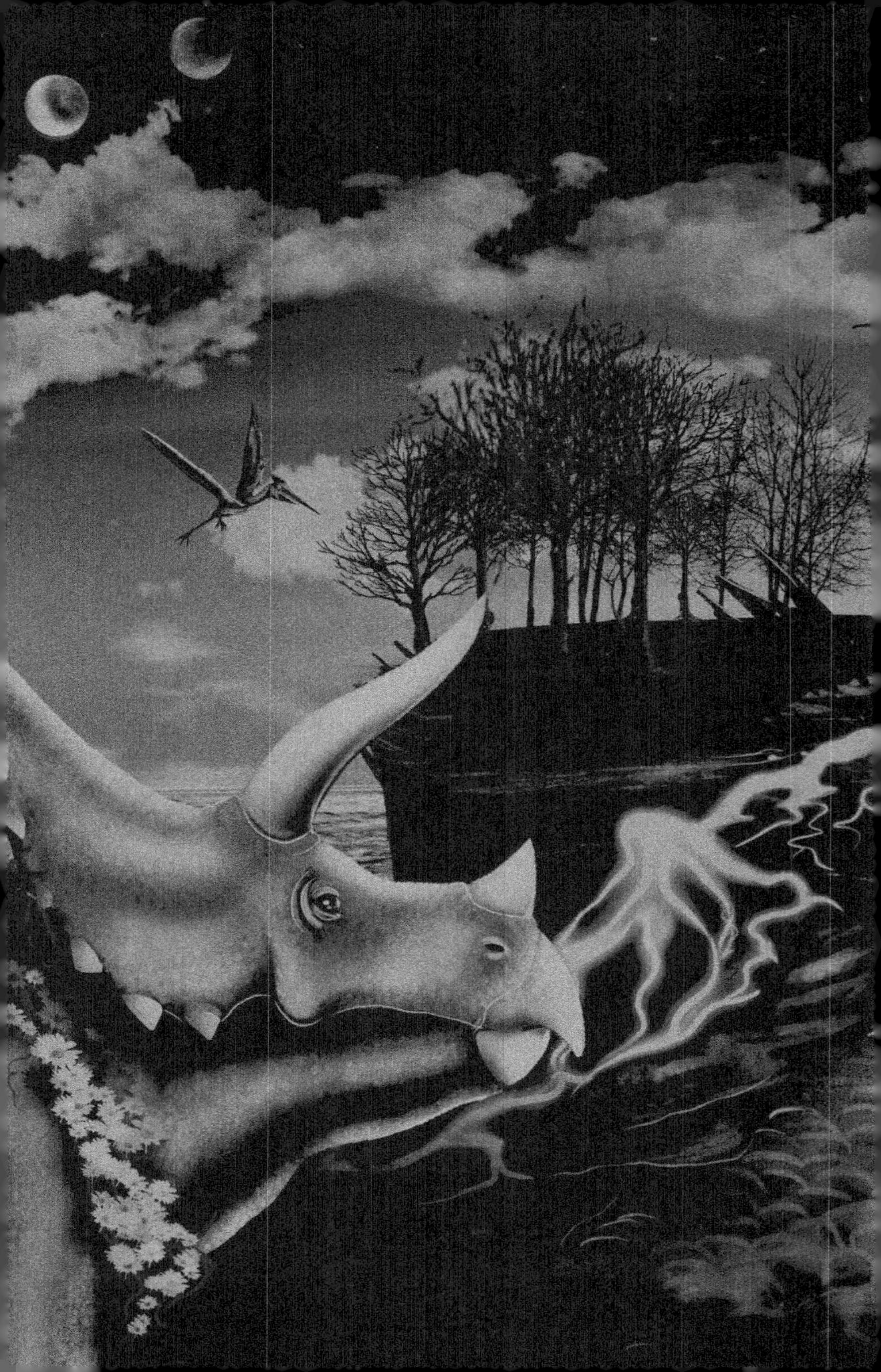

CHAPTER ONE: STELLA

*T*here had never been a point in my life when things felt...right.

Now here I was in Vegas, with bright lights, chaotic chatter, and a horrible pit in my stomach.

Something bad was going to happen.

Oh, enough of that.

I massaged my temples with the tips of my fingers. Nothing bad was going to happen. Evera, one of my few friends who kept in touch from time to time, had called to say she was in Vegas and had a hunch I might be there too since I often headed west in the autumn. Sure enough, she'd been right, so we'd agreed to get drinks at a party in a bar called The Portal.

Nothing bad was going to happen.

Not even if this hotel lobby threatened to overwhelm my senses.

Was I even in the right place?

Intricate mosaic tiles adorned the floor, and warm light flowed from the glittering crystal chandeliers. A pianist in a suit sat on a red velvet bench, swaying in time to the music as his fingers danced across the keys in a soothing yet sophisticated song that was sharply at odds with the hustling hum of guests and ringing bells of gambling games farther away.

Taking a deep breath, I noted so many scents: polished leather, magnolias and rum, woodsy cigars, lily of the valley and freesia, rosemary and cucumber water, fresh bread, rich dark wines, and amber whiskeys. So much, all clawing for my attention.

And, of course, I'd chosen to walk through a super-fancy hotel casino—in my fuzzy, soft triceratops hoodie and Starry Night leggings and sneakers.

Still, it was Vegas on Halloween, so most folks didn't pay me much mind.

So many costumes, though. Mostly elegant with long lines and crisp colors. There might have been a formal gala tonight by the looks of some of the dresses.

I neared the large marble sculpture of a waltzing couple. Evera was supposed to meet me here. Wow—there were so many more people here than I'd expected. Guess I should have thought more about what Halloween in Vegas was like.

Last year, Evera and I had both wound up as waitresses in a themed diner. Making friends wasn't usually something I did, not because I didn't like people but because eventually I just bled awkwardness and sadness. That never bothered Evera. She was as kind as she was beautiful, and she could convince me to do almost anything. That included coming out for a party at this bar.

"Stella!" Evera's cheerful voice cut through the smoky haze of strangers milling about. She wore a Red Riding Hood costume that set off her golden skin and dark hair to full advantage, her emerald-green eyes sparkling.

I bounced forward and hugged her, her arms already circling me. "Hey! You didn't mention how huge this party would be. I mean seriously, it's like *everyone* is here!"

"They probably dropped a flier under every possible door." She chuckled with a shrug. "I'm surprised you didn't get one."

I hesitated, wondering if I'd just missed it. I'd been feeling so off lately. Even when I sketched to relax, it felt like something was just not right. Who knew what else I'd missed? And she was looking at me like she was worried. Of course she was, but I didn't want her to be. "Maybe they weren't doing the motels? It might just be the hotels on the strip."

Her gaze flicked over my face once more as if weighing my words. Then she seized my hand. "Come on. Let's grab a drink. I need one after this week."

I nodded in agreement as we made our way toward the bar. We'd barely squeezed into two black and gold seats before a bartender appeared before us. With a bright smile and a flourish, he looked at us both. "How can I help you, ladies?"

His name tag read Carlos, and Evera offered him a bright smile as she relaxed against the high-backed chair.

"My friend and I will both take a glass of champagne. We're celebrating."

"We are?" My eyebrow lifted as I looked at her, surprised at this. Good as it was to see Evera again, I had no idea what we were celebrating. I couldn't help the smile that tugged at my mouth. She had always been such a bright spot. She never felt like she fit anywhere exactly right either, but that didn't stop her from being this positive force of nature no matter what she was doing.

Carlos snatched up a green bottle with gold foil, giving it a small flourish as he looked us over. It had a pretty label, and, if I remembered correctly from the restaurant I worked at a few months ago, it was an inexpensive brand with sparkly floral notes. Good for get-togethers where you just wanted to sip something without shattering the bank roll. "Anything important? Or just life?"

Evera twitched her shoulders, her dark hair standing out against her red hood. "Just having a night off from work and being with friends."

"Well, that deserves several drinks on the house." He slid two glasses across the sleek black surface and then put the bottle into an ice bucket in front of us. "Cheers, ladies."

Smiling a little, I picked up the flute of champagne and studied the pale bubbles as they rose and burst at the surface. "Do you know him?" I looked at her curiously.

The way she picked up her own glass and grinned warmed my heart. "Nope, but he could probably tell we needed a drink."

Damn. Evera had such an easy charm that folks were just drawn to her. In this case, it got us free drinks, which was great because I wasn't sure I had much money for alcohol. At least not if I wanted to eat something besides beans and rice out of my mini hotpot.

Still, it was worth it. Sometimes we all just needed to live a little beyond existence, and from the way Evera held herself, there was a lot more going on with her too.

"What's going on?" I asked.

She remained silent for a couple breaths, her arms folded on the marble slab of a bar top. Her mouth pinched. "Honestly? I am working over sixteen hours a day consistently. I am making almost no money because rent has gone up, and my boss is an absolute creep...so lots going on, and none of it fun."

A sigh tore through me. That rawness in her voice...I got it.

"I'm sorry. That sounds horrible, and I definitely understand. Honestly, I'm out in some cheap motel until I figure out where to go next. I only headed out this way recently since it's been warm here consistently."

Her eyes widened. "Shit, you should have called me. You absolutely could have stayed with me."

I took another sip of the champagne, savoring the fresh

apple and lemon notes as the more floral flavor transformed, and then shrugged with a smile. "You're a great friend, but I didn't want to be a burden. It sounds like we both have a ton of stuff going on. Besides, I'm trying to figure out what I'm really looking for, you know? Everything just feels...off. Maybe I'll head toward the ocean. Anyway, I'm just glad we were able to meet up."

She clapped her hand down on the bar. "You're right. You're completely right, and this bottle is *not* going to finish itself. Drink up. We can absolutely ignore all of these problems until tomorrow."

Evera and I talked for what felt like hours, sipping champagne in a fancy bar in our strange costumes. Life hadn't been easy for either of us, but rough times made for good stories with friends. We caught up on the highlights of what had happened in the past year, including the bugs and wrinkles.

I even admitted to her that I'd just left my own crappy job on instinct—as if something had called me out here. It was hard to explain, but Evera seemed to get it. At the very least, she didn't judge me.

Time flew as we chatted. We moved on from champagne to frozen spicy strawberry margaritas. And then, as we both realized how late it was getting, we hugged each other close, promised to keep in touch, ordered a drink for the road, and went our separate ways. The alcohol had already started to hit me, but I could still walk straight. At least for now.

Carlos, bartender of the year and total sweetheart, put the frozen spicy strawberry margarita into a fancy to-go cup with a spiral straw. I hadn't realized that a place this fancy would have that. I slipped him an extra tip on top of what Evera gave him. It wasn't easy working in a place like this, but hopefully, tips on a night like Halloween would make it easier for him.

It really was a busy night. I wandered down a long lobby that connected with another casino, not really caring where I was going so long as I was moving. As I nursed the spicy margarita, I finally found and curled up on a leather-covered bench beneath a tree that might or might not be fake. So many people and I was completely content to disappear.

Oh…maybe not completely. Oh, no. This wasn't good.

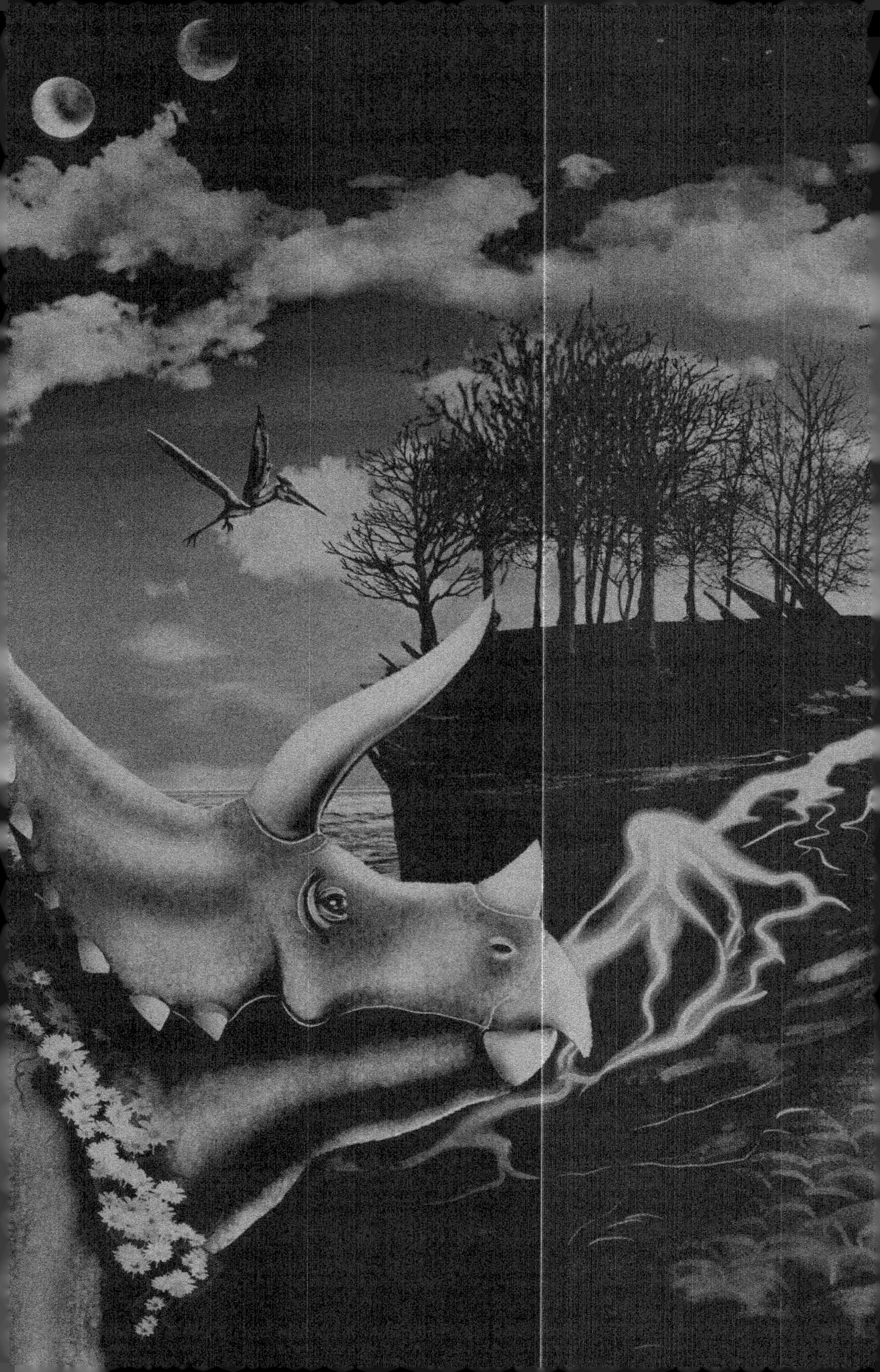

CHAPTER TWO: STELLA

*J*ust a few feet away, a tall blond man with brown eyes flashed me a grin that should have set my stomach somersaulting, yet all I did was give him a polite nod back and hope he didn't come over.

I had no idea why. It wasn't that I didn't like men in theory, but I always felt like I was looking for someone in particular and had never managed to spot him.

Just one more item on the list of reasons I didn't belong here. The question was, where did I belong?

Certainly not here.

I drew my sneakered feet up under me, then remembered I was out in public. Dropping my feet back down, I sighed.

Life sucked. I was in my mid-twenties.

If life hadn't clicked by now, then things were never going to feel right.

Ihlkit!

That made me roll my eyes again. Who even talked like that? Other than me. I didn't even know what "ihlkit" meant. That and a few other phrases like "horns' sake" and "abyssal damnation" just popped into my mind from time to time as if they were totally normal.

But they weren't. I wasn't. None of this was.

The blond man sidled closer, smile broadening. His musky cologne wafted through the air, a potent combination of cloves, maple, and some earthy scent I couldn't place. There was nothing wrong with him. He was perfectly fine. Everything about him from his curly hair to his confident stance to his stylish clothes insisted he was at least a decent starting possibility, but instead of feeling drawn to him, I instinctively scooted away.

"Quite a crowd tonight, huh?" he asked, giving an even bigger smile as he tipped his head. Apparently, my unusual attire did nothing to dissuade him.

I gave a small shrug in response, not smiling but not scowling either. My head swam a little from the alcohol.

"Not much of a talker, are you?" He leaned in closer, invading my space.

I fought the urge to recoil and blinked back at him. "Oh, um, yes, quite a crowd," I mumbled back in answer to his first question, dropping my gaze.

He chuckled, his hand massaging his glass before he took another sip. "Ah, the subtle, silent type. I like a challenge. First time in Vegas?"

I nodded, glancing briefly away from his intense brown-eyed stare. Something about the way he looked at me made me feel...on edge. Hostile. Cold.

He arched a brow, seeming amused by my flustered response. "Ah, thought so. You've got that wide-eyed look about you." He chuckled. "Don't worry. I don't bite. Unless you ask nicely, that is." He winked.

My eyebrow flicked up, and I just looked at him.

Why was this so awkward? Why did I feel nothing but... Oh, horns' sake, I was still staring at him!

It wasn't that I hated flirting or pickup lines. Honestly, I admired anyone who had the guts to pull out a cheesy one-liner and keep a smile on their face, but that wasn't me, and this dude's flirtations left me cold as the last frozen margarita. He was just wrong. All of him. From the top of his curly blond head to the soles of his polished black dress shoes.

"I'm messing with you." He chuckled after a too-long, awkward pause on my end. "Couldn't resist teasing such a pretty girl, but hey, at least I got you to crack a smile."

I pressed my lips together, wondering whether I had involuntarily smiled to be polite. Who even knew? My foggy brain screeched at me to leave.

"I, uh, I should get back to my friend," I mumbled, standing and then edging away from him.

That had been painful.

This was why I would always be alone.

I wandered to a colorful drinks vendor, ordered another frozen spicy margarita, and sipped it as I walked down the too-bright hall. The juxtaposed flavors flowed over my tongue, but it all dulled inside me.

Little round lights brightened and flared to the left as someone struck a jackpot. Happy screams followed.

Yay. Someone was having a good night.

I took another long sip. My mouth tasted like oversweet strawberries and tequila with a hint of habanero. I pulled the soft grey triceratops hood up over my head. Time to go—who knew where?

Did it even matter?

I didn't want to go back to my room. It was a bit of a walk. Better than an Uber, cost wise. I probably shouldn't have gotten the margaritas. Especially not the second. But right now I didn't care.

With the alcohol swirling in my blood, I just wandered.

Wandered like I did more and more. Searching for something that probably didn't exist.

Eventually, I found myself in one of the gardens, one with dual fishponds, all quiet and serene.

How did I get in here? Not really sure. Again, did it matter? Nope.

All I knew was that one minute I was walking down the hall, and the next I was leaning against the clear plastic separator with the silver railing and overlooking one of the two koi ponds.

The water looked so peaceful. So tempting.

Not that I was drunk enough to jump in.

No. It'd been a long time since I was that drunk.

But it was nice to be in the shadow of a desert willow with its pale leaves and wiry branches. The waning gibbous moon didn't provide much illumination. The lights of the casinos and hotels drowned out the natural starlight and moonlight.

It was even bright enough to read the little sign that announced they had just rearranged the koi exhibit and provided additional enrichment options for the fish.

Good for them.

I sighed and pressed my hands to my forehead, the alcohol not doing a good enough job of numbing my mind or the emotions that twisted through me.

Good as it was to see Evera, part of me wished I hadn't come to Vegas. I missed the ocean. I missed the wind in my hair. The richness of starlight. The wholeness of a home I had yet to find. For years, I'd been looking for something I'd never been able to put into words. How messed up was it that I always felt so wrong that not even the night sky felt right when I looked up at it?

"Is anything ever going to fit?" I murmured. "Maybe I should just give up."

Something splashed in the artificial pond.

I turned. My eyes widened.

One of the red and black speckled koi had splashed up on the shore, its massive body flailing. Bits of mulch and mud flipped up around it. And somehow, it was going in the wrong direction. It was heading farther up the bank. It was going to die!

Clumsily, I flung myself over the edge of the railing and fell on my butt. My sneakers skidded on the slick earth. Huffing, I struggled back up, knowing I'd probably stained my leggings and triceratops hoodie but not really caring.

The red and black koi flopped farther and farther up the bank, halfway over the earthen bridge. I scuttled up to it, hands outstretched as it inched along. "Come on, baby. Imma help you."

Almost slipping, I managed to scoop up the koi. It smelled like algae and fish. My nose wrinkled as it wriggled back and forth in my arms, as slippery as a...as a fish. Bits of leaves and streaks of dirt clung to the front of my fuzzy grey hoodie.

I almost turned to deposit it back in the pond it leaped out of. Then I stopped, catching sight of a white and gold koi in the pond on the other side of the separator.

A pang of realization struck me. Had this one been trying to get there? The black and red fish flailed harder, its mouth gaping and its black eyes bulging. Its tail nearly slapped my face as I staggered.

"Don't worry. I can help." I carried the koi over to the other pond. Just those few steps and twice, I almost fell, but I finally lowered it clumsily into the water.

The gold and white koi glided in tightening circles around the newcomer, seemingly delighted. Then it flicked under and against the red and black fish as the black and red fish mirrored its movements.

"You found your friend." I cupped my hands over my mouth, tearing up. "Oh!"

The two fish swam away, side by side, disappearing beneath the bridge and into the darker chasm of black waters, hidden from prying eyes and the assault of the neon lights and pale moonlight.

I'd almost put that poor fish back into the wrong pond.

More tears rolled down my cheeks.

This was stupid.

Yes, I was being totally ridiculous, but tears traced down my cheeks nonetheless. Dammit, I hated my life. Why couldn't I find the right pond for me?

"Crying over a fish? Can't say I'm surprised, Bug. You always were soft-hearted. It's good to see you haven't changed in all your time here."

The warm, earthy voice startled me. A spike of familiarity stabbed me. Not just the voice but the name. No one had ever called me "Bug" before, yet it felt as if someone had. If anything, it sounded like something a big brother or a cousin or someone like that would call you.

I turned, sniffling and scrubbing away the tears.

His eyes bored into me.

I froze.

Gold eyes.

Actual gold eyes. Almost like a hawk's or a snake's but so warm and friendly.

Contacts, maybe? No. Somehow, I knew that. Why did they seem so familiar?

The man's face brightened when I looked at him, his pleasant mouth curving into a broad smile. He had a lean but strong body with a triangular face, and there was a sharpness in his gaze that might have seemed menacing if not for that smile and all his warmth. Azure curls framed his face, almost too perfect to be real. He wore loose light-blue robes with a braided cloth belt around his narrow waist. Indigo serpent tattoos coiled up his forearms and disappeared beneath the sleeveless tunic and robe. Dark-blue gladiator sandals completed the ensemble.

He spread his arms wide, his smile a touch more tentative and his brow a little furrowed. "Come on, Bug. You remember me, don't you? Kine!"

I wiped my hands on my colorful leggings and backed away from him, nearly losing my footing again. "Never seen you before in my life."

Strong arms clamped around my waist, coming up behind me and pulling me into a tight hug. "Stella!"

I squealed, swinging my arms and legs. A warm scent engulfed me, but it wasn't familiar. Vanilla and raspberries and cedar.

"Off! Let go!" I tried to pull away, glaring at him as best I could from over my shoulder while the whole world rocked and swayed. "Don't touch me!"

"Elias!" Kine scowled. He flung one lanky leg over the barrier and hopped over. "Don't scare her! It looks like she doesn't remember us."

Elias set me down and steadied me as I swayed on my feet. He tugged my triceratops hood back by its little white horns, letting my blonde hair spill out. "It's been too long, Stella. I've missed you so much."

"I don't even know who you are," I growled, fumbling at the arm that remained tight around my waist.

"We're going to bring you back home, Stella," Elias said, excitement shining in his dark-blue eyes.

Kine ran up to me, putting his arm around my other shoulder and shooting a glare at Elias. His face broke back into a smile as soon as he looked back at me. "Listen, I get that you're scared, Bug, and I guess it makes sense you can't remember everything yet, but—"

"I'm not scared. I'm mad! I decided I don't want to be around anyone, and here you two are making me be around people." My words slurred a bit as I blinked. Now the alcohol was making things difficult. Great!

Elias laughed at this and then put something around my neck. It was cold. A necklace. A necklace with a dark-blue charm that looked like a... What even was it? I scrunched my nose as I tried to focus on the strange bit of marble dangling from the chain.

"What this?" My vision blurred. Two charms appeared in front of me.

"It's just for good luck and reminders of friendship," Elias whispered in my ear, giving me a friendly pat on the shoulder.

I glared at him. "We are not friends."

Kine rolled his eyes at Elias. "Come on. We need to keep focused. Stella, listen to me. We don't have much time. The veil is at its thinnest right now, and we only have a limited amount of time to get you back. If we don't, you'll be trapped here for years and years after that, but we're here to take you home."

The way he spoke... Elias's voice did nothing to me. His voice was as unmemorable as a random NPC in a generic video game. But Kine's... I'd always wanted a brother or a cousin or someone to look out for me. Somehow, when he spoke, a small part of me wanted to trust him, predator eyes and all.

"I don't know you," I said again, slower this time. "Are you... are you family?"

It was possible, wasn't it? I could have a family out there. Obviously, I had parents. I just hadn't ever met them.

Elias let out a huff of disappointment.

Kine chuckled at this. "Yeah, Bug. Kind of. You're like my kid sister, and I always promised I'd look out for you, so here I am. Elias and me both. We're going to get you home to the rest of your family. It'll come back. You'll remember everything. I promise."

I jerked back then. Maybe I was drunk, but I wasn't that drunk. I didn't have a family. I'd remember if I did. How could I have been stupid enough to fall for that feeling? It had almost felt true despite being impossible.

Bitterness filled my mouth. I remembered every part of my life perfectly, every bland and untethered day, every insipid moment of not belonging and pining and wishing. There weren't any gaps that Kine or Elias or anyone else could fit into unless it was before my first memories.

Balling my fists, I glared at them both.

Kine's eyes widened with concern. Elias took a step forward, reaching for me.

I pulled farther back. "No! Don't touch me. Don't lie to me. Don't you dare! Don't either of you dare."

Kine opened his mouth to protest.

I snapped my fingers at him. "No!"

It shocked me how firm my voice was. Maybe it was just because I was drunk, but I didn't usually sound that authoritative. Even with my words slurring, it was clear I was in no mood for any of this. It was like they had figured out what would hurt me most and had come here to taunt me.

Kine bowed his head. He then held up a small teal orb and covered it with his long, tanned fingers. It looked like a buzzer. "I know you're scared, Stella."

"I'm not scared. I'm angry. You think I don't want a family? You think I didn't want one? What kind of assholes are you? Did you stalk me? Is that how you know I don't have any family? Too bad for you, I'm not an idiot."

Usually. I continued to move away.

"Stella, we're running out of time. You don't belong here," Kine said, glancing around as if afraid someone might see us. "We've come to take you home."

I scoffed, shaking my head. He felt familiar for an instant, yes, but something was...wrong. I kept my fists balled. Neither he nor Elias were supposed to be here. I wasn't... What was going on? My head pulsed as blood thundered in my ears. Everything swam around me.

Kine stepped closer, hand still extended. "Just let us take you home."

"No!" I shouted. My hands clutched at my hair, knotting the fine strands like string. "No, stay away from me. No! I can't go back!"

The words slipped out, hanging there.

Can't go back?

Kine's eyebrows lifted, his golden eyes brightening. "You do remember then, Bug? You remember, and you don't want to go back? Why? Is it because of the curse?"

Elias shook his head. His dark-blue eyes hardened as his brow furrowed. He squared his broad shoulders. "No. No matter what you remember, you have to come back. We'll figure out a way to handle the curse. I promise. I won't let anything happen to you. I am your friend, and nothing will change that."

My mouth had gone dry. My tongue felt like a brick. What did I remember? What was it?

Nothing more than a heavy sense of dread. A vital promise. A deep terror. And eyes. Not gold eyes. Not brown eyes. Not blue eyes. Red eyes. Deep red, like heated rubies and pomegranate gems. Beautiful red eyes staring down at me, pleading with me, begging me.

"You cannot come back."

Who had said that?

Why did I know?

Why couldn't I go back?

It didn't matter.

I just had to escape.

I bolted for the railing, my heart pounding as panic flooded me.

Elias put a hand on my shoulder to stop me, but I cringed

away and ran. All that mattered was keeping that promise. I had promised not to go back until it was time.

"Stella, wait!" he called after me.

"Stella!" Kine cleared the barrier and flung the teal orb at the wall. It crackled and pulsed, sluggish light pouring out from it. Static electricity lifted my hair and popped against my fingertips as I seized the opposite railing.

Elias lunged after me. His hand seized my arm and jerked me back. "Stella, stop!" he said, wrapping his arms around me.

Kine caught hold of me too. "I know you're confused and scared, but you have to trust us. We're your friends. We're family. Please, Bug!"

I struggled against his grip. "Let go!"

Flashes of those red eyes danced through my mind, accompanied by a sense of urgency and danger. Tears stung my eyes.

Elias buried his face against the back of my neck. "I can't let you run from this, Stella," he said through gritted teeth. "We've got to get you home. This is our last chance for another fifty years!"

The energy from the portal swirled faster, pulling at the very fabric of reality.

"It's gonna be all right," Kine said, moving in front of me and seizing my wrists. "I promise you, Bug. I've always watched out for you. I'm not letting anything happen to you. You're just gonna be scared for a little bit longer, and then you're going to start to remember."

With that, he and Elias dragged me three steps forward and leaped into the portal.

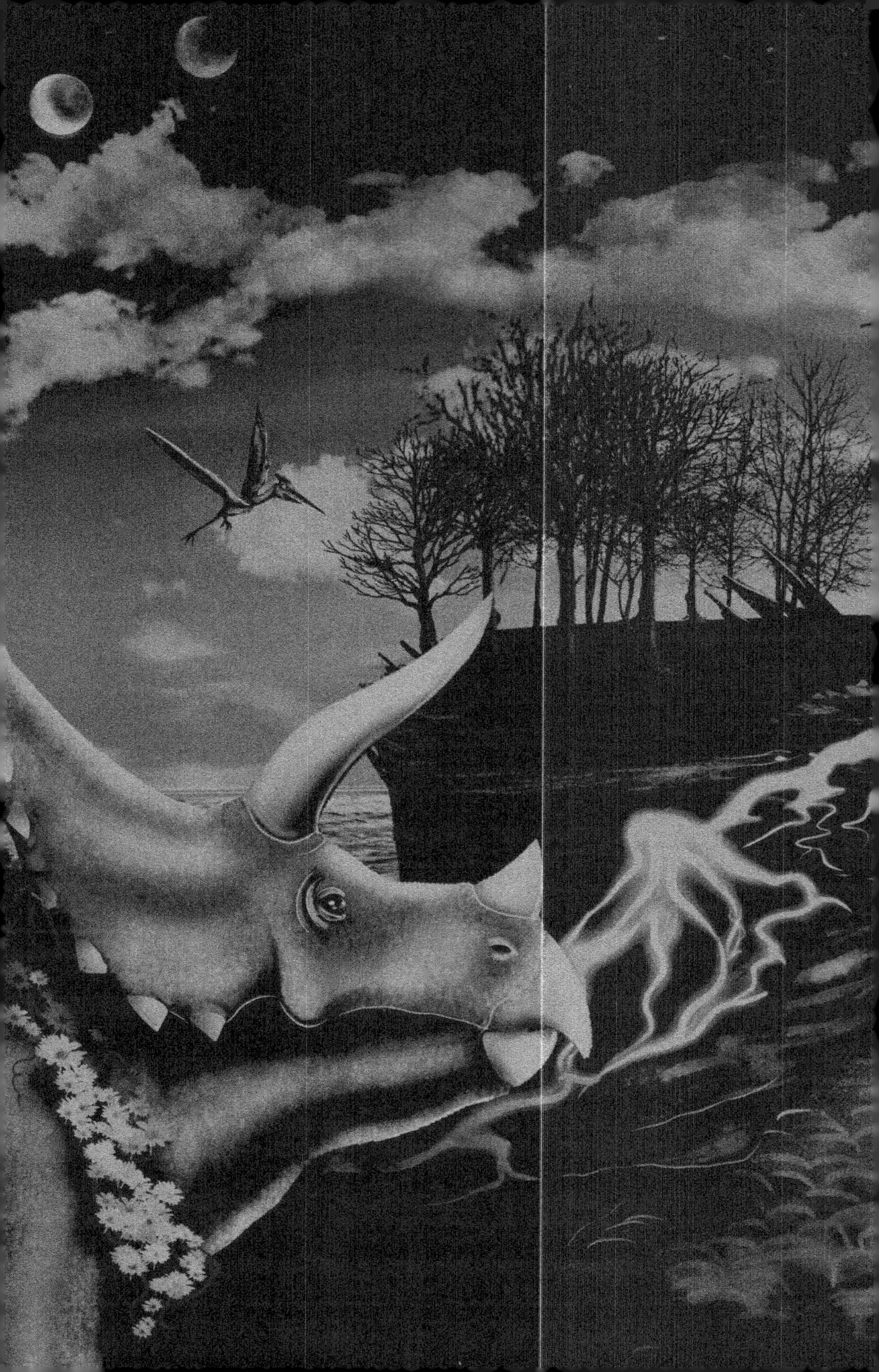

CHAPTER THREE: STELLA

~~~

The portal's swirling energy was cold and slick, engulfing and chilling me. My limbs went heavy as if twenty-pound weights were bound to each of my joints. It squelched and slid along my body. Then I lurched forward and fell onto a black stone floor.

Kine and Elias rolled out beside me. Kine struck his head on the wall, collapsing with a groan, his hand flying to his temple.

My body locked. There was something familiar about this place. It was a black stone chamber. Regular grooves made it seem that it had been hand cut. Was it jet? Obsidian? Why did it seem so familiar? A cold metallic scent filled my nostrils, a scent that was ancient stone but also some sort of energy.

Familiar energy.

The back of my skull prickled. Goose bumps formed over my skin.

It was hard to breathe.

"You promised. Don't come back. Even if you find a way, Stella. My heart, my love, my everything, don't come back until I've fixed this."

I struggled to my feet, my head swimming. The ground

swayed beneath my feet. I had to... What did I have to do? My limbs were heavy, my strides uncoordinated. Pits opened in the floor at odd intervals and in the walls as well, like great chasms. Were those real or my imagination?

"Stella." Kine staggered as he struggled to stand, wincing. Blood dripped down his forehead. He moved out of the silver ring on the floor.

Elias had likewise fallen. He blinked, a dazed expression on his face as if he struggled to remain conscious.

Kine grabbed for my wrist. "Let us explain. You're almost home."

I shrugged him off, stumbling forward, and ignoring the pull of whatever Kine had done to me. I couldn't stay here. I couldn't! This was wrong!

Those pleading red eyes flashed in my mind again. I had to keep that promise, no matter what.

I had to—

"Bug!" Kine's desperate shout echoed in the cold, dank halls. "Wait!"

I ran faster, my limbs no longer clumsy. Adrenaline pumped through my veins. I couldn't be here!

Darting around a corner, I urged myself forward. Faster, faster, faster. Kine's and Elias's voices faded. All that mattered was getting away.

The floor abruptly turned downward. Shrieking, I tripped. My hand whipped out, fingers hooking on a corner to keep myself from falling flat on my face, but then I found myself facing a great passage of inky darkness. My momentum carried me forward, and I plunged into darkness.

The stone floor fell out from under my feet. My screams stuck in my throat. The darkness was suffocating. It was like I had fallen into cold, slimy Jell-O. Disgusting!

My heart hammered in my ribcage. The darkness swirled

and deepened. Then a flicker of orange-ish green appeared before me.

My muscles tensed.

Those were eyes.

Orange and green, full of malevolence.

Energy similar to the portal's coiled around me, suffocating me, sticky and thick like tar.

"Look at who returned," an icy yet familiar voice cooed.

The cold, tar-like substance pressed over my mouth. It seemed to reach all the way into my heart. My breath cut off. Terror spiked through me.

"I am so glad you're back. So very, very glad." The voice drew closer, metallic and feminine. It seemed to be all around me, each syllable scraping over my mind and chilling me to my soul. "I always knew you would. You wouldn't be able to stay away, no matter what you promised. In the state you are now, I could kill you with little more than a thought. Do you know that?" A low, simmering chuckle followed. "I want you to know that, but…it will be so much sweeter when he is the one who kills you. Make the most of what time you have, my darling. The game has finally gotten interesting."

The orange-green eyes vanished. The tar pulled back.

The darkness deepened.

My stomach lurched as I resumed falling, scraping against stone as if I were on some demented slide, spinning and whirling around as if the amusement park ride had gone off its tracks. No sense of up or down. My limbs flailed helplessly over the frigid surface. The impressions of shapes and itching sensations over my body overwhelmed my mind.

A pinprick of light appeared far below my feet. It switched back and forth as if someone was turning a light from a gold to a silver setting. After each flash, it got closer.

The pinprick expanded. With each shifting flash of color,

more details came into focus—the smooth edges of the passage, the glints of silver mineral veins.

As it grew brighter and then dimmer at alternating paces, I realized I wasn't moving that fast. In fact, it was more like I was dropping bit by bit, slower and slower as the pinprick grew to the size of a dinner plate, then a manhole cover. With a soft swish, I dropped out onto a grassy knoll.

Ihlkit! What was that?

My eyes widened. What was this?

The terror of the strange entity and the urgency of my promise faded. Someone must have put something in my drinks. It seemed to be night, but everything was too bright, too vivid, yet there was a softness to it. Obviously, this was a dream.

Two moons hung in the sky, both brilliant waxing orbs. I'd have thought I was seeing double if not for the fact that one was the usual silver-white and the other was teal.

Dream. Yes. It had to be. A drunk dream.

The air had a sweet, salty scent to it, the breeze caressing my face. It was as if the sea had met a meadow of sweetgrass, and it enveloped me here at the base of this butte.

Loud splashes caught my attention, and I turned.

What in all the horns and blessings?

Dinosaurs? Triceratopses! They splashed in and around the river like hippopotamuses. Parasaurs too. And other types I didn't recognize. Even a few actual hippos. One triceratops shook its head and lowed. Tall cattails lined the sparkling river. The night sky was a deep shade of indigo-violet, and the light of the dual moons made this place almost as bright as day.

The air buzzed with some kind of energy. Pterodactyls flew above with smaller pterosaurs darting in and out. Little striped songbirds sitting on branches and twittering their hearts out.

I was… I'd never drunk-dreamed like *this* before.

The triceratops beside me shook its dark-green head. It stared at me with soft doe-brown eyes.

I grinned like an idiot and held my hand out. "Hey, pretty baby." I giggled a little. All feelings of danger evaporated as I looked at this gorgeous impossibility.

The triceratops thrust its snout up and rubbed its jaw against my hand. It huffed a heavy breath on me.

"That's a pretty baby." I couldn't help but giggle more. Maybe it thought I was a triceratops, too, because of my hoodie. Maybe it was whatever I wanted to be because this was so obviously a dream. I leaned against it and kissed it on the edge of its rich-green frill. "You were always my favorite dinosaur growing up."

The triceratops huffed, not at all impressed. It continued to graze on tall, white-tufted clumps of grass beyond the speckled border.

Maybe I could ride it. That could be fun.

No. Something was wrong with it. It wasn't the one I was looking for.

Pulling back, I scowled at myself. What was wrong with me? Did it matter?

My feet sank a little into the springy grass as I stepped back. A chortle rose to my lips. What had I been worried about?

Something pulled within my gut. Calling me. Urging me. *Come this way*, it whispered.

Come.

Come.

Come.

The wind tugged at my hair. A blue ribbon flashed in front of my face, sticking to my lips. Reaching up, I tugged it away then flinched, a sharp pain in my scalp.

Wait.

I drew the thread—no—my hair. It was my hair.

At least it was attached to my scalp, but it was blue. Cerulean. One of my favorite colors. I'd always wanted to dye my hair this shade, but I'd never been able to justify the money.

What a dream this was.

I almost laughed as I slid my hands into my hair. It felt almost exactly the same, yet it was blue.

Crossing over to the river, I peered down. The triceratops and salamanders playing and bathing farther downstream sent ripples up through the water, though they paid me no mind. My reflection danced over the bright surface, taking a moment to come into focus.

I jerked back.

Was that... How was that possible?

I leaned forward again, hands pressed against my thighs as I peered down.

I had shoulder-length blue hair now and golden eyes. My skin had become an almost ethereal golden brown, and my ears were long and pointed like an elf's or a fae's.

My heart beat faster, hammering within my ribcage.

Not fear.

No.

This was me.

This was really me.

All the times I had looked into a mirror before, the eyes and face peering back at me had been wrong. Even though I couldn't see all the details of my face, I saw enough.

My heart raced faster, my breath catching in my throat. Gently, I tugged out a strand of rich-blue hair. Yes. I'd always known I wanted this color, but, costs aside, no dye ever looked like it would come out right on Earth. I felt like I did the day I changed my name from Margot to Stella. Stella was who I was, and Stella had gorgeous blue hair.

I almost laughed as I stood. *In vino veritas*, perhaps. Or in margaritas clarity.

Digging my fingers into my scalp, I stared down at my watery, rippling reflection. If only there were a real mirror here. I had to remember this when I woke up. I wanted to memorize every detail.

This was me—the me I was supposed to be.

And I'd become *her* again.

Again? That was an odd thought. I'd never been this person before, had I?

No, that wasn't possible, but when I woke, I would remember, and I'd become whoever this woman was.

A strange urge intensified within my gut and rose into my chest, a plucking, like someone was playing a series of strings coiled around my very heart.

Come in. Come deeper.

A dark-green triceratops with black patches on its back shambled by me, munching on mouthfuls of the tall, sweet-scented grass. As I passed it, I pressed my hand to its hindquarters in an almost absent-minded pat. As if this were normal.

Somehow, it felt as if this made all the sense in the world despite so much of my brain struggling to comprehend this. It was easier to simply let it be.

Go along.

Breathe.

Follow.

Why did this have to be a drunk dream?

If I didn't feel so calm, I'd be sobbing, begging for this to last forever.

But no amount of tears would make it last, so I should enjoy it while I could.

Off I went. There was no path exactly, yet I walked beneath the broad-limbed trees with delicate dark-red and white flowers, similar to cherry blossom trees. The ground beneath my feet had strange thick veins gouging and clawing throughout—black or dark green or even dark purple maybe, depending on how the light hit them. Wherever they were, the plants had withered a little or lightened.

Similar veins occasionally stretched out in the night sky above me, like a fork of lightning moving in slow motion, but there was no trace of thunder, only the heavy steps of the dinosaurs and the loud sloshing of the shimmering waters. When the wind changed directions and caressed my face, both a soothing floral scent and a bitter acrid odor struck my nose before disappearing into the rich earthy aroma of the riverbank.

Nothing acted as if I didn't belong. A dark-eared rabbit, almost the size of a cat, hopped out from a red-berried bush, studied me, and then hopped away just as fast.

An aching howl rose in the distance. A wolf? Certainly wolf-like.

The hairs on the back of my neck lifted, yet I knew I wasn't in danger. Not here. Not now.

Something had summoned me, and within me, it burned, called, pushed, and begged.

It was more important I find that source than any of the danger I might face. Danger was not something for me to concern myself with now.

It was so easy to just keep walking. My feet seemed to know where they wanted to go. I was content to marvel at the beauty around me.

Far, far ahead, I glimpsed clusters of towers, maybe? Or perhaps they were narrow, triangular mountains? Possibly buildings on mountains? I squinted, trying to make them out.

Why had my first thought been towers? They didn't look like any tower in the mountains I'd seen on Earth.

I quickened my pace.

That was where I needed to be. I had to get up out of this valley and into those towers. Answers awaited me there.

The wind changed again, carrying with it a different scent. My body tensed as I slowed beneath a dark-red blossomed tree. Oranges, smoke, leather, and bergamot. Ihlkit! My blood heated. That smell was beyond divine.

My feet rooted to the pebble-strewn ground. Boulders and ridges of earth rose in intervals, but this portion was flat and tan with precious little grass. Farther out the river bent, triceratops and hippos swam in the deep waters. The waters sloshed. A reptilian cry cut through the air.

But that heavenly smell dominated my consciousness.

A muscular arm wrapped around my waist, snapping me up against a hard body. Another hand rested against my throat. My heart clenched, my spine stiffening.

"You swore to me," a rough baritone voice growled, his hot mouth against my ear. "You swore it. Now you're back, and I'll have to kill you."

Holy night, I knew that voice!

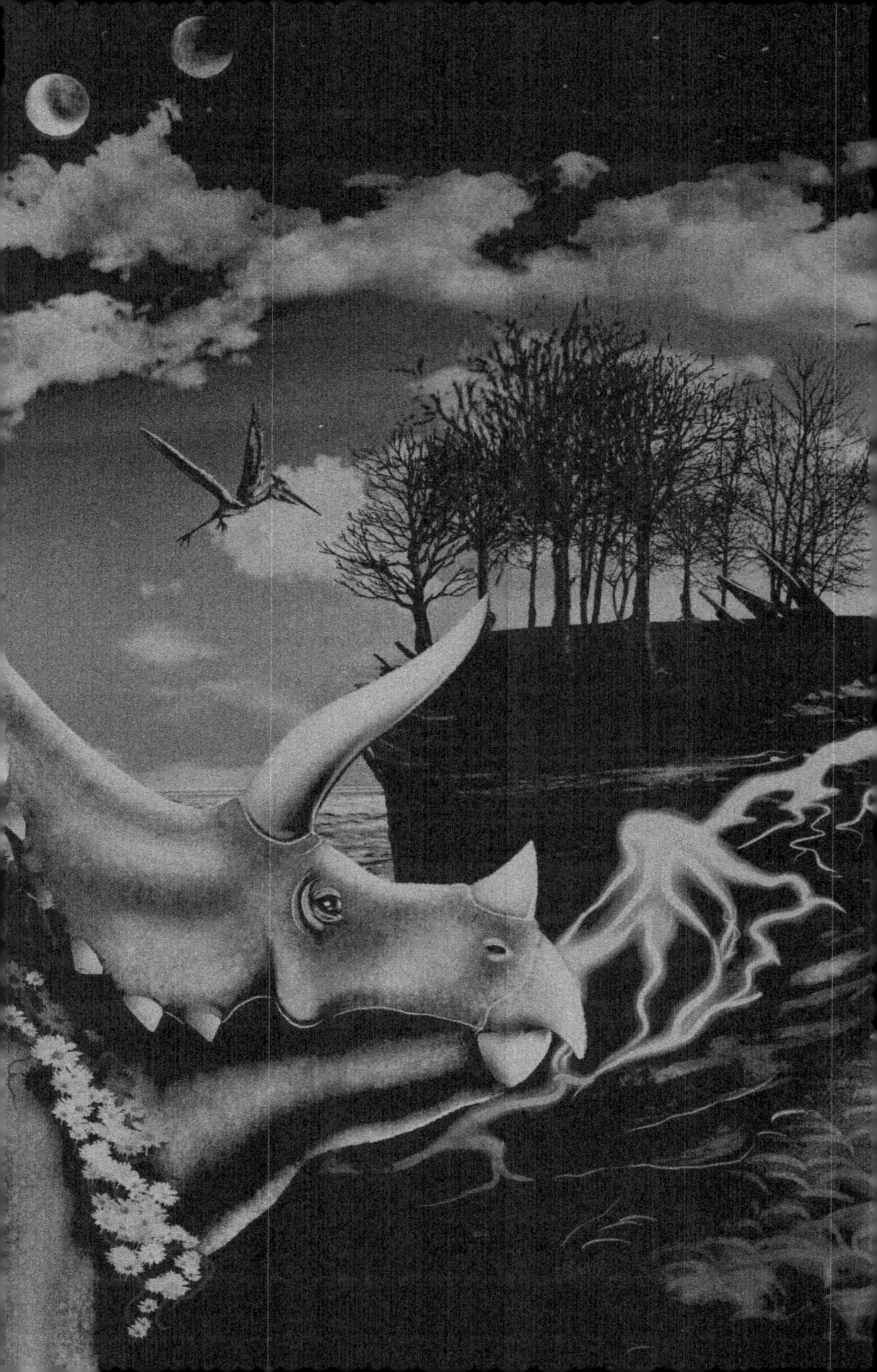

CHAPTER FOUR: STELLA

The stranger held me tight, his other hand moving over my throat, but instead of squeezing, he stroked a thumb along it. "Stella..." His voice thickened, rumbling in my ears. The heat of his breath made my skin prickle. "When they told me you had been brought back and that you had run, I thought you ran because you remembered enough to keep your promise. I hoped, oh gods, I hoped!"

The groan that followed weakened my knees and set a tornado of butterflies fluttering in my stomach.

This. This was all a dream. If ever I had needed proof that this was a dream, this was it. There wasn't a chance it could be anything else.

My heart raced as the hand gripped my throat and continued to stroke. I should have been terrified. Yet...yet there was something in this that felt...not right. Right was not exactly the word I wanted, but as if there was something here...

And I could do something. I could have broken free because he wasn't holding me *that* tight.

He nudged me with his nose. "I have to kill you," he whispered, his voice a low, hoarse rumble. "I have to..."

The line he drew along my neck and up to my ear... I didn't move. All I wanted was his touch. Desire warred with fear, and desire trounced fear as much as I wanted to pounce on him, so I stood there, waiting, listening, feeling.

"Why couldn't you stay away until we found an answer, Stella?" he whispered in my ear. The arm around my waist pulled me tighter.

My skin prickled with goose bumps. It took all I had to not press my butt against his groin as he held me there. What was going on? I wasn't usually this stupid! All those dumb blonde jokes had always made me mad, and here I was, acting worse than those jokes, acting like he turned me on.

Which he did.

So much.

But why?

Why wasn't I terrified?

He nuzzled me again, his breath rough against my neck and in my ear. "You should be running from me." Another low growl followed as he seemed to almost want to hug me closer. "I don't know why you aren't running."

That voice of his was setting me on fire. I tugged free, spun around, and...found myself staring straight into his eyes.

Red eyes. Red like ancient rubies. Red like cauldrons of dark flames and smoldering embers.

These were the eyes I'd remembered in the jet cavern.

Was this who that evil-voiced monster was speaking about in the cavern? The "he" coming to kill me? Thank you, evil monster lady!

All my fear evaporated into nothing but giggling jittery need. Laughter bubbled out of me. My "attacker" was gorgeous. Tall, broad-shouldered, tattooed, red-eyed, eyelined, black-and-red haired, pointed ears with piercings.

Yes, please!

Heat flared through me, blossoming in my face as I laughed

so hard I snorted. Ihlkit, I had never felt so high and drunk all at once.

I tried to clap my hand over my mouth but instead found myself touching the muscular planes of his chest. "I know I'm drunk, but I don't know how you can exist. Where have you been all my life, you big spicy strawberry margarita man?"

He looked down at me, his brows first flicking upward, then down, then up again as he cocked his head. "What?" He blinked. "What did you just say, Stella?"

More giggles followed as I practically collapsed against him.

This *so* wasn't me. I was sensible. Skittish. Shy. Solitary.

I needed to stop, but I leaned closer, laughing even more. As I ducked my chin and staggered, my triceratops hood flipped up over my head.

He started to put his arm around me, then stopped. He lifted his hand, his brow furrowed. "You should be taking this much more seriously, Stella." He frowned as I adjusted the hoodie. "And what are you wearing?" His upper lip curled. "Did you skin a...stunted, deformed triceratops?"

"Oh." I shrugged, lowering my eyes as I shifted my weight back. I stuck my hands in my pockets and swayed. "It's a triceratops hoodie. It has pockets and little horns. Kind of looks like a triceratops ate me though. You can touch it. It's soft."

His eyebrow raised sharply. "Stella..."

"Come on. Feel me."

"Stella, you need to stay away from me. I'm dangerous," he growled. "I'm cursed to kill you. I don't want to do it, but we both know the curse will seize me and force my hand."

It was all I could do to keep from purring at him and giggling simultaneously, and somehow, that turned into an utterly bizarre snorting laugh that would ordinarily have embarrassed me. "Yeah, you are. Slay me with those looks. You're so tall!"

I was making an utter fool out of myself. I should really be more worried about this, but that little voice in the back of my head wasn't as compelling as everything that was happening in my body right now.

He stiffened and took a step back, nodding once. "I am tall, yes."

"I want to climb you like my favorite rock-climbing wall." I slapped my hand over my mouth. Had I really just said that?

The corners of his mouth twitched. "Stella," he said, slower this time. "Stella, please. You really need to fear me." He struggled not to smile as his gaze raked up and down my body.

Even with me in a baggy triceratops hoodie with Starry Night leggings, he thought I was appealing.

"The only thing I'm afraid of is how attracted I am to you right now." Another snort and giggle followed. Part of me just wanted to die, but it wasn't the part of me that was talking. "If you're so dangerous, you walking red flag, you, then why are you here? Hmmm?"

"I'm drawn to you. I can't stay away. No matter how hard I try." Agony was etched into his granite jaw and marble cheekbones. A low growl erupted from his chest. "My instincts take over my will."

Hmmm. Instincts. My eyelids shuttered involuntarily, my insides rebelling against my better judgment and melting into heated desire. Goose bumps rioted over me. Why did he have to make that sound?

"If you really want to make me run away, you need to stop growling at me, whatever your name is."

He pulled back as sharply as if I had struck him. The air grew cold between us. His thick brows furrowed. Pain flared in his dark-red eyes. "You don't remember."

"I know...I know that there's something." A clawing panic driven by his expression chilled me, and I stiffened. *No, don't be mad at me. Don't be mad at me, spicy strawberry margarita man.* That didn't feel good at all. "I just—I'm fuzzy on the details."

He rubbed his hand along the back of his neck, up the left side of his curly mohawk fade, and then back down his neck. "Hold on..." His brow knit even more, the heavy eyeliner around his eyes making his gaze all the more intense. Then he looked at me. My knees weakened, and my head swam even more. "You actually don't know what happened between us? You don't remember my name, but you look at me and you're not afraid? You don't fear me?" He set his muscular arms akimbo, snake tattoos on full display over his magnificent biceps and coiling down his scarred forearms beneath his bracers. "Really?" The last word was spoken so low it set my insides on fire.

"That's a future Stella problem, margarita man," I quipped, leaning against him. Being apart from him would destroy me. We had to be together. I might love him.

"You need to take this seriously, woman," he snarled at me, making my head and insides spin even faster. Something else danced in his eyes though. "Do you expect me to be soft with you?"

More giggles tore out of me. "I'd rather you be hard."

He snapped back, his eyes wide as he looked at me as if I had grown horns. Which was fitting. I was horny. I descended into more giggles. No matter how much I pressed my hands to my mouth, the giggles wouldn't stop.

It was ridiculous. Every part of me was melting. *Look at him. Just look at him!*

Yes, look at the big scary man glowering at me. Or maybe he was trying not to laugh. Maybe both. He glanced down at the orange charm on his necklace. Then he tucked it away and stepped toward me.

"What did you just say?" he asked, leaning closer. His hot breath caressed my skin. His gaze ran up and down my body before settling on me. "You aren't exactly the same, are you?"

Those words and the heated gaze that met mine seized me

fast, sobering me more with the jolt of awareness. The disappointed anger earlier had sliced deep and chilled me. This look—that statement—it coiled out of him and speared me in place as if threads anchored us to each other, threads that made me awake despite the dreaminess.

Ihlkit. I was in trouble. This didn't feel so playful any more even as the humming continued in my ears.

His eyes shuttered. A ragged breath trembled from his lips. "You look upon me now, and you do not know me, yet some part of you does. I know this. The part of you that remembers what happened and why you must not be near me. Why, no matter what, you have to stay as far from me as you can." His voice changed, severing the memory's connection to me. The déjà vu ceased, though he remained as temptingly familiar as before. "Because I *will* kill you."

My heart sped faster. "No, you won't," I whispered.

Fear stirred in my blood for the first time. He wouldn't—he would. A deep, gnawing sorrow swelled within me, and I wanted to weep. Emotion knotted in my throat as tears burned the backs of my eyes.

"I can't stay away from you. Even though I knew you were gone, I couldn't stop searching for you or hoping," he said roughly, his voice thick with desire. The muscles in his angular jaw jumped. His broad shoulders tightened. His hand went to the leather band with the strange charm on it and pulled it out again. The dull orange color had gotten a little brighter. "But you have to go. The way between the worlds may be shut now, but if you go in the opposite direction of those towers and past the forked hill, you'll find Auntie Runa's. Her magic is strong enough to—"

The ground rumbled. It vibrated beneath my feet.

Earthquake!

The triceratops in the river bellowed and fled as the river surged. Deer bolted across the grassland. The trees rocked and trembled. Everything swayed and shook. Lurching forward, I collapsed in his arms.

He hugged me tight against his leather-vested chest, bracing himself and leaning forward, his muscular arms wrapped tight around me.

Then, just as swiftly as it started, it stopped. Everything stilled. Even the lowing and bellowing of the dinosaurs.

Slowly I relaxed, looking up at him, my arms pressed firmly against his chest while he held me snug against his incredible body. Whatever words I wanted to say dried up. All that mattered was here. This moment.

Straightening, he continued to hold me, his shoulders squared as he drew himself up. Something soft and impossibly warm filled his eyes as he set me on one of the boulders.

The smooth stone provided support. I leaned back on it as I stared up at him, daring him to keep going.

There was no question that there was history between us. We had been lovers. Perhaps we still were. Perhaps we could be again?

He hooked his finger through the band of my new necklace and pulled it taut. His fingers curled around the dark-blue charm, his gaze fixed firmly upon mine.

My breath snagged in my throat. The warmth of his body against mine, the tight circle of one arm at my waist, and the tension in the necklace as he held me there—oh, yes, whatever he had in mind, *yes*! A gentle hint of something sweet and fruity—like cherries—reached me, caressing my senses.

His thumb stroked the stone of the charm as he leaned closer. The charm around his neck started to glow. His strong thighs pressed against mine. "Get away from me, and don't look back. Resist the pull. Be better than me."

My breaths trembled through my parted lips. All I could do was stare up at him. I didn't want to be better than him! I wanted to kiss him. Now!

His dark-red eyes bored into mine, his pupils large and dark. He edged closer. His heat overwhelmed me and pulsed within my core.

Yes. Kiss me.

I couldn't form the words, but if I could have willed them into his consciousness, I would have.

He leaned in even closer, his thumb still stroking the charm as he stared deep into my eyes. The soft cherry fragrance intensified.

Yes, whatever he wanted, *yes*. I reached up to slide my hand along the back of his neck.

Light flared in his eyes, his pupils shrinking into pinpricks. His shoulders dropped as his jaw jutted out. Rage blazed in his face. "You must die," he bellowed, his hands seizing my throat and squeezing.

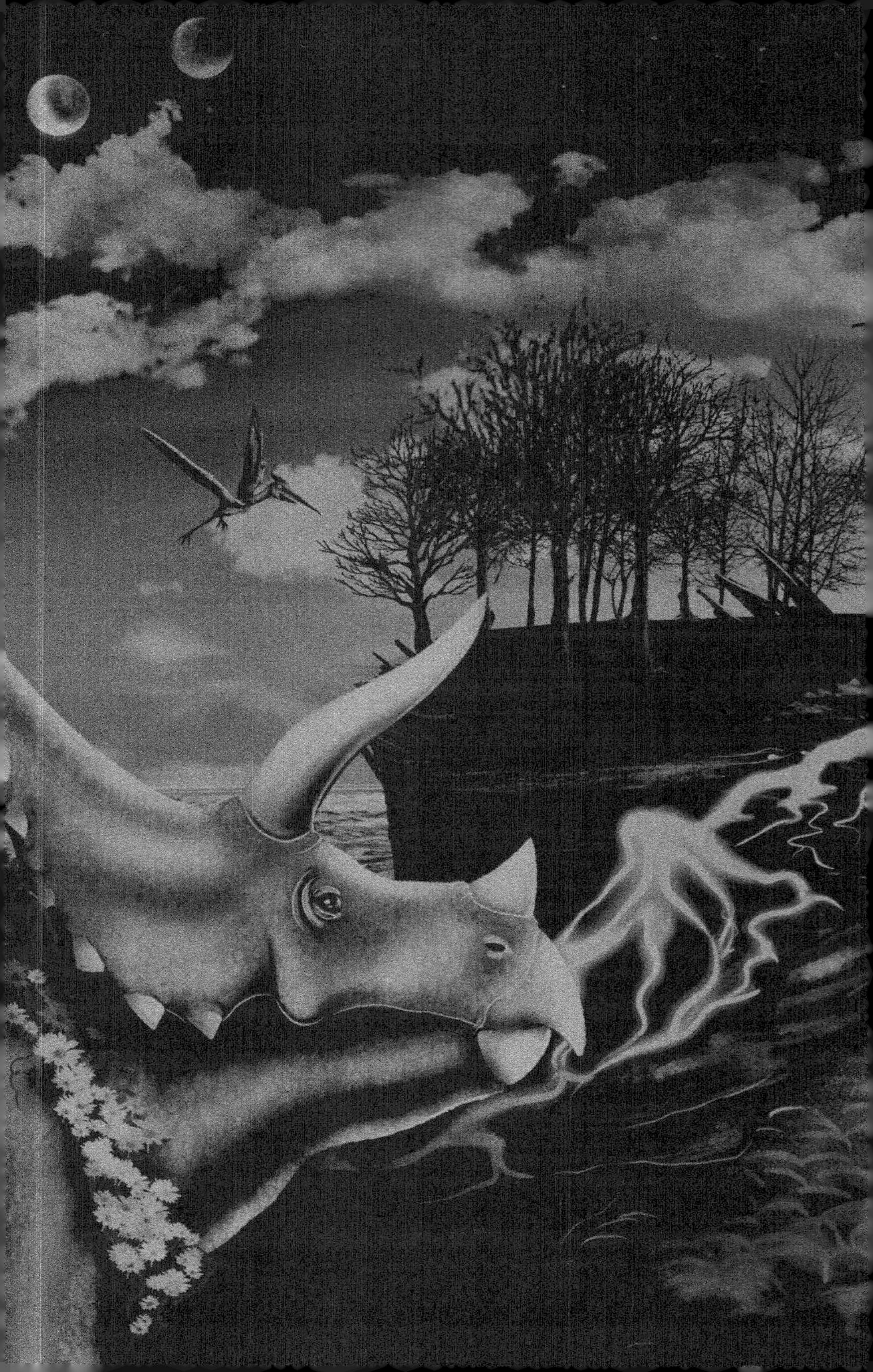

CHAPTER FIVE: STELLA

*H*e really was going to kill me!

I gasped and choked, my hands flying to his. Those deep-red eyes were no longer warm and friendly, the lines in his face now terrifyingly sharp. His gaze burned with fury, his fingers tightening like iron bands.

I clawed at his hands, trying to pry his fingers from my throat as he squeezed tighter. My lungs burned for air, and black spots swam before my eyes.

No. No! Something had gone wrong. *It hadn't warned me. The charm turned yellow too fast. We had more time!* My thoughts grew more confused, not fully making sense. *This isn't the man I love.*

Flailing, I struggled to free myself. Memories danced like the dots in front of my eyes, all hovering just out of consciousness as if to lure me in.

He was going to kill me.

And I couldn't stop him.

I aimed my palm at his nose and hit his cheek instead, the blow glancing off. His thumbs crushed along the sides of my windpipe.

Something struck him, the force vibrating through me as it

dragged him away. "Get off her, Brandt!" Kine's voice cut through my hazy mind.

The ground shook. Thunderous beats filled the air as the world turned upside down. I rubbed my throat, gulping in harsh, burning breaths.

Strong arms scooped me up as easily as if I weighed no more than a bag of eggshells. Tears blinded me. Harsh coughs racked my body.

Elias carried me to the other side of a cracked grey boulder with sparkles of pyrite beneath the broad-limbed, red-leafed tree. Kneeling, he placed me against the trunk between the roots and leaned close.

"You're safe," he whispered in my ear, his breath hot. "You're safe. I've got you. You're safe. The others are coming."

"It didn't turn yellow first," I blurted out, struggling even to speak.

My own words made no sense, but they erupted out of me like that was the actual betrayal. Something was supposed to go yellow, and it went yellow at the wrong time. The charm? It had glowed yellow when he was strangling me.

Fear, anger, sorrow, and grief—they all pulsed within me. My hand remained at my throat, my breaths shallow and ragged. Tears rolled down my cheeks.

No.

This was wrong.

Brandt lurched back, striking the ground. His gaze fell on Kine with nothing but pure hate. "Traitor!" he bellowed. His eyes blazed like fire, his jaw seeming to distend.

The intensity in his voice and his words seared me.

"Why don't you fear me, seer?"

His voice echoed in my head. A foreign memory pressed at my mind. As if he was asking me the question in another place at another time. But I saw the two of us standing in a throne room.

Did I fear him—*Brandt*.

The trembling in my body intensified as I spoke his name within my thoughts.

My heart clenched.

My Brandt.

My love.

Elias crushed a gooey purple berry against my shoulder and pressed a bottle to my lips. "Drink this," he murmured, his other hand against the back of my neck. His bracer pushed down farther on his wrist, a dark circular tattoo peering up from the wavy leather cuttings of his protective armbands. A pungent but sweet scent like currants filled the air and my lungs, masking his cedar, raspberry, and vanilla cologne. "The medicine will help you heal and counter the effects. The berries will mask your scent."

A guttural roar followed.

Had Brandt made that sound?

I pushed the bottle away, my gaze snapping back to him. That sounded reptilian rather than human.

Brandt leaped back up, his boots crunching on the soil. His face distorted with rage. The words staggered out of his mouth with great effort, his body lurching to the left. "You condemned her!"

Another roar tore through him as Kine crouched into a stance that reminded me of wrestling. Brandt doubled over then, snarling. The veins and muscles in his body strained and contorted.

Then, like boiling water poured onto ice, Brandt's body tore apart and lengthened. His eyes bulged and became large as mugs, his arms and legs fusing to his body. The black and red of his leather garments vanished into black scales with red stripes running the length of his body. Another reptilian roar, deeper and angrier this time, broke from his now massive body.

He'd turned into an enormous red and black serpent with a broad, spiked crest and long red whiskers.

Kine's muscles tightened. His brow furrowed, fear flashing through his golden eyes. He clenched his fist, then struck the silver ring on his left hand against his palm. Blue light arced briefly over his fingers, a burning scent similar to electricity filling the air. He dodged, rolling as his shoulders struck the ground.

Brandt lunged. His blunt snout struck the rocky soil. He didn't even react. He just snapped back, hissed, coiled, and struck again.

Elias gripped me tighter, his muscles tensing. "We may have to run. Something's off with Kine's shifting. Everything's off tonight."

I struggled to my feet. "We can't leave Kine here," I managed hoarsely, my throat still burning.

Elias held me back, his arms tight around me. "If you go in there, Brandt will focus on you. He'll catch your scent again, and then he'll try to kill you. Do you think you can survive if he goes after you like that?"

My heart sank. No. No, this was wrong.

"Right," Elias said firmly. He thrust the bottle against my lips again. "Now drink this. It'll help you heal. If we have to run, you need to be stronger."

He dumped some of the amber liquid into my mouth this time. A salty, bitter flavor choked me. Drawing back, I covered my mouth, spluttering. It burned all the way down, but the pain in my throat eased, along with my breaths and the tension in my chest.

I couldn't tear my gaze from the fight before me. Kine lunged and jumped. Each time he hit the ground, he rolled or spun and struck the ring on his finger again. Each time, energy burst forth. Occasionally, his features twitched. His arm almost fused to his side.

Brandt attacked again, eyes blazing. The roars mixed with words, but none of it made any sense. It was too garbled, or maybe I just couldn't hear.

The thunder intensified, the ground shaking as the sound drew closer. Not an earthquake but like hundreds of horses stampeding.

My heart clenched, squeezing with agony as I watched. It was like a rattlesnake going after a jumping mouse. Did Brandt have venom? It felt like maybe he did. He kept striking within a hairsbreadth of Kine.

"We have to help him!"

Elias was unrelenting. "You need to hold still and stay back. Kine is guiding him away and keeping him occupied. Movement will attract him more than sound when we've got your scent masked with the punji berry. If we have to, we'll run. The others are almost here, though. So just wait. We can't risk drawing his attention. The curse has taken over, and, no matter what he wants or intends, it will make him kill you!"

Brandt lunged at Kine again. This time, his jagged teeth nipped Kine's indigo sash. Kine kicked Brandt in the snout with a broad sweep of his leg and struck the ring again, and as if a light had suddenly come on, Kine's body elongated and poured into a blue and silver serpent form with gold eyes and gold speckling along his chest.

Brandt buried his fangs into Kine's side.

A long, loud snarl of pain tore from Kine as he squeezed his gold eyes shut.

I clapped my hands over my mouth. Elias held me tighter, one arm around my waist, the other around my shoulder.

Brandt opened his jaws and then bit down again. Blood ran down Kine's silver scales, but instead of lunging away, Kine twisted around and bit just at the base of Brandt's neck.

An enraged growl erupted from Brandt's jaws, his teeth still stained with Kine's blood. He recoiled just enough for Kine to shoot away from him. He narrowly escaped Brandt biting him again. The wound in his side started to heal from left to right in uneven surges like a ragged heartbeat.

The hoofbeats and thunder grew louder as riders crested the hill. Warriors on triceratops and parasaurs. Over a dozen of them.

They wore simple cloth and leather uniforms, dark blue, almost black, with red cord and ornate sashes that depicted interlocking water serpents of red and blue with silver and gold highlights throughout. Their dark bracers had scales etched into them, and the pommels and hilts of their bladed weapons had waves carved into their fluid designs.

Some of their faces looked more familiar than others. A statuesque woman in pale blue and bright pink strode out from the arriving warriors and into the fight. She cracked her knuckles and then her neck.

"Oh, Candy's here." Elias sighed with apparent relief. "Well, that may help calm Brandt. Those two are very close. Nobody gets Brandt the way she does."

Candy? My eyes practically bugged out of their sockets. Jealousy flared through me at the way he said that, a vicious heat that seared me in place, overwhelming my fear.

She looked like a princess in her shimmering garb. The leather and silk caught the moonlight and made it dance. Her long, pointed ears had interlocking gold chains that chimed in the wind. Excessive but pretty. And her silver-white and purple hair had been bound up high on the top of her head, giving her the most epic ponytail of anyone I'd ever seen. She wore a simple flared skirt with layers of silk, and the top portion was further accentuated with a dark-pink bandolier belt. Who was she to Brandt?

Like a dancer leaping across a stage, she became a pink and white serpent with a deeply curved crest tipped in magenta, softening in shade as it went down her back. "My turn," she said, her tone firm yet almost playful. Even her voice was beautiful!

Kine swiveled in her direction, narrowly missing another attack from Brandt. Brandt didn't even seem to hear her.

Candy swept up alongside Brandt and body-slammed him. He glimpsed her and tried to dodge, but the edge of her crest still clipped him a second time.

The newly arrived warriors formed a semicircle around Brandt and Candy. Their expressions were grim. None had their weapons drawn.

Kine shot away from Brandt and through the semicircle. He dropped out of his serpent form at once, gasping. The bloody wound in his side sealed up and vanished as his body shook.

I hurried toward him. This time, Elias didn't object.

Kine shook his head at me as I approached. "I'm fine...fine," he said, his voice shaking. "Don't get too close, Stella. The punji berry might not mask your scent if you get too close, and he isn't out of full bloodlust yet. It's going to be a bit."

One of the warriors—the largest and most elaborately clad—stepped toward Kine. "You need medical attention?" he demanded, his voice gruff.

A sense of familiarity rushed over me.

I knew him. His name—Hoarding Muscles. Hoard of Muscles? He wore reptilian skull caps on each of his shoulders, and his black and orange hair had been shaved at the sides similar to Brandt's but then combed and bound back in a single thick layered braid. The long panels of his tabard reached past his knees. He looked a lot like Brandt. Perhaps a brother?

A heavy thud followed as Candy dodged and led Brandt to smash his face against one of the stones.

I winced out of instinct, cringing at the pain Brandt must have felt. He shook his head, slower now, then lunged again.

"Careful, Candy," the familiar man called out, scowling. "We just want to wear him down."

"I know what I'm doing," she called back. She circled Brandt with easy confidence, her lithe body swaying. "Come on then, Brandt. Let's get this wrapped up. We both know how this goes." She paused as she reached the point farthest from me, her crested brow lifting and her purple eyes seeming more human than before. She lifted her head in greeting even as Brandt hissed and coiled back to strike. "Good to see you again, Stella," she called out, her voice unfairly melodious even in serpent form. "I was afraid you weren't going to make it back. Can't wait to catch up with you." It seemed as if she was smiling.

"Always such a charmer," Elias chuckled. "It's good Brandt has someone he's that close to. Candy is one of a kind."

"Is she your girlfriend?" I asked, praying that that was why Elias praised her so profusely.

He laughed at this, shaking his head. "Nah, she'd never have eyes for someone like me. Brandt's the one who's got all her attention these days."

My upper lip curled instinctively as I strode toward Kine. Whoever Candy was to Brandt and whoever I was to him, it didn't matter at this point. I needed to focus on my wounded friend or family member or whoever Kine was to me.

"Kine, you need help." I crouched beside him. I still felt off balance, more agitated than elated. My throat no longer hurt, but my heart throbbed. So many thoughts and feelings warred within me. That amber liquid had sobered me up fast.

Kine shook his head. "I'm fine," he said, his voice strained and his face pale. He gripped my hand, though it seemed more to comfort me than help him. He gave me a weak wink before he released me and let his arm drop to his knee. "Don't worry about me, Bug. Sometimes you've got to know when to let go."

From the way he teased me, I knew he wanted me to laugh, but all I could manage was a small smile.

The man who looked similar to Brandt helped Kine to his feet. "You'll need some good rest. You're lucky he didn't kill you."

He paused as his gaze fell on me. "Damn. You really do look like Stella."

A few of the newly arrived warriors glanced back at me. Some raised their eyebrows. Others murmured back and forth. I frowned a little at this. "Well, I am a Stella," I said, folding my arms.

"Doesn't just look like Stella. She *is* Stella." Elias stood at rigid attention, his storm-blue eyes blazing.

The gruff man kept his arms akimbo, his tone stern as he looked me up and down, taking in every aspect of me. He clicked his tongue. "You remember me, then?"

I hesitated, then lifted my shoulders apologetically. "Your face is familiar, but I don't know your name."

"Hord."

"Arch General Hord," Elias added, his tone sharp. A clear note of disapproval rang in his words.

"Just Hord here. If it's really Stella, then we were all friends once," he responded, his gaze moving back to me.

A softness entered his burgundy eyes, a softness I hadn't expected. Or maybe it was sadness.

His breath hissed through his teeth as he sighed. "Looks like you. Sounds like you. Is it really you, though? And why would Brandt have attacked you and Kine? There were at least eight hours before the curse was to take hold again. How do we know this isn't some other manifestation of magic? An illusion preying upon our desire for Stella to return."

Kine stepped closer. "We don't have time for this," he said, hand still over his freshly healed side. The tunic and sash did not appear to be damaged either, and no more blood dripped through his fingers. Was that because he had been wounded in the serpent form? "Something is wrong with the magic. Maybe the curse is drawing out the magic once more. Maybe it's something else, but the curse took hold, and he was trying to kill her. This is Stella. Our Stella. Our queen."

Queen? My eyebrows flicked upward. Had he just said I was a queen?

Brandt struck another boulder with his snout, an angry roar following. I cringed and covered my mouth, my eyes starting to squeeze shut. That had to hurt! I couldn't look away—couldn't really focus on much else.

"We've got to get her out of here," Elias said firmly, standing as close to me as he could without touching me. "The destabilization of the magic puts Stella at risk any time she is near Brandt. It could happen again! And if the others find out that she's here... We just need to get her somewhere safe."

"The Master of Sight's sanctuary," Kine said with equal conviction. "We'll need her help. Stella doesn't have her memories back. She's only got impressions. Maybe it'll come back in time. Maybe that chasm she got stuck in messed with her head. We don't know, but Auntie Runa can help us."

"I need proof. Just because our magic is weakened doesn't mean other magic isn't strong or that it couldn't mask this," Hord said firmly. "This could be some elaborate ruse to undermine the king's authority. We could all be deceived."

"How can we prove it?" Elias demanded, stepping between us. His hand moved to his belt, but there was nothing there. Not even a sheath. "After all she has been through, you would put her in harm's way and demand proof?"

Kine placed his hand on my arm protectively, his eyes narrowing as well. He was looking stronger by the second. A low sigh followed. "Hord, I know you're doing your duty, but these are strange times. We have to get her to the Master of Sight. Would you be willing to take her word for it if she testifies that Stella is who we claim?"

Hord considered this, though his expression suggested he did not like the thought of letting us leave. "You and Elias are both still criminals for your actions," he said. "If you all return with us to the palace, we could send for the Master of Sight."

"We can't risk going back to Castle Serpentfire or any of the other locations," Elias said sharply. "One among the factions may decide to eliminate Stella just to see if it ends the curse. The one thing Brandt was right about is that we can't let Stella's return be known by any more than it already is, especially not when there are still so many important questions to answer."

As they continued debating, my gaze remained on the fight between Candy and Brandt. The arguing voices faded. My insides clenched. The way Candy and Brandt darted and battled was like a dance, one where he chased her and she responded with grace and poise.

Bile rose in the back of my throat. Yes, he'd tried to kill me. Yes, it had hurt. Yes, I was scared. But I didn't want to go. I didn't want to leave him here. Tears rose in the back of my eyes. I was supposed to be with him, and he had replaced me?

Was that the right word? Replaced?

That was what it felt like, even if something inside me warned that the word didn't exactly fit. Fear made that word appealing. It slipped into place so easily.

He was mine, and I was his. There was a word that wanted to form on the tip of my tongue, but I couldn't find it quite yet.

The way he had held me in those brief moments… The playfulness he had brought out in me… He'd gazed at me in the way I had always wished a man would. The thought of him looking at anyone else like that soured my stomach.

"Wait." Hord lifted his hand, the sharpness of his deep voice snapping my focus back to him. His eyes narrowed though the faintest hint of a smile curled at the edges of his broad mouth. "I know how to fix this. Magic can't fool some creatures, and there's one reason Brandt was out here tonight." He gestured toward the hill. "Buttercup."

Elias and Kine looked at one another. Their brows smoothed.

It sounded significant, but my heart tightened again. Buttercup? Who was Buttercup? Did Brandt have *another* possible girlfriend? First Candy, now Buttercup. Heat flared in my cheeks even as I tried to talk myself down from it. Jealousy wasn't a good look on anyone, and I didn't have any reason to feel or be jealous. What was wrong with me?

"Oh." Kine hesitated, then nodded. "That'll work. No magic or spell could fool that girl." He chuckled and gave me a reassuring pat on the arm.

"I don't want to leave," I said as firmly as I could. "I don't know what I am to him or what all is going on, but whoever it is, bring them here. I don't want to go. I...I belong with Brandt."

"Buttercup won't like seeing Brandt like this," Hord said. "No one does, and if you are who you seem to be, then we need to get you away from here to somewhere safe until we have a better solution. Don't worry. If you really are Stella, we'll have you back with your husband as fast as we safely can."

"My husband?"

Yes. Yes, that was who he was. No, more than that. He was my mate.

My chest tightened, my breath sealing in my throat for a heartbeat.

My mate.

Yes, that was the word I'd been searching for.

I mouthed the word, unable to even speak it aloud yet.

Elias nodded. "Yes, before your death, he was your husband."

My death? My eyes widened. Wait. I died?

"He could be her husband," Hord said.

"*Is* her husband," Kine corrected sharply. He gestured toward the hill Hord had indicated. "But if Buttercup's here, let's prove it, and then get Stella to safety. We really don't have time to waste."

I shook my head, protesting. "No, don't make me leave him. Please. I know I sound like a fool, but please, don't make me leave him!"

Some of the guards looked at us again. The raised eyebrows and whispers continued. Candy continued to lure and bait Brandt in their exhausting dance. His snout had bloodied and healed several times at this point.

Kine stepped closer to me, lowering his voice. His golden eyes were soft with concern. "Bug, trust me, please. This is for your own good as well as his. I promise that I'll explain everything I can. I believe in you and Brandt both. I support you both, and I swore to you then what I am swearing to you now—I'm going to help you two find a way to be together again."

Tears rose to my eyes as I ducked my head. I didn't even know what to feel in this moment. The twinge in my heart told me I'd trusted Kine before. He wasn't lying to me.

He gently took my hand as Elias kept his arm firmly around my shoulders, and we started to walk away. My feet were leaden. It took all my strength not to turn around and run back to Brandt. The distance made the siren's call of returning to him more and more potent despite the risk. Kine, Elias, and Hord continued to speak, but their voices jumbled in my ears. Nothing mattered right now. As much as I hated it, nothing mattered at all.

As we reached the top of the hill, I glanced back one more time. Brandt was still a monstrous black and red serpent. His jaws snapped at Candy's scales, his teeth slicing through the air, and all I wanted in that moment was for him to look at me and know me, even if that meant he would kill me.

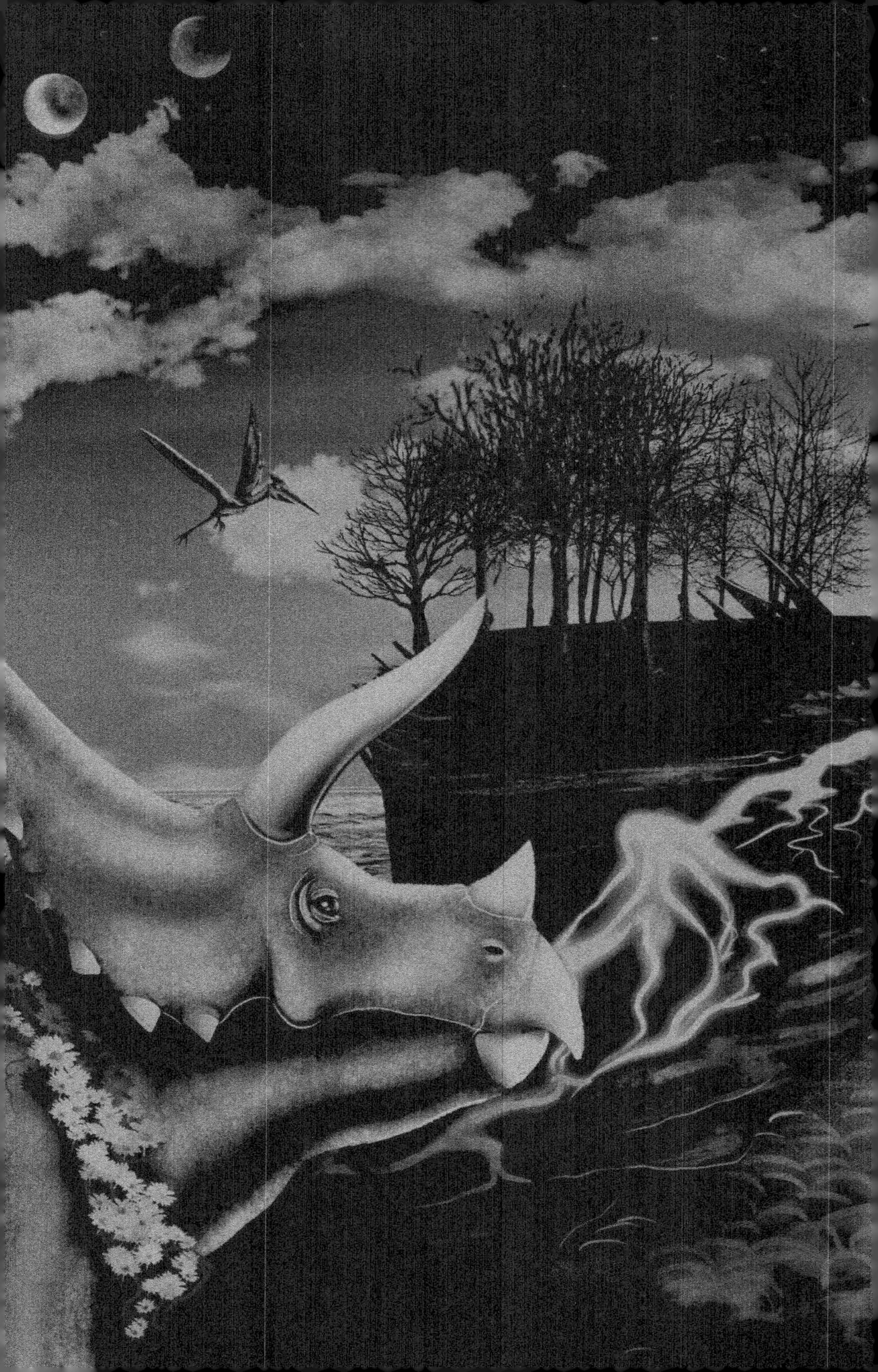

CHAPTER SIX: STELLA

Kine kept his grip on me firm as we continued over the crest of the hill. He then gave me a side hug. The smell of blueberries, charcoal, and lemongrass grew stronger. "It's all right."

It didn't feel all right. My whole being was numb, detached, as if I left part of myself behind with Brandt. A dull ache had already formed in my chest. It was hard to walk, even though we were now moving downhill over short grass, and the incline wasn't even all that steep.

And there was one small problem.

"So...I died?" I asked quietly.

Kine managed a faint smile. He brushed the hair out of my face. "Yeah, Bug. You and seven other royal women laid down their lives to save this world from a great threat. You were all reborn on Earth. When the veil was thin enough here and we knew the truth about where you were, we came to get you and bring you home."

Elias shook his head as Hord walked with us in silence. "It should have been sooner. It took too long. We should have found some other way."

Kine gave me another encouraging hug, his touch and warmth familial and surprisingly comforting. "It'll all make sense in time. You'll keep getting back your memories in bits and surges. I know it's probably shocking—"

"No, actually. I... Life never felt right for me. It was like I was always missing something."

His words settled over me, pressing against my consciousness. It wasn't nearly so hard to accept as I would have expected. I'd died here and been reincarnated on Earth where I had lived. Now I was back. Bizarre. And yet...with all I'd seen this night, I could believe it.

The hill continued down into another relatively flat valley. Oaks and maples were scattered about, most standing sentinel around the river until the forest that rose on the foothills around us. Dark-green bushes heavy with blue and red berries clustered in thick batches along the steeper riverbanks. The earth was softer down here in this valley, rich and dark, smelling more like warm black mulch than turned topsoil.

Hord glanced back at us. His steps slowed. "What went wrong exactly? Was it just the timing of the attack? Or was there more?"

The silver and teal moons cast enough light on the grass dotted with clumps of wildflowers that it was almost as bright as if we carried torches. His stride was heavy and firm, leaving behind deep prints on the soft springy grass.

"Don't know," Elias said flatly. He gave me a worried look, and several thin lines appeared on his brow. He moved with quiet purpose, a somberness clinging to him. "But it's been odd since we brought her back. Very odd. It worries me."

"Seems to me the magic in general has become even more unstable," Kine offered with a broad sweep of his arm. "Maybe it's just because of how much the Gola Resh and the Babadon stole before the curse's progress stopped, or maybe it's changed. I don't know, but I struggled to shift, and my ring was fully prepared. It isn't as if I would have been using it in the dungeon."

Hord grunted in agreement. His brow furrowed more.

"Curse? Gola Resh? Babadon?" All of it was so familiar. Infuriatingly familiar. I rubbed my hands over my temples. All the giddiness from before had faded, and everything crushed in on me. I had so many questions. Too many. "Brandt was talking about being cursed to kill me. I don't remember that happening. I don't remember...but it's familiar. What is it doing?"

"There are two curses at play," Kine started.

Hord held up a scarred hand, tilting his head. His square features had taken on a particularly grim cast. "Let's wait to tell her everything until we've confirmed she is who you say she is."

"What could we possibly tell her now that would help anyone? Even if she was just pretending to be Stella?" Elias demanded, his voice far sharper. His hand clenched into a fist, proving he was nearing the end of his patience.

Hord gave him a studied glare. "I do not know. This is far beyond my area of expertise, but until we confirm her identity, we should all be careful. You both should have offered a better solution before you brought her here."

"We would have come up with another one if we had had a chance," Elias snapped, "but as soon as she got here, he had us thrown in the dungeon for—"

"Stop. Just stop. All right?" Kine shook his head, releasing a tight breath. "None of that matters right now. We need to prove Stella is who we say, and Buttercup can do that."

"You were thrown in the dungeon?" My eyes widened. "Was it because I ran in that dark place?" My heart sank. Everything felt so wrong now, worse than it ever had on Earth. Maybe it was just because it had come so close to being right, and now... now, that had been torn away.

"Yes. No. Not exactly." Kine stumbled over the words. He raked his hand through his loose azure hair and shook his head.

"I mean, there were concerns after you disappeared in the Shadow Hall."

Elias gave him a dark look, his expression tightening as if he disagreed.

"The king had his reasons for those decisions," Hord said firmly, "and we will not speak about what happened further, not until we know what we are dealing with. It is as simple as that."

"How far do we have to go?" Elias asked, clipping his words.

"Brandt brings Buttercup out here to her favorite meadow at least once a week," Hord explained.

Elias grunted at this.

Who exactly was Buttercup?

My head hurt. It was becoming so hard to think, and that gnawing need to return to Brandt somehow intensified. It swelled within me like a thirst.

"It's going to be all right, Bug," Kine said. "Seeing Buttercup again will do you a world of good. I bet you'll remember her in a flash."

"She isn't… She isn't a person, is she?"

All three of them laughed at this, their voices booming in the relative stillness of the night. The mood lightened at once.

"Not at all, and I trust her senses better than mine," Hord said. A hint of a smile returned to his face. He then stopped as the hill leveled out.

A flicker of excitement rose inside me as I looked in the direction he'd indicated. A large oak with branches wide enough to hold a whole house stood near the base of the hill beside a river. It wasn't just grass down here. The short grass turned into dense dark-green clover with little flowers, but instead of the delicate white globes on Earth, these were pink blossoms that resembled rosebuds. Several had opened up, revealing delicate silky petals, each one half the size of a tea rose.

A deep, plaintive bellow sounded from the other side of a

tree, rising above the river's burbling. A man in a uniform similar to the warriors who had come to our aid stepped out and away from the enormous trunk, holding a golden glowing lasso. He pulled it taut and called out something in a gruff voice.

That bellow was deeper than I remembered but so familiar my skin prickled in response. "Buttercup?"

Some of the darkness receded within me. My steps quickened.

Another low, grunting bellow followed.

"Koigrim," Hord called out. "Is Buttercup secured?"

The warrior stepped out into the moonlight. His green-and-black hair had been woven into a single-layered braid, though the sides of his head were not shaved. He tightened his grip on the glowing gold rope. "She's having a rough night, Arch General. Something's got her all on edge. Like she smells something." He staggered to the side as another heavy bellow came from behind the tree. "Eid, hold her steady."

I quickened my pace, glancing about. The grass sprang back under my feet, erasing my footsteps as I hurried forward.

Koigrim frowned a bit. "Who's that with you?"

"Did anything strange happen about two hours ago?" Hord asked.

"There was a surge of energy. Buttercup got real agitated. The king left. Told us to keep her safe, and if he didn't return by midnight to take her back to the stables before the predators came out."

Koigrim tilted his head as I approached. His expression did not change when he saw me. There was no spark of familiarity for me either, but the huffing snort that came on the other side of the tree, that sound I knew!

"Careful," Hord hurried in front, putting his arm out to stop me from running. Kine and Elias were close behind. "She's a big girl, and when she gets excited, it's hard to make her settle." He gave the guard a nod of assent to let me pass.

I nodded, my breath catching in my throat. "Buttercup," I called out.

Another huff followed, and a large crested head with three horns poked out from behind the tree.

My eyes widened. Buttercup was a triceratops.

Of course she was!

A gorgeous yellow-orange triceratops with dark-brown splotches and speckles on her back.

Oh. Be still my heart.

Koigrim held the ropes taut and moved out to the side a little more, whistling low and then calling out, "Easy, Eid. Give her a little leeway."

The energy enchanting the ropes hummed softly, releasing a warm scent similar to burning hay and smoldering incense.

Buttercup stared at me as I walked closer. She stopped lowing and struggling, her manner growing more alert. Slowly, she blinked.

Never in all my life had I seen a triceratops as perfect as her. Her large frill sported two great horns that glimmered in the moonlight like cloudy smoky quartz. The third one on her snout was a little darker, closer in shade to the beak of her mouth but still a creamy grey color. Her gorgeous eyes were as big as tea saucers and the most beautiful shade of mahogany I'd ever seen.

All had gone silent.

Breath catching in my throat, I held my hand out so she could sniff it. "Hi, Buttercup," I whispered, smiling so much my face hurt.

Unlike the triceratops I met at the river, she didn't respond with calm curiosity or casual disinterest. Her nostrils flared, and then she fell back into an almost crouching position, dropped her head, and let loose a loud series of honking bellows. She pranced in place and shook her head, the enchanted ropes likely the only thing keeping her from charging me right then and trampling me in excitement. Moonlight danced over her horns.

"Yes, baby girl! It's me!" All the pain and even some of the heartache from my encounter with Brandt vanished. I held my hand out again and slipped closer.

"Easy there. Easy," the deeper-voiced attendant on the other side called out.

Koigrim immediately stepped out farther to the left and pulled the magic rope as the triceratops tilted her head. "She gets a touch excited, and you don't want this one trying to jump on you."

I'd said there was no way Brandt could hurt me, and he'd nearly killed me. I would be a little more careful with Buttercup. Still, I couldn't stop myself from smiling as I edged even closer and pressed my hand to her snout. "I missed you, Buttercup."

Buttercup let out another honking bellow and then thrust her snout harder against my hand. Her heavy steps shook the ground as she wriggled with happiness.

"Calm down, baby girl," I said, stepping out to the side and coming in a little closer. "Just calm down."

Another happy honk followed, longer this time.

I gently scratched from her jaw down her neck. Her scales were so smooth and warm. Happy tears filled my eyes. "That's a good girl."

This was my triceratops. I actually had a triceratops! I was her guardian and caretaker. The knowledge itself more than actual memories flowed into me, and the sensations made my heart fill with such joy and excitement I could scarcely bear it. Unlike Brandt, whose presence had brought me a myriad of emotions, Buttercup just filled me with joy.

Kine chuckled, then sighed, his shoulders squared. "You know, maybe we should have sent Buttercup to bring you back here." Grinning, he scratched her scaly side.

Elias laughed at this and set his hands on his hips. "Might have been hard to pass her off as a Halloween costume, though."

I laughed as I hugged her head. She'd grown up while I was gone. Memory reminded me that she had been a fair bit smaller when I last saw her. "All you had to do was tell me that you could take me somewhere with dinosaurs, and I would have bolted through that portal." I rubbed my nose against the top of her beak and giggled. "Did you grow up, baby girl? You got so big!"

Buttercup stomped. She nudged me again, surprisingly gentle for a creature her size, though she still nearly toppled me with that head nudge. When I squeezed my eyes shut, I remembered hugging her and my arms fitting all the way around her neck. Not now though. Baby girl was bigger than a car!

"Satisfied?" Kine asked Hord.

Hord nodded, hands still braced on his braided belt. "Don't know that it'll be enough for the advisers, but it's good enough for me." He dipped his head in my direction. "Good to see you again, Stella. Or do you prefer I call you Your Majesty?"

Your Majesty? Right...

I blinked, shaking my head. Brandt was a king. He was my husband. I was a queen, if that Candy hadn't displaced me. Another pang of jealousy twisted in my gut. Still, being called queen didn't settle well with me. It felt off.

"Just call me Stella." That name sounded right. It always had.

"Stella then." He grinned, but his smile faded as he glanced up at the moons. "I assume Brandt would want you safe in the palace, especially after what's been happening with the factions."

"I don't know anything about factions, and I have lots of questions," I said, still stroking Buttercup's snout. "But Brandt wanted me to go to Auntie Runa's. He said that before he changed."

His name was strange on my tongue.

"Yes, it's the safest place for her," Kine said, and Elias nodded.

"Please. We must keep her return as quiet as possible. We don't need more assassination attempts. The Master of Sight was Stella's mentor instructor for years before she became queen. She will make sure she's safe, and we need her counsel."

"Very well, but hurry. It sounds like it's taking longer to kuvaste Brandt into a quieter place. His energy is even more elevated than the first time the curse manifested." Hord sighed as an especially loud bellow tore through the air, and Buttercup shook her head. "If we don't find a way to end this curse..." He shrugged as if not wanting to finish that statement. "Well, if we don't get answers soon, it won't make a difference. We'll all be dead."

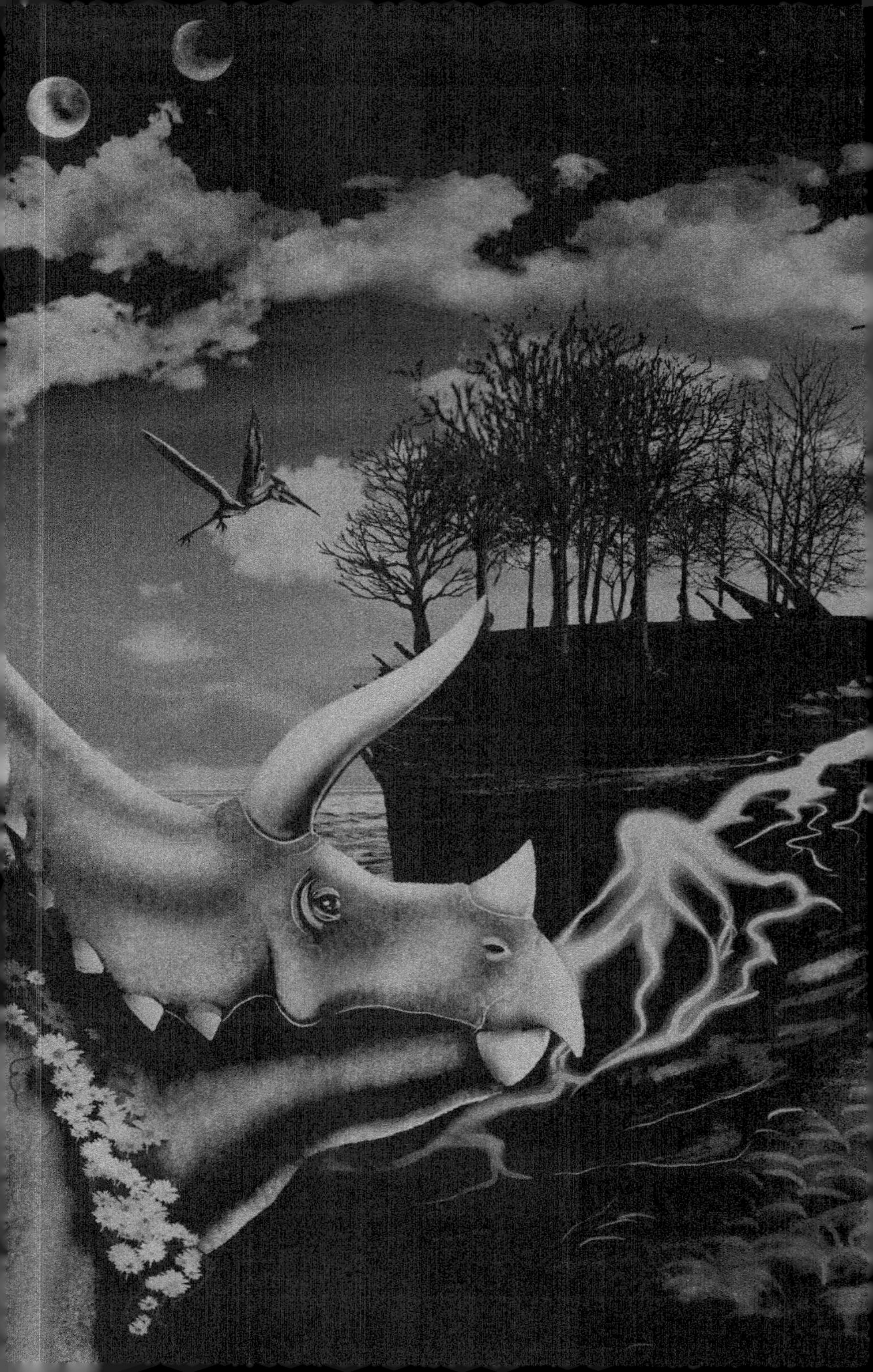

CHAPTER SEVEN: STELLA

My head was swimming with all the information and all the changes. Elias pressed the flask into my hand and encouraged me to take another sip. The liquid was still burning and harsh, but it was doing something. Each time I swallowed, my head cleared a little more.

The guards unfastened the ropes on Buttercup at Hord's command. He and Kine spoke quietly.

Elias moved along beside me. "You're doing incredibly," he murmured.

"Thanks. I...I don't quite know what I'm feeling," I admitted. As I fidgeted with the necklace charm, I caught a hint of cherries once more, but it was smothered by Elias's scent.

"Once we get you to Auntie Runa's, I'm sure you'll get all your questions answered. Or at least most of them. But I know I'll feel better once you're somewhere safe."

Being safe and having answers sounded good, especially if those led to my being able to be with Brandt again.

Within the next fifteen minutes, the plan had been made. Kine and Hord had come to some sort of agreement, and Hord summoned two parasaurs with quarterstaffs fastened to their sides. They had similar speckling patterns on their backs. The one Elias scratched was juniper green with a blue crest, while Kine's had a yellow crest and chestnut-brown hide.

"If the Master of Sight requires anything to resolve this matter, inform us," Hord said. "Even with the magic disrupted, the water mirrors in her sanctuary should work for a time. At worst, they'll be delayed."

"Need any help?" Elias asked, watching me with a raised eyebrow as I stood next to my girl. He started to shift forward as if preparing to lift me up.

"No." I grabbed onto some of the stony growths on Buttercup's side and easily climbed up on her back almost without thinking. Muscle memory must have transferred because I found myself just doing it as if I had done it a thousand times before. I probably had. It felt good. Natural. Easy.

Kine chuckled from the back of his parasaur. He looked like I'd done exactly what he expected, as if it was the most natural thing in the world for me to recall.

"Looks like your memory is coming back." Elias stared up at me, admiration shining in his dark eyes.

"Some things feel familiar." My cheeks flared with color, but I was pleased nonetheless.

Every aspect of riding a triceratops felt habitual to me. The leggings I wore were surprisingly appropriate and comfortable, just coarse enough to make it easier for me to grip Buttercup, and my dingy grey sneakers with the tattered laces weren't so bad, even if part of me wanted to kick them off and run barefoot over the soft grass.

Buttercup's warm, scaly hide shifted beneath me. She shook her head and then gave another honking call. My hands settled into place on her crest as if this were something I did every day.

"Now that we're heading out, it's vital that you do exactly as you're told. These lands are dangerous, especially after midnight. The predators come to hunt on nights like this as the prey gets weary after overfeeding. If we get separated, we're headed to Auntie Runa's," Kine said. He clicked his tongue. The parasaur lowered itself so Kine could place his hand on my shoulder. He directed my gaze in what seemed like a generally northern direction and indicated a forked hill and a trio of rock columns near a blue-grey rock formation that resembled a sea turtle. "That's where you want to go. If the river is too fast and broad to cross, just keep heading south. It narrows eventually, but be careful of the ridge. There are some points where you could get trapped pretty easily. Other than that, aim for those pillars. It's decently easy to get to."

Well, hopefully we wouldn't be separated for me to figure that out.

For a time, we simply rode. It was surreal. The coolness of the night surrounded me. Bright moonlight made it easy to see. Kine led the way, a few paces in front.

Elias rode alongside me. His parasaur put him a little higher than me, but not by much. "Do you need more medicine for your throat?" he asked. "Or anything else? You were trapped in that chasm in the Shadow Hall for a while."

"I'm only a little sore, but that wasn't really from the chasm." My voice thickened. Stroking the top of Buttercup's crest, I drew in a deep breath. "I felt like I had fallen into darkness. Then this slimy thing told me a man was going to kill me. I'm guessing she meant Brandt."

Elias stiffened. "What slimy thing?"

"I don't know. It was a woman's voice, and she mentioned a curse and how Brandt was going to come kill me when it was time, though she didn't say his name or hers. It was rather terrifying."

"You're sure about that?" Kine swung around on his parasaur, blocking my path. His brow furrowed. "What was the voice like?"

"Cold. Kind of metallic. Feminine. It was familiar, but I couldn't place it. She had orange-green eyes."

Kine's jaw clenched. "I knew she wasn't dead!"

Elias drew his hand over his mouth. The worry lines returned to his brow. "No, she's dead. We saw her die."

"Who's dead?" I looked between them.

"It's the Gola Resh," Kine said tightly. "I'm certain of it. She escaped somehow."

Elias gave a heavy sigh, his shoulders dropping. "How did she escape then? If she survived that, that changes everything. It means... No. No! She's dead. She has to be. If she isn't dead, that means we don't actually know how to kill her."

Kine shook his head, no longer listening. His loose blue curls bounced with the movement, contrasting sharply with the hardness of his eyes. "That may even be why you were trapped, Bug, and that may mean..."

My eyes widened. They'd mentioned the name before. "May mean what? Who's the Gola Resh? What is she?"

"The Gola Resh is one of the primary beings responsible for the curse binding Brandt to kill you as well as the curse draining our continent to death." Kine's words had taken on a sharper edge. "She was supposed to be dead. But if she isn't... Tell me what happened. Every detail."

I told them both everything I could remember. It didn't seem like much.

"That sounds like the Gola Resh," Kine said at last. "Somehow she survived."

Elias prodded me once more with the flask. "You still need more," he said, his manner almost apologetic. "Especially after she trapped you. It probably made you feel even drunker than you were. You poor thing! No wonder you were so off."

I had certainly felt...off. Even now, my head swam a bit, and my pulse beat steady as a migraine. Taking the flask, I managed a couple more sips. It burned all the way down, but it cleared my thoughts even more and left me aware of an uncomfortable tension.

"We're fortunate the Gola Resh did not decide to destroy you. Or perhaps it's part of the curse," Kine murmured. He scratched his head. "She never does anything good, but she usually has some sort of reasoning for what she does. So if she didn't kill you, that means she has something else up her sleeve. But we've got time. We can figure it out. We'll find a way to destroy her."

"I still can't believe the Gola Resh is back, but it does make sense. Magic has been messed up for a while, and lately it's gotten worse. It's distorted. Not just here, but everywhere." Concern bit Elias's features.

I frowned, mulling this over as I took another burning sip of the salty liquid.

Even as my thoughts cleared, some of the knowledge made no sense. One I couldn't precisely explain. The yellow had been wrong, the yellow light of the charm. It was not timing out the way that it should have, and everything was off balance now, even my mood. I wanted to laugh, cry, sleep, run, and hide all at once. What I needed was information and clarity.

"And what happened after I disappeared? From your perspective?" I asked.

"We got in a great deal of royal trouble." Elias gave a tight smile, his gaze lifting to mine.

Kine cut him off. "It was understandable. As far as anyone knew, we had lost you. We didn't bring you through, but we knew you weren't dead. I'm sure you can imagine how that would cause a great deal of distress for everyone who loves you. There were consequences for that, but it will all be resolved. In the end, we all want the same thing."

"And what's that?" I asked, wanting to make sure that I did, in fact, want the same thing. Even though I trusted Kine almost implicitly, I wasn't just going to assume we agreed.

Kine's smile went crooked. "To end the curses, restore our land, and all live quite happily ever after."

"Is that... Is that the queen?"

A small group of robed people stood on the lip of a low hill, looking down. How had I missed them? Had they been there this whole time? Their surprised murmurs rippled out.

The queen? I looked around with surprise, startled at the calls. Who were they talking to?

Wait. Me. Yes, that's right. I was the queen. I was once a queen. Was I still a queen? Did I just pick that up again after being gone for years? How did that even work? There was so much to absorb. And I had been dead too. Apparently. I pinched the bridge of my nose.

"Stay here and be calm. Don't confirm anything," Kine whispered, his eyes narrowed. He clicked his tongue and urged his parasaur forward. It didn't even hesitate before it bolted up the hill, dark-clawed forearms tucked against its sides.

"That doesn't sound good," I said.

"Just act natural," Elias responded, scratching his parasaur's shoulder. "All they need to be told is that we're travelers. Kine will find some reason to explain why he is approaching them alone rather than all of us going to talk with them. He's very good at that, but perhaps you should find something to occupy your attention, so it isn't so apparent."

I stroked the charm on my necklace, appreciating the smooth texture of the warm stone and the smooth metal along its back. My nerves prickled. Look casual, basically. Unfortunately, that wasn't one of my strengths.

Noticing some berries similar to black raspberries, I slid down. A wave of fear rushed through me as I realized I was falling, but muscle memory brought me into a soft fall position so it didn't hurt. It was a little unnerving to feel instincts taking over like that.

"You two have had to deal with a lot of this?" I ask. It felt odd to think of them like a rescue duo.

Elias shrugged, chuckling a little. "Only when it comes to getting you back. Kine doesn't want me to say anything, but..." His gaze softened as he looked at me. Then he pressed his lips into a tight line and forced a smile. "It's been hard, you being gone, Stella. I swear to you now what I swore to you then—I will not let any harm come to you. I would die to save you."

"I don't want you to die," I said, ducking my head. That sort of declaration made me uncomfortable.

"Thanks." Elias chuckled a little. "But I vowed it long ago. You don't have to like it, but I wanted you to know. Whatever it takes, I will protect you."

Those words struck me hard, but what could I say?

I plucked a handful of the berries and brought them to Buttercup. She tried to scoop them up with her tongue and slimed my hand.

"Oh...oh..." I grimaced.

"Careful. She won't bite your hand on purpose, but she might take it by accident, especially if you offer her grapefruit. And don't ever come between her and a honeydew or watermelon." Elias leaned his forearms against the parasaur's neck.

I wiped my hand clean on my leggings, narrowing my eyes at her. "I didn't think that through." Instincts weren't filling in all the gaps.

My gaze drifted over Elias. He was another point where my instincts and memories offered nothing. I didn't feel anything at all when I looked at him. Nothing good. Nothing bad. He might as well have been a stranger, but the dedication in his voice and the sincerity with which he spoke to me... Shame flared within me. I didn't deserve that kind of devotion.

Biting the inside of my lip, I stared down at the tufts of fragrant grass. "Do you think my return is what disrupted the magic?"

"Not alone. It was just something that happened at the same time everything else started going insane." His shoulder twitched. The lines in his brow deepened as he continued to watch Kine. "It fits, I suppose."

"So my return has caused a lot of problems?"

"Not in a bad way." His eyes widened as if he realized he'd suggested something other than what he meant. "Just in a way that is noticeable to anyone who knows of you."

"Of me specifically?" My brow lifted. That was rather hard to believe. "Does everyone have such a distinct feel?"

He offered a faint chuckle and shifted on the parasaur's neck. His eyes narrowed as he continued to watch Kine and the strangers. "Well, it's not so much that you have a distinct feel to everyone. It's just, well, word leaked out that you were coming back. Then it leaked again that you had vanished. And tonight when you fell through the rest of that passage, everyone who is sensitive to it could feel the pulse of Kropelki." He paused. "You're Kropelkian, by the way. Not sure if you remember that."

I shook my head.

"Sepeazia is two nations united in one kingdom. Kropelki and Ognisko. Some people could feel the stirrings of Kropelkian magic returning through you."

"How long was I gone?"

"Since we tried to bring you back? You were gone weeks in the Shadow Hall." Elias sighed. "Don't even ask me how it's possible. It just is."

"And they came to find me?" I jerked my head toward the people who had appeared on the hill.

"My guess is those are just travelers who happened upon us." His brow furrowed a little more. "I don't know, though. Seems to be taking Kine longer than usual. We don't want to raise suspicions if we can avoid it, but we can't just keep hanging around here." He sniffed the air and glanced around. "It feels off. Do you feel it? Do you sense anything?"

Drawing in a deep breath, I tried to analyze the layers. Fresh river water. Vanilla cedar cologne. Tart, smashed berries. Green crushed leaves. Animal droppings. Fresh hay. A trace of cherries. And something metallic. Something oddly sweet. Sickeningly sweet. Just a trace.

A sharp sensation gripped me.

A warning.

Everything slowed. A pressure filled my chest.

I stepped to the left, crouching down. Something cold slashed toward my cheek as I moved. At the same time, that sickening sweet odor strengthened as a chilling shriek sliced through the air. Buttercup bellowed in response.

Elias's eyes widened, exposing the whites all the way around. He seized the quarterstaff from the parasaur's side and spun it around. Blue-white energy crackled along it.

My body twisted, and I narrowly avoided the sweet-scented blade. The attacker's momentum carried him through, leading him to fall as I lunged to the side. Catching myself on the chunk of granite, I sprang up, spun around, and faced them with the boulder between them and me.

Two masked warriors stood behind me, flanked by five grey and black deinonychuses approximately a dozen feet away, waiting as if for the next command. The grey and black reptiles had long curved claws and jaws filled with sharp teeth.

"Surrender," the farthest attacker hissed. "Surrender or be torn to shreds."

Elias brought his staff down on one of the assassin's heads as his parasaur shot between the assassins and me. He slammed his foot down. Yellow-white energy like lightning arced from his hands.

"Run, Stella. Go!" He brought his staff down once more.

The way he barked that order made me realize I had to obey. I scrambled onto Buttercup's shoulders. As one of the assassins tried to grab me, Buttercup body-blocked him and bellowed.

"Come on, girl!" I cried out, climbing high and wedging myself down behind her crest. My fingers knotted around the knobs on her crest.

Buttercup thundered forward. Out of the corner of my eye, I glimpsed Elias continuing to fight the assassins. He struck another black-garbed man between the shoulders and sent him down.

A third darted up from the grass, blade flashing in the moonlight. He whistled several sharp notes and pointed in my direction.

The deinonychuses' attention snapped toward Buttercup and me.

"Kill both," the assassin commanded.

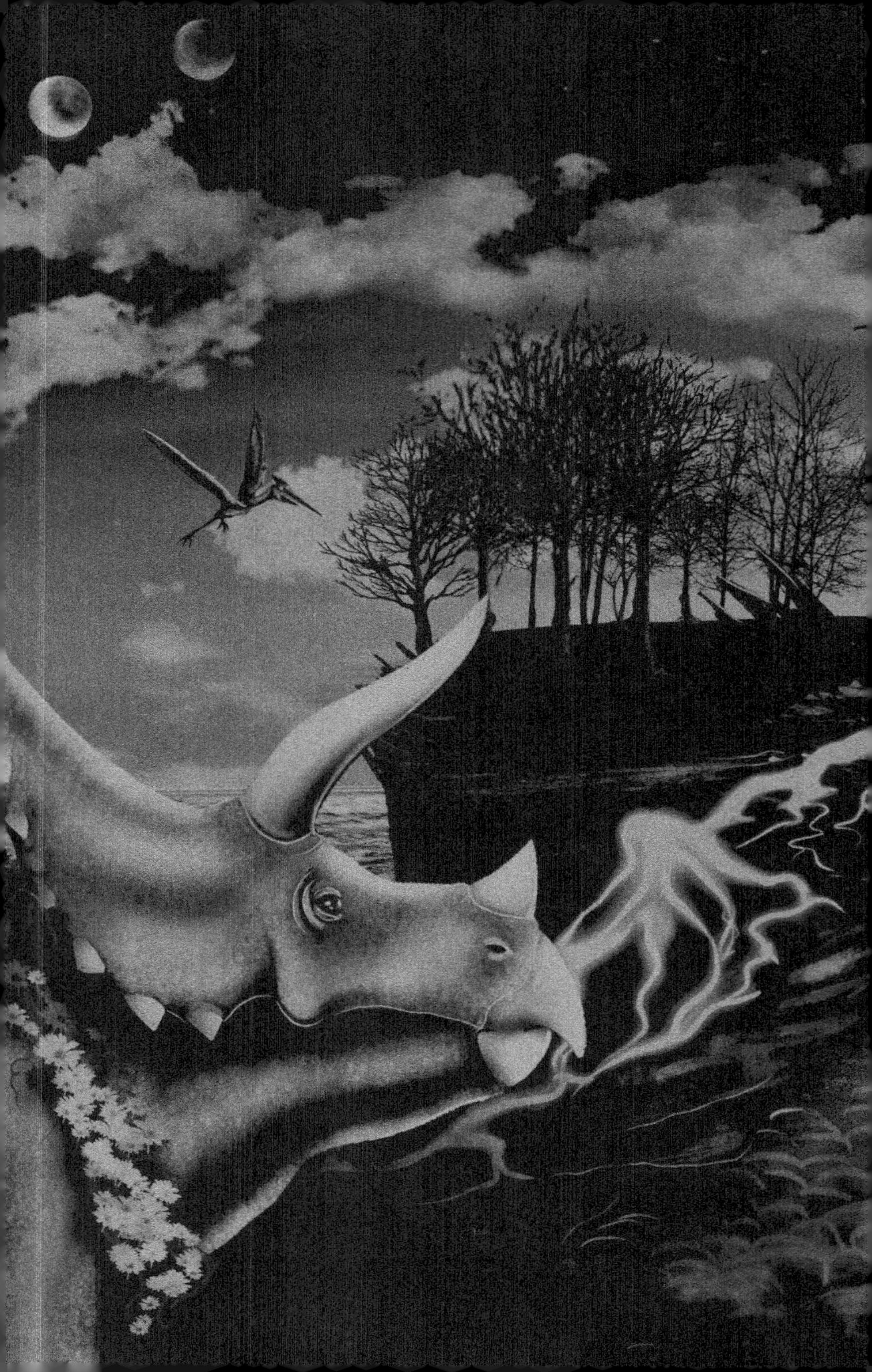

CHAPTER EIGHT: STELLA

"*R*un, Stella!" Elias shouted again. "I'll hold them off!" My jaw clenched tight. I didn't want to abandon him, but when I glanced back, preparing to argue, I saw the deinonychuses. They were racing after us, heads low and in perfect alignment with their spines. Their muscled hind legs allowed them to race forward at a terrifying speed, the large center claws spearing the soil. Claws and jaws like that would let them tear through Buttercup as easily as cream cheese.

Kine appeared to still be engaged with the travelers some distance away. His head snapped up at the sharp cries of the fight as Elias fought the assassins with his staff and parasaur.

It felt even more like a trap than before, and there was nothing to do but run.

My heart hammered against my ribs, my lungs tight as Buttercup's powerful legs carried us away and tried to put distance between us and the deinonychuses. Her thunderous footsteps pounded the earth. Clouds of dust rose with each footfall. My legs gripped her tight, holding me in place as I steadied myself on her crest.

Faster.

Faster!

The wind whipped my hair back from my face, and the sounds of the clashing metal, cracking wood, grunting attacks, and angry parasaurs' calls faded. It all smelled of fresh night air and green crushed leaves now.

At last I dared a look over my shoulder. The deinonychuses were steadily gaining on us, their lean frames built for speed.

The nearest one released a terrifying, ululating shriek.

Terror chattered down my spine as I leaned lower on Buttercup's crest. "Come on, baby!"

My girl continued to gallop at full strength, crashing through bushes and crushing the delicate flowers and clovers underfoot, cutting close to outcropping rocks so the deinonychuses had to fall back.

The deinonychuses remained relentless in their pursuit. They now called out, back and forth, shrill, piercing voices echoing in the air around us.

We broke through a thick copse of berry bushes into a wide-open field. Briars whipped against my legs. The thin thorns raked over Buttercup's scales harmlessly but tore at my leggings and skin like needles. Yelping, I curled forward. "Come on, girl!"

She huffed, her sides rising and falling with rapid breaths.

We still had what felt like miles to go before we reached Auntie Runa's, the forked hill and spires not seeming any closer than they had been.

I glanced back; my stomach dropped. Why was I even surprised?

The deinonychuses were right on our heels, not even breaking a little. That narrowest lead we'd had when we'd started was fading away with each breath.

Outrunning them was a losing battle. Triceratops could run at around twenty to twenty-five miles per hour, assuming what I'd read was accurate. Deinonychuses could run at the same pace. Now it was about endurance, and these deinonychuses didn't seem to be slowing.

No. They were herding us.

But where?

Ahead of us, the land dipped. We were heading toward a large segment of stone. The terrain up ahead grew rockier, and it looked like it moved into a bowl-like valley with stones all around, forming a wall.

A sharp awareness sliced through me, almost as painful as a real blade, rising up through my gut and flaring through my chest with a powerful weight. I tapped my hand against Buttercup's shoulder and directed her to the other side. Her tail flicked and nearly clipped one of the deinonychuses.

They immediately barked and snarled. The ones on our right quickened their pace, snapping at her side and tail. They didn't like that, hmmm? Well, I didn't like the fact I had no weapons and we were still thundering into the night.

Another glance over my shoulder revealed no trace of Elias or Kine behind us. All I could do was ride. My jaws itched and ached, my arms tightening. It was like I was missing something.

The nearest beast snapped its jaws inches from Buttercup's flank, making her bellow.

"Get away!" I shouted, waving my arm at them. The urge to bite and snap my jaws back flashed through me.

What was that?

The closest two surged in and snapped their jaws at the air like traps, dagger-like teeth clicking loud. The ones on the left started veering away while the two on the right moved in closer. They were trying to herd us toward that rock wall at the base, a jagged line of unyielding stone that would easily trap us and let the deinonychuses split up, with half pinning us to the wall and half getting the high ground.

Up ahead, there was a larger, stony outcropping. Beyond that was the river. The outcropping was large and layered, sandy and earth-covered, easily as long as a house. The river behind it was a dark ribbon, snaking across the landscape as the call of the rushing waters grew louder.

Dust and grit filled my mouth, but I hunched down and urged Buttercup away from the easier-to-reach basin and toward the uneven outcropping. If we got close enough, the deinonychuses on our right would have to fall back or get crushed. So long as they didn't get ahead of us, we wouldn't be snared.

Buttercup's trunk-like legs propelled us closer, but the deinonychuses were unrelenting. They snapped and hissed, still trying to force us toward the stone basin. I glanced back again, hoping against hope to see Elias or Kine, but there was no sign of them.

Gritting my teeth, I held on tighter. Buttercup continued at her swift but heavy pace. Her sides heaved in and out with effort. We'd been running too long.

The ground sloped down toward that basin by the rock wall. As she started to veer toward it again, I pressed on her side. That deep flare through my chest intensified, clarifying into an impulse. "No, Buttercup! Not down there."

I clenched my knees into her sides and tugged on her crest, pulling her to the right at a much sharper angle.

With a startled bark, she almost stepped on one of the deinonychuses, but there, just where her feet would have been seconds ago, the ground collapsed inward along a broad track as if a giant mole had been digging. One deinonychus fell in, disappearing from sight. Another staggered and flipped. A third circled back, barking and shrieking as it nudged its fallen comrades.

"Yeah!" Oh! That was amazing. Leaning against her crest, I urged her forward and closer to the outcropping and away from the basin.

Light glinted at the top of the rocky stone wall. Someone

was up there. Probably the other members of the assassin team. Whoever killed me would need proof of the deed's completion.

My heart sank. The two other deinonychuses still raced along behind us.

All at once, Buttercup halted.

The deinonychuses peeled back, chattering and shrieking.

Cold shuddered through my veins.

Buttercup turned from the river and the forked hill and the natural tower Kine had told me to get to. She shook her head and huffed, halting by a granite rock formation. A short distance away were clusters of termite mounds looking like ancient altars and icons. The moonlight was dimmer now, lengthening the haunting shadows.

"What's wrong, baby girl?" I leaned against her crest and rose up on my knees. Even though I asked, I felt it too. What was *it*, though?

Something was wrong.

The air had changed.

All was still.

The sensation wasn't as strong as the moment before the assassins or the mole tunnel. But it was there. Farther away though.

The silence deepened.

A predator of some sort. Dangerous even to the deinonychuses.

My ears strained as the wind picked up, combing through my hair as if shifted to the west.

The forest to my left and the tall grasses beyond the river... We needed to avoid those. And we still had to get to Auntie Runa's.

Leaning forward, I stroked her crest. "Come on, Buttercup. We'll find another way. Let's take it slow."

I nudged her farther to the right, avoiding the flatter portion near the river. The trees dipped closer there, branches heavy and low. The land leading down into the river sloped flat and muddy, as if something large came up and thrashed about. No triceratops, hippopotamus, or other large creature was apparent. The waters themselves ran dark and still.

"We're not going into the river here," I reassured her, rubbing her side. My own words fell flat, so soft it was as if they had not been spoken aloud at all.

The silver and teal moonlight took on a far more sinister cast, the lack of insect and birdsong now devastating. Not even the earthquake had silenced that much of the nighttime noise, and this...this silence was one of the most haunting things I had ever heard. Every lap of the river filled my ears. The entirety of this valley breathed malice and danger now.

Buttercup's sides heaved, rising and falling from our desperate race.

I looked back at the jagged line of rocks now a fair distance away. Something dark skulked along the top. The jagged stone wall leered at me like a broken mouth. Not friends. I knew that as clearly as I knew danger lay within the river.

Something was watching us. I could feel it.

Still no sign of Elias and Kine. Were they all right? Had they escaped?

Buttercup snorted.

"Yeah, let's go." I guided Buttercup away from the river but not toward that jagged rock line. There was a narrow path between the two. Somehow we'd find a safer way. Some of this area felt familiar, like a remnant of memories, nothing specific. They fluttered at the edges of my mind.

Buttercup's steps were slow, deliberate. She huffed again.

"I don't suppose I could just tell you to go to Auntie Runa's," I murmured. She was smart enough that maybe she would understand.

Another snort followed along with a toss of her head.

The moonlight dimmed further still. The shadows stretched across the grasslands and the forest beyond them.

A low, guttural growl grated over me.

I froze.

It wasn't coming from the river but across from it.

Amber eyes glinted in the darkness.

Buttercup halted.

Those eyes…they were over fourteen feet off the ground.

Reptilian.

Another growl followed as the branches parted and a large green snout appeared. The leaves separated and shifted as the enormous creature emerged.

My mouth fell open.

A tyrannosaur?

Why was I shocked? What else could it be!

Did holding perfectly still keep the tyrannosaur from seeing us?

Buttercup tossed her head and snorted, her right foreleg striking the ground.

Ihlkit!

The tyrannosaur roared. The branches around it cracked and swayed violently as it strode forward with heavy steps. It bared its massive teeth.

Buttercup's eyes rolled up to look at me as if asking, "What're you going to do about this?"

She was scared. More scared than she was of the deinonychuses and the assassins.

Rage swelled in me. No one scared my baby.

Flinging myself off her crest, I landed on the soft grass between Buttercup and the river with the tyrannosaur on the other side. Spreading my arms, I roared back.

The tyrannosaur straightened. Its jaws snapped shut as it cocked its head, its amber eyes narrowing as it studied me.

I lifted my chin, swallowing hard. My body hadn't changed. I wasn't—wasn't bigger. I was supposed to be a lot bigger. And have teeth. And venom. My mouth, though itching, was decidedly...human right now.

Yup.

I pressed my hand over my lips.

Very, very human.

Buttercup huffed again and stomped her foot on the ground. Dust kicked up beneath her heavy foot. The side eye that girl was giving me was next level. But how could I blame her?

Obviously both of us had thought I could do something, and clearly I wasn't doing it.

The tyrannosaur tilted its head again. Then its eyes narrowed, and it roared, stalking down closer to the river's edge.

Spinning around, I ran back to Buttercup and scaled her side.

"Go!" I half expected her to take off before I was safely positioned, but she didn't even flinch until I settled back. Not even when the tyrannosaur bellowed again and started forward.

Then she lunged diagonally from the river.

Another bellowing roar tore through the air, the ground shaking beneath its feet. It reached the river and stalked through, sending out crashing surges through the muddy waters.

Something large—something below the water's surface—snapped its angular jaws at the tyrannosaur's hindquarters, more a warning than a threat, like the tyrannosaur had gotten too close for comfort. The tyrannosaur only snarled at it and kept moving through the river.

The ground shook beneath it as water sprayed in all directions. Whatever creature lurked in those muddy shallows wanted nothing to do with it.

My palms sweated as I gripped Buttercup's crest tighter. She galloped at full speed across the grasslands, aiming for the narrow stretch that went between the sloping hills of the jagged rock line and the river with the seemingly impenetrable forest on the other side. If we weren't careful, we'd get pinned.

Behind us, the apex predator's thunderous footfalls battered the earth. Twisting about, I saw it bearing down on us.

"Come on, Buttercup," I urged. My hair whipped back and forth, streaking wildly across my face and into my eyes.

No flashes of inspiration or knowledge struck me. My heart clenched and pulsed, squeezing adrenaline through my veins, each breath a knife.

The landscape passed in a blur. How much longer could Buttercup keep up this pace? Her sides heaved against my legs.

Human-like shapes moved on the top of the jagged line of stones. Flashes of silver suggested they had weapons. If they wanted to see me dead, then this tyrannosaur after us in hot pursuit was about to do them a big favor.

The grasslands sloped upward, becoming more rugged. The dark earth and the grey and charcoal boulders made the incline all the more treacherous. Pebbles, clumps of soil, and tufts of short-rooted grass kicked back in the tyrannosaur's direction.

Buttercup's breaths rasped, huffing with increased intensity. Her heart thundered in her chest, the rapid beat palpable against my leg, her feet striking the loose rocks. Several clattered down, kicking up small puffs of dust and debris.

The tyrannosaur thundered up the hill after us, snarling and snapping heavy jaws.

A strangled cry escaped my lips. The path along the top of the embankment might be broad enough for us to run on, but one false step and we'd both go plummeting down. Even worse if the ledge ended. Was there a way beyond it? Dull knowledge bit into my mind. If there wasn't, this was it.

Another bellowing roar shook the ground, so close foul rotting air struck the back of my head.

Buttercup cried back, her voice more a wail now. She tossed

her head. Her eyes rolled back in her skull as her legs struggled to gain traction on the incline.

I hunched down close to her ear hole. "I'm so sorry, baby!" I whispered hoarsely. "I don't know how to fix this!" Reaching down, I grabbed for a rock, ready to throw it at the tyrannosaur.

The monstrous reptile lifted its head, lunging forward, massive jaws gaping wide.

A brilliant wall of light shot up, cutting off the tyrannosaur from Buttercup and me. Buttercup ground to a halt, her forelegs digging into the pebbled soil. I flung my arm out to cover her eyes and put my other hand over my own.

"Well, well. Here you are at last," an elderly woman's resonant voice spoke straight into my mind. "Glad to see your death didn't take."

Even without a formal introduction, I knew who this was: Auntie Runa, the Master of Sight.

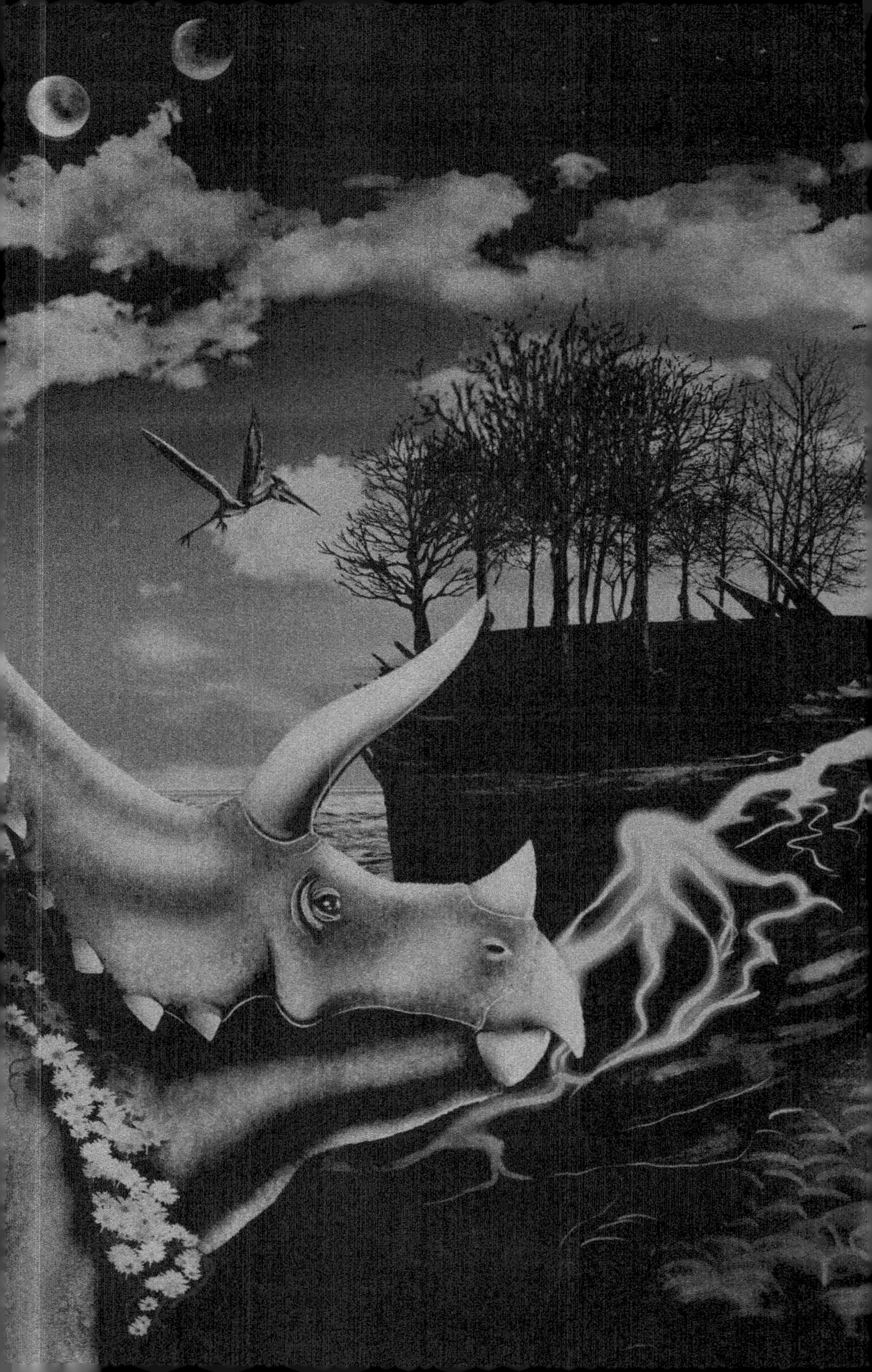

CHAPTER NINE: STELLA

*B*uttercup and I were no longer on the precarious ridge, sliding back toward gruesome death. We now stood in soft grass surrounded by gentle hills with a large river slicing through the fragrant earth. The moons had disappeared as well, replaced by a single golden sun. The sky, however, was still a deep, almost purple-blue. It looked to be midmorning...somehow.

An elderly woman stood in front of us. She was a couple inches taller than me, her body thin but surprisingly muscular for a woman her age. Her golden-brown skin had faint lines of gold in fern-like patterns branching down her face, some of the markings darkened or lined with russet sun spots. Strands of rosemary, sage, and dill had been woven into the coils of her pinned white hair. Even from this distance, the bright green fragrance reached me. Her murky eyes were a dark gold, ringed with deep brown, and flecked with caramel. Her heavy blue eyeliner made them stand out all the more, the crisp wings a little smudged at the edges.

Relief flooded through me. I clambered off Buttercup and flung my arms around the old woman. The smell of fresh herbs, celery, and lemons struck me like a wall, and I burst into tears. "Auntie!"

A thousand sensations and memories erupted in my mind, pouring out of my bones and heart.

She wrapped her bony arms around me and stroked my hair, her calloused palms cold against my scalp and neck. "My darling girl came home," she whispered, her soft voice thick and hoarse with emotion.

Her rings caught in my hair, but I didn't mind. I just hugged her.

My mind swam, and I sobbed, my face buried in the shoulder of her indigo robe. I was six and ten and thirteen and sixteen and twenty and twenty-five all at once. Afraid. Sad. Angry. Safe. No single memory or image clung to my mind. Instead, it was as if all of them poured over me and into my consciousness. These were arms that had held me many times over the years and reminded me that there was hope.

I could have disappeared into that comforting warmth of memories and simply savored them. Images—no—sensations flashed through my mind. Soft blankets and fuzzy cloths wrapped around my shoulders and legs, steaming soup making my mouth water and my lips pucker at the strong dill and savory chicken, cold water streaming over my fingers, sketching with charcoal and graphite, feeding something and its thick-whiskered mouth pressing against my palm.

Another desperate memory thrust itself forward. I gasped, stepping back and grasping her hands. "I had two friends. We were separated. Kine was dealing with some people who stopped us, and while he was talking with them, assassins attacked Elias and me. They sent the deinonychuses after Buttercup and me. And we got into tyrannosaur territory." The words came out half blubbered, and I scrubbed at my face like a child.

Auntie Runa nodded, her gaze gentle and understanding.

She patted my cheek, her well-trimmed fingernails lightly scraping my skin when she pressed my hair back. "Yes, I know them both, my dear, and don't worry. They'll be here soon. I saw the trouble starting and sent help. The factions are hard at work to fix the problems in the way they think best, even though they will only make it worse. Your two companions will be fine. I couldn't risk using my magic to pull them in, so they had to take the long way. It's far too unstable these days, but I'm sure it won't be long until they're here soon. Come. Bring Buttercup. Let's get you some food and fresh clothes." She flicked her hand in the air, giving Buttercup an affectionate glance as she turned back toward the hill and made her way down with firm strides, steadying herself with her polished cane, a large sapphire set on the top for the handle.

"So Elias and Kine are all right?" I asked.

Auntie Runa chuckled as she continued down the hill. Buttercup followed along behind her, her steps leaving heavy impressions in the soft grass. "Oh, yes. Magic may be unpredictable lately, but I still have a few tricks up my sleeve. You'll see, my dear. It's all gonna work out."

"And time...it jumped forward for me?" It looked like several hours since we had been on the ridge, though, similar to when I was trapped in the Shadow Hall, it did not feel as if hardly any time had passed at all.

She nodded. The sunlight shone on her soft white hair. Numerous wrinkles lined her face, making her expression all the more serious. "Oh, yes. Or, rather, you were brought forward in time. Time and magic have not been the best of friends lately. At least not in our land. I don't think it's the same for the other continents. We can thank the Gola Resh and the Babadon."

"Will you tell me who the Gola Resh and Babadon are?" I asked, hurrying along beside her. "Why are they doing this to us?"

She lifted her hand, chuckling a little. "Oh, so many things to remind you of," she said.

We passed beneath a large, sprawling tree with tiny circular leaves. Amber pear-like fruit with little shining white orbs hanging from their swollen bases brightened the darkness of the branches. Buttercup tilted her head back and took one in her jaws.

Bees buzzed around my head, not coming too close. They were each as large as my thumb, shaped more like bumble bees than honey bees, but with colors more vibrant than any I'd seen on Earth. Butterflies fluttered among the flowers. Once the land flattened and we passed beneath the tree, there were more fragrant fruit trees and tall golden apiaries.

A river chuckled across the land as well, branching off into several paths. One went straight to a large broad structure as if it were a part of it. Numerous arches and paths led to the house, each one easily large enough for two triceratopses to walk side by side. Clover and tiny white spire flowers lined the river stone path. The stones weren't even. Several had cracks in them.

The earthquakes.

Earthquakes were part of our life here before. That sounded right, but…they had gotten worse?

Something else to do with the magic, probably. The dark cracks and marks in the ground were here as well. Deep gouges with a lightening or yellowing of the plant life that touched them as if they had been weakened. They reminded me of a predator's claws sinking into the flesh of its prey before it tore them apart.

My gaze narrowed on the structure ahead. This building, like the others, had been built to withstand the earthquakes, combining magic with architecture. It had a broad base with specially constructed bricks and various components to allow it to move with the land when it trembled.

Auntie Runa indicated a large archway and an open side

door. "Straight through there and into the door with the blue and gold sea serpent and the gold crest at the center. Don't enter the rooms with eyes marked on the doors. I'll see to Buttercup here." She patted Buttercup on the snout, then plucked an amber fruit from the tree and offered it to her. Buttercup pretended to be a dainty princess and took it gently from her hand.

I smiled a bit, feeling as if I had walked into a dream. So strange to feel that I knew and loved this place. My eyes widened as I took it all in.

This house was so unlike anything I'd ever seen on Earth. Comfort swept over me as soon as I stepped beneath the thick stone arch and toward one of the side doors as Auntie Runa indicated. It smelled like fresh water and incense, smoky fruit and green plants.

The walls all appeared to be made of interlocking stones, the masonry exquisite. I brushed my fingers over the cool stone.

Most of the stones were pale, shades of cream or white or opal. Someone had hand-painted little designs over them, mostly water lines, sea snakes, and currents. I felt as if these had once held a far greater meaning for me. Had I painted some of these designs? A few of those squiggles looked like ones I'd made in my sketchbook. Especially the serpent with the crooked head and two triangular eyes and one with a triangular pupil and the other with a diamond.

Beautiful. Haunting. Familiar.

The coolness of the house enveloped me. Water lapped somewhere nearby. It sounded like a pool was somewhere in here, or maybe it was just the river.

If I closed my eyes, I could almost see it or at least part of it. Reflections dancing on the water and casting funny shapes on the walls. A home more vibrant with life than any I'd ever seen in Nevada or Ohio or California or North Carolina or Florida or anywhere else I'd traveled.

The door Auntie Runa indicated was one of many, yet I walked straight to it. My feet remembered better than my mind.

I'd stayed—no—I'd lived here.

The small bed in the center of the room had an old quilt on it, each triangle or square of fabric embroidered with serpent and water designs in interlocking waves and starbursts. It looked old. Decades, perhaps. The whites had gone a little dingy, and some of the old threads holding the blocks together had started to fall apart, so tinier new stitches had been worked into the fabric, the lighter threads standing out, little reminders that someone had deemed this quilt worth saving again and again.

A single round window looked out from the bedroom into a garden of flowering herbs and fruiting plants. This room was all in shades of blue. A small table sat beside the bed, a shallow stoneware basin of water beside it. A stoneware pitcher and basin with a towel hanging over the edge was on the dresser on the other side of the room. The coarse texture revealed that the blue was not painted on. The clay itself appeared blue. Or maybe it changed colors in the firing.

I washed and put on the clothes that had been placed on the foot of the bed—a pale-blue dress with a gold sash and an asymmetrical hemline. There were short leggings underneath to allow me to retain some measure of modesty if I had to bend over or spin—or if I fell while trying to rescue a koi or launching myself off a triceratops at a tyrannosaur.

Scoffing, I shook my head. Still couldn't believe I'd done that. Rubbing my jaw, I wondered why it had been so instinctual. And why did it still feel like I should have long, sharp teeth?

As I tied the sash, I bumped into the wardrobe. The door jarred open, revealing the flash of a mirror. Drawing it open farther, I stepped in front of it.

My breaths tightened.

I'd already seen myself in the river's reflection, but that had been through the haze of alcohol and rippling water.

Was I... Yes.

My heart leaped when I stepped in front of the mirror, my hand flying to my mouth.

Yes.

Yes!

I recognized myself.

A giggle rose to my lips.

This was the person I had been searching for in the mirror all my life.

The eyes that peered back at me—warm gold with dark brown and soft honey flecks—were my eyes. This rich-blue hair that cascaded to the tops of my shoulders like a waterfall was my hair. The shape of my face had not changed, but its coloration had. Faint streaks of gold marked my cheeks, the sides of my throat, and bits of my forehead, as well as my forearms, similar to the fern markings on Auntie Runa. They were almost invisible at times, depending on how the light struck me. Even those long, pointed ears were right somehow. The only thing missing were the earrings for the multiple piercings.

But this... I choked, my hand pressing against my throat. This was who I was supposed to be. As terrifying and tumultuous as all of this had been, at last, it was becoming real. Things were somehow starting to feel right even if they did still feel wrong in some respects.

I was becoming who I had always been meant to be.

Then I noticed the bruises where Brandt had choked me. Despite the magic of Elias's medicine, they were not fully gone. The piercing pain and crushing ache returned. The bruises had darkened and faded significantly, but they were there, dull marks on my skin.

His eyes flashed back into my memory. Not the rageful heat

when the curse took over. Mournful eyes wet with the tears of loss and sorrow.

Pressing my hand over my heart, I sank down onto the edge of the bed.

I felt empty inside.

Brandt.

For the first time, I was able to sit and contemplate what had happened. His name was heavy on my lips and tongue. My eyelids shut as I shielded my throat.

He had tried to kill me.

That didn't feel right, but it had happened. It didn't feel real, but it was. As right as everything else was, that had been wrong.

The hollow ache intensified. I wanted to be with him.

My hand pressed harder over my heart.

I had to reach him again. I needed him.

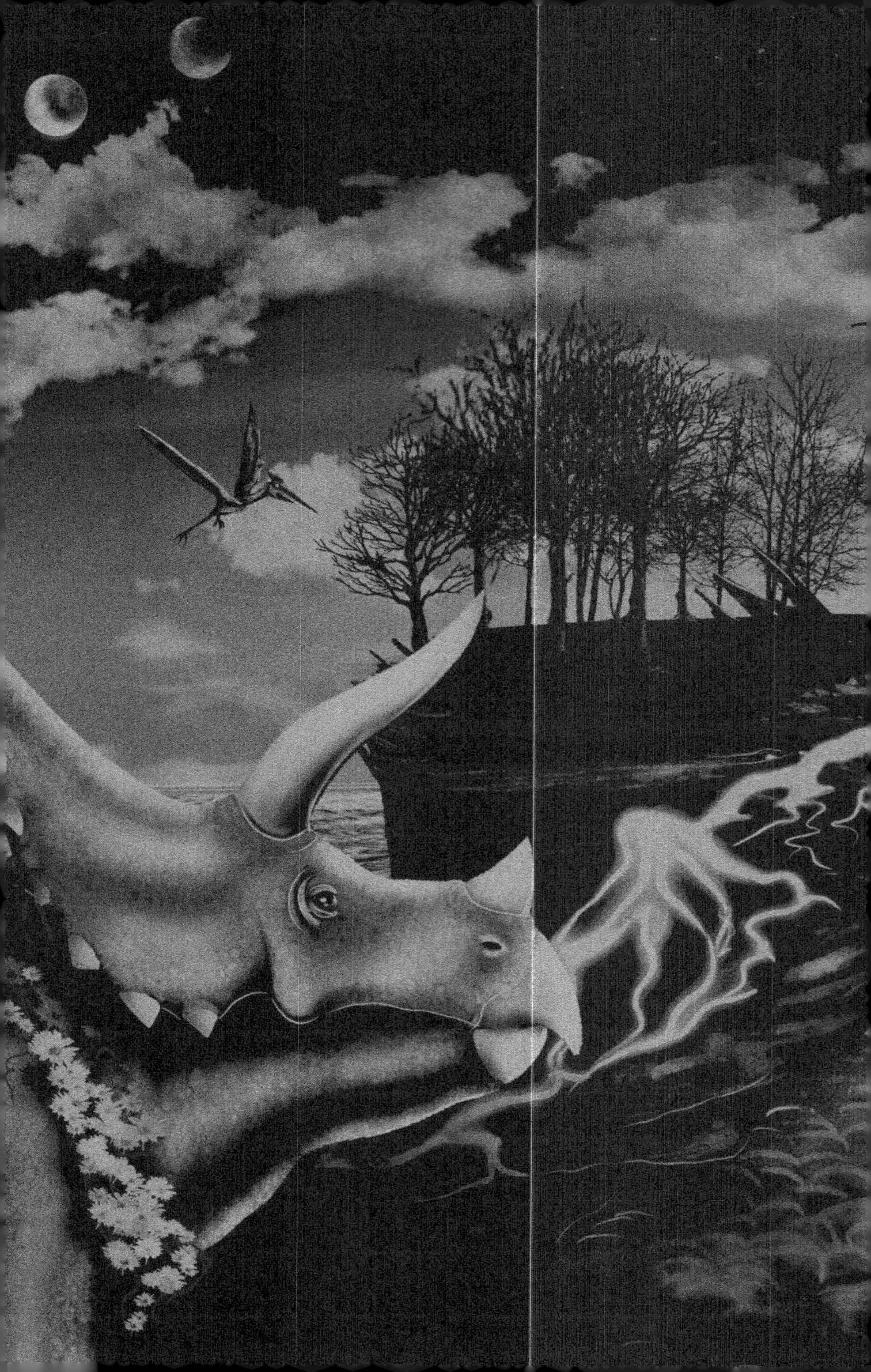

CHAPTER TEN: BRANDT

Scarlet, a red and black mini raptor, nudged my knee. Her ruby-like eyes glittered, and her narrow charcoal-speckled jaws nipped at my leather trousers. Absently, I dropped my hand down and stroked her triangular head as the droning dialogue continued in the inner throne room of Castle Serpentfire.

A council representative—Tile, an older, fire-haired arcanist with a cleft in his chin and a nail-bitingly dry voice—spoke on about the dangers to Sepeazia. He stood in the center of the room, gesturing with one arm toward the assembled council members.

My head thundered as if a triceratops had kicked me full-on. I could barely focus—my mouth dry, chest heavy, vision blurred.

Tile's heavy droning pressed in on my ears and fuzzed around the edges of my mind.

Stella.

I'd almost killed her.

My heart. My love. My all.

The one whom I had vowed to protect with my blood, soul, spirit, marrow, bone, and sinew.

The dark walls of the throne room merged with the floor. The black stone hid the creases and cracks caused by the curse devouring the very life force and magic of our land, but they were there, the curse simmering in the very souls of both Kropelki and Ognisko, the two nations that made up the single kingdom of Sepeazia. Many things had united us over the years, but this curse was one of the worst. Though torches and bronze braziers cast golden light upon the scooped and sculpted stone, the chamber had a red cast from the lava suspended in columns and contained by magic that wove and propelled them through the specially cut shafts into the floor and ceiling.

If ever our magic failed completely, the castle would become a death trap. That likely would not come until the end when the curse devoured the last of the life force of Sepeazia and undid the heartstones as it had with Taivren, our former capital.

Every fiber of my body ached and pulsed, aware of the emptiness that came from being separated from her and knowing that if we didn't find a solution, I would either murder her or go insane. Perhaps both.

Somehow, in the midst of this, we had to find a way to end that curse and the one that loomed over the entirety of Sepeazia. Even if I found a way to save Stella from myself, we were all going to die if the curse against Sepeazia resumed, and we couldn't stop it.

Scarlet nipped at my fingers. The other mini raptors and tiny pterosaurs that clustered and fluttered about the throne room were in similarly bitey moods, nibbling and nuzzling as they struggled to understand the source of tension. Two red-and-orange-feathered mini raptors hopped around on the massive hourglass that displayed the curse's progress.

Not the curse that condemned me to murder the one I loved above all others.

No, no.

Because one curse from the Gola Resh wasn't enough.

The abyssal-damned curse that started it all off was draining the life and magic out of the land and air of Sepeazia. It was the whole reason we had killed the Gola Resh and Babadon, but their curse remained. And it had ticked down steadily downward for days, even after their deaths.

The hourglass had appeared here before this castle became the capitol. It sat proudly in the center of the black iron table, approximately three feet in height. The sands were a mixture of red and black, teasing stripes of color and darkness. The bottom half had two bulbs. The smaller interior bulb held a replica of the first capital, Taivren, the former capital of our dual monarchy.

The first time I saw the hourglass, my blood had chilled. It was a threat. I had known that then, even before the seers spoke.

The sands had filled that inner bulb first, creating an effect that looked like the replica had been engulfed in toxic fire.

When that bulb filled, the entire capital city and the strip of neutral territory upon which both kingdoms had pledged peace, cooperation, and understanding all plunged into the sea and the very waters turned toxic.

The violent screams of the earth as it had torn itself apart echoed in my mind, stone shattering and land splitting, filthy waters surging. Stone walls, seamless and unyielding as the sea itself, had risen, trapping the toxic waters and displaying in vivid horror the fate that awaited our people and the rest of our lands.

Had it not been for the seers and arcanists, it would have been a bloodbath. Some died that day. More than should have. Not as many as would have, thanks to the seers, rescuers, and our allies.

Tile droned on, making the same points he had for the past three months.

My gaze flicked to my right where she had once sat beside me. That was her place. My queen. My love. Right here on the same throne.

This throne had been carved from a great chunk of stone that had been found on the boundary line of the two kingdoms. It was ungodly large, cut to seat two. When we weren't holding court, she often curled up beside me and complained that her side was too small, so she had to sit on my lap.

Or she'd put her icy feet on my thighs and pretend not to understand why I was annoyed.

The throne had been rescued before the fall of Taivren. Dromar and his sons had dared the toxic waters and plunged beneath the surface to rescue it when the first attempt to retrieve it had failed. A few others had rescued other items. Ultimately, all that had mattered to me on that day was Stella.

That toxic vortex had nearly ripped her from me while she was in the middle of a rescue. Despite being a water seer, when swimming, she lacked strength and endurance. I had let the blessed Sword of Kairos—pride of our people—fall into the devouring depths to seize her.

It had been worth it.

That day...that was the day I knew I would rather die than lose Stella, the day I pledged to make her my wife and queen.

My hand flicked over my brow to wipe away the sweat. The heat from the lava coils usually kept the castle comfortable in the autumn and winter months. Yet I was sweltering.

Everyone else was at ease. Hands folded in their laps or resting on the carved arms of the low-backed bastion chairs, each member of the various councils paid adequate attention. Not even Hord, my cousin and arch general, appeared even slightly flushed.

It was just me. I imagined my appearance was even more haggard than usual. Heavy bags under my eyes. An unhealthy flush at my cheeks and throat. The years had been harsh.

The curse we faced was even harsher.

Being away from Stella was worse still.

But she had come back.

Abyssal damnation, she'd come back!

And I didn't have any more answers for her now than I did when she had laid down her life fifty years ago.

The hot ball of rage in my chest burned stronger, settling deeper.

Answers. There had to be answers. And soon.

If Stella had come back, it would not be to her death. I would die before I permitted that.

Somehow, we would find a way.

Scarlet nipped my finger.

Snapping my hand back, I glared down at her.

She cocked her head and chirped.

Little beast.

My eyes narrowed.

She chirped again and thrust her head at my hand, even as my finger bled. I screwed up my mouth at her, then resumed petting her.

Tile continued to speak. "There has been no change within the hourglass to suggest that the curse has resumed its cruel continuation," he said, grasping the lapels of his dark-red robe. "Nothing has changed on that front. Not even with the stirring of the Kropelkian energy."

"There has to be some way to undo the curses of the Gola Resh." I clenched my fist, my weight heavier on the arm of the throne. Scarlet hopped up on my left side and curled up on my lap like a scaly cat. "No magic is permanent. Nothing lasts forever."

Tile inclined his head to the left, his mouth pinching. Obviously he disagreed.

Dromar rose. He was one of my kinsmen, one far enough removed that he was not in my family home while I grew up.

His red and black hair had been plaited into an elaborate braid that reached down to the middle of his back. "Perhaps the solution could be found if Your Majesty were willing to accept another bride. The Vampire Queen herself wed the new Vampire King for the good of the nation, despite the fact that he was the son of her first husband."

The harsh laugh that escaped my mouth startled Scarlet. She scurried away and glared at me, tiny claws clacking on the smooth black dais and then the carved floor.

I straightened and then gave Dromar a lazy glare. Between him, Osvar, and Kendrall, my dealings with the council had become exceptionally challenging. The other council members had differing perspectives, but they were not so vocal.

"The Queen of Sepeazia remains unchanged." I enunciated each word with painful clarity as I stared them down.

"It has been fifty years," Osvar said, his tone harder. "You have flouted custom in many areas and received far more tolerance on the matter than any other king in all of Sepeazia's history. We are in exceptionally turbulent times. It is not just the vampires and the mages that are in turmoil. The dragon kingdoms—"

"Dracon," Kendrall corrected, lifting his hand.

"Dracons," Osvar said, shooting Kendrall a sharp look. "Their lost princess has returned and is rumored to love the brother of her betrothed while her father, the king, is going mad. Do you think that will be resolved without conflict and bloodshed? Do you think they will hesitate to eliminate the royals who fail to do their duties?"

"Except she is not here to fulfill her role. Even if the rumors that she has returned are true, she has not been serving as queen, has she?" Dromar bit out. The respect in his voice and on his face were the minimum required for this situation. "And the matter of the curse remains. One curse can be removed, even if the second remains. The curse has not been moving forward, but we know that will not last forever. If there is the opportunity to end the curse that threatens to drain all life on Sepeazia before the countdown resumes, we should take it."

Kendrall straightened his shoulders and lifted his chin. His oiled blond beard shone in the red-orange light of the lava and torches. The tiny raptors darted about, a few pouncing on stray insects that made their way in and the others playing. The volcano slugs moved along the columns, their movements silent but steady, like the machinations of those who worked against me.

"If you have something to say, Kendrall, say it," I said gruffly.

"As a Kropelkian, I understand and respect your attachment to our former..." He dipped his head forward, his eyes closing with respect. "...to *the* queen, but the truth remains that she laid her life down once. If the rumors are true..."

He halted a beat as if to allow me to confirm or deny Stella's return. I looked at him without blinking.

He cleared his throat. "The queen's return may be the blessing and stroke of fortune we need."

I lifted my chin, sensing the underlying challenge of his words. "Her return would be a blessing indeed."

Go ahead, I dared him silently.

Say it.

Say it!

My fingers dug into the stone of the throne's arm. I knew where he was going with this already and hated him for it.

"This land and the others of this world were saved by the queen and seven others spilling their blood in selfless sacrifice. Rumors abound, not only here but abroad, that all of them have returned. Each one has had to face trials and challenges. The mages themselves may be turning to evil and cruel methods once more. The crown prince of Magiaria may have even abducted their sacrifice, and I am not sure how she will survive him. War will almost assuredly break out. The demons of

Isramorta despise the vampires now because the vampires abandoned them even though they were once vampires themselves. Who knows how that will end except in further bloodshed for their chosen and others? Every continent is being rent with torment and conflict. None of the women who sacrificed themselves have returned to easy circumstances. In truth, from what our allies say, I fear most—perhaps all of these women will die yet again. It may be that our very own queen returns to sacrifice herself to end this curse and restore your sanity and save Sepeazia."

The rage boiled within me as I straightened on the throne. "The Gola Resh did not say that the curse against Sepeazia would be lifted. She said she might lift it if I killed Stella. The curse condemning me to madness is separate. The Gola Resh is dead. We slew her in the Grand Hall. Her corpse was vanished without a trace. She can't very well end the curse when she's dead, can she?"

Not that I believed for a single moment that she would have ended it early or allowed some mechanism to end it. The Gola Resh was vicious, heartless, and incapable of compassion.

Dromar's upper lip curled, disgust flaring in his eyes. "Yes. Had she lived, it might have been possible to end both curses. To plead with the Gola Resh for mercy and spare both nations this torment. But in that, our king did not put Sepeazia first."

"She was lying," I said, forcing my voice to a deadly calm. "Her sole purpose was to torment us."

But it was true I had struck the Gola Resh too soon. She had already wounded herself grievously, but my rage had taken over when she'd threatened Stella. If we'd kept her alive long enough, we could have undone hers and the Babadon's magic and ended the curses entirely. But I'd failed. A reality which tormented me daily.

"If Stella returns, she will not be slain. She will not be sacrificed a second time," I said. And I was not going to confirm her return to anyone any more than I had to.

"*If.*" Dromar repeated the word.

Evnal leaned back in his chair, shifting his weight. Though a neutral force among my advisers and council members, he did not speak often. Lately, his patience with the entire matter had worn thin. Even the usually immaculate kohl lining his eyes and the markings on his cheeks lacked their typical crispness, smudged in the creases of his eyelids and the wrinkles that feathered along his cheeks and temples.

"The rumors have strengthened," he said. "There are reports. Rumors. Not just of the queen's return, but also that her brother and his ally have broken out of the dungeon. Rumors too that the reason they were imprisoned was for bringing the queen back."

"Kine and Elias do not have to be held any longer," I said coolly, resting my chin on my palm. "Their imprisonment served no further purpose at this time, and I am certain that there are many rumors, especially given the intensity of yesterday's earthquake and the stirrings of Kropelkian magic in the air. Who could blame them?"

Two of the younger mini raptors hopped on one another. They hissed and chirped. Scarlet darted in and nipped at the larger of the two. They immediately scattered. Sometimes I wished I could use her methods to quiet my council on days like this.

"Your Majesty..." Cura, another councilor who typically supported me, leaned forward. Her red-and-black lined lips pursed. "We are aware that prisoners were brought in. They were captured by Arch General Hord, and some have said that these prisoners were actually assassins from one of the factions sent to target the queen. Allegedly."

I crooked my finger as I pressed it against my lips. "Factions with designs of assassination are not new," I said, "and they will be dealt with as we have dealt with the others. So far as them coming for the queen, it may be that they have heard rumors as well and wish to be prepared. But allow me to be clear. I have no tolerance for any who would seek to undermine Sepeazia. And..." I leaned back, my gaze drifting around the assembled council members. "Allow me to remind all of you that while some aspects of the larger curse are nebulous, one thing is true. I have to kill Stella to satisfy this specific curse." I indicated the charm that hung around my neck. The bauble in the center was a dull orange, signaling many hours until the next madness that would seize me. "If she dies before we figure out how to end the Gola Resh's curses and not by my hand, then this curse may never be ended." It was a bluff and a guess, but one I was willing to hold to.

Those words hung heavy in the air. The hissing of the lava coiling through the vents kept the silence from being truly oppressive.

I held their gazes for a breath longer, then inclined my head forward. "You will all continue with your tasks. Research and develop various methods and possibilities for ending both curses. The curse that devours the life of Sepeazia still has not resumed." I indicated the hourglass with the days etched into the glass. "Make the most of the time we have. Prioritize that above ending the curse that hangs over me."

Dromar's face had gone as sour, as if he had shoved a whole lemon in his mouth. "After more than fifty years, we have exhausted all options. Unless you have something new for us to provide the various practitioners and scholars and sages, or perhaps another theory for us to examine, we are wasting time. There is nothing new or significant for either case."

"Then order them to start at the beginning," I barked. "Unless they would all rather hurl themselves into the Blight Sea to make our destruction easier at the end."

My words echoed in the chamber.

A bubble within the lava popped and hissed. All stared at me. I lifted my hand. "If there is nothing else…"

Even if there was something else, I doubted they would bring it up then. They disappeared in a rustle of robes, silks, leathers, and cotton, colognes and perfumes fading until all that remained was the spice of the incense and the pungency of the lava that escaped the magic's hold.

My mood darkened as the footsteps faded. I let my elbow fall over the cold, carved arm of the throne, then gripped the silver goblet. Stella's goblet sat beside it, filled with tart, woody autumn wine. It rippled out, the light reflecting off the dark-red surface.

Scarlet hopped back up beside me, chirring as she tilted her head at me. Baro and Tad, two others, circled at my feet. Baro shoved his face against my boot and gave my trouser leg a tentative nibble, as if that was all I needed to rouse myself.

I stroked their heads one at a time and tickled their jaws, my movements absent as my gaze fell once more to the hourglass that held the time left before Sepeazia's doom. The sands had not started shifting even though Stella was back.

Was it possible that her sacrifice had been enough? That the curse had been forever stopped, even if the weakening of the land itself and the signs of the toxic drain upon our very soil and stone remained?

I wanted to believe it was so, but all any of the seers had seen was nothing. I had spoken to every single one, including the ones Auntie Runa said she wouldn't trust as far as she could throw them. No matter how much I longed for hope, I knew better than to believe this silence and stillness was anything more than a pause.

Somehow, though, I'd find a way to save Stella.

Even if it cost me everything.

Rising, I crossed to the water mirror in the back of the chamber. I brushed my fingers over the still waters to make them ripple out. The reflection turned dark, revealing another chamber.

"Belligerent asshole," I muttered.

There was silence until another deep voice responded, "Insidious blight."

I stepped back, smirking.

Footsteps clattered outside the chamber.

Cahji stumbled in, his silver eyes wide, his silver hair all askew. The youth stumbled over his feet and nearly crashed into the wall. The mini raptors scattered, hissing and flicking their tails.

Cahji was close to being an adult, and yet in that moment, he looked more like a child, his eyes wide and white-rimmed and his breaths panting. "Your Majesty, there's word on the queen!"

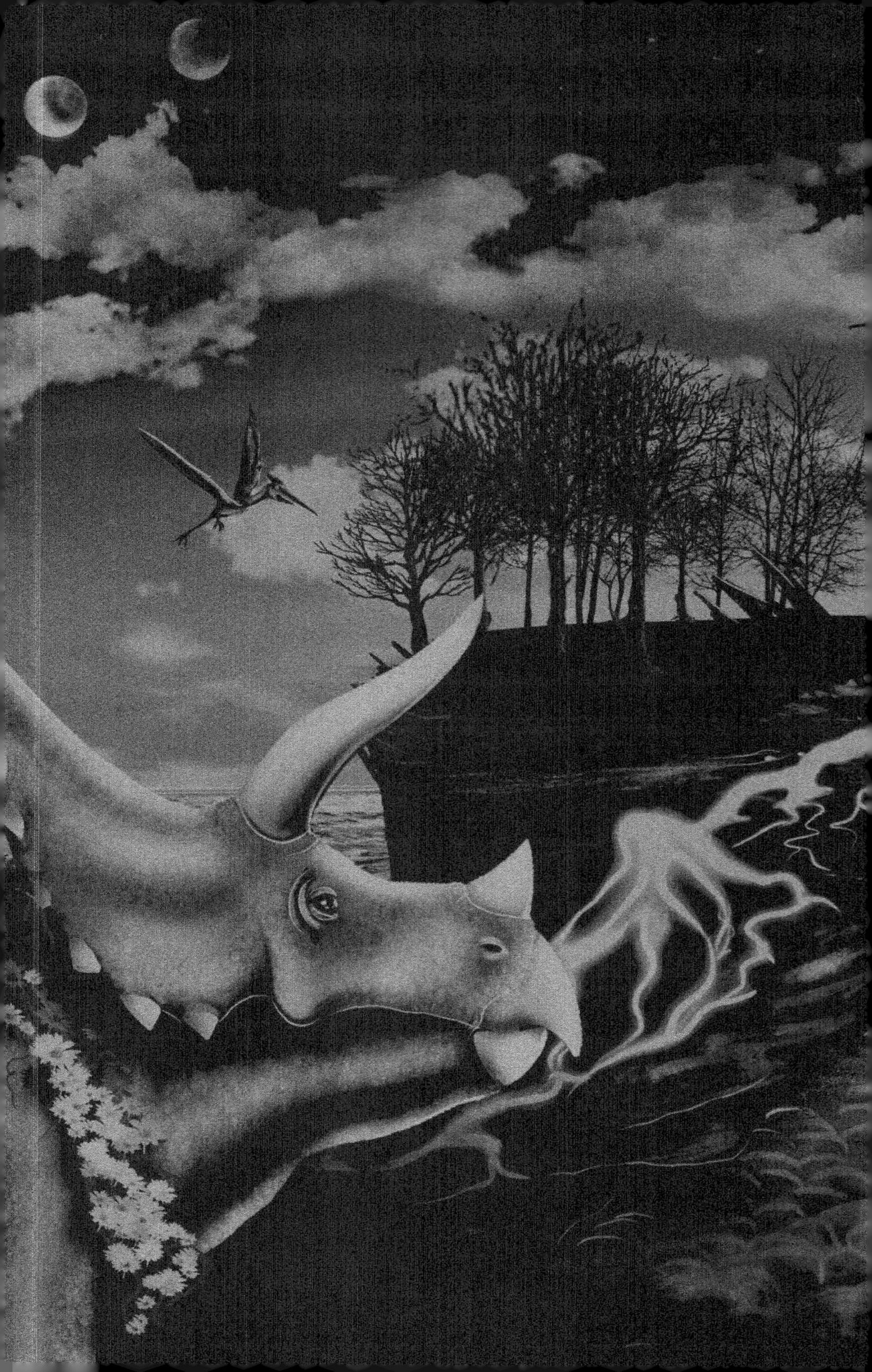

CHAPTER ELEVEN: BRANDT

Cahji barely caught his balance before I was charging toward him. "What news?" I demanded, seizing him by his pale-blue tunic.

His silver eyes widened even more, making him look even younger than he was. "F-Father—I mean, Arch General Hord is in the inner dungeon," he stammered. "He said it was important and confidential."

I swept briskly toward the staircase.

Not dignified. Not formal.

Didn't matter.

Scarcely anyone was about. My boots echoed on the stone floor. Kine hadn't responded to my summons through the water mirror when I'd first tried this morning, which meant that he hadn't yet reached Auntie Runa's or another place where he could make a report. Hord's warriors had caught the attackers and brought them back, but Kine might have made it back to Auntie Runa's between that time.

The heavy iron-bound door creaked open, and I went down the staircase. As I descended into the depths of the dungeon, the air grew cooler. The bright slickness from the sound-devouring gel glistened on the walls. Torches set in metal sconces cast ominous shadows.

Cahji followed after me, padding down the steps at an uneven pace.

The stairs curved down and around. Down, down, down. At the very base stood another black iron-banded door. With a swift gesture of my hand, I tossed it open and strode inside.

Hord, my arch general and cousin on my father's side, stood with his back to me, facing the nearest cell. He hadn't changed out of his clothing from the night before, the sash over his tabard still stained with blood and grass and his boots streaked with mud.

He bowed his head. "Brandt." As we were in private, neither of us worried about formalities. He kept his arms banded over his broad chest. "Two things."

"Speak, then." I stopped in front of him, setting my arms akimbo with my hands braced against my belt. Cahji had not followed me into the chamber, instead waiting on the stairs. The door at the base of the stairs snicked shut.

Hord nodded and jerked his head toward one of the more secure inner chambers so we could talk. Like the others, this one was simple, the door banded with iron and secured to block sound from leaving it. This was a smaller interrogation room, holding a single heavy-legged table and two rickety chairs. The torch sputtered on the wall, the red oil in its basin low and smelling of must and grime. Hord closed the door at once, pressing his hand to it to ensure it was closed.

"What news?" I demanded again. "Are the prisoners talking yet?"

The would-be assassins had been dragged here shortly after Candy and Hord had brought me back. Exhaustion had kept me from speaking with them in any rational fashion. If I'd had my way, I'd have ripped out their throats.

Hord's dark-red eyes met mine, his expression like granite.

Once again, he was the stable voice of reason. He braced his hands against his belt, his left hand grazing the hilt of his sheathed hunting knife. "Kine has reached Auntie Runa. He was terse."

My eyebrow lifted. "Really?"

Kine was usually a chipper, cheeky bastard. The fact that he had added no element of fun or play told me almost as much as the message. Even after I had him imprisoned, he had retained that annoying wit, though he'd slowed down. He'd even remained confident that his decision to go and get Stella before we had the answer was right. So for him to be terse meant something was wrong.

"What has happened to make him so? Is Stella not safe?" I asked.

"No. She's there. She's safe, but they believe she was attacked by the Gola Resh."

My shoulders squared. Rage clenched my heart in an iron grasp that my beloved had been attacked. Then Hord's words settled over me. The Gola Resh had survived. Somehow. Fear and hope alike warred within me. The Gola Resh had survived? Hope and disbelief roared within me.

"What did he say?"

"Not much. The reason that Stella disappeared in the cavern was because of the Gola Resh's interference. At least that's his theory. Stella said the Gola Resh taunted her." Hord glanced at the door, as if worried someone might overhear us. "Which means that the Gola Resh has been waiting for Stella's return as well. The halting of the curse was simply to ensure that the Gola Resh could inflict the most pain and sorrow possible."

If that was the case, it meant Kine and his ally had doomed us even more by bringing Stella back before we found a solution.

Dragging my hand across the back of my neck, I closed my eyes and drew in a deep breath.

No.

No, we weren't falling into the Gola Resh's trap. We were going to find a way to undo her. Even if this was a trap, we would figure a way out.

"We have no proof that the Gola Resh is alive beyond the encounter Stella had—" Hord started.

"The Gola Resh lives. What else could it be? There's nothing else like her." I paced to the other side of the room, turned, and paced back, my steps steady. I didn't need any more proof than that, but we would find it. The Gola Resh was planning to finish her work, perhaps even to twist the knife a little deeper.

Somehow, she had lived.

Someone must have helped her.

One of the factions, perhaps? Who had that kind of power? And why would they have done it when the Gola Resh was a threat to our very existence?

"We need to inform the Council," Hord said. "Despite their opposition to Stella remaining queen, they will understand the gravity of the challenge the Gola Resh presents. And if Stella is indeed back, then she could be reinstated."

"The Gola Resh still being alive may give the sages, scholars, and arcanists what they need to find a way for ending these curses," I muttered. I pressed my hands harder against my belt. "And these assassins, did they have anything to do with the Gola Resh? Have you finished interrogating them?"

"They claim a seer helped them. They don't know the name, but the seer told them that the queen had returned and where to find her," Hord responded grimly, "and that her death was essential. Should forces be sent out to return Kine and Elias to the dungeons and Stella to the palace?"

That look of disapproval was one of those times Hord's manner alone indicated we were family. He had my father's way of curling his upper lip and wrinkling his nose ever so slightly when he disapproved of something even when he tried to hide it. Hord hadn't agreed with my imprisoning those two at the start.

"No."

As much as I longed to hold Stella in my arms once more, I could not risk her. I would rather never see her again and know she was safe rather than see her and harm her. Sometimes, the need that rose within me was so strong I could scarcely breathe. And sometimes the curse compelled me to seek her out. Being away from her cut me to my soul.

But for now...for now, I could refuse its urge. I could remember how vital it was that we not see one another. We would wait, and I would not see her. Not until I knew I could be contained. Not until I knew why I had snapped early. Not until I could end this curse, or at least predict when the madness would seize me with more accuracy.

"Then do you want guards sent to the Master of Sight in case additional assassins attempt to harm her? If the factions who want her dead know that she lives or even if some of the people become panicked, then it may be needed."

I stroked my jaw. Auntie Runa had recently declared the entire surrounding territory of her land to be one free of weapons. No weapon—magic or not—could be wielded in that place. Something to do with strengthening the protective properties of her sanctuary. And the people of Sepeazia were far more preoccupied with day-to-day life. As far as they were concerned, the curse ending our land and destroying our lives was still held back. They'd gotten numb to its presence over the past five decades, even with the deep gouges in the earth representing the start of the Gola Resh's draining magic at work. Best to keep everyone calm for now. Let them focus on the ordinary tasks. It wasn't as if they could do anything at this point anyway.

"Select a few trusted warriors to go to the corners of her land, but do not permit them to cross the barriers. Inform the Master of Sight that they are present should she have need." I hesitated. The curse had not included my issuing orders while in its grasp thus far, but with the time surge, could I really risk that remaining true? Other facets of the curse might change as well. "And bind them to take no action against the queen. No matter who commands it."

Hord scowled. "May I ask why?"

"To keep her safe," I said gruffly. "Make sure it is done."

My intelligence plummeted in the throes of the curse. Sometimes I could speak. Sometimes I couldn't. Mercifully, I remembered little, but Hord and Candy as well as a few others—the ones I trusted with my life—told me I became more brute than man. Not being able to remember was both a blessing and a curse.

Apparently, all I managed were threats. Poor ones, at that. It gutted me to know that friends and allies as well as threats could be harmed in these times. No matter how hard I tried to fight it, it always won.

The dread that trickled down the back of my neck and seized along my spine before I lost control might as well have been all my cunning and willpower draining like wine out of burst wineskins.

Neither my full council nor my people knew how often these attacks came now. Only Hord and perhaps a few others knew the full extent of it. I used the charm to ensure I was isolated as much as possible when they came. But last night—something had changed. Maybe it was Stella's return. Maybe it was something else. Maybe the Gola Resh playing games, now that we knew she was alive.

Setting my jaw, I dug my fingers into my arms. The serpent tattoos that coiled around my biceps and forearms twitched.

Hord inclined his head, his tone even more serious. "The other matter is that we cannot contain word of the queen's return for long. There are already rumors because of what magically inclined Kropelkians felt. The seers have been speaking of it, and there was enough knowledge from all of this to prompt one of the factions to try and end her life. The only reason my men were able to intervene and help at all was because we heard Kine's and Elias's distress calls."

I leaned back against the cold stone wall. Though it looked slick, it was dry. Strong and secure as this fortress was, it was useless when it came to protecting Stella.

"No. We don't change our stance so far as the people go. We may have to inform the council, but they will be sworn to keep it secret. The more people who know she lives before this curse is ended, the more who may choose to take it into their own hands," I said.

"We should increase the guards on you as well—"

A sneer twisted my mouth. "It doesn't matter. Any assassin who comes I will deal with as I have dealt with the others."

Hord inclined his head to the side, concern etched into his usually stoic features.

I continued, not allowing him the time to interrupt. "As for the current prisoners…have they said anything else?"

"Nothing we didn't already guess or know," Hord said. "I recommend you rest—Brandt!"

I had already crossed to the door. They'd tried to kill Stella. Maybe I couldn't protect her from everything. I could barely protect her from myself, but I could get vengeance on them for daring to harm her.

Flinging the door aside, I continued out to the landing and then down into the inner dungeon. The dungeon itself was made of long halls with narrow cubicles, every inch of the stone drenched in the essence of silence. No screams could penetrate these doors or walls, even if someone stood just on the other side.

On the long table at the opposite end from me sat instruments of torture: wicked curved blades, icy thin needles, vials of dark potions. These items were mostly for show and intimidation.

The two prisoners had been separated into adjoining cells. Both men cowered, shrinking even from my shadow as it crossed the seams of the floor. The chains about their wrists and ankles rattled. Their black garb was tattered and torn, their masks ripped off but the indentations still apparent on their skin. Bruises and markings covered their faces and peeked through the rips in their garments. Blood spattered over their flesh and garments. One was missing two fingers on his left hand. The other had a makeshift bandage wrapped around his thigh.

My jaw clenched, and my right fist tightened. Only two of the assassins who had attacked my beloved survived, and here they were.

"Who is the seer who told you where to find the queen?" I crossed my arms over my chest, my fingers digging into the serpent tattoos once more.

Both men eyed me with caution.

Hord approached from behind and took his position on my left.

"Answer me!" I bellowed.

The man with the missing fingers staggered to his feet. The chains visibly bit into his wrists. "We don't know who the seer was. The messages were anonymous, but the need is clear. The queen must die, or else everything—"

I struck the stone wall. The stones rattled. Fiery pain blistered through my knuckles and up my arm as I glared at the man. "How many of you believe this? How many are there?"

Both men stared at me, stupefied. These men were clearly amateurs. One of the homegrown factions of allegedly well-intentioned nationalists who lacked true skill.

"Answer me!" I bellowed.

The assassin with the bandaged leg spoke, his voice shaking.

"There are many scattered about. The curse must be ended, or else all will die."

Rage boiled inside me. "Fools," I spat.

"We did it to protect you," Missing Fingers pleaded, "to protect Ogniskoan interests and the Ognisko line. If we do not slay her, then other factions will slay you. We are on your side."

"If you try to kill your queen—*my wife*—you are not on my side," I snarled.

Lunging forward, I reached in, seized Missing Fingers by his black tunic, and dragged him forward. He whimpered, dropping his gaze and struggling to pull back.

"I want the names of everyone involved." I slammed him up against the bars. My voice echoed and faded almost at once within the stark chamber. Fear shone in the man's bloodshot eyes.

Bandaged Leg hunched back, clearly hoping he was out of reach.

"Tell me!" I loosened my grip on his ragged black tunic to let him fall back just enough before jerking him forward and striking his face again.

Blood gushed from Missing Fingers's nose as it cracked against the metal. The chains rattled and clanked.

Hord stepped forward. "Interrogator Lodin will be coming to conduct the interrogations to gain all this information," he said, his voice calm, "and both these men will speak better if they are...alive."

It occurred to me that I might kill one and let the other speak, but who was to say who actually had relevant knowledge?

With great effort, I released the man. He staggered to the ground, then collapsed, weeping as he held his bloodied face.

I glared at him, contempt filling my very being. "Fine."

Hord followed me to the staircase out of earshot of the prisoners. "When we are finished with the interrogations, should they be placed in the general prison for trial—"

"Kill them. Make sure the bodies are never found. Do the same to all involved with that faction," I said, not even glancing back over my shoulder.

Hord halted, his boots squeaking on the floor. "No trial?"

"I am the king." I spat the words out with ice. "They had their trial. There is nothing any of them can say that will change what they have done. Get the information we need from them. Find the rest and then make sure they aren't found. There is no mercy for anyone who would harm my wife."

That went for me as well. I turned my back on them and left.

No matter what it cost, I would keep Stella safe.

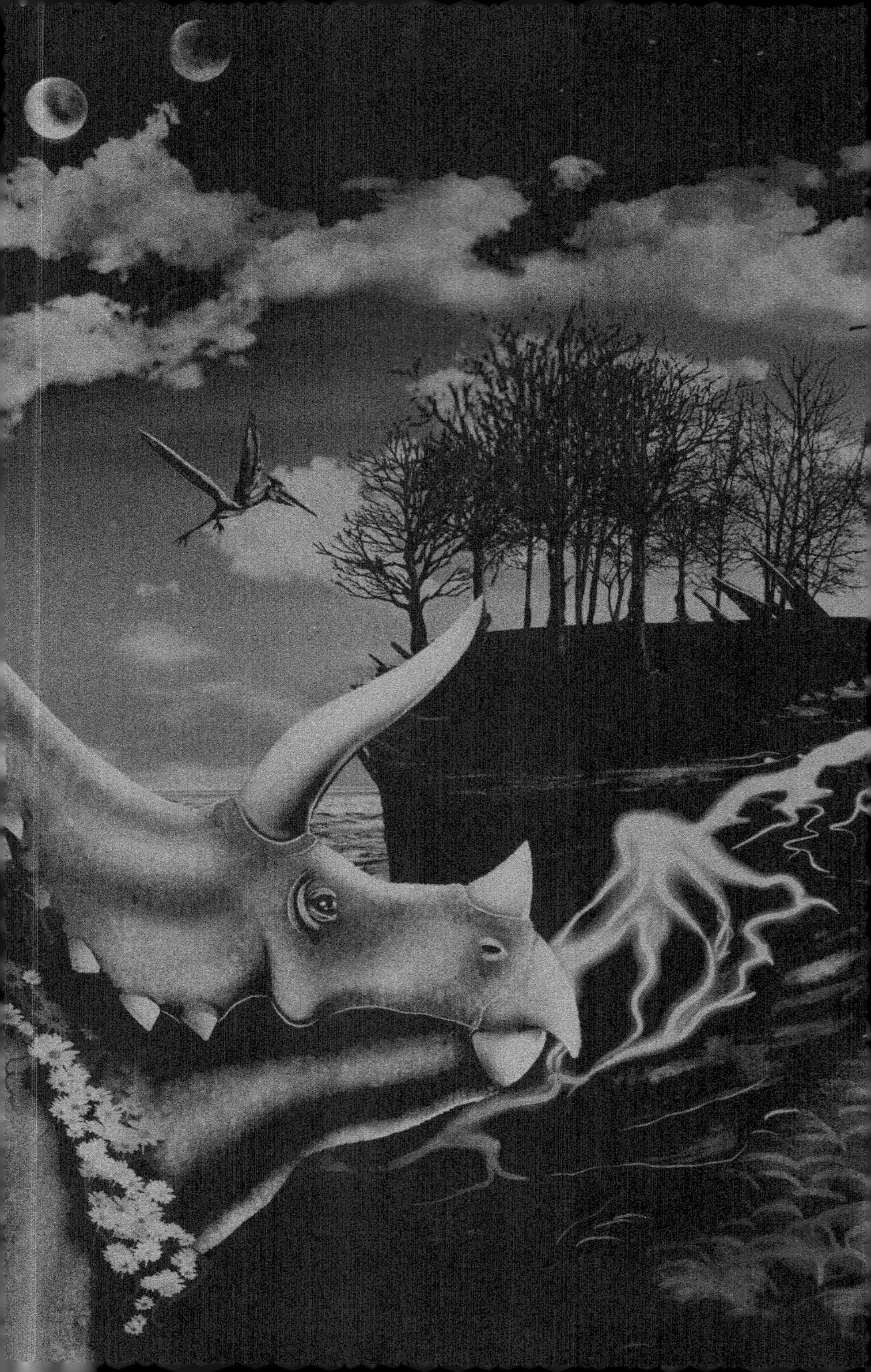

CHAPTER TWELVE: STELLA

As I stepped out of the room into the hall, voices echoed toward me. Male voices—one warm and earthy, the other smooth and quick. Kine? Elias? Thank goodness they made it! They spoke quietly, their words muffled.

Quickening my pace, I slipped forward. The polished tiles were cool beneath my feet, each one hand-painted in delicate designs. Little waves. Tiny fish. Glittering serpents.

It was so strange to be walking through this place. It was as if the memories stood just beyond a curtain, and I was almost in arm's reach.

My fingers traced a line across the cool stone wall. As I emerged at the end of the hall, I opened my mouth to announce myself, but Kine must have heard me coming because he was suddenly in front of me. His golden eyes were white-rimmed, his brow lifted.

"Bug!" He grabbed me in a great bear hug and lifted me off the ground. "I am so sorry," he whispered, squeezing me so tight I could scarcely breathe. "We should've asked Hord for that escort. I didn't think we'd get into that much trouble so fast. I thought it'd be easier to get you here with fewer people drawing attention."

This man gave good hugs. Even if I'd been so inclined, how could I stay mad at him?

"It wasn't your fault." I squeezed him back.

He felt so much more familiar now. We'd been in this place together before. I could almost hear him in my mind, talking about something with shifting and water and hot cakes. The scent of his cologne—blueberries, lemongrass, and charcoal—stirred even more memories here.

I pressed my cheek to his shoulder. "I'm just glad you're all right."

"Me too." He set me down and then stepped back, lightly cuffing my cheek. His brow remained furrowed, the concern apparent in his features. "Elias said you and Buttercup rode out like a greased serpent in a jet chute. Glad that bit of memory kicked in for you and you remembered how to escape on your noble steed."

I laughed at this and nodded, my hand still on his shoulder. His azure tunic and the much darker blue bandolier highlighted his golden-brown skin. Was he actually my brother? Was that who he was to me? He'd said he kind of was.

"I guess riding a triceratops is like riding a bike."

"Sure, sure. Whatever a bike is." He grinned, but his gaze still traveled over me as if to make sure nothing had gone amiss. His breath caught in his throat, and his brow puckered.

"She's going to be fine. She's stronger than you give her credit for." Elias stepped up behind him, shaking his head. His smile was much softer, his dark-blue eyes likewise surprisingly gentle. His expression warmed as soon as he saw me. "I knew you could do it. Looks like you're healing up good." He gestured toward my throat. "Those'll be gone in no time at all."

My hand rose to my neck, heat striking my cheeks. "I'm fine."

A spark of fear flared within my chest. And yet...yet I still craved Brandt. As good as it was to see Kine and Elias, my heart beat for Brandt. Being away from him stung. The heaviness in my chest intensified.

"Do you know... Do we have any way of knowing if Brandt is all right?"

His name was still so strange on my tongue. My heart skipped.

Elias frowned slightly at Brandt's name.

Kine nodded, squeezing my hand. "Yes. He's safe. They took him back to Castle Serpentfire. Got a few knocks, but no serious injuries or lasting harm. His inner court is used to kuvasting him."

I remembered that word! It was a type of combat and conflict resolution that could to the death or just until one party yielded. It was for resolving disputes. Brandt had been good at it. That bit of recalled knowledge somehow made my insides flutter.

Elias gave a soft laugh as he folded his arms. "Candy knows how to wear him down. Don't know what he'd have done without her."

Heat twisted in my belly. Candy. I hated her.

"Well, don't stand on ceremony," Auntie Runa called from beyond the hall, her voice firm but playful. "Let the lady breathe. Come in, darling girl. See if you remember this. You certainly spent enough time here when you were a youth."

Kine and Elias both stepped back, giving me space to enter the enormous open layout of the rest of the house.

My eyes widened. This place was like something out of a fairy tale. Whole sections had actual waterways cut through the floor, but it wasn't like a pool running through the home. It was as if the river entered the house in tributaries and became a part of it. There were structures and interlocking stone columns that seemed designed to provide support even if the earth shifted, and portions of these canals had decorative sluice gates.

Plants grew with abandon. Large domed windows allowed sunlight through. Some looked as if they didn't even have glass. Ferns and vines cascaded down some of the walls. Sculptures adorned the enormous room at random. Colorful mats and blue-green bag chairs formed comfortable seating arrangements at intervals throughout the spacious room with polished tables in between. Dark woven rush rugs were set out along the stone floor and earth floor, most stretched out in immaculate rectangles with a few scrunched a little to the side.

The waters lapped at the stone-sided canals, and the air was thick but fragrant like a greenhouse, a sauna, and an oasis all at once. The interlocking stones had been painted with vivid delicate designs, even on the pillars with broad bases. In a few places, large, jagged juts of something like black mortar cut through. I frowned. Not part of the design. Something more sinister. Like the gouges I'd seen in the earth. Here, in the walls, the stone seemed a little more brittle rather than lighter, but there weren't any fissures or spiderwebbing to suggest deeper structural damage.

"Honk."

"Buttercup!" I laughed a little as she paced out from another hall and approached me, her steps shockingly delicate, as if she understood she was indoors and needed to use her inside feet. She walked through this place like she owned it.

Auntie Runa shook her head as she approached me from the other side. "I haven't seen Buttercup this happy in ages." She set her hands on her bony hips, her wrinkled fingers contrasting against her smooth, colorful sash. "Boys, go fetch the trays I set out. They're in the kitchen. Not a full meal but enough to take the edge off and have ourselves a little chat."

The water splashing and a series of excited chirps drew my attention back to the canals. Were my eyes lying to me?

Those weren't sculptures. They were animals, living here in this home.

On the short thick stone wall nearest me rested a real mata mata turtle with a triangular head and dark shell, sunning itself in the shaft of light from the broad circular window. Fish swam in one of the channels, whisking back and forth in a shimmering school, brilliant silver even in the shadows. Two other triceratopses lounged in the water as well. Both were grey and blue with shorter snout horns and deeper curved crest horns. A tiny one, barely the size of an elephant calf, paddled in the water like a little baby hippo. Manatees munched on large clumps of bright seagrass and shiny kelp.

Two of them lifted their heads as I drew near. The largest, with heavy black mottling on its head and an opaque white eye, lifted its whiskered snout out of the water. A series of rapid chirps followed, each one seeming to mount with excitement. The second one, longer and sleeker with a scar along its left shoulder, poked its head out of the water and then blew more bubbles that mixed with the quick calls. They swam toward me, bubbles streaming along them as they vocalized what seemed like excitement.

Buttercup leaned against me as if jealous.

For a moment, I staggered under the unexpected weight. "Whoa, hey there." Reaching up, I stroked along her jaw. "It's all right, baby girl. I'm just saying hello."

The snort that followed suggested Buttercup did not appreciate that answer.

"Don't be a jealous jabber, old girl," Kine scolded, patting her on the side with a soft *thwap-thwap*. He held the tray he'd brought back with one hand as Elias placed the other on one of the small tables near the water's edge.

Buttercup gave him an annoyed glare and huffed again, but she relented when Kine started scratching behind her frill.

I knelt on the edge of the canal. Names came to me easier now. Bubbles and Bobbles. Bubbles had the opaque white eye. Bobbles had the long scar.

I dropped onto my belly and put my hands out, gently stroking each of them. "You remember me?"

"They always remember," Auntie Runa said. "Just like your big, spoiled baby there." She pointed toward Buttercup with her cane.

Buttercup snorted again.

Auntie Runa continued as if she didn't hear the triceratops's commentary. "Their true names are Maikiao and Dochana, but you just called them Bubbles and Bobbles when you swam here as a child. Not entirely certain what your thought process was with those name choices." Her smile softened as she shook her head, obviously recalling some sweet memory. "Magic can fool folks like us easy enough. We're all susceptible to it. But beasties like them and your baby—well, magic won't fool them."

It was hard not to feel a pang of sadness that I couldn't remember the specifics, only the vague sensations of connection and home. Here I was getting greedy, though. For once, I was feeling like I had returned and I almost belonged. As if things were heading toward right. That was good. This was progress, and I was thankful.

I leaned my face down closer to the water, continuing to stroke the slick skin and bristly whiskers of both the manatees. How many times had I done this in the past? Probably countless. Bobbles liked the underside of his jaw scratched more, while Bubbles liked that little spot right on the center of her forehead. More memories lurked on the edges of my mind, teasing me.

"They all live here with you," I said slowly. "But they're not allowed in all the channels."

"Well, we can't housetrain the manatees," Auntie Runa said with a wry smile, "but the triceratops and all the rest are housetrained. They know to leave. We rotate the channels to keep them clean."

"Buttercup..." I hesitated, realizing I had been about ready to say she was trained, but was she?

Auntie Runa smirked. "She is."

"My memories are returning so oddly," I said with an apologetic shrug. "I don't even know how to explain it. It's like...they just are here in my mind or waiting on the edges."

"It's probably rather disconcerting," Auntie Runa agreed, "but just continue on with it. You should trust your instincts."

Instincts were odd things. If I listened to them, they would have me riding a triceratops again, dodging pits and holes while at the same time launching myself at a tyrannosaur, throwing myself into Brandt's arms, and kissing him until neither of us could see straight. It might also involve pushing Candy off a ledge.

Auntie Runa handed me a white plate with two chunks of bread. The center of the plate dipped, cradling a fragrant combination of oil, greens, herbs, and salt. "Here. Have something to eat, love. Now I'm sure you have many questions. We're going to have to take this cautiously. Your memories haven't fully returned yet, and, well, no one here knows precisely how to manage something like this. In general, when it comes to other forms of magically induced amnesia, it's considered best to allow as much as possible to return naturally rather than forcing it or inundating you."

"Except we're dealing with curses, and apparently, my husband is set to murder me."

"Yes," Auntie Runa said with a dry smile. She passed out the plates to Kine and Elias as well and then sat on the soft blue bag chair. "That does tend to complicate things."

"And there's the matter of Stella's safety," Kine said. "Even keeping Stella's return as much a secret as possible, those assassins will not be the only ones. If others come here, we will be in trouble. I humbly renew my request that you permit us to bring our weapons into this place as well as the shifting rings."

Auntie Runa leaned back on the cushions. "The curse is weakening all forms of Sepeazian magic throughout the entirety of both continents. To protect this space and honor of the Creator of All, I have recently dedicated it to non-violence."

"That...that makes the magic stronger?" It sounded idiotic once I said it aloud, and I cringed.

Auntie Runa nodded slowly. "It seems to be working for now, but also it means that the focus is on defense rather than fighting. Nothing can get in unless I permit it, except in a few places that might be a drop or so weaker."

"Or something breaches the barrier," Kine said gently.

Auntie Runa's thick white eyebrow arched, but she nodded nonetheless. "Yes, well, we'll keep the breach points secure. I assume you want to train Stella in all the old ways," she said.

"Will that weaken the spells?" Kine asked it as calmly as if he were inquiring as to the weather. "You did require that we leave all magically infused items in the lead box."

"I still have the training rings in the Scrying Chamber below. It's the most secure with the wards and the safest so long as the lid to the well remains on after dusk. You may use those to teach her until she is familiar with shifting once again. By that point, I may have another solution. She must be trained if she is to have any chance against the Gola Resh and what is to come. And who knows how fast the memories and skills will return," Auntie Runa responded. Her shoulders sagged for half a breath, but her eyes remained bright and fixed on me. A small smile broke over her face. "It is so good to see you again, Stella."

I smiled at her as well, feeling that same swell of emotion as before. "Can I ask... Who are you to me?"

It felt rude to straight out ask if she was family, but the way she looked at me...it was the way I'd always imagined the grandma I'd never met looking at me.

"I'm the Master of Sight, the seer of seers, and when you were very young, you came to study with me." She pressed her finger to her cheek, smiling. "I knew you before Brandt but not before Kine. Kine came with you. There's quite a lot to tell you, but let's start with the important bits. You, my dear, are a water serpent shifter and a seer, and you got on the wrong side of a powerful pair who were deeply in love and intent on destruction and vengeance. In fact, you were part of the reason their love was destroyed. Do you remember them?"

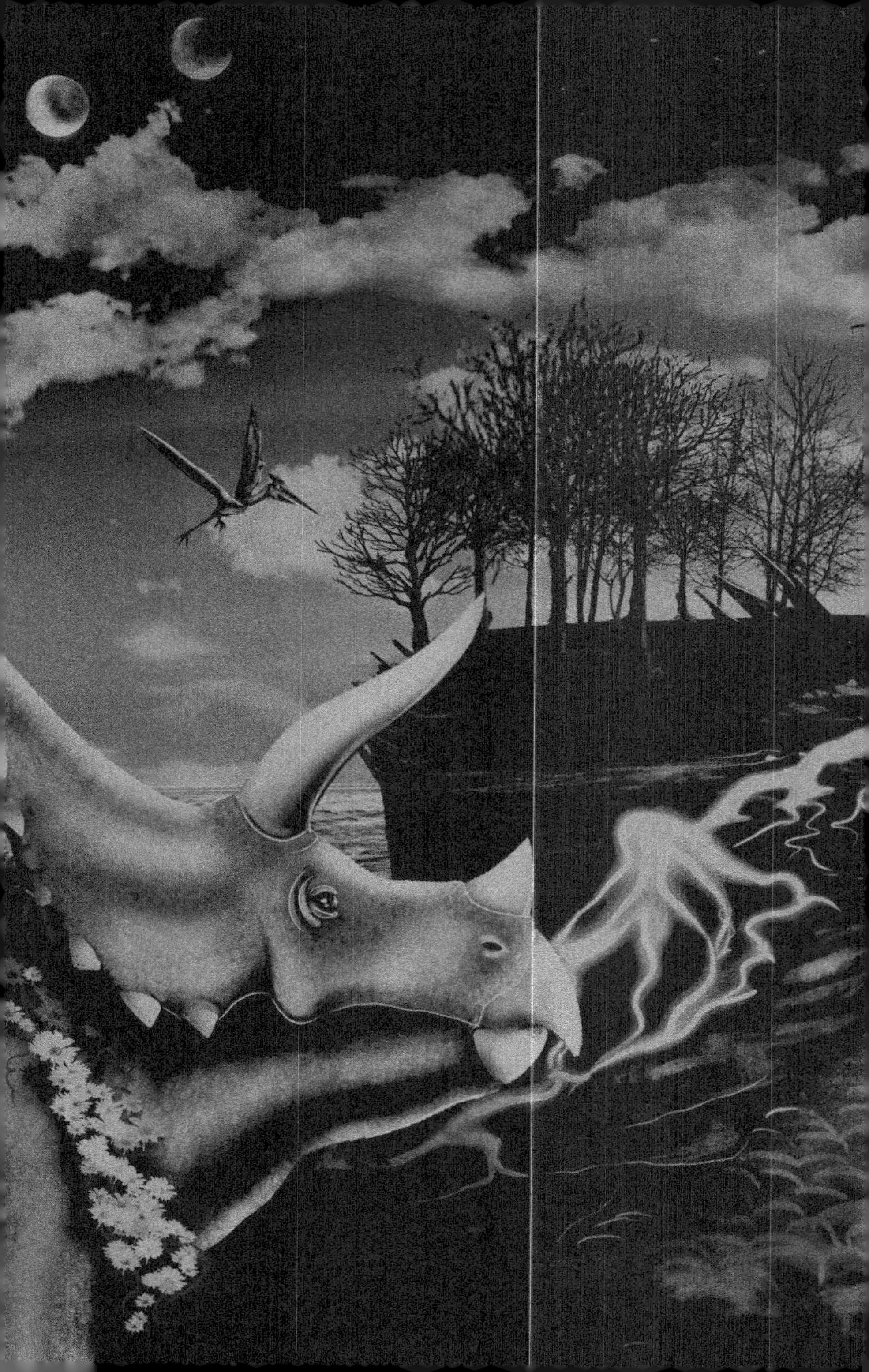

CHAPTER THIRTEEN: STELLA

I swallowed hard. Had I destroyed someone's love? "Yes. I...I don't really remember the specifics. Anything you can tell me would be helpful."

The Gola Resh were part of that magical couple unless there was another pair I'd pissed off somehow. Ihlkit, I hoped not. But if I'd destroyed her bond with her beloved, then maybe that was why she hated me.

Crossing my legs beneath myself, I situated myself on the dark-blue cushion.

Kine looked at Auntie Runa expectantly. He cradled the teacup in his palm rather than holding the handle. Elias appeared almost bored, his gaze fixed on the circular window above as the sunlight slanted through in a golden shaft.

Auntie Runa tapped her fingers against the handle of her cane. Her mouth went a little crooked as her gaze softened. "It started decades ago. The Babadon and the Gola Resh are ancient entities unlike any we have ever encountered. They came to our world seeking a way to strengthen their power. To accomplish this, they placed a curse upon our islands and the seas that surround them to drain them of all their life and magic. They did not intend to stop until they siphoned everything from everything in this place. That curse is still present to this day. And if it ever resumes its countdown, then all who live in Sepeazia will be destroyed."

"I take it we can't flee? We can't run to one of the other continents?" I shifted my weight, uncomfortable. An unsettled feeling grew in the pit of my stomach. Surely we had friends. We couldn't be all alone out here. Could we?

Auntie Runa shook her head. She stroked the baby triceratops that nudged her leg. "Afraid not, dearie. Our people are tied to the magic of this land. The curse the Babadon and the Gola Resh enacted against the two kingdoms of our united Sepeazia is such that it would take all the life from everyone and everything. Every creature. Every plant. Even the bacteria and plankton. Even if we ran, we'd drop dead in our tracks when they completed this curse. We have friends in the other nations who have tried their best to help however they can, but none have succeeded in breaking it. They set this curse upon us approximately fifty-three years ago. We all fought it as best we could. Times grew desperate. The countdown to the destruction of Taivren, our capital, and then of all of Sepeazia. Taivren fell. Then, when there were forty days left of the curse's countdown to destroy Sepeazia, you had a vision that gave the answer." She gave me a knowing look.

My shoulders stiffened. Whispers nudged at the edges of my mind. Brandt had called me a seer. I had just passed over it earlier when Auntie Runa had mentioned it, but now it settled over me. I was a seer.

Auntie Runa stroked the baby triceratops, her voice soft. "Because of your vision and the combined might of our warriors and the killing blow of your beloved, the Babadon was slain and the Gola Resh was captured. To undo the magic of the Gola Resh and the Babadon, at least one needed to be killed in a particular way to end the power of their curses. Ideally, we needed to kill both in that fashion. They needed to be eradicated and consumed. With the Babadon dead and the Gola Resh swearing even crueler vengeance, our people had to find a way to undo her magic. A tall order even for sages, scribes, and scholars as gifted as ours. Not even we seers could fully see the path forward. All that we knew for certain was not all hope was lost."

Buttercup huffed and nudged my arm. With a quick glance to confirm how indignant my triceratops was, I stroked her snout. "Hope sounds good."

"It usually does," Elias said grimly, and Kine gave a somber nod.

Auntie Runa chuckled. "Well, in this case, the hope was not entirely gone, but it also was not fully in the right place. The Gola Resh gave herself a critical wound to free herself to her mortal form and enacted one final curse, the curse that now hangs over our dear Brandt and you. She even gave him a charmed necklace to show the countdown. The one you saw around his neck, I'm sure. For every period he has not killed you, he goes mad for a time, desperate to end you and willing to destroy anyone who gets in his way. It started off happening every eighteen hours, but little by little, it has shortened, though not so badly as this last time. This last time, it leaped forward several hours, as if they didn't exist at all."

"The charm turning yellow..." I whispered, covering my mouth. The plate nearly slipped out of my hand.

Auntie Runa nodded. "Now, going back to that fateful night, she claimed that if Brandt killed you, she would consider ending the curse against Sepeazia. Brandt responded with rage and slew her. Or so we thought. It would seem she has escaped that. But it also seems that she shed the physical body, if what you described is accurate. Something has happened to change her form."

My shoulders dropped, and a weight pressed in upon me. "To end the curse against Sepeazia...he has to kill me."

"Ah, ah, ah, child. That's not what the Gola Resh said, now is it?" Auntie Runa's sharp white eyebrow of hers arched again. "People keep twisting it around, insisting that the Gola Resh meant it as an even trade, but she was quite clear. She would only consider it. It's all rather classic, I suppose, slaughter the queen and the monster relents, but the curse she placed was for vengeance. She set it upon Brandt and you because of her rage. The people have been trying to make sense of all of this, and things change over time, especially decades." She tapped one long, wrinkled finger against the stone tile. "You'll have to stay in hiding, my dear. Some are convinced that all the Gola Resh wants is your death and that magically it will undo the curse."

"But if she said she'd consider it, how do we know for certain she won't? What if there's some mechanism in the curse that would make that happen automatically?" I asked.

My stomach clenched. It wasn't that I wanted to die, but it seemed a fair and vital question to ask. Already feelings of something I could only describe as concern and patriotism were rousing within me. This was my home. These were my people. My people. My creatures. I had been a queen. I was a queen!

Auntie Runa's eyes narrowed. They seemed to grow even darker and murkier for a second. "When the curse was first enacted, my dear, you and Brandt came to me, hand in hand, terrified but prepared. On that day, Brandt showed great wisdom. He was actually the one to insist you seek the seers rather than flying half-nocked into death and destruction. You forgot that, as a seer, you should not look ahead to your own fate in that manner, and you had already given up hope. You believed that it was the only way. Were it not for the fact the Gola Resh had said plainly that it had to be by Brandt's hand that you died, I suspect you might have taken matters upon yourself. Thank the Creator you did not. Brandt asked me to look into the future again and seek the truth of the Gola Resh's promise. It was exceptionally difficult, but eventually, I succeeded."

I leaned forward, my breath catching in my throat. I could practically feel Brandt's hand wrapped around mine, his warmth and strength wrapped around my palm and fingers. Sparks of an old argument flared back into my thoughts. My grip on the teacup tightened. "And what did you see?"

"Betrayal. Darkness. Mourning. The life of everything we hold dear drained away like the remnants of Taivren when it and the strip of land it stood upon slid into the sea, blackened and ruined. The sky went dark from the oppressive force that covered us. It sealed us in like the tephra from a volcano. The waters turned dull."

I bit the inside of my lip. It seemed rude to ask her how she could know for certain, but wasn't it possible there was a misunderstanding?

Auntie Runa's mouth quirked up. She tilted her head forward slightly, her eyes narrowing. The skin around her eyes wrinkled even more. "A reminder in lessons from long ago, my dear. When a seer or a prophet receives a vision or foresight, the clearer and more vivid it is, the more certain it is to happen and the less likely there is to be deviation. So if we ask a question and the Creator deems to answer us in a vision bold and vivid, it means…"

"It means it only ends in one way." My shoulders straightened, and my spine stiffened once I remembered. "It came to you in oil paints?"

Auntie Runa nodded. She sucked her teeth as she settled back. Her lips pressed into a hard line. "It was so clear it was like living it, as if I stood on the marble cliffs at Southern Fire Point and watched all the life be drained out of our lands and waters like a giant sucking it up with a straw. So real I felt my own life leaving me. It burned like fire in my veins until it turned cold and froze me there as all our world became ash and death." She fixed her gaze on me. "The Gola Resh cannot be trusted, girl. She gains power untold through draining Sepeazia of all its life. She won't release it. Remember that."

"She was toying with me in the cavern. It's a game to her."

She snapped her fingers at me. Her murky, golden eyes narrowed as she leaned closer to me. "Not a game. Revenge. Never forget that, my dear. Always remember her motive. This is about vengeance, pure and simple, a desire to cause the most harm and pain possible. Her and that Babadon were going to take the life force of all who live in this place, and they would have succeeded if not for us. They are cruel and vicious, greedy, and above all, concerned only with their own comfort. Now that her love is taken from her, there is no comfort, only sorrow, and she is intent upon spreading that to all she can. That motive is second to her desire to thrive and increase in power. Were the Babadon still here, she might give up her plans for vengeance if she could be reunited with him. That is the only thing she might want more, but with him gone, remember that it is about power and vengeance."

"Do I...do I have visions like you?" I asked cautiously. It didn't feel like something I had. My gift was subtler.

Auntie Runa chuckled. She patted my hand. Though her hand was wrinkled and thin, its strength and warmth could not be denied. "Not exactly. Or not usually. You were never particularly strong with imagining scenes in visions. You feel more than you see in your mind's eye with a few exceptions, usually objects. The world is something you experience through sensation and emotion, and your foresight would either involve an object or an impression. Generally something that needed to be done in the near future rather than far future. In the past, you described it to me as an impression and weight in different parts of your body."

"Hm." I frowned at this. "When I was with Brandt, I felt that weight, but I wanted to be with him."

"Yes, well, not all pressures and weights are the same. It doesn't surprise me that the Gola Resh's magic is warping your own intuition and intensifying your more...physical desires."

"So how do I tell the difference in pressures and sensations?" I asked, leaning forward. "How would I tell how vivid it is? It seems like that isn't like watercolors versus oil paints."

Auntie Runa just chuckled as Kine offered a shrug of commiseration. Elias shook his head, a small smile tweaking at his mouth.

"Intuition, dearie," she said. "You're just going to have to keep practicing and listening. You'll get it wrong sometimes. You'll get it right others." She strode over to one of the shelves and removed a polished wood box. The lock snicked open, and she removed a leather-bound sketchbook with pressed leaf pages. She then fished out something that resembled a blackwood pencil. "Here. You should practice drawing your intuitions and whatever you see. Even if it doesn't reveal anything to you, it will help you calm and process the world around you and learn better what you are sensing."

"That sounds like my foresight would be hard for others to verify." I frowned as I accepted them. The pages had a soft yet almost coarse texture to them that would grip the graphite well. I'd always loved doodling and sketching random nonsense. But it hadn't ever meant anything. How could I have ever hope to gain mastery over a skill like this when I couldn't even draw what I saw?

"Precisely." She returned to her seat and lifted her teacup. "That is why your mastery requires that you act on it and prove it. All must be proved, but it is so tricky for those like you. Not impossible, though. None of this is impossible. Just stay aware and listen."

I opened my mouth to ask another question. The ground shook. Silt and dust sifted from the ceiling. Everything swayed.

I froze, my eyes widening.

"Earthquake?" Elias started to his feet, looking around as if it were off somehow.

Kine steadied the teacup before it spilled over onto the baby triceratops. Auntie Runa simply stiffened, her gaze turning to the well and the thick mist that coiled up from it. The animals did not move though the waters churned in the canals.

The shaking ceased within seconds.

Something was wrong. The space between my shoulders and down my neck burned like an electrical shock.

Auntie Runa collapsed onto one of the dark rush rugs. Her body twitched as her eyes rolled back into their sockets.

"Auntie Runa!" The teacup fell from my hand and smashed on the stone. I dropped beside her and swept my hand beneath her head and tried to cradle her as her body convulsed.

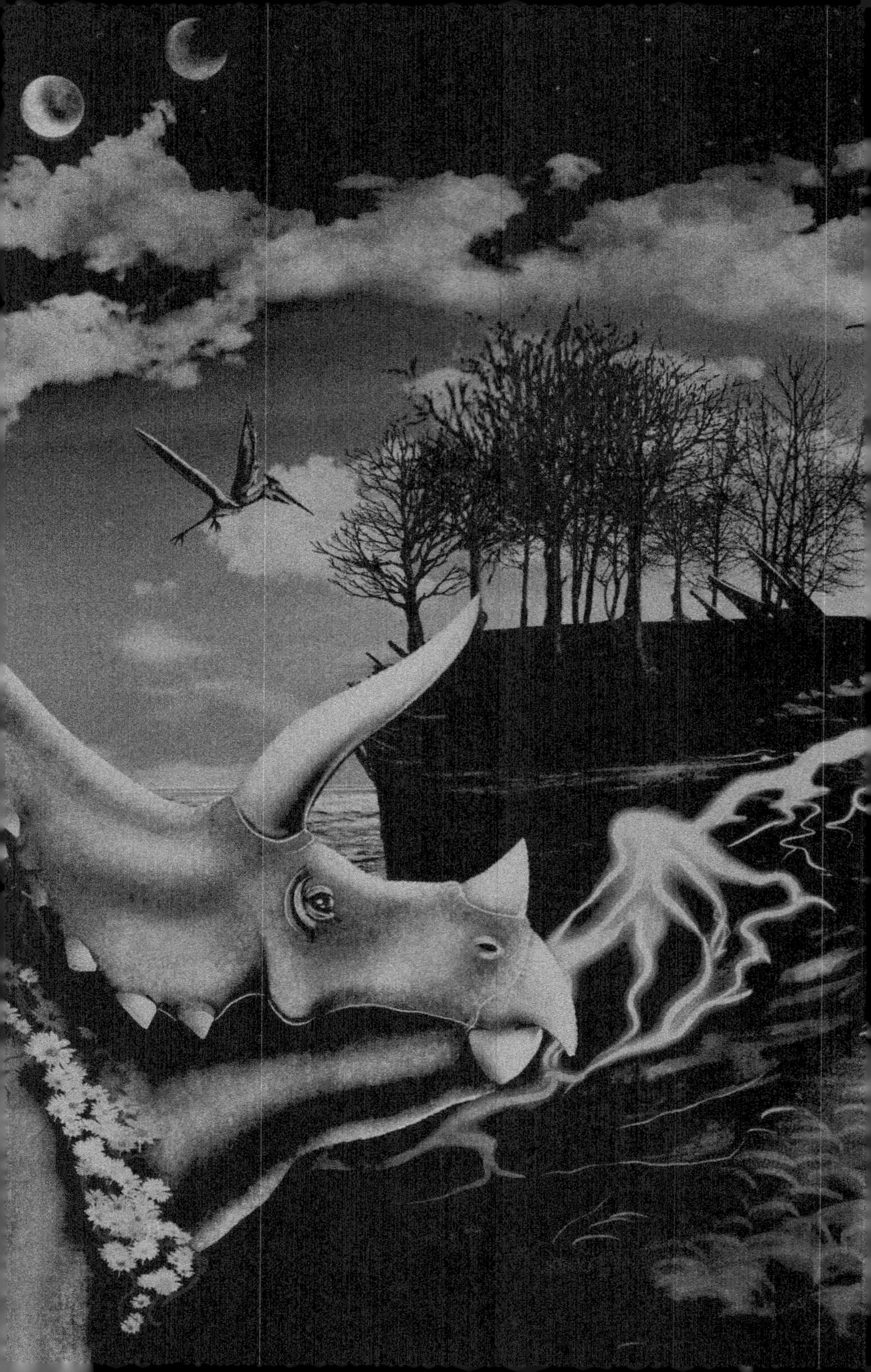

CHAPTER FOURTEEN: BRANDT

I'd sent Cahji to fetch the council heads again. They weren't going to be thrilled about another meeting, but with word of the Gola Resh's return, there was new information that would perhaps transform our search. It had to be so. By all that was good and holy, it had to be so.

Hands clasped behind my back, I paced.

This second discussion with the council members was not likely to be brief. Informing them of Stella's return still felt like a mistake. For now, there was plausible deniability. Sort of. Enough.

I halted. It was the fifth day of the week. Crossing to the back of the room, I returned to the shallow basin that held the water mirror. Swishing my hand over the surface, I focused on the corresponding water mirror. Its tenuous connection attached to mine, the magic far stronger and stable than any water mirror here. The waters swirled in response. My reflection wavered, the waters shimmering. Then another chamber was revealed. An almost unearthly stillness spread through the connection.

I clasped my hands behind my back. "Fine?" I asked the water mirror.

A deep voice with a cool edge spoke out of the water mirror. The waters rippled with each syllable. "Fine. Fine?"

"Fine."

I watched as the waters stilled. Perhaps I should use the mirror to speak with Stella as well. She was with Auntie Runa now. I could apologize for almost killing her. See her face. Ask her how she was. If she wanted to speak with me.

My fingers brushed the cool rim of the basin, and I brought Auntie Runa's water mirror into my thoughts, but there was no pulse of magic, no connection to indicate that magic was present in the water there. She'd probably cut off the connection to reduce ways for the Gola Resh to slip past the wards. Wards and other protective magics not cut deep into the very heartstones of our people had become trickier to maintain.

Perhaps I could send a message another way. Perhaps—

The entire castle shook. The stone walls and foundation had been built to both absorb and withstand tremors, and this one didn't feel as strong or large as most of the earthquakes, but something was off with it. A strange burning sensation moved across my body, rippling out through my muscles as if it coursed in my veins.

As I seized one of the ledges fixed into the wall, another tremor rocked the castle foundations. I clung to the slick surface for support as screams and shouts echoed from the courtyard below, the water in the water mirrors sloshing and spilling.

The tremors passed.

The hairs on the back of my neck prickled, a dangerous heat spreading over me.

This wasn't an earthquake. Not a true earthquake.

There was a charge to it. Similar to when the Gola Resh summoned the hourglass before the collapse of the capital.

The hourglass.

The mini raptors fled the chamber, hissing and calling out, all except Scarlet, who bolted to me. She hissed and dropped low to the ground, her ruby eyes fixed behind me on the iron table and the hourglass.

Dread surged over me like a tidal wave as I turned to face it.

It stood where it always had, but the otherworldly glow had returned. The light of the iridescent sand surrounding the representation of the consumed city glowed. The red and black sands had returned to their vivid colors, and the sands hissed down into the lower bulb.

My blood went cold.

The curse against Sepeazia had resumed its countdown. The sand resumed sliding down past the lines that marked the days that remained.

We had twenty-nine days before all was destroyed.

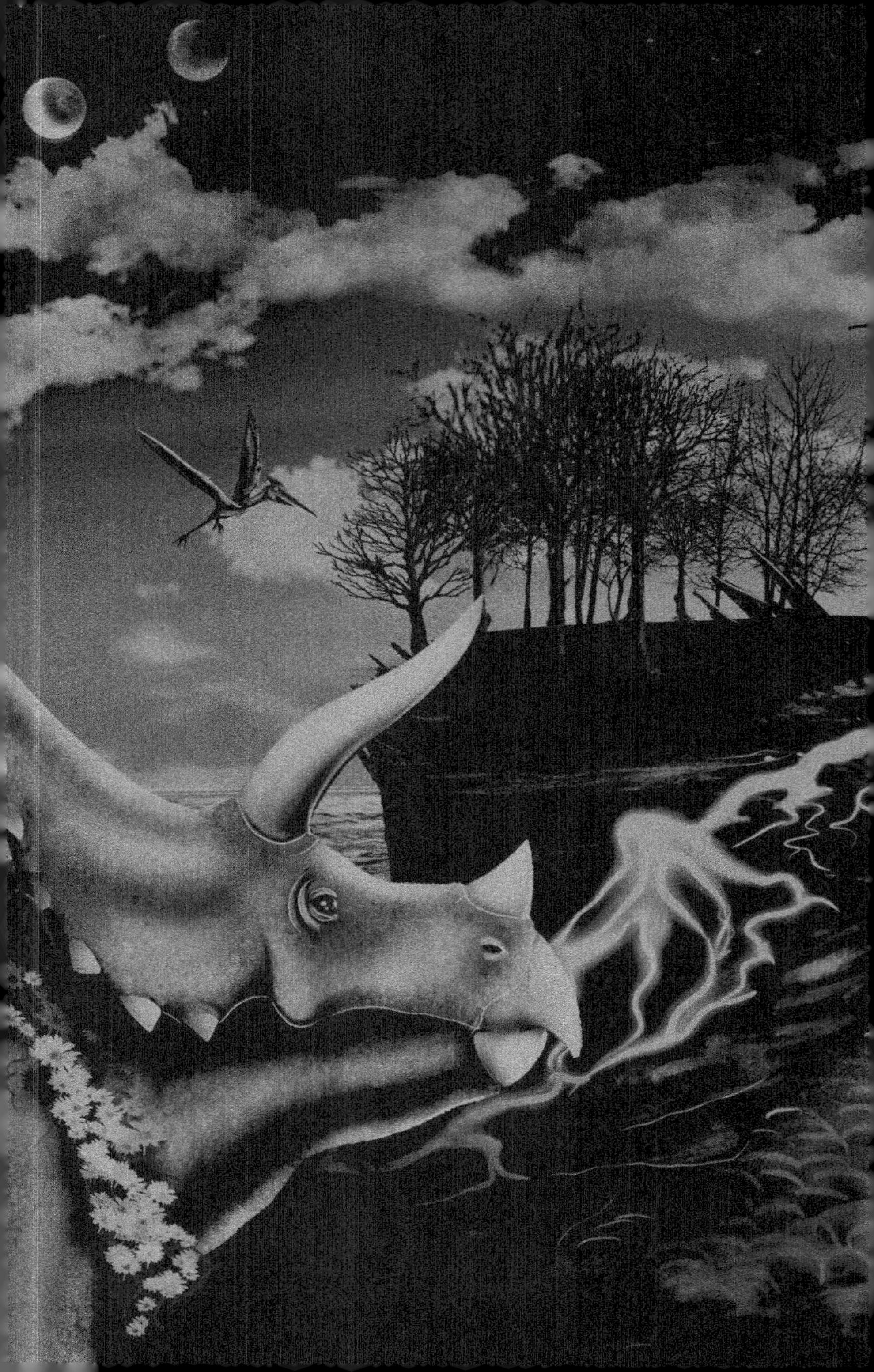

CHAPTER FIFTEEN: STELLA

As I supported Auntie Runa's head, Kine took her pulse. Elias brought wet cloths and placed them across her throat and forehead.

"What's happening to her?" I cried.

"It's a seer trance," Elias said, shaking his head. He cupped the side of her face as he examined her. "She's receiving a vision, most likely."

Kine nodded in agreement. He finished checking her head to ensure there were no wounds or cuts. "She could be like this for a while."

The trembling and shaking had stopped, and her pulse had steadied. Whimpering, baby triceratops nudged her. The other creatures did not appear as concerned. It was as if this happened rather frequently. Even Buttercup just gave a soft whoosh of her breath against Auntie Runa's forehead.

"Let's get her to her room," Elias said. "Once she starts to recover, we can move her into the waters to ease the vision's arrival."

"Agreed." Kine clicked his tongue. His brow remained knit.

Together, he and Elias lifted Auntie Runa's now still body

and carried her down the hall to a cozy bedroom with circular windows like mine.

I turned down the embroidered quilt and stepped aside as they placed her on the bed. The room smelled like water lilies and clear running water, peaceful and pleasant as the stone fountain that spilled water over its ladder. It seemed untouched by the jarring or earthquake or whatever it was, aside from some trinkets that had crashed to the floor and a couple of pictures that had fallen. Like the other pieces of furniture, the bed, dresser, and tables were bolted to the floor.

Elias drew the covers up over her and placed the back of his hand against her forehead. "The onset was far more intense than most I've seen, perhaps because of whatever caused that earthquake, but...I think she's all right."

"Then why isn't she waking up?" I knelt beside her, gathering her hand in mine.

She looked so frail right now, her features drawn and her eyes shuttered. Her beautiful wreath of snowy-white hair had slipped loose from its silver pins, the fragrant herbs and greens sliding onto her shoulders and the pillow.

"This is part of the process for a vision like this and a seer like her," Kine said gently. "She isn't in danger right now. We need to let her rest. Whatever vision she is receiving, it will take its time in appearing to her."

"What do we do?" I asked, biting the inside of my lip. "Should I make her some tea? Or get her some medicine?" Surely I was supposed to do something.

"Let me take care of her," Elias said. He cupped his hand along my elbow, his gaze soft. "I don't mean to be rude, but she'll recover faster if she has peace and stillness."

Kine gave a nod of agreement. He tugged gently at my arm and drew me out of the room. As we entered the hall, Elias shut the door. The lock snapped into place with a soft click.

Hugging myself, I drew in a deep breath. Several doors lined this hall, each one marked with a distinct crest and secured. A few had elaborate eyes painted on them.

"Do we just wait out here?" I asked.

"She's probably going to be resting for a while. If you're up for it, we should probably get started on training you to shift." Kine placed a hand on my shoulder. The worry lines on his brow eased. "It's all right, Bug. This sort of thing happens to seers. Usually with more warning, but Auntie Runa is going to be all right. She's been through far worse."

His grip comforted me. I ducked my head, then pushed my hair back with both hands. "Kine, I'm trying so hard to remember, and I'm sorry—"

"You don't have to apologize. Listen, this is new for all of us. I know I'm supposed to be careful about what I tell you so we don't overload your memories with everything else that's coming in," he said gently, "but if there's something simple you want answered, you can ask. I don't think there's any harm in it. Some pieces may be better if you hear them from, say, Brandt, but other than that...maybe it would do you good to think of something else than all that's happened."

There were a lot of things I wanted to ask Brandt, a lot that I still needed to know, but Kine was right. I wanted to hear those words from Brandt's lips. Like how did we meet? What would it take for us to be together again? What was our first kiss like? Did he like to cuddle? How did he propose to me? What were our fights about? Who was Candy? Why was Candy around?

Ihlkit!

What I wouldn't give to see him right now.

But he wasn't here. Kine was.

And I had questions for him as well, starting with the way he looked at me, not with the passionate, brooding hunger of Brandt but with a gentle, rueful affection.

Kine continued to study me, his brow furrowed. "Your

favorite color used to be periwinkle and yellow because you never liked having just one. You still like both those colors?"

My mouth quirked a bit at that. That was such a ridiculous thing to ask, but it kind of made me like him even more. "Yeah."

"When we were kids, you used to try and trick me into cleaning crabs and fish. Do you remember how?"

I shook my head.

He gave a short huff, then tilted his head. "Well, I don't know if I should tell you because I don't want you pulling it on me again. Whenever it was time to clean the fish and crabs, you'd always have an accident. All the greens for the compost would fall over or the corn bin would topple. And you'd ask me to get started on the fish and crabs while you cleaned up. Usually by having a triceratops or the manatees eat it. Sometimes you didn't even actually spill anything. You just told me you did." He raised an eyebrow at me. "And you always disappeared when it was time to wash dishes. It was annoying."

More memories rippled over me. My smile broadened. "You didn't really fall for it though, did you? I don't think you were really fooled."

"Eh." He shrugged. "Maybe. Maybe not. You'd get on a roll. And you never knew when to let a bit go. Sometimes I was just curious how long you'd keep it up. Besides, I don't mind washing the dishes."

"Okay... So, who are you to me exactly?" I tilted my head, studying the laugh lines along the eyes and the smile lines around his jaw. "We're—we're family?" He *felt* like family.

"By choice rather than blood." He tapped my nose. "Your folks took me in when I was a kid, and you were barely able to read signs in the water. They gave me a home. You were so excited to have a big brother. You told me all the rules, all the things I had to do. I think maybe some cousin or something out there connects us by blood, but your folks gave me a home because I needed one."

"What happened to my folks?" Those memories loomed at the edge of my mind, mercifully vague and dark. "They...they're dead, aren't they?"

He raked his hand through his loose, blue curls and then sighed. "Yeah. I'm sorry, Bug. They passed a while back, before we knew what was going on with the Gola Resh and the Babadon. At that time, all we knew was that magic was starting to fail or falter at random points if it wasn't cut into heartstones or something similar. Your folks got caught in one of the freak monsoons before we could save them and a bunch of the others. Couldn't get there in time, and our magic failed. It was one of the first times we started seeing just how bad the Gola Resh and Babadon's magic interfered with ours." His eyes misted with tears as he looked at me, his brow furrowing. "But you know, it was funny in a way because your folks, they weren't seers like you. They couldn't have known what was coming, but the last thing your momma told me was that I needed to make sure you stayed safe, and your da told me the same. Asked me to swear to it. So I did. I swore I'd see you got to old age and had lots of grandbabies and great-grandbabies. Your folks were proud of you, Bug. Real proud."

A knot of emotion choked me. Tears burned the backs of my eyes. I dipped my head forward. It wasn't an actual memory that pressed itself into my mind, just something gentle within my awareness, and the words sprang to my lips as if they had been summoned. "I think you mean our parents, Kine, and I know—I can feel it—they were proud of you too."

He brushed his hand along my cheek. "I won't break my promise to them or to you, Bug. No matter what, I've got you. I'm rooting for you and Brandt both, but if I've got to choose, I don't care that he's king. I'm siding with you."

"You won't have to make that choice." I said that with all the conviction I could, and I meant it.

His smile went a little crooked. "It's good to have you back, Bug. Now let's get started on reminding you of just what you're capable of."

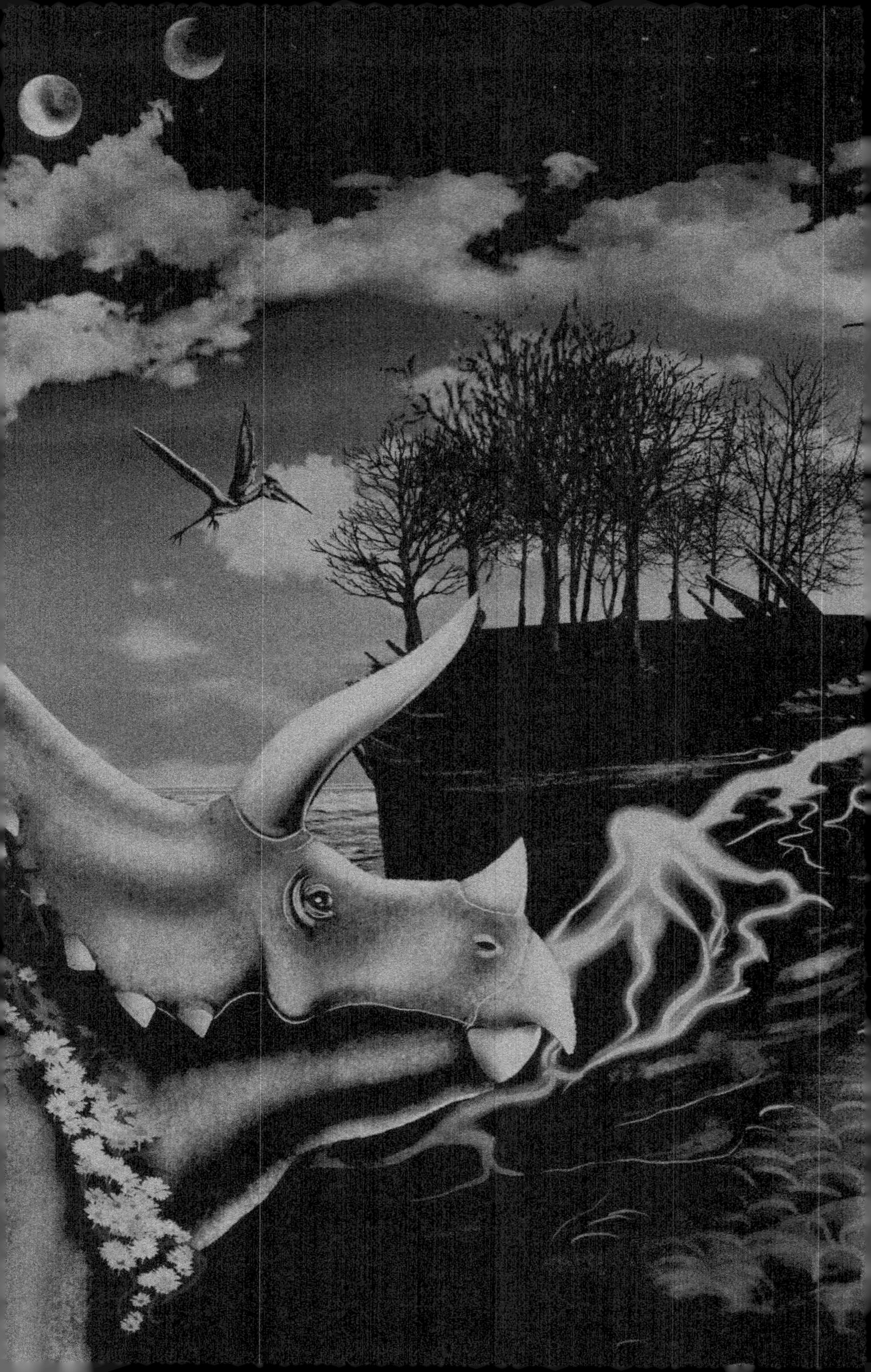

CHAPTER SIXTEEN: STELLA

*K*ine pushed the door open and gestured to the stone staircase that wound down into the glowing blue light.

The chamber he led me into was cool and quiet, seemingly undisturbed by the tremors earlier. Instead of a floor of stone though, it was sand. The air smelled like stone and...electricity maybe? I wasn't sure. My bare feet sank into the pale-grey sand, fine as the white sand in Siesta Beach. It was a sharp contrast to the hard stone walls surrounding us.

I'd been here before. My nerves prickled with anticipation, excitement curling in my belly.

Blue light flowed from the swirling river that curled across the back third of the chamber. It flowed swiftly, the azure glow casting dancing shadows across the sandy floor that did not seem to be connected or attached to anything. The water flowed out through a dark, narrow chamber, splashing and gurgling.

A large well stood in the back corner, similar to the one in the back of the main room on the first floor at the back. This one had a large wooden lid fitted over it. An ethereal azure glow leaked out along the seam, and thick waxy vines grew along the back of the well and up the wall. They crept up the interlocking stone wall into the vent. Perhaps they were connected somehow? This was the well Auntie Runa said had to stay shut. Perhaps all of them had to.

"Now, I know a lot has happened, and I should have asked this before we went down all those stairs, but are you sure you want to start now?" Kine asked. "We could get some rest and start tomorrow morning."

He meant that offer, though he obviously felt we should start now, and I agreed. We didn't have time to waste. That certainty hardened in my gut.

"We can get started. Let's get as far as we can tonight."

"All right," he said, cracking his knuckles. "We're going to do a little bit of double work here. This is the Scrying Chamber. It's used for training, and the sand is good for strengthening the shifting and softening falls. We'll only be able to do the basics because of the wards and spells Auntie Runa's set up, but it'll get you back into a groove."

He strode over to the stone wall and removed one of the blocks. It slid out like a puzzle piece. He removed a thick silver ring from the box. It was unadorned, but light seemed to emanate from it for a moment.

"You put this on your fourth finger on your left hand," he said.

As he dropped it into my palm, a surge of energy coursed up my arm. A tang of pain and discomfort as well as excitement too. I slid the cold metal onto my finger, shivering. There was something familiar stirring in my veins and pulsing in my fingertips.

He continued, "Now, all you do is focus on what you want to become. In this case, this is a training ring. It won't allow you to assume a full form, but it will let you start flexing. Your first task is to become a rectangle."

"A rectangle?" My eyebrow arched as I studied the ring. "You just want me to turn into a rectangle?"

His mouth quirked up. "A rectangular prism, to be more precise. You'll need volume. We're going to do shapes just until you get the feel of shifting energy again. Full-form shifting is excruciating if you don't do it properly. Even just shifting a portion of yourself. So when you're strong again in the basics, it'll be easier. Maybe it'll even ground your memories and make the more complex forms effortless. Sort of like a bridge with a good foundation. It may help if you close your eyes."

Drawing in a deep breath, I closed my eyes, envisioned a silver rectangle, clenched my hand into a fist, and—

Oh!

My body tore apart and came back together, jagged shards of ice and fire cutting through my veins. My field of vision collapsed entirely, but I wasn't blind, just aware in a different way. The edges of my consciousness and my rectangular form were the most sensitive, the temperatures playing along them with uncanny nuance. More to the center was only a weight and dullness. Sound ceased to exist, but vibrations spoke about the world around me.

It was hard to put into words, but some of it was familiar somehow.

The form fell away, and I staggered to my feet, gasping. "I was a rectangle!"

Kine chuckled. His head dipped forward as he nodded. "Yes, you were. You up for more?"

"Yes!"

Maybe it was stupid, and it certainly did sting, but turning into shapes was surprisingly entertaining. Laughing, I clenched my fist once more and became a rectangle.

Giddiness was not the emotion I had expected to experience, but there was something almost fun, childlike, and comforting in shifting. It was almost like play. It tapped into something old and ingrained within me, something that reveled in being let out.

Kine encouraged me with each shift, urging me then to become different shapes. I could only hold each for a few seconds, sometimes ten, if I was particularly focused.

But I did it.

Again and again.

Each shape had its own sensation and...voice? Was that it?

Voice didn't fully encapsulate the sensation, but each one had something about it. Triangles? Itchy. Rectangles? Curious. Circles? Hilarious and sometimes terrifying if I started rolling away.

Kine switched his teaching instructions based on my form. He didn't use words when I was a shape—at least none I heard. A simple tap-tap near one point. Another tap-tap at another. A firm hand or a foot if I started to spiral away.

When I returned to my human shape, he gave me pointers. "Tuck your elbows in before you shift" or "draw three breaths before you start so you have enough air in your lungs." Sometimes he explained more about how to connect these forms into the larger water serpent form.

Each time I changed, it got easier.

To exist simply as a shape while remaining conscious in some manner...it wasn't a language I could speak, but it was something. Like a dance I could once have done in my sleep. A dance I had once loved. A dance I was returning to and whose flow swept me up in its passionate embrace.

After what felt like hours, I dropped out of another rectangular prism. That time, I had managed to hold the form for thirty seconds.

"How exactly does this work?" I wiped the sweat from my brow and combed my fingers through my hair. "The rings and shifting, I mean."

"Our shifting abilities are a gift from Vawtrians. You might call them true shifters," Kine said, arms still crossed over his broad chest. He had paced back and forth on the sandy floor, leaving grooves and footprints. He seemed pleased with my progress, his manner even easier and calmer than before. "They can turn into whatever they want, heal from almost any wound, and can take only one mate their entire lives. They also wander and explore. Before they found us, we weren't water serpent shifters at all. Some Vawtrians fell into our world. They needed our help, and we gave it. Quite a lot happened, but the short of it is that they channeled their magic into reservoirs for us and showed us how to make rings that would allow us to change but only into water serpents. It was fitting, as we had used the water serpents we tamed to help save them."

"Do all Sepeazians become water serpents then? Or do only some of us get the rings?"

"Each of us has to prove that we are worthy and capable of the form first. The rings allow for a certain number of transformations before they must be returned to one of the sources and filled with the energy again. The rings are kept within the well for a night, and then they are returned."

"Is it—is it like in those werewolf stories? I have an inner water serpent?" That idea sparked quite a bit of interest for me, but it didn't feel quite right.

Kine chuckled. He raked his hand through his hair as he tilted his head. "I mean, sure, maybe you personally have an inner water serpent, but that isn't how it is traditionally. Traditionally speaking, the water serpent form is a representation of you as a water serpent. You're still you inside, just sometimes the outside changes its shape. It's always the same one, and that's good. It makes it much easier for when you do go to shift again. We don't have to worry about adapting the form or changing it in some other way. It becomes woven deep into our minds."

"Oh." That didn't sound quite as magnificent as having an

inner water serpent. Then again, if I had had an inner water serpent, it probably would have shown up or said something to me during all my years on Earth. "What does mine look like?"

"As a water serpent? You're blue and gold, like Brandt is red and black. Kind of funny, really. It's why both kingdoms in Sepeazia thought yours was a blessed and fated match. It all came together so naturally."

The pang that cut through my heart made me wish more than ever that I could be with Brandt again. It hurt, even into my lungs and my spine, like an ache that was only going to grow.

I hugged myself tight. "That's rather beautiful."

"There's a lot beautiful about what you and Brandt were," he said.

Were? My eyebrows lifted.

He lifted his hand as he shook his head. "Still are. Sorry, Bug. Don't read into it. Brandt has never stopped loving you. I can promise you that."

"Really?"

I wanted to believe him, but Candy's face flashed back into my mind. Elias had said she was good at calming Brandt down and comforting him, that she had been there for him. Heat coiled in my belly, but it wasn't fair for me to be jealous. After all, he had to be lonely. But something felt wrong about it, no matter how reasonable I wanted to be.

"Yeah. I don't think he ever really gave up hope that you'd be back," Kine said gently. "Not really."

A sharp scoff cut through the air.

I turned sharply.

Elias stood at the halfway mark on the staircase, arms folded over his chest.

Kine's eyebrow lifted. "Everyone had moments of doubt, including me."

"I didn't." Elias's lips pressed into a tight line. "I never doubted. I knew she would make it back. I knew she would make it back from the chasm in the Shadow Hall too. And—" He cut himself off. His expression twisted, his dark eyes blazing. "Doesn't matter. Just came down to say Auntie Runa woke enough to tell me what she needs, so I'm making red soup, and I'll take care of the animals as well. We'll eat in a few hours. If training lasts that long." He turned and stalked away.

My brow tweaked as he strode back up the stairs. He didn't make a sound at all, but anger and offense rippled off him.

I kept my arms wrapped tight around myself. "What was that about?"

"Just..." Kine shook his head, raking his hand through his curls. "'s nothing. We all love you and care about you, Stella. Sometimes we don't all agree about how it's shown, but we're all on your side and on Sepeazia's side. Let's get back on the training. We don't have much time."

I cast one more glance over my shoulder at the staircase as Elias disappeared.

It was strange. He cared so much, yet when I looked at him, I felt nothing. No familiarity. No connection. No awareness. Not even a hint.

And that felt deeply wrong.

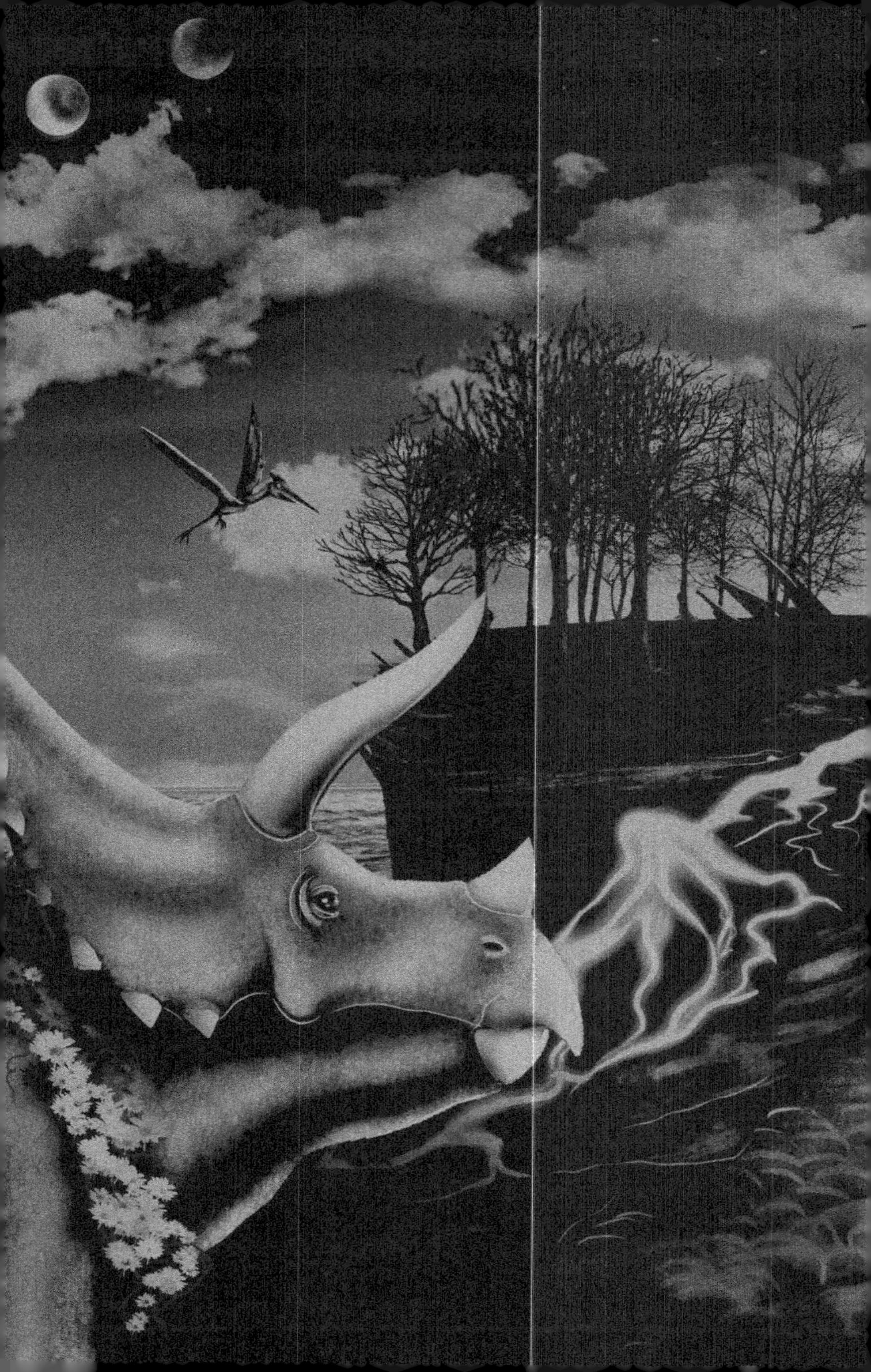

CHAPTER SEVENTEEN: STELLA

Kine refused to talk anymore about what had happened and instead focused on the training. He encouraged me to continue with the exercises, and we practiced until my muscles screamed and my brain ached from focusing. He was a patient teacher.

The remaining time flew until Elias called us to join him for dinner. He had already fed Auntie Runa who was still half in the dream state. The red soup tasted familiar. It reminded me of hearty coconut, tomato, and chicken broth with walnuts, basil, sweet potatoes, corn, and dark leafy greens.

"You did an incredible job, Elias," I said, hoping to draw a smile from him.

He sat hunched in his chair, cradling his bowl with one hand. When I spoke, he glanced up and gave me a faint nod.

Kine ate in silence.

What was going on here?

I frowned. "Is Auntie Runa all right?" I asked, even though I'd already asked that when we'd first come up.

Elias managed a small smile. "Yes. She's as fine as she was ten minutes ago." He set his bowl down on the plate. The dishes clinked against one another. "How did the training go? I'm sure it's all coming back to you."

"It is, actually, but we're only in the beginning stages. Do you shift as well?"

Elias shrugged. "Not at all."

"Elias is a type of seer." Kine rose and brought the pot back from the kitchen. With practiced care, he ladled out more servings for each of us. Fragrant steam wafted around us. "More foresight than visions. Charcoal sketches mostly. Sometimes pencil. Strong lines. That about sums it up, wouldn't you say, Elias?"

Elias nodded, his manner calmer.

"There's so much to learn," I said, grateful that the tension was easing. "What does it mean though? More foresight than visions?"

"There's a difference between sight and prophecy," Elias explained. "Prophecy is connected to the divine and much rarer. Foresight and the like—what we seers usually do—is the awareness of possibilities. There isn't necessarily a divine will associated with it. Strong intuition allows you to see through it to what is most likely, but sometimes it's more. I see through intuition that I put on the page. You feel your intuition."

"How do you know if it's more?"

He twitched a shoulder in response, offering an apologetic smile. "It's probably not what you want to hear, but being a seer isn't like being a shifter. It's more instinctual—"

"Instinctual," I said as he said it. Sighing, I laced my fingers together on the top of my head. "Great. Right now, I feel like my instincts are split between good and bad takes, and I have no idea which is which."

"Auntie Runa will help you get back on track," Kine said gently. "She's probably going to be in and out of this vision state for another few days."

"What brought the vision on? Was it the earthquake?" I asked.

"It wasn't an earthquake, at least not one of natural causes." Elias took another spoonful of soup. The fragrant steam rose around his face. He shook his head.

Kine made some odd noise of affirmation.

Elias's gaze remained fixed on the soup. He lowered his spoon to the bowl without tasting it.

"What?" I frowned.

"It's the curse," Elias said quietly. He shook his head, wiped his mouth with the cloth napkin, and rose. His fists were gripped tight. "The countdown has started again."

"Perhaps—" Kine started.

Elias struck his fist on the table, jarring the dishes and sloshing the drinks. The muscles in his jaw jumped. He started to say something, then stopped, unclenched his fists, and sighed. "What else can it be? You are the one who said the Gola Resh had returned and was not dead, that she is the one who trapped Stella in the chasm. She stopped the curse. Now she has started it again. It makes too much sense. Just because we don't want it to be so doesn't keep it from being true. The curse starting its countdown again is what makes the most sense. And worse still, she's no longer bound to a physical form."

Kine nodded slowly. "Fair enough."

An uneasy sensation welled up in the pit of my stomach. Curling my fingers around my cloth napkin, I cleared my throat. "How...how long do we have? If it turns out that the curse's countdown has resumed, I mean."

"Twenty-nine days." Kine pushed his bowl of soup aside. As he looked up, some of his mask slipped, and I saw the raw, painful emotion in his eyes—the fear, the uncertainty. He opened his mouth to speak then shut it.

"It could be less, especially if the magic continues to become more unstable," Elias added. "I doubt that Auntie Runa's vision will bring us much comfort either."

"Did she say anything?" I whispered.

He shook his head. "But you can tell by how she's lying there, it's drained her badly, and she's sad. When I fed her some broth, she had tears in her eyes. She didn't even want to eat at first."

Kine released a slow breath. He stood, his hands braced gently on the tabletop. The embroidered tablecloth scrunched beneath his fingertips. "True or not, it doesn't matter," he said evenly. "For now, what we must do has not changed. Stella, we need to get you through as much of your training as possible so that when we know the next step, we can act. We're going to have to trust that it will be enough."

"She needs rest too," Elias murmured. "Ihlkit, this has been a horns-damned nightmare."

Kine gave a faint nod.

Before he could say anything, I tightened my grip on the napkin. "I—this doesn't feel like we're doing enough."

"It's all we can do for now," Kine said.

"Can I see Auntie Runa?"

Though Elias started to object, Kine nodded. "Yeah, we'll clean up. Then I'll come get you so we can train a little more if you're up for it."

The hall to Auntie Runa's room was two halls from my own. My footsteps light and quick, I slipped inside.

Outside, it was dark, moonlight spilling through the window and shadows stretching long beneath it. Memories of little footsteps, heavy thunder, and scrambling up onto the bed overtook my mind. I could practically hear Auntie Runa shushing me. *"Don't you cry, lovely. Could be the spirits playing a game of pins and balls. Or could be a good cleansing storm. Nothing to fear."*

If only all I had to fear were storms and thunder.

Auntie Runa lay motionless in the bed. Muscles fluttered in her face and neck.

Kneeling on the rug, I placed my hands over hers and leaned closer. "I hope you feel better soon," I whispered. "I don't remember you well, but I'm so scared right now. I don't know how I'm going to be enough to fix any of this, let alone what to do. All my life I have never felt like I fit or like I was in the right place. Now…now I am finally starting to feel like I am where I should be, and the curse countdown starts again. It feels like it's all going to be snatched away. Worse than that, like it's going to be completely destroyed."

Auntie Runa's fingers twitched beneath my hands, and tears rolled down my cheeks. Sniffling, I ducked my chin.

It was so quiet in here aside from the chuckling of the water fountain. My moods had been up and down all day. Now all I wanted to do was bury my head in a pillow and hide from the world.

What kind of person was I? This poor old woman had suffered something similar to a seizure, and here I was complaining to her. If ever there was proof she had been like family to me, perhaps this was it. But I could do better. I would.

Drawing in a deep breath, I pressed a kiss to her wrinkled hand. "It'll work out. I know it will. Even if I don't know the specifics."

More tears rolled down my cheeks. That had to be true. I'd make it true.

I don't know how long I was in there, holding Auntie Runa's hand, but eventually, Kine came to fetch me. He took me back down to the Scrying Chamber and put me through the paces once again. Neither of us spoke about the curse.

After another hour or so of training, I decided to go to bed. Before going to my room, I bid Buttercup goodnight. She rested in a large woven bed in the main chamber with the other creatures. Most just looked at me with large, sleepy eyes or ignored me in understandable disinterest, but Buttercup thrust her snout under my hand and huffed in happiness. Bubbles and

Bobbles rushed up along the edge of the canal to ask for scratches.

There was something comforting about all these animals living in peace, but as soon as I lay down in the bed, the ache within my chest intensified.

Not just from the uncertainty and the fear.

Brandt.

Oh, ihlkit, it hurt. Drawing my knees up to my chest, I clenched my eyes shut.

I had made it home, more or less. Found the right appearance. Found part of my family. Found the answers to so much of what I felt. And yet a great gaping hole remained within me. Sorrow and pain flooded it.

Brandt's face played in my mind's eye as memories danced just out of sight. I could practically brush my fingertips over them, but whenever I focused, they vanished.

Soon, I drifted to sleep.

~

I stood in a crystal grotto with magnificent towers of amethyst and all kinds of quartz. The very ceiling dripped with them as if they were icicles, and the air smelled crisp and rich with life. A hazy dread filled me. The waters shimmered. Their reflections danced on the walls of the cavern. And I...I waited.

Waited with my heart thundering in my rib cage and dread pooling in my belly and coiling up around my heart.

Brandt gathered me into his arms. He held me close, his arms binding me so tight I could scarcely breathe.

I clung to him, leaning up on my toes. "Brandt."

"Stella." He cupped my face between his hands and pressed his forehead to mine. A long, ragged moment followed as he gripped me tight.

I struggled to find what to say, but emotion choked me. There was no easy way to say this: I had to die. The words were like poison in my mouth.

Before I could speak, he nuzzled me. His soft lips pressed against mine. "I'm so angry with you. I'm furious," he said hoarsely. "I can't believe you agreed to—"

"Please," I whispered. Tears streamed down my face. "This is the solution."

He scoffed. "You expect me to just accept this? That you and seven other women have to go and die at the roots of some tree to save the entirety of Terrea? Not just one nation or kingdom. The entire world." His voice broke at the end, as if pleading for me to say that there wasn't yet another thing that wanted to destroy me.

I curled my fingers along his cheek and chin. "It's true. And Gola Resh won't matter if the entire world is destroyed, and perhaps with this, you won't have to..." My fingers dropped to the charm at his neck. The stone glowed yellow-orange, ruddier than when it was dangerous. A knot formed in my throat. Time was moving too quickly.

He grasped my hand in his large one, scarred fingers holding mine together as he brought them to his lips. One at a time, he kissed them. "I swore I'd protect you." His voice was barely audible. "I swore I'd lay down my life for you."

"That's why she did it. To make us live her pain." Tears streamed down my cheeks, blurring my vision. I struggled to hold back more sobs, ducking my head. "But this way...this way you won't have to be the one who kills me. It may satisfy her curse too. At least it will stop it if we complete a binding ceremony beforehand."

He pressed his forehead to mine and seized me. Our bodies pressed flush against one another. Bergamot, smoke, leather, and spice filled my lungs as I clung to him.

Tears glistened in his eyes. "It's wrong. All of this. You are my heart, my love, my queen."

"This will work," I responded. "Auntie Runa saw it in a vision, and I felt it in my soul. This will slow the curse. Not stop it completely."

"There has to be something else. You haven't even gotten your tattoos yet. This can't be finished before that. There has to be something else."

"There isn't." I slid my hand up along his cheek. The squared muscles of his jaw pressed against my palm. The dread pulsed stronger. "This only ends in death, Brandt. I feel that too."

"It cannot. I won't let it." He gritted his teeth and hugged me closer. "I'd drag you back and lock you up in the dungeon if it would keep you safe. I'd chain you up—"

"What a pair we'd be. Both of us chained?" I tangled my fingers in his hair, tugging on the curly coils and then on the straightened waves. "It's unfair, I know, but this is better. This way doesn't end in flames."

"What is that supposed to mean?" Brandt demanded roughly. He pulled back, his dark-red eyes wild. "What does that mean, Stella? What did you see?"

I bit my lip as I stared up at him. It was all I could do to hold back the sobs. "Brandt, if you don't let me go...if I am here at the end of this curse and this curse is fulfilled, you have no idea how horrible it will be. I saw—"

I jolted awake, cold sweat drenching my body. Gasping for breath, I sat there staring at the stone tile wall. My fingers clutched at my hair. "What?" I rasped, my tongue heavy and my throat parched. "What did I see?"

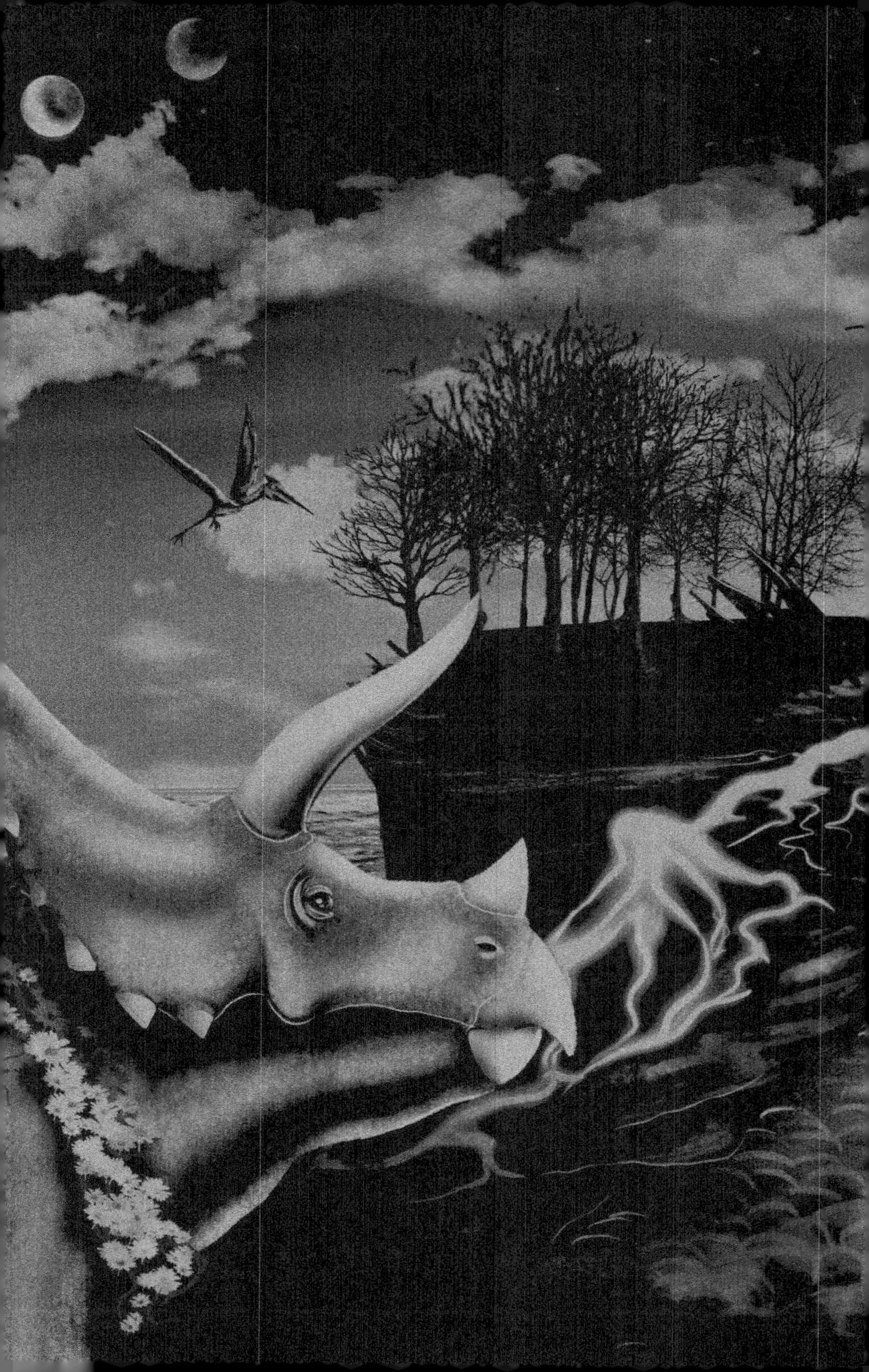

CHAPTER EIGHTEEN: STELLA

The dream haunted my thoughts, but no matter how hard I tried to remember the last part, it did not come to me. Only a terrible sense of dread.

There had been a reason Brandt told me not to come back. Other bits of that memory returned to me. Most especially the way Brandt told me he knew this wouldn't be the end. How he had held me so tight and made me swear that if I found a way to come back to life, I couldn't return until he had figured out some way to end this curse.

My insides churned. That hadn't been a promise I was able to keep.

Here I was now, present but without all my memories and without any knowledge of how to stop either of the curses that plagued us. And apparently the Gola Resh, our arch nemesis, had assumed an entirely noncorporeal form which was going to make her significantly harder to defeat.

When I came out of my room, Elias was already working on breakfast while Kine fed the animals. I checked in on Auntie Runa and changed the water in the vase before going out to help

Kine. Buttercup provided commentary on her breakfast, nudging me and demanding extra alfalfa.

Kine, Elias, and I ate our breakfast in near silence. The heavy focus of the previous night remained. As soon as the dishes were cleared away and the food put up, Kine took me back down to the Scrying Chamber. More shapes and forms.

As I practiced, my chest tensed. The ache inside me grew stronger and stronger. Not only the fear but the pining for Brandt.

Somehow, that was getting worse.

It had become a physical pain.

Perhaps because of the shifting.

Each time I tried to tell myself that, the lie stuck in my throat. I couldn't even think it without recognizing it for what it was.

We broke for lunch, a simple meal of brown bread, fish, and greens with spiced walnuts and blueberries. Then more training until I could no longer focus and my entire body hurt as if it had been beaten.

"Maybe Elias can run you through some of the basics of being a seer again. If that's possible. I'm not really certain. You might also try working with your intuition and sketching. That would help some," Kine suggested as he helped me up the stairs. "You're doing great, Bug."

His words were meant to be encouraging, but I barely heard them.

Later that afternoon, I found Auntie Runa up and swimming —or floating, rather. She lay on her back in the water, her loose aqua-blue dress flowing around her like some ethereal painting. Her silky white hair was down about her shoulders as well, half of it floating in the waters around her. Her breaths were slow but focused as Bubbles and Bobbles swam up and nuzzled her and then dove down to the bottom of the canal.

Her murky, golden eyes focused on me. The tightness in her

jaw loosened, and she unclenched her left hand. "Oh, my darling girl."

Were those tears misting her eyes?

I drew closer and stooped down at the edge of the canal. The cool tiles pressed up against my knees and palms as I leaned close. "What's wrong? What did you see?"

She blinked and sat up in the water, her movements lithe and graceful, far stronger than what I had expected. "It is…" She shook her head. Bubbles popped up beside her and pressed under her arm. "I am not certain what this vision was precisely. There is a great responsibility that comes when one receives a vision. It is also vital to know with whom to share and when. Sometimes when giving the vision, one can start to feel as if no other choice is permitted. In the end, so often it is about faith, in trusting that the Creator will bring all together for good so long as we are faithful."

A chill gripped me. I leaned down closer. "What did you see?" My voice trembled as I reached for her hand. Was it the same thing I had seen before I went to my death?

Her tongue licked at her chapped lips. Her tanned skin had gone paler. "It is nothing you need to know right now, sweet girl." She squeezed my hand and patted it firmly. Unshed tears glistened in her eyes. "It will work out. I believe—I know this."

The dread expanded within me. "I…" Swallowing hard, I gripped her hand.

Tears rose in my eyes too. A vague unease swelled inside me as well, a silent warning I understood. Visions and foresight were dangerous. They had to be treated with care.

"All right," I said. "I trust you will tell me when I need to know."

"You're a good girl, Stella." She gripped my hand tighter. Her smile trembled, her voice reedier than before. Reaching up, she tucked a strand of my hair back behind my ear.

"Do you want something to drink? Some tea?" I whispered.

"No, love." Auntie Runa gripped my hand again. "Knowledge is a precarious thing, especially knowledge of something that has not yet happened. Never forget that we are mortals. No matter how long we live, we all have an end. Our minds are finite, as are our wills. Everything that we perceive is filtered through our senses and our experiences, and love is precious, but it takes many forms. No one form of it should dominate your life."

"I wish you could tell me more plainly what I should do. This whole thing makes me uncomfortable," I said. "It feels like I'm… doing nothing."

"You are being faithful in what you are called to be," Auntie Runa said. "You are relearning the skills you once possessed and honoring your path of double proficiency as a shifter and seer. Young Brandt is also seeing to what he must do, and he had his sages and scholars searching for the answer for all these years. With your return as well as the Gola Resh's, they will find something. Do your part now while you can so that it is easier on you when your time does come. Hard as it may be, it is better than doing nothing and being caught unprepared. You must remember this."

I leaned closer, taking in every word.

Her grip on my hands tightened. "Love…it is not the only reason for living, my dear, and when it is corrupted, it can trick you into thinking that there is nothing else worth living for. It makes you believe there is nothing but darkness and destruction outside of it." She fixed me with a stern gaze, her gold eyes uncommonly hard. "And you must not let yourself lose sight. Don't let the lies consume you."

"What lies?"

"Love takes sacrifice, my dear. It always will, but it is not destructive. If your love makes you think you should give up everything in life because there is nothing else for you or makes you willing to destroy everything to keep it, that is not a good love." She gripped my hand and patted it. "I don't know what path this is going to take, my dear girl. I wish I did. But please… remember that Brandt is not the only part of your life that matters. Your love for him and his love for you can only remain healthy if you remain grounded."

My shoulders dropped. Had she seen straight into me? Tears pricked my eyes. "I know. I do know that, but I just…I miss him so much. All I want to do is see him."

It wasn't that I didn't want to save Sepeazia or that I didn't care about anyone else. No. It was just…needing to see Brandt was consuming me. This could so easily tip over into obsession and destruction.

"I know. You and Brandt have a powerful mate bond. It has survived death. It has survived loss, but it is influenced by the gift the Vawtrians gave us so that we could shift in any fashion, and the Gola Resh's magic has tainted it."

"What does that mean?" I frowned. Kine had mentioned these individuals before.

"Centuries and centuries ago, a small group of Vawtrians were trapped here. They were separated from their families. They could not take mates or bear children in this place. After decades of trying to escape, they accepted their place here. Because we had cared for them over the years, they looked upon us as part of their family. Well," she chuckled a little, "'weaker cousins' is probably a more accurate term. They decided that if they could not pass on their skills and abilities to their children, they would use those abilities to create tools that would allow us as much of their powers as they could. It wasn't the simplest of transfers, and they put more of themselves into the energy than they intended." Her fingers curled tight over mine.

"What does that mean exactly?"

I studied her face. She didn't look ill, just tired. Her hand felt so delicate beneath mine, the bones fragile. Numerous little scars worked their way across her fingers along with age spots and darker gold patches.

"It means that while you are not a Vawtrian, you have an infusion of their skills and energy and some of their weaknesses. Your mate bond is affected by that."

Uh-oh. Maybe my seer instincts were kicking in, or maybe it was just that obvious, but my gut twisted, warning me I wasn't going to like the next part of this conversation.

She continued, still holding my hand. "You have to understand that when a mate bond snaps into place, Vawtrians get... Well, to put it gently, until they get their sexual urges satisfied, they get stupid. Because of what the Gola Resh has done, her magic has affected this mate bond. The Gola Resh's curse preys on your need to be together. It contaminates it, and when you are together, it's much easier for you to ignore the danger you pose one another, making it easier and more likely for the curse to be fulfilled."

My mouth pulled into a frown. Definitely didn't like it.

No.

I guessed the rest of what she was going to say. I started shaking my head.

After all this time, I'd finally found someone, finally learned that there was someone just for me. And he was perfection—except for being cursed to kill me. But that was manageable, wasn't it? There had to be some way to end the curse without him killing me. We could work through it. Together, Brandt and I could work through anything.

"I'm not a Vawtrian, though, right?" I bit the inside of my lip. "Maybe there's some way we could counter part of it."

"No." Auntie Runa laughed a little, though her gaze was sad. "And you can be glad you aren't. They only have one mate for the entirety of their lives, and, by mate, I mean sexual partner. We aren't bound like that. Their mating bond is so powerful it can scarcely be resisted. We do have the choice. You could pick someone else if you really wanted another lover."

My brow furrowed. A sharp pain twisted in my stomach. "Never."

"I'm not saying you have to." Her mouth tipped. "I'm just saying we differ from them in many respects, but that doesn't mean we are fully immune. The mate bond will make you stupid, my dear. You have to guard against that. I don't even need to ask whether your first encounter with Brandt upon your return proved it. You have to understand that it intersects with what the Gola Resh has done. You've experienced this."

I lifted my chin. "It was the alcohol." My cheeks burned as I recalled my ridiculous conduct.

Auntie Runa scoffed. "Really?"

"Yes..." I cleared my throat as I thrust my fingers into my hair. Pushing my hair out of my face did nothing. I immediately moved it to the other side as if to fix my part. "Alcohol. Margaritas. Spicy strawberry margaritas." My cheeks burned. "That was it."

Her expression wavered with something between amusement, annoyance, and concern. "Dearie, listen carefully. You've been out of our magic and our way of life for a very long time. You're becoming who you were always meant to be at a rapid rate. The old memories are flowing back, but you aren't fully braced for it. It's a lot for anyone to handle."

My bad pickup lines and the snorting giggles all flashed into my mind so fast. The giddiness. The utter glee to see him.

"You're saying what I felt wasn't real?"

Her gaze softened. "Oh, no, my dear. No, not at all. It's real. It's just...you won't be your usual self when you're around him, and he won't either. You both want to be together. It will continue to be that way. It certainly would be to her advantage if either of you were, shall we say, dumber. Especially you, my darling girl. It will keep you from being aware of danger or solutions. It will take extra effort for you to find your voice."

A weight pressed down on my shoulders. "I don't want to be dumb."

"Then you need to stay away from him until you have a handle on your abilities once again, and you should not have sex with him."

My cheeks heated. "What?" My mouth fell open as I debated denying even thinking about it.

"Don't be coy with me, child," Auntie Runa said, her eyebrow arching. "I know what you've thought of. I have had such love myself. You must assume that the Gola Resh will have done all she can to destroy you both, and if she can destroy you through your love of one another, little would make her happier. I suspect that if you two were to be together in that way, the urges and the need would become far more intense. The stronger those urges, the harder it will be for either of you to focus. It's why I've told Kine we aren't even to use the water mirrors unless it's an emergency. You and Brandt must avoid one another. Hard as it is, it will only get harder the more time you spend with one another."

"But what do we do?" I asked softly. "How does my learning how to be a seer and a shifter help stop the curse that will suck all the life out of everything?"

"I'm not sure yet. Just know that you need to." Auntie Runa indicated a stack of parchments with numerous sketches on one of the tables. "Other seers have confirmed. None of us know precisely what this will require. Your task is to be faithful in what you can."

It was hard, but I returned my focus to training. The novelty of it started to fade as Kine continued to put me through the paces. Shapes and then textures. Promises of the serpent form that would soon come.

For the next few days, it was nothing except training with

Kine and learning with Auntie Runa and sketching my thoughts and feelings. Lots of those sketches were of Brandt. His hands. His eyes. His face. His arms. His body. Everything I could remember about him.

Not that that helped me feel any calmer or more connected to anything except missing him. A couple times Auntie Runa caught me sketching him, and I blushed like I was a teenager again.

After her recovery, she spent most of her time in the secret room with the crest with a blue and silver eye. She called it her sanctum. None of us were allowed inside.

Whenever I passed the door of her sanctum, an electric hum of interest pulsed within me. Questions surged.

What was this vision she had seen? Could the knowledge really be so dangerous?

Each time I asked that, my chest tightened. The memory of the dream about the grotto and the horror it had brought swept over me as strong as the earthquakes that shuddered through the land each day.

Every night, without fail, I dreamed of Brandt. Most of the memories that returned were small and comfortable. Little moments. His hand cupping my cheek. Me biting his lower lip and teasing him about being so ferocious. Him throwing me over his shoulder and then chucking me into the river with the manatees and triceratopses. His mouth whispering sweet words in my ear and then threatening if I put my icy feet between his thighs ever again.

I woke up each morning missing him more, and that longing only grew, pulsing and building like an infected wound.

In the afternoons, I rode Buttercup out in the meadow, putting her through her paces. She honked and lowed with delight, her great footsteps making the earth shake. Sometimes, the other triceratops joined us. Three times, Kine joined me, demonstrating different battle tactics, including the Coiling

Serpent Duo, a special technique in which a water serpent shifter paired with their steed for an effective launching attack maneuver.

My eyes widened when he launched himself off the back of the triceratops, shifting into a water serpent in midair. That! The Coiling Serpent Duo was what I had been trying to do when I had been facing off against the tyrannosaur.

"You'll get the hang of all this again," Kine promised. He flashed me that bright smile of his. "If you want her to stop abruptly and snap her head down so you can launch yourself, you shout 'komul.'"

"Komul," I repeated.

He beamed at me. "Exactly."

No matter what, he always tried to keep that cheery persona, but all of this had to weigh on him as well even though he did not show it.

Elias, on the other hand, clearly struggled. He grew quieter and more withdrawn, his shoulders hunching down as if a great weight pressed upon him. More than once, I found him in front of Auntie Runa's private chamber staring at the eye crest, his mouth pinched and his brow furrowed.

That was where he was on the sixth night. Just standing there, staring.

I massaged my aching shoulder, my whole body pulsing with the pain and discomfort of intense, prolonged shifting and the vague memories of old routines. "Is everything all right, Elias?" I asked.

He turned sharply, his finely plucked brows lifting. A small smile tugged at his mouth. "It is what it is."

"What do you mean?" I drew closer. My footsteps were muffled by the thick woven rug. Tension filled the air.

His gaze dropped as he turned his head. "Auntie Runa has forbidden us from seeing the vision. She's drawn it and sketched it many times, and there have been others. I heard...I heard her speak of part of it. I saw glimpses. But..."

I folded my arms tight over my chest. A chill slithered up my spine. "You saw part of it?"

He nodded. The muscles in his neck corded. "Not all of it but enough. And...I'm afraid."

"We all are," I admitted.

"No!" He turned on me, his dark-blue eyes blazing. He dragged his hand through his silky, dark-red hair and scoffed. His usually smooth voice became ragged. "No, I am afraid for you. It wasn't enough that you died once. At this rate, you'll die again, and I can't bear it. It's wrong, and—" His hands balled into fists. He lowered his voice. "There is so much I want to tell you, Stella, but I don't want to make it worse."

"Auntie Runa reminded me that part of the burden of being a seer is that we have to use wisdom about what to share and what not to share." The words felt stupid coming out of my mouth, but they were true. I lifted my chin, steeling myself for his response.

Elias only nodded, his hands still clenched at his sides as if in great turmoil. "Once words are spoken, they can never be taken back. The same is true of knowledge. I know this." He bowed his head.

I bit the inside of my lip. My own curiosity warred within me as my gaze darted once more to the door. "Is this what's had you so quiet these past few days?"

In addition to the end of our world, of course.

"Mostly," he admitted. "Kine and I disagree on what should be said and when. We both care for you. We both want you to—" He paused, his gaze soft and vulnerable as he looked at me with those big dark eyes. "Forgive me for being so forward, but have you had any memories of me return at all?"

The abrupt change in tone startled me. My mouth fell open. "I..."

A pang of something I couldn't place struck me. Regret? Sadness?

I could lie.

No.

It was...it was nothing. I knew I should feel something. Not anger. Not closeness. Not friendship. Not family. He was purely neutral. Comforting if I didn't focus too much on the alarm of nothingness.

He dipped his head closer, his brow furrowing as he studied me. "What's wrong? Oh..." He closed his eyes. "Let me guess. You don't remember me."

That last phrase had an added measure of pain to it.

I shook my head. "I'm sorry, Elias."

He gave me a warm smile that didn't quite reach his eyes. "It's all right," he said, his voice surprisingly gentle despite the sadness in his gaze. "There are so many other more important people and matters for you to remember. It truly does not surprise me. Besides, our bond...it was different."

"How so?" I frowned a little at this statement. That made sense. It didn't stir memories, but that part of what he said...it felt like truth.

He leaned back, folding his hands behind his head. His fingers threaded through his thick, soft hair. "It's a lot to summarize, and it happened swiftly. But it started when Taivren fell."

A pulse of recollection cut into me. Not about him but Taivren. "That was a dark day," I whispered.

"It was. I don't want to overwhelm you, so I won't tell you what happened. Just that that was when our bond began. I owe you everything, Stella. Because of that, I will do anything for you. To protect you, preserve you, please you. Whatever you want from me, it is yours. I would risk anything for you. Without you, my life is meaningless."

My eyes widened at his frankness. "You shouldn't say that."

A chuckle fell from his lips, followed by a heavy sigh. He undid the leather straps wrapped around his wrist and showed me the tattoo I had glimpsed earlier. The indigo ink appeared almost black in the low light. "You saved my life. You helped me find purpose," he said frankly.

As I stared at his wrist and that bold mark, all I could do was shake my head. "I never wanted you to do that." No memory pressed at the edges of my mind. Just a certainty that this was not what I would have asked of him or anyone. "I never asked you to do that."

"No. You didn't. I did it myself." He dipped his head forward, his hand clasping his wrist and his fingers cradling the mark. "It was the only thing I could do to—" His eyes shuttered. "I meant what I said. I would do anything to protect you, Stella, even break my vow as a seer."

"I'm not asking you to do that—"

"I know," he said, his voice sharpening. He stopped, that muscle in his jaw jumping once more. "I know," he repeated, softer this time. "You would never ask that of me, but I made my choices. I made my choices long ago. For better or worse."

The way he looked at me held an intensity. A hunger that frightened me.

I lifted my chin. "Please don't do anything that would violate your conscience or destroy yourself for me."

His gaze grew melancholy, suggesting it might be too late.

I had to go. I had to go, or else I was going to ask him to tell me, and then I would have that on my head too.

I spun on my heel and hurried back down the hall. No sooner did I turn the corner than I realized my room was in the opposite direction.

Ihlkit!

Well, I wasn't walking back down there.

"Stella," Elias called after me. "Where are you going?"

"Back down to the Scrying Room to practice," I said with as much enthusiasm as I could muster.

Before he could respond, I scurried down the staircase and closed the door behind me.

I'd never been down here after dark. Even though it shouldn't have changed all that much, the chamber seemed darker, the blue of the river more electric, the air sharper.

I flopped down at the base of the stairs with my back against the wall. What was I supposed to do?

"I don't have a clue," I moaned, holding my face in my palms.

"Stella."

I stiffened.

The question of who had said that flashed into my mind and faded along with one observation.

The lid to the well now leaned on its side against the stone.

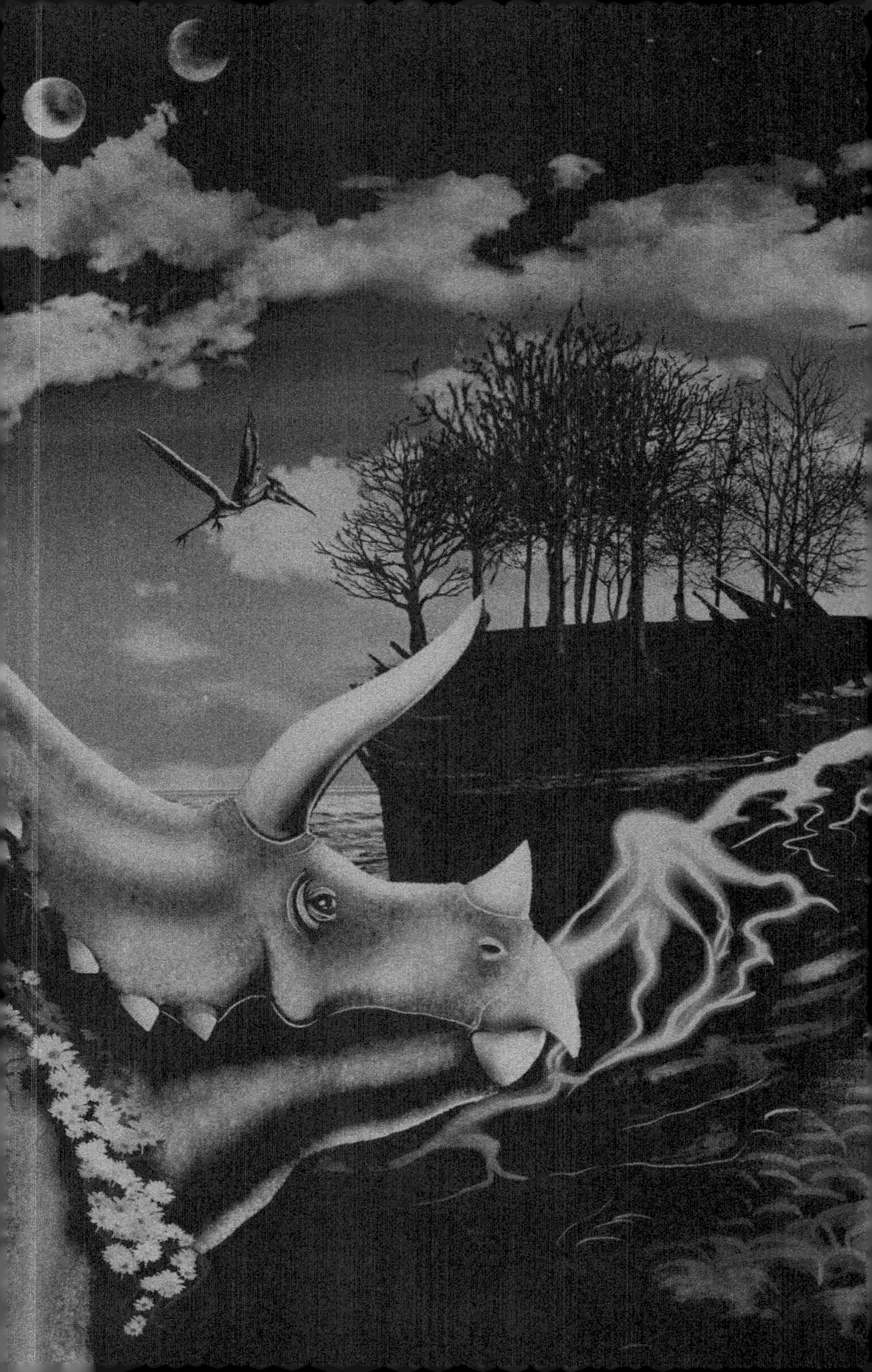

CHAPTER NINETEEN: STELLA

Cold shards of fear cut into me, icy needles in my veins. That lid should have been on the well. It was always covered down here unless someone was scrying.

But the voice enveloped my senses, and the well called to me, bright yet heavy. Intoxicating. I could practically feel arms wrapping around my waist and drawing me toward it.

Whatever words I might have spoken died within me, sticking to the sides of my throat.

The voice whispered in my ear, coming from all directions at once. "Stella."

Everything else faded, all sounds and scents, everything except the well and the empty warmth that twined about me like steam. Its grasp tightened. My feet scraped across the floor, my senses hazing.

"Stella."

This—this was wrong.

Alarm flared in me.

I had to stop, had to stay away from the well.

But my feet wouldn't listen. I lurched forward, my hands

striking the coarse stone that fashioned the well. Blue light danced on the walls and ceiling, coiling and arcing.

Dread settled in my stomach as I leaned forward and peered down into the well.

The stone walls opened into a chasm of glistening, raw white stone. As I leaned forward, though, a pair of orange-green eyes glared up at me. A malicious smile formed in the ether.

It rooted me in place.

The cold sensation of the slime from the chasm whisked along my memory.

The paralysis.

The fear.

The eyes.

The Gola Resh.

"Hello, girl."

My mouth went dry, my fingers digging into the stone. I tried to pull away or even blink against the humming force that dragged me forward. My shoulders slumped, my elbow striking the edge of the stone as I leaned forward.

No. I had to stop.

Had to scream. Had to call for someone.

My voice stayed frozen in my throat.

A face appeared in the mist. "How does it feel to be so close to home and yet so far from your heart?"

I renewed my struggles. My hands scraped on the stone. Sharp pain bit along my palms, but I pressed harder. My tongue still wouldn't work.

The Gola Resh smirked. Her face was ever shifting, becoming something terrifying and ethereal. Skull-like and effervescent beauty. Shadows streamed around her face as she rose closer to me. "What happened to your voice, little seer?" She blinked her eyes slowly, her smile cruel and cloying. "Did something happen to you? Oh, whatever will you do?"

I struggled to swallow. Her eyes burned into me.

"Your devoted Master of Sight has tried so hard to keep me out, but not one of you fully understands what you're dealing with. Especially not when I have grown into something even stronger than before. You are nothing but algae and bugs."

Sometimes, bugs were deadly.

Anger flashed through the fear. "Let go of me," I said, struggling to regain control of myself. The heat of my ire strengthened me even as the fear fought to paralyze me.

A low laugh followed. "Are you afraid, scum girl? Don't worry. I'm not here to kill you. I wouldn't dream of sparing your beloved that fate unless I could assure myself of something far more horrifying, though your death is tempting. You have no idea what you stand over."

A shadow-like claw appeared over me, seized me, and dragged me forward.

My voice eked out of me in a strangled cry.

I dug my palms harder into the stone. The rocks gouged deeply.

"Your death wouldn't really soothe me. You are such a stupid girl, but you do feel," the Gola Resh whispered, her voice tickling my ear and worming into my brain. "Perhaps I will offer you a way out."

She waited for half a beat as if to let her words sink in. The smirk spread over her shadowy features, the smoke around her undulating and transforming and making her always changing.

"I can be reasonable." Her shadow claws raked along my cheek, stinging though they did not cut. "Now that the Babadon is dead, there is really only one thing I want. If you can give it to me, I'll give you your life."

"What?" I gasped. What would it take? And would it end both curses? "Will you free Sepeazia from your curse?"

The Gola Resh just laughed. "No, but I'll spare you and one person you love if you give me what I want. Oh, come now...

you can figure this out. Think hard. What did you take from me, you tedious little disease?"

"I didn't take anything from you." The words scraped out of my throat.

It took all my strength to hold myself up. She wasn't even touching me, yet the force that gripped me was unrelenting.

My foot slipped. I jammed my hand against the coarse rock of the inner well, cutting my palm. The wall dug into my stomach as I struggled to keep from falling in.

The Gola Resh laughed, her voice becoming darker and more metallic as it thrummed through the air. "But you did. Even if it could be undone, what you did... You vicious little seer, I will never forgive you unless you know my pain. You didn't hold the blade, but you called the place. I have thought about it long and hard and changed my mind so many times, so who knows? By the time you figure it out, maybe I'll have changed my mind again." Her eyes narrowed, becoming more sinister. "I doubt it."

Bits of stone grated beneath my palms. It trickled down into the well, disappearing into the mist. "What do you want? Just tell me!" I shoved my knee against the rock.

She rose, the smoke and mist bitter and acrid as she circled me. "In the end, just one thing," she hissed. "Your suffering. It could take so many forms. As long as I get the most suffering from your wretched life that I can, I can fade, happy."

The shadow-like claw appeared over my head as she spoke. It sliced through the air, striking the back of my head, tangling in my hair, and hauling me down.

"No!"

I flung my arm out to stop myself, but I tipped forward and plunged down into the maw of the well. Blue light and white smoke swept up around me, filling my nostrils. Screaming, I flailed my arms.

Down, down, down, I plummeted into the well, the Gola

Resh's laughter echoing around me. I flung my arms out desperately, my palms grating and scraping over the rough rock.

Icy water slammed up around me, swallowing me. The air cracked out of my lungs as frigid liquid rushed into my nose and mouth.

Frozen.

Immobile.

Move. Kick! Swim!

Anything!

The cold choked and burned as I wriggled. The water pressed harder against my face, threatening to steal the last gasp of oxygen from my lungs. An aching chill speared into my marrow.

No. No! Not like this.

Forcing my eyes open, I moved my arms. Which way was up? Was I even facing the right direction? People could drown swimming the wrong way. It was bright all around me. The blue water glowed. No one direction was more correct than the others.

My lungs burned as her laughter rang in my ears.

The waters sparkled, a beautiful crypt. Panic every bit as cold as the waters clutched me tighter.

No. I wasn't going to die here.

I kicked harder and faster. I closed my eyes and listened. No words came to my mind. My instincts said to twist around. A deep, quiet pressure that moved from my gut up around my heart. Bubbles streaming from my mouth, I kicked around and forced my eyes open. The waters weren't as bright here. It felt—

No. No more arguments.

That pulse of knowledge intensified. I sliced my legs faster through the waters. Stone rubbed along the back of my neck and against my feet as I shot forward.

My body was so heavy, my fingertips going numb. It was like daggers into my cheeks. Gritting my teeth, I pushed forward.

Each kick and slice through the water took me deeper into inky darkness. I couldn't go much farther.

Then—no warning, no sight, nothing!—the waters broke away, and I emerged into darkness. Gasping and choking, I sucked in a breath that was half water and half air.

Air! Blessed, blessed air!

I flung my arms over a rock and heaved myself up, coughing and sputtering.

I'd made it. For now.

My whole body ached, and my hands throbbed, but I was breathing. Where was I?

It took several moments for my eyes to adjust to the darkness of the cavern. There was a bit of light to my left. Something soft, almost purple-blue, provided just enough illumination for me to see as I sat on a broad stretch of stone.

My teeth chattered, and my body shook. If I didn't get warm soon, I would be dead as surely as if I'd stayed in the water. Clumsily, I pushed my sopping hair out of my face.

There had to be a way out. With that thought, the familiar tugging sensation returned, urging me toward the gentle light. There was just enough to reveal the slick obsidian stone I rested on.

My body still trembling, I edged forward. No way was I falling back into that ice bath. The gentle lapping of the waves against the stone sounded almost soothing. No signs of predators or even anyone else here. Not that I wanted to imagine what might be lurking in here.

Another shudder trembled through me as I drew closer to the soft glow. Its light intensified, revealing the slick stone that was almost the opposite of the uncut stone on the inside of the well. It opened into a larger passage. A soft humming filled my ears as I stepped into the soft light.

There was something familiar about this place.

Blinking, I lifted my hand to shield my gaze.

Wait.

Wait!

My eyes widened as I realized where I was. The crystal grotto from my dream, but far more vivid this time.

Towering amethyst crystals jutted up from the cavern floor, glowing with an ethereal violet light. Their smooth facets reflected and refracted the light, scattering it across the cavern walls in mesmerizing patterns. Interspersed with the amethyst were rose quartz crystals, their pink hues contrasting beautifully with the purple. The crystals sang with energy, a soft hum reverberating throughout the space. Their soft hues bathed the chamber in ethereal light. Great formations of naturally forming wands tapered into columns of marble and granite. A crisp mineral tang flavored the air, biting my tongue and burning my nostrils.

Water ran off me in rivulets, leaving shining puddles on the glossy rock. Another river sliced through the dark-purple stone of the crystal grotto. The sound of whispering water came not from the river behind me but the one before me. Just like the well, this water glowed, blue in portions and purple in others. It caught the vibrancy of the amethysts and quartz and shimmered in its own dance.

"Stella?" A rumbling, sensual voice came from my left.

My breath caught in my throat as I turned in his direction.

Brandt.

As if he had been waiting for me here all along.

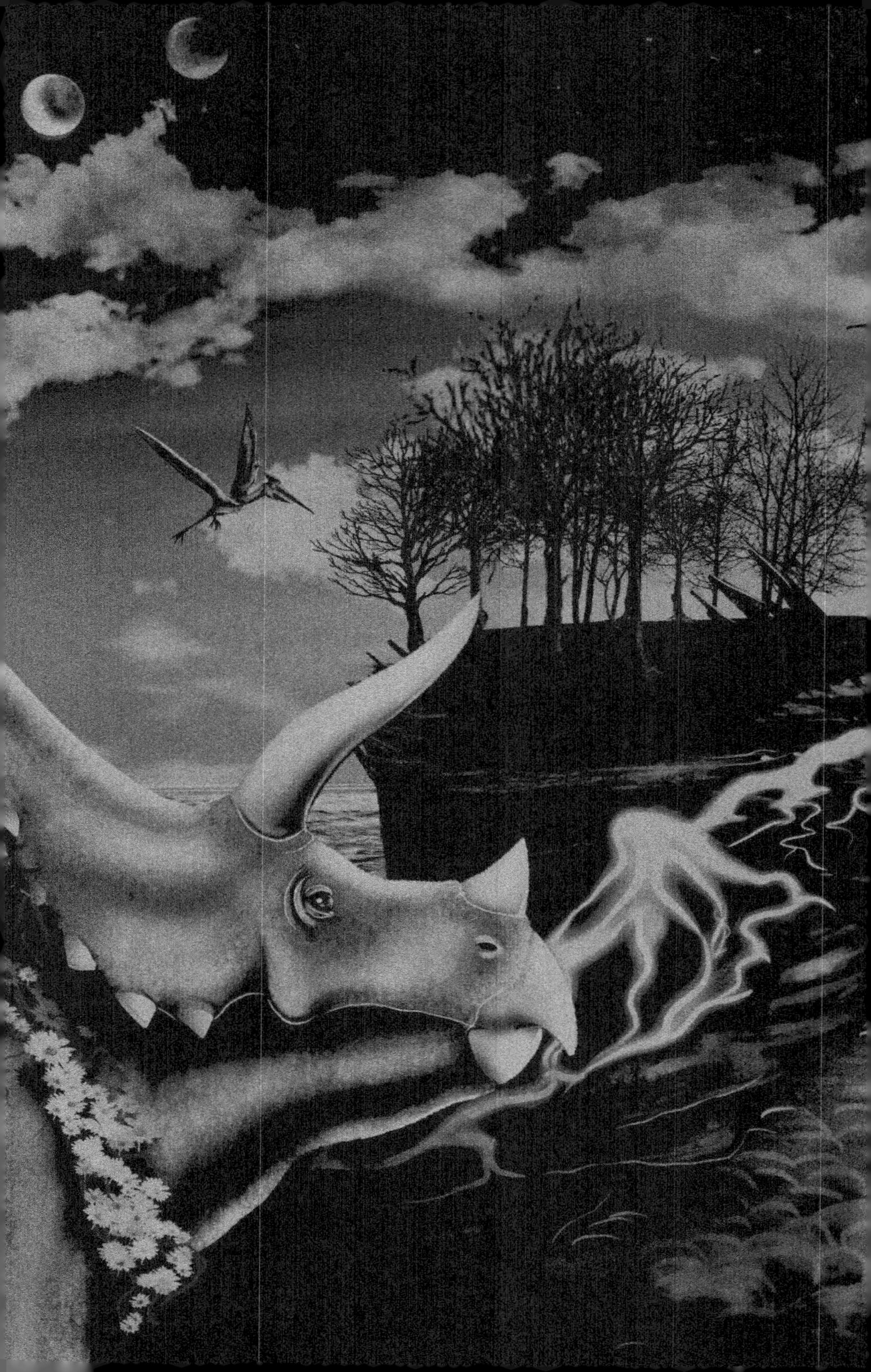

CHAPTER TWENTY: STELLA

My eyes widened. "Brandt."

He loomed on the other side of the river, hands clenched. The charm around his neck was bright orange. He must have been standing behind one of the large amethyst formations. It sparkled like the most incredible dusk, catching the light of the glowing river. His muscles were taut, his eyes so dark in this lighting they seemed black. His gaze raked over me.

Another chilling shudder cut over me. I couldn't tear my gaze away from him now. Auntie Runa's warning rose, then faded within my mind.

How could I ever stay away from him?

We just stood there and stared at one another. His magnificent masculine scent reached me through the crispness of the grotto. Something inside me sparked, heat rising within my belly even as I shivered.

He wore clothing similar to what he wore when we met in the valley. His black tabard and the crimson belt were stark in their contrast. The dancing of the light made the serpent tattoos on his arms seem to coil and pulse. And his eyes…they made me shudder again but this time not from the cold.

He was dangerous. He had been cursed to kill me.

Memories of his hands around my throat returned. The pressure of his thumbs choking the breath out of me. The rage and animalism in his eyes.

And yet, I wasn't afraid.

Somehow.

I should have been.

He was strong enough to snap my neck if he chose, and the charm on his neck warned that he was even closer to being consumed by the curse in that wretched rotational countdown than when we had met before, though allegedly there had been hours yet to go. This river wasn't going to do much to protect me.

But those thoughts were just noise I tuned out as I stared at him as if in a trance.

"You're bleeding." Concern filled his voice.

I blinked, his voice bringing me back to more present needs. I dropped my gaze back to my hands. Cuts and scrapes covered my palms and forearms, blood dripping along with the water onto the glossy stone.

"The Gola Resh."

I hugged myself, tucking my hands against my torso. The blood would probably stain my white dress, but the dull burn that raged along my skin grounded me in the moment along with the cold. I shuddered again.

What was he doing here? Had the Gola Resh set us up? Was it possible this was just chance?

Fear tried to assert itself. This was too good to be true. She wanted us to suffer. She wanted both of us to feel pain, and she wanted me dead to amuse her. This was not just a chance meeting.

He stepped closer to the water. His shadow stretched back, disappearing into the darkness. A muscle twitched along his neck.

"You're in bad shape." Though he spoke like someone also fighting against a trance or just waking from a dream, he removed his tabard and then tossed it toward me. It flew in a smooth arc over the sparkling waters. "Here. Sorry I don't have any sleeves, but it's heat-woven. It should help keep you warm."

Reaching up, I caught the garment. It smelled so much like him it took all my strength not to bury my face in it. The heat of his body still warmed it, and magic had been woven into it to assist with healing. The energy prickled and tingled across my body.

I hugged it close for half a breath, then wrapped it around my shoulders. "You never wear anything with sleeves if you can help it."

A half smile tugged at his oh-so-kissable lips. He licked them briefly, dropping his gaze. "No sense covering the ink when it's done this well." As he spoke, he spread his arms and turned them to show off the detailed serpent tattoos that coiled all the way up his biceps to his shoulders.

"Or the muscles." Haziness rose within me. A pleasant warmth. My breaths deepened and yet became uneven.

That smile of his rose higher, hints of redness returning to his cheeks. "You're incorrigible, Stella."

The intensity of his features was softened by that smile. It was an invitation for me to draw closer. If not for the river, I'd have been in his arms already.

"Yeah..." I shivered again, my eyes squeezing shut. "I guess when all is said and done, I'm just really into you." I couldn't resist the smile spreading over my own lips.

"Ihlkit," he swore as he dragged his hand up into his hair. The spiky bits of red and black crunched beneath his fingers before he trailed them down to his neck. "You've got to go. Can you—"

"What were you doing down here?" I blurted out. Hugging his tabard tight around myself, I willed myself to be strong. This wasn't accidental. I had to go, but I also had to know. "The Gola

Resh pulled me down into the well, and I wound up here, but I...I remember this place. It was in a dream. I just—I can't remember what it is exactly."

His brow furrowed. Frustration and longing filled his dark-red eyes. "I had to come. This was where I learned I would be the happiest man alive and then later where I learned I was the most cursed." He ran his fingers through his hair once more and then shook his head. "Listen, we're both adults. We're intelligent. We're...we are smarter than this even if we're getting played with by some wretched entity set on vengeance. You know this wasn't chance. She dragged you down here. She probably lured me here too, or maybe I just have bad luck."

"Probably?" I shivered more, my body practically trembling. Still, I smiled seeing him. He was so ferocious. The wicked scar that slashed thinnest just above his eye down to his jaw seemed even starker in this light, contrasting sharply with his skin. It made him look oh so dangerous.

He looked me up and down, his gaze so ravenous I wanted to pounce on him and demand he show me what he was thinking.

Ihlkit!

Auntie Runa was right. It hadn't been the alcohol.

Horns, stars, amethyst caverns, and whatever else could sparkle in the sky above, I wanted this man. I wanted to be with him more now than I did when we first saw each other.

This was embarrassing.

Or should have been.

The shame might as well have washed off me when I climbed out of that icy water. Even that wasn't enough to cool me off inside, especially not while holding his tabard.

He pointed behind me. "If you can walk, then go. Take the passage to the left and keep your hand on the wall's left side. Never break contact with it. It will wend and wind, but eventually, it will take you back to the surface. Then you've got to get back to Auntie Runa's. Don't let any of the factions see you. They've been roaming. My guards can't keep them back all the time. A few might slip through."

"Whatever the Gola Resh is doing, we can trust it's nothing good for us." I struggled to speak the words. They were true. I knew it, but I didn't care. I hugged his tabard closer, the warmth and healing of the black fabric encasing my shoulders.

"No, it's not," he agreed. "Our sages and scholars are close to finding the solution, I think. A little while longer, and we'll have an answer." He swallowed hard, his throat bobbing. "We'll find a solution. Just—"

"Just what?" The pounding of my heart quickened as I stared at him, unable to tear my eyes away, barely able to even blink. I knew I needed to leave this cavern immediately, but my feet remained rooted in place.

"I don't know how we missed that the Gola Resh was still alive and capable of existing fully incorporeal," he said. "No one has given me a good answer. Maybe it was her magic, but I think we've missed something or someone. There may be a traitor on my council, but I don't know who. No seer can tell me either. All they see when they look is darkness or emptiness. You need to get back to Auntie Runa's. Even though I can't see you while you're there, it's worth it to know you're safe."

My own muscles clenched in protest.

We held each other's gaze. The longing intensified. The pulsing within my chest was like a wound. Just seeing him wasn't enough. I couldn't move.

He dragged his hand through his hair again and rubbed the back of his neck. "You need to run, Stella," he murmured. He pressed the base of his palm to his temple, turning his face from me. The muscles and veins along his arms tightened, standing out like angry lines.

No.

I needed to run, had to run, but I stood there, hugging his tabard close.

"I am sorry for hurting you," he said hoarsely. His eyelids squeezed shut to block the sight of me. "And I don't want to do it again, so go. Please."

"I don't hold it against you," I said softly. "I know this isn't you. When I was looking into your eyes, it wasn't you."

The haziness intensified as I drew in a deep breath. His arms looked so strong. It would feel so good to feel them wrapped around me. To feel his heart beating against my cheek. To hear his powerful breaths.

The few shreds of commonsense I had frayed. If I walked away, it would get easier, wouldn't it?

I forced myself to look back at the passage he'd indicated. The passageway loomed at the back, narrow and cold. My feet refused to move. A shiver coursed through me.

I had to. For both our sakes.

Swallowing hard, I pushed the heat down within myself. "Do you want your tabard back?"

"No." His voice was strained. It sounded as if he was in pain. "No, just go. Now. I can't hold myself back from you much longer."

I managed two steps before I stopped. Then I turned back to look at him. My heart raced faster.

Leave.

That was all I had to do.

I gripped Brandt's tabard tighter. As I turned, my eyes traced over his sculpted jaw and broad shoulders, desire rising within me like heat from a flame. He'd clenched his eyes shut as if it took all his strength to remain there.

Amid the haziness, a rawness developed. "Being away from you is one of the most painful things in my life," I said.

His jaw tensed. His arms braced as if he was physically fighting himself to stay back.

I wanted to laugh, sob, wail, scream, and dance all at once. All the emotions intensified.

"My whole life on Earth felt wrong," I said, my voice so thick it was hard to speak. "It was...hard. Nothing stable. Nothing solid. Nothing but group homes, shifting dynamics, and longing. Perpetual longing. When I looked in the mirror, even the face that looked back at me was wrong. When I saw you again... everything started to feel right in a deeper way. I found out that I died and was reincarnated, and all of it made sense to me. I'm not even struggling that much to leave Earth behind. And that's because I look at you, and I know I am in the right place. I am finally where I am me. I am so close to being back exactly where I belong and with the people with whom I belong. And now I have to leave you?"

"I'm sure you found others there in your new life," he growled, his gaze still fixed on the stone. His hands balled into fists. The muscles along his forearms tensed. "And I would not have held it against you. All I want is for you to be all right, even if it is apart from me."

"There's no happiness for me apart from you, Brandt. When I look at you, I am reminded of what I was looking for every day I was on Earth." I couldn't make myself move away. The fogginess was growing, pulling me in deeper. "I love you."

His jaw tightened. "I love you too, Stella." The words were little more than a growl. "More than anything."

His tortured expression sliced through me.

This was ridiculous. How could anyone demand that I leave him behind? He was my mate.

A week ago, I hadn't even known that I had a mate, but here I was now, incapable of living without him.

I glanced about the chamber once more. The river was narrowest four feet away. I could leave. Yes.

Or...

I ran over and leaped across.

Brandt's eyes widened. The war that raged within him turned to terror and desire. "Stella."

Oh! It was incredible. Just being near him made my blood ignite. I squared my shoulders as I drew in his scent, and I giggled. "Did it hurt when you fell from heaven?"

His eyes widened. "What?"

I swallowed, my cheeks burning. So much for blaming the alcohol, but oh, it felt so good! "You heard me."

He lifted his chin. "Stella…"

The way his cheeks flushed a little bit made my stomach somersault. I edged closer. "Did you sneeze just then? I'd ask God to bless you, but looks like He already did."

He set his jaw. A smile twitched over his lips as he sighed. His cheeks reddened more. "I can't believe you aren't taking this more seriously. I almost killed you last time."

"You might as well be a camera because every time I look at you, I grin."

"This is so inappropriate."

"I'm your wife." I batted my eyelashes at him. "See what I'm wearing? The smile you gave me. Don't you want to wear what I gave you?"

It actually felt good to just go with it. Had it always been this way between us? I felt utterly stupid and entirely entranced and…happy. All I wanted to do was tease him, kiss him, and keep him. Why did he have to be cursed to kill me?

He held up his hand. "Stella…"

"Yes?" I tilted my head. I didn't care how dangerous this was. I didn't care that I might die at any moment. My head spun a little already. It hurt so much to smile, but I couldn't stop. "I understand why you're worried. There's something wrong with my eyes."

"Oh?" He frowned. "What?"

"I can't keep them off you." I burst into another fit of laughter.

His shoulders dropped as he raked his hand across the back of his neck. His mouth twitched as if he fought a laugh. "Stella."

This was dangerous beyond all reason.

The charm at his throat was orange. If it turned yellow, he would attack me again, but I stepped closer, drawn to him like a stupid moth to a vicious flame. And oh, did he make me hot.

"I think I need someone to warm me up."

He placed his hand on my shoulder, his thumb stroking up the curve of my neck. "You *are* cold." He stepped closer, towering over me. Leaning closer, he pressed his forehead against mine.

My breath caught in my throat. As he nuzzled me, I bit my lower lip. His masculine scent consumed me like the heat that radiated off him.

Hold me.

Kiss me.

Take me.

Kill me.

I didn't care.

"How long do we have before the curse overwhelms you?" I gasped.

His lips grazed my cheek. "Six hours. If it doesn't leap forward again. You stubborn, ridiculous, horrible little seductress."

I splayed my hand over his chest, drawing in a sharp breath. "Then stop wasting time—"

He gripped the back of my head and kissed me, his lips crashing into mine with a desperate urgency. One hand slid around my waist, pulling my body flush against his muscular form while the other tangled in my hair, holding me in place as his mouth claimed mine. The kiss obliterated every thought, all sensation fading away until there was only Brandt—his warmth, his taste, his scent.

My fingers dug into his shoulders, nails scraping against the taut muscle as I tried to eliminate any last speck of distance between us. Our mouths moved together feverishly, tongues twining and dancing in a dizzying rhythm.

My knees grew weak, and I clung to his shoulders, my fingers digging into his hardened muscles. He groaned into my mouth, nipping at my lower lip.

His kiss consumed me, enveloping my senses until the rest of the world faded away. Our lips moved together with escalating urgency, making up for lost time and the unknown number of moments left between us. His fingers tangled roughly in my hair as he held me against him, my body molding to the hard planes of his chest.

I was dizzy with desire, my heart racing wildly. My nails raked down his muscular back, and he shuddered, his tongue delving deeper to taste me fully. We strained against each other, both desperate to eliminate the space between us.

The entire world shook, shuddering and groaning.

His grip around me tightened as he lurched forward, staggering against me. "Earthquake!"

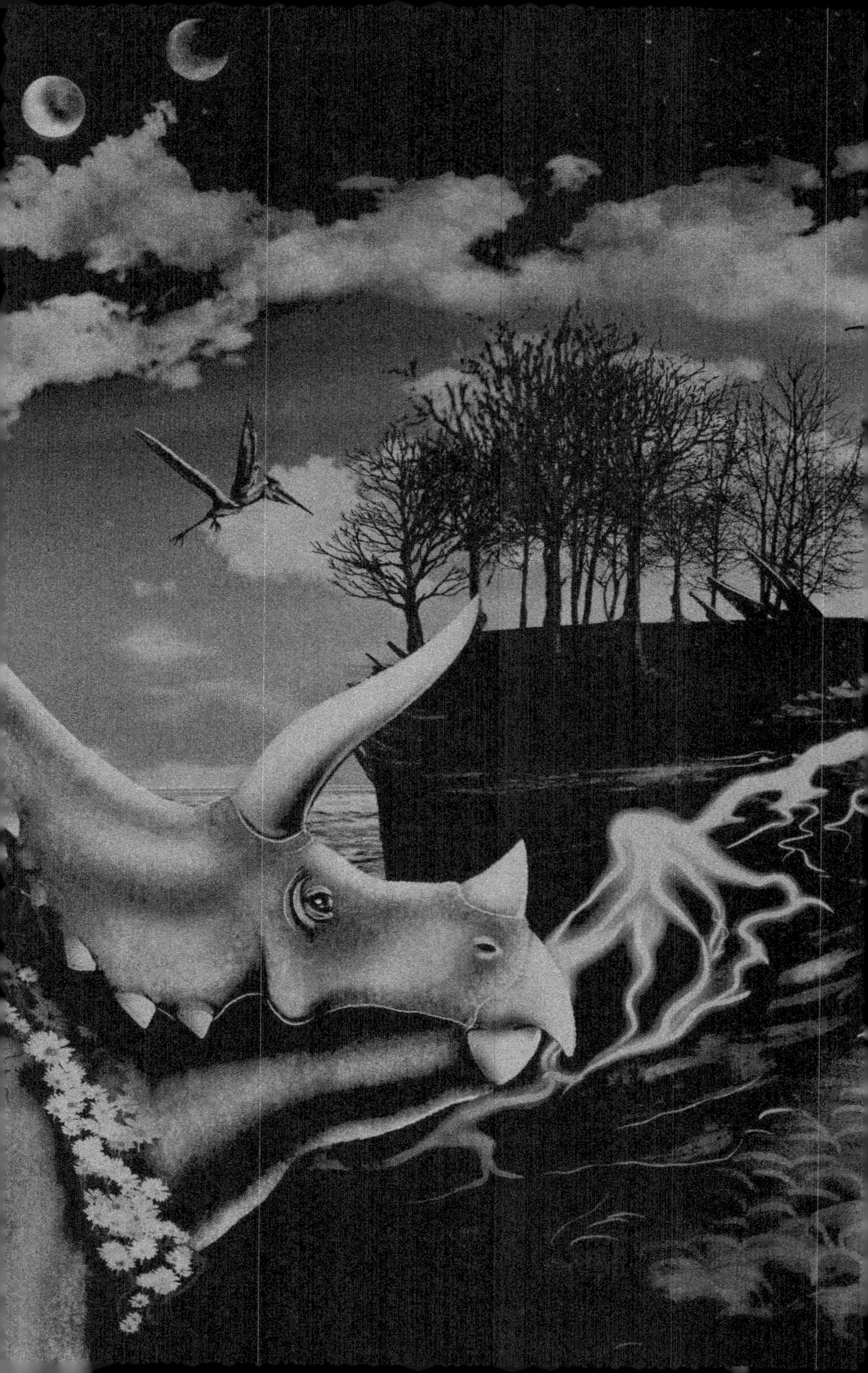

CHAPTER TWENTY-ONE: STELLA

My mind spun, struggling to comprehend his exclamation as I clung to Brandt. The ground rumbled beneath our feet. The crystal walls of the grotto shook all around us, their humming intensifying.

Brandt dragged me under one of the thicker marble arches and knelt over me, shielding me with his body. The amethyst and quartz cracked, silt and dust raining down in a kaleidoscope of violet. The hum of the crystals became a roar.

Then, as swiftly as it started, it stopped.

I remained frozen, heart pounding. His body stayed pressed over mine, protective and warm. I slid my hands up his back, feeling the rapid rise and fall of his breath and grounding myself with his presence.

The elation of being near him faded as I looked around, fighting to catch my breath.

"Are you all right?" he asked.

I nodded, though my legs still felt like jelly. "I think so."

He helped me to my feet, keeping one arm around my waist to steady me. I leaned into him, grateful for his strength.

"Do you think it's over?" I asked.

He lifted his head, eyes scanning the grotto walls. Dark cracks had formed in some places, but the formations were largely whole. No large chunks had fallen away except for a large sheet of stone that had cracked away and covered up the passage he'd told me to follow before. No chance of me leaving here that way now.

"For now," he said, his voice dark with concern.

The hum of the crystals had resumed. The notes had changed a little though, a touch rawer. Or perhaps that was just me.

My brow furrowed as I looked at the dark cracks. "That doesn't look good."

He nodded, drawing me out from under the arch, his hand firm beneath my elbow. "It's not from the earthquake. Those are the effects of the Gola Resh and the Babadon's magic."

Oh. I glanced back up at him. "They were in Auntie Runa's house," I murmured.

Another nod. His hand gripped my elbow tighter. "Yeah. They're draining the life out of everything. They're everywhere now, getting deeper and stronger by the day until the point when they drain all of every scrap of life away. I don't know if it will worsen again soon, or if the Gola Resh will focus it again as she did with Taivren. But I fear what happens when it is strong enough to destroy our heartstones."

My heart dropped into my stomach. This vile magic was spreading like a deadly fungus. Heartstone magic would last the longest because of how deep and grounded the magic was. It was reserved for the most sacred and protective measures.

I took a deep, steadying breath as I turned to face him. His jaw was set, eyes dark with determination. He gave my arm a reassuring squeeze, and a sensation of déjà vu swept over me. We'd been here before. Had a conversation so similar that I feared our conclusion was going to wind up being the same.

I opened my mouth to speak, and suddenly the belief that I had nothing of value to add overtook over me.

He smiled a little. "We'll figure this out," he said in that deep sexy voice that probably sounded more confident than he felt. "We'll find a way to defeat them before..." His arm got tighter around my waist as he drew me in. "I won't let you die again, Stella," he whispered in my ear. Hot breath caressed my skin.

The haze was starting to return. I swallowed hard, knowing that we were running out of time in more ways than one. I could practically feel the stupidity returning as the adrenaline wore off.

All I wanted was to be with him.

He dipped his head forward, a wisp of laughter escaping his incredible lips. "I feel it too," he whispered. "It's taking everything I have to not throw you down right now and strip you naked."

"Damn you! Why do you have to talk that way?"

"You've got some nerve chastising me for talking a certain way," he said, a note of teasing in his voice. "I thought I put a smile on your face."

A smile twitched on my lips. The way he held me made me feel safe.

Ihlkit!

"Your charm," I whispered, my shoulders tightening. "It's changed."

He glanced down and then swore. Raking his hand along the side of his head once more, he shook his head. His jaw tensed. The charm had gotten significantly brighter and lighter.

"How much time do we have left?" I couldn't tear my gaze away from the orb. It glistened, the light mocking.

"Four hours at most," he said, his voice tight. His arm wound around my waist once more. "Kine's probably noticed you're missing by now. He'll be looking for you. If he sees the lid to the well is off, he'll know the Gola Resh pulled you in here. I can—"

He pressed his forehead to the top of my head, breathing in my scent.

Oh, help!

Heat surged through me.

How could just the sound and feel of his breath be such a turn-on?

He held me closer. "Since walking away from each other feels impossible, I'll take you up the main way. We'll sort it out when we reach the surface."

The tip of his nose grazed my neck. Heat flared in me, and a moan escaped my lips.

"You really think that's going to work?" I murmured, leaning against him, my eyelids sliding shut. His intoxicating scent made my head spin.

He grunted, his body tensing in frustration. "Hord is up there. I told him I had to come here to meditate. He…he'll help you get back. Ihlkit, how do you smell this good?"

I giggled a little. "You smell like trash. I want to take you out."

He growled at me, but his heart quickened, the beat faster against my ear. "What got into you on this so-called Earth?"

"Are you seriously telling me that I wasn't flirtatious with you before this?" I asked, peering up at him. My arms remained tight around his steely frame, my body flush with his.

"No, but it was different." He dragged his hand along my neck, his gaze softening.

A knot formed in my throat. He was going to kiss me. And it would be heaven.

But Auntie Runa's words echoed in my mind. We couldn't afford to be any more stupid than we had already been. Here, pressed up against him, that tiny shred of consciousness felt and understood why it mattered.

A splinter of my will surged up. "We've got to go," I whispered. At least in this, we were still near one another. I wasn't walking that long, dark passage alone.

"You're right," he said softly. His breath mingled with mine as his tongue darted out to moisten his lips. Then he straightened. "Let's get out of this cave."

I mourned every inch of space between us, the cold of the cavern so much fiercer now. His tabard remained draped over my shoulders like a cloak. Tears pricked the back of my eyes, threatening to spill over.

I really wanted to flirt with him. Desperately longed for something to say to make him smile. I had to subdue the giddiness.

"Do you think the earthquake made the curse's timeline for you advance?" I asked, my voice thick.

He guided me down the passage. "I don't know. Both times, it happened when we were near each other, but there were also earthquakes at both points. It wasn't until the earthquake, though, so that seems like it's more likely." He glanced down at me as we walked. "It's a bit of a maze to get you out of here now. I'll get you up to where it's a straight shot. Then you can tell one of my guards to escort you back to Auntie Runa. They have orders to protect you."

I could get lost in those soft, dark-red eyes. Walking side by side with him, his arm around me as we moved through the passage was beautiful torment. The intensity had almost settled out because we were in contact, but if the curse advanced again and crushed Brandt into insanity, I would be helpless. A shard of fear pulsed through me.

"Councilor Tile's theory is that agitation and stress advance the curse." His powerful shoulders shrugged. "Some of the others agree…they're studying it more. Hopefully we'll have answers soon."

Our footsteps echoed down the passage. Even as my eyes adjusted, it was challenging to see. The light came from bioluminescent fungi on the walls. On Earth, my friends had always said I'd had uncannily good eyesight in dark places, but this location put that to the test.

I glanced up at him, managing a weak smile. "Maybe I'm a special kind of stress that tipped the rest over the edge."

Or maybe the curse was advancing because we were nearing the end.

His smile went a little crooked, a hint of red reaching his cheeks. "Yeah, you are a pain in the spine. I've been so strained since you arrived I can barely walk without cracking."

A low growl rumbled through the air.

The joke that sprang to my lips faded as soon as I realized that wasn't him. He tensed too.

My pulse quickened. His arm tightened around me as he scanned the shadows behind us.

"What else is down here?" I whispered.

"There are three rivers that run through this cave system," he responded in hushed tones. "Could be any number—"

Another snarl ripped through the darkness, deep and gurgling. Much closer this time too. My breath caught in my throat. Claws clicked on the stone. Three pairs of eyes reflected in the darkness.

Brandt grunted. "Kapis." He pushed me behind him and farther down the passage.

The air sharpened. In the darkness, I glimpsed large reptilian forms. I couldn't remember what kapis were, but the gurgling rumbles coming from the passage didn't sound like they were friendly.

Brandt shook his head. "They shouldn't be awake."

"Sounds like they are, though."

"Apparently." He drew a deep breath and shook his head. His boots scraped on the stone as we continued to back away down the passage. "Great. You remember how to fight these?"

My eyebrow cocked. "No."

"Of course you don't." He turned to glance back at me. Our

eyes met. His gaze softened. Then he gave a wry chuckle. "You got any weapons?"

"I was on my way to bed before I fell through the well!"

"And you don't sleep with a dagger anymore?"

"No! Am I supposed to?" My heart hammered against my ribs as the kapis slunk from the shadows. Their scales glinted in the dim fungal light, glistening yellow eyes fixed on us.

"Heh. You used to be such a badass," he said with a grunt that sounded almost amused.

"Bastard." Was he seriously teasing me now? I shot him a glare. The adrenaline was driving back that desire.

"Oooh, did I hit a sore spot?" He smirked as he continued to press me back.

More hisses and rumbles followed from the passage ahead. Maybe there were four now. Even five. Were kapis pack hunters?

"Why does it feel like this is the first time you've relaxed since I came back?" I demanded.

"Because it is." He glanced back at me, mischief sparkling in his eyes.

"So imminent doom and bodily dismemberment gets you laughing, while flirtatious banter makes you tense. You're a piece of work, Brandt."

"We've both got our own brand of crazy, love."

"Well, don't call me 'love' unless you want me scaling you like my favorite rock wall." I grabbed at his belt.

"Stella!" he started.

I pulled one of his daggers free and brandished it with a smile. "Just grabbing a weapon. What did you think I was doing?"

He narrowed his eyes at me. "If you distract me too much, we will both die horrifically." His smile twitched in amusement.

"I actually just grabbed and then realized I knew where your spare dagger was," I said with a smile, feeling some of my own tension easing away.

His brow quirked. "Yeah, but you still don't remember how to fight kapis. Good news is it sounds like they're more bored and curious than hungry and angry. The earthquake probably woke them."

His muscular arm swept out and guided me farther into the passage. We moved beneath a broad marble arch. The light expanded as water trickled and chuckled behind us.

"Yeah, well, bad news is kapis sound like creatures that like to bite things when they're curious," I said.

Brandt rewarded me with another of his deep laughs, sending a confusing mixture of delight and caution up my spine. His arm remained firm against my back as he steered us into a larger cavern. The light from the luminescent fungi and crystals danced across the glistening walls and the shining waters.

We now had plenty of room to maneuver.

The slick stones here were more blue and black than deep purple. There were fewer chunks of crystal compared to the one I'd found him in, and the river rushed through far faster, the currents powerful, slicing around the broad rocks that jutted out of the white-capped waters.

Brandt still hadn't grabbed either of the other daggers strapped to his waist. Then I saw the kapis.

"I guess now I know why you didn't draw your dagger," I murmured.

These kapis resembled the ancient kaprosuchus from Earth, long-legged crocodilian creatures. Each one was at least twelve feet long. The largest had one opaque eye and a long, jagged scar that ran down its grey-white hide. It opened its jaws and uttered a hissing gurgle.

Brandt glanced back at me, his smile curling crooked. "You noticed how useless it'd be, hmm?"

"Are you going to rub it in my face?"

"I could."

"Why are you in such an infernally good mood?" I demanded.

"I'm just remembering how to breathe. And how much I love you."

"We used to fight kapis, didn't we?" I narrowed my eyes at him, conflicting emotions flaring through me.

"One of our first dates, brash seer. This time, instead of me testing to see what your skills are, I'm desperately hoping you remember."

The way he looked at me set my heart pounding faster.

He leaned closer, his posture still strong and guarded as he remained aware of the kapis. His voice lowered to a conspiratorial tone. "But this time, I'm not threatening to leave you. I'll die before I let anything happen to you here."

"Funny thing to say," I smirked, unable to help myself. That giddiness was starting to take over me again. Not so unmanageable. The terror seemed to balance it out. "Especially when we're on a countdown before the curse takes over and you kill me."

"Fair." He inclined his head, his eyebrow arching. "But seeing you again, I'm remembering again just how much we've already been through. All the impossible things we've already done, Stella. I don't know how, but we're going to make it through this." He nuzzled me, his nose tracing a line from my cheek to my neck. "Now...do you remember why this chamber we're in is the better location for fighting kapis?"

I shivered, my gaze fixed on his face. Despite the familiarity, I couldn't catch any specifics within the stream of my mind. "Tell me, arrogant king."

His smile went absolutely devilish as the gurgling, hissing grumbles of the kapis intensified. They were getting closer.

"There's one thing this chamber has the passage did not—room to be epic."

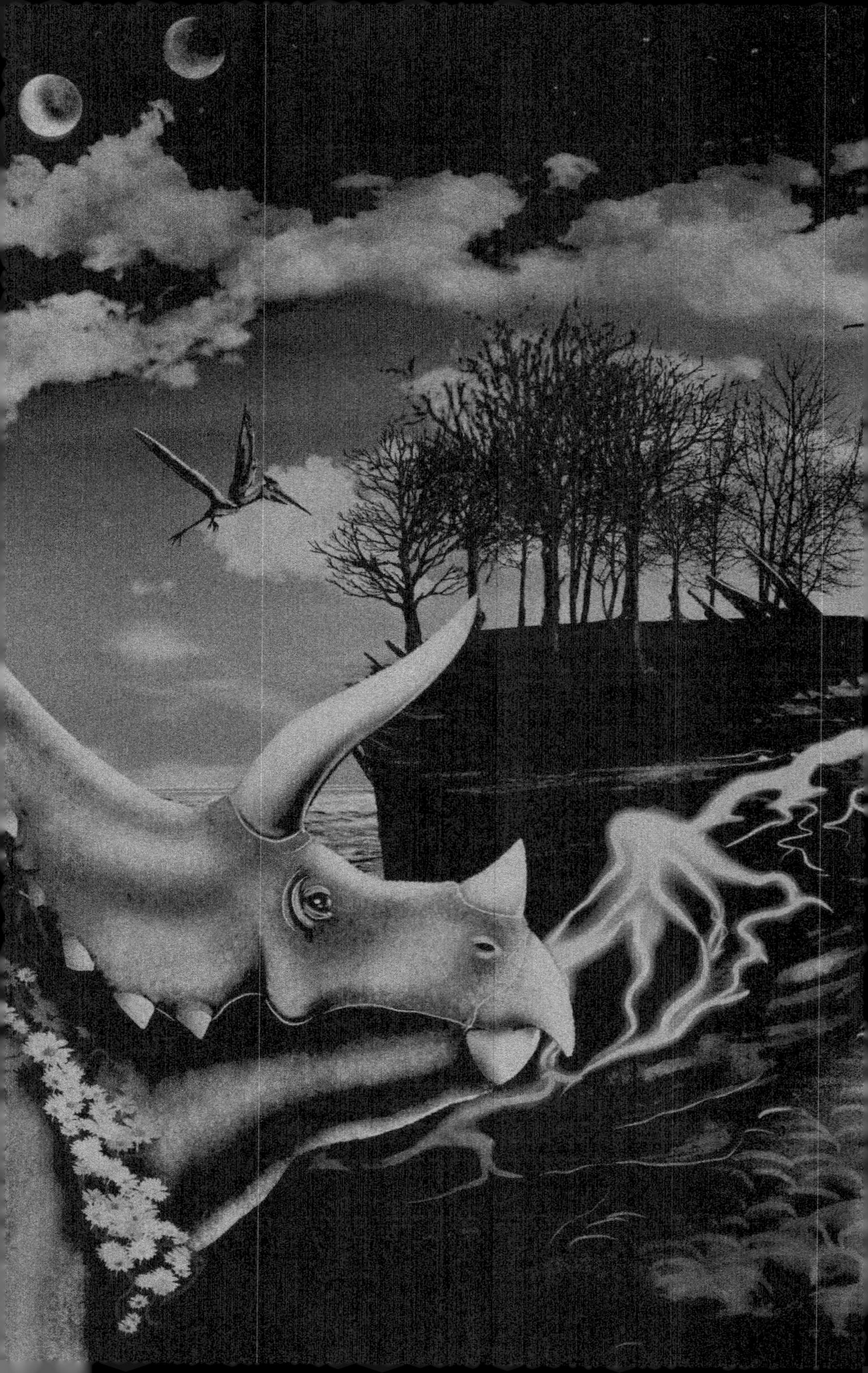

CHAPTER TWENTY-TWO: STELLA

As Brandt winked, his body tensed. Blue energy arced out of the red and black ring. Muscles rippled beneath his garments as his body lengthened and stretched, melding effortlessly into the black-and-red water serpent form. He tossed his head back and roared.

The kapis lurched away, the leader crouching down as its long scaly tail swished back and forth.

Brandt tossed his horned head and leaned forward.

Damn. That man was sexy even as a gigantic water serpent, especially when his attention was focused on the kapis ahead of us and protecting me rather than murdering me.

At the same time, a deep pang of loss struck me. Another memory of sorts. An impression. As if I should be right there with him. Like a less terrifying echo of what I felt when I'd launched myself off Buttercup's back at the tyrannosaur.

My jaws and skin itched. My muscles tensed. An image flashed into my mind. Was it a vision or a memory? I saw myself side by side with Brandt, both of us in water serpent form, draped over one another in a bold, dual-sided attack formation.

Yes, that was where I belonged. That was where I belonged.

On his right. Part of the arch. Part of the battle. The yearning to fight at his side was almost as strong as the desire to be with him.

As Brandt struck at the air in front of the kapis and drove them back, I knotted my fingers in the soft fabric of my dress. He let out another thunderous roar as he reared up, towering over the crouched kapis. His long, serpentine body undulated as he lunged forward, jaws open wide. All but the leader of the kapis scattered back with grunting hisses, but the leader braced its legs against the ground and straightened. Its head moved down into a straight line with its spine as its jaws moved open.

Brandt lashed forward, moving his massive body between the kapis and me. His powerful jaws snapped menacingly, razor-sharp teeth glinting in the dim blue light.

That beat and pressure inside my chest returned. I followed its tug, moving to a marble column with chunks of pale stone like popcorn clusters. My heart raced faster.

Once again, Brandt charged forward and snapped, driving the kapis back. The leader closed its eyes, its body tensing as another guttural groan followed. It had almost flattened itself against the cavern floor, but it wasn't moving back. The other three halted in the passage.

Brandt coiled and stretched out again, his massive, scaled body forming a living barrier while also showcasing his size. He snapped his jaws with a heavy click.

The lead kapi tensed, then lunged for Brandt's throat.

"Brandt!" The scream tore out of me. I dropped to the ground and gathered up loose stones. Maybe I couldn't be a water serpent, but I could help.

I'd no sooner straightened than Brandt had whipped his head down and seized the leader in his jaws. His coils spun around the creature, twisting it about so that its heavy jaws snapped shut on empty air.

The kapi thrashed in Brandt's grip, writhing and twisting but unable to break free.

The other kapis milled together back in the passage. Their yellow eyes glinted and narrowed. As one darted forward, I flung a rock. It struck the beast between the eyes, startling it just enough it hopped back.

That had worked.

Not the best but sufficient.

Still, Brandt cast an approving glance in my direction, his dark-red eyes shining. "See? You remember the spirit, Stella!"

"The spirit?" I raised an eyebrow as I picked up more stones. "What's that supposed to mean?"

"Kapis aren't that bad if there aren't too many, and you've got enough room to maneuver, and you're significantly larger and more powerful than they are. Is it coming back to you, Stella?"

The pulse in my chest grew more insistent, and my fingers twitched with the urge to transform. Flashes of memory teased my mind of hunting alongside Brandt, our serpent bodies twining together in a deadly dance. I ached to release the transformation, to unleash my water serpent self and fight by his side. Yet there was only hollowness where that urge remained as if my mind could perceive the form and yet something was missing to let me fulfill it.

This wasn't what either of us wanted exactly, but I chucked more rocks at the attacking kapis.

Brandt continued to tighten his coils around the leader. The kapi wheezed, claws scraping helplessly against Brandt's thick, sleek hide. Its struggles grew weaker as its eyes bulged. It gurgled a final hiss before going limp in Brandt's clutches, unconscious.

Brandt released his grip, and the kapi's body slumped to the cavern floor. The remaining kapis shrieked their fury, baring knife-like teeth. Muscles bunched under their heavy scales as they prepared to attack. The nearest one charged forward. Brandt darted around it, coiling it up and squeezing.

Another kapi darted forward, jaws gaping. I snatched up a shard of marble and flung it hard. The heavy stone struck the kapi's neck, and it reeled back with a choked hiss.

The whole cavern shook.

Another earthquake!

I stumbled, barely catching myself before I tumbled to the ground. The walls trembled, stones raining down. One struck my shoulder, and I cried out.

Brandt flung the half-conscious kapi away and swept his tail around me, shielding me from the falling debris. His scales brushed against my skin, smooth and cool. I leaned into him, fingers curling into his hide as I ducked my head.

Two earthquakes so close together?

Fear speared me as silt rained down on us.

The remaining kapis hissed and huddled against the stones as rubble tumbled from the quaking cavern walls. Brandt stayed coiled protectively around me. The stalactites swayed as the ground rocked.

The tremors intensified, the rocky walls of the cavern groaning as the crystals screamed. Cracks spiderwebbed through the dark stone as more debris pelted us. I turned my face down, clinging to him.

If the cavern collapsed, we would be buried.

A thunderous crack split the air. I jerked my head up as a section of the cavern wall crumbled away. Beyond was a churning rush of water, another channel of the underground river that ran alongside the cavern. Filthy, raging currents burst through the gap, crashing into the cavern in a foaming torrent.

Brandt's muscles tensed all around me. His coils tightened.

I couldn't move. A deep heaviness pressed on my chest, encasing my heart with an urge to leap so intense it paralyzed me. My mouth went dry. The formerly calm river crashed and surged.

He spun around, seized me in his jaws, and lunged forward onto the highest of the outcropping boulders. His massive form closed around the dark-blue boulder as he dropped me at its center. The slick surface offered me no purchase. I flung my arms around his sides again and pressed my face down. Grey froth splashed up around us. The icy waters struck me like a giant's fist, flattening me and ripping the breath from my lungs.

The quake ended as suddenly as it began. An eerie silence fell over the cavern, broken only by the groans of shifting rock. Dust clouded the air even as the river settled. I coughed and spat grit and foam.

Slowly, I lifted my head. Chilling fear lanced through me, the light eerie and intermittent as some of the bioluminescent lichen had been destroyed.

Brandt's sides heaved. "You all right, Stella?" he asked, his voice heavy and rough.

I swept my gaze over Brandt's serpentine form resting protectively around me, his scales glinting in the eerie bioluminescent light. The cavern trembled and groaned in the aftershocks intermittently. Some of the crystal clusters still vibrated, their hum uneasy. The waters were no longer rising, but the currents were powerful. Only strong swimmers could brave them.

"I'm all right. What about you?" I scrubbed my hands over my face and hair, squeezing out the silt-filled water. The grime and cold seeped into my bones.

"We've got to get you out," he said hoarsely, all traces of play gone.

Blood oozed from his side as a few of the punctures and cuts from the stones slowly healed. It trickled into the river and turned into red spirals that vanished into the dark depths.

"There's never been two earthquakes back-to-back. Could be

a third. I... You have to go now." He moved his horned head back and forth, scanning the broken rocks and passages. "Serves me right for getting cocky. Shouldn't have enjoyed that moment. Thanks to the rock slides, I don't know which paths are safe. Your seer instincts, do you feel anything?"

I pushed myself up shakily. My feet slipped, and my cheek bumped against his side. His heartbeat had quickened, throbbing throughout his body, but it wasn't from lust or need. All I felt now was fear. Awareness that something was wrong.

I placed my hand over my collarbone and pressed the necklace down hard against my skin, fighting to calm myself. If the earthquake had been responsible for the curse advancing in time before, could it—

Brandt's body shook. He ducked his head, his black-and-red scales glistening. The long whiskers drooped. "Stella—" His voice became more guttural, his coils tightening around the rock.

Low growls echoed up the dark chamber. My gaze jerked up as Brandt's head remained down. His horned eyelids slid shut. Over a dozen yellow eyes glittered in the dirty waters, swimming against the current with impossible grace and strength.

Kapis.

Their powerful tails sliced through the current, their bodies submerged except for their eyes. The churning and swirling eddies meant nothing to them.

Thrusting my hand against Brandt's side, I pointed with the other hand. "The kapis are back, Brandt. Brandt?"

His breaths had grown more ragged, his head drooping, though the rest of his body had gone rigid.

Dread chilled me more than the cold waters. No...no.

The kapis' glowing eyes drew closer, their guttural growls louder.

"You can fight it, Brandt!" The words slipped out of my

mouth as I helplessly pressed my hand to the red stripe running the length of his body. Could he? Who knew?

His head lowered again as if a great weight pressed upon him. Pure fear glowed in his eyes even as the rage and madness crept in. He shook his head. What little fragment of him remained fought desperately to retain control. It was like watching it swallow him alive, sucking him down into a narrow vortex of hate and rage. The fear intensified, pulsing in those brilliant red eyes, and that fear was only for me.

Tears stung my eyes. I couldn't move. Couldn't will myself to speak. We both knew jumping in the water was a death sentence for me. Without my water serpent form, I had no chance of surviving, especially facing over a dozen kapis. And as soon as the curse seized him, it would take only one bite.

The haze swept over me again. I placed my hand flat against his scales and stared up at him, watching as he struggled and shook. Dread pounded within me. I didn't want this. Dying was one thing, but to know he would have to bear it for the rest of his days? His fear sliced into me even deeper, sinking its hooks into my consciousness.

All I wanted was to say I loved him, that I forgave him. This wasn't him, and it wasn't his fault.

He kept his gaze locked on mine. Then—with great effort—he lifted his heavy head once more, took a sweeping glance around the chamber, and grunted. He drew his tail up out of the water and snapped it around me.

The coils pulsed tighter. For one devastating moment, I thought he was going to crush me. But then—as the kapis swam closer—he looked me dead in the eye and flung me toward the ledge that led from the passage.

"Brandt!" His name tore out of my mouth as I sailed through the cold air.

He didn't follow. The last remnant of his humanity vanished

from his eyes as he released his grip on the stone and launched himself back into the frothing waters at the kapis.

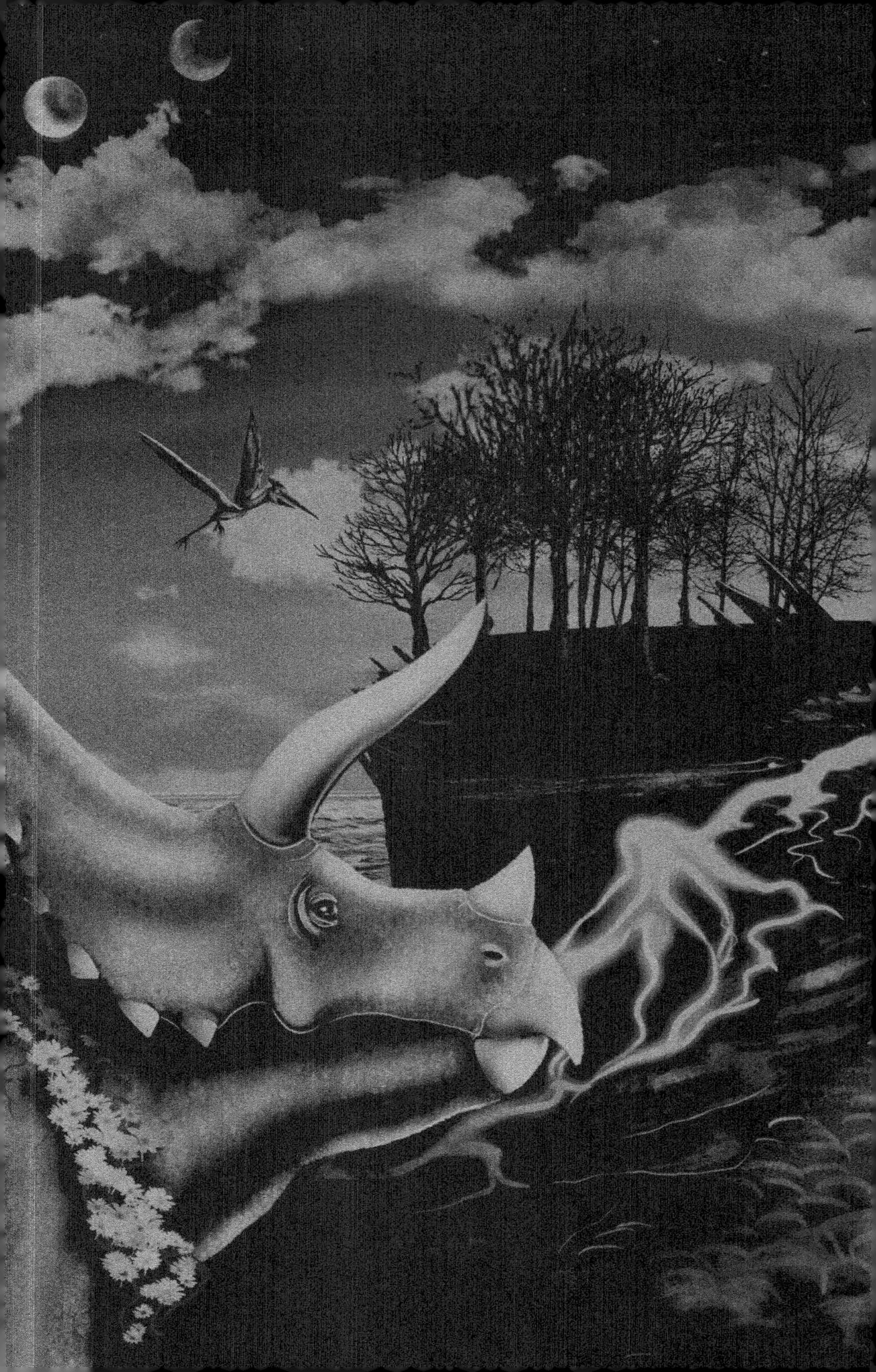

CHAPTER TWENTY-THREE: STELLA

The narrow ledge of stone that connected to the main passage hit me hard. My ribs protested, taking the brunt of it along with my right arm. My legs splashed into the rushing waters. Instinct alone gave me the presence of mind to seize hold of it with my left hand. Sharp pain jarred up my side, but the ragged cry that tore from my lips was for Brandt.

He vanished entirely beneath the frothing grey waves. The glowing eyes of the kapis blinked out as they dove after him.

"Brandt!" I sobbed, my voice weak and broken. My lungs cramped, rebelling against my pleas for air.

Another chunk of a crystal formation broke off and crashed down into the water, sending up filthy streams of water. Red swirls, bubbles, and froth rose in the water.

No.

By all that was good in this world, this wasn't how it was going to end. It couldn't be!

Shaking, I dragged myself up the ledge and to my feet.

The waters dipped and then returned. Brandt surged upward, a bloody kapi corpse in his maw. His powerful jaws snapped left and right, crushing the kapis between razor-sharp teeth. Blood filled the churning waters as he whipped his muscular body back and forth, slamming the creatures against the cavern walls and rending with his claws.

They mobbed him, lashing out in attack. Their teeth and claws cut and scraped, and once they found a wound, they focused on it.

The kapis kept coming, a never-ending swarm of crocodilian fury. They slashed at his sides, working in concert. He thrashed about, dislodging some and seizing another in his jaws. With a roar that vibrated through my very core, he surged back into the frothing waves, tearing through the snarling beasts. In seconds, his massive form erupted from the churning waters that were now more red than grey.

I couldn't wrench my gaze away. My body trembled from the cold. He couldn't keep this up forever, but the kapis also couldn't keep coming forever. Once he finished going through the kapis, he would turn on me.

But how could I leave him?

Another sob choked me.

He trapped kapi after kapi in his teeth, crushing them effortlessly in his jaws. Crimson blood swirled through the waters as the kapis' rageful, dying shrieks echoed off the stone and reverberated over the water. Brandt dove down again with another kapi in his jaws. He heaved above the waves, farther downstream. Three kapis clung to his back, and another ten trailed after him. He flung himself at the jagged cavern walls, shaking the stalagmites even more. The rock face crunched beneath him, crushing the life out of two of the kapis.

Ducking my chin, I hugged myself, cradling my bleeding arm.

Think, Stella. Think!

What good was I doing down here?

Nothing.

I couldn't save him, not from the kapis and not from the curse.

He'd found the strength to push that curse back enough to give me a chance. Now, I had to find the strength to get out of here and trust that somehow he would survive while I found help and escaped.

It was the smart thing to do.

If I could get out, I could find Hord and the rest of Brandt's warriors and send help. Perhaps they were already on their way down.

It was like resisting the pull of a powerful magnet while walking waist-deep in sludge. The entirety of my being fought me.

Wounded arm clutched to my chest, I willed myself forward as the frothing, bellowing rage in the churning river continued. I struggled into the dim light of the narrow passageways. None of it was familiar, and soon, the paths branched.

Which way?

Even when I closed my eyes and searched my impressions, nothing stirred. No one passage seemed better than the other. There weren't any traces of light farther down nor hints of a fresh breeze. The scents of the river and all that blood as well as Brandt's cologne still filled my nostrils as if the memory held me in its thrall.

No. Go back. Go back to him. Don't leave him there.

I swallowed hard. My throat remained tight. What kind of seer was I if I couldn't find my way out of a series of underground tunnels I had once known like the back of my hand?

Even if my instincts were trying to say something, the voice in my mind wouldn't give me peace. It just kept going. I staggered toward the tunnel on my right, carried more by momentum than any sensation that it was correct.

Just go back.

He could die.

Do you want him to die?

He'll die alone. Would you really do that to him?

My body swayed as I stopped at the edge of the passage before it split. My senses darkened.

Go back to him.

Go back now.

Run!

The air sliced through my lungs like icy blades. It burned its way through me. The mineral-rich scents of cave water, blood, and something electric reminded me how real this all was. His cologne had faded. The absence of smoky bergamot and leather seared through me, leaving a deeper rift of longing.

When I closed my eyes, his face flashed back into my mind. Those dark-ruby eyes. The fear of hurting me mixed up with the torment of the curse itself. And that curse had devoured him.

If he caught me here, he would tear me to shreds. When he woke from the haze of the curse, he would mourn me.

Even so, the urge intensified, digging into my consciousness.

The passageway narrowed, water dripping from the ceiling. Brandt's roars lessened, but the roar within me intensified.

Go back to him. Now!

"Get a grip!" I whimpered, clenching my eyes shut.

I wasn't stupid. I really wasn't. What could I do back there? Really? Nothing except die! And for no good reason.

The weight pressed harder upon me, my legs as heavy as if they'd been bound to the very core of the world.

Just go. Keep going.

Why was it so much harder than in the valley?

I braced my good hand against the damp stone wall, my breaths ragged. My fingers scraped along the smooth surface, seeking something to ground me. Cold sweat formed on my brow.

I wouldn't go back.

Couldn't.

Shouldn't.

I bit my lip so hard I tasted blood.

Once I had been a woman strong enough to lay her life down to save a world. Now, did I have the strength to keep walking away from the man I loved even if going back would get me killed?

Nope.

The weights fell away from my limbs as soon as I admitted the truth. I could run again. I was free. Free to return to him!

Blood thundered in my ears, the hum intensifying and blocking my ears.

"Brandt!" I shouted, not caring who heard. "Brandt, I'm coming!"

That was all that mattered, getting back to him.

I'd barely made it to the curve of the passage when strong arms covered in purple tattoos grabbed me and spun me around.

Ihlkit! I found myself looking up into Candy's purple eyes.

The tall woman gasped with relief and hugged me tight. "I found her!" she shouted over her shoulder. "She's down here! And I think I hear Brandt. Something's wrong."

I struggled to break free, shoving her arm away. "Let go of me! I have to get to Brandt! He's in trouble."

Candy crushed me tighter. "Don't worry. We're getting him out. The others are on their way."

Anger blossomed inside of me. Candy was several inches taller, but by sheer force of rage, I would get out of this. I had to.

"Stop!" I screamed, thrashing harder. "You can't keep me away from him!"

"Not keeping you away from him, hon. Just keeping you both alive until this curse is gone, all right?" Candy pressed her head against mine and squeezed me tighter, pinning even my wounded arm as I struggled. Horns! She was stronger than she looked. She was a real-life Amazon!

"You can't keep me from him, and you can't have him for yourself!" I snapped.

"Have him for myself?" She tilted her head, her immaculate brow arching dramatically. Even her freaking eyeliner was perfect. "You really are talking out of your head, Stella."

Before I could respond, a splinter of pain embedded in my consciousness. "Ah!" I gasped. It exploded through my arm, dragging me roughly back into the moment. I tried to double over as she held me. "My arm. My ribs!"

"Oh, sorry." She adjusted her grip but kept a firm hold on my other arm. She winced as she studied the bloody scrapes on my golden-brown skin. "You hit this hard. Is it broken?"

Go to him now!

The urge reared up again, but the pain usurped its authority. I stared down at the bloody wounds and the gouge along my elbow. It was hard to pull in a full breath. Had it been this bad the whole time?

More footsteps thundered down the passage.

I knew Kine was there before I saw him, recognizing the rapid tread of his boots. "Bug!" He skidded to a stop in front of me, his gaze searching. It immediately fell to my arm. "You're hurt."

"Nothing serious." I struggled to speak.

The need to return to Brandt's arms welled within me, begging me to turn back and run, but it was no longer so overwhelming in its destructiveness. The intensity of the pain had broken through the magic and made it hard for me to process much beyond it.

"It's Brandt." Shoving my hair back, I gasped, struggling to stay steady. Embarrassment flooded me as much as the pain. "He's in trouble. The curse claimed him again. It went forward. For a second time! After the earthquakes."

Tears leaked down my cheeks. It hurt so much I could barely think clearly.

Candy's head snapped back in the direction I'd come, her sleek ponytail flicking with the movement. She then looked to Kine, her gorgeous eyes wide. "You got her? I can get Brandt calm."

"I got her. Go help Brandt." Kine put his arm around my waist as he pulled me to the side of the passage. "Damn, Bug. Looks like you broke your arm or came really close to it." He examined the limb, wrinkles forming around his eyes and over his brow.

Candy bolted, her feet rapid and light on the stone.

Wrath bristled through me as she left, screaming at her intrusion. I should be the one helping her!

"Relax, Bug. She can help more than either you or I can right now," Kine said.

That didn't make me feel much better.

Other warriors raced past. I didn't remember most of their names, but their faces were familiar. My head ached, throbbing with so much knowledge that couldn't fully rise to the surface. It was like almost recalling a language in which I had once been fluent.

Most of all, I fought the demand that I return to Brandt. My own ragged breaths continued. Bowing my head, I whimpered, struggling to hide my tears.

"Come on, Bug." Kine pressed a gentle kiss to my temple. "We'll get you back to Auntie Runa's and get this fixed. It's all going to work out."

His soothing presence countered the demands more than I would have guessed. It was as if he grounded me even though I recoiled and considered bolting after the others.

"How did you find me?" I asked weakly.

"We realized the Gola Resh took you and how she took you. That well is one of the few weak points in Auntie Runa's wards.

At least when the lid is off. Not sure how that lid got off, though. I could have sworn I made sure it was closed before I went up to care for the animals. Even with her strange magic, the Gola Resh couldn't have pushed the lid off." He guided me up the passage.

A chill jolted through me, pulsing with intense longing. The need rose again even stronger, so strong I could barely breathe.

I dug my heels in and halted. "Wait, no. Please, I don't want to leave without knowing he's all right."

"He will be fine." Kine tightened his grip on my wrist, his voice sharper than usual. "You being here makes this harder. The more you two are around each other, the stronger those impulses become. I know this is hard, but if you don't want to be an idiot, you're going to keep walking out. Brandt will be fine. Even if there were thirty kapis, he could hold them off, especially in his rage state. It takes his warriors at least an hour to wear him down when he's like this. Those kapis don't stand a chance, not in the water. That's where we water serpents are at our best. Now come on."

The firmness in his voice brooked no argument, yet my heart felt as if it was being ripped out.

He tugged me forward.

My wounded arm throbbed in time with my footsteps. Pain in my knees and across my shins flared as well. Tears filled my eyes as he guided me up the long, sloping passage into the silver-white and teal light of the dual moons beyond the cavern.

Several more guards and warriors stood at the entrance. They bowed their heads to us, touching their spears or swords to their foreheads in respect.

Kine also bowed his head as he guided me along. "The arch general and his warriors will be bringing the king up shortly. Remain here."

"And what of the queen?" one of the guards asked gruffly. "Does she require medical attention?"

"I am taking her to safety," Kine responded. "The king's orders regarding the queen have not changed."

He guided me forward toward the foothills. The fresh air filled my lungs, rich and powerful. Rose clover, hop grass, valley sage—all cleansing scents. My head still thundered, and the pain throughout my body hadn't diminished, but there was a merciful clarity up here.

Kine led me to the top of a low hill. As we crested it, a familiar lowing greeted me.

My eyes widened. "Buttercup?"

Buttercup raced up to me. She honked and hopped, shaking her head. The ground shook beneath her feet, bits of grass and earth kicked up.

I dodged a thrust of her horn and embraced her with one arm, feeling a little more like myself in her presence and Kine's. "Did you miss me, baby girl?"

She huffed. Her breath steamed my hand as I scratched her favorite spot.

Kine scratched the base of her jaw. "Yeah, of course she missed you." He dipped his head forward as he lifted my chin and examined my face. "You're not looking as bad now that you're up here. Feeling more like yourself?"

I nodded. The pain and need to be with Brandt remained, but my own awareness had been restored. Whether this was an aspect of the curse or the mating bond or a combination of the two, I'd narrowly escaped death.

"Yeah. Thanks for helping me back there." Thanks to him and Candy.

"It's my job." He started to give my elbow a playful swat, then caught himself. "Come on. Let's get you home."

He helped me up onto Buttercup's back. This time, he climbed onto the back of her neck and situated himself behind her crest. After directing me to put my good arm around his neck, he urged Buttercup forward.

It didn't take us much time to get there. By the time we did, my whole body ached and throbbed. I'd become so stiff I practically fell off Buttercup's back.

Kine caught me and lifted me down. "I think you need a hot bath and a long sleep."

"Is there any way I can get confirmation that Brandt is all right? Surely they've gotten him out of the cavern by now," I said, cradling my injured arm to my chest.

"We'll get you inside and get you fixed up. Then I'll ride out and see." He slowed as we neared the entrance with Buttercup trailing behind us. With a sweeping bow and elegant motion of his arm, he opened the door.

Loud voices echoed from inside Auntie Runa's peaceful sanctuary.

"I had no other choice," Elias shouted.

"It was a violation," Auntie Runa countered, her voice startlingly sharp, almost shrill.

I froze, rooted in place at the entrance of the home. What had happened while I was gone?

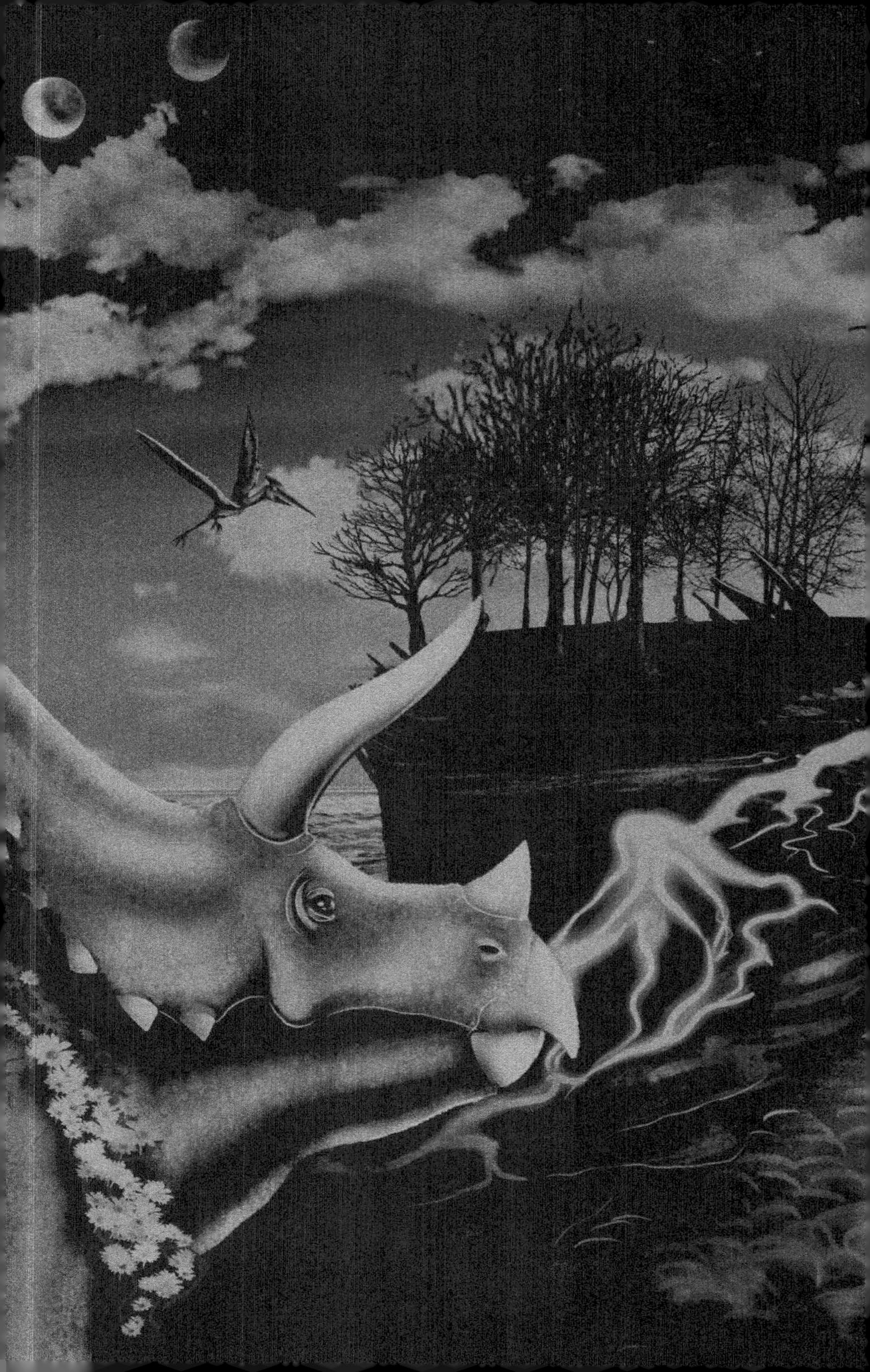

CHAPTER TWENTY-FOUR: STELLA

I halted at the edge of the hall, uncertain how to proceed. To hear either of them yelling was strange. Especially Auntie Runa. It felt like an intrusion that was made all the worse because of the subject. Kine's raised brows and startled gaze also suggested this was rare.

Auntie Runa and Elias faced off in the main room, Auntie Runa gripping her sapphire-topped cane and Elias standing with his arms folded over his muscular chest. His dark-blue eyes blazed, yet a defensive air surrounded him.

"You had no right to invade my private sanctum." Auntie Runa's voice was tight with anger. She brought the cane down with a hard crack, her fingers gripping the rounded handle so tight her knuckles whitened.

"I only went in there because I saw a lizard slip under the door. I was trying to catch it before it could get lost in all your things and ruined your materials. It could have contaminated your paints." Elias's usually pleasant mouth twisted, a muscle leaping in his jaw. "I never intended to see the representations of your visions, especially the last one. The last thing I want is a burden like that. Just because I'm not a full-sighted seer doesn't mean I don't understand the responsibility of those visions."

"The sanctum is forbidden for a reason," Auntie Runa snapped. "Its protections are not to be trifled with, especially not in times like this."

"But the lizard—"

"You should have left the lizard in the sanctum. It couldn't have been a large one if it got under the door. You could have told me about its presence. You could have asked, but you didn't."

He bowed his head. Two more muscles in his jaw twitched, and the pulse in his neck leaped. "Forgive me, please. I Intended no harm. I never intended to intrude upon your privacy or the purity of your sanctum."

"The harm is done." Auntie Runa drew in a long breath, shaking her head. "You will show your worth and the cut of seer you are by how you handle the knowledge you obtained."

My mind flitted back to the conversation I'd had with Elias earlier this very night when he'd admitted he'd seen part of the vision. Was that what Auntie Runa had just discovered, or was it a second encounter? Had he entered the room after I left?

Kine cleared his throat and stepped out from the hall into the main room, announcing our return. I followed much slower, allowing him to take the lead and explain what had happened.

Auntie Runa's anger morphed into concern as she hurried over toward me and began her examination, interjecting questions directed to both Kine and me. While I avoided telling her about how I had almost been incapable of walking away from Brandt or how I had behaved with him, I did tell her about the well and the double earthquakes and everything else. Kine offered his own observations, but he said nothing of my struggle. Not that I could or would hide it forever. I just couldn't bring myself to speak about it now.

Elias remained silent, standing at the edge of one of the channels, hand against the back of his neck and his gaze distant.

I avoided looking directly at him, wanting to give him some measure of privacy. He had meant well, almost certainly, and now my own curiosity was even more piqued. What had Auntie Runa seen? What part of that vision had Elias seen? What possible knowledge could be so devastating that it was dangerous?

No sooner had I asked that than my mind obliged, supplying numerous terrifying options.

Brandt's horrifying descent into madness and death.

The end of our people and land as a whole.

Destruction of everything we cared about.

Eternal hopelessness against the Gola Resh.

The return of the Babadon combined with hopelessness against the Gola Resh.

Some new force or enemy making everything even worse.

A new curse that would make everything worse.

I clamped my hand to my temples and shook my head, willing the horrors back.

No, stop. No.

"Don't worry about changing your clothes. Just get in now," Auntie Runa said, indicating the channel with the manatees. She held a large wooden bowl filled with pink and red flower petals against her hip.

"Do you need to check to see if my arm is broken?" I asked, lifting it slightly.

The pronounced swelling and purple-black bruising with puddles of green mottling my forearm had expanded to cover most of it, wrapping around my wrist and extending all the way to my elbow. The blood from the scrapes and cuts had mostly dried. Based on the dull, constant ache that made me want to gnash my teeth the more I focused on it, I'd probably broken it in more than one place. My ribs were probably cracked. Candy having to hold me back like that certainly hadn't helped.

Auntie Runa scooped up a handful of the fragrant petals and tossed them into the gentle current. Bubbles and Bobbles as well as the other manatees swam about, dipping beneath the surface and sending out ripples and masses of bubbles. The petals spun and floated, releasing a soft floral scent like roses and magnolias before the manatees ate some of them, whiskers twitching as they munched.

"Doesn't matter. The water will help you just the same. It'll even push the broken bones back into place. Only time we have to be more careful is if it's snapped off or the bone's protruding or something like that." She gestured toward the channel with her chin. "Go on now. Get in."

My body aching and stiff, I sat on the edge of the stone channel and dipped my feet in. The water was as warm as a soothing bath, and the manatees swam alongside me, their whiskers tickling my sensitive skin.

"All the way. Try to relax. Let the waters do their work. You're safe. There's no one here you need to worry about protecting," Auntie Runa said, her tone gentle.

The harshness from her confrontation with Elias had faded. Both Elias and Kine had left. For now, it was just me and Auntie Runa. As much as I cared about Elias and Kine, their absence meant a release of pressure. Auntie Runa probably already knew everything I was struggling with. She'd been absolutely right about my relationship with Brandt and how it affected me.

Yup. Embarrassing as it was, she had been right all along. It was just me being a horny idiot.

With a grunt, I pushed myself off the edge into the warm, fragrant waters. Like an eel diving into the depths, I disappeared beneath the surface. The sharp change in sensation and temperature overwhelmed my senses for a second before relief seeped in. My feet brushed the bottom of the stone channel as I forced my eyes open. Soft hazy beams of lamp light filtered down in golden shafts. The manatees' calls took on a different, clearer cast below these waters. A smile tugged at my lips when the baby triceratops dog-paddled farther down the channel, its chubby little legs swiftly kicking.

The weight and pressure of the water soothed me. More memories pressed on my mind, mixing with all the times I had dove into pools and lakes and ponds and gone as far down as I could. A part of me had remembered all along how much I loved being far beneath the water with all of it against me in a massive warm hug.

Far too soon, my lungs burned, the need for air forcing me upward again. I kicked up off the floor and sliced my arms through the water. Already the stiffness and pain in my arm had reduced.

If only all my problems could be swept away this easily.

When I lifted my injured arm from the water, some of the pain returned. It vanished as soon as I submerged it again. That was familiar. The cuts and scrapes had even started to stitch back together.

Buttercup huffed as she lay down at the edge of the canal, close enough to keep an eye on me.

"Keep yourself under at least as far as your neck." Auntie Runa continued to cast more flower petals onto the surface. "It'll take a few hours."

"Brandt was able to heal almost instantly." I massaged my arm beneath the warm waters, my fingers pressing along the sensitive points. Dull and sharp pricks and lines of pain spiraled into my wrist and up into my shoulder, but already the improvement was marked.

"Brandt is fully seated in his powers as a water serpent shifter, and his ring is full of shifter energy. After the chamber is unlocked and your ring is restored to you, you will start to regain your healing abilities as well. With time, of course. You'll need to rebuild your endurance, but all your training with the basics is going to pay off there." Auntie Runa's eyebrow arched as she gently prodded Bubbles. The manatee continued to scoop up mouthfuls of the flowers. "Don't eat all the petals, you greedy thing. There's still plenty of lettuce and mango from breakfast."

"You were right. It wasn't the alcohol, Auntie Runa." The words were bitter on my tongue, but I forced them out nonetheless. My cheeks burned as I recalled how I'd practically swooned over Brandt and how swiftly my own desires had pushed me toward very poor decisions. "How do I stop being stupid around him?"

Auntie Runa sat on the edge of the canal. She tucked her blue skirt up around her knees and dangled her bare feet in the warm waters. "Oh, girlie, there's no real way to keep from being stupid around the one you love when it's like this. You just have to stay away from each other as much as you can, though that might not be possible if we want to get this all resolved. The Gola Resh is a cruel one. She'll likely orchestrate it so you two have no excuse but to be near one another. All you can do is ground yourself. Remember what matters. Don't let Brandt be the center of your world, no matter how much you want him, and remember, temptation's much easier to fight when it's not looming over you in the room."

Yeah, but I wanted Brandt looming over me, pressing on me, climbing on me—

I clapped my hand over my eyes. "I hate this!"

My hand dropped to the necklace as I rubbed the charm, tugging at it as I did. The cool stone offered no comfort, nor did the steel on the other side. The faint scent of cherries returned, sparking more memories I couldn't quite bring into focus.

"These are difficult days," Auntie Runa said.

Auntie Runa's more basic observations brought out my sarcastic side, but I bit my tongue instead of contradicting her. Besides, she was right. Sometimes the truth was simple.

"What was your vision about, Auntie Runa?" I tread water, my gaze focused on Bobbles as if the ancient manatee was the most fascinating creature in all of creation. Truly, he nearly was, especially when he was eating chunks of lettuce and watching me with those big dark eyes, but there was one other thing that was even more compelling.

My question hung in the air as the silence intensified. At last, I glanced back at Auntie Runa. My eyes widened.

She didn't have the same calm visage as usual. The look in her eyes...the tension in her hands...the tightness of her muscles...

She wasn't sure if she was doing the right thing.

That didn't make me feel so good. My insides churned.

"You must understand that this is not a vision that is lightly shared." Auntie Runa's mouth pinched. "I understand your curiosity, but you must not press this matter. This knowledge—I fear that it will..." She bent her head forward, then shook her head again. Her fingers pressed to her lips.

I nodded slowly, avoiding Auntie Runa's gaze. As much as I wanted to know more about her mysterious vision that had so upset Elias, I knew better than to push her. A sharp bitterness filled my mouth. What had she seen? It must have been powerful if she did not want to share it. Or horrifying. Probably horrifying.

"I understand. I won't ask again." Dipping my head down, I continued to tread water.

Auntie Runa's expression softened. She leaned out and squeezed my shoulder, affection shining in her murky eyes. "You're a good girl, Stella, and you're a smart one, even if you don't always feel it and sometimes don't act it."

I sucked as a queen, though. The woman I had once been sounded incredible. A powerful seer who could easily turn into a water serpent. Who marched into the king's chambers and challenged him with her predictions and her insights. And she had been right about her predictions too. She had also been willing to lay her own life down along with seven others. The more I learned about who Stella was before, the less I felt like I could measure up to her spirit and skills.

None of that rang true to who I was now. Whatever steel and fire had existed within me had been muted in my time on Earth.

I'd gotten dorky and goofy.

Curse or no curse, I was boy crazy. Well—man crazy actually. Brandt was no boy.

Old Stella would have rolled her eyes at that, probably. I would have rolled my eyes at current me at any stage in my life after twelve. Horns, I used to be a judgmental know-it-all.

I startled as the surface of the water rippled. Bobbles bumped against my arm gently. Her wise eyes met mine, and she let out a soft rumble.

Smiling sadly, I reached out and stroked her large, slick head. "You're right. Worrying won't help," I murmured.

Bobbles blinked slowly at me. Bubbles came up under my other arm, demanding attention. For a few moments, I forgot most of my troubles and simply stroked and scratched the manatees as the healing waters worked their magic on my wounds and fractures.

Sighing, I sank deeper into the soothing warmth until the water covered all of me up to my ears. As much as I wanted to be the bold, fearless queen I had once been, my new life had softened me. The struggles and heartaches of Earth had sanded away my strong edges, leaving me raw and vulnerable. Even if my memories returned, I would always be different from who I once was. I would never again be the unflinching seer-queen who had looked doom in the face and sacrificed herself. That Stella was gone for good. She really had died.

How pathetic was it that she had died, and I had come back, and yet it was as easy as slipping into water to believe that this was who I should be? It wasn't that I was in the wrong body any more. It was just that I didn't measure up.

I shuddered despite the water's warmth, a knot of dread forming in my stomach. I had to get serious about collecting every scrap of knowledge and skill if I really wanted a chance of stopping the Gola Resh. She'd hauled me down into that well as if I were nothing at all. Maybe that would have still happened even if I had been a water serpent. My skills didn't immediately scream a connection to stopping the Gola Resh, but Auntie Runa said I just needed to be faithful in training for now. The rest would come later.

So...I was faithful.

That, at least, was something I was good at. Steadfast and consistent. And I could hold on even if I couldn't see.

∽

FOUR DAYS PASSED.

Kine rode out and returned with word that Brandt had indeed survived and been returned to Castle Serpentfire without any serious injury. My spirit and body alike yearned to return to Brandt. Everything ached in his absence, but at least with this much distance, the horrible weight and pressure to run to him had not returned. Just a deep, unyielding longing.

I spent time practicing my forms, working with Auntie Runa on instincts, sketching my thoughts and feelings, and riding with Buttercup. Each day at some point between late afternoon and midnight, an earthquake rocked the land. No more double earthquakes though. The dark cracks spread a little farther and deeper each day, widening at their bases and spreading out their tendrils as the curse marched forward. Elias remained far quieter, his expression dark and downcast.

On the fifth day, I took Buttercup out early, when the sunlight glowed through the mist. Old trails and paths had become familiar once more, along with her favorite patches of clover and the locations of star leaf bushes. She ate enough that anyone else might be fooled into thinking she wouldn't want breakfast, but that was all just a snack. Once I brought her back, I fed her and helped Auntie Runa with the others while discussing more seer methods.

Being a seer—at least a seer who had lost her memory and needed to recover it—was like being told to just feel again and figure it out from there. At least shifting had specifics. Being a seer was like sorting beads in the dark and then drawing what you thought you saw.

I made my way back down into the Scrying Chamber to work on forms again. No more than an hour later, footsteps pounded down the staircase.

"Stella!" Kine shouted.

That was odd. He rarely called me by my given name.

I set my hands on my waist, tossing my blue hair back over my shoulders. My feet settled into the grey-white sand. "What?"

He grabbed me by the shoulders as Hord followed him down. Before I could acknowledge Hord's presence or that oddness, Kine grinned and gave me a small shake. "They've figured out how to stop the Gola Resh. The scholars have a solution!"

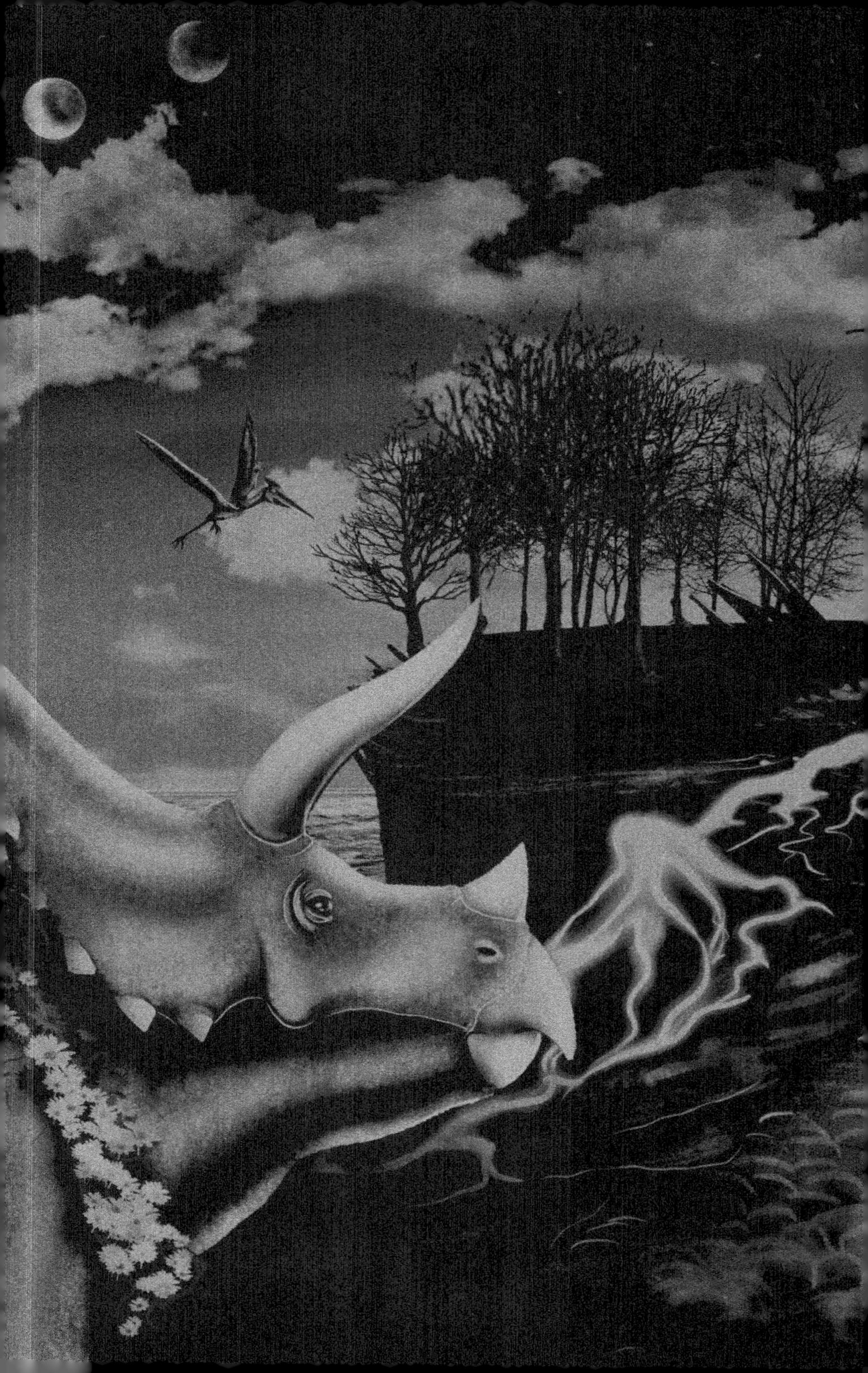

CHAPTER TWENTY-FIVE: STELLA

My eyes widened, and I nearly collapsed with relief. They had found a solution?

I didn't even remember saying anything. The next thing I knew, I was running up the curved stone stairs, gripping the railing to drag myself up faster.

I burst into the main room where Auntie Runa sat sketching with her feet in the water and the manatees clustered near her. "Auntie Runa! They found a solution. We're going to break the curse."

Auntie Runa looked up from her sketch pad, her fingers smudged with charcoal smudges. She lowered the stick to the page. "What's this?" One of the sprigs of rosemary woven into her hair drooped over her ear.

"They've found a solution. Brandt's sages and scholars. They know how to stop the Gola Resh. We're going to be free!"

Auntie Runa glanced behind me at Hord and Kine. Elias looked up from the back corner of the room where he sat beneath a flowering ivy, working on his own sketches.

"You know how to stop the Gola Resh?" She didn't sound as excited as I thought she would.

Hord stepped forward. He gave a polite bow. "Yes, Master of Sight. They have all but finalized it. The king wishes Stella to join them at the council where they will lay out the plan. There are a few minor details that must be managed, and they will go more swiftly if Stella is there."

Auntie Runa set her book and the charcoal aside. With practiced grace, she rose to her feet, water dripping onto the stone tiles as her skirt clung to her calves. "This is not wise. It is unsafe. She should not go. Not unless it's absolutely necessary."

I drew back as if I'd been slapped. "What?" How could she say that? "Auntie, we have a chance—"

"It is dangerous. I haven't had a vision or seen something regarding this, but this is tempting fate. The kind of curse that works against your mate bond is perilous to both of you. If they have the solution, surely they do not need you there. Let them find this solution, implement it, and then you two can see one another. This smells like a trap."

Hord frowned. "The king has asked for her presence. He wants her to be informed, and she will be necessary."

One of Auntie Runa's thick white eyebrows cocked as if to imply she didn't care what the king asked for.

Kine sighed, threading his fingers and resting them on the top of his head. "Auntie Runa, it will be safe. They have the solution, but they need Stella's help to finalize this plan. That much was made clear. It will go faster if she is present. We don't have much time."

Concern and something like anger flashed in Auntie Runa's eyes, cutting paths over her wrinkled brow and along her jaw. "Really? He wants to see her just as much as she wants to see him. You two are playing into the curse. Mark my words, the Gola Resh will do something. You cannot resist one another forever if you are together, and if you come together before the curse is removed, it will only make matters worse for both of you!" She shook her finger.

"I agree. Even if it isn't a trap, the Gola Resh *will* do something," Elias said from the far wall.

It was the first time he'd said more than three words at a time since his altercation with Auntie Runa. He set aside his drawing materials and strode toward us, his dark-blue robes swishing with the movement. A small coral snake coiled around his neck like a necklace. "This feels dangerous. I will do all in my power to protect Stella, but...Brandt is a threat to her. Even if he does not intend to be. The curse draws them together and traps her there until he can resist no longer and tries to murder her."

"We guarantee that the queen will be looked after." Hord remained beside Kine, arms crossed and voice strong. His hair glistened in the soft golden light. "My guard will protect her with their lives, and the king's cycle was concluding as I left. We have hours before it returns."

"The Gola Resh has controlled too much of our lives." I took Auntie Runa's hand in mine, my thumb pressing to the back of her hand.

A heavy, almost painful confidence had risen within me. Yes, I desperately wanted to see Brandt again, but time was of the essence. This was the right thing to do. This was what I needed to do.

"Girl, can you tell me that this isn't simply because you want to see your beloved?" Auntie Runa asked, her golden eyes hard and her brow furrowed.

The temptation to lie rose at once to my lips.

Just deny it.

Deny everything.

Reassure her that I was clear-minded. But...no.

I shook my head, managing a small smile. "Of course not. I want to see him so much. Just the thought of not seeing him makes me feel like I can't breathe." My voice shook a little. "But that doesn't change that deep in my core, I know I need to go. We have to resolve this. Any extra time that this might take is time we don't have. You said only if it was necessary, and before this, you said that it might be that, in the end, we would have to work with one another. That's what is happening now. Trust me. Please."

Auntie Runa clasped my face in both her hands. Her eyes searched mine, her lips pinched in a tight line. Then she pressed her forehead to mine. "My darling girl..." Her fingers dug into my cheeks as she wrestled with some deeper question. At last, she shook her head, patting the side of my face gently as she stepped back. "I trust you, but even though I trust you, this won't be easy."

Kine stepped forward, his head bowed with respect. "Auntie Runa, they are also convinced they understand why the rotational element of the king's curse keeps advancing. They believe it comes when he is feeling agitation. The intense earthquakes make this far worse. He has not had any significant skips forward in the curse's seizure. Both times happened after the earthquakes, and in both cases, the force of the earthquakes was unusually high."

"Did a seer spot this?" Auntie Runa asked, her voice tight.

"No," Kine admitted with reluctance, his smile fading as he glanced at Hord for support. Hord simply shook his head. "No, but the sages are relatively certain." He gave a broad shrug. "There has been so much darkness in this time, Auntie Runa. Many seers have hardly been able to see anything when it comes to the Gola Resh and anything attached to her, but the sages are convinced."

"It's because our magic is being drained," Elias murmured. "I can feel it. Reduced to little more than impressions. Next to nothing is left unless it's divinely granted. It goes faster by the day."

"All the more reason for us to get this resolved," I interjected, squeezing Auntie Runa's hands. "We're going to figure out how to stop this curse and the Gola Resh, Auntie Runa. I know we are."

She gripped my hands as well. Tears misted her eyes, but she forced a smile as she took a moment to collect her thoughts. When she spoke, she spoke with only the faintest quaver in her voice. "Remember, love is a powerful thing, my dear. It can be cruel and destructive as much as it can be good and beautiful, and it is not available only to you and your allies. Keep yourself grounded. Don't let it sweep you off your feet and into its current, or else you will be consumed by it, and remember also that not everything has a single solution. Sometimes there will be more than one, and until death, there is hope." She paused as she studied my face, then shook her head. "I got charcoal on your face. Hold still."

Licking her thumb, she scrubbed off the marks. I grimaced but didn't protest. Of course she would do this.

With a soft smile, she kissed me on the cheek. Then she embraced Kine and Elias, kissing both of them and whispering something to each.

Elias's shoulders eased as she hugged him. He nodded, dipping his head forward as he whispered something back. Whatever it was, she must have appreciated it because she patted him on the arm.

Then, after gathering a few items, we were off.

Hord led the way on a green-backed triceratops with amber eyes and ebony speckles. Four of his other warriors accompanied us. Kine and Elias both rode their parasaurs. As for me, Buttercup barely had to be encouraged to run. She surged ahead so fast I nearly slid out from behind her crest.

The sun shone brightly as we set out, bathing the grasslands in a comforting golden glow though storm clouds built in the east. Dark and heavy as they were, it looked like we would be getting a bad storm in a few hours. Still, the brilliant rays warmed my skin, and the purple cast to the sky seemed a little darker even compensating for the storm.

The grasslands blurred past as Buttercup galloped along them, her powerful legs kicking up small clouds of dust with each thundering step. My heart pounded with exhilaration and nerves.

Hord took us on a roundabout path, actively avoiding anyone who might spot us. If there were any roving factions out and about, I didn't see them.

We hugged the tree line except when we neared the river. Once there, he led us into the shadows of rocky outcroppings. It took almost an hour to reach Castle Serpentfire.

The black castle had been built on a great dark-red cliff above a white sand beach. It was more obvious here than it had been at Auntie Runa's, but the structure was built with a massive foundation and base and tapered toward the top, giving the towers an odd pyramid shape. The bricks had similar interlocking panels despite being made of stone. The terrain sheared off in deep cliffs leading down to the beaches. Woven ladders hung down the sides. Staircases had been fastened at the treads and sides with a railing that appeared to be wooden, and then a series of ropes and handholds had been fastened and carved into the sides as well.

A harbor of sorts curled around the beach. Large double-hulled ships of dark wood with bright sails were moored in the center, each massive sail painted with a series of crimson and azure symbols, all including some variation of the water serpent. Large metal rings had been worked into the sides of the ship well above the waterline. The prow of every ship, regardless of size, had been carved to resemble a different water serpent. Even from this distance, I could tell that the craftsmanship was exquisite.

The sea breeze tasted of salt and algae, bracing and familiar. A softer citrus undercurrent was what really brought me into the moment, the scent I had been looking for all my life. Scraps of memory pulsed over me—scraping my knees on the coarse red stone as I shimmied down the cliff walls, running onto the docks, feeding the sea birds and ocean reptiles, watching the sun turn vermilion as it sank below the horizon, and diving into briny waters and letting the warm waters engulf me.

Gulls and pteranodons wheeled in the air above, some diving down to snatch up morsels from the ships and docks. Thunder grumbled as storm clouds built in the distance.

The closer we got, the more I recognized, though it did not feel like home, exactly.

The soaring obsidian towers, the crimson banners snapping in the sea breeze. They felt familiar.

Hord guided us along a narrow strip of grassland into a tight, arched passage. We filed into the castle. I kept my hand on Buttercup's golden frill. Excitement built within me, mirroring the storm outside. Soon, I would see Brandt again. Soon, we'd have an answer.

Attendants in blue robes and black leggings waited for us. They took our mounts without question. The red-haired girl who whisked up beside Buttercup slipped her a large red apple and led her away like they were good friends.

The air got much smokier and heavier the farther we went indoors. Hord and the attendants hurried us along, up an inner spiral staircase. The staircase wound higher and higher, the smooth stone steps worn down in the center from centuries of use. Torches in sconces along the curving walls cast flickering light as we climbed. My nerves escalated with each step.

At last, we reached a landing, and Hord led us down a long hallway, its walls hung with vivid tapestries depicting serpents and seascapes. Candles flickered in alcoves, filling the passage with warm, dancing light.

Hord stopped before an ornate black iron door. His gaze raked over me and then to Kine and Elias, a question in his eyes.

My hands bunched at my sides. "I'm ready," I said.

I had to see Brandt. The aching hollow within my chest intensified until I could scarcely bear it.

Hord gave a small nod, then three sharp raps on the door. His hand gripped the great circular ring pull and tugged it open.

Part of me half expected Hord to announce us. Instead, we just walked in as if we were expected, as if this were nothing more than a social call.

Then again, maybe he had.

It wasn't as if I heard or saw or felt anything except…Brandt.

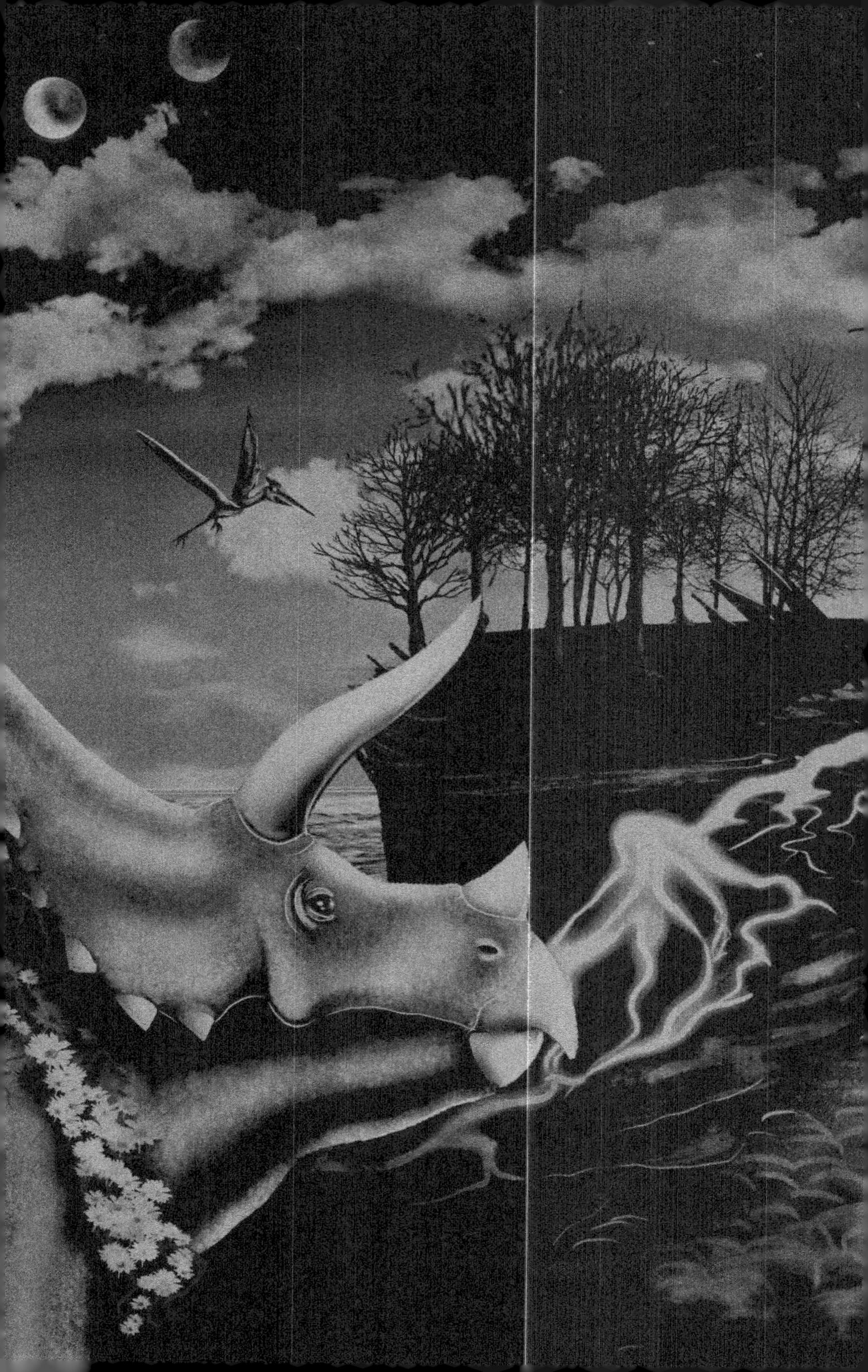

CHAPTER TWENTY-SIX: STELLA

My entire world narrowed to a heartbeat. Brandt was lounging on a massive obsidian throne, elbow pressed on the armrest and his cheek resting against his fist. Then, in slow motion, his dark-ruby gaze lifted to mine. His breath hitched as his shoulders rolled back, and he straightened on the throne.

Ihlkit!

My mouth went dry.

Brandt's eyes smoldered, his chiseled features set in an intense expression that weakened my knees and heated my core.

A hand plucked at my elbow.

No, no.

Not now.

I resisted the call, eyes locked on Brandt.

Something sharp cut into my leg. My gaze snapped down. A little raptor stood at my feet, peering up at me with indignant eyes. Blood trickled down my shin where she'd nipped me. Just a tiny little cut. She tilted her head and squawked.

Crouching down, I stroked her delicate, triangular head.

"Little bitey princess," I murmured. A small laugh rose within me.

Other miniature raptors scampered up to me, none taller than my knee. They chirred and clicked their jaws, each one thrusting closer and demanding my attention.

They knew me, and I knew them, especially the largest one. All black and red with the attitude of royalty. Yes, I might be queen, but she was the empress.

Slowly, the rest of the throne room came into focus. This was my throne room. But it was a replacement for a place far grander and steeped in far more lore and history. The circular room was sculpted and carved from sleek black stone. Its size and craftsmanship were significant, the ceiling high and domed. The dais supported the enormous throne.

Actual lava coiled up from the floor in columns, moving into ventilation shafts. Volcano snails glided along the magical barrier and on the walls. The mini raptors and tiny pterosaurs added more sparks of color and movement.

Over a dozen council members or advisers or whatever they were stood in a semicircle fanning out from the dais, each one before a padded leather curved bastion chair. They stood in elegant, shining robes with their hands clasped before them, eyes fixed upon me.

One, a flame-haired man in pristine white and charcoal robes, spoke, his voice humming in my ears as the words took a moment to register. "Time is of the essence."

I straightened, fidgeting with the neckline of my blue and white dress. My fingers grazed the edge of the charm necklace, brushing the metal side, its cool surface grounding me even more firmly in the moment.

Kine now stood directly to my right, his manner protective. "Then I suggest that we skip the formalities and focus on the most essential matters. Eliminating the Gola Resh in the proper manner will eliminate her magic as well as all active curses."

Brandt tore his gaze away from me, his expression downcast. He gripped the right arm of the throne, his powerful muscles working as he dug his fingers into the stone ridges.

I understood.

I shouldn't be looking at him either.

My blood was heating. It was hard to focus.

Hard to think.

Hard to do anything except stand here with my fingers working against my palms.

I drove my fingernails deep into my skin, and the sharpness brought clarity back to my mind, not enough to shake off Brandt's effects or the desire to fling myself at him and mount him on his throne, but enough to at least pretend to be a mature, composed adult.

One of the attendants slipped alongside me and gestured to four empty chairs at the end. I took a seat in the farthest one directly across from Brandt, smoothing my skirt down over my legs.

A muscle jumped in Brandt's jaw as he looked away. The carved black throne he sat on was oversized. Large enough for two. The goblets had liquid in them and were both fastened to a side. Did he just like to have two beverages?

No. Even without his saying so, I suddenly understood.

My heart swelled, my breath catching in my throat.

I forced myself to look around the chamber once more, taking note of the people present as Kine and Elias sat next to me. Hord refused to sit but strode to the left of the dais next to Candy.

I frowned. Yes, Candy was here, but she sat in a curved bastion chair between a red-haired councilor and Hord.

Interesting.

Despite my jealousy, Candy didn't seem like a rival. She wasn't standing close to Brandt, nor was she seated with him on the throne, and when she lifted her hand and smiled at me, that smile reached her eyes. Little wrinkles even formed along the creases of her eyes. She wore lavender today with a red tabard and a black belt, the red and black the primary indicators of her connection to Brandt.

I forced myself to look back at the older, flame-haired man. His name was Tile. I knew I had liked Tile. He was dry and a little prone to wordiness, but he'd been a good man.

His nose wrinkled as if he were about to sneeze, but he seemed to be agreeing with something. "Yes. The queen's identity has been established sufficiently for me."

"Not for me," one of the others said. His dark-red eyes glistened like his oiled beard. "You've always been biased toward the queen and the king's indulgences with her absence. This is all too convenient." His focus shifted to me. "You were named Stella when you were reborn in the other world as well?" The man's shaggy brows lifted.

A woman in dark red—another I knew even if I couldn't place her name—stared, her mouth pinched with disapproval.

No one looked pleased. Elias's fist knotted.

Annoyance flared through me, but the growl that followed didn't come from me. Brandt was glaring at them. Had he just growled at them?

My brows lifted. Then I cleared my throat, finding it easier to choose a more diplomatic response. "No. On Earth, I was named Margot Joy, but it didn't suit me. I chose the name Stella for myself after I turned sixteen, about eleven years ago. It felt…right."

And it had been right in ways I couldn't even understand.

"Enough." Brandt struck his fist against the arm of the throne, his gaze dark, his voice little more than a growl. "The purpose of this meeting is not to interrogate her. I know who she is. Her beast knows who she is. Her brother knows who she is. The Master of Sight knows who she is. The other seven royals who sacrificed themselves over fifty years ago have also been returned. There is no reason to believe that Stella is not who I say she is. *She* is my queen." He jabbed his finger in my direction.

My stomach somersaulted. The way he said that... If I'd wanted to climb him before, then I wanted to jump him now. Or let him jump me.

Heat flared in my cheeks. Thank goodness no one here was a mind reader.

I lifted my chin and avoided looking at him. "I understand that this is difficult and everyone is struggling with our countdown, but finding a way to stop the Gola Resh and her curses is most important. In just a matter of days, nothing else will matter."

"Well said." Another older man—one with dark-blond hair and silver eyes—bowed his head. He spoke in a more familial way, as if we shared some sort of connection. I wanted to call him Kend or something like that. "The Gola Resh's purpose is torment and vengeance, and there is no purpose in wasting further time."

Several of the others murmured their agreement.

A black-and-red-haired man who looked like he might be an older uncle to Brandt lifted his chin. "And what if all of this is a ruse from the Gola Resh to capitalize upon our desire for the queen's return?"

"Then we die," Brandt said dryly.

Frustrated murmurs started as the advisers bickered.

The humming in my ears intensified.

The hourglass sitting on the black iron table. That...that brought back a terrible tumult of memories. A nauseating, stabbing ball formed in my stomach. The overwhelming dread and terror. I'd wanted to collapse, had dug my fingers into the wall and fought to remain standing, and then composed myself because I knew people were watching. I hadn't been a queen the first time I saw that hourglass.

The black and gold chess table in the back—that was familiar too. It was in the middle of the game, but whoever's move it was, the blue seer was set to topple the red rook.

Tile lifted his arms. "If I might interject, even if this woman is not the queen, slaying the Gola Resh is entirely separate." His long, dark sleeves swung with the movement as he gestured from the glowing hourglass to me. "I hope you are indeed the queen, dear lady." He bowed his head, his chin tucking against his chest. Genuine emotion stirred in his voice. "You have been greatly missed, but regardless, so long as you are not in the service of the Gola Resh, then even if you are only a reflection of what we wish to be true, then we can move forward. Surely you can concede this, Councilor Dromar."

The one who looked like Brandt's relative offered a faint lift of his shoulders, his middle finger resting against his cheek. "So long as she is not restored to a full position of authority and she does not receive a shifting ring, then we can move forward."

"She gets her ring back," Brandt hissed. His tone allowed no debate. "In the absence of the Master of Form and as the reigning King of Sepeazia, it is my right to determine how these are disbursed. The ring, and all of the magical energy which it will require upon its being used and restored, has always been hers. Before his passing, Master Tasnal indicated his wholehearted support in reserving it for the queen to be bestowed upon her after she returned once the restoration cycle had concluded. Last night, the restoration cycle completed for all the rings. She gets her ring back."

Several of the council members tensed. Dromar's jaw clenched. They'd likely had this argument many times before.

Dromar extended his hand, his fingers curling in an almost pleading gesture. "What good does her having the ring returned to her do? It detracts from the energy reserve, and she will not have had time to regain her former abilities."

Kine cleared his throat and bowed his head. He kept his

words clipped. "I have seen to her initial training. Or perhaps I should say her re-training. The queen shows exceptional recall. She has made significant strides toward regaining her former skill. Once her ring is restored and she has time to acclimate, I am confident she will be at full fighting strength within ten days. She could probably assume her water serpent form now for a few seconds or so if need be."

"She is who she is." Brandt glared at them, his voice taking on a harsher tone. "She will receive her ring."

An adviser with a long, elegant plait stepped aside, cutting into Brandt's right. Rage twisted over Brandt's face. He glared at the adviser. A low growl rumbled in his chest before he stopped. The adviser stepped aside at once, his face turning bright red as he bowed his head.

Everyone was staying away from Brandt's right side.

My gaze darted back to him. Oh. Oh, ihlkit, he was looking at me.

A giggle rose in my chest.

No! Please not now.

I tried to swallow the flirtatious giggle and the heady need. My fingernails dug into my palms.

His slow, sensual smile tugged ever so slightly at the right side of his mouth.

My heart fluttered as Brandt's gaze held mine. Even as the council continued bickering around us, it felt like we were the only two people in the room.

Please, if any divine being is listening, don't let me make a fool out of myself here. I didn't want to be stupid. I just wanted him, and I didn't want to shame him or me by calling him a spicy strawberry margarita man or offering to climb him like a rock wall.

I dug my fingernails deeper into my palms, trying to ignore the heat pooling insistently in my lower belly. Sweat formed on my forehead. Now was not the time to indulge in fantasies, no matter how tempting. Everything depended on us stopping the Gola Resh.

Brandt growled again, striking his fist against the throne. "Enough! The queen receives her ring. As soon as the well is opened, her ring will be restored to her. There will be no more discussion of this. If anyone opposes it further, they may kuvaste me at their leisure. Councilor Tile, what has been determined regarding the Gola Resh?"

Councilor Tile bowed his head as he rose from his curved chair once more. With a graceful gesture toward all those present, he stepped forward. Though he had a dry way of speaking, it was almost soothing after the tenseness of the previous debate. "Honored assembled members, the Gola Resh's continued existence remains a mystery, but my sages have concluded that because she lives, the proper elimination of her and all of the Babadon's remaining elements must be done in the heart of the Ember Lord's Crest. The ritual itself will allow us to make her corporeal and capable of being harmed with our weapons once more. And so long as everything related to both the Gola Resh and the Babadon are destroyed completely in the heart of Ember Lord's Crest, the curses they have woven and which are not yet completed will be ended."

"The Babadon was slain and all life of his destroyed," Dromar protested sharply. "Councilor Osvar can attest to that." He indicated the man with the silver rings on his left. "He swore it before this council. How could his remains cause problems? Is the Gola Resh bound to them?"

"From what we have learned since the revelation of the Gola Resh's continued existence, there is something of the Babadon that yet lives as well, despite all efforts to drain out the magical remnants of life," Tile said. He gave an almost apologetic look to Osvar. "The heart..."

Brandt's eyebrow lifted.

A sharp memory thrust itself forward—a horrible squelching, mopping up buckets of blood, and sterilizing stone. A question about the heart. A pungent scent: sulfur and iron. An attempt to replace something precious that was lost.

Blinking, I pressed my hand to my forehead.

The black and red mini raptor hopped up onto my lap. She chirred and then settled herself over my heart with her narrow jaws resting against my collarbone. Absently, I stroked her sides. Her sleek scales soothed me.

The Babadon. I'd been responsible for knowing where to slay the Babadon. I'd told Brandt exactly where to stand. Where to strike. It was my foresight. My vision. In memory, I heard my voice whispering those words. Saw my hand sketching out those images on an unevenly cut page.

A long keening wail filled my mind as memory dragged me back. The Gola Resh with her orange-green eyes weeping over the body of her fallen mate. The mate slain by the hand of my beloved and with my insight.

Elias leaned closer to me. "Are you all right, Stella?" he whispered. "You've gone pale."

I nodded, biting the inside of my lip. Drawing in a deep breath, I curled my arms around the little raptor in my lap. She chirped again, then nudged me.

"Everything was destroyed except the heart, and that was drained," Brandt said. "You assured me that so long as the heart was drained properly, there was no risk."

Osvar tipped his head forward, his brow furrowed deeply. The arrogance of his former manner fell away. "To the best of our knowledge, that was true...unless something happened with the process." He cast a helpless look around those assembled. "Unless something changed it."

Most remained silent, only staring.

Tile gave a faint nod, his expression quirking in a sympathetic manner. "Perhaps the Gola Resh is simply capable of manipulating the last traces of magic that remain. It is hard to say, but as we now know for certain she lives, we can set about destroying her in a way that will eliminate all of her magic and curses."

"The heart of the Babadon was divided into three sections," Brandt said. "We gave one to Arjax and Lorna for that spear. The other two pieces were used to create other items to represent peace and for unification purposes."

Those names flashed into my mind with shocks of familiarity. Powerful arms. Even bigger hugs. Terror birds. Grey and brown feathers drifting on the wind. I tilted my head, trying to make a more concrete connection.

Kine leaned closer, his elbow brushing against mine. "Old friends," he whispered, his earthy voice husky in my ear.

Hmm. That explained the memory of hugging.

Kine then indicated the raptor sitting on my lap. "And her name is Scarlet."

"One was sent to the Chimera Caldera near the land of the vampires, less than four days from here," Tile said.

Brandt nodded. "Yes. The second is right here in Castle Serpentfire. It was molten into the base of the Peace Goblet to serve as a reminder of our unification and what was lost in the fall of Taivren."

Scarlet nibbled at my collarbone. This was familiar too. Bratty little empress.

She seemed to know what I was thinking as she tilted her head up and then nipped at my necklace. Her teeth clicked on the stone. I sighed, giving her a slightly annoyed look as I pressed her jaws back. She nibbled at my finger. Her teeth set lightly against the skin but did not pierce it.

"We must gather all three talismans and bring them to the Ember Lord's Crest," Tile said.

"A volcano beyond the ruins of Taivren on the coast," Kine whispered. His hand brushed over Scarlet as he gave her a small smile.

Tile continued, unaware of the hushed clarifications, "When these items, along with the necessary reagents, are cast into the heart of the Ember Lord's Crest where the magic and the sulfur make the flames burn blue and red and the river is fire, then the Babadon will be destroyed forever. The Gola Resh's body must be cast in as well. Living or dead, it does not matter. The particular energy of the Ember Lord's Crest and the combination of all the chemicals and elements will be such that their hold will be thoroughly destroyed. All the curses which have been cast and not completed will be undone, but caution must be taken. The magic that flows through the Ember Lord's Crest may restore as well as destroy. She may weave new curses there or attempt to cause additional harm."

The Gola Resh's words flashed back into my mind.

"These three items," I said, my own voice startling me. Was I actually speaking up like this? My heart leaped into my throat, my pulse thundering, but the words had a mind of their own. "Was what happened to the items created from the heart common knowledge before this?" When the councilors shook their heads, I closed my eyes. "And is it possible that the Gola Resh could bring the Babadon back if she were to have those items?"

Silence fell.

All eyes remained on me, but I kept my gaze steady, chin lifted. "The Babadon was the Gola Resh's mate, the one whom she loved more than any in all the worlds. We know that what she wants is to inflict pain and vengeance upon us. I am not having a vision or any sort of second sight with this. At least I don't think that that's what this is. But...my instincts say that there is something related to bringing the Babadon back. That just as the Gola Resh has returned, the Babadon will return too."

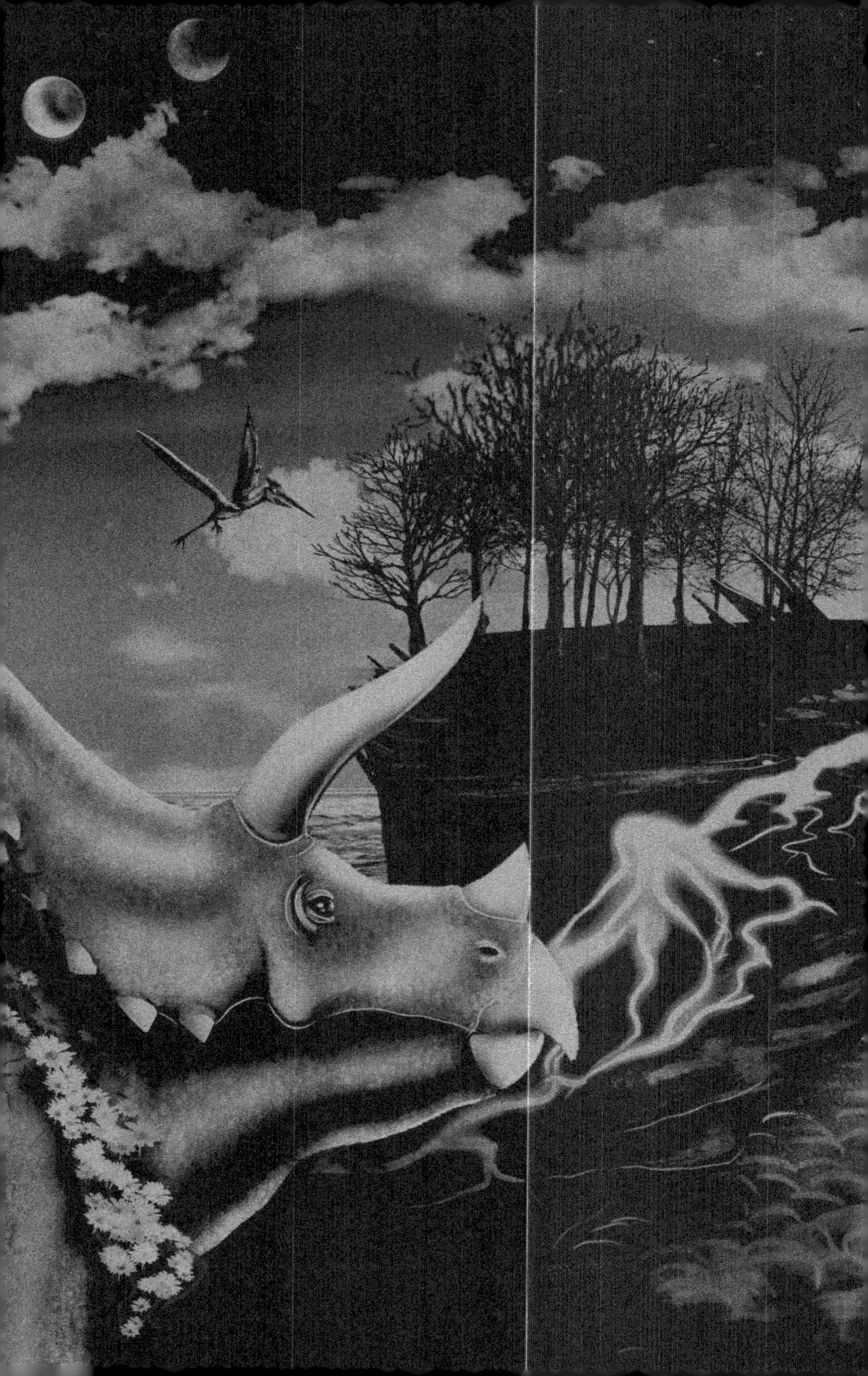

CHAPTER TWENTY-SEVEN: STELLA

Murmurs rippled through the chamber. Brandt's expression darkened, thunderclouds gathering in his eyes. He stroked his chin. His gaze dropped to the hourglass. The sands sifted into the lower bulb, relentlessly steady.

Tile cleared his throat. "It is...difficult to say for certain whether the Babadon can return, but we would be fools if we did not at least consider the possibility. If we succeed though, we can slay both and destroy them fully. It is, in truth, our only option."

Kine leaned back in his chair, his posture now crooked. "Would the Gola Resh not have known about these items? Were these kept secret enough?"

"The Goblet is sealed away for ceremonial occasions. The Great Axe made in Chimera Caldera was sealed in a labyrinth for separate purposes." Osvar shifted in his seat, his eyebrow lifting with annoyance. "None of these would be readily available to the Gola Resh. Their enchantments and wards were set in ancient heartstones already available."

If there was a traitor who was helping the Gola Resh, then they were likely beyond that individual's reach.

"And who knows where Arjax and Lorna are," Dromar muttered.

Brandt released a slow breath as he drew his hand over his mouth. "The Wild Lands. Reasonably, assume three or four days to get there with the currents and wind staying average. Two if we're lucky. At least a day with Arjax and Lorna, either because of delays or getting the timing right for the Keening Pass. One day to return if we draw the ships ourselves and take the Keening Pass. Half a day to get to the Ember Lord's Crest. Then however much time is needed for the ceremony. The Great Axe is more straightforward as long as whoever gets it can navigate the labyrinth. It's a day and a half there, a day and a half back. Maybe half a day for the labyrinth."

"It's not an overly complicated ceremony," Tile said. "One simply gathers the items and reagents together and throws them in the center of the Ember Lord's Crest in the primary chasm. You might call it the heart of the heart. It's impossible to miss with the sulfur and caldride essence forming that outer circle and turning it such a bright shade of blue."

Thunder rumbled outside, distant but growing steadily louder, matching the ominous beat of my heart.

The councilor with red lips leaned forward. "What is the likelihood that the Gola Resh knows this and is trying to find the location of these items or remove them from their holdings?"

"So long as whoever has assisted the Gola Resh is not in this room, I would say little chance," Tile said. He cast another long look around the room, his gaze fixed on his fellow council members. "And I trust these men and women. Even in our darkest hour, none of us would side with the Gola Resh because we all know that to do so would mean certain death for all in Sepeazia. There is no escaping that truth."

Grunts and murmurs followed. Some appeared ashamed. The words struck deep.

My gaze drifted back to Brandt. His expression remained stoic, his gaze set on a few of the council members beyond Candy, his jaw set.

Thunder cracked loudly outside, making me jump. Scarlet squawked in disapproval and buried her face against my neck. A relentless drumming pounded against the walls. Rain. The steady roar reminded me of late summer nights.

"Bad storm," one of the men robed in blue said.

"Bad omens," a woman clad in black and red countered.

The door creaked open, the sounds of the worsening weather intensifying. An attendant in silver entered with a large square box. Dromar and Osvar murmured their disapproval. All the rest were indifferent.

Brandt indicated me with a casual wave of his hand, though he did not look at me. "Return the ring to our queen," he said.

The attendant approached me, his footsteps echoing in the tense silence of the chamber. He held the carved wooden box reverently in his hands. Scarlet sat up straighter, tilting her head as if contemplating nipping him.

The attendant offered it to me, not moving within Scarlet's reach. "Your ring," he said, bowing his head as he opened the box.

My breath caught. Nestled inside on a bed of black velvet lay a silver-white ring with a single blue line along its sides.

Dozens of memories raced through my mind. The cold of the silver. The blue arcs of energy. The sting and ache of transformation. Echoes of the previous Stella and her water serpent form who had once been and who might yet be.

Steadying the box with one hand, I lifted the ring out with the other. My skin prickled with goose bumps almost at once. Slipping it onto my finger was the most natural thing in the world. It settled into place. My blood heated.

For the space of a breath, the blue line glowed, burning with magic.

Everyone was watching me, but Brandt's attention was all I cared about. Looking up, I met his intense, dark-red gaze. Slowly, I held up my hand and spread my fingers.

Brandt's jaw tightened as he lifted his chin. The barest hint of a smile played at his lips.

Heat flared through me. Oh, that man. By all that was—

Scarlet nipped my finger, her teeth scraping my skin and the metal.

A startled yelp escaped my lips. She peered up at me indignantly. I scowled at her. She bobbed her head again as if what she was demanding was obvious.

Little bratty empress indeed. I stroked a line down her neck as she settled again. One thing was certain. Nothing killed the hazy seduction of romance like a mini raptor biting you.

Brandt cleared his throat. "Councilor Tile, ensure that a list is prepared of the necessary reagents and everything else that will be required for this ceremony. We will separate and send forces to retrieve each item. The meeting point and timing will be designated among the parties involved. No one is to speak of this outside of these walls or anywhere the Gola Resh may hear of it."

My eyebrows lifted a little as I continued to stroke Scarlet. The Gola Resh had been able to send her cursed hourglass into this place. Auntie Runa had secured the sanctuary from her as well, but that hadn't kept the lid over the well from jostling off and the Gola Resh somehow getting up through there. The truth was that none of us fully knew what we were dealing with. Who was to say she wouldn't surprise us yet again?

Brandt then dismissed several of the council members. All that remained were myself, Elias, Kine, Hord, Candy, Tile, and three others I did not know.

Once they had gone, Brandt resumed speaking. "Hord, you and Candy will take three whom you trust to find the Great Axe. You will also see to it that guards are stationed at random throughout the castle to ensure that the Goblet remains protected without drawing direct attention to it. Tile, you must ensure that every other aspect is prepared. Kine, you may choose whoever you like to go with you to retrieve the spear from Arjax and Lorna in the Wild Lands. The ships can be readied as soon as the storm ceases. Stella, I would ask that you go with him. You may not remember them yet, but Arjax and Lorna were friends of ours. I'd also appreciate you considering remaining here for the night so that you can depart early in the morning."

The thunder cracked even louder, shaking the castle like a giant's footstep.

"Of course," I said.

Scarlet chirred again, burying her face against my dress and biting at my neckline and the necklace once more.

Cradling her, I untangled the necklace, my finger swiping over the leather band and the charm, almost unfastening it. "Shh, shh," I whispered.

She shook her head and nipped at me.

Thunder bellowed even louder this time. The hourglass itself rattled on the table, the sands rushing faster. I cringed, lifting my shoulders toward my ears.

Someone screamed.

Suddenly, Kine seized my arm. "Stella, move!" he shouted.

The force of his grip nearly sent me reeling out of the chair. My head snapped in Brandt's direction. He'd fallen out of the throne and clutched at his chest, his fist wrapped around the charm at his neck. Yellow light glowed like a beacon of doom.

"Get out," he said, struggling to speak. The veins stood out across his temples and along his neck.

No.

No!

How could it be happening again? There had to be some sort

of mistake. There hadn't been an earthquake. Surely the thunder wasn't that strong!

My breath caught in my throat. That horrible weight pinned me into place, sealing me there to await my death.

Kine's fingers dug into my arm as he tried to drag me from the wood and leather seat. I couldn't move. Couldn't even twitch.

Brandt.

The thudding of my own heart filled my ears, drowning out everything else. The thunder. The rain. The screaming. The footsteps.

My whole world spiraled down to him. He writhed in agony, baring his teeth and fighting against it as if, even more than before, he could feel its claws seizing him and dragging him into the vicious mire.

The council members fled the room.

Candy lunged toward Brandt, dropping to her knees and skidding beside him. "No, no, no," she cried, grabbing him by the shoulder. "Why is this happening again? What's going on, Brandt?"

His charm glowed bright-yellow against his heaving chest as the curse seized him in its merciless grasp. He let out a guttural yell, back arching off the floor.

The sound tore through me like a knife, snapping me out of my frozen state. I wrenched my arm from Kine's grip and rushed forward, Scarlet squawking in protest as she tumbled to the ground. She and the other raptors scrambled away, shrieking.

"Stella, stop!" Kine bellowed, reaching for me.

Elias tried to fling his arm around my waist, but I dodged both of them. All that mattered now was being with Brandt.

Nothing else mattered.

Nothing else registered.

Go to him. Go to him now!

My heart pounded as I fell to my knees beside him. His face was contorted in agony, veins bulging in his neck. Horror and need warred in his gaze as he stared at me, sweat pouring off his brow.

"Don't," he forced out through clenched teeth.

The world slowed. I placed my hands on the side of his face as his jaws clenched and gritted.

Candy's eyes became white rimmed as she stared at me, her mouth open.

My fingers trembled against his fevered skin. His eyes were wild and feral. Yet behind all that, his eyes were full of that yearning gentleness that was truly him.

"I'm here," I choked out. Some part of me screamed to get away.

Or maybe it was Kine or Candy or Elias.

Brandt's hand found mine, squeezing with desperate strength. Our gazes locked, speaking words we did not have time to say. I was trapped as I leaned over him. Pinned. As incapable of moving away from him as he was incapable of fighting the curse.

The wind howled outside, rattling the very walls and braziers.

His eyes snapped, all traces of my Brandt fading. The panicked struggle to hold fast was replaced with rage and loss.

My stomach sank. The great weight pressed upon me all the harder as tears spilled down my cheeks.

His grip on my hand tightened painfully, his face becoming reptilian as fangs appeared in his mouth. I gasped, trying to pull away, but his preternatural strength held me fast. For half a breath, he glared at me. Then he lunged for my throat, yanking me closer.

Alarm spiked through me. My fists clenched.

I was *not* going to die.

Candy and Kine shouted warnings, their voices muffled by the roaring in my ears.

Pain tore through my body but not from fangs. No, it was all over my body. Burning. Tearing. I rose up in the air, everything shrinking down and spiraling away.

Shifting. I was shifting! I was becoming a water serpent!

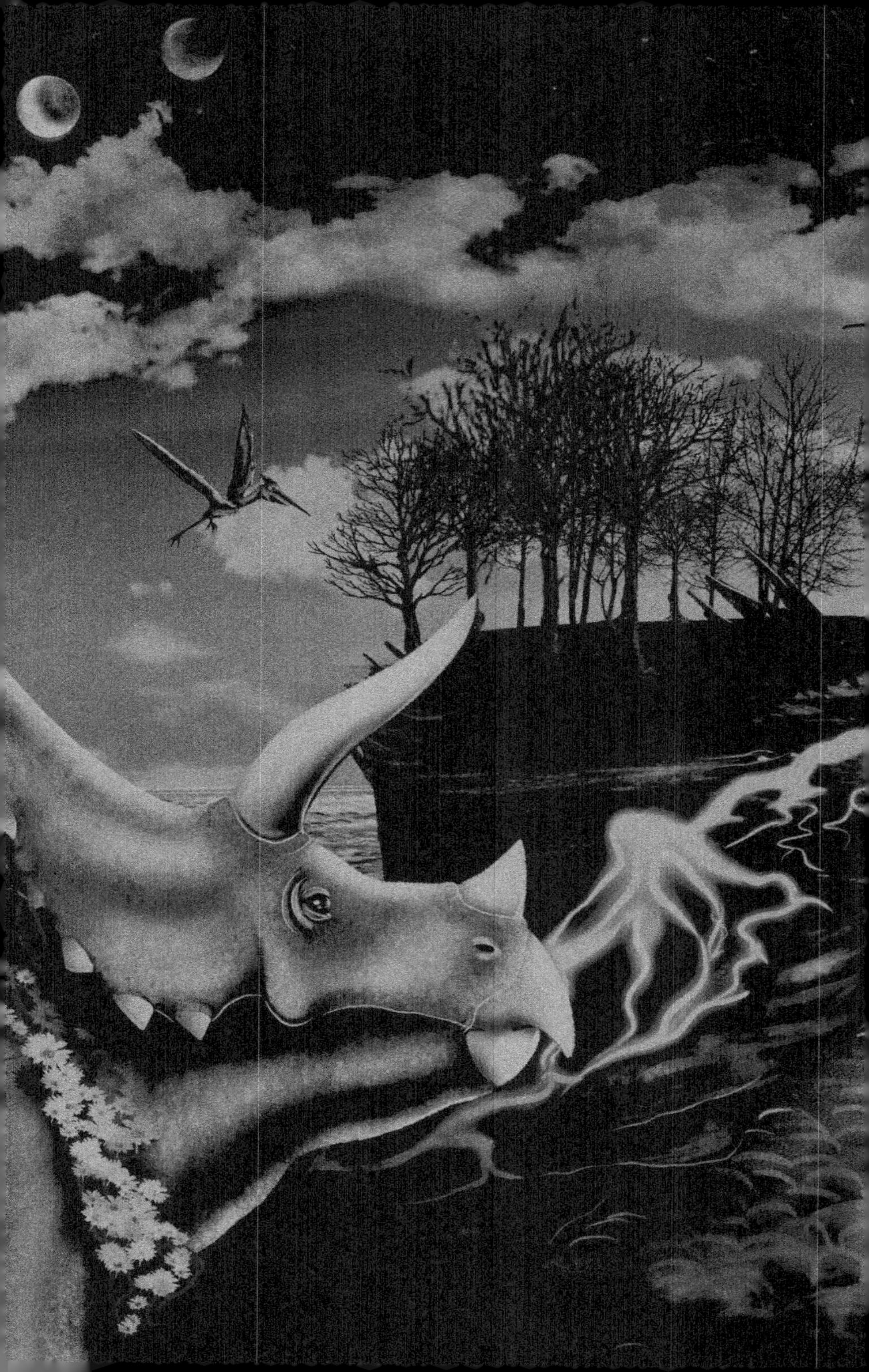

CHAPTER TWENTY-EIGHT:
STELLA

How? How had I turned into a water serpent? Had I triggered a latent memory? Or was there something else at work?

Did it even matter?

The transformation didn't feel like it was taking focus at all. Scales erupted along my skin as my body elongated into a sleek serpentine form. My vision sharpened, colors becoming more vivid and details leaping into focus. Scents intensified in bursts, filtering through my mouth. So many tastes and scents rolled over my tongue with each new breath. Charred stone. Bitter iron. Tangy soaps. Heavy hair oils. Floral perfumes. Spicy colognes. Citrus, leather, smoke, berries, and so much more. My eyelids jerked shut involuntarily. It was just so much.

Oh. My head.

It was heavy.

Horns.

Right.

I had horns. I remembered now. The whiskers swinging off my snout tickled and made me want to sneeze.

The blue and gold hairs on the right felt heavier than the left.

But I was...I was a beautiful water serpent. Rich blue like my hair colored my back with a pearly white belly and speckled gold stripes running down my sides. My jaws itched, and my mouth had become heavy.

"Stella, focus!" Kine's voice jolted through me.

I took in the entirety of the room once more, my gaze snapping back to Brandt. He had arched away, sleek black and red scales forming along his powerful serpentine body.

Candy struck her hand repeatedly. Her form didn't change, but blue energy arced over her fingers.

Brandt wasn't looking at her. His focus was all on me, his hulking reptilian body coiling up to strike. His eyes were devoid of reason, consumed by the curse's feral bloodlust. He hissed menacingly, baring fangs the size of daggers.

My serpentine body coiled defensively as I swayed back and forth. A shudder rippled down my now-massive spine. I lowered my head. My tongue flicked out, taking more of the rich, bright, and varied scents.

A low growl rumbled from Brandt's chest. He lunged. His tail caught Candy in the chest and struck her against the wall. She cracked against the interlocking stones like a dry walnut. Blood blossomed from the wound.

I dodged, knocking over several of the low-curved bastion chairs. Wood clattered and snapped against the stone. My smooth scales let me move across the carved stone floor with exceptional ease. I slid beneath the iron table and shot beyond one of the curling columns of magically contained lava.

Brandt's enraged roar resounded through the chamber. The deadly dance between us had resumed. He bashed through chairs and furnishings, hellbent on the hunt.

I flowed like liquid around the dais, flinging myself forward. He matched me turn for turn. His tail caught the throne and flipped it. The tart-smelling wine spilled over the floor. The world was at once both too crisp and blurred. I shot up the wall, rolling and coiling as he struck at me again and again. His snout bloodied when he struck the stone. I spun back, tucking my tail in before he could snap it up in his jaws.

Elias knelt beside Candy, pressing a large cloth to the wound on her head. Kine shoved away one of the chairs that clattered toward them in Brandt's chaotic wake.

Terror and elation flooded me at once. It was like realizing I could fly. If it weren't for my husband trying to rip my throat out, I'd be laughing. This form felt so good! It was like sinking into hot water after a long day.

I swirled around another pillar, my body moving gracefully despite my leaning a little too much to the left. The horns dragged me down.

He lunged forward, massive jaws open, aiming for my neck. I dodged, flattening myself so that he sailed over me. His body collapsed atop mine, burning like fire as he lay over me, stunned. His black and red scales shimmered in the red-gold glow of the lava.

I shot out from beneath him and up the wall. My belly scales clutched at the scooped black stone. A dull ache like a stitch formed along my left side.

Brandt roared again. He shook his horn-crested head and bolted up after me. The rain poured down in a deafening cascade as thunder shook the entire room. Whipping myself up, I narrowly snatched my tail out of his jaws before he snapped again.

My muscles shook. It hurt. Badly. Fire coursed through my veins. Nothing bent. It was like being frozen.

He bit at me again but caught only air.

My tail had vanished.

I had shrunk!

What? Ihlkit! Why? Why had I lost the form?

My fingers scrabbled at the walls, desperately seeking a

handhold. My water serpent form had vanished, and I was falling.

Brandt's thunderous roar echoed through the chamber as he reared up, massive claws raking the air inches from my feet.

I jammed my legs against the wall and kicked myself back, shooting past Brandt's jaws. My back arched.

Instinct commanded me to put my hand out. I obeyed and snagged one of his horns. I whipped my other hand out to grip the other and landed on the back of his neck with a thud. My bare feet skidded across his scales until I found a foothold in his spikes.

Brandt stiffened, then growled.

Damn it! I'd said I wanted to climb him, but I didn't mean like this.

I burrowed down against his back behind his head, holding tight.

He jerked his head around, hissing and snarling as he tried to spot me. The guttural growl vibrated through me. This one definitely wasn't sexy. I clung to his horns and the spines, using my legs and arms and even tucking my chin down.

Thrashing back and forth like a creature possessed, he snarled and frothed at the mouth. The chamber spun as he tried to throw me off. I held on for dear life, my breaths coming in panicked gasps. It took all my strength to hold on.

Someone shouted my name. Kine maybe. The words were a blur in my mind, the wind rushing in my ears.

A great force slammed into the side of Brandt's neck and body. A deadly streak of black and orange shoved him up against the wall and nearly crushed my leg. The two serpents collided and fought. Hord—that was who the black and orange water serpent had to be.

Hord drove Brandt back as Brandt writhed with increased violence. I clung to his spine with my hands knotted around his horns and my thighs gripping his neck. Ihlkit!

Brandt reared. His body lengthened, shooting backward in a flash of black and red glory.

Realization sliced through me like a dagger. He was going to crush me against the wall.

No time to think.

I let go.

He cracked against the ceiling as I plummeted toward the stone ground.

Kine shot underneath me, twisting onto his back so that I struck the side of his belly and slid the rest of the way down. The wind gusted from my lungs. Flopping onto the stone, I tucked my legs in before my ankles struck the iron table.

Up above, Brandt staggered, the force of the impact leaving him reeling. Hord attacked from the side and forced him back. Paintings and tapestries fell from the walls as he slid to the ground.

I had to get up. My lungs struggled to fill. Frigid stone pressed against my body. Wait, wait. Where were my clothes?

I'd barely registered this when Kine pounced on me. He threw his outer robe over me and then swept me up into his arms. Quick as a serpent, he carried me out of the room as Hord continued to fight, draining Brandt of his strength and driving him to exhaustion.

A protest rose in my throat, but my body ached. I struggled to process everything. The fall, even broken by Kine's placement, had left me stunned. Worse, I was naked. Well, would have been naked except for Kine's robe wrapped around me like a blanket.

"I need to fix this," I said hoarsely. "Where are Candy and Elias?"

Four other guards hurried into the chamber. Chaos continued within the throne room, chairs cracking and stones grating. My heart quailed. Brandt. The knot in my throat threatened to choke me.

"Elias got her to the physician. She cracked her skull pretty good and probably broke her arm." Kine set me down in the hallway beside one of the blue-and-white embroidered silk screens and turned to give me privacy.

Rain spattered through the window onto my bare skin. The storm raged outside. These windows were just openings with shutters, so weather was able to penetrate them. My movements were stiff and halting as I pulled Kine's robe on. The dark-blue material with light-blue and silver accents was a couple of sizes too large for me despite his narrow waist and hips. Thank goodness he wore his clothes looser, or I would have been in trouble.

I hugged the garment tighter around myself. "What happened to my dress?" I asked as I stepped out from behind the screen. My knees trembled as if I had spent hours swimming.

"You probably absorbed and purged it in the transformation," he said. "I don't think it was protected against shifting like your jewelry."

He pulled up my loose sleeve and crushed a cluster of tart punji berries against my arm. The purple juice ran down my bicep, staining the fabric before I could roll it up high enough.

"Kind of embarrassing," I said, swallowing hard. Heat flared in my cheeks.

"Don't worry about it, Bug. It happens all the time, especially during shifting. You used to be real good at keeping your clothes intact. I'll bet you get it back in less than a dozen shifts." He tossed the remains of the berries into the little bin beside the screen and the table.

I hesitated, about to ask what the other circumstances when one absorbed clothes were, but the question died. My gaze locked onto the doorway into the throne room.

Kine tugged at my elbow. "Come on. There's nothing more to see. They're going to wear him down, and then they'll take him back to his room to rest and recover."

I hugged myself tighter, shaking my head. "I can't help him, but I won't leave him."

It wasn't the way it had been previously. No magical haze or heavy hum burned within me and rooted me in place. Maybe it plucked at the edges of my mind like a discordant harp, but it had changed again, its presence muted by pain and sorrow. Now, I just had to see him. I had to know he was all right. It wouldn't hurt anyone for me to stay. The berry masked my scent. The door hid my presence. I had to stay.

Kine relented, his hand still on my arm.

After what felt like hours but was likely only a matter of minutes, they filed out, carrying Brandt on a stretcher. A plain red blanket draped over his body, his chest rising and falling at an achingly slow pace.

My hand flew to my mouth. Tears rose to my eyes. His humanity had returned to him, but he was spent. Exhausted. Turning my face, I wiped away the tears.

My Brandt.

He was ferocious and powerful, but he was not a brute. This curse made him something he wasn't, and it kept changing in little ways. It was as if someone tweaked it each time it surged into its power. As if the Gola Resh taunted and undermined us, showing that nothing was secure. This curse was fluid, and the Gola Resh was determined to take everything from us she possibly could.

Part of me wanted to ask what more could she take when she was already draining the life from Sepeazia and had set my mate against me in such a horrid way, but it didn't take much for me to realize that she could still make things worse. Much, much worse.

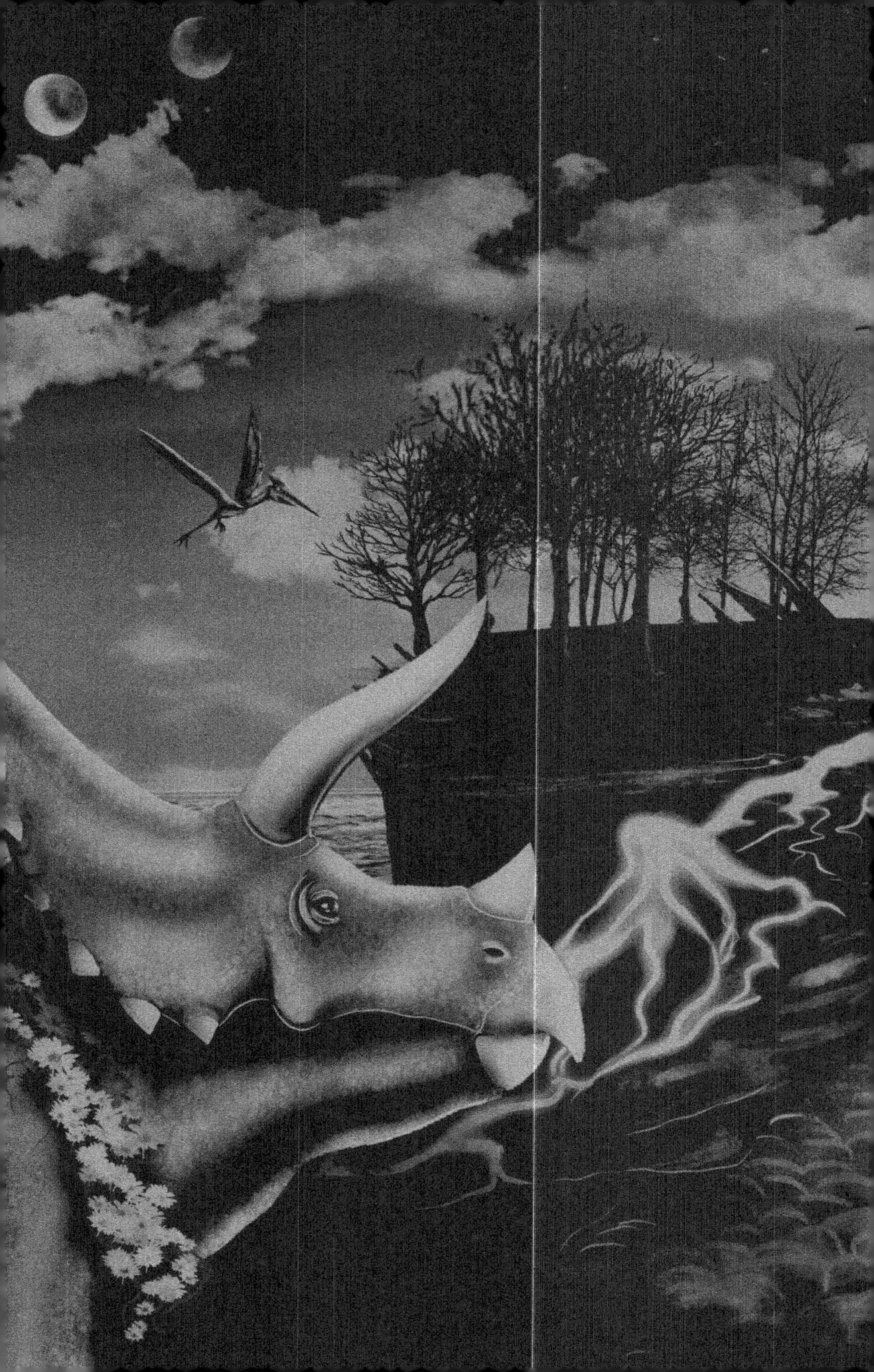

CHAPTER TWENTY-NINE: STELLA

The wind and rain howled outside the castle. Thunder shattered the sky. Lightning lit it up to reveal high-peaked storm clouds, their chaos reflecting my thoughts. The elation from shifting had faded. Now, I was left empty and aching as I tried to process what had happened.

"It's all so strange," I whispered, my voice breaking. My fingers pressed into my arms as I hugged myself. "Each time I see him, it feels a little different. The curse, I mean. It's like being drunk and drugged and emotionally raw and desperate. I hate it, but I can't stay away from him."

As the heavy tramp of the guards' footsteps melted into the silence, I turned to Kine. He looked almost as lost as I felt.

"I know you were trying to get me out of the throne room before everything went insane. I just...I couldn't move."

"Yeah. I know." Kine pinched the bridge of his nose as he shook his head. For a moment, he seemed far older and wearier than he had in all the time I had known him. "I know. It was strange. Had to be the curse. It was like...it was like you got heavier. Physically. I couldn't move you." He gestured toward my arm. Purple and green bruises shaped like fingerprints marked my bicep and forearm where he'd tried to drag me away. Even now, I barely felt it. The ache in my lungs and in my heart dominated my focus.

Covering the bruises, I swallowed hard. "I'm sorry. I just...I couldn't stay away from him. I had to be close to him. It was like...if I could touch him, somehow it would be all right, even though part of me knew it wouldn't. In the back of my mind, I always knew." My breath snagged. "This magic makes no sense," I said hoarsely. "What part of it is magic? What part of it is..." I shook my head, tears rolling down my eyes. "I'm so confused, Kine! And I feel horrible. It's not like I want to die, and I don't want him to die or go insane."

"It's not your fault, Bug," he said.

It felt like it was. Surely I could have chosen to strengthen my will in some other way. "Every time it happens, it's harder in a different way, and it's impossible to prepare for it."

Auntie Runa's warning flashed into my mind. We were fortunate that some subconscious part of me had remembered how to shift, but being lucky wasn't something to count on.

"Your instincts are something to be proud of though," Kine said. When I opened my mouth to protest, he gave a sharp shake of his head, azure curls dancing. "No, Bug, I mean it. That was actually a good sign. All your practice with the base forms? It really paid off. I've rarely been happier to see someone shift, and you remembered your old form like you'd done it yesterday. Your horns and whiskers were crooked, so your balance was not on point, but it wasn't too bad."

"I turned back into a human halfway up the wall—"

"You held the full water serpent form for over two minutes, and you stayed out of his jaws. You also managed to respond swiftly in the crisis and not plummet to your death." Kine bumped me with his arm. Concern and torment marred his eyes, despite the comforting smile he offered. "It wasn't flawless, but it was a fine start."

"I didn't even think about being a water serpent. It just... happened, but then Candy couldn't shift at all. What's that about?"

"No idea. It's just something that has started happening. It happened to me in the valley and several others in different scenarios," Kine said. "It's been this way since your arrival, especially after the Gola Resh released you from that chasm." He braced his arms against the balcony and stared out over the storming sea.

"Will she be all right?" I asked.

Elias strode around the corner, steps slow and expression heavy. His dark-red hair hung limp around his shoulders, one section especially ragged. He tugged on it and smoothed it back behind his ear, but when he turned his head, the hair slipped back over his eyes. "Candy is fine," he said hoarsely, "or will be but barely. They've got her fixed up and resting, though she definitely doesn't want to be left on her own." He lifted his gaze to mine, shaking his head. "You're damn lucky, Stella." His focus turned to Kine. "And why didn't you shift? Could you not either? Or were you just watching to see what happened?"

Kine shook his head, his lips in a tight line. "It's becoming too unpredictable."

"We should leave even with the storm." Elias glowered at the window.

The torrential sheets of rain had not let up at all. The torchlight barely illuminated a foot or so beyond the tall window, though when the lightning brightened the sky, the churning sea was clearly visible.

"It isn't safe here for Stella." He raked his hand through his hair again. "It isn't safe for anyone."

"I am afraid I have to advise against leaving." Hord's deep voice rumbled from the doorway.

I turned in his direction. Lightning forked across the sky

behind him beyond the lancet window, illuminating his imposing silhouette.

"The seas are treacherous, and the land is even worse," Hord continued. "You'd never make it in this storm."

Kine frowned, folding his arms across his chest. "We may not have a choice. If Stella stays, who knows what will happen next time Brandt loses control?"

"We agreed to get Stella out of here before the next earthquake." Elias scowled as he moved closer to me. "What happens when Brandt's curse is triggered again? What if we can't figure out what this other trigger is?"

Hord shook his head. The light played over his dark-orange and black hair. "If I may speak bluntly, it is more important than before that you remain. This storm is harsh and powerful. It will last through the night. The king has been restrained and can do no further harm in this cycle, even if something should trigger the curse again. The plan should move forward as originally intended. If the storm has passed, you may depart in the morning."

Elias stood beside me, stance wide as he glared at Hord. "How can you be certain that Stella is safe?"

"The king has been restrained in chains strong enough to hold him regardless of the form." Hord paused. A muscle in his jaw jumped. That flash of pain in his eyes spoke even more than his words. "He regained consciousness enough to speak of his desires moving forward. Until the curse is broken, he intends to remain chained in his lower chambers unless absolutely essential. He has additional concerns regarding the advancement of the curse."

I fidgeted with the necklace, stroking the charm faster as I worried my lip. "This is wrong."

"Perhaps so, but it is all that we can do to ensure everyone lives." Hord's shoulders drooped, and he rubbed his nose. "The curse has become too unstable. We just don't know enough."

"Maybe the thunder was like the earthquake this time," Kine suggested.

"Perhaps the Gola Resh is tampering with her own magic," Elias muttered.

"Regardless," Hord said. "In the fifty years of the queen's absence, this did not happen. The intervals between the curse overtaking his mind varied by an hour or so as it shortened the window little by little, but the charm itself provided enough of a warning that he could trust it."

"And since my return, that has changed," I said.

"Everything has changed since your return, but this does not make you responsible," Hord said firmly.

"He can't just stay chained up though. He's not an animal!" I hugged myself.

"Most of the sages believe that if Brandt became agitated, that might escalate the timeline," Kine interjected. "The last time, it happened with the kapis attacking along with the second earthquake. The earthquakes triggered agitation and protective instincts. The thunder was loud…but was it that loud? There must be something else we're missing here. Maybe it was some of the council resisting the idea of letting Stella have her ring back."

"I think he's just starting to lose his mind," Elias said, his tone dark. "He practically crushed Candy. It's a miracle she's not dead."

I kept my arms folded tight over my breasts. My body ached, throbbing and pulsing with the remnants of energy. I felt like I wanted to run and scream and crawl under the covers and hide. Fragments of my transformation energy still burned in my fingertips.

"He isn't beyond hope any more than I am," I said flatly, biting back the urge to snap at him. "The Gola Resh wants us to suffer. Do her powers allow her this much leeway? It seems like it's so fluid. Or is there a loophole we could exploit?"

Kine shrugged helplessly. "The Gola Resh and the Babadon have always had magic beyond this world and beyond our understanding. They maximize momentum. We've been figuring it out as best we can, but we just don't know. Since we're here for the night, I'll speak with Tile to see if there's any other scrap we can use to sort this out."

"He'll be glad of the company and to discuss his theories with someone," Hord said, "but I don't anticipate much help coming from it. The truth is, the Gola Resh is doing what she wants because she wants to."

"And we have to be willing to accept that the erosion of Brandt's mind may be too much." Elias stared at the window.

Part of me wanted to throttle him for daring to say that, but he spoke the words with such heaviness it suffocated me.

Instead, I covered my mouth and shook my head. "It isn't."

"So long as he lives, I will not give up hope," Hord said, arms braced on his hips but his head down. "Our family is strong. He is strong. There is a way out." His mouth opened then closed as if he was about to say something else, some final gasping declaration of hope.

The weight upon my head and shoulders pressed down even harder.

Hord squared his shoulders as he ran his thumb over his nose. Then he straightened. "We have guest quarters set up with everything you need. I'll show you to them myself. Then in the morning, we'll continue with the plan. Difficult decisions await us."

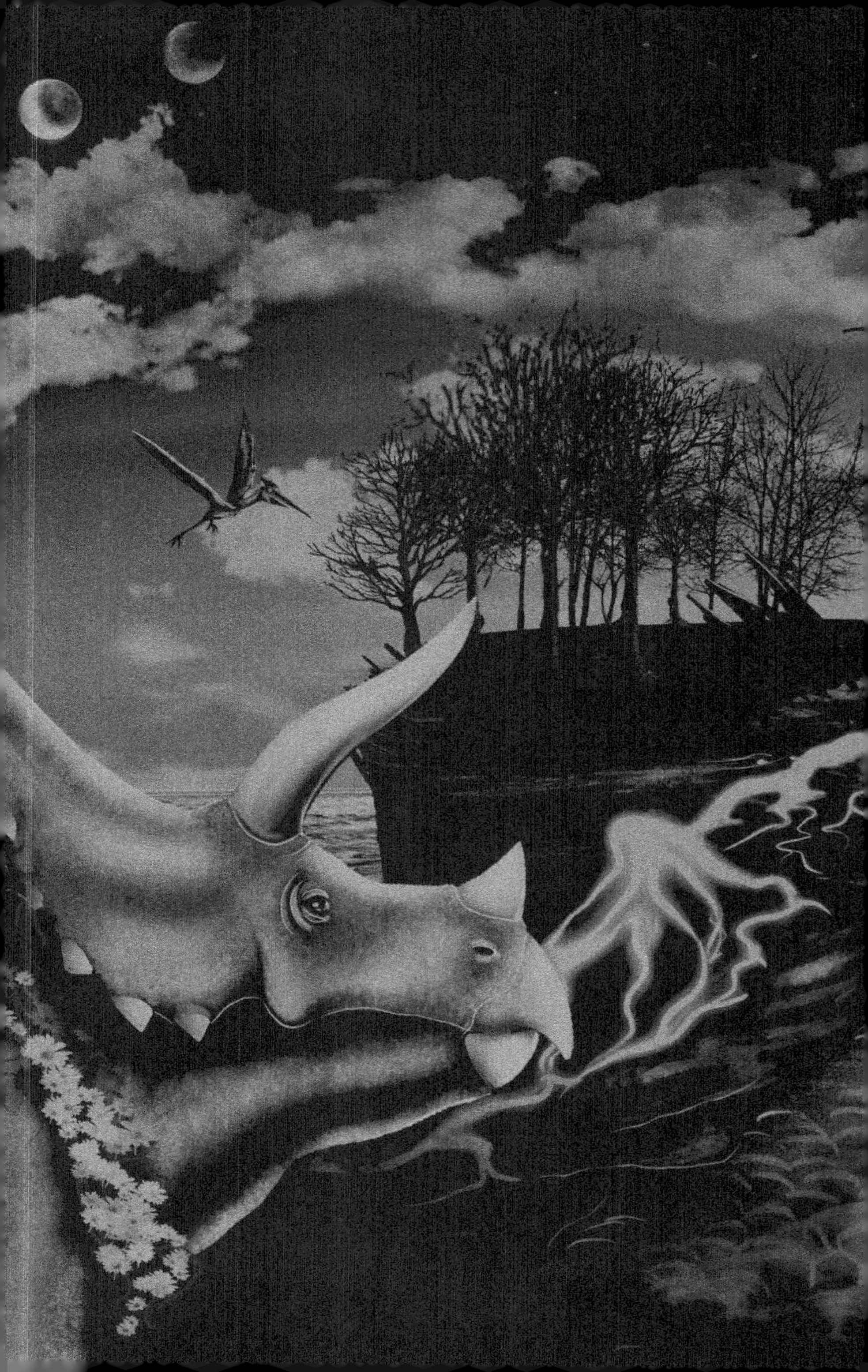

CHAPTER THIRTY: STELLA

"**D**ifficult decisions" was an understatement. The soft torchlight flickered as Hord guided us through the castle, his steady footsteps echoing off the carved walls. Once or twice, my feet almost carried me in a different direction entirely, as if my memory had kicked in and knew where I was supposed to go except we weren't going that way.

The room Hord led me to was not mine. It was lovely in its own way, simple and beautiful. The same dark stone composed these walls and floor, but the light came mostly from tall, globed oil lamps. Garnet-red oil glistened in the wells, shimmering in the light.

The focal point of the room was a large luxurious bed with an embroidered red quilt and black pillows. The bed frame, like the rest of the furniture, resembled mahogany, but the room smelled of sandalwood and lavender. No fireplace or other source of heat was present, but the large vents in the ceiling and floor made me wonder if they used lava for heat here.

Elias cleared his throat from the doorway. Kine must have gone on to speak with Tile. "May I have a moment?" he asked.

I nodded, arms still folded over my breasts. Kine's robes were too long for me and trailed on the floor. "Of course."

He glanced around, his gaze flicking from the wardrobe to the bed to the lancet window to me. "I don't like us being here tonight. I don't have a good feeling about it, but since we can't leave, I just..." He gestured toward the window and then dropped his arm, his jaw working.

"Do you feel like something specific is going to happen?"

He shook his head, then shrugged. There was a wildness in his deep-set eyes. "I don't know. I don't think so. Just...it's uncomfortable." He crossed into the room and scanned it. His hand brushed along the wall and pressed against the curve of the oil lamp. "I know they will have been strengthening the wards to protect against the Gola Resh's entry, but they won't be as strong as they could be. I know that everyone here will do everything. I know I will do everything I can." His gaze fixed on me. "Do you want me to stay with you tonight, Stella?"

My eyebrows lifted. "What?"

"Even without the silencing oil, it's hard to hear anything in these rooms. The stone absorbs sound on its own," he said, continuing to circle and glance around. "I'm in the room next to yours, but if something goes wrong—"

"You're really on edge tonight." I turned along with his circles, keeping an eye on him.

He nodded. His deeply tanned skin had paled. Sweat ran along his hairline. "I don't have a vision giving specifics, not even foresight right now. Just fear." He shook his head and then rubbed the back of his neck. "If you don't want me to sleep in here, I understand. I just want you safe. You and your happiness mean everything to me, Stella."

"I'll be happy when the curse is removed. Both of them." I tilted my head as I watched him. "As far as safety, I don't know what else can be done."

He removed a slim polished stone from inside his tunic and

held it up. It resembled a moonstone. "This is just a flash stone. It's connected to my consciousness. If you grab it and squeeze, it'll let me know you need me. If I can't get to you, I can at least sound the alarm."

I accepted the stone and held it in my palm. Smiling a little, I glanced up at him. "You're very kind."

His brow remained furrowed, his gaze pained. "It's the least I can do." He edged closer.

Was he going to kiss me? Surely not. I frowned, drawing the robe tighter around myself as I stepped back.

He didn't look rebuffed or even shocked. Just attached the moonstone to the charm on my necklace. "I know you can do this, Stella. You are strong enough to survive. You will get through this. Just take care of yourself, please. Don't keep running to Brandt while this curse is eating his mind. Even with Candy there to comfort him, it isn't enough to counter all that has happened."

Footsteps sounded outside the open door.

He glanced over his shoulder and sighed. "I think I need a walk to clear my head. If you change your mind and want me to stay here or even if you want Kine to sleep in here, I'm sure he would. We both want you to be safe." He dipped his head forward then and left the room, giving me one final look before he disappeared.

Bad feelings abounded. I had to admit, now that I was alone in my room, an odd feeling struck me. It was like I was being watched.

Glancing at the window, I took a moment to listen. The storm hissed and boomed outside.

Elias was right. They were strengthening the wards here, but the Gola Resh was something else. Maybe I shouldn't be alone.

Regardless, I needed to get dressed.

I pulled the wardrobe open on instinct. Halfway through, it occurred to me that there was no reason for my clothes to be in there. Then I realized that some of them were. Someone had taken the time to choose clothing for me and bring it here.

Hmmm. Scents of strawberries, grapefruit, and salt water with hints of orange, smoke, leather, and bergamot transported me back. Not to this room, but to another, lush with silks and velvets and a massive four-poster bed with red silk sheets and a black coverlet. Heavy curtains hung over the windows, blocking out all traces of sunlight.

Our bedroom. Our marriage bed. Our...

Tears rose to my eyes.

Ducking my head, I drew in a sharp breath. More memories crashed over me. Gentle touches. Ferocious kisses. Trailing fingers. Ihlkit.

Did Brandt sleep in our old room? In the same bed?

My heart clenched as Elias's words washed back through my mind, bitter and bile-filled. Candy had been the one to comfort him.

Except...no. I drew in the scent from the wardrobe once more as I pulled out an indigo dress with a silver waistband. It didn't feel right. Comfort did not mean sexual. Closeness did not mean romantic intimacy.

Would the man who had insisted I remain queen and had refused to let anyone else take my ring have taken another lover? It didn't seem like something he'd do.

Not that he was incapable of cheating. Anyone could cheat. But still...

I cringed inwardly as I recalled the way his tail had struck her. Her violent strike against the wall. Her crumpled form. Concern spread through me.

After Elias's offer and his obvious dislike for Brandt, I didn't want to ask him about it again. No. I needed to go check on her. It wasn't like I could sleep anyway. It was too early.

I needed to hear it from her own mouth if she could speak. There were so many things that this could mean. Maybe it was just one-sided on her part. She might have had eyes on Brandt. Even if she did, that didn't mean she deserved to suffer. Besides, visiting just felt like the right thing to do.

Shadows danced on the way to the infirmary, my own rippling and halting along the wall. The few attendants I passed bowed and nodded. Some offered to escort me to the infirmary or to bring me food. One told me where to go, but it simply confirmed what I had thought. The infirmary itself was on the third floor.

I peeked my head through the first of the doorways.

"Stella!"

Candy lay in the bed, her face lighting up as if she had been waiting for me. Half her head had been bandaged, and her right arm was in a woven cast. Her lips weren't purple from lipstick, though. The bruising along her face and neck and chest from Brandt's tail flinging her was vivid. She winced, shuddering as she realized she couldn't sit up.

"Is it all right if I still call you that? I didn't think to ask," she said.

Even injured, her smile was absolutely infectious. Now that we were alone in this room, it felt different than when I'd seen her before. A lightness flowed from her. A sincerity.

"You can call me anything you like." I walked up to her bed. The cut lemons and herbs set out in small saucers with fragrant oils gave the room a pleasant fragrance.

Up close, her injuries were even more apparent. The stones had sliced her up, and it looked as if Brandt's tail had crushed part of her body. His scales, too, might have been sharper than I initially thought based on some of the smaller cuts along her unbroken arm.

"You aren't healing anymore," I said softly.

Candy shrugged with one shoulder. "The magic's been off," she said, trying to smile. She held out her good hand, her fingers shaking a little. "I'm glad to see you, though. There's been so much happening. I thought I was never going to see you again."

I stepped closer and wrapped my fingers around hers.

Her eyes squeezed shut. Tears trickled down her cheeks. "Got to admit," she said, her voice rougher now. "I gave up the idea you were coming back, and I'm sorry."

Shaking my head, I sat on the edge of the bed beside her. "No, Candy, no... I mean, how could you have known?"

"Some believed. It isn't that I didn't want to see you again. I love you like one of my cousins, and what you and Brandt have is so special, but I thought...you know, all good things...they end. It was cut short too soon. Damn tragedy. And..." Her mouth pinched as the tears rolled down faster.

The storm thundered outside.

I patted her hand. "I don't think I'd have believed either, and I definitely didn't really remember anyone."

Candy swallowed hard, sniffling. "I'm just glad you're back. I hope you know that."

"I do now." Smiling, I squeezed her hand.

The longer I studied her, the more I felt aware of other things we had shared. She was a tall woman with a gentle presence despite her playfulness. Memories seeped in. Stomping out patterns in the beach before the waters rushed them away. Carving wishes into seashells that we cast into the sea. Testing our triceratopses' speeds. There was an easy comfort in her presence. A soft warmth that radiated from her even in this state of pain.

She wasn't my rival. She was my friend. Brandt's friend first but mine as well.

My shoulders drooped. Why had the memories about Candy been so slow to return? It didn't seem like there was anything complicated in this.

I paused, and Elias's words rang in my ears. Had my own

jealousy shrouded who she was? Was it possible I had misunderstood him? I worried my lower lip.

"This might be awkward for me to ask, but I still can't remember a lot of things. You and Brandt aren't…"

Candy's eyes widened, and her brow lifted until she winced. Then a rolling laugh escaped her lips. "No. Brandt and I would murder each other in minutes if we tried being a couple. His parents and mine were close friends. We grew up together. He's like a brother to me, the same as Kine is to you." She chuckled again, her eyes sparkling. "Oh…I guess if you couldn't remember, I can see how that might have seemed odd. Mark and believe though, Brandt and I are no good for each other that way." She gagged. Then she paused, her mouth screwing up. "Wait. You thought maybe I was moving in on him, angling to be queen or just taking him as my own, and you still came to check up on me?"

"I mean, you were hurt." I shrugged, suddenly uncomfortable. It was hard to look at her. Guilt rose within me. I was nosy and suspicious too.

"Yeah, don't take this personally, Stella, but if I thought you were moving in on my love, I don't know that I'd be coming in all sweet and friendly to check on you." She grinned a little at this. "What I'm saying is…extra thanks for doing that."

My shoulders twitched. "I've been feeling jealous of you."

She giggled at this. "Yeah, I'm a looker right now." She swallowed hard. Her jaw clenched a little as her fingers worked against her palm. One of her nails had been torn off at a bloody angle. The others remained mostly immaculate aside from a couple chips in the pale lavender paint of two. "Really stunning," she said.

"You are, and you're going to heal up. When Kine got hit hard, it took him a while too. It has to be part of what the Gola Resh is doing."

"It is." Candy sighed as she relaxed against the bed. "Thank all that is good and kind in this world for sedatives and teas. Otherwise, I'd be so much more miserable. As it is, I'm just sad I can't join in on the fun and find a way to help unless the magical healing properties of Gershwin's elixirs returns."

"They're not working right either?"

"Meh." Candy sighed. She managed a weak shrug. "Not fully. Everything went insane tonight. I couldn't even get my ring to activate enough to give me the healing beyond keeping my skull from cracking the whole way open, and it was at least half charged, but this has happened more in the past week than ever. It'll stop working, and then everything will zip back to what it should be. Well, most of it." She bit her lip, concern in her purple eyes.

"What?" I tilted my head.

"Just...some people are afraid that maybe we're going to lose all our magic before the end. The thing is, the shifter rings aren't Sepeazian magic. They were supposed to be safe. And after all those rings were lost when Taivren fell, there should have been more power to strengthen them. Not less. It just makes no sense. But the Gola Resh is draining everything, and nothing is as stable as it once was. What if..."

It suddenly made even more sense why some of the council members hadn't wanted my ring restored to me. I glanced down at the silver band around my left ring finger.

"Don't think that way." Candy tried to sit up and then fell back, sighing heavily. "That's your ring. Brandt saved it for you for years. Never let anyone take it. He kuvasted people to save it for you. Fought them all off even when the curse hadn't taken him. He has always fought for you. He refused to let anyone else be queen, and there has been all kinds of pressure for him to do that."

"Really?"

"Yeah. Always keeps your wine glass full with your favorite wine whenever he drinks. Doesn't let anyone be on his right side if he can help it. Except Scarlet, but you can't tell that one anything unless you want your finger bitten."

I covered my mouth, but the giggle still escaped. "Yeah. She's something."

She nodded, her gaze even softer now, almost hazy. The medication must have been reducing her discomfort. "This is hard. I know it is, but Brandt is a good man."

Yes, he was. I had no doubts. The fact that this curse tormented him so was horrifying.

I worried my lower lip as I considered everything. "As far as you know, has the curse ever surged forward like this before?"

She shook her head. "The time gets a little shorter every so often but never like this. Just a matter of seconds each day. Maybe the thunder was like the earthquake in this case."

"Maybe."

Everyone had a theory. No one knew for certain.

Sighing, I stood. I smoothed out the white sheets and stepped back. "I should probably head out now. Pleasant dreams."

Outside, the storm continued to rage. Thunder boomed so loudly the vase and oil lamp on the bedside table rattled. This storm showed no signs of stopping at any point soon.

I had almost reached the stone doorway when Candy spoke again, softer this time, her voice rich with affection. "I'm glad you're back, Stella, even if I did struggle to believe it was possible."

Her smile pulled the corners of my mouth up higher. "I wouldn't hold it against anyone who stopped believing."

"Brandt never stopped believing you were alive somehow, not even once. What you two have is special."

"Thank you." My voice was little more than a whisper. Her kindness shamed and encouraged me. "I'm grateful for you."

My gut twisted. How could I have thought she was a rival?

Actually, there was one reason I had suspected her. Maybe it was all innocent, but the fact remained one person had consistently pushed me toward seeing Candy as a rival, and that was someone I needed to speak with as soon as possible despite the tension between us.

It took only a few minutes to track down Elias. He stood in front of one of the large woven tapestries of Sepeazia, his arms clasped behind his back. As I approached, he glanced at me with a tender expression on his face. "Everything all right?" he asked in that velvety soft way of his. "Did you change your mind about me staying the night?"

Lifting my chin, I stopped beside him. "Can you tell me something?"

"Depends." He smiled at me, but sadness was behind his eyes. He tipped his head forward. His elbow grazed the edge of the vibrant tapestry that depicted the forging of a great sword with runes carved in its handle. Lightning flashed in the window behind him. "What would you like to know?"

I folded my arms over my chest, shifting my weight onto my left foot as I faced him. "You've said some things about Candy and Brandt...suggesting that there was something going on between them. Do you know if something is going on between them?"

"Hm." He tilted his head, glancing to the left before he shook his head. "I don't know anything for certain. Just that they're close. I guess it's hard for me to imagine a man and a woman being that close without developing feelings for one another. I was never a part of the royal court or the inner circle. I've never really belonged anywhere until you and I became close."

"So just because they are close, you assumed there was something else at play?" I frowned. That was possible, but it didn't feel accurate. "Why? Kine and I are close. You and I are close."

"Kine is your brother, adopted perhaps, but your brother nonetheless." He paused, then lifted his shoulders as his gaze turned to the window. The rain poured down in a relentless torrent. "You should ask Candy. I think she would tell you. She's a good person. A little thick sometimes, but good."

Had he seen me leaving her room? Maybe he already knew or suspected.

I paused, startled at the harshness of my own thoughts. What was going on with me?

I massaged my temples. "Yeah. That's a good idea. I just wanted to know your thoughts. It seemed like maybe you were suggesting Brandt had..."

What exactly had he implied? That Candy had taken my place? That Brandt was unfaithful? But how could Brandt have been unfaithful when I had been dead?

"That Brandt was cheating on you?" A half smirk returned to Elias's lips as he shook his head. "Brandt might be a flirt, but I can't imagine that he would do anything if he had the chance of being with you again. As for Candy, like I said, she's a good person. She'd never get in the way of a mate bond, even if she did have feelings of her own." He swallowed hard. "But...what I will say is that you deserve better than Brandt."

"Brandt is—"

"I know. You still deserve better." His jaw tightened, his expression even more downcast.

I clenched my hands into fists. "Don't speak ill of my husband." I almost reminded him that I was the queen, but those words died on my tongue. It didn't feel right to say, even if it was true. What counted was that I was married. Maybe not legally, if our marriage vows ended at death. But in spirit.

None of that explained what had happened here though.

The tension grew heavier, burning and prickling in the air.

He gave a tight nod, then started to turn away.

"Elias, who are you to me?" The question snapped out, trembling in the air before us. I wanted to ask him if we had been romantically involved before Brandt. There was just something about the way he looked at me even if I couldn't remember anything about him.

His dark-blue eyes softened. "I have longed so much to tell you everything, but some things... Stella, you'll just have to remember on your own. Trust your instincts. You are a seer at heart as much as you are a water serpent shifter."

"When I look at you, I don't remember anything," I said, my voice tight. I clenched my hands into fists. "There's no memory there. It's as if you have been wiped away completely. Why is that?"

His brow lifted more. Sadness flashed across his face. Then he forced a smile. The corners trembled. "I—I don't know. I would have thought..." He bit the tip of his tongue before he glanced at me once more. "It doesn't matter. Everything you need to know, you will know when it's time. I have faith in you, Stella, and what happened between us—what we were to each other—it's not important right now." He swallowed hard. "I know you love Brandt. I'm not saying Brandt is evil, either. I just... If you knew everything, then you'd understand—"

"Don't say that!" I snapped. "If you're just going to walk away and not explain, then you don't get to say that."

He gave a slow nod. "Then I apologize for leaving."

With that, he strode away.

I watched him go, confused and angry. Why did this feel so wrong? Why couldn't I remember even a trace of Elias? Everyone else was coming into focus. It had taken time with the others, but I had seen him every day since my return, and there was just nothing.

Was he an ex? Was he hinting that we had had a relationship?

Something had happened at Taivren. But even in thinking about that—it didn't connect exactly to him. Just with an intense sensation of loss and fear and cold.

Slamming my fists down at my sides, I fled back to the guest room. Finding an attendant, I told her I wouldn't be attending dinner. I didn't want to be disturbed. All I wanted was to sleep. Then I slammed the door.

"Why does everything have to be so hard?" I cried out.

I ripped the loose dress off and scrubbed myself clean with a fury that left my skin raw and red. My hair received no better treatment as I clawed at my scalp and yanked the brush through it. Everything was so close to being right, and yet happiness was darting out of my grasp. Everything was going to fall apart. Everything—as perfect as it had nearly been—was about to collapse into complete annihilation.

And I didn't even need it to be perfect. I just needed it to be real. To have my family back. My husband. My home. That was what I needed.

I ripped off my necklace and ring and tore out the earrings, dropping them into the glazed blue bowl on the dresser.

"What makes that so hard? Why are we so cursed?" I jerked an orange silk nightgown out of the drawer and pulled it on. One of the seams snapped and ripped at the hem.

The uneasy sensation intensified. My skin crawled.

What was going on?

"You know, I must admit, I'm disappointed, dear. I gave you that little challenge almost a week ago, and you still haven't answered it."

My feet fused to the stone.

No.

How?

How had the Gola Resh gotten into my room?

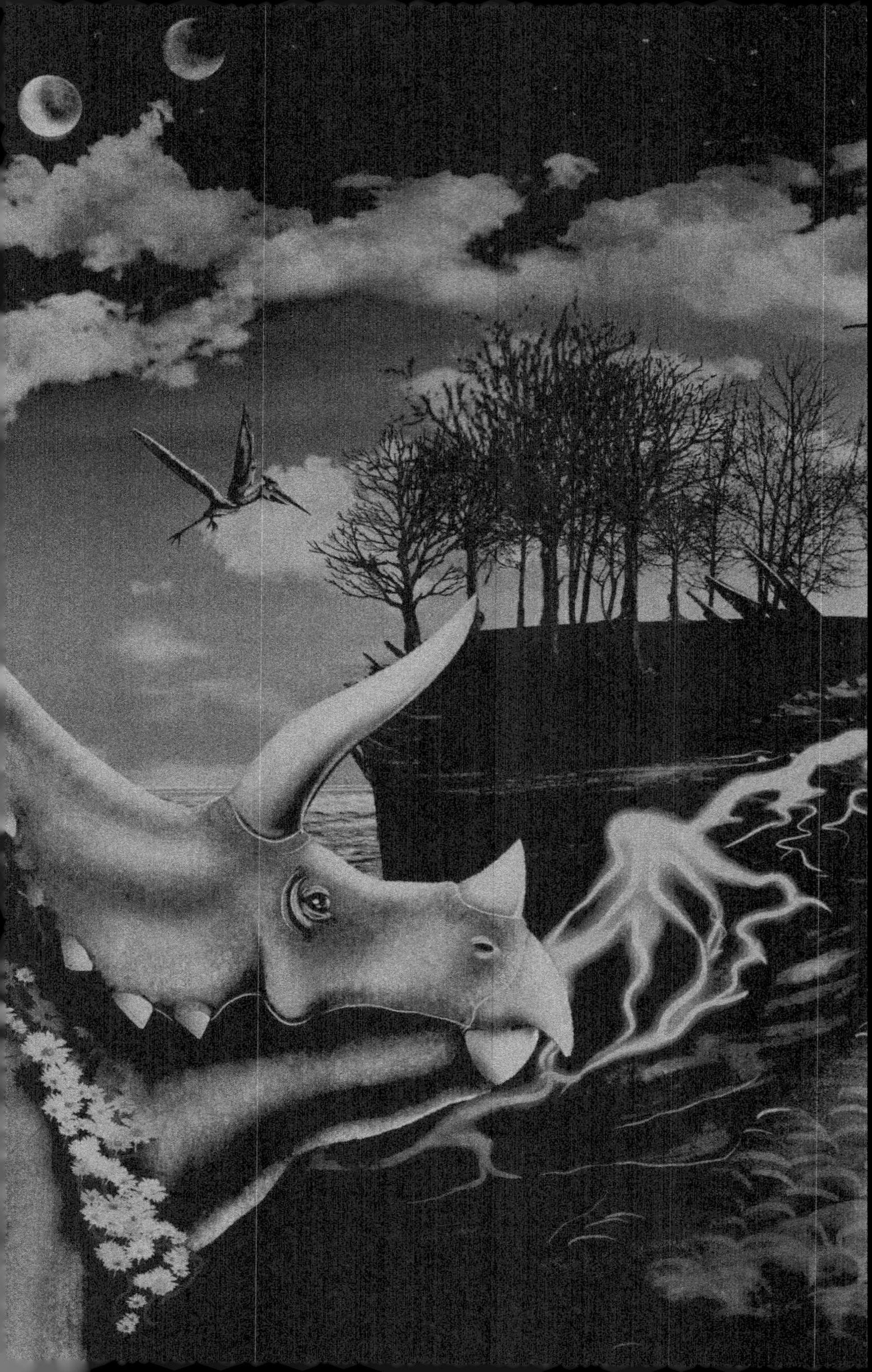

CHAPTER THIRTY-ONE: STELLA

The silver-framed mirror. It was directly in front of me, but I couldn't bring myself to look at it yet. I already knew what I would see.

She was in here.

Watching me.

The hairs on the back of my neck lifted. My gaze darted up to the mirror. Nothing but my own reflection stared back.

"It hurts, doesn't it?" Her voice lowered, coming from everywhere at once.

My heart pounded against my ribs as my mouth went dry. Her eyes bored into me from somewhere.

"What hurts?" I whispered, lifting my chin. "And how did you get in here?"

Did she know what we were up to? Our plan to destroy her? To make her vulnerable and gut her of her power before we destroyed her in molten rock?

She laughed again, her voice seeming to draw closer. A wisp of shadow appeared before me and then vanished before I could focus on it. "I have friends, my dear, friends among your kind.

There are those who understand the truth about me, about my beloved."

"And what truth is that?"

"It was always you or us. We only took from you because we had no other choice," she said, her voice dripping with self-righteousness. "Your magic was necessary to heal my illness. Otherwise, I would have perished."

"Forgive me, but I'd rather you die than all of Sepeazia." I gritted my teeth.

I wondered if hers was the presence I'd been sensing for the past few hours. Was it possible that she was the one turning the curse forward?

"I disagree. As did the Babadon." She chuckled, though the sound contained a hard note. "We were both beyond your comprehension, my dear, and yet because of you, that brute of a mate of yours knew how to harm my beloved." Cool air tickled my ear and rustled my hair.

I tried to watch her through my periphery. She seemed to vanish each time I looked in her direction, but her presence intensified.

"Why would any Sepeazian serve you?"

"Because they understand that in serving me, they serve something greater than themselves. Your people are not as devoted to you as you might hope."

I could practically envision the cruel smile curling over her lips and the flash of her sadistic eyes.

"The truth is, my dear, I have become rather fond of a few of you. As cruel as you were to separate me from my beloved, I am willing to give you a little…knowledge."

Clenching my jaw, I braced myself. There was nothing to be gained from gazing upon her, but some deep compulsion within me wanted to look her in the eye and prove I was still going to stand up to her in spite of, or perhaps because of, my fear.

"What knowledge?" I spun around, scanning the room.

Every shadow seemed to jump and twitch, swaying just out of my sight.

"Are you looking for me?" Another low laugh followed. "You flatter me, mortal."

The shadows by the wardrobe swept forward and stretched out, vaguely taking the shape of a woman with a skeletal face. She reminded me of the banshee or a wraith in some of the old lore books in my foster family's home except her hair wasn't stringy. It flowed in great, soft curls around her face.

"What is this knowledge you're offering me?" The words stuck in my throat. "Are you the reason for everything going wrong?"

"That's quite a lot to put on me." She pressed her palm to her cheek as she crept closer. Her form remained airy and shadowy, though some parts dripped and sagged. Her voice raked over my ears. "There's perhaps one other thing I should tell you. It isn't as if there are an unlimited number of times Brandt can enter the cursed state without losing his mind. It takes a toll."

"What do you mean?"

The Gola Resh drew closer. Her orange-green eyes blazed like venomous fire. "Do you really want to know, dearest?"

"Tell me." My fingernails dug into my palms.

She laughed again, mirth dancing over her wavering features. "Well…it's amazing how many hundreds and hundreds of times Brandt has gone through this and retained his sanity. The truth is, your Brandt is far stronger than I gave him credit for, but you see, my dear, all things must come to an end. He can only make that shift another eight times before he…" A slow smile bloomed on her cruel mouth.

I stiffened. "You said—"

She cut me off with a sharp swipe of her hand. "I don't really know what you're going to counter with, my dear, and I don't especially care. Did you truly believe that he could just resist it up until the end of Sepeazia or that I would let you two die together with the end of Sepeazia? No. There are consequences for failing to obey the curse's demand, however…I might be willing to offer you another solution."

"What? You want me to kill myself?" I said it with as much defiance as I could muster.

Truth was…I'd do it. If it would save Brandt, I would do it.

Another grating laugh escaped the Gola Resh's mouth. "Oh, my dear, sweet, little girl, do you really think I'd let you be a hero again so easily? I was actually rather amused that you did go through with sacrificing yourself, even a little grateful because of how you destroyed your poor love's heart. That's why I halted the curse's progress while you were gone."

"And all you want is our suffering?" I demanded, my voice shaking. "You and your beloved came here to kill all of us, and he got killed, and now you feel entitled to torment us? He deserved to die!"

Her eyes blazed. "You had no right to slay him," she growled.

"You had no right to destroy us!"

"I have every right to take what I want."

"Then we had every right to slay the Babadon in self-defense."

Her breath hissed between her teeth. The shadows became like claws. Then she stopped, lifting her chin. "You are a fighter. I will give you that. Meaningless as you are, you are willing to struggle. So…let me give you another gift."

A chill passed through me.

Before I could tell her I didn't want any more of her so-called gifts, she inched closer. "I will spare your life, little queen, if you are willing to understand me. Not that you could fully understand me. I am far beyond your comprehension. But you could try. A solid step forward."

Rage built within me. It burned deep inside my chest. I had no desire to understand her. I only wanted her corrosive, draining magic gone from Sepeazia.

An acrid burning filled my nostrils, turning my stomach as she loomed closer.

"You see," she said, lifting one dripping hand. "I've been debating who I hate more, you or your beast of a mate, so let's allow fate to decide. If you kill Brandt, I'll let you live. As I said before, I'll even protect you from the death of Sepeazia. You can pick one person other than Brandt and swim away, free from harm. Flee to the lands of one of your princess friends now that you're all back from the grave. Rebuild your life. Start a new nation. Begin afresh. You'll still have your shifting magic because it isn't part of Sepeazia. It's a better deal than I offered him."

My fists clenched. "I will never kill Brandt." I growled the words at her, rage overwhelming my fear. "We will find a way to stop you."

Her laughter echoed off the walls. "My poor deluded girl, you still don't understand. There is no stopping me. Like your shifter magic, I am not of your world. All your plans will fall apart."

Her shadowy form drifted closer, tendrils of darkness reaching out to caress my face. I jerked back, suppressing a shudder.

She smiled, baring shadowed, pointed teeth. "If it helps, you'd be doing Brandt a favor. Do you know how much he suffers? Perhaps I should show you. Just a taste, of course. Not the full thing. Goodness knows Sepeazia couldn't take two of you being this way for long."

My muscles tensed. I stumbled back as she brought her hand up. Her index finger thrust between my eyes. An icy jolt tore through me, knocking me back.

Darkness engulfed me, and a howling roar rang in my ears. All the energy that had surged within me when I shifted now returned a dozen fold. I couldn't bear it. None of this!

I tore at my hair and screamed. Icy anguish, burning sorrow, endless aching. Blood thundered in my skull. The room lurched and screamed around me. Colors bled across my mind.

Flinging my arm out, I tried to find the wall. Something, anything to support myself. It all blurred and howled around me. Was I still screaming? Red light streaked across my eyes. The world spun.

I had to kill him. He needed to die.

It was as simple as that.

Like breathing. Like blinking.

Natural.

Brandt had to die.

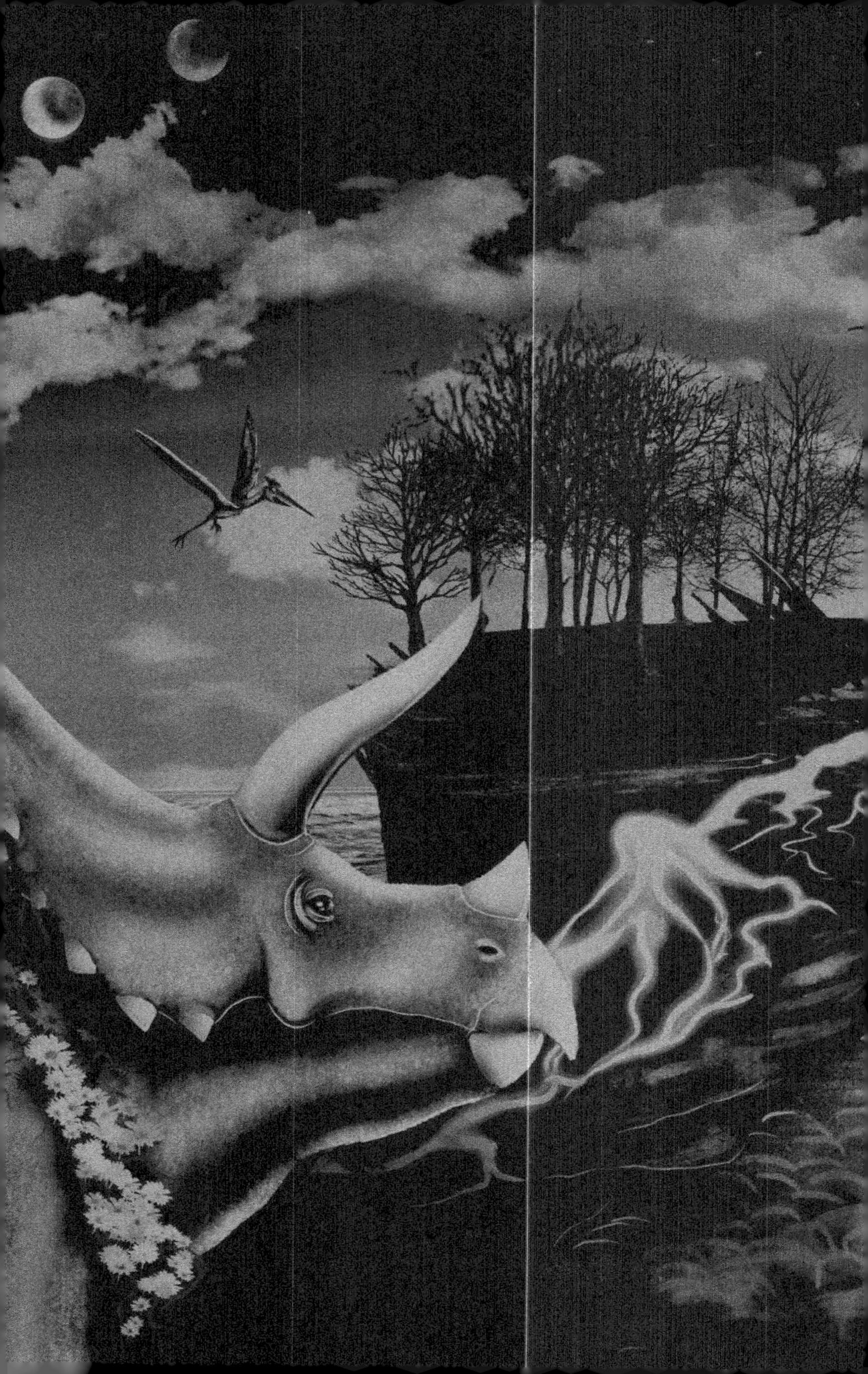

CHAPTER THIRTY-TWO: STELLA

Everything had become so much more intense. Cold spikes of water hammered the back of my head. The ground beneath me swayed and spun, barely visible in the darkness. Everything was shades of red. The whole world throbbed like an infected wound.

Somehow, I had fallen to my knees. My stomach dropped and lurched like I was falling.

Maybe I was falling.

A ragged roar exploded from my throat. My lungs ached. Everything hurt. There was only one way to find relief.

That rageful pulsing intensified within me. My sense of smell intensified, each scent strong enough to club my brain—sharp rain with saltwater, iron-rich blood, ancient stone.

And him. The scent of the one who had to die. Rich and smoky. He had to die. It was the only way.

Die.

Die.

Die.

The stone was slick beneath me. My fingernails scraped across the grooves. Water ran down my hair and face. My breath came in pants and gasps. The stones eventually evened out. The cold wetness on my face and body ceased.

I would do it. I had to. It was the only thing that made sense anymore.

I just…

Had.

To.

Find him.

A column of light appeared before me. The need to kill crackled through me, absorbing every trace of energy and focus. I lunged at the column, my hands flying up.

"Stella, I know you. Stella, wake up. Stella!"

The words cut through me, hot as fire. My head snapped back. My mouth fell open.

What? How…how was this possible?

I stood in front of Brandt, my hands clutching his throat. For one horrifying moment, I stared up into his face. The light around his face solidified, revealing the richness of his eyes, the sharpness of the kohl, the prominence of his brow and nose, the vibrancy of his red and black hair. He was restrained against the wall, black iron chains shackling his wrists and his ankles to the dark stone. He had little more than a few inches of give in either direction.

I fell back and dropped to the floor, holding my head. A wail of sorrow escaped my throat. "Brandt," I moaned. "Oh, Brandt. I'm so sorry!"

A wry chuckle followed before he sighed. "Don't blame yourself, Stella. That curse… Well, I guess you know now."

"If you hadn't pulled me out of it…" I whispered in horror, my forehead pressed to my knees.

Why hadn't I been able to help him that way? He'd always seemed deaf to any calls for him to return, and yet he had been able to do it for me. Thank all that was good he had!

He clicked his tongue. "Stella, look at me."

Tears blurring my eyes, I lifted my head.

His smile was soft and surprisingly comforting, his voice even gentler than before. "Don't go there, sweetheart. It was like that for me at the start. The first few times, you could call me out of that cursed state, and you did that as long as you could. Over time...the curse got worse."

Yes. Much clearer flashes of memories snapped into my mind. Holding him. Nuzzling him. Whispering against the column of his throat as I dared to be close to him. Pleading for someone to save him.

Tears rolled down my cheeks. I really did want to be closer to him. Not just in memory but in reality.

"If I could hold you and comfort you right now, I would." The low rumble of his voice enveloped me.

"Look at the pair of us." My voice grated in my throat.

"We are rather striking," Brandt said softly.

Blinking, I scrubbed the tears away. The oppression of this cell wore upon me even though I had barely been here five minutes. Three lancet windows with arched tops lined one wall. The rain beat its insistent pattern outside, and heavy water marks showed that someone had crawled on their hands and knees over the ledge.

Someone?

Me.

"I climbed in through the window?"

He nodded. "You climbed in like a lizard, but you did it without shifting. We're facing the sea on this side too. Had you fallen... Well, I don't recommend you go out the way you came." He tilted his head. "You're wearing your ring. Maybe it changed your hands or your stomach. Regardless, terrifying and impressive, my love." He winked at me as if this wasn't utterly appalling.

My stomach somersaulted. Those gorgeous ruby-red eyes smoldered with an otherworldly fire. All I wanted was to flee into the shelter of those powerful arms, but the shackles held him there so cruelly, and I didn't want to make things worse by touching him.

"You're all right?" He studied me, his furrowed brow softening with concern.

I gave a small nod. "I think so." The shame threatened to choke me.

"What happened?" he prompted. "I'm guessing the Gola Resh?"

"You don't even sound a little surprised."

"I'm not. Besides, she has been the reason for most things going wrong," he said with the faintest hint of a smile. "So what did she do? Or say?"

"She said she would let me have a taste of what you're going through, and she said..." I hugged myself, my gaze dropping back to the scuffed stone floor before I scanned the room.

This was where my beloved...slept? Except there was no place to sleep. The cell itself was a bedroom that had been cleared out of everything but the wardrobe and a couple tables as well as a wash table with a basin and pitcher. Chains and shackles hung from black anchor rings drilled deep into the wall. They held him fast without even the slack to scratch his nose.

"What did she say?" He leaned forward as much as he could. The chains clanked. His shadow shifted on the wall.

The words almost rose to my lips before I could stop them. She wanted me to kill him, and what would he say? He'd tell me to do it.

I swallowed them down and shook my head. "She does what she does to torment us, to show me what you experience." There was one part of that he should know. "And...the curse will only take you eight more times. If you don't kill me before then, you'll lose your mind forever."

"What?" His eyebrows rose.

I took a deep breath before speaking again, my voice trembling. "The Gola Resh told me that the curse seizing you will only happen ten more times. After that, if you haven't..." I trailed off, unable to speak further.

The weight of her words pressed in upon me. I struggled to breathe. Tears burned the backs of my eyes and choked me.

He looked like I slapped him.

My shoulders shook as I drew in on myself. The thought of him going mad without any chance of aid or healing destroyed me.

He scoffed, his voice low. "I always assumed..." He shook his head. "Well, that was foolish of me." His gaze tilted as he gazed at me. "What else?"

I bit the inside of my lip. "Who says there's anything else?" I whispered.

"You don't lie particularly well, Stella. Never have. You always bite the inside of your lip when you're confused or hiding something. We both know you're hiding something."

Thrusting my hand over my mouth, I rubbed it briskly as if I could scrub the words away, but I couldn't. I couldn't deny him.

"She said if I killed you, then she'd spare me and one person of my choice. Then she touched my forehead, and I went mad."

The silence hung between us, heavy and smothering. Chills crept over my body.

"She wants us to know her loss," Brandt said quietly. "As if she and her so-called beloved didn't visit loss upon hundreds, not even considering those who are yet to come."

"I refused her offer," I said sharply. "I will not kill you, Brandt. I don't know how we're going to stop her, but we will."

He nodded as his gaze drifted over me. "Good thing we have a plan. Did she offer to free Sepeazia as well if you killed me?"

"No. No, just me and one other person," I said, my voice thick with emotion. I hugged myself tighter, resisting the urge to draw close to him and his warmth.

His mouth twitched as he studied me.

"What?" I frowned. A chill pierced me.

"Stella, eight cycles of the curse isn't even a week. They're sixteen hours apart now, and if the curse is triggered early again...I don't think you can make it back in time."

"What?" My mouth fell open. "Of course we can! We will. I know we will! We have to!"

He shook his head. "Three days to get to the Wild Lands on average. One day there to track Arjax and Lorna. One day back if we take the Keening Pass. That passage cannot be rushed, and it can only be entered at set times. Half a day to the Ember Lord's Crest. If we're lucky, we could shave a day or so off, but we'd have to be very lucky and go straight to the Ember Lord's Crest."

"See? It is possible. We could just make it!"

"Stella, we don't know what causes the curse to leap forward. It's been using up time. That means it could happen maybe once and we'd be all right. With how the Gola Resh is interfering, you know I will turn at least once, if not more, especially given her goals."

I pressed my lips into a tight line. "We still have a chance." Turning, I dug my fingers into my scalp. "I have to get out of here! We have to leave tonight."

"Stella, there's no way that you can leave tonight. The storm is too strong."

I licked my lips, then bit them. "You said maybe it could take us two days!"

"If we're very fortunate."

"And Arjax and Lorna. If we tell them what's going on and if we get lucky when we get there, they'll help us in less than a day, right?"

"If it were just up to Arjax and Lorna, then of course, but it's a matter of winds and tides, and taking the Keening Pass will require that we be at just the right place at just the right time or else everyone could die."

His words struck me hard. There was practically no room for anything to go wrong.

My mouth had gone dry. "It's still possible."

The way the side of his mouth twitched stabbed me through the heart. Was he giving up?

"Besides!" I spread my arms wide. "Even if it does, if we kill her, her curses lose their hold, right? You'll be healed."

As soon as I said that, I knew I was wrong. Of course, everything a curse had done couldn't be pulled back. If the curse completed, then...

I looked up at him, desperate to see some sort of contradiction.

That wasn't what I saw reflected there.

If I went to the Wild Lands, I might never see him in his right mind again. If we didn't get the spear and conduct the ritual in time, the man I knew and loved would be gone forever.

How was that possible?

"Brandt..."

My mind flashed back to Auntie Runa's vision, to what Elias had wanted to tell me he had seen, to my own prophecy. Was it dread or foresight that now spoke into my mind and whispered, "This only ends in death?"

That night in the grotto snapped back into my mind.

That instant when I had told him what I saw.

Death.

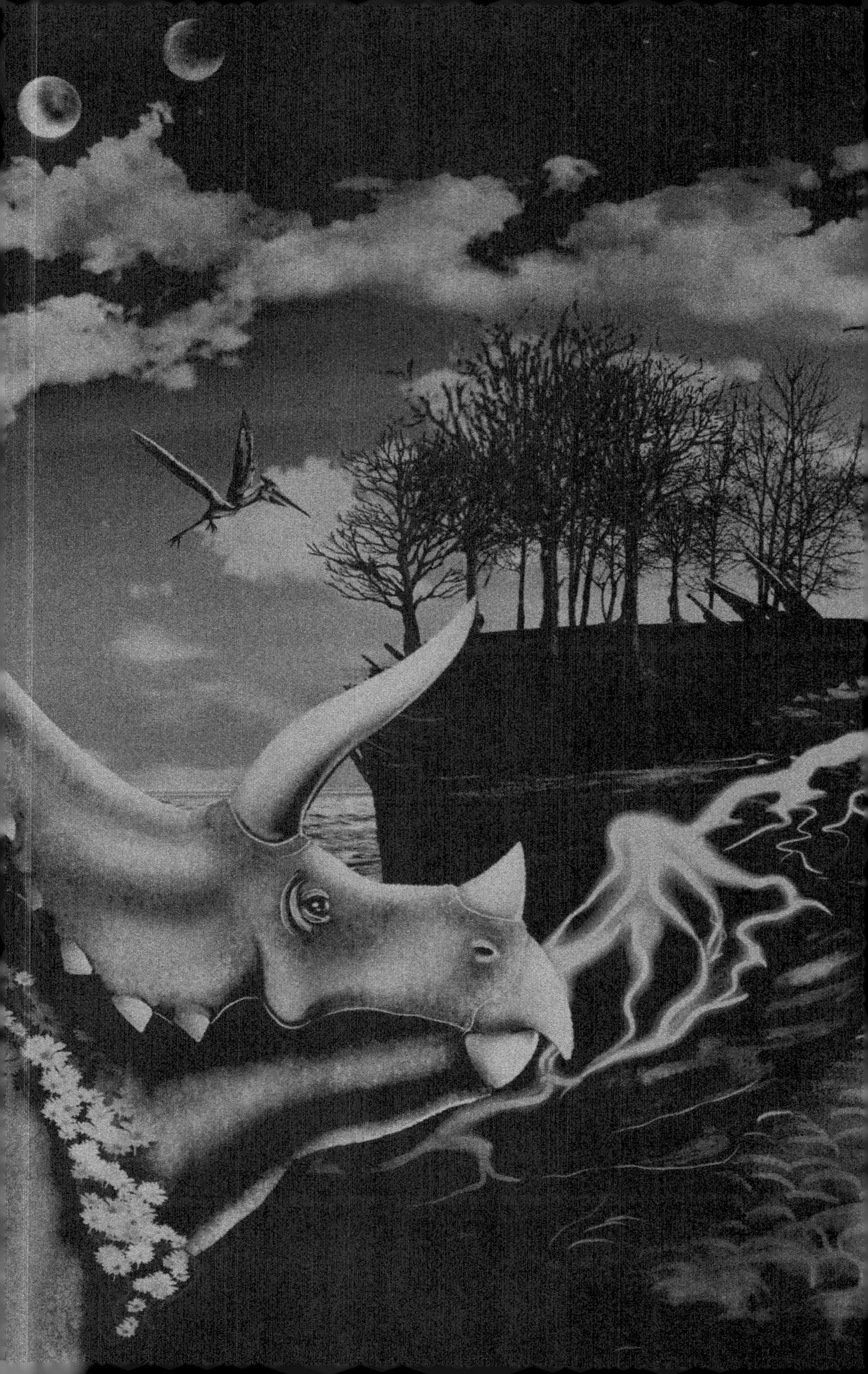

CHAPTER THIRTY-THREE:
STELLA

*N*o. I couldn't accept that there was no hope for our relationship. The quietness in his gaze infuriated me.

"Don't tell me you've given up!" I snapped, my voice harsher than I intended. "This isn't—No, Brandt!" A ragged sob dragged up my throat. I slapped my hand over my mouth as I shook my head. "Maybe the Gola Resh lied! She loves to lie and spread dissension. Maybe there's something else. You aren't going to die. We're going to find another way around this."

While I ranted, he remained silent, arms spread wide and fastened to the wall. His gaze followed me as I paced. The wind wailed outside with the pattering of the rain.

I just kept repeating myself. I couldn't stop until at last I flung my arms up in the air and turned to face him. "Say something!"

He scoffed, but his dark-red eyes remained soft. A hungry glowing fire burned but not a fight. "If this is my last night to see you, then I'm glad you could be here, that we could have this time together alone when I don't have to fear whether I will harm you. What the Gola Resh intended as cruelty is instead a blessing."

"No." I held my finger up to his lips, shaking my head. Tears leaked down my cheeks. "No! This isn't our last night. I'll...I'll—"

"What? You'll stay here with me until the very end?" He gave me a wry smile. "Arjax and Lorna will hand the spear over even if it's just Kine who goes, but you were closer to them, and while I'm not a seer, I know you should be there. It will comfort you."

"You just don't want me to see—" I swallowed hard.

No, that was unfair. Of course he didn't want me to see him succumb to madness. Who would want that? But Auntie Runa was right. Our being close to one another would make everything harder.

Maybe there was something else. Auntie Runa had always described foresight and visions as coming to us on their own, but I closed my eyes and reached out into the darkness of my thoughts, begging, pleading for some kind of answer. Some alternative.

There was nothing.

The minutes dripped by, only the beating of the rain against the stone outside to mark them. My own breaths shuddered.

Nothing.

Nothing.

Nothing!

"Hm." Brandt cleared his throat.

When I opened my eyes, he was studying me, head tilted, gaze half-lidded and soft. "What happened to my brash, fearless seer?" he asked, meaning to tease me.

The pressure throughout my chest constricted even tighter, choking me as I fought desperately not to cry any more than I had. "I can't see anything about us. I can't feel anything about us except fear. Fear of losing you. Are you just giving up?"

The last question was more of an accusation, and it wasn't fair, especially not when he was chained down like this.

He smirked. "No, Stella." His gaze traveled up and down my body. "I'm just recognizing that this could be the last night I see you, and I've got to say...abyssal damnation, woman, look at you."

"Don't try to change the subject. Don't you dare start flirting with me!"

His eyebrow arched, his mouth quirking. "Oh...now we aren't flirting? Would it be...inappropriate?"

I folded my arms tight over my breasts. "I'm not in a playful mood."

He got flirty at the weirdest times.

He twitched his massive sculpted arms. His gorgeous serpent tattoos glistened in the torchlight.

Dragging my hands across my face, I tried to compose myself. For now, the magnitude of the haziness and the humming that had been present in my other encounters with Brandt had not returned. The need was controllable, but how long would that last? Besides, I had to warn someone about the Gola Resh. Someone had to know something. Anything!

"We're going to find a way out of this, Brandt."

"I love you, Stella."

"Don't you dare," I whispered hoarsely, clenching my fist against my mouth.

"Don't dare tell you I love you?" He chuckled.

"You know what I mean." Dashing the tears away, I started for the door. "We've got to strengthen the wards or do something to keep her away. There has to be something we can do."

The handle refused to turn. It was locked.

Of course it was.

"Hey!" I banged my fist against the door. The cold metal greeted me. Stopping then, I pressed my fingers against my scalp, remembering what Elias had said. "No one can hear us."

"Probably not." Brandt's eyes shuttered. "I'm sorry, Stella."

"Elias gave me…" My hand reached for the charm and met only warm skin. Ihlkit! I dropped my head to my chest.

"What?"

"I just…" I shook my head. "I thought I had a way to get help."

"They'll be here in the morning."

I stared at the black iron-bound door, my jaw set. Then I spun on my heel and charged toward the lancet window. My hands struck the window ledge. Rain spattered beyond the overhang.

"I don't recommend you try climbing out there again," he said. "That's a sheer drop at least a hundred feet on this side straight into the ocean. Even with years' experience, I wouldn't recommend those waters at this time in this weather."

More tears choked me. Shaking my head, I hugged myself tight. The cold wind made my skin prickle as it howled through the windows.

"Looks like you're stuck with me till morning," he said, "but you don't have to worry about me hurting you or anything. I'm completely tied down."

I dashed the tears from my eyes once more. This was wrong on so many levels, and that low rumble in his voice made me go weak in the knees.

"I'm not afraid of you hurting me. I just… There has to be someone we can talk to who can figure out something."

"We have figured out something." He gave a small shake of his head. "Hm."

"What?" I kept my hand pressed to my temple.

"Do you remember our last night together?"

"In the grotto?" I left my hand up, unable to look at him. "When I told you that there was no way that this ended except in death?"

His shoulders lifted. "That wasn't actually the part I was remembering." His smile went crooked.

My heart raced faster. Highlights of memories swept along

my mind, fragments and sensations, but that dream and memory ended with the knowledge that I had to die. At the time, I'd believed with my entire being that this was it. Yet here I stood.

I turned my face toward the window.

"We made love one last time," he said. "Right in that cavern."

"And what does that have to do with anything?" I refused to look at him, staring instead into the darkness beyond the window. Indigo-black waves with lilac foam crashed and rolled in the sea beyond.

That low chuckle of his followed. Soft. Intimate. Underpinned with sadness. Almost as if he were whispering in my ear. "I tried to take you against the amethyst, but we had to keep stopping and find a place where the geodes wouldn't scrape you. We wound up on the stone beside the river, and I thought I could make love to you all night, but the grief... It was so intense. As if we were both being dropped from a great height and crushed all at once. I felt like I was drowning. All I could think about was the fact that, in a matter of hours, you would walk to your death, and I couldn't save you. I had to let you go. It was all I could think about as I held you for what I thought would be the last time."

I shuddered, closing my eyes as if that could block the memory from returning.

The heat of his body against mine.

His tongue pressing between my lips.

The taste of salt from tears and sweat.

Frantic in our need for comfort and release. Desperate to make the seconds last forever. Clinging to one another and mourning the loss that was yet to come.

"I made you shake and scream. You made me howl. I kept thinking this can't be the end. How could someone so perfect... so wondrous...so beautiful... How could my mate have to lay down her life like this?"

I shook my head, the tears stinging. "No. I came back. You knew I was coming back. Before I died, you made me promise that if I found a way to live again, then I wouldn't come back until we knew how to end the curse."

"I hoped," he whispered, his voice rough. "That was all. Hope borne of desperation. Hope with no actual basis in reality."

"Then have hope for you, please! Even if you can't see a way through." I knotted my fists as I forced myself to meet his gaze. "Brandt, please! Don't give up on me. I can't...I can't lose you again!"

"You have to go forward without me. You can't waste time thinking about whether or not I am going mad," he said. "What I am telling you is hard. I know. I lived it. I carried on as best I could, holding you in my heart and praying for a miracle, but I had to live—"

"No! I spent my whole life on Earth feeling like everything was wrong, as if I was only a shadow in the wrong world. Everyone else was separate from me. Evera was one of the most real people I ever encountered. But even then, I just... I couldn't. It was horrible. And now, now I finally have found you and the life I am supposed to have. My family."

The memories assailed me, amorphous and cold. They battered my mind. The person who I was searching for was here. Bound and chained, prepared for death.

"You expect me to give this up now?" I asked.

"You are a queen. My queen. Always. Forever. You have to let me go, just as I let you go, and then you will lead our people. You will find a way to save them. I'll always have faith in you, Stella."

"And I'll never let anyone sit on my left," I whispered.

"What?" He tilted his head, his brow raising.

"You never moved on from me." I lifted my chin slowly, forcing myself to look at him through the sheen of tears. He'd never let anyone sit on his right or drink from my goblet. He'd never moved on, and yet he wanted me to let him go?

"I never said I did. I haven't always been the best king, and I may have kuvasted a few more than I should have." His gaze grew more intense. "And I never stopped loving you, but there's no way back for me. You made your sacrifice, and you were brought back because you and the others sacrificed yourself to preserve that sacred tree. But that was magic Abba could control. Magic she could overpower." He referred to the priestess of the goddess.

"I could ask Abba to bring you back—"

"We already asked, love," he said softly. "She was powerless. Stella, love of my life and breath of my being, we have asked everyone. The Gola Resh is beyond us all. Beyond our magic. Beyond our knowledge. Our friends in kingdoms far from here have done all they can to save us, and no one can do anything. This plan to slay the Gola Resh, it's all we have left. You have to go. Even if I am beyond saving."

"Don't say that."

His voice sharpened. "Stella, I adore you. To see you again, even like this...it brings me comfort, but I did not always handle this as well as I should, and it has been lonely. So swear to me that when I am gone, you will find a way to live."

I needed him. Craved his touch. Longed for his love.

I forced myself to turn, trying desperately not to imagine his full lips against mine, his taste on my tongue, his heat encompassing me.

There wasn't the same cloudiness as there had been in our other encounters. No dimness obscured my thoughts. Just desire. A pure and potent desire that begged me to run back to the arms of my beloved. But somehow I held back, arms tight over my breasts, Auntie Runa's warning echoing in my ears.

"I swear to you that I am not going to give up on you so long as there is breath in my lungs." My voice trembled. "I didn't ask you to give up on me. Sometimes letting go is wrong."

In my mind, though, I did hear myself asking him to let me go. It played out before my eyes, vivid and painful. Tears in my eyes, tears in his. This wasn't the same, I told myself.

"Don't you dare give up on me, Brandt. I can't imagine how hard this has been for you, to have had to endure with this curse eating at your mind and chipping away at your sanity. You waited for me fifty years, but please, even if you can't believe for you, know that I still believe we are going to find a way. There's no one else for me. Only you. Always you. Even on Earth, no one was right."

The air grew heavy around us.

The corners of his mouth pulled up softly, that hint of a dimple returning. "I wish I could make love to you one more time—"

"It doesn't matter," I whispered. "Auntie Runa said we should not be together like that, that it would just make things tougher."

"I have no intention of leaving this room until I'm cured. I'm too much of a liability," he said, his voice guttural, his expression heavy with need. His gaze raked over my body, heat blistering in it. "Stella...I need—"

My name was barely out of his mouth before I flung myself at him, my lips slamming over his.

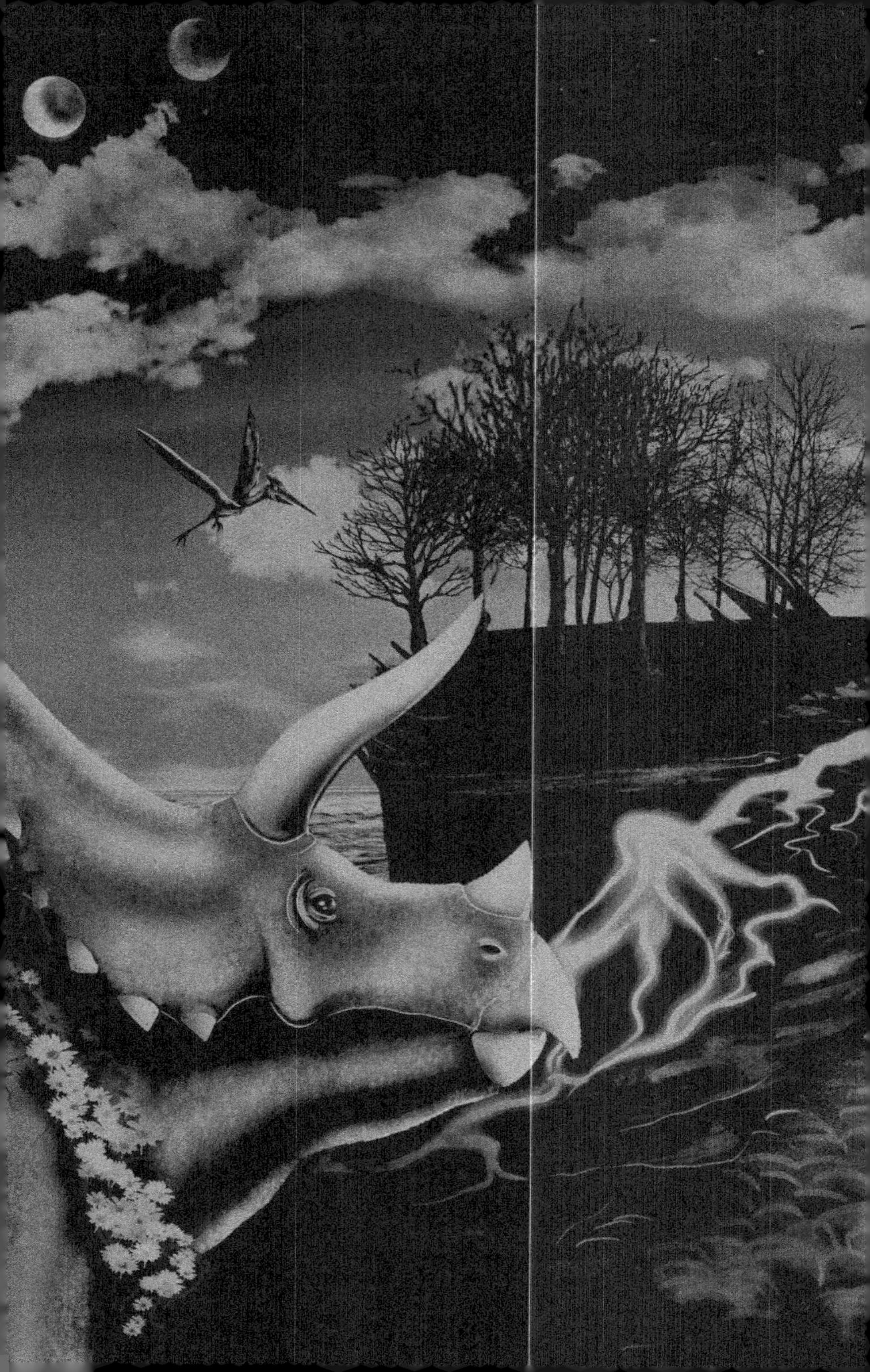

CHAPTER THIRTY-FOUR: STELLA

I had to feel him. Had to be with him. Had to taste him.

My mouth crashed over his, my body flush against him. Already, he was hard as marble. I thrust my fingers up along the planes of his face as I leaned up and kissed him as if my life depended upon it.

Brandt groaned into the kiss. "I want you so badly," he growled when I pulled back to gasp for breath.

I pressed my lips to his once more. The kiss turned wilder, deeper, but it was lacking. His hands weren't on me. They weren't in my hair. As heavenly as his scent was, as devastating his heat, it was torment to not feel his arms around me or to twine myself around him.

"I want you," he repeated, his voice guttural. "I need you."

More.

I needed more.

I rubbed up against him, feeling his taut strength and powerful form, all the more infuriating for being restrained, but I kissed him nonetheless. His mouth worked against mine, wild and fierce, drawing me in.

It still wasn't enough.

It was never going to be enough, not when he was chained up like this.

My eyes dropped to the shackles and the anchor rings with their heavy locks.

His gaze followed mine. "Don't you dare unshackle me," he growled.

I lifted my chin, my heart pounding furiously.

He was right.

Some part of me rebelled at this. I wanted to feel his arms around me. Memories of what we had once shared—especially that night in the grotto—swept back over me. Whatever happened this night, it needed to be special.

Not a commemoration of his madness or the risk that he posed.

An idea sprang into my mind. A slow smile spread over my mouth. "That's not the only thing the anchor rings are used for."

I pressed my hand to my collarbone as I tried to collect myself, my breaths practically coming in pants. The last time we had had sex, it was about mourning. This one would not be. I refused. We both needed release. We both needed to relax. Maybe I didn't feel as befuddled as I had before in the valley or in the cavern, but I did know a few other things.

"I know just what to use these rings for."

He tilted his head, his eyes narrowing. That throbbing pulse in his throat was even faster now. "What exactly do you have in mind?"

I stepped back, forcing myself to draw in a deep breath and calm a little.

This was my husband. My mate. My most beloved of all. If this was our last night together, then I would make sure it was memorable for both of us. He had comforted me and made love to me so that when I walked to my death in that sacred pool, I could think of him and revel in his love. I would comfort him and make him laugh and moan even as we grieved.

"Can't you guess?" I tilted my head, letting my hair slide down one side of my face as I dropped the strap of my silky orange nightgown.

A breath hissed through his teeth as he shook his head at me. His smile returned too. "You are such a tease."

Laughing breathlessly, I curled my fingers into the fabric of his red shirt. "You think this is being a tease?"

He narrowed his eyes at me, his words rumbling in his chest. "That wasn't a challenge."

"But I accepted it." Grinning, I leaned against his body, delighting in the planes and lines of his body.

Another growl vibrated in his chest. His hips bucked against mine, ensuring I felt him.

Good. We were headed in the right direction.

Rising onto the tips of my toes, I kissed him deeply. My hands slid down his muscular chest, fingers tracing each ridge and valley. His muscles strained, and his breaths grew labored.

"Ihlkit!" he swore.

More swearing followed as I brushed my lips in feather-light kisses across his jaw and down the column of his throat.

His nostrils flared. "Oh, I will make you pay, woman."

I stuck my tongue out at him as I continued to rub against him. "Good. That means you'll have to keep fighting so we can do this again."

"I will. I will make you pay so much you won't be able to walk," he promised, his eyes blazing. He chuckled darkly. "I'll tax every muscle and sinew you have."

"Oh no. I'm terrified."

"You should be." He grinned, pausing as he lowered his gaze to mine. "Do your worst, woman."

Biting my tongue at him, I slipped closer. It was so easy now to dance and tease and play and taunt.

Sliding my hand down, I stroked his length through his black trousers.

He tensed against the chains, a guttural moan rising from within him. "Seems like you haven't lost your touch," he said, the words far tighter than usual. "Impressive."

I unfastened his belt and then slid him out, my hand wrapping around him. "You're the one who is impressive." Ihlkit. I stared at him. "Just look at you."

"Look at you," he rasped. "I don't know why I thought you'd be shy."

"Neither do I. I'm quiet, not shy." I gripped him tighter, smiling up at him.

I'd done this many times before too. Those memories were like echoes, taunting me with what Brandt and I had once had while urging me to make this even better.

His breaths became shallower, nearly panting. "And what exactly are you going to do now, you little tease?" he demanded, baring his teeth at me.

"Is 'Tease' my new nickname?" I tilted my head at him as I moved my hand up and down.

"You've certainly earned it." His mock glare honed in on me. He shifted his weight as much as he could, straining to push against me.

"Patience, my love." I swished my hips and moved back a bit.

He grunted in response.

He really was quite tall, and that was going to make this next part a little tricky. I rubbed up against him again, sliding down his body with a sensual moan. His body stiffened against me even more. Once more our mouths collided, his tongue pressing eagerly between the seam of my lips.

The heat coiled tighter within me as I ground my hips against his. I could disappear in these kisses, his heat, his scent. Though he could not move far forward and the chains clanked with every shift of his body, his mouth demanded my surrender. He bit at my lower lip and swallowed my moans.

My eyelids slid shut. That heavenly, heady combination of bergamot, smoke, leather, orange, and sweat filled my lungs. This...this was a moment I would always remember, that he would always remember too. This was worth remembering.

Everything in me stilled as I leaned against him. What if this was our last time?

My first time in this life.

Our last time for forever.

I—I couldn't do this. My body froze.

He pressed soft kisses to my cheek to the shell of my ear. His breath caressed me. "Stella."

My heart lurched. I forced my smile to return, drawing in a deep breath. If this was our last time, I couldn't think of that. I was comforting him and bringing him release. He had held me and comforted me on that night long, long ago, and those memories had carried me forward, along with so many others.

If he stayed stuck here for the next few days, I would make sure he had something exceptional to look back on. And then—then we'd make more memories. Because we'd be together.

Drawing in a deep breath, I took hold of the anchor rings near his shoulders and gripped them with my hands. Then I jumped so I straddled his waist, my feet braced against the wall as I positioned myself.

His eyebrows arched, genuine surprise reflecting in his eyes. "I never did anything like this before?"

The slow smile curled over his lips, his dimple becoming more prominent. "Not like this, no." Tension radiated through his body. "Maybe it's not so shocking how you climbed down that wall."

"Told you I was gonna climb you like my favorite rock wall." I lowered myself against him, my eyes locked with his. I was so ready for him. Curling my hips, I pressed up and down, teasing my entrance against him.

He growled at me again, his eyes lighting up. "Yes, you did." A rasping groan escaped him as his body tensed even more. He shifted his hips, moving along with me.

Years of yoga and rock climbing had certainly given me an excellent grip and magnificent balance, but I'd never actually anticipated using either like this. I rocked back and forth, building the friction and heat between us. His eyes rolled back, and his body shuddered.

The heat between us intensified, the air thick and close. My body trembled against his as I moved against him, my core tight. The pleasurable torment intensified. I kept my grip on the anchor rings tight, leveraging my weight and position.

Between his growls and my grinding and gasping, we formed our own sensual pace. He nipped and bit at my neck each time I came closer. Darted at my breasts but had to pull back because the chains held him fast. He grunted in frustration before I could sweep my mouth back against his.

Yes.

This was worth remembering.

Then I wrapped my legs around his waist, and he was in me. My back arched. I gasped. His skin was so hot against me that my whole body trembled in response. Ecstasy washed over me, and the burning in my arms and legs was no longer a distraction. It melded into the perfection of this moment.

"You are magnificent," he breathed, his head falling back as he drew in a great heaving breath.

The friction built between us, my arms taut and my legs tight around his waist. I rode him with abandon, twisting and grinding as he thrust and strained against me and the manacles that held him in place. My thighs squeezed tight against his waist. The tension between us rose and rose.

I moaned his name.

He tightened beneath me, a guttural snarl following that. He erupted, and I clung to him harder, pressing tighter and clenching, riding the waves of his passion until I followed.

The orgasm shattered me, pouring over my body in its own frenzied storm. My body sagged against his, my legs trembling as I dropped back to the ground.

"Incredible." Sweat gleamed on his face and rolled down his neck and chest. He stared at me with hungry, awestruck eyes. I had never felt more powerful.

"As are you." I smiled up at him dreamily. My lungs filled with the cool air as the storm outside continued its angry path.

"I'm far more impressive when I'm not chained up like this," he said softly, nudging me with his nose once more. His teeth grazed my lips as he turned his mouth to mine. "It's a good thing I am chained up, though. You know it's the only way you'd get a reprieve tonight. It'll be so hard to let you go tomorrow."

"Who says I want a reprieve?" I cut my eyes up at him, trailing my fingers over his chest.

That smirk of his returned. "Really?" He chuckled. "You surprise me yet again."

"I'm full of surprises."

With that, I devoured his mouth with mine, kissing him fervently.

I spent the next few hours kissing him, worshiping him, and tending him as we both came apart time and again. Our lovemaking became slower and slower with each passing hour. At last, I simply leaned against him, drenched in sweat and panting.

"Not being able to hold you is a torment," he ground out. "But you...you—" That ragged breath nearly had me melting against him again. "If these restraints weren't holding me up, I'd be on the ground. I'd be on you."

"Well..." I draped my arms around his neck. "You're just going to have to make good on that promise as soon as you can. I eagerly await your attack."

He chuckled. "I do have to add if what you did to me is what you did to your favorite rock wall, then your life on Earth was quite obscene."

That wicked grin of his only broadened as I smacked his shoulder lightly. He dropped his head forward to nuzzle me. I leaned up and pressed the tip of my nose to his.

"How dare you." I raised my eyebrow at him.

He sucked his teeth, his dark-red eyes sparking with mischief. "Did I insult your honor, my queen?"

"Yes, and to make amends, I require that you find me in one week, and...well, I hope you'll use your imagination, Your Majesty." I waggled my brows at him and then snuggled in closer.

He chuckled. "Hard as it will be to bid you goodbye, I'll see you off at the docks. My guards can ensure if anything goes wrong that you escape safely, but I do intend to kiss you so hard you see stars."

"You'll make everyone blush if you do that." I tapped the tip of his nose with my finger.

"Let them blush." His jaw rubbed against the top of my head, the little roughness of stubble making my scalp prickle with pleasure. A deep sigh vibrated from his chest. "You are my heart, Stella."

Tears pricked the backs of my eyes once more. I swallowed hard. "And you are mine."

Dread pooled within me as I realized we were getting close to saying goodbye. The storm had ceased outside. The wind whistled against the stones, and the salty tang of the storm's passing filled my nostrils. I buried my nose in the crook of his neck to breathe in his scent instead. I never wanted to let him go, but as the dawn sky lightened, I knew I had no choice.

Not really.

But I wasn't giving up. I would fight for us both.

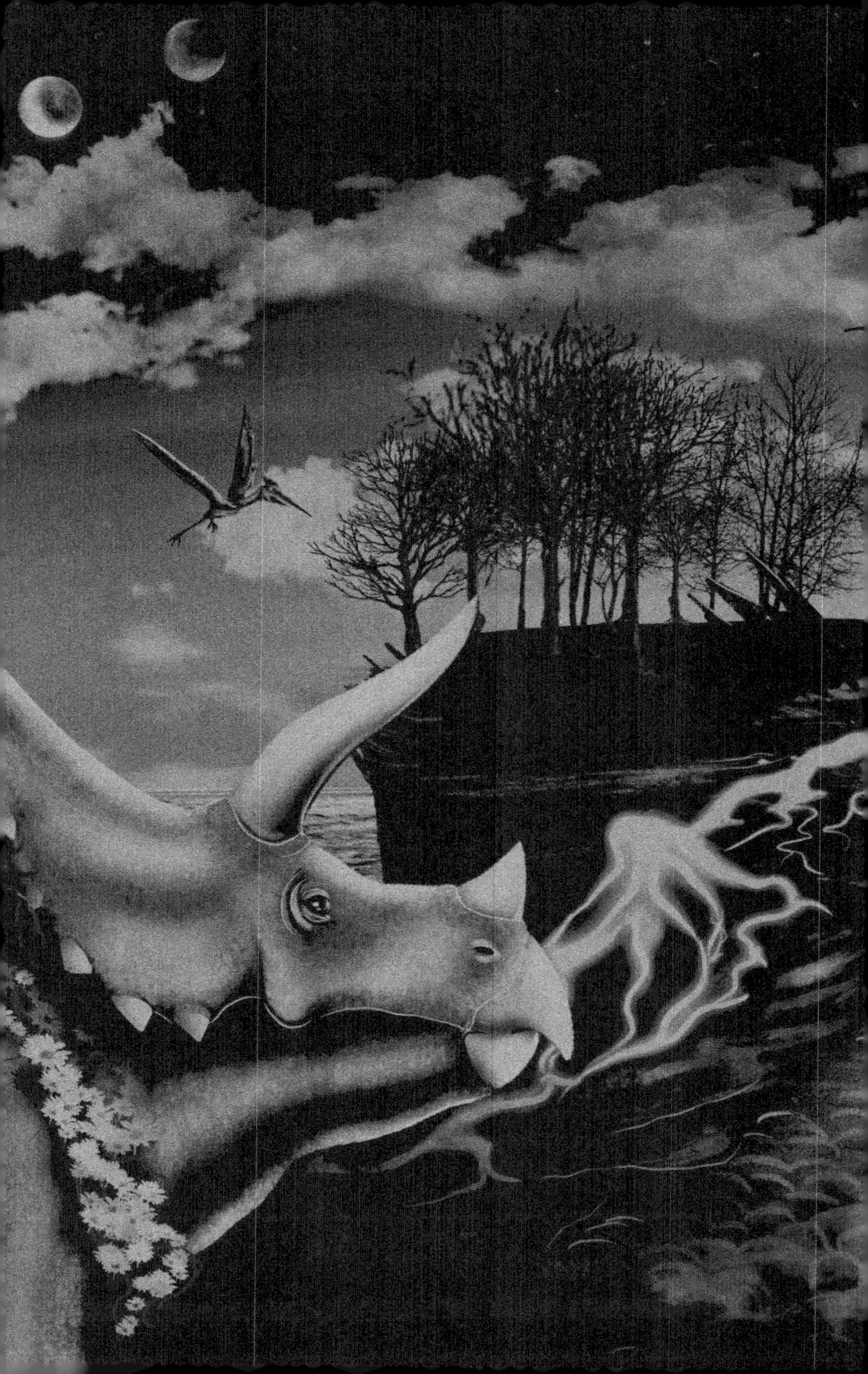

CHAPTER THIRTY-FIVE: STELLA

*A*s the dawn neared, I helped Brandt clean up and get dressed. We drank half the water in the pitcher and used the rest to wash up.

I'd never done a walk of shame before. Not that there would be much walking. We simply waited for Hord to discover me in Brandt's room.

Oddly, there was no shame here, even knowing that soon we would be found. There was a heaviness, a sadness that was not hard for me to delve into, but each time, I swallowed those feelings down and hugged Brandt as tight as I could.

Somehow, Brandt drifted off. I massaged his muscles and tried to provide support so that he could rest at least some. His sleep was fitful, his body awkwardly slumped against the shackles until I flattened myself against him to give his limbs relief.

The lust of our passion had dimmed. All I wanted now was to bring him comfort.

His sleep seemed fitful, but it was something. What little rest he got in this state had to be precious. With gentle strokes, I wiped the sweat from his brow.

After maybe an hour, he startled awake. He looked about the room, his eyes wide. His throat worked as his gaze fell to me.

"What's wrong?" I gazed up at him, my hand along the plane of his jaw.

He drew in another shuddering breath. "Nothing," he gasped. "Nightmare. Nothing serious. Don't want to talk about it. Glad that you're here." He pressed his chin to the top of my head, his heart hammering.

"I don't see why you have to be so uncomfortable in here," I said, my cheek resting on his chest. "Surely you could have a bed to lie in rather than being chained this tight to the wall."

"Mostly because I broke free a couple times," he said softly. "Sometimes, the need to be with you...it's just too much for me. Or almost too much. It's not exactly like the madness of the curse when it takes me, but it's hard to think around it. Tile and Hord think it's from the Gola Resh. Maybe it is. Maybe it's just because we aren't meant to be apart."

And yet we had to be.

Auntie Runa's warning echoed in my ears, but I burrowed closer. His heat bled through my thin orange nightgown. All I wanted to do was hide in his arms.

My eyelids slid shut. "Every time I see you or think of you, I feel like where you are is where I must be."

"Because you are," he whispered roughly. "It's just...for now...where you belong is too dangerous." He set his jaw and spoke with more effort. "And if the worst happens, you'll find someone else who—"

"Shut up." I squeezed him closer, my whole body aching as much as my heart. "You don't get to talk to me like that." Anger stirred deeper within me. How could he even say such a thing?

"Very well." His low laugh rumbled up, weakening my knees again...except there was another note to it. Something was off. Something was on edge.

Dawn's golden light spilled over the windowsill and onto the dark stone floor. A lark's song sailed on the wind along with the gull and pterosaur calls.

I played with the red and black hair that curled over his shoulder. "At least I'll feel your arms around me once more before we leave."

He set his jaw. His throat bobbed. "We say our goodbyes here, Stella."

I huffed at him, scowling. "What? You were going to come down to the docks. You were going to kiss me and make everyone blush."

He shook his head. "This goodbye here is perfect—"

"You can't think you'll snap and attack me again," I said sharply. "You have to come down to the docks."

"I don't want to risk hurting you or damaging the ship. We can't afford any delays."

My lips pressed into a tight line. What had made him change his mind? I didn't like this.

Or maybe I was just greedy to be close to him.

"What changed? It will be all right. Look at your charm—"

"I just...I had a chance to think about it. How often has the charm been wrong, Stella?" He tipped his head forward, his expression hardening. "We say our goodbyes here. Once you leave, don't come back into this cell."

"You don't have to fear yourself that much." The words came out sharper than I intended, but the feeling behind them was the same. "You are not a monster. You never have been. This is a curse, and you are still the king."

"Can our goodbye here not be enough?" he asked, his voice low as his gaze searched mine. "And if you are successful, can our reunion not serve as our reward for succeeding?"

Anger seared through me even stronger, rising in my heart. Something had changed in his eyes.

"What happened?" I demanded. "What happened in that dream?"

He shook his head. "Just a nightmare, but its warning is wise. I cannot play games with your life, Stella. You mean more to me than anything."

"You would not be risking my life if you came down to the docks. Your warriors are there. Kine and Hord have handled you countless times!" A slight exaggeration, but true in spirit. "You can't let fear control you."

"Don't fight with me on this, Stella. Please. Let our night together close peacefully. Let me just enjoy your presence."

My lips pursed, my muscles tightening. Tears spilled down my cheeks again, but why argue? We were down to our final hours, and I couldn't bear the thought of fighting with him.

I burrowed my face in his chest and sobbed.

The sun had barely warmed the stone when Hord arrived. To his credit, his face registered only minor surprise before he schooled his features and asked if either of us required anything. I swiftly explained what had happened relating to the Gola Resh while Brandt listened with minor amusement, still bound firmly to the wall.

Hord's brow rose at the statement that the Gola Resh had gotten in. He immediately sent for an attendant with orders to begin scouring all the wards and strengthening them. Despite this, he agreed with Brandt that the only thing for us to do was move forward with the plan. We would gather the necessary components and meet directly at the Ember Lord's Crest, saving us a half day's travel and the potential for more delays. He and Cahji would leave shortly after Kine and I departed. Tile would oversee the Goblet with Candy's help.

I dragged my hand through my hair as I studied Brandt. His solemn expression. His muscular planes. His gentle eyes even when he tried to keep the emotion from them. Who would have known that red eyes could be so expressive? Despite our lovemaking last night, part of me felt as if he had already given up.

"We could take you with us," I offered. "Then you would be with us for the final battle."

"Three days at sea at minimum with a water serpent shifter going insane," Brandt growled, rolling his eyes. "You're smart enough to know why that wouldn't work."

I was, but that didn't mean I was happy about it.

I then returned to my room but not before Kine caught me in the hall. Unlike Hord, his expression was teasing, but that soon faded when I explained to him what had happened, leaving out once again what Brandt and I had done to pass the time as well as the offer the Gola Resh had made me. No sense in sharing what I would never accept.

The rest of the morning passed with something akin to numbness. Elias avoided me. Kine spoke with Tile and others.

Hord informed me that someone had chipped off a portion of the wards that had prevented the Gola Resh from entering. Something else must have been used to draw her in, but they weren't sure what.

Alarm spiked through me at once. "What's going to be done to keep that from happening again?" I asked. "Who did it?"

"If I had to guess, one of the factions," Hord said solemnly, arms akimbo. Weariness remained etched in his features. "You will have to continue to be careful. We've kept your presence here as quiet as possible."

"Why would the factions try to kill Brandt or me? Why would anyone even worry about this right now? Our entire race is at risk!"

He lifted his broad shoulders. "I have never understood it, but I am not a politician. We have been working to engrave more protective wards into the heartstones ever since we learned that the Gola Resh survived."

"And they still don't know how that happened?"

He shook his head.

"Please...I don't know what Brandt will say to you regarding his protection, but if the Gola Resh came for me, I am afraid she will come also for him." I pressed my hand over my chest. That pulsing sensation had returned, but I spoke before I registered it.

His eyebrow quirked as he studied me.

I offered a small shrug in response. It was hard for me not to worry even more, especially with Brandt being vulnerable. "I don't know for certain. These could just be concerns. I know he does not feel worthy of care because of all that has happened, but—"

"I will ensure that proper precautions are taken," Hord said. "There are a few whom I trust in this."

"Thank you."

It wasn't just the Gola Resh either. Assassins could also find him vulnerable and attack. He knew this, though, so I bit back my concerns and continued with the preparations.

By late morning, we were on our way. Apparently, as water serpents, our people were seafarers. We had systems in place to allow us to provision our ships. I helped however I could. My thighs and biceps scolded me sharply each time I had to bend or flex after last night's exertions.

Buttercup and the other steeds and companions were loaded onto the ship as well. None of them seemed even mildly concerned. Buttercup tossed an annoyed glance over her thick shoulder at me, then lowed long and slow.

I crossed over to her and stroked her crest down to the base of her jaw. "It's going to be all right, sweetie," I whispered.

The ship bobbed up and down as the waves lapped at the sides.

"We're almost ready," Kine said as he passed by me, a large bag slung over his shoulder. Elias had yet to make an appearance. "The sky is clear, and the sea is open. We'll make good time." Kine clapped his hand to my arm before he strode away.

My insides squirmed as I cast my gaze up to the looming

castle above. I desperately wanted to slip back up there and hug Brandt one more time. The need was already building. A hollow ache started in my heart.

"You all right?" Kine asked, frowning.

My eyes burned as I tore my gaze away. "Yeah," I mumbled. "I'm fine."

He chuckled. "Are you going to go say goodbye to Brandt?"

I shook my head, my lips pressed in a tight line, my gaze on the planks of the dock. Fish darted below the boards, little shadows in the dark waters. "He was clear about not wanting me to return to his cell."

"Yes, well, he's right there." Kine pointed over my shoulder, smirking.

I turned. My heart leaped.

There Brandt walked, flanked by his guards, wearing fresh clothes. The charm around his neck was still orange. It hadn't progressed forward at all, but there hadn't been any earthquakes either.

If I hadn't known better, I would have sworn he was in perfect health. He came forward with a powerful stride, shoulders squared, face stoic. Oh, my heart. He looked every bit the arrogant young king that stirred my memory, despite the gentleness in those eyes and the masked schooling of his features. Folding his arms over his chest, he halted at the edge of the dock.

Tears burned the backs of my eyes. He'd done this for me. He'd relented and come to say goodbye despite whatever fear he held.

Kine was already walking back up the dock to him as Brandt spoke to the captain and some of the assembled warriors and sailors. His manner remained firm but calm, a slight smile on his full lips.

My whole world narrowed to him. All I could think was how grateful I was that the Gola Resh had not even thought to give me the choice of keeping Brandt alive and sacrificing everything else. Most likely, it was a signifier of what a poor queen I was or would be that I was tempted by the thought, but for him...for him, I could imagine abandoning everything just to stay in his arms forever.

His gaze fell on me. The wind tugged at his hair.

My heart raced faster. I lifted my chin, trying so hard to think of something witty or wise or amusing to say, to at least keep up the pretense of dignity. I was a queen, after all.

Then spread his arms.

I ran to him. Just like that, I was back against him, my face buried in his chest. He held me close, his muscular arms clasping me tight.

I melted. "We're going to make it in time," I whispered, tears choking me. Burrowing closer, I couldn't bear to look at him yet. All I could do was feel and breathe and hope. "You'll see."

He grunted. His arms tightened around me, lifting me off the ground. "Last night..." He nuzzled my cheek, tracing his nose up along the side of my face. "You were exquisite."

"Remember, you promised to get even with me. You can't do that if you kill me or if you die." I nudged him back, trying to smile up at him through the haze of tears. "Don't you dare give up hope. Please. Keep fighting. For both of us."

His mouth twitched a little, but he nodded. "Brash seer," he growled. A veil of tears shone in his eyes.

"Arrogant king."

"Always my queen." He pressed his forehead to mine.

We held one another. Then, though I flailed and screamed inside to stay in his arms, I pulled away. It was time for us to part.

I'd no sooner stepped out of his embrace when I felt the cold and the pain of our separation. One look into his eyes told me he felt it too. I steadied myself, knowing we were both on the verge of breaking as everyone watched.

"I'll take a rain check on that kiss," I said, forcing my voice to be steady. "You'll have to find me later and kiss me then."

He nodded slowly, setting his arms defiantly on his hips. "That seems to be two things I owe you then, Your Majesty."

"So you do. See to it that you honor your word." I dipped my head forward, turned my back, and marched toward the ship. Somehow, we would find a way through.

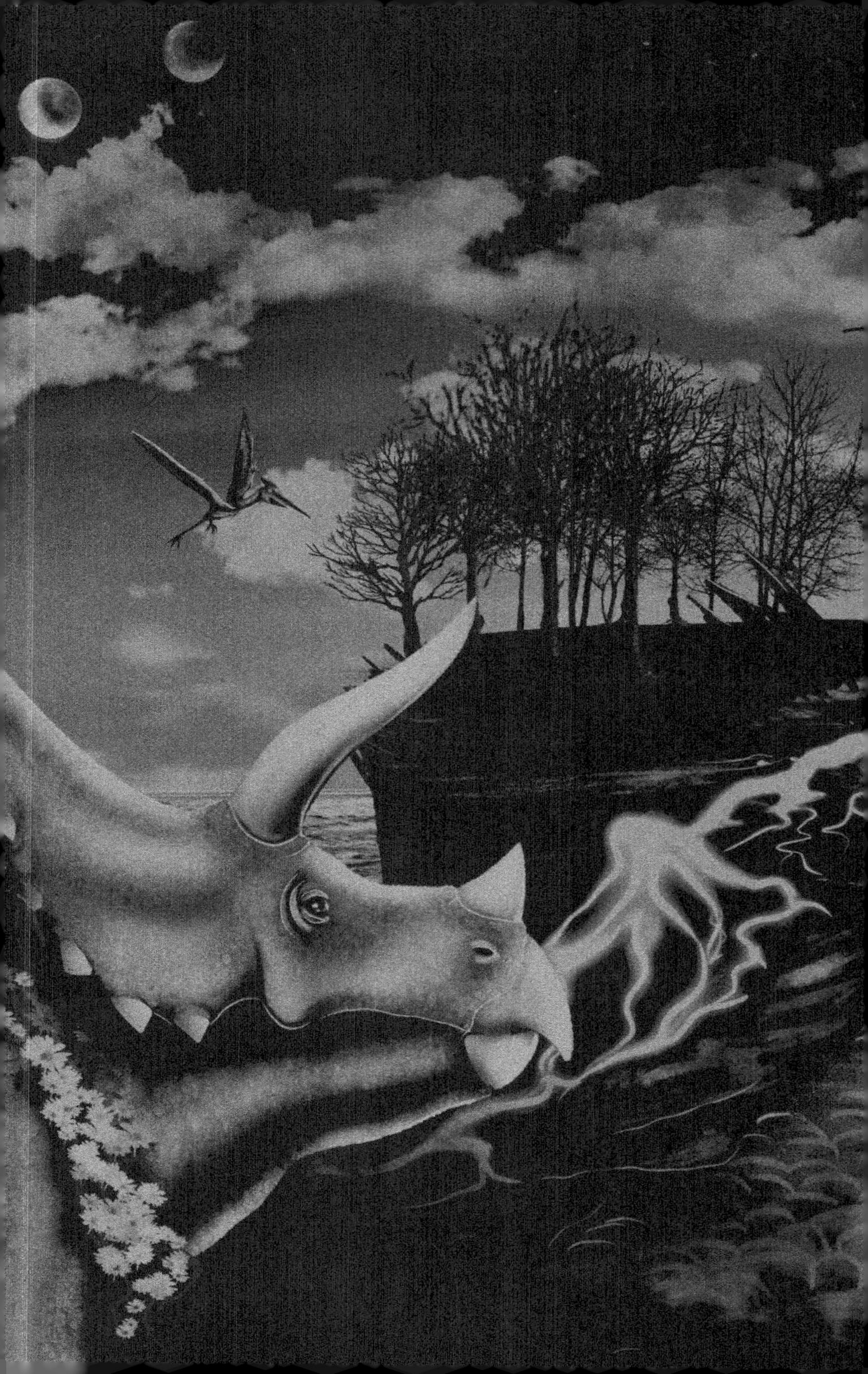

CHAPTER THIRTY-SIX: STELLA

It seemed to take hardly any time at all for the ship to pull away from the dock. I kept my eyes locked on Brandt, and he remained at the edge, flanked by his guard, watching. His tall, powerful form stood motionless as the wind caught in his hair. The charm remained steady, not turning yellow or even flickering in color.

I imagined his arms around me once more. Imagined being held as we celebrated the elimination of the Gola Resh and the saving of Sepeazia. Envisioned that kiss he'd promised me.

He remained there until we were out of sight, and I did not move from my spot as we left the harbor. We would be united again. We would stop the Gola Resh. We would survive. This was not the last time I would see him.

Once we left the harbor, Kine and five other warriors split into two groups. Each one took up a position between two of the rings set in the sides of the ship with a sort of rope harness in hand. They put these harnesses over their chests and then dove into the water, shifting into water serpents as soon as they entered the waves.

The ship glided forward, the warriors pulling us steadily

through the current. I stood at the prow, the wind whipping through my hair as we picked up speed. The sunlight danced on the waves, sparkling and glistening like millions of diamonds. The salty spray caught me directly in the face. A laugh bubbled up in my chest as memories of play and fun surfaced.

Elias leaned against the railing. "No ship faster than a Sepeazian ship. Especially with Sepeazian water serpent shifters drawing it."

I glanced at him, my eyebrow lifting. Our previous conversation flashed through my mind. "I suppose so."

My curiosity intensified. It was so strange. I still felt no stirrings of recollection when I looked at him. There was an absence about him but also, as I studied him, a comfort. It was easy to pass over him, easy to accept his presence.

Except now I was suspicious, or maybe I was just raw after what had happened between Brandt and myself. His last-minute change of mind still troubled me. Though he had come to the docks to bid us farewell, he had not explained what caused it. Nor had he seemed fully there.

Elias took a sidelong look at me and then reached into his pocket. His fingers fumbled in the dark-red fabric. "I apologize for how I ended our previous conversation. It was unfair." He removed the necklace with the charm he had given me. "Please. Forgive me for my affront, but I beg you to wear this. It's for your protection." He placed it in my palm, his fingers pressing along the charm and the moonstone.

I stared down at the necklace and the dark stone charm with the metal backing. I had been so overwhelmed with everything that had happened that I hadn't really considered it much. It weighed little more than a silver dollar in my palm.

"You gave this to me when you found me in Vegas. Why?"

He closed his eyes, scoffing. As he leaned his long arms against the railing, he stared out over the rolling sea. "It's a protective charm. At least in my people's tradition it is. Not likely that it works as well as I hope, but..." He shook his head. A muscle jumped in his jaw. "I know you had to grow up alone on Earth. Away from all of us. Away from everyone who cared about you."

"How exactly do you think this charm helps?" I did not move to put it around my neck, but I didn't set it aside either. "What makes this so significant?"

He bowed his head. "It's...it's just a protective charm. Probably nothing more than old superstition, but sephorite is supposed to help with the restoration of memories and ward against evil."

"And what is it you need to tell me?" My fingers curled over the necklace. That faint cherry scent returned. It was less fruit-like than I'd remembered. More like my favorite ChapStick when I was a teen. Pleasant as that smell was, Elias was not telling me all he should.

He shook his head. His tongue pressed at his lips. Then he turned his gaze back to mine. "You can ask Kine to verify anything I tell you. He won't be happy about my telling you, but it *is* the truth."

"Tell me, and I will verify it with him," I said, not allowing any weakness into my voice.

He stared down at the waves striking against the golden-brown hull. The fine spray coated his face, but he barely blinked. "I realized you were coming back during one of my meditations early on, that you were trapped on Earth. Brandt had mentioned during nearly insane ramblings that perhaps you might come back. He refused to let anyone claim your place as queen, but there was no evidence of it. I saw—I saw in the waters when you were born on Earth, and I set to learning how to get you back. The years passed slow and long. I am not powerful by any metric, but you..." His mouth twisted as he covered it. "You gave me another chance at life. I vowed to protect you, and I failed because you had to die.

Then, when I saw you in those waters, I realized I had a second chance. I saw how lonely you were. How hard life was for you."

"Others had it far worse." I dropped my gaze to the shimmering waters.

"That doesn't mean it wasn't hard." He remained silent for another beat, his gaze darting up to the cloudless sky above. "I couldn't be there for you. Couldn't help you. Couldn't do anything except look for a way to bring you back." He clenched his jaw. "I wasn't a member of the court. I convinced Kine to help me, and he agreed, but Brandt refused to let us go fetch you because we didn't have the cure for the curse. We'd waited fifty years. It was the first time we could get to you, so...we went anyway. We intended to bring you back to Brandt, but...you sort of ran and vanished for weeks."

"And he imprisoned you both?"

Elias nodded, arms still folded over the railing. His tunic and tabard had been dampened by the salt spray, but he did not move back. "I've rarely seen him so angry. He believed we'd condemned you, but it would have been even worse to abandon you there on Earth, to leave you alone in your misery. He was willing to leave you there for another fifty years."

My stomach knotted. "Brandt was trying to keep the curse from destroying me, from destroying this kingdom too. We didn't have answers. My coming back here forced the curse to resume."

It had put everyone at risk.

Elias shook his head. "We could have done so much more. You were trapped there. Abandoned. Isolated. No one to protect you. That was wrong." He lowered his head, the ragged sigh that followed merging with the hiss and call of the waves.

Maybe what he said came from a good place, but it angered me nonetheless.

"Everyone did what they could. My life on Earth was not the

easiest, but it wasn't the worst either. I survived, and I am here now. That is what matters."

The sharpness that had entered my voice did not sound like me. Or rather, it sounded more like another version of me. Perhaps the old Stella. The one who understood that being a ruler was about making hard choices. Or maybe the one who knew her husband loved her with all his heart and was doing the best he could.

Brandt's pleading gaze returned to my mind's eye, his voice so startlingly gentle and heartbroken.

Elias's jaw tensed, but he nodded. "You're a brave woman." His voice softened though he did not look at me.

"I'm not. Not really. I just love and trust my husband, and that is Brandt."

He nodded, his head still down. "It is not my intention to undermine your relationship with Brandt."

"My marriage."

"Your marriage," he conceded. "I just... You gave up everything already, Stella. If there's any chance for you to be happy—"

"There is no chance for that if Sepeazia is destroyed."

"You are worth so much more than Sepeazia," he said, his gaze still on the sea below us as the waves rushed and sliced along the hull. "Even if you were the only one who could be saved, it would be worth it."

"It would not be worth it to me." My voice sharpened. "I am not worth more than all of Sepeazia. I have hidden away and scraped to gather what I used to be. I am not worth more than anyone here."

His jaw tightened. "I don't know how to convince you that that is not so."

"You don't have to. It isn't even important to this discussion." I knotted my fist and pressed it against my chest, holding the necklace tight. My thumb stroked the smooth stone. "I am no more important than anyone in all this. Queen or not."

"Please. Hear me. You are to the people who love you," he said quietly, "and sometimes too much is asked of those whom we love."

A weight pressed within my chest. Not that I was a good lie detector, but he seemed to be speaking the truth.

I placed the necklace in the pocket on the side of my butter-yellow dress. "I am going to speak with Kine about everything and confirm what you have said. Then I will decide whether I will wear this."

He nodded. "Please do."

I slipped away, taking up a position on the other side of the mast, peering out to the east. At this point, we were far enough away from Sepeazia that I could see we had been beneath some sort of barrier.

The magical force that was draining us maybe? Whatever it was, it looked like a purple dome over the top of Sepeazia. My blood chilled, and I shivered despite the heat of the sun against my head. That sinister energy, I hadn't even noticed it really before we left, but now…how could anyone miss it?

A vague memory stirred in my mind. I recalled seeing this before. The day the sky had started to change color. The tang in the air. The dryness. The first day those dark marks in the land appeared.

It was odd regaining memory in this fashion, to brush against reminders and realize that there was more there than I initially realized.

The weight in my chest intensified. All of this…all of this would die because of the Gola Resh.

I remained there, staring out over the sea until Sepeazia vanished from my sight. After that, I went to help prepare food, another old task that my hands remembered well.

Sen, the ship's cook, didn't flinch at all, nor did he refer to me as "Your Majesty." He was an older man with an oiled and beaded grey-white beard. Unlike most I had seen, he wore only green and turquoise instead of incorporating black, red, blue, or gold. He simply grunted at me, indicated the pile of sweet potatoes, and offered me a small knife, as if my coming here to help was the most natural thing in the world.

I suspected that it was, and that comforted me. The wood-handled knife fit easily in my hand as I began on the sweet potatoes. The thin orange peelings dropped into the bucket while Sen prepared a large salmon-like fish.

The smell of the savory fish stew brought back even more memories of mundane activities. Despite the rocking of the ship and the splashing of the waves, I did not find my stomach unsettled even a little. The wild fresh air of the sea as well as the steady motion brought me only a sense of awareness that this was indeed where I belonged.

After a couple hours, Kine found me in the galley. Maybe it was my expression. Maybe he just knew me that well. Maybe it was obvious. But he nudged my arm and tilted his head forward, his other hand resting on the belt of his robe. "Do you need to talk about something, Bug?"

"Is now a good time?"

"Now is as good as any other," Kine said. "Can you spare us a moment, Sen?"

Sen shrugged. "She's the queen. Won't force her to stay until the potatoes're peeled."

"Very good of you, Sen." Kine cupped his hand beneath my elbow and drew me out to the narrow hall and then to one of the cabins. "So what's going on?"

"You know something's up, then?"

His mouth quirked. "Just a feeling." He opened the door to a cabin that, based on the dresses hanging on the hooks on the wall, was likely mine. It was small and cozy but clean.

I contemplated my words for a moment, then sighed. "Can you tell me who Elias is to me?"

Kine shrugged, his golden eyes contemplative. "Don't know. Just know he's been as loyal to you as blood."

"So you don't know him?"

He shook his head once more, his loose azure curls set off by the golden tan of his skin. "He said the life bond happened after the fall of Taivren. You and I weren't in touch as much then because our duties took us in separate directions for a time. You saved many people. Most likely his family was among them. He resembles the Lenven family in the Mylko and Kairos lines. I think he referenced them once."

It made me uncomfortable to think of anyone owing me such a life debt.

My arms folded tight beneath my breasts, I paced. "Elias said that you and he are the ones who wanted to get me and that Brandt opposed my return."

Kine swore under his breath and then rested his hands on the top of his head. His mouth pursed in disapproval. "Bug—" he started.

I held up my hand. "Listen, I'm not angry. I know Brandt loves me. I trust him. I trust you." My shoulders drooped as I curled up on the small green settee. "I remember Brandt begging me to not come back before you all had the answer."

Kine perched on the settee beside me. "Brandt wanted you back more than anything but only if it could be done without risking your life."

"So you and Elias came to get me." I didn't want to offer much more than that in case there was a hole to be sussed out.

Kine nodded. He rubbed the side of his head, then sighed. "Elias was the reason I found out you were even still alive, that you'd been reborn on Earth. He was determined to get to you as soon as possible, but no other method worked until the veil was thin on what you called Halloween."

"So he told you that I was alive. Is that the whole reason you trusted him?"

"Not the whole reason. See, I knew he couldn't hurt you. The tattoo, the one that indicates the life debt—it's magically formed. It's sacred. If he hurts you, he hurts himself. He was crushed when you died. I do remember him at the official funeral. It took months to get that set up because Brandt kept opposing it." He offered a small shrug. "When I saw the life mark on his forearm, I knew that Elias could be trusted to get you back."

My brow arched at this. Perhaps that did make sense.

My gut twinged. "But he and I never had... We weren't romantically involved, were we?"

"Not that I'm aware of." Kine chuckled. "Brandt rather dominated your focus once you two met, and before that, you were obsessed with your dual proficiencies."

"Do you think I should be worried about Elias?"

"Are you worried about him?" His brow lifted as he studied me. He looked at me with an expression that said he trusted my concerns more than the tattoo.

"I...I don't know. I'm worried. I feel like there's something I should feel when I speak with him, and I don't, and it bothers me that when I look at him, there's just nothing. No recall. No twinge. Just an awareness of his presence."

"Odd, but not impossible," he said, his arms still folded over his chest. "The bond you and I share is long-rooted. Obviously your bond with Brandt is intense and of a deeper level even than that of the family you grew up with. Did you mention your worries to Auntie Runa?"

"No. It didn't seem important given how much else I don't remember. I just...I feel like I'm missing something with him."

Kine nodded slowly. "He's a private individual. All I know for certain is that the very magic of Sepeazia binds him to protect you. Even if..." He frowned, shaking his head.

"Even if what?"

"The only advantage that he would have to press with you

would be that if Brandt died and you chose him as your husband, then he would gain the power of the king. There'd be no value in that, though, because Sepeazia is dying. He couldn't escape that. No one can. But he also couldn't really gain the full powers of the kingship because those powers mostly relate to shifting. Elias can't shift even with a ring. Not that the king has to be capable of it, but it's generally expected."

I scowled. "Why would I have to choose someone to replace Brandt?"

"To ensure the balance of the two kingdoms that make up Sepeazia. Brandt cultivated great disfavor in his refusal to declare you dead. It was seen as unreasonable and offensive, but he is one of the strongest water serpent shifters in Sepeazia and had enough support to hold them off even though it did get bloody sometimes."

"I wouldn't have asked him to do that," I said quietly, staring down at my arms. The fern-like patterns reminded me of waves dancing across my golden-brown skin.

Another memory resurfaced—Brandt's promise that we would go to Hadeon's palace and get my tattoos.

"I wouldn't have asked—"

"It doesn't matter. You are dearly loved. We all love you." Kine leaned closer, his hand brushing mine as the ship rocked. "I just don't want you to think that Brandt didn't care—"

"I know he did." I spoke firmly, startled and touched by the warmth I felt in this moment. My smile grew. "And you have cared about me as well."

He chuckled. "I love you, Bug. From the day you first walked into my life and became the perturbing hellion of a little sister I never knew I needed, I have loved you, and I would give anything for your happiness." His expression grew somber. "But if we're being honest, I fear that perhaps I have doomed you and everyone else by putting that love and the desire to see you home above all other considerations."

"How do you mean?" I frowned.

"Could we have found the cure or a way to open the portal before the fifty years?" His expression grew more downcast. "What if in trying to save you and bring you home, I simply condemned you? You didn't remember us. You didn't remember Brandt. You had a life on Earth."

"Setting everything else aside, the life I had on Earth...it was wrong." I gripped his hand in mine, startled at how raw he sounded. I hadn't realized how much this troubled him. "If I must die here, then it will be with the people I love."

"Oh, Bug, you could have found happiness in time. I'm sure of that, but I was selfish. I was so desperate to bring you back and make you a part of this family again that I didn't think about the very real possibility that doing so would put you and Sepeazia in more danger."

"If you and Elias hadn't brought me back, I'd have been stuck there for another fifty years." I ducked my head and pressed my forehead to his shoulder.

How odd was it that with Kine I wanted only to offer comfort and excuse what he had done and with Elias I wanted to remind him that I was not more important than the entire nation?

I shook my head at him. "Besides, you didn't know that the curse wouldn't have picked up again when you couldn't reach me. Then there wouldn't be any hope at all. Right now, we've got a little hope."

He hugged me tight, his lips pressing into a tight line as he pressed his forehead against the top of my head. "A little hope and a lot of knowledge. If I was wrong to bring you back...if I cut your life short—"

"No, there's nothing to forgive. At least not on my part." I pulled away, my hands against his shoulders. "You did what you did with the best of intentions, and I know you would never hurt me."

I did know that. I trusted him more than myself.

"And thank you for helping give me clarity," I added.

He really had helped me so much, even if I did still feel like I was being split in two.

I resumed helping Sen cook in the galley. We didn't talk at all, and that was fine. There was plenty for me to do, and it gave me time to think.

Come late afternoon, I sought out Elias. I found him at the rear of the ship, sketching in his book once more. He straightened and stood as soon as he saw me.

Though I nodded in greeting, I did not wait for him to speak. "Let me be clear. I accept your friendship, and I appreciate how you have fought for me and tried to help me get back here. I would not be here if not for you, so thank you, but our relationship will never be a romantic one. My heart belongs to Brandt. Can you accept that?"

"Yes." His expression did not even flinch. He simply met my gaze, his voice steady.

"And I do not ever want to hear again that you think I could do better than Brandt or anything that even remotely suggests that I should not be with him."

He started to nod, then hesitated.

"Is there something else that you need to tell me?" I raised an eyebrow.

Though he'd hesitated, he shook his head. "No." He dipped his head forward. His head remained down. "There is no valid justification I can share for my words. I can only ask your forgiveness."

I bit the inside of my lip. There was still nothing when I looked at him, nothing except what I had experienced with him in this life, and as Kine had said, Elias had been a faithful friend.

"So long as we understand one another."

"We do."

"Then I am glad to call you friend." I pulled the necklace

from my dress pocket and fastened it around my neck. "Thank you for all you have done for me, Elias."

"It has been my honor." He removed the bracer from his wrist and turned it up so that I could see the dark tattoo on his tanned skin. "My life is yours, and I will gladly give it if it will save you even if it is a fool's hope."

I paused. The marking on his arm had changed. There was now a skull woven within the design.

"What did you do?" I grabbed his wrist.

He twitched his broad shoulders. "If you die, I die."

"Elias, I never asked you to do that. Why did you do this?" I stared up at him in shock.

"I just needed you to know that I am doing everything that I do for you and in your best interest. I don't care what it costs me so long as you can thrive, Stella," he said hoarsely. "And while I may think you could have found someone better than Brandt—someone who would have saved you from Earth and the misery of your existence there—I will fight for whatever it is that you want. That includes fighting for you to be with Brandt. Whatever you want, Stella. I'll give all I have to give you the best."

With that, he strode away.

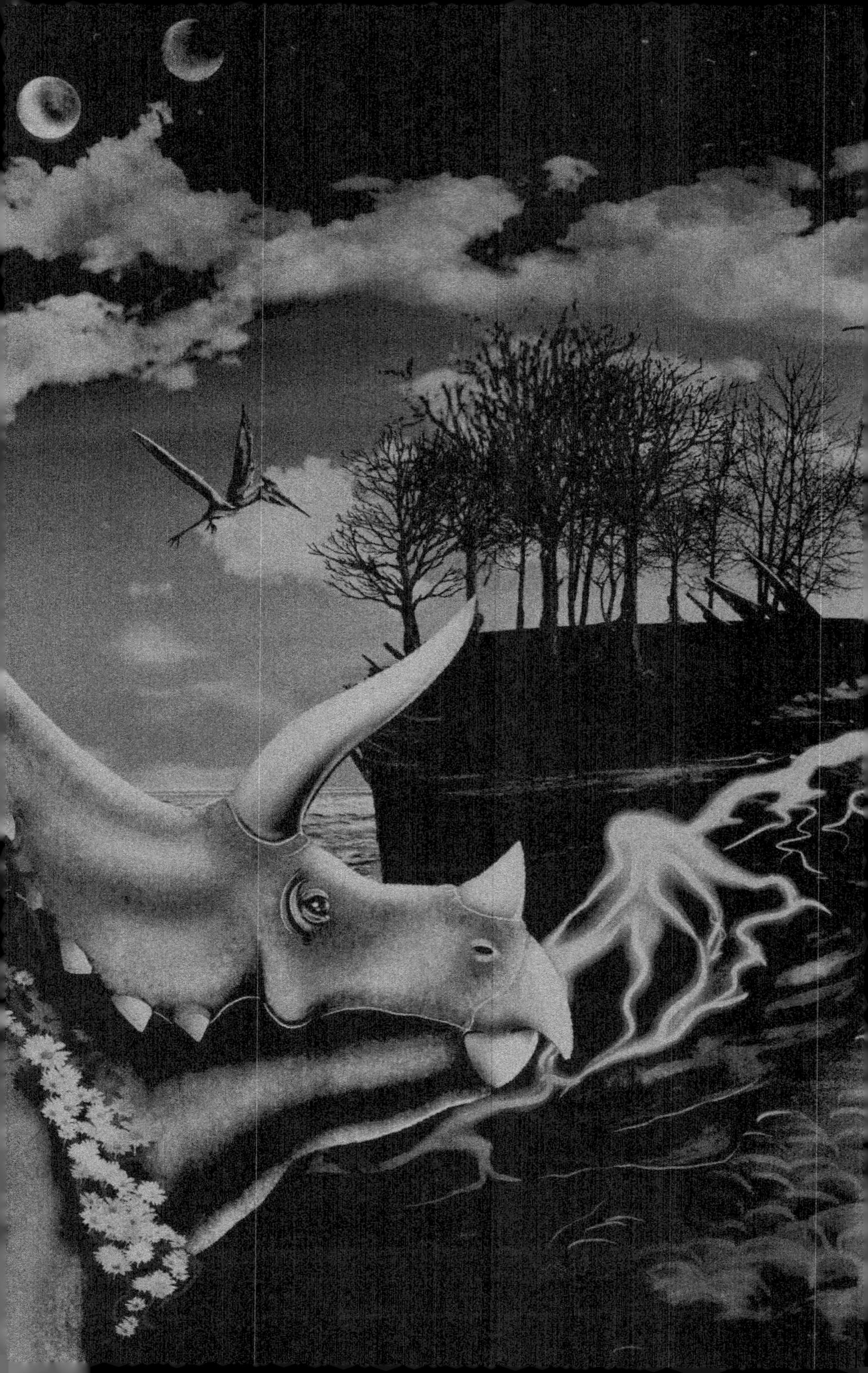

CHAPTER THIRTY-SEVEN: STELLA

*D*espite the darkness that loomed within my thoughts and the crushing timeline that we were up against, I found myself enjoying our voyage across the seas. The salt air filled my lungs and brought bouts of memories rushing back.

The sailors we traveled with apparently knew me as well, men and women who had perhaps traveled with me before. None made me feel awkward. They simply reintroduced themselves, sharing little snippets.

My time was split between sketching out my memories, assisting with tasks, working on my intuition, and practicing my shifting. At my suggestion, Kine even allowed me to become a water serpent and help draw the ship along. It felt good to be able to aid the speed of the ship. Even Elias mentioned that it seemed like we were moving faster than we anticipated.

Kine remained my faithful protector and steadfast brother. He even swam alongside me when I became a water serpent. Whenever the form slipped away, he darted down to seize me and bring me out from under the double-hulled ship. If my dress did not reform, he either brought me another or hid me from sight until I could get clothing. Each time, he coached me on how to keep my clothing intact without even once making me feel shamed and as I regained the finesse I once had.

The warm, surging waters covered and cradled me the way I'd always craved. The water serpent lungs gave me the strength I needed to delve into the depths, but it also allowed me time to practice.

Buttercup did not think much of my towing the ship. But she only lowed and stomped her feet when I was gone too long. Her distinct knock-knocking as I swam along soon became the signal I needed to resurface if my own muscles hadn't given out.

That night, the dreams returned, bold and vivid but fragmented, like streaks of oil paint across a white canvas. The need to be with Brandt intensified. Auntie Runa had warned me that it would be harder.

It was.

It hurt now like an infected wound, but it had been worth it for that night.

I couldn't bring myself to regret the closeness Brandt and I had shared. What I regretted more than anything was that we had not had more time together. But there would be more time in the future. I promised myself that.

If sheer strength of will could make us go faster, then we had it. Whatever good there was in the world seemed to favor us. Kine whispered to me in the morning that we were making excellent time and might even reach the Wild Lands early.

Halfway through the second day, we neared our destination. A heavy fog embraced the island, creating shadowy silhouettes of the jagged cliffs and dense forests. The craggy shores offered countless hiding places for predators and sentient enemies. The fog grew thicker as we approached, blanketing the island in an impenetrable haze. I strained my eyes, searching for any sign of danger, my nerves on edge.

The sailors worked quickly and quietly, faces grim. Even Kine was subdued, constantly scanning our surroundings as the captain guided us to a rugged dock stained with algae, heavy slick weeds wrapped around portions of the coarse wood. Dark fish wove in and out of the shadows, most no larger than my forearm.

"How much do you remember?" Kine asked. "Do you remember Lorna and Arjax?"

"A little. Like vague shapes. I remember that the Wild Lands are always changing, and Lorna and Arjax aren't like us. They're Vawtrians, full or true shapeshifters. Their ancestors are the ones who gave us the rings so some of us can shift. We're the 'little cousins.'" The facts rattled off my tongue, not really hiding my nerves.

"Right." He squeezed my shoulders, but that cautious timbre remained in his voice. "There are all kinds of monsters here. Most of them are large. This side of things and this time of year..." He shrugged. "Terror birds and boars, the five-tusked kind. Basilisks farther in. Seven-clawed raptors, of course. Magic changes it up a fair bit depending on who is here, but even that isn't always consistent."

"So basically, danger." I moistened my lips.

"Yeah, that's the sum of it." He gave me a worried look. "You sure you don't want to wait on the ship until we find them? We can lead them back here, and then you can talk. I didn't know them as well as you, but they trust me."

I shook my head, my mouth tightening. "No. I don't want to risk wasting the time. We got here early. We're getting this done as fast as possible. I want to be through the Keening Pass today if possible."

He chuckled, but the worried expression remained in his eyes, darkening his golden eyes. "If we don't have the spear by mid-afternoon, we won't be leaving until morning. There's no way into the Keening Pass after that. Not until dawn, but don't let it trouble you. We're over a day ahead of what we'd planned. Brandt's still got a chance."

"Yes, well, let's not squander it," I muttered as the crew set the wooden ridged plank walkway down from the ship to the dock. The pieces slid into place with a heavy thud and a jarring knock.

Kine had given me weapons, a short sword and a dagger this time. Both were strapped to the belt of my dress, even though I wasn't convinced I knew how to wield them. They were there in case I needed them and my water serpent shifting didn't work. Best to be safe. I pressed my hand to the hilt of the short sword, reveling in the cool metal and smooth leather of the hilt.

With Kine by my side and Elias following close behind, I strode down the gangplank. My footsteps reverberated through the wood, echoing over the water. A large carp-like fish poked its whiskered snout above the waters, tasting our arrival.

The coniferous forest remained shrouded in mist, the jagged cliffs looming above us in all their dark-grey and dark-red glory. Gnarled tree roots snaked across the ugly beach of pebble-packed earth. This place felt ancient and forbidding, as unforgiving as the Gola Resh. The tendrils of mist coiled about smooth grey-blue stones and sharp coarse white rocks alike, but the gloom seemed all the more pronounced as it reached the tree line. This forest was something primordial.

Buttercup tromped down the walkway, her strides purposeful and regal. She tossed her head, unperturbed by the eeriness of this place. She gave me a small nudge with her grey-beaked snout. The dock creaked a little bit but did not shift.

"Yeah. We're here," I murmured, stroking her front horn. "We're here, baby." I kissed her cheek and guided her forward.

We used to come to this place all the time. Brandt and I had made love in some of these groves and nooks. A shiver traced down my spine, the memory of his lips against my skin and his teeth grating over my shoulder and throat as we pressed against one another vivid.

We walked down the dock. The old boards groaned in response to our weight, especially once both Kine's and Elias's parasaurs were set free, but still, the old dark wood did not shift. Whoever had built this and reinforced it had known we would be coming with multi-ton beasts of burden, and we came here with these creatures intentionally. The larger beasts of burden made us less tempting targets for the smaller predators. Even larger predators would think twice about a pack of such size and scale.

Fog curled about the island in great loose formations. The air had grown chillier as well, thick with humidity that clung to the skin. Maybe not all of the pale mist was fog. Some of it might be smoke. Guttural roars and unearthly shrieks echoed up from the shrouded interior.

I shuddered.

Most of the crew remained behind on the ship except for a couple whom Sen sent out to find provisions "just in case." An old tradition and a wise one. Who knew what treasures or even just supplies this strange place held?

More memories spattered through my mind as we paced toward the tree line, random factoids. Moss with red flecks was poisonous. Lorna and Arjax had multiple camps. Basilisk venom was a powerful reagent.

I noticed then that I was walking with Buttercup on my left. Kine and Elias had their parasaurs on their left as well. Someone had taught us that.

I looked to Kine as an especially loud howl pierced the air. "Where do we look first?"

"One of their base camps is up on Bald Ridge near the hot springs," Kine said, gesturing north. "There's a white stone marker that shows the main way if you know how to find the paths. If we keep walking, they'll catch our scent sooner or later. There's none better than Vawtrians when it comes to catching scents."

Elias chuckled darkly. "Part of what sometimes makes them more beast than beast shifter."

Kine shook his head, then turned to me, his gaze serious. "Just remember, whatever you do, don't call them skinchangers. That's a big slur for them. They're shapeshifters."

Immediate revulsion filled me. "I'd never call them that. They're our friends."

"Good." Kine nodded, his posture relaxing. He then glanced around and gestured toward an opening in the tree line where the trees most resembled redwoods. "That way."

"Seems as good as any to me," Elias said.

My seer instincts said nothing except to keep moving.

We strode into the ancient-looking forest. Strips of black moss clung to some of the trees like rotten garlands. The mist coiled about trunks as if it were a living being. Somehow, it seemed that the fog even muffled our footsteps yet made our breaths louder, or maybe it was my imagination.

As soon as we were fully within the forest, though, that seemed inescapable. My blood thundered in my ears. It smelled of old water, ancient wood, rotting greens, and decaying bones, but there was comfort in the scent. This was a place that had existed long before any of us, perhaps longer than anywhere else in this world. Likewise, it would exist long after we had passed. Even if Sepeazia fell, it would go on.

Deeper and deeper we went into the forest, following an invisible path or Kine's instincts. The sunlight filtered through the trees, grey and silver with pale bits of gold. Up ahead, the trees thinned out into a clearing. I could see the glimmer of a frothy river.

Kine held up a hand, his eyes narrowing.

I drew closer to him, leaning toward his ear. "What's wrong?"

"Trap," he murmured.

As if summoned, a bloodcurdling shriek split the air. Giant shadows erupted from the fog, circling us and darting just close enough for me to get a glimpse. They were nearly as tall as a man with cruel hooked beaks and claws larger than an ostrich's. Terror birds.

My heart clenched. Buttercup bellowed her disapproval, shaking her head and stamping her left hoof.

"Ambush," Elias growled.

"Keep close," Kine responded. He leaned forward and sent up a reptilian call, a coughing grunting sound that was far larger than him.

The terror birds backed away. The largest snapped its black and gold beak at the air.

"Grip your ring and roar," Kine whispered to me, gripping my hand and guiding it into a fist.

I balled my fists up tighter and obeyed. A great roar reverberated out of me, somewhere between a dragon, a lion, and an angry woman. It shook me to my core.

Kine roared as well, and the terror birds shrieked in surprise, flapping their enormous wings as they retreated several feet. The largest, a brute with dark blue plumage and grey stripes on its back, shook its feathers and stomped forward. It cocked its head, its muscular neck bobbing.

Shafts of grey sunlight speared through the canopy above, casting everything in an ethereal glow. The mist swirled around our feet like spectral dancers. The terror birds had us surrounded. Kine and Elias roared again. I joined in again.

It wasn't deterring the birds. The smallest one was easily six feet, the tallest probably closer to twelve. They scratched and clawed at the earth. Buttercup snarled in response. She stamped her feet against the ground and snorted.

"It's all right, girl," I whispered to her. "I've got your back."

She huffed, giving me a dark expression that suggested she had my back rather than the other way around.

I cut my eyes at her and summoned my water serpent form. It was much heavier to be a water serpent on land than in the sea, but already, I felt so much stronger. A terror bird lunged in at me, and I snaked back just in time.

Elias swept his quarterstaff around and clubbed one on the side of the head.

Kine had also transformed. He struck and snapped one of the terror birds in his jaws, dropping it to the ground.

Mimicking his pose, I lunged at the next one.

My aim was poor. A grey-green terror bird leaped at my back, and its beak dug into my spine. Pain erupted through me like branches of fire, burning a path up my back and across my lungs.

Kine launched himself at the terror bird as Buttercup charged at a second.

I flattened and then coiled myself inward. The wounds were healing. They itched as the flesh knit back, creeping and crawling, but they healed!

I snapped once more at the nearest terror bird. My jaws caught only air. Feathery bastard was fast.

Buttercup took down the one at my left.

More and more circled, darting in with snapping beaks. I bit one and nearly took a beak in the eye before I recoiled.

Ihlkit! They were slick.

Heavy footsteps jarred the ground, sending out ripples in the glassy puddles and jarring the little stones. A dark-orange spinosaurus pounded into the clearing, followed by a second dark-red one.

The parasaurs and Buttercup dropped back, flattening their necks and bellowing. Their tails snapped out like defensive weapons, but the spinosauruses lunged at the terror birds. Their roars reverberated through the ancient forest as they charged our attackers, their massive frames like impenetrable walls of scales and muscle.

The largest terror bird screeched in defiance, unfurling its wings in a show of dominance, but it was too late. Razor-sharp teeth glinted in the filtered light. Massive jaws closed, feathers puffing into the air, bones crunching. The spinosauruses had the terror birds outmatched in both size and ferocity. Feathers and blood flew as each spinosaurus dropped a corpse and seized another. The remaining terror birds scattered, their claws cutting the dark earth and flinging up pebbles and soil.

I fell back, jaw agape, preparing to run. There was no chance we could fight off two beasts like that.

But Kine hadn't retreated. He'd dropped back into his human form, his hands resting against his thighs as he shook his head. "It took you two long enough."

Elias dropped off his parasaur and ran alongside me. When he looked at me, his dark-blue eyes were soft and comforting. He waved his hand as if to indicate it was all right despite his rapid breaths.

The dark-red spinosaurus snapped the neck of one of the attacking terror birds and turned on Kine. "Well, well, did we miss your announcement informing us you'd be stopping by?" a gravelly male voice boomed from the spinosaurus's jaws.

The dark-orange one laughed, tilting her head as a much softer but no less intimidating voice rang out. "They thought they would just drop in."

I released the water serpent form as well. My dress started to fling off this time, but it didn't vanish at least. Clutching it in place, I stared at the two. "Arjax? Lorna?"

The dark-orange spinosaurus's amber eyes widened. She dropped forward, her form collapsing into a powerful woman's shape.

Unlike me, she had no difficulties maintaining not only her clothing but the intricate beads and feathers in her hair and bracelets and bracers on her wrists. She was seven feet tall with a muscular yet feminine build, wearing leather and cotton in all shades of brown and ecru. Her deep-brown skin had reddish undertones mirrored in her red-black eyes and contrasted with her golden-brown hair. An intricate silver cuff marked her left ear—a lithok, a piece of jewelry that marked her expertise in shifting.

Lorna.

Yes, of course.

The dark-red spinosaurus dropped, becoming a man who was easily seven feet tall, perhaps seven and a half. His thick hair was bound back in multiple braids, woven with great care, leather thongs securing it in place. His dark eyes glittered, sharp and insightful against his dark olive-brown skin. He also had feathers tied and stuck at random in his hair, as if he had just put them in there rather than having had to shift and reform with all these little details.

Arjax.

How could I ever have forgotten these two?

Before I could do anything more than gawk, Lorna stooped down, her face almost directly in mine. "Crespa, look! It's Stella! Lookit her!" The enormous woman seized me up like a rag doll and spun me around, laughing.

I gasped, laughed, and nearly collapsed as she set me down. I'd barely caught my balance when Arjax grabbed me in an even tighter bear hug.

"You're back, girl!" His deep voice boomed in my ear, louder than Buttercup's bellows. He set me down on the ridge and slapped me on the back so hard I nearly fell off. "And you don't look a day over—is it sixty? Seventy?" He cast a helpless look at Lorna who was busy hugging and manhandling Kine. "Well, whatever your age is, you haven't changed since the last time we saw you. Where's that veskare of yours? Did you come alone?"

Veskare. I recognized that word. It was their word for their mate. The most beloved of all.

I set my hands on my waist and nodded, trying to catch my breath. "Brandt is in Castle Serpentfire, but he sends his best." I noticed them glancing at Elias. "And this is Elias. He's a friend of ours and one of the main reasons I'm back."

"I already know who you are," Elias said, stepping forward as he offered his hand. "I'd rather not be picked up and shaken if that's all right."

Laughing good-naturedly, Arjax seized Elias's hand in a strong grip. "Fair enough. Good to meet you. You're an Ogniskoan who fights with an oak quarterstaff and smells of cedar." His brow twitched. "And your hair is in a single color?" He glanced between Elias and me.

Elias gave a small smile and then lifted the binding on his arm. "Life debt to Stella. I honor her in her Kropelkian traditions."

I hadn't thought about that aspect of him. But now that he mentioned it, I realized he was right. Most—maybe almost all?—Ogniskoans dyed portions of their hair while Kropelkians did not. And once that had been a source of great dispute between us. I cleared my throat, shaking my head before I could get distracted. "And I am deeply grateful to both Elias and Kine for their kindness and faithfulness to me. But this isn't a social visit, I'm afraid."

"It isn't?" Arjax asked, his heavy brow lifting.

Kine hung limply in Lorna's arms, half sliding out of his outer robe. "You can set me down any time, darling."

Lorna raised her eyebrow and shifted positions so she held him bridal style. "You prefer it this way, baby blue?"

"Much better." He gave her a thin smile, then crossed his arms. "But you should listen to Stella. This is important."

I nodded, their eyes burning into me now. All had fallen silent. "I am so sorry, but we have come for the spear. We need it as soon as possible so that we can return and destroy the Gola Resh's power."

"The spear?" Arjax folded his arms over his barrel of a chest, the feathers in his hair rustling in the wind. Lines furrowed his brow. "The one you and Brandt gave us in tribute of service or the one for spearing electric bog eels?"

"Tribute of service, I think. Whichever one is the one made from a third of the Babadon's heart." I winced. Recollection told me that Lorna and Arjax were difficult to offend, but something in the way they looked at one another and the tension in their posture alarmed me. "Please," I said, extending my hands. "It is no insult to either of you. We are grateful for all that you have done for our people, for giving us the gift of our shifting, but we desperately need it so that—"

Arjax held up his hand with a sharp snap of his wrist as he shook his head. "There is no offense given or taken. The spear is yours, little cousin. The only problem is...we don't have it."

My heart sank. It was as if someone had struck every member of our group.

Elias staggered back, falling against Buttercup. "That's not possible," he whispered, his eyes white-rimmed. "You must—you must have it! Everything will fail without it."

Arjax shook his head, his long thick braids swaying with the movement. "Now, now, not all hope is lost. We just have to get it back. It's here in the Wild Lands, probably not even that far. It's just we lost it in our last scuffle. If it means saving you and Brandt and the rest of our little cousins, mark our words, we'll find it. It'll just take some time."

"Time is the one thing we don't have," I said, my voice shaking. "We've only got a few more cycles before Brandt is lost forever. Please. Tell me you know where it is."

Arjax and Lorna exchanged glances.

Arjax bobbed his head and shrugged. "Possibly. How much time can you give us?"

"We have to leave in the morning," Kine said, still draped in Lorna's arms.

"We'd prefer sooner than that. In the next couple hours," I said firmly, knowing every hour counted.

Arjax grunted. His gaze drifted up into the sky and then back around to all of us. "Bit of a tall order, but we'll make it work anyway. Come on. We're going mischief hunting."

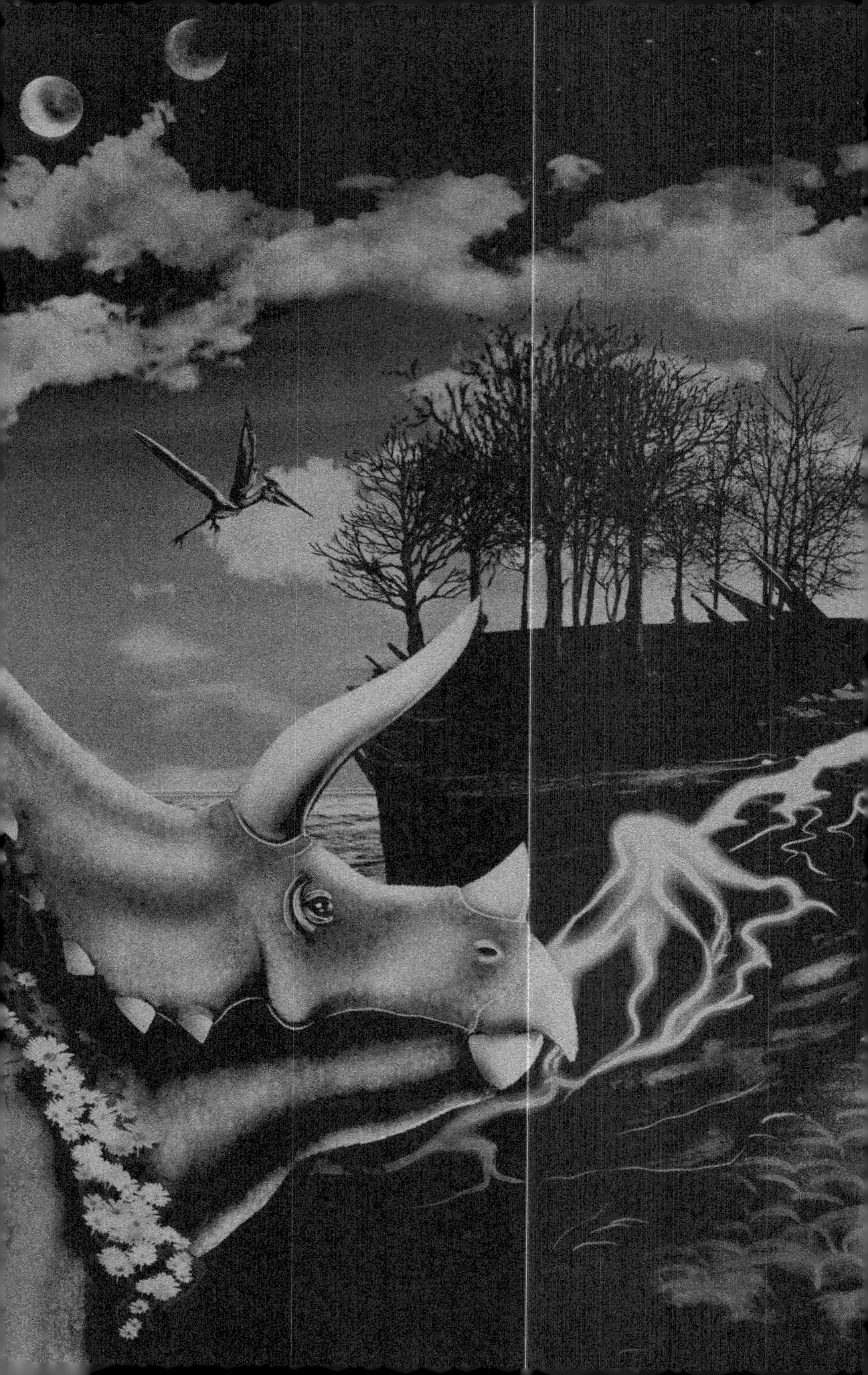

CHAPTER THIRTY-EIGHT: STELLA

he energy around us changed as soon as Lorna and Arjax agreed that we were, in fact, going to get the spear back. My heart beat faster, my breaths lightening. It was like running into old friends from school, only to find that they were even more fun and full of life than when you last saw them.

I explained swiftly what had happened, with interjections from Kine and Elias.

"Curse is moving again." Lorna deposited Kine back on the ground and set her arms akimbo. Her hands balled into fists. She scowled. "Well, let's get the spear. You can tell us all about what's new."

"Yes, little cousins." Arjax scooped the air with his arms. "I don't know if we can accomplish this in the next couple hours, but we'll do our best."

"Where do you think the spear is?" I asked.

"Basilisk nest. Almost definitely." Lorna shook her head, her mouth twisted in a wry smile. "Mischief."

My eyes widened. Mischief. That was a name. The basilisk's name?

"And lucky for you, we're on the hunt for her anyway," he said. "Friends are coming, friends in need of basilisk venom. Not to mention it's time. She stole the spear about two weeks ago. Loves shiny things, that girl does. Almost certainly took it back to her nest with all the other treasures she steals. Once we're done gathering venom, we'll take the spear. You three can head back to our camp and wait for us there if you like."

"Would it go faster if we accompanied you?" I banded my arms tight around myself, my fingers digging into my biceps. "Maybe there's a way we could help?"

"You want to be the bait?" Arjax's heavy eyebrow arched. Then he guffawed, hands resting on his muscular stomach.

"Would it help you get the spear faster?"

"Stella!" Kine shot me a ferocious glare.

I shot him a glare right back.

Ihlkit, if I had any doubt that Kine was my brother, adopted or otherwise, it was gone now. He had a way of saying my name in that disapproving tone. It wasn't the first time he'd chided me, but this time, it certainly held an added edge.

"Please don't be bait." Elias pinched the bridge of his nose.

"Answer my question," I said, my gaze fixed on Arjax.

Arjax exchanged looks with Lorna, then burst into another deep, hearty laugh. "If you're that determined, there might be a couple ways you could help it go faster."

"What will it require?" Kine gave me a sidelong glance but spoke in a serious tone, obviously willing to go along with whatever it was. He seemed resigned to accept that this was the best way. A weight hung over him as if this wasn't easy.

"Doesn't matter. If our participation will help and speed up the process, then we'll do it. I'll do it. I'll do anything, even if means being bait," I declared.

Arjax chuckled, shaking his head. "Well, you'd best be careful where you're making offers like that. Lucky for you, we're basically kin and wouldn't hold it against you. Come on, Lorna.

Let's take them to the spot." His voice wobbled and deepened as his body stretched and strained, dark-red scales emerging and new muscles and bones forming. A powerful fin erupted from his back as his face lengthened, a long snout filled with jagged teeth jutting out.

Lorna transformed as well, her own process far swifter and smoother, her eyes turning reptilian and amber at the very end.

Buttercup tilted her head, utterly unimpressed with the spinosaurus forms that both shifters assumed. A fierce toss of her head assured me she could take both if necessary.

The two parasaurs took a couple more moments to sniff and adjust to the presence of the false apex predators.

Elias remained beside his parasaur, shaking his head. "I just hope this doesn't make them comfortable around predators."

His parasaur's nostrils flared, and she bobbed her head.

"Our smell is different on purpose," Arjax responded. "Your beasts won't confuse us with the real thing."

I couldn't smell much beyond the scents of dark mud, fresh blood, rotting plants, and something a little more bitter.

"Are there really spinosauruses here?" I raised an eyebrow, not certain whether I was concerned or intrigued or both.

"Oh, yes," Lorna said, "but they don't come into basilisk territory that often, especially not a big gal like Mischief."

"Most don't go anywhere near Mischief. She's ornery," Arjax said.

"That's putting it mildly." Lorna clicked her tongue.

I climbed up on Buttercup's back, giving her a reassuring scratch along the top of her frill. She lowed again. "Yeah, I know, baby," I said with another pat. "We're going as swiftly as we can."

We were going to get that spear. Then we were headed back. We would finish before nightfall.

We started along the rocky path, single file. Kine brought up the rear while I rode along behind Lorna and Arjax. The two peppered us all with questions about our homes and families as well as what was happening with the curse and the Gola Resh. We brought them up to speed as best we could.

"How do you intend to slay the basilisk?" Elias asked from the back. The terrain inclined upward. "That's a fairly tall order."

"Oh, we're not slaying her," Lorna said, glancing at him with a sidelong grin that was quite perturbing in spinosaurus form. "We're catching her and milking her venom. She's an old girl, so her venom has special properties."

"Milking a basilisk," Kine repeated, the trepidation apparent in his voice. "Why?"

"Sounds like that's more dangerous than just slaying one," Elias said.

I hated to admit that I agreed. Somehow, it hadn't occurred to me that we were going to leave her alive.

"Definitely is," Arjax responded. "You can slay a basilisk from a distance if you know what you're doing. Dragon fire dart right to the eye will pierce the brain and end one at two hundred yards if your aim is good enough, but Mischief's an ornery, angry old woman, and we aren't going to dart her with anything. We're building a pinch trap. Won't hurt her, but we've got to lure her in, bind her eyes shut, and then milk the venom."

Arjax ran us through the basics as we moved through the forest, pausing when his and Lorna's footfalls were too loud, or repeating himself if they crushed a log or boulder. Not only did we have to lure Mischief into the valley, but we were going to have to wear her out and then spring the trap to secure her. All of this would have to be done without looking her in the eye or getting caught by any of the venom leaking from her fangs or on her breath.

"And keep an eye out for the mirror-tail foxes," he added. "They run with the basilisks and help them spot and distract prey. They're not real dangerous on their own, but they can mess things up. Besides, we really don't want to hurt them.

They're basically her family. Or her pets. Depends on how you look at it."

Once we reached the spot, they set to work. The pinch trap didn't take long for them to put together, and Arjax dug out a deep trench within seconds just by turning into a massive badger. Lorna put Buttercup and the parasaurs over into another little clearing a safe distance away.

Lorna smashed up a blue pill and sprinkled it in a circle. "Rels," she explained simply. "They keep predators at bay so they won't come near your pack beasts." She picked up some and wiped it on Elias's shoulder. "They won't come near you either. You call out and whistle about what you see, right? Keep it simple, and don't make any big flailing moves even if you are safe back here. Basilisks hunt based on movement and sound."

Arjax strode along the edge of the valley, scanning up and down. Up above, birds called. Some darted and soared on the wind currents. The humidity intensified here. My hair tangled and curled around my neck despite the strap I'd used to tie it back. Horrible snarls awaited me tonight, but if that was the worst I endured, then I would be lucky.

"So what is the plan exactly?" Kine asked, stopping at the edge of the valley's center where the lush grasses gave way to sludge and muck. Boulders rose at intervals like rounded teeth.

I cringed. The mud down here had an unpleasant odor. Some sort of biting bile burned my eyes, worse than excrement and vinegar. I sank down almost ankle deep.

"Lorna and I are going to wear Mischief out. Then we'll lure her into the center, and we'll spring the trap that'll hold her in place. You two..." He gestured to Kine and me. "You just keep those mirror-tails off our backs. There'll be six. Trap them in that trench over there. Keep your head down around the basilisk and make sure your scales are tight if you shift. It helps if you keep your gaze soft so you can scan the area and not focus directly on anything. She's getting old anyway, so her vision isn't as good, which means she's not as fast to paralyze folks, but don't get sloppy. It's important that we don't kill any of the mirror-tails or wound them. They're sneaky little bastards, though, especially when Mischief is in a bad state like this. Just remember they're always trying to trick you so they can flush you out for her to catch."

Another plan that was all about tiring someone out. Great. I could manage that.

Arjax and Lorna put up bait stations at the end of the valley right before the mud slick. The trench was about fourteen feet deep by ten feet. The ground at the bottom was the same slick mud.

Each of us got into position. The air grew thicker and heavier. I crouched behind a boulder near the edge of the ridge that led up out of the valley, my hand resting against the coarse surface.

The air thickened. Something called deeper in the forest.

Then I glimpsed it. A mirror-tail fox.

The silver fox was approximately the size of a golden retriever but with distinctly foxlike features, including a slender jaw, a triangular face, and high, pointed ears. Iridescent bands of color fanned out across the dual tails, catching the light and sending out prisms.

Another one appeared. Then another. They were bigger than I'd expected, and their eyes glowed an unnatural blue.

I glanced over at Kine, who nodded. He'd spotted them as well. If they were here, then the basilisk would be close behind.

Arjax and Lorna had disappeared completely. Whether into the edges of the forest or into another form entirely, I wasn't sure.

The mirror-tail foxes crept forward, ears erect and twitching. They walked with such delicate grace. Part of my brain said they were just puppies. I wanted to pet one! The smarter part of me knew that they were dangerous predators in a symbiotic relationship with a ferocious basilisk. Petting them was off the table.

Lorna had told us to wait for the mirror-tails to either make an aggressive move or for one of us to spot the basilisk before we started gathering them into the trench. If we caught them before the basilisk made her showing, she might realize what was going on and upset the plan.

The foxes moved forward. Three pairs. Sparks glistened on the striping along their tails. They darted out. One pair investigated a bait trap. Another pair wandered the perimeter. The third stopped across from me. Their tails twitched.

Elias gave a sharp whistle. My gaze snapped up and around when something shifted and rustled, catching my attention.

There she was. The basilisk.

The enormous serpent was at the valley's edge directly across from me, hovering over a rich blue flower of some sort.

I froze.

Wait. Wait. No. That wasn't right.

I was looking right at the basilisk directly head-on…and I was fine?

No.

Those two foxes had their tails up, forming a frame. The basilisk had lined up with it perfectly.

They were directly across from me. That was my hair in the reflection. Ihlkit! The little bastards had tricked me. The basilisk was right over my head!

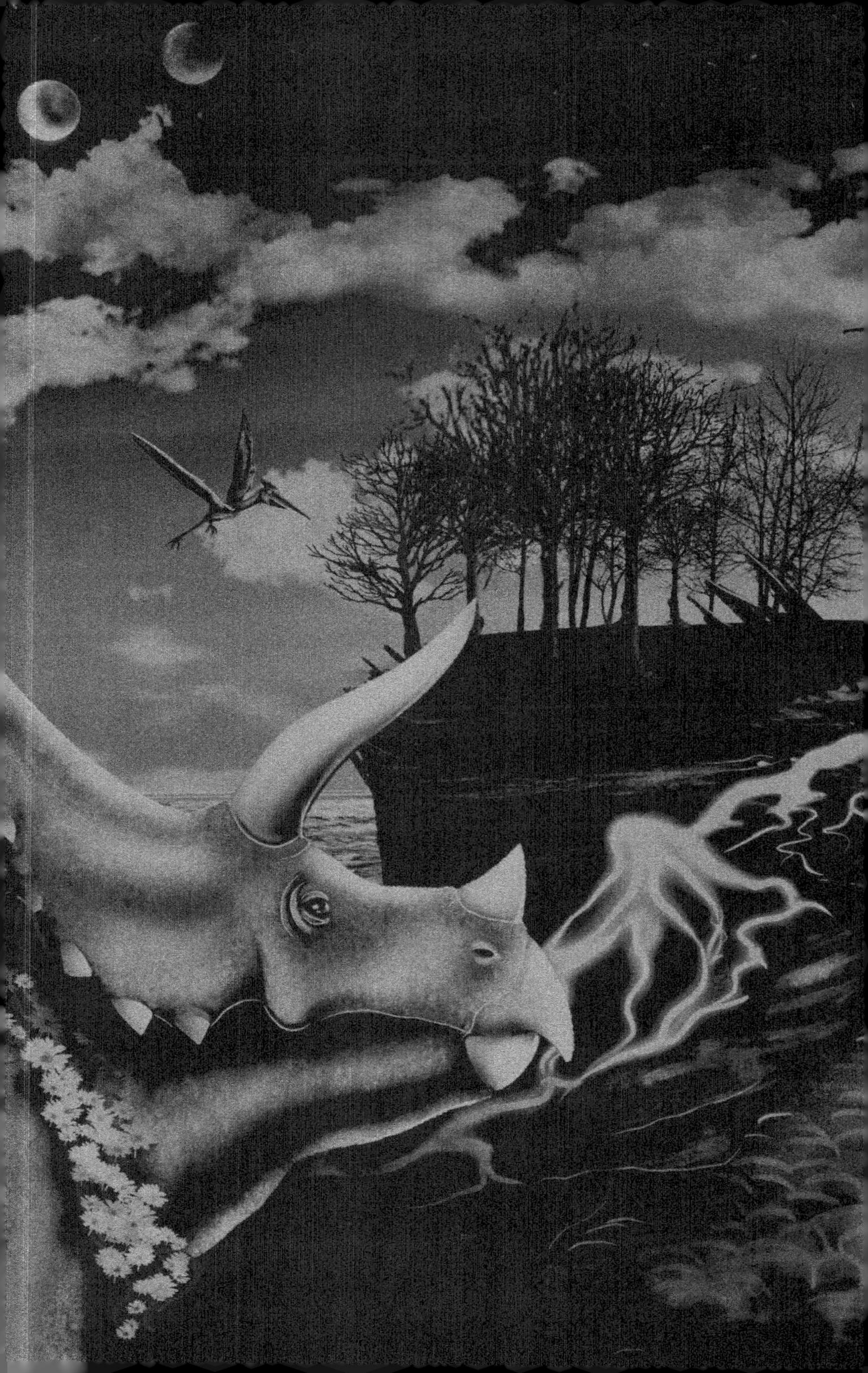

CHAPTER THIRTY-NINE: STELLA

My eyes widened, and my mouth went dry. Had she seen me?

No. Of course not. If she had, I'd be dead.

My breaths remained locked in my chest, my body rigid.

The mirror-tails directly across from me continued to hold their tails out, creating the mirror illusion. From this angle, I had an exceptionally good look at her. My gaze hinged upward.

It was much more terrifying from this vantage point.

The basilisk did not appear to have noticed me yet as she loomed out over the rock shelf that led to the valley. Her scaly underbelly was within arm's reach. Her green-scaled hide was weathered and scarred with patches where the scales were duller than usual. A few of them appeared damaged. On the top of her head was a horned ridge similar to a crown. Just at the base of that crown was a white dot the size of my fist.

Her tongue flicked out as she tasted the air and swung her head back and forth. The low hiss that emerged from between those dagger-like fangs vibrated through the air into every cell of my body.

I held my breath as I glanced around. The mirror-tailed

foxes continued their sinister illusion, framing the basilisk's reflection so she appeared to be across the valley.

Kine stared at me from the other boulder, his hand lifted as if to encourage me to stay put. Right. Like I was going to run with the basilisk right on top of me.

The basilisk continued to slide forward, its body suspended in the air over me. She paused, flicking out her forked purple tongue.

The wind changed. Oof. She smelled worse than the mud, acidic and foul.

Where were Lorna and Arjax?

Elias whistled again.

Yes, I knew the basilisk was right over me.

A pair of the foxes ran up near me and barked. The basilisk tilted her head and then reared up. The foxes twined their tails into a frame. Energy arced between the iridescent strips on their tails within that frame, forming a reflection. A reflection of me and the ground beneath the basilisk.

The basilisk's head swung around, those burning yellow eyes fixing in my direction. Another hiss rumbled through her chest as her lips curled back, exposing rows of dagger-like teeth. Venom dripped from her fangs.

My muscles tensed, my body begging me to run.

This wasn't what I had envisioned when Arjax had said the mirror-tails helped with prey. I frowned as I considered what was happening here. Something deeper rooted me into place.

These foxes were clever, but so were my friends.

No one had freaked out yet.

Lorna and Arjax still hadn't emerged. Kine was just watching with his hand up, not motioning for me to move.

This was an ancient basilisk. I eased my gaze up, keeping it soft but not looking directly into her eyes. Yes, they were murky. She probably couldn't see me, and I wasn't making a sound.

Right. The mirror-tails were trying to scare me into bolting. Then it would be game over.

Clever babies.

The two foxes gave rasping barks. Their tails pulsed, the energy along the edges crackling. They stepped closer, bright-blue eyes narrowing as if daring me to run.

The basilisk slid farther out, swinging her head back and forth. Her tongue flicked out faster. Her nostrils flared.

Kine kept his gaze fixed on me, but he had angled more toward the trench. The other four mirror-tails started to draw closer as well.

I held my ground, refusing to move out of the basilisk's shadow as she continued to ease over the side of the ledge. She was so close I could see the individual scales lining her pale-green underbelly.

One of the pairs neared the trench, and she let out another rumbling hiss.

The foxes barked again, tails crackling with energy as they framed the basilisk's reflection. She reared up, following their illusion. Her massive head swung down, yellow eyes blazing.

I dropped my gaze, my breath snagging.

A deep, grumbling roar speared through the silence as a dark-orange spinosaurus seemed to suddenly appear. Lorna. Finally! Her shoulders and backfin lurched into position as she snapped her jaws and entered the fullness of the new shape.

All the mirror-tail foxes spun around. They chittered, a couple of them prancing in place as the energy arced faster between their tails. Two started producing a much higher call.

The basilisk arched up, baring her massive fangs. Droplets of venom dripped from the tips. Each droplet burned into the mud, leaving a painfully bad scent in its wake.

Lorna roared again, extending her neck and gnashing her massive jaws. She then lunged out onto the edge of the valley. Her heavy footsteps shook the ground.

Kine shot out, his own body transformed into his serpent shape. He caught the two mirror-tails nearest the trench right in the side, clotheslining them into the pit. They yelped as they fell into the slick mud.

The basilisk snarled, her cotton-white mouth gaping open. She swiped her head back and forth, but Lorna stomped forward. The basilisk surged at her, flinging her body out like a sidewinder.

The mirror-tail foxes raced forward, the pairs splitting. Silver-white energy pulsed along the iridescent rings on their tails.

I darted forward, flattening myself as the basilisk's body shot over me and letting the power of the water serpent tear through me and remake me. Pain ripped along my body as I curled inward and forced myself to stretch out. The momentum of the transformation carried me forward until I struck the mud. I gasped, the wind crushed from my lungs as I gulped for air. I tried to draw myself back, then cringed.

Oh! Mud in the scales was disgusting! I shivered and shuddered. Ihlkit! This was vile. I hadn't kept my scales tight enough, and some of it had gotten stuck. It felt worse than a wet sock sliding halfway off while you were walking, and sidewinding made it so much worse.

One of the mirror-tail foxes nipped at my tail. Its teeth glanced over the scales. It felt like nail files rubbing the wrong way. Not painful but annoying.

I flung my body around and encircled the nearest mirror-tail. It bared its white teeth. As I tried to coil around it, it jumped up, escaping. I coiled again, twisting a little more. If only I could have my arms and fingers! It would be much easier to grab things. I could practically feel phantom digits futilely trying to close around the fox. The fox slipped out with a chastising bark and bolted away.

Damn it! It had seemed easy when I was coiled on Buttercup and practicing that launching maneuver.

Arjax stomped out from the other side of the valley. His steps were so heavy I felt them reverberating through the mud into my body. He straightened his neck and sent out a great echoing bellow that nearly deafened me.

The basilisk swung around, rearing up.

Two of the mirror-tails darted forward. The rings on their tails sparked, brightening in color. Bolts of light shot out.

I body-slammed one of the mirror-tails into the pit. It shrieked and looked at me with such betrayed eyes as it flew through the air. Guilt seized me. I had to race to the edge and peer inside just to make sure it was all right. It was. Down below, they all snarled and barked.

Kine snatched up another of the mirror-tails, moving with lithe grace. He looked like a baby snake stealing something from its mother as he darted past the basilisk.

The mirror-tails were light enough that they barely sank into the muck, but the trench walls were slick enough it offered them no way to climb out.

I chased after the last one until my water serpent form slipped away again, and I collapsed with all but one arm plunging into the mud. So, so gross.

Kine hurried to me and hauled me up. "Easy there, Bug," he said with a light laugh. "This mud isn't the best for facials."

So disgusting.

Lorna and Arjax had transformed their feet so that their claws could twist and break the suction of the mud and allow them to run better. Back and forth they went, like this was some demented game of tag.

Even more mud slid into Mischief's scales, slowing her further. She halted, uttering a deep, guttural cough. The mirror-tail foxes all called out from the trench, their low voices keening and rasping. One clawed at the edge and almost dragged itself out, but Kine bopped it back in. Shrieking howls rose from the pit.

I cringed inwardly.

The basilisk shook, and her scales vibrated, making a shivering sound like a massive rattlesnake.

"She's getting ready to change!" Lorna shouted.

The words had barely left her mouth when the basilisk's form coiled and sprang into a long-bodied rooster with a great red comb and a serpentine tail. Glistening spurs clung to her yellow heels. Head cocked, she let out an ear-piercing cry, her wattle quivering.

"Crespa, she's a sassy one today." Arjax dropped back into his human form, his stance broad. He spread his arms as he gestured toward her in a chastising fashion. "Come on now, Mischief. You know us. We're just here to help." He stood between her and the pit of mirror-tail foxes.

The basilisk bobbed her head forward in a defiant gesture, her reptilian tail snapping around like a whip. She looked between Lorna and Arjax.

More shrieking howls swelled up from the trench.

She charged Arjax. He leaped back into his spinosaurus form, moving backward and luring her to the end. Lorna raced up behind her and sideswiped her.

The basilisk swung around, baring her fangs and trying to strike but missing. She shuddered and dropped back into the serpent form.

Back and forth they led the basilisk along the valley. The mud squelched beneath their claws, but she seemed to struggle with it more. She wasn't meant to be in the mud like this.

Kine crossed over to me, half his body coated in the slick mud. He started to rake his hand through his hair, then stopped, grimacing.

"Got an itch?" I held up that one hand that was somehow still clean and wiggled my fingers.

He chuckled, then leaned his head to the side, indicating the spot over his ear. I gave it a light scratch. "Thanks," he said. "I hate messing up my hair."

His hair had emerged remarkably unscathed.

"How are we doing on time?" I asked, gesturing toward the sun with my head. "Can we make it to the Keening Pass if we get the spear and go?"

He glanced up, his brow furrowing. "If we can get it in the next two hours, maybe. But, Bug—"

"Is that a hard two hours?"

"It gets more and more dangerous the more time passes," he said reluctantly. "If we aren't back on the ship within an hour, I wouldn't recommend we go until after the sun rises. You don't remember it, but it's not the easiest of passages to navigate. At some points, it's practically a death sentence."

"What matters is that we get this and go to the Ember Lord's Crest as quickly as possible," I responded sharply. "We can't delay. If we hurry, we can save Brandt—"

"Let's just see how long it takes us to get the spear and then cross that bridge," Kine said. "Hord and Cahji still have to navigate that labyrinth. Assuming everything went perfectly, they'll be on their way to the Crest now, but you and I both know that it probably isn't going perfectly."

I nodded, but I had made up my mind. We had made it here early, and we were going to salvage every scrap of time we could to get back to Brandt. The Keening Pass was fearsome. I recalled great boulders and rapid waters. But we could manage it. We were water serpents. I would draw the ship myself if need be.

The foxes barked and whined from the bottom of the trench, their voices coarse and raspy. They looked utterly miserable down there, trying to climb on top of one another as they desperately tried to reach their basilisk.

The basilisk at last slowed. Lorna shouted for us to strike the trap, and immediately, I hit the pad. The trap sprang up, wrapping around the basilisk like a cocoon with small tines pressing against the scales so that she could not keep going. Arjax leaped forward immediately and placed a blindfold over her eyes as Lorna pressed something pink and round onto the basilisk's tongue.

The basilisk thrashed and struggled a moment longer, her body writhing against the confines of the trap. After a few breaths, she went limp.

Arjax checked the blindfold and patted the basilisk's heaving side. "Yeah, there's a good girl. Bet you're feeling better."

Lorna rubbed the basilisk's snout. "She's much calmer. I think she was suffering a lot more than usual. Next time, we need to come sooner."

"Agreed." He crossed over to the edge of the valley and brought back a large vat with a leather covering. He waved his arm at us. "Let them up. They'll see she's fine. Danger has passed. More or less." He gestured toward the plank near the trench. "Get out of the way as soon as that plank is in, and they won't hurt you. They just need to see she's all right."

Carefully, Elias and Kine lowered the plank down into the pit. The mirror-tail foxes bounded up, baring their teeth at them but turning their focus to the basilisk. They ran up alongside her, sniffing and barking. They split into two groups, three on each side. Then they cozied up around her heart and throat as if to stand guard.

They gave Arjax side-eye, but the vocalizations softened. A couple dipped their head at him and Lorna as if to acknowledge their presence.

Lorna continued to examine Mischief, running her hands over the thick interlocking scales and searching her for any signs of injury.

"Why aren't they attacking us?" I asked, confused.

They licked at her sides or groomed one another, fluffing up their silver fur. The iridescent bands around their tails had gone almost pure silver. Surprisingly, none of the mud had clung to them either, except at the lowest points of their paws.

"They can tell she's relaxed, so they're relaxing." Arjax continued to stroke Mischief's side. "She recognizes us best after she's gotten that itchy venom out and her glands cleaned. At her age, it's hard for nature to take care of it all. Normally, snakes dispel their venom on their own, but after a basilisk reaches a certain age, if she doesn't dispel it, it builds up and makes her gums itch and her tongue burn." He gave her another gentle rub then glanced at me, eyebrow lifted in a conspiratorial manner. "You want to pet a mirror-tail?"

"I can pet one?" My eyebrows lifted. "I—No, we need to go get the spear. I don't have time—"

"Nonsense." Arjax crossed over to a mirror-tail that had a black diamond on the back of her neck. He squatted down and scooped her up. "Come here, little girl."

The mirror-tail wriggled and licked at his throat and face like a little dog. She might as well have been in his arms. He chuckled as he carried her over and crouched down to make it easier for me to pet her.

I pursed my lips, then relented. Tentatively, I pressed my hand to her head and stroked her. She was so soft! There was a hint of vanilla mixed in with the smells of earth, blood, and filth.

"She really is cute."

"I love 'em," he said with a grin. He patted her on the head and stroked between the ears, tilting his head back as she tried to lick his face. "They mostly tolerate the affection, and you'd best not be getting too close to the cubs if you don't want to lose your fingers, but some, like this girl, like being babied, especially when they know Mischief is fine. If you lean in real close, you can hear her chuff a bit."

I scratched her throat and behind her ears a little longer until Buttercup bellowed from the clearing above the valley.

Apparently, she disapproved.

"You're making your girl jealous." Arjax chuckled. He continued to hold the mirror-tail as he scratched her chin.

I laughed at this. Stepping back, I placed my hands on my waist. "Yeah, well, we'll be leaving soon enough. Where's the basilisk den? Maybe Kine and Elias and I could check the hoard while you and Lorna are gathering the venom."

Arjax gave a jerk of his head toward the cracked ridge. "Just beyond that forked tree split by lightning. You can't miss it, but mind the walls. Basilisks stick stuff in the nesting material on the outer layers, and they love shiny things, so daggers, swords, all that sort may be in that lining or the pellets."

"Got it."

And soon I'd have the spear as well. We could get out of here early.

It didn't take long for Kine, Elias, and me to approach the basilisk burrow. The forked tree stood to the right like a dark sentinel. Bright red and yellow birds sat on the branches, peering down. Their song pierced the hazy humidity, stark and cheerful despite the ominous feeling of this place. The mouth of the burrow yawned open, a gaping maw ready to swallow us whole if I listened to the fears nudging the back of my mind.

"All right," Elias said, rolling up his sleeves. "Any ideas how to make this more efficient?"

Kine shrugged. "It'll be in with the other shiny things the basilisk's stolen."

I was already slipping down, butt sliding across the cold mossy stones and making me glad the dress had shorts.

Ihlkit! This was vile. I repressed the gag that rose within me.

The descent wasn't too steep at least. The mirror-tail foxes could run in at this angle, and I didn't have to watch my head. Brandt might have if he were here.

Dull light filtered through the entrance. My eyes swiftly adjusted. This den was only a little wider than the basilisk herself. The mirror-tail foxes might have been able to flank her and provide additional protection, but there would be very little room left.

The passage into the burrow flattened and then sloped downward. The light lessened, and, while I stopped seeing quite as many colors, my eyes still took it in.

The basilisk hoard was not entirely what I had expected. Unlike dragons that put their hoard in the center, the basilisk had woven a sort of nest that was more akin to a bird's. Bones and plant matter as well as sparkling items had been thrust all around the sides in a winding pattern. It smelled of rot, filth, blood, metal, and soggy incense. My eyes and mouth burned.

Horrible place.

I crept deeper into the basilisk's den, the stench overwhelming my senses. My eyes watered as I scanned the piles of bones, shed skins, and glittering treasure.

We had to search for a fair bit until Elias spotted the blue glow of something magical. He pulled out a heavy, furry chunk of something none of us wanted to analyze. The glow intensified, resembling the eyes of the Gola Resh more and more.

There lay the spear, embedded in the other treasures and materials. It had an otherworldly green shade to it, bright even in the darkness. My fingers closed around the shaft. Kine and Elias helped move away the rotted debris and bones to make it easier for me to remove.

The intricate carvings along the wooden handle told a story I could not discern. It was easily over twenty feet in length, the dark wood light but sturdy and enchanted. The blade affixed to the tip was longer than my hand, shining like liquid silver despite the filth, and a gem had been fastened at the base of the spearhead.

The Babadon's heart. It was the source of the blue glow. It startled me to see how small the gem was, barely larger than my thumb. A rune had been carved into its center.

The first of three talismans. I gripped it closer, my heart hammering. When I closed my eyes, I saw Brandt.

I've got it, my love.

We had a chance. Now all we had to do was risk the Keening Pass. If we could get lucky again, we would make it.

My stomach knotted. Luck wasn't something we should be counting on, but did we have any other choice?

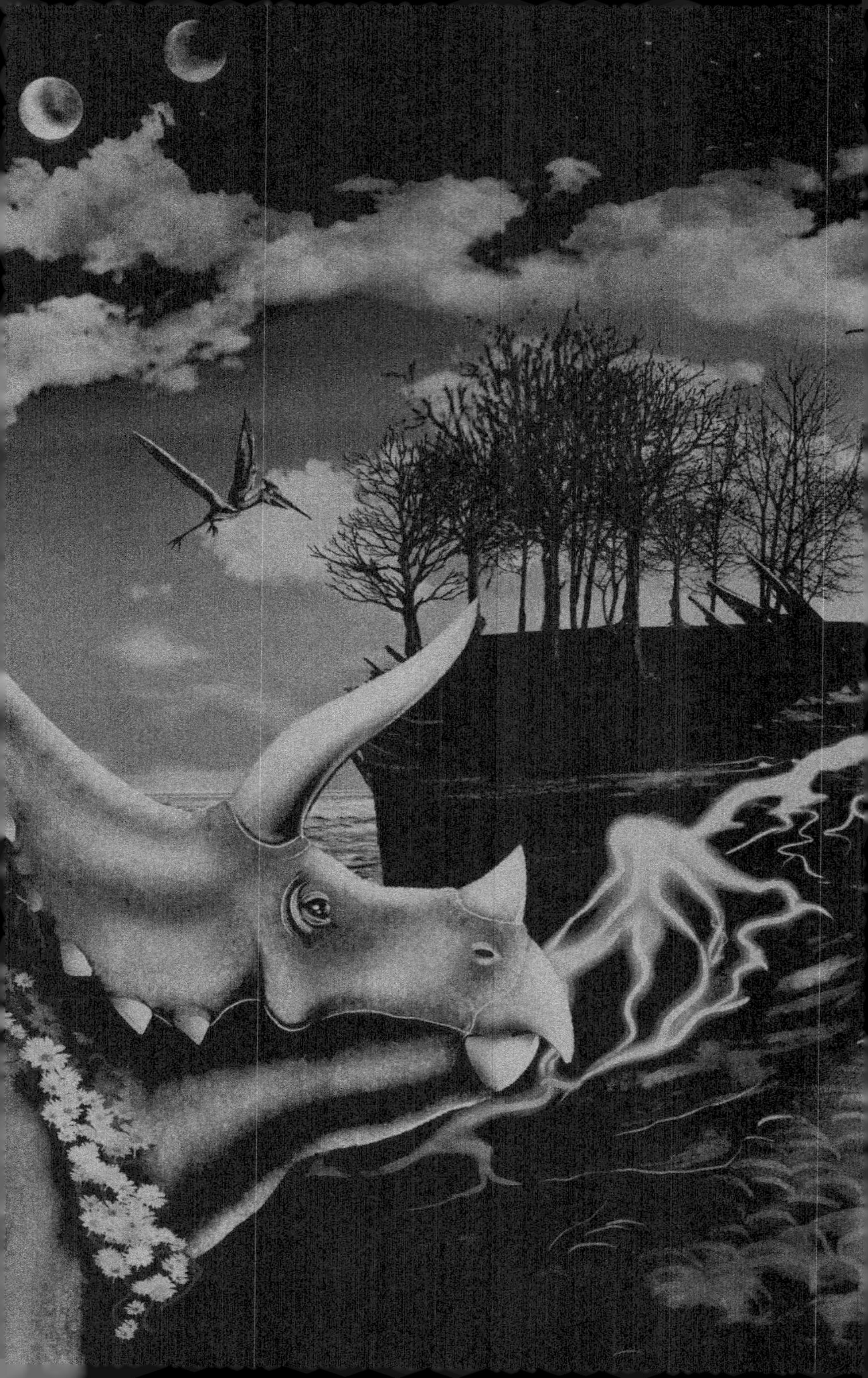

CHAPTER FORTY: STELLA

We clambered out of the burrow as Arjax and Lorna approached. They dragged Mischief between them with all six of the mirror-tails trotting along beside them. A couple of them still appeared more tentative than the others, but, just as Arjax had explained, they were now calm and friendly, especially compared to what they had been.

"We're gonna get the old gal down to her nest. She'll sleep until morning. Venom expulsion is a tiring thing, and she's probably had pretty poor sleep with that itch in her gums and glands. We were a little later getting to her than usual." Arjax put the ropes around her massive form and gave her a solid tug.

Lorna assisted him. I set the spear against the lightning-struck tree and then tugged at the ropes as well, but it made me feel like a child "helping" her parents in a way that was, at best, just not getting in the way too much.

The rays of sunlight slanted long in the sky, suggesting that it was nearing late afternoon. My insides tightened. It wasn't too late, though. The Keening Pass didn't simply cease to exist because the hours were late. It was just trickier, but we could do it. We'd been so fortunate this far. Our luck would hold out a little longer.

Except...death.

It was going to end in death.

A chill passed through me. I closed my eyes, shuddering.

No. Not from the Keening Pass.

I hadn't dreamed about it at all. Really, I could scarcely remember anything about it aside from the darkness and rush of water and speed we would travel at. It was a dark place. A frightening place.

Kine, Elias, and I waited above the massive burrow. Arjax and Lorna fussed over Mischief some more. They even took down two boar carcasses, presumably so she would have something to eat when she woke even if the mirror-tail foxes decided to feast beforehand.

"They didn't become anything smaller?" I asked Kine as they slipped down for the second time.

Both Lorna and Arjax were so large and muscular. I couldn't imagine that the basilisk's den was a pleasant place for either. As true shifters who could become practically anything they wanted, shouldn't they have shrunk down to something more...appropriate?

Kine shook his head. "Apparently it's easier to become something bigger for most Vawtrians. They like being bigger." A bit of a smile curled at his mouth.

"What?" It looked like he had another story, and I had to admit I could use something to make me smile. The angsty nervous energy in the pit of my stomach roiled stronger.

"The rumor is Vawtrians like them make themselves taller than any sentient they meet if they think it'll intimidate them or something. They can change their state of rest—what they call their normal form—a fair bit. Height is easy for them."

He then told me how he, Brandt, and I had once tried to trick them into proving this one way or another.

"Not that it was especially well thought out," he said, "and we forgot to take into account their exceptional ability to detect and distinguish scents. We looked like a trio of idiots, just trying to pretend like we were some nine-foot monstrosity."

"And it didn't work?"

"Well, Arjax did make himself bigger, but he made himself into a giant baryonx with those fish hook claws and threatened to slice us in quarters, so it didn't exactly work. And Lorna got us from behind."

I couldn't recall the memory, but the laughter and warmth returned to me. It wasn't hard to see why Brandt had wanted me to come here. It had seemed so important to him.

"Did we often come to visit Lorna and Arjax?"

"Most everyone does when they can," Kine said, "especially those of us who have the skills to become water serpent shifters. They come to Sepeazia's capital at least once a year to check the rings and ensure that the energy well is working properly. Not that they have to. The ancestors who created it set it up to be self-sufficient. It's the whole reason that water serpents were the form chosen. Well, one of the main reasons, I suppose, but they still come. We never know when, but when they do, it's always a big party. And so much food."

Those memories felt a little closer. I could practically taste the roasted meat with heavy spices, the coconut shrimp soup, the fried bananas, the broasted fowl, and the chopped meat pressed in geometric forms.

My mouth watered. "We need to eat soon. After we're on the ship. After we leave."

Lorna helped fasten the containers of venom to Arjax's side. Then she resumed her spinosaurus form. They led the way to camp.

Nothing in the Wild Lands bothered us as we returned. Our path seemed lighter despite the unease in my heart, the sunlight more golden and the colors bright. I gripped the spear so tight my hands hurt, the shaft lightly pressed against Buttercup's crest.

Lush ferns and towering trees surrounded us on all sides. Strange calls and rustlings sounded from the underbrush, but nothing strode out onto the paths before us. Deer and boar studied us from the shadows as well as creatures whose eyes I did not recognize. Whether predator or prey, they certainly weren't interested in fighting one spinosaurus, let alone two.

Palm-sized dragonflies zipped in and out, their wings glinting in the shards of light. The earthy scent of moss and rich soil permeated the woods. It took a little over an hour to return to their camp. The soil became darker and rockier, the incline steadier as the humidity fell away and a refreshing coolness settled over us. Spruce trees rose high above all the rest.

We reached the white stone marker that indicated the parting of paths.

I squeezed Buttercup's neck lightly to indicate we needed to halt. "This is where we should part ways," I said as firmly as we could. "If we're going to get to the Keening Pass, we need to hurry."

Kine's brow raised at my statement. Even Elias looked surprised, shaking his head as he remained on his parasaur's back.

Lorna and Arjax exchanged glances as if I were some child.

Then Lorna looked at me, her face breaking in a great smile. "I have a better idea. Invite your crew up to join us for a night of feasting and celebration. It's been far too long since we've had guests. It won't be safe for you to take the Keening Pass until tomorrow at dawn. No sense fighting it."

"No," I said, shaking my head fiercely. As the queen, I could order our ship to leave early, couldn't I? I held the spear fast. "Listen, we can't afford the extra time. We have to go. Surely there's some way for us to leave early."

Arjax knelt down, his expression pinching as he studied me.

He placed a heavy hand on my shoulder. "I understand the mate bond that plucks at your soul and demands you run to him," he said. "We Vawtrians honor that above almost any other bond, but you must do what is best for your veskare now, yes? And that means taking the route that makes it most likely you get home. Not the one that feels faster just cause you're moving."

I squirmed under his grasp, tears burning in my eyes. "I don't want anything to happen to him. If we're late… If anything happens to him, he'll lose his mind forever. The curse is going to take him."

His gaze softened, and he nodded.

Lorna spoke from behind him, her voice as firm and authoritative. "And he won't want anything to happen to you either. He'd tell you to take the Keening Pass when it's safe. No sense in throwing yourself into death or near death without purpose. Your love isn't worth sacrificing everyone. That isn't real love."

The desire to go worked within me, powerful and nearly unyielding. It took so much effort to nod, even though, deep down, I knew there was no way that I could do it without their permission or aid.

Arjax squeezed my shoulders as he peered down at me like I was some sort of wayward child. That sympathy in his gaze somehow didn't feel patronizing, but it left me feeling exposed.

"It's eating you alive. I know it, girl, and it's just as bad for him. Maybe worse cause of the curse. But you two, you'll make it. That ache will call you together. You'll learn to fight through it and fight for each other."

"Hard to fight through something that makes him want to kill me," I muttered, hugging myself tighter.

He poked my shoulder. "But you do it anyway, and so does he. You and he, you're both strong. You'd have found each other even without the shifter mating bond. Now that's something special, and it deserves to be cherished. It also deserves a fair chance. That means not sacrificing yourself on a fool's journey or turning it into something cruel."

"You'd cost yourself even more time if you left now and risked the lives of everyone for no added benefit." Lorna kept her gaze fixed on me. "You're a seer, aren't you? Do you really think this is a one-in-a-million chance where it works out?"

My shoulders slumped. I hated being called out like that.

I shook my head. No. There was only darkness when I looked at it.

"But they say you shouldn't look to your own." My gaze drifted to Elias.

He gave me a helpless shrug. "This isn't the one in a million."

Kine gave an enthusiastic nod, his manner firm and not in any way apologetic. "Agreed. We'll get back to Brandt in time, Bug."

I hugged myself as I stared down at the ground. "And if there isn't a one in a million, it'll mean..." I looked up to them, already guessing the response.

"People are injured or die," Lorna said, her voice calm. "Is your love worth sacrificing these men and women? The creatures on your vessel?"

The heaviness bloomed within me, crushing down on my shoulders. I shook my head. If it was only my life, perhaps, but with everyone else's?

I swallowed hard. "We'll stay."

Kine breathed with relief.

Arjax leaned closer, drawing in a deep breath.

I pulled back slightly, startled. "Did you just... Did you just sniff me?"

"Yes. There's something off about your scent." He leaned back, his brow furrowed as he looked me up and down. "I've been smelling something since you've arrived, but it has been hard to pinpoint. I'm now certain it's coming from you. It may even be the reason the basilisk focused on you. The smell is odd."

"She still smells of that Vegas place and Earth, the world she was reborn into," Elias said. "The scent has lingered."

My brow raised. "I wasn't aware I smelled that different, especially not after all this time. Wouldn't the smell of Vegas and everything else have faded by now?"

Elias twitched his shoulders. "Not as far as I can tell. Then again, I have a sensitive nose, and I thought that city smelled vile," he offered. "Some of it's the Gola Resh too. Stella got trapped in her magic for days and days."

Arjax continued to stare at me, his brow heavy. Wrinkles creased around his eyes. "I know the Gola Resh smell. That's not what this is." He sniffed again, then shook his head. "Were you involved in various magics in this other world?"

"Not that I know of." This was starting to get a little uncomfortable. I stepped back half a pace. Elias gave me a sympathetic look.

Arjax tapped his finger to his scalp as he contemplated me, then shrugged. He straightened. "Odd. We'll sort that out later. You're staying, yes?"

I gave a slow nod of assent. It was the right thing to do, but I squirmed inwardly.

"Good!" Arjax clapped his massive hands together. "We'll tell the rest of your crew to join us at the camp. You can bring your vessel to Scale Rock to put you closer to the Keening Pass and us. Then we will celebrate with meats and wines and all the best the Wild Lands has to offer."

Lorna went to extend the invitation while Arjax led us back to camp. It did not take us hardly any time at all to make it there. The camp was far larger than I had expected, especially with it being for just the two of them, and yet it was familiar too.

More than one firepit sat in the center of camp. Large

carcasses—some boar as well as other creatures—hung from trees over a ravine on the east side. On the west, the ground angled up into rockier terrain. Drying racks stood at intervals with strips of meat hanging on them. Hides had been tacked up in the back portion for curing. Pots of salt and a few other minerals clustered near the hides. A few large tents suggested either that there were more of them here, or they were prepared for guests.

Guests most likely. Yes. That sounded right.

"You can clean up in the waters up there," Arjax said with a broad gesture to the ridge on the opposite side of camp. "There's six or seven hot pools up there, plenty of shrubs and greenery. No magic to help with the healing, but the waters feel good."

I took him up on his offer. By the time I returned, Lorna was back as well with promises of the coming crew. They would all be here before nightfall, and those who needed to remain with the ship to keep it safe would take leave in turns with plenty of food and wine sent aboard so no one felt left out.

Arjax prepared the pot of venom and then set it on the ground with care, wedging it between two large stones so that it would remain safe.

It was hard for me to remain still though. I clutched at my arms and paced.

"Unato tradition," Arjax said, sitting on the boulder. His long legs folded up, scuffed and bruised and slicked with drying mud. He leaned forward and painted a white symbol on the side. "My mam was Unato. If there's a medicine that comes from nature, you take what you need and then you give away the extra. It's a way to give thanks to Elonumato, Creator of All for forming such bounty."

Unato...that was a group of people. Healers and poisoners.

"Only if it's from nature like this?" I asked.

"You're more or less free to do with other medicines whatever you like," he said with a grin, "but it's most important when it involves something like this. The basilisk venom is powerful and rich with healing properties and antivenom. It can be used in many potions and anti-venom concoctions, though it must be treated with great care. It's worth its weight in liquid gold. My mam would be thrilled with such a bounty. She'd spend hours and hours on those anti-venom concoctions. Three drops of this steeped with blood root and vulture bones and a few other reagents and a month of rotation and proper care and—boom."

"That sounds complicated." I raised an eyebrow.

"And his mam would never charge much even when it was complicated," Lorna said.

He tilted his chin in agreement. A flicker of sadness passed through his black eyes.

He missed his family. Both of them did. They'd been here in our world for so long.

I opened my mouth to speak, but Arjax shook his head. "In time, little cousin. We'll find our way home one day. Until then, Mischief and all the rest have need of us, as do you. So we just make the best of what we've got. Fix what we can. You'd be amazed at what's really possible out there."

Lorna strode up to me, fixing me with a stern gaze. "Show me that water serpent form of yours again."

I straightened my shoulders and obliged, feeling the surge of energy and sting of transformation.

"Stop." She pushed her hand into the center of my chest.

The sharpness of the blow startled me more than it hurt. My form fell away before my dress had even merged with my scales.

"You can interrupt shifting?" I staggered back, staring at her in shock.

She smirked, hands on her waist. "I can." She held up her finger, then tilted her head. "Now." Drawing in a deep breath as if to demonstrate, she lifted my shoulders and then pushed them back to open my chest. "This has to stop. You're hunching in when you go to shift, girl. Push your shoulders out and back. Deep breaths. You need the air. Fill your lungs."

Kine had told me to take three deep breaths before shifting, so I did that as well.

Lorna nodded, her gaze moving up and down my body as she considered me. "After this, when you have time, you need to build the muscles through here." She put her hands on my back and then pushed against my core. "You're strong, but you could be stronger."

While Arjax made the preparations, Lorna worked me over, examining and criticizing my form. She praised my stance and examined my pressure points. The hardest one was her focus on my spine.

"You little cousins always want to pull in. It lessens the pain. I know that, but you've either got to have your lungs and blood full, or you've got to keep open. It shortens the shift. Now draw more from your core like this. It'll help you when you try to coil and be more fine-tuned with your movements."

She had me continue to shift and change while Arjax worked on the venom. Kine watched while Elias sketched. He'd nearly filled up yet another book, his pencil now little more than a stub and his red sleeves smudged with graphite.

Kine kept his arms folded as he watched Lorna work with me.

She analyzed every aspect of my shifting, critiquing my posture and my stance most of all. "You'll be strong enough eventually to shift even when you aren't in perfect formation, but for now, if you take the proper stance, you'll have better energy throughout and better control."

The shifting had eased my tension as well, wearing me out.

She turned toward Kine. "What about you, baby blue?"

Kine offered the ring to Lorna. "Can you see any reason why this would stop working? The Sepeazian magic is separate from yours, but the rings—well, something has disrupted it. Our scholars believe it is because of the overall curse and how it affects all the elements. They think maybe it's because something in there is blocking the Vawtrian energy, but perhaps you could tell us better?"

"How long has this been an issue?" Lorna accepted the ring.

"It started a few weeks ago as best I know," Kine said. "Before that, there had been odd fluctuations but nothing alarmingly out of the ordinary, especially considering what had been happening."

Lorna gripped the ring in her hand and clamped it tight. Golden energy surged and crackled from her hand into the ring. It smelled like lightning on metal.

Oh, wow. "What was that?" I asked, my hand still gripping my arm but no longer working out the tension.

Lorna chuckled. "The well that you put these in to recharge is filled with Vawtrian energy, but here you are at the source. Well. Not exactly. But Arjax and I count as sources even if we aren't the only ones." She scowled as she gripped the ring tighter, thin lines forming over her brow. She tilted her head as she looked at Arjax. "Hold this." She tossed him the ring.

He snatched it out of the air and turned it over in his palm. He'd barely curled his fingers over it when he snapped his hand up. "Someone poisoned the energy." A deep frown seared his brow. "This isn't coincidence. Someone has been trying to steal your shifting as well."

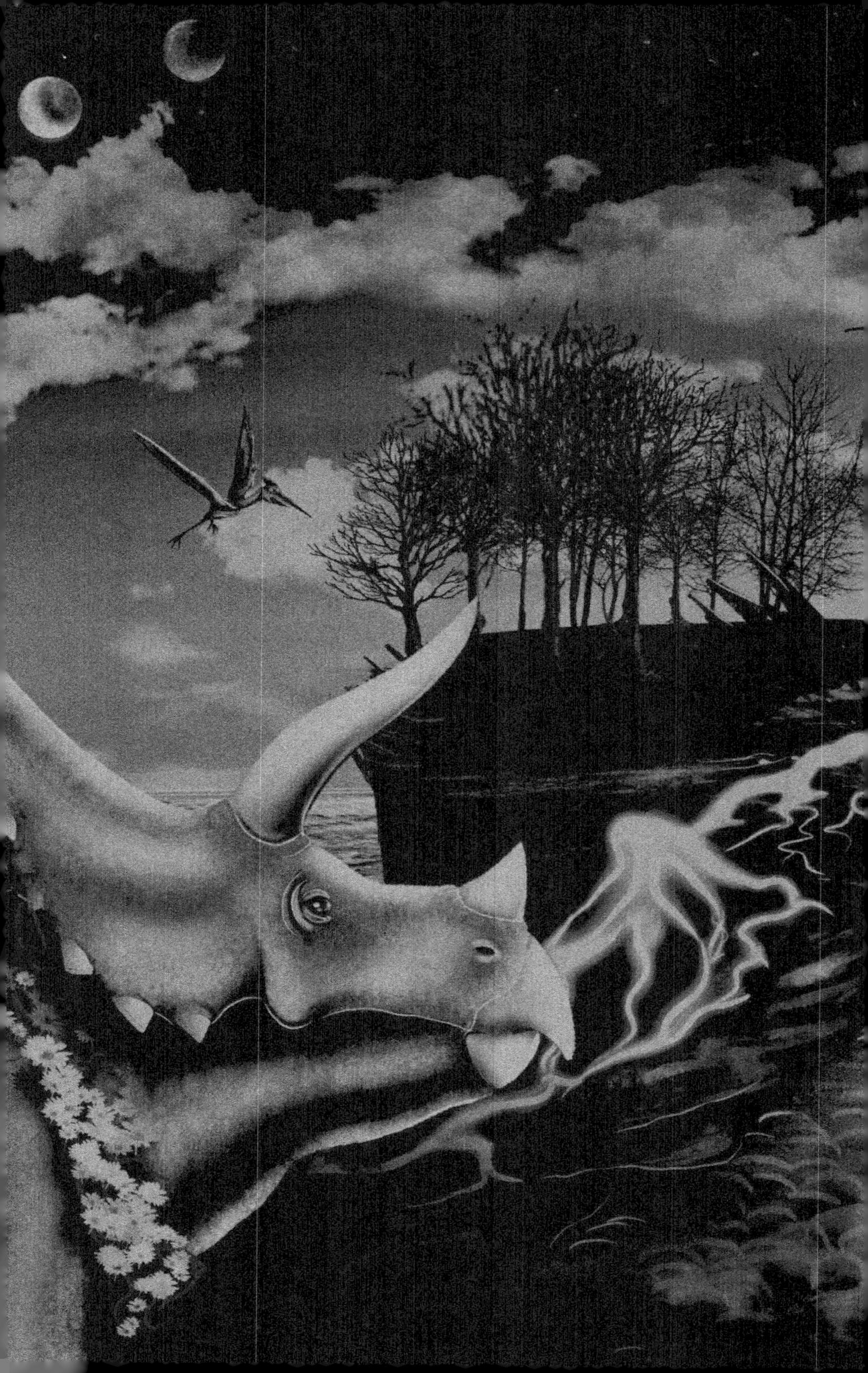

CHAPTER FORTY-ONE: BRANDT

That dream had been so real, and it wasn't the first time I had had it either. Cold sweat soaked my skin.

I stood against the wall, iron manacles holding me fast, muscles burning and aching from the unrelenting pressure of the position. They dug into my wrists and ankles, but the pain grounded me in a manner that provided comfort. So long as the metal dug into my flesh and gripped my bones, I wasn't risking following my urges and tracking Stella down.

Again and again, this dream had come to me, bursting through the darkness of my sleep. It had come after the grotto and on the night Stella had come to kill me. It filled my mind's eye, though I had barely dozed off.

Now it returned. It was never fully the same, though its core message was unchanged.

Dread spun in my gut and warned me as surely as if I were a seer myself that there was something far worse coming.

I had not told Stella that I had felt the claws of the curse even then, scraping across the back of my mind. The Gola Resh's warning stirred some deeper knowledge within me, reminding me just how precarious our position was.

The need to be with Stella burned in my chest, barely muted by the nightmare, but that nightmare showed me what I did to her. What I always did to her.

I willed the images out of my mind. The late afternoon wind scratched and whispered across the stones.

My charm and its lurching forward tormented me from deep umber to bright yellow in a breath to Stella beneath me, neck snapped, eyes glassy.

The truth was that ever since Stella's return, the curse had worsened at an alarming rate and in ways that could not be denied.

Memories of our lovemaking and of her death cycled one after another, faster and faster. And this last one... In this last one, I had found her in some hot spring, naked and vulnerable. She'd looked up at me with those big golden eyes, her expression soft and tentative.

And she had stayed.

She didn't run.

She wouldn't!

My muscles clenched as I tried to push the dream from my thoughts.

It wasn't going to happen. There were no hot springs anywhere near Castle Serpentfire, and she was on a ship nearing the Wild Lands.

Yet the dream had been so insistent. The way she stared at me even as I tried to force the words out, to beg her to leave...

In the dream, we made love. It felt almost as real as when she had pressed her slender body to mine here in this very room, her skin salty and sweet at once. I inhaled her scent in that dream, unable to fight off my lust. She clung to me, kissed me, and offered herself to me.

My eyes shuttered as my breaths went ragged. If only the dream had ended there.

But it didn't.

It continued as the need to kill her intensified more than it ever had before, as if the curse had crept deeper into my body now and taken hold of my very form before its time. Our coupling grew rougher. She slipped under the waters. I clutched her tighter.

Then it all blurred and sped by until she lay beneath me, dead.

I wanted to retch, shaking my head as if to remove those images. They weren't prophetic. They couldn't be. Every time they came, they were different in settings, even sometimes in time and tone.

Just nightmares. That was all these were.

They'd probably worsened because all I had to think about was keeping her safe.

Thank all that was good she and I were so far apart right now. I hated myself and what I had become, and I did not know how to fight it any better.

The pulsing ache in my wrists and thighs felt stronger, more insistent now. The manacles' biting embrace stung. I focused on each point of discomfort.

This was the cost to keep my beloved safe.

This was what I had to endure.

It had been hours since the curse had claimed me, leaving me writhing and frothing like a mad man. My limbs had healed from my twisting struggles and raging bellows, but the hollowness within me had not.

I licked my lips, staring at the shadows as they inched across the floor.

I wanted Stella back so bad that I didn't trust that I wouldn't go in search of her. Powerful as my need for her had been before we made love, it had become an inferno after that night. Instead of easing my torment, it worsened everything, like eating salt bread instead of drinking water when dying of thirst.

The hours were interminable, but at least they passed.

A heavy thud sounded outside the door. The scuffle of boots on stone. The metallic, sweet scent of blood.

I tensed.

A metal key scraped in the lock. The door creaked open, a dark masked form now standing in the doorway, wave blade drawn.

Tau's body slumped across the floor, blood running down his tattooed arm onto the smooth stone floor. Etano was likely dead as well. Rage boiled within me.

The assassin wiped the bloody dagger on his trouser leg.

A growl rose in my chest.

The insignia made it clear. This was one of the faction members. From the marking on his shoulder, he looked like one of the faction members who had tried to murder Stella in the valley.

Odd. To avoid civil war, most would insist on killing only Stella or myself. If he was here to kill me, then that meant Stella was likely safe. Something had changed over the past few days to make them change their mind. Something didn't sit right, though.

"Today you die," he said, waving the blade at my face.

A snarl curled at my lips as I stared him down. At least this way I would die without hurting Stella. Her life would continue.

"You slew five of my blood," he said coldly. "You kuvasted one to death in two blows for daring to challenge you when he said that a new queen should be chosen, and that is aside from those whose lives were lost when Taivren fell and the legacy you threw away."

I met his gaze, unblinking. "If you are here to kill me, then do it." The thought brought a sick relief.

He drew closer, blade clutched in his right hand as he studied me, mask covering all but his eyes. Ihlkit. Those eyes... they burned deep red, like my own.

His eyes flashed at my words, his stance tightening. Slowly, he stepped closer, his boots light on the stone floor. "You humiliated them. Fought them and snapped their necks for all to see."

"They challenged me in open council. They formally demanded kuvaste," I said, not certain which of his kin he was referring to. There had been many who had attacked me over the years. "I defended myself, and if they died, then they died. They should not have attacked. If you wish to kill me for that, then do it."

"You showed the world that your power was greater than theirs. Now I will show the world that my power is greater than yours." The assassin growled the last words. "You are not worthy to be king."

"Do not unshackle me," I warned. "Unchain me after I am dead, not before, or else I will kill you."

His eyes narrowed, his grip on the dagger tightening. "You think you can threaten me, bound as you are?" He let out a harsh laugh. "Do you think I fear you, cursed king?"

It would be humiliating to die at the hands of this weakling.

I glared at him. "You should fear me."

He picked up the keys from the iron circle and dangled them as if to taunt me. "You will fight me in kuvaste, and you will die, and then we'll take your queen." He chuckled darkly as he unfastened the first of the shackles on my arm.

"What?" My gaze darkened.

He scoffed as he moved to the second set of restraints. This idiot assumed I valued the honor of rightful kuvaste more than I did protecting my wife from myself. "We know where the queen is and how to take her. Our leader wants her for himself. Claims it's his right, but we'll all have our turn."

I seized him by the throat, lifting him off the ground with one hand. "You threaten *my* woman?"

My muscles were stiff, my fingers clumsy, but rage coursed through me.

I dragged him closer, baring my teeth. "Who is behind this?" I growled.

His neck and spine cracked beneath my grip.

Ihlkit!

I flung his body aside, rage pouring through me.

Bastard couldn't even assassinate me properly. That hadn't gone well. The blood surged stronger through my veins, my wrist and arm tingling as the circulation intensified the sensations in my fingertips.

With one arm free, the temptation to break loose intensified.

I clenched my eyes shut, shuddering as I struggled against the pull.

Go to her.

I needed to go to her.

I had to hold her once more.

That was all. I'd hold her. Kiss her. Tell her goodbye.

No!

Jerking back, I pressed my free hand to my chest. No matter how the mate bond compelled me—no matter how much my need for her intensified—I wasn't going to endanger her.

Mocking laughter filled the room and seized within my chest. My head snapped up.

The Gola Resh floated above the ground, her form swaying and twitching. Those malevolent orange-green eyes blazed at me, smirking with malicious delight.

"So amusing." She chuckled, her shadows dripping down the wall like sludge. "You thought you could keep this from happening. You thought that binding yourself with these flimsy metal straps would keep you from the doom I have planned. Well, let me tell you, brute, either you or your little rutting mate will be dead before the curse makes its final claim. You *will* know my pain."

"I am ready to die to save Stella and Sepeazia." I kept my

hand tight against my chest, fingers digging into my pectoral. "I am not your instrument of destruction."

"Oh, but you are, and yes, you'll die. I'll see to that. You destroyed my beloved. At least most of him." Still laughing, the Gola Resh lifted her hand. The darkness dripped from her, erasing her fingers and then returning as they grew once more. "But if you don't know what you're doing, you can't hope to make that permanent, now, can you?"

"If you require my death, then kill me now," I snapped. "I give you my life. Just free Stella and Sepeazia."

"No. There's a third bargain in play, my dear. See, I knew you and your stupid little slut weren't ever going to take me up on my offer, but that doesn't mean you can't suffer. Just knowing you held the knowledge was enough. Part of me had hoped she might try to hide more of it from you so that I could reveal it with a flourish and make one of you think the other had betrayed you, but that isn't how it works with you two, is it?"

Some small part of me stirred with pride. Stella and I had our weaknesses, but even after death and years of torment, we did our best.

"Don't look so self-satisfied," she chided, chuckling. Her hand swished through the air, the sharp metallic scent intensifying. Her eyes burned like poisonous fire. "All that means is that it is far easier for me to wound you both and ensure both of you will suffer, and watching you here just a moment ago made it so clear what must happen. I will ensure that your beloved is given to another."

I scoffed, glaring at her. When I opened my mouth to respond, she swiped her hand up near my mouth, the cold darkness of her form choking me.

"He has already spoken to me of his desire for her, not that she will accept him. He thinks she might. I'm sure he'll believe that when he takes her too. Think of that. Your mate with another, not even happy to be with him."

She smirked, holding up one dripping finger as she tilted her now-skeletal head. Drawing closer, she smiled. Her fingers danced dangerously close to my skull.

"I wasn't missing for those fifty years. I was watching, nursed back to health by one who has come close to understanding my value. I learned that not all is ugly and small with you Sepeazians. In truth, there is something that some might consider beautiful within you." Her mouth grazed my ear. "You wanted her happy. It's how you comforted yourself. Not even with the thought that she was searching for you and pining for you. You took comfort in the belief that she would find someone who would make her happy enough to give her a good life away from you. If you don't kill her, Stella will live. Your beloved Stella will watch you go mad and die. You may even get the chance to kill her a time or two before the end, and that will make the memory of you harder to bear. Hopefully, you'll hurt her, badly, and if she survives that, then I will see to it that she is handed over to another. He will take her, believing that he can force her to love him, but we both know that that won't happen. He will feel righteous and good because he will believe that through him Sepeazia will be saved. Not in full but in part. I will spare him and ten of his choice, including Stella. A remnant of Sepeazia will survive. One without magic of any type, but survive they will."

I sneered at her, masking the terror that clenched my guts. "You've allied with one of the factions."

"There were so many to choose from," she said with a wry smile. "You have made so many enemies over the years, little Brandt. Refusing to take another queen? Refusing to let anyone use her ring? There are consequences for that. If it weren't for your cousin and the strength of your inner court, I suspect that you would have been overthrown by now. How fortunate for you that no faction or *living man* could tempt your cousin to aid me." Her voice turned smug, leaving obvious implications.

"Hord would never cooperate with you."

"Really?" She lifted her chin, smirking. "His beloved passed in Taivren, did she not? All he has left is his son, Cahji. Well, other than you and the rest of your kin, for what that is worth. Cold comfort for the loss of a beloved. You do not know what it is to love as a parent, and you cannot know what else I promised him if he did not do as I commanded. Then again, there is so much you do not know." She plucked at the manacles on my right hand. The metal squealed beneath her touch, the screws in the stone loosening as the bands weakened like wet paper.

"I don't believe you."

All she wanted was our suffering and our pain. Hord was one of my closest friends and allies.

"Hm. You will. If you survive this, you will." She smirked. Her fingers dragged down the chains. They started to warp beneath her touch. "My powers are returning even as Sepeazia's are fading. You consider why. What was I given that has allowed me this resurgence? What special nourishment was I given to let me escape the jaws of death and become what I am?"

Her taunting words crept under my skin. Already, they worked along the edges of my mind like claws digging into the softness of raw flesh.

"What were you given?" I growled.

"I'll let you figure that out." She seized me, dragging me up into the air. With a burning roar of orange-green fire, she swept her other arm in a circle. A portal appeared in the air, the flames turning purple, tinged with red as it pulsed. "Give Stella my very best."

She flung me through.

The energy arced and burned along my flesh, sucking and biting and singeing. The world around me blurred and hissed. Rocky soil struck me in the shoulder and chest. Dirt filled my nose and mouth.

Coughing, I struggled to lift my head. A myriad of scents

enveloped me: invigorating spruce, chalky stones, mineral-rich waters, and fresh roasted meat. The cool night air kissed my skin, whispering lies that all would be well. Drums pounded in the distance in some sort of celebratory Vawtrian dance rhythm. Laughter and singing carried on the breeze.

No. My fingers dug into the earth, my limbs shaking as the need intensified and my thoughts blurred.

No.

Anywhere but here.

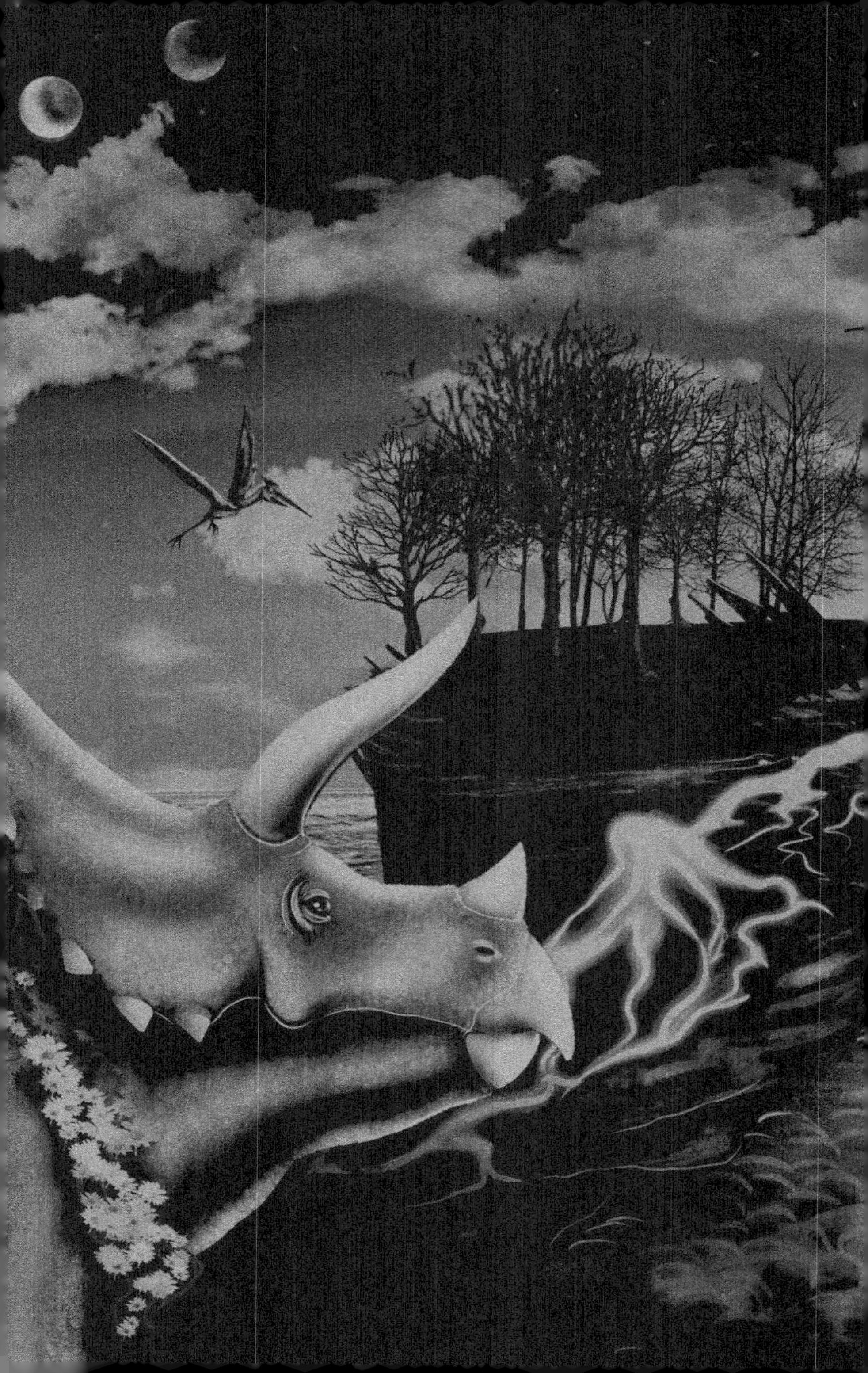

CHAPTER FORTY-TWO: STELLA

Silence fell over the camp. I gripped the necklace, my fingers locking around the moonstone and charm. "Poison?"

Kine crossed over to Arjax and peered down at the ring. "What do you mean someone is stealing our shifting?"

Elias's eyes widened. He glanced down at his sketchbook, flipped to a page in the center, and then stopped. "Wait. What? Where...where did the theft happen? When? How?"

Lorna spread her arms as she looked at Arjax, the feathers rustling in her hair. "Clumsy theft, really."

Arjax gave a slow nod. He handed it back to Kine, then gestured for me to give him mine. "But damaging enough." His voice became a dangerous rumble.

Elias turned through the pages, shaking his head. He ran his hand through his hair. "It can be stopped, yes?"

"Now that we know it is present, yes." Lorna paced back and forth, shaking her head. "We can fix it so long as we stay strong, but this is an insult."

Kine placed the ring back on his finger and studied it. "Can you estimate when the energy was poisoned?"

"It feels as if someone drew off the energy and then started to thread it in as a replacement, which means that this happened long before Stella returned," Arjax said. "This is siphoning."

"Did any of the rings go missing?" Lorna continued to pace. The scowl on her face deepened.

Kine rubbed the back of his neck. One of the logs on the fire crackled and snapped, falling into the fire pit amid a burst of sparks. He stared down at those embers. "It's possible. Several rings went missing shortly before that in one of the attacks. Also when Taivren fell. But we assumed those were simply lost in the sea and the toxic waters that came afterward."

Elias lowered his sketchbook, his eyes wide with concern. "Is it possible... Could someone have used the magic in the shifter rings to save the Gola Resh's life? Is that the missing piece?"

"That would explain a few things," Arjax admitted. "It means you are dealing with someone who understands more of the matters of magic and how they work together than you assumed."

"Someone chillingly intelligent," Elias muttered. He flipped back through the pages of his book, swallowing hard. Sweat formed along his brow. He stopped at one page in particular, his hand flattening over it.

"Is it something that you can share?" I asked.

He hadn't said what it was, and seers knew better than to pry too much, but I couldn't resist asking. My insides were already squirming. Was this what Auntie Runa had seen? And if so, why had she not shared it? These visions always brought with them such a burden, but this knowledge seemed important. Wasn't it?

Elias's jaw worked. He closed the sketchbook and set it down. "I am not sure how much I can say except that yes, I think we are on the right path. It gives me hope that this has been discovered. I—I'll spend the night in meditation and contemplation to see if anything more comes to me."

Arjax grunted as he gripped my ring in his hand. Golden

light flared and flowed around it before it calmed. "There's a way out. There always is."

Neither Lorna nor Arjax pressed Elias to share. They were familiar with visions and foresight. I was too, and I did know better, but...I desperately wanted to know.

The temptation burned in me now with a strength almost as great as the need to see Brandt.

But Brandt wasn't here.

Kine continued to stare at the fire before he gave a slow nod. "Well, we have no way to go but forward. There isn't much to be done now—"

I swallowed hard, then stepped forward, interrupting him as I looked to Lorna and Arjax. "You have already done so much for us, and we are all so grateful, but please, I must ask you another favor. Will you come with us? The Gola Resh almost assuredly knows we are going to the Ember Lord's Crest, and we must be prepared for her. If she has started to drain our ability to shift, would—"

"We were already planning on leaving with you, little cousin." Arjax placed the ring back into my hand, his smile warm and gentle.

I turned it over slowly, tears pricking my eyes. "I don't know how we'll ever thank you enough for everything."

"You don't have to. You're our family. We can't be with our veskaros or veskares here. We don't have our cadre, but we have our little cousins and the beasties we've taken in." Arjax nudged me with his elbow, almost toppling me. His smile had that sad note to it again, as did Lorna's.

Kine chuckled. "Were you just going to stowaway or something or surprise us in the morning?"

"Do not underestimate my abilities to hide, baby blue." Lorna patted Kine on the head as she walked past him toward the tree with the carcasses.

"Figured we'd cover that after the party," Arjax said, still smiling. The concern remained apparent on his face, in the wrinkles around his eyes and on his brow. "But there's no more to be done for the end of Sepeazia tonight. Tonight, we celebrate life. We feast. We dance. We laugh. All right?"

Kine agreed wholeheartedly while Elias nodded, his manner subdued. I forced myself to grin and offered to help.

It felt good in a way to be able to focus in on the preparations for tonight's feast, basic as Arjax and Lorna insisted it would be. The simple work occupied my hands, though my thoughts remained discordant and agitated. Elias rolled logs out to serve as stools and tables. I busied myself gathering herbs and digging roots with Kine while Arjax and Lorna butchered the meat and set it to roast. From there, we chopped up the herbs and mixed them with the salt to rub on some of the meat. The roots were similar to potatoes. We buried them in the embers of one of the fires and left them to cook.

The sun had begun its descent, casting the forest in molten gold by the time the crew arrived. Sen carried a large pot of something steaming and fragrant that resembled the sweet potato chowder from the other night. He beamed when Lorna swept it from his arms and planted a kiss on the top of his head.

The quantity of wine that these two had in casks in the camp probably should not have startled me, especially when I recalled that Vawtrians didn't drink wine the way we did. Their wine was different, and this wine... Well, it wouldn't get either Lorna or Arjax drunk, but they had still kept it for visitors.

The sun soon sank below the horizon, leaving the fire as our only source of golden light. Its smoke rose and snaked out of sight, the air fragrant and rich as the meat roasted on the metal spits. Fat dropped and sizzled in the flames, and the charred scent should have made my stomach rumble.

Soon after, Kine dug out the roots we had buried. They were charred and black on the outside, but they split open to reveal creamy soft goodness inside. I managed a few mouthfuls with sprinklings of fresh herbs, but mostly I just enjoyed how happy everyone seemed. Most everyone seemed able to forget what we were up against and enjoy the reprieve that this little celebration permitted.

Then it was time for the dancing. While more meat roasted, Arjax set up three drums as well as a rattle and called out for volunteers. He soon had them. Cheers followed as two brothers and a sister set the pace for the dance.

What a night.

I wanted to enjoy it. It was good. Arjax and Lorna had blessed us with uncommon kindness. The crew—my crew—reacted to them as if they were family. No one seemed out of place or troubled. You wouldn't have guessed that in less than two weeks, we would all be dead if we failed in this mission.

And yet, I couldn't bring myself to smile. Hard as I tried, part of it still felt wrong to me. This celebration too felt familiar, but it was missing pieces. I wanted Brandt's arms around me, to lean back against his chest and tease him with my hips before prancing off to dance around the fire.

Kine came to stand beside me, arms folded over his broad chest. "You should come dance. Sulking doesn't fix a thing."

"It doesn't feel right without Brandt," I said with a shrug. The aching pulse within my chest had intensified so much it was like a physical weight. It held me down.

"True, but sitting out here like this won't make it any better. You'll feel better if you dance. Work out some of the nerves and sorrow." He nudged me with his elbow. He pulled a sour face at me, then looked to see if I would smile back.

I only gave him a halfhearted smile in return. "I may go soak in the hot springs and see if I can get the depression off me."

He laughed and held his hands out. "Come on. You can soak in the hot springs after you dance."

The heaviness within me intensified, but Kine was relentless. Gripping both my wrists, he yanked me into the dance circle.

My feet staggered into the steps as I remembered, the beat familiar as my own heart. The steady rhythm of the drums guided me. My stiffness eased even if my heartache didn't, and somehow laughter came as well.

If all dances had purposes and voices, then this one was simply to celebrate being alive. It was madness and play with no instruments except the drums and a rattle and laughter. Some danced with rhythm, some without.

Arjax and Lorna were such show-offs. They transformed in mid-dance, slipping between shapes and varying colors and patterns of flesh and scales and hair and eyes as effortlessly as breathing. Snakes, dragons, eagles, terror birds, gazelles, horses. When they weren't shifting, they were pounding their feet and slinging anyone around within arm's reach.

Most of the crew joined in. No one had brought fancy clothes, but a few had brought ribbons. Lorna and Arjax shared their feathers and shells. Half the time Lorna and Arjax danced, the feathers and bits of plants they'd collected fell out of their hair, but they always kept them in when shifting. Probably to show that they could.

With Kine's encouragement, I let the dance take me. He whooped and grabbed my hands, twirling me around. Lorna seized my other arm, then swept me up and spun me out. Someone else caught my arm and guided me back as we stomped and bent and spun.

Everyone danced.

Except Elias.

Elias remained outside the dance circle, his knee propped up and his sketchbook against his leg. The contemplative smile and slight frown on his face contradicted one another, and his eyes... There was something odd there. He'd angled himself away from everyone and put his back to one of the stacks of boxes so that unless someone climbed up on top of the crates, no one could see his work.

We seers did require privacy. It wasn't easy to process what flashed into our minds and discern what our sight told us, but some part of me wanted to know. I craved the knowledge. It tugged at me as my dread increased.

What was he drawing? Was he seeing something?

Stop thinking about that.

I dragged my hand through my hair, pressing it back from my sweaty face.

"What are you thinking about?" Elias called to me from his seated position.

I strode over, arms still crossed, fingers digging into my biceps. "Just everything."

"Hm." His eyebrow flicked upward. "That's quite a lot."

"You aren't dancing."

"Not really in the mood tonight," he said with a faint smile, "but I may take a walk to clear my head."

He stood. As he did, his sketchbook dropped, and a vivid sketch in Auntie Runa's colors slid out, a picture of a couple descending into the heart of the Ember Lord's Crest, swallowed up by lava and clinging to one another as they died.

I gasped, frozen.

That...that was Auntie Runa's vision.

Elias's gaze snapped up to mine. He shook his head as he grabbed up the book. Other pages slid out.

I couldn't tear my eyes away. It felt as if we had become a world all alone from the rest and not in a good way. "Elias."

He shook his head. "It's not what you think." He sounded miserable, his words soft and forlorn, almost drowned out by the drums.

"Then what is it? Why did you take Auntie Runa's sketch?"

"To see if there was any way for me to disprove it or to see something beyond it," he said tightly. He pressed his hand over it, his brow pinching as if he sought to block it. "I have tried...I have tried so hard to see some way around it. There has to be a meaning in it other than the obvious..."

My head spun. "I wasn't aware you could do that," I said, my voice shaking.

"My abilities have been changing," he admitted reluctantly. "They're expanding. I can...I can do and see more than ever before, but it's dreadful." He glanced around the camp, his hand gripping the back of his neck as if afraid that someone would overhear. "I can't explain it exactly," he whispered, "but it's intense. There are periods when I see so much and then others where there's nothing." He placed the book in my hands.

My breaths sharpened. Was he really giving this to me? I'd always felt reluctant to let anyone look at any of my drawings and sketches. "Did you tell Auntie Runa?"

He nodded, his mouth pinched. "She said to embrace the gift but remember its weight."

I still held the book, not turning through the pages despite the curiosity burning in me. It was so heavy in my hand, and he was willing to let me look. All I had to do was ask.

But Elias... His guidance hadn't always been good. My instincts weren't always good either, but I knew to question them. I had to question his as well.

Yet the curiosity burned.

Elias continued, softer now, "I had been having strange visions of the end of all. I wanted to see whether it was the same as what she saw."

My body tensed, my lips pressing into a tight line. I shouldn't ask.

"Do you want to know?" His gaze remained fixed on the ground.

My mouth had gone dry. I wanted to shake my head as the drums beat on and on, to tell him no, of course not. To know what might be could lock a person into that path. It was a heavy burden, and I didn't need more burdens. Did it make a difference after all that we had learned?

"I can make it easy for you. All you have to do is look away," he said softly, his voice in my ear.

Then he opened the book.

I didn't look away.

He showed me page after page of sketches of the Gola Resh and Babadon in various forms, of darkness spreading across Sepeazia. The emotion and depth of skill that he had woven into these sketches and drawings took my breath away.

So did the fear rooted within me.

All I saw was their power. Their strength. Their ferocity. Symbols and marks flowed across the page. Portals opened in ink. Destruction wrought in charcoal and graphite.

"If what I have seen is accurate, then the Gola Resh and the Babadon came here because she was dying," Elias said quietly.

I recalled the Gola Resh referring to an illness. It had breezed past my consciousness at the time she had spoken of it. A frown tugged at my brow.

"They could not bear the thought of being separated. They planted their spells deep in our soil and waters to drain the power out of them and grant her new life. They took enough before we noticed for her to regain a fair bit of her strength, but to cement them in eternal life together, they had to finish taking all our life. Those gouges we see are channels. They're draining us even now."

"Ridiculous," I murmured, my fingers brushing over the page, yet my insides twisted at the thought of being separated from Brandt again. I could understand the fear. The pain.

"I think you're right that the Gola Resh intends to summon the Babadon," Elias said softly, "to bring him back from the grave. I suspect, too, that the shifter magic is the last bit that she needed to give her the strength to keep going. Otherwise, she would have faded. Something has kept her alive and changed her. I think that's what did it."

"Someone has kept her going," I said sharply. "Probably more than one."

"Yes." Elias nodded firmly. "And her love for him as well, most likely."

I scoffed, wanting to deny that what the Babadon and Gola Resh shared was love, except it was. A twisted, cruel love. A love that could justify anything so long as it allowed them to be together.

"I keep hoping that there is some way to reason with her. That when the time comes, it will turn out she is willing to be reasonable. That she'll realize our suffering is enough and gives her nothing." His fingers stroked a line down the page, tracing the patterns of the sigils. "But I haven't found that answer. I don't even have an idea for how to convince her to not take everything."

"Ask her to take half of us and spare the rest," I murmured, the words bitter on my tongue. "Condemn half the population."

"If it would save the people I love, perhaps. People do terrible things to save the people they love." He swallowed hard, his gaze fixed on a sketch of heavy darkness rolling across the sea and the cliffs like a fog. "Whoever betrayed us, she had to have offered them something." He kept his gaze fixed on the page. "I'm sorry." He dropped his gaze, his shoulders slumping as if beneath a great weight. "I-I haven't seen any visions that show the two of you together and alive. I'm sorry, Stella. Whenever I look to your future with you and Brandt, all I see—"

I held up a trembling hand. Nausea roiled inside me. Death. Death was all he saw.

"I'm sorry," he repeated.

I shook my head as I backed away. When I closed my eyes, I saw that livid image of the lava. It was the Ember Lord's Crest. That was where we died.

"Stella, please don't leave," he whispered. "Please."

"I need to be alone." My voice shook.

I hurried to the edge of the camp and then up to the ridge. I had to get myself under control. I had to figure out a way to deal with all of these emotions. My whole body trembled.

Water. I needed water. Needed to feel it rushing over me.

I climbed the ridge, pulling off my necklace and tossing it and the shawl onto a bush. I scarcely remembered to check for anyone else in the area before I pulled my dress off and dove into the hot spring.

The steaming waters were almost too hot to bear. They burned my eyes and reddened my skin at once, the sharpness of the minerals filling my lungs, but I plunged beneath the surface, and the heat encased me.

Heat, powerful and surging. Heat like the lava that would devour Brandt and me somehow. Heat like what thundered in my core.

I emerged and flung myself back against the rocks, gasping.

The need inside me was intense. Heat. Nothing but heat and want.

Curse it all.

The vision was a weighty one. There were so many things that that image might be. So many possibilities.

Fear gripped me tight, choking the breath from me.

There was no escape.

Brandt and I were going to die.

Why couldn't he be here?

Maybe this meant he wouldn't go mad? Not that the sketch actually revealed Brandt's state of mind. It hadn't even shown our faces. We were only charcoal, burning together in the molten flow. I couldn't even say for certain who was who. I just knew it had to be us.

Because this ended in death.

That was the only thing that would satisfy the Gola Resh.

I leaned my head back against the heated stone, staring into the night sky filled with stars.

The water's heat seeped into my bones, the steam into my lungs. There had to be another way. Auntie Runa had not wanted me to know that vision, and that meant it wasn't guaranteed. She didn't want me locked into it, but what other answer could there be?

Biting the inside of my lip, I closed my eyes and tried to see something. Anything. All we had was faith and hope that we could find a way.

If only Brandt could be here.

How pathetic was I? I longed to feel his arms around me. I could practically smell him even now.

A low growl echoed over the water.

My core tightened.

Brandt?

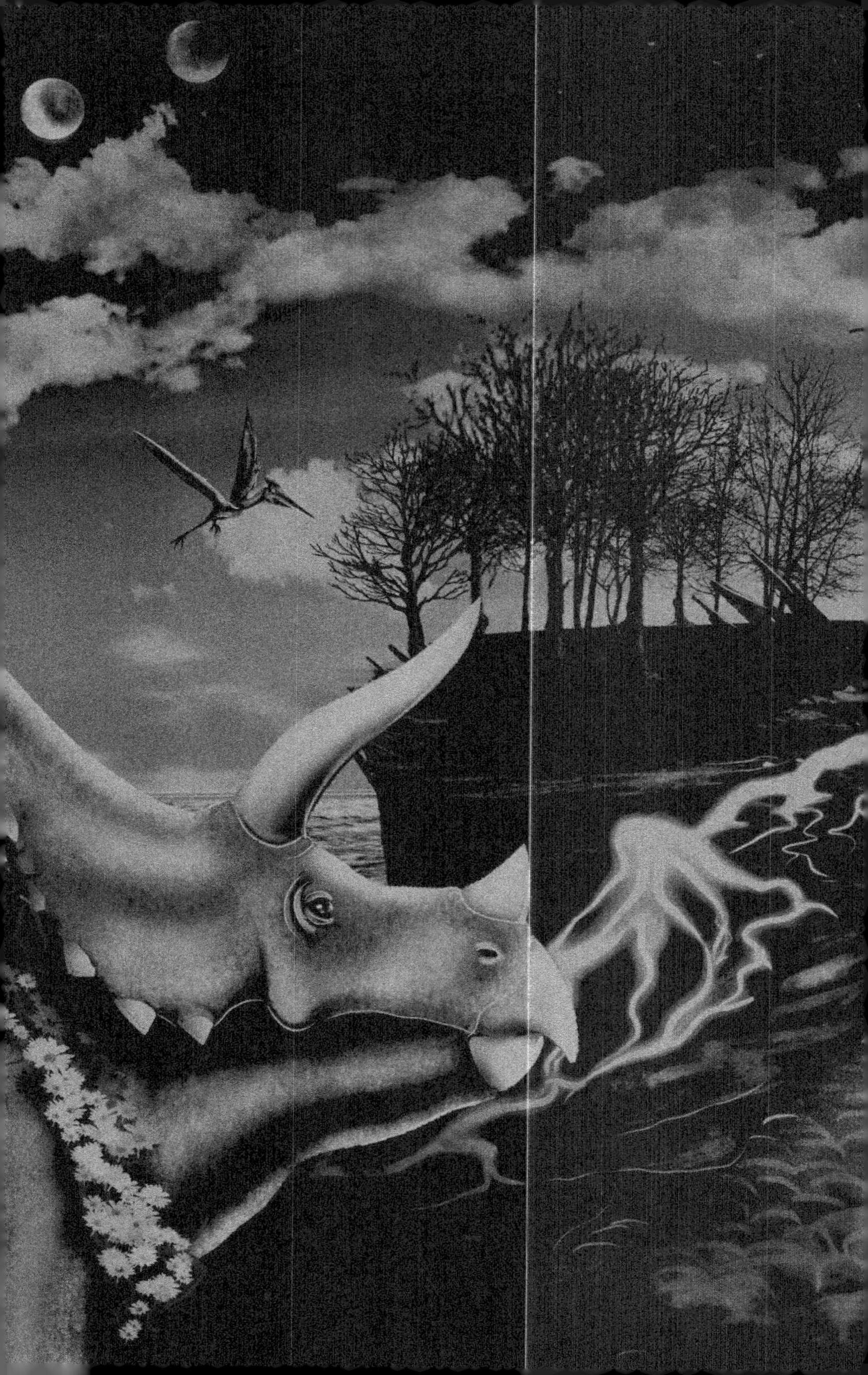

CHAPTER FORTY-THREE: STELLA

My eyes sprang open as my breath hitched in my throat.

It was him. He stood at the edge of the hot spring, his gaze fixed on me, his body like granite. All of his years of training, all his discipline, all his strength. All of it honed in on me. His deep-ruby eyes blazed bright, pupils wide with lust.

I sat up in the hot waters. They swirled about me, whorls of white and silver in the dark blue amid the bubbles. My mouth went dry despite the steam surrounding me.

The charm around his neck was a rich orange, like the sun setting in autumn.

He stepped forward, his cut muscles taut.

My head spun, and my heart pounded in my ears. The steam continued to rise, framing his massive muscular body. How had he gotten here?

His throat bobbed, his gaze fixed on me, unblinking.

This was bad.

Dangerous.

Little warnings scrabbled at the back of my mind, begging me to listen.

The thrum between us intensified, pinning me in place. Maybe I could move if I wanted to.

But I didn't want to.

The drums beat in the camp below, relentless and steady. It filled my ears like the pounding of my blood.

There were so many things I should ask. The questions surfaced at the edge of my consciousness, but I thrust them away. Nothing else mattered.

It wasn't alcohol this time. No giggles rose to my lips. I just remained there, resting, naked beneath the steaming water.

He stripped off his tabard and tunic and tossed them on the coarse rocks. Serpent tattoos coiled along his sides and arched over his stomach, highlighting his chiseled form. The shadows played along his body, drawing attention to the hard lines and long planes.

Ihlkit.

Hold me.

Kiss me.

Take me.

Destroy me.

I wriggled a little beneath the waters, my hand rising to graze my collarbone as I arched back. My breasts teased just at the surface of the water.

Clicking his tongue, he then growled. He slid into the water. It lapped up to his narrow waist, then up to his muscular chest as he strode toward me.

Part of me wanted to tease him for not taking his boots off. Or his pants, for that matter.

But the words got stuck inside me. They curled in my mind and evaporated as I remained frozen, simply watching as he approached.

That look in his eyes—oh! His gaze raked over me with rabid hunger. If I hadn't been sitting, my knees would have buckled.

A dull roar filled my ears as he leaned over me, his arms caging me against the slick stones. A whimper escaped my lips.

Tilting his head, he brought his face to mine, his dark-red eyes searching, his mouth so close to mine we shared breath.

The burning need practically consumed me.

He ripped off his trousers and boots, still staring at me with such fierceness I could barely hold a single breath.

His thighs pushed into mine as he thrust against me. I gasped, then moaned in response. He thrust his mouth against mine, another low growl rumbling through him. A second moan escaped my lips.

I wanted more. More of his hardness. More of his weight. More of him. I wanted him with me, in me. I wanted him imprinted on my bones and soul. This bond of ours had sealed us together years ago. Now I wanted it crushing over me.

He braced himself against the stone and moved against me, ferocious and unrelenting as he unleashed himself on me.

Yes! My voice caught in my chest as I arched up against him, bucking and driving my hips in response to him. My toes curled. I clutched at his neck and his back, dragging my fingernails over him. My eyes slid shut as I gulped in air.

Nothing but delicious heat and wonderful pressure.

Deeper and faster.

His hands cupped, clutched, and grasped. The steam swirled around us both, misting past his face and around my cheek.

Yes.

Yes!

I needed him as much as he needed me.

The tension and friction built between us. Building. Burning. Searing.

Growling, he intensified his pace, setting a punishing rhythm.

The beating pitch of the drums intensified as Brandt climaxed. His guttural moan vibrated through me as I followed swiftly behind. The intensity racked my body and stole my voice. All I could do was pulse and writhe, my eyelids fluttering.

For several breaths, we lay there with each other, his body pressed over mine, my arms still around his neck.

We'd gotten another night together. Somehow, he had gotten here. Who was I to question it?

Except this wasn't... It wasn't good.

His mouth moved. I tilted my head back to try to see him, but my own voice ceased working. All I could do was cling.

Blissful relief spread through my body, pulsing through me in rhythm with the drums, but there was still unease, something that curdled even the pleasure within me.

Dangerous.

That frightened little voice scraped at the back of my mind, begging me to listen. The weight intensified, crushing down upon me and constricting my breaths.

I couldn't move.

He stared at me, his lips parting as if he struggled to say something. His breaths huffed against my face, his brow creasing.

"Run," he whispered hoarsely. "Please." He pressed his forehead against mine.

The brokenness in his voice cut deeply, spearing me into place as I stared up at him. I...I couldn't move.

A trap.

This was a trap.

Tears spilled down my cheeks.

I knew it, but I couldn't. I held on to him, but my body had detached from my consciousness. We were here together. I was as powerless to run from him as he was to not kill me.

The vision's interpretation had been wrong. I would die here.

Life suddenly felt so raw and fragile, so delicate.

"Stella, your necklace fell in the bushes." Elias's voice called up from the path leading to the hot springs. "Don't worry. I won't look. I'm going to set it here on the stump with your dress."

The wind changed, blowing toward us. Elias's cologne and the cherry scent of the sephorite stone mingled with the sharp bite of the steaming mineral water.

Brandt groaned, lurching forward. His shoulders thrust back. His neck arched up. Strained gasps escaped his lips. He was fighting. Struggling.

I pressed my hands against his shoulders. My whole body moved slowly, as if I were trapped in hardening tree sap. There was no strength in my palms. Every part of me had gone so heavy I just wanted to slide beneath the water.

"Run," he whispered thickly. "Scream."

He battled against the curse, the muscles in his neck straining and a vein along his forehead bulging. All I could see were his eyes. That desperate struggle. The light flaring as he faded.

I could barely move. The weight pressed me down more than him and made me like lead.

It was a nightmare. My mouth wouldn't work. My voice had no strength. My tongue was a brick.

A weak "help" struggled from my lips, dying in the steamy air, my hands still against his shoulders but offering no resistance.

His hand gripped my throat. The muscles in his jaw tensed and ground.

"Stella? Did you say something?"

How had he heard that?

Brandt twitched, sweat pouring off his brow as he struggled to form a strangled shout. "Here."

His hand clamped over my throat.

My gaze snapped to his.

The panicked look in his eye. The terror. It all vanished, swallowed up by madness and hate.

Please, Brandt, fight!

"Quickly!" Elias shouted. "Come help! He's trying to kill her again!"

Brandt's grip tightened on me. He plunged me beneath the steaming waters, fingers digging into my throat. Burning. Dark.

My blood pounded, my bones groaned, and my throat screamed. I was helpless, my own hands weak. My thighs and hips grated against the stone. The surface was mere inches away, but I was pinned down, blurred, distorted, paralyzed.

Bubbles streamed upward as hot water filled my mouth.

Time ended. It was only this moment. My last breath suffocated within me, an endless scream locked inside.

The curse wore Brandt and pulled his strings at the Gola Resh's command.

Something massive plunged into the water behind us. Strong arms ripped me out. Brandt came with me, one hand locked around my throat, the other arm tight around my waist. His thumb crushed my windpipe.

A loud crack was followed by an agonized snarl of rage and pain.

Tears and water streamed down my face, blinding me. I gagged and choked, but I was still reaching for Brandt.

Lorna stood in the center of the pool, arms latched tight around him. His arm was broken but already starting to heal. His black-and-red ring rolled across the earth as if she'd ripped it off and tossed it away.

The massive arms that clutched me tight pulled me back. Arjax. His hand wrapped over my left one and guided me to clench my fingers and squeeze the ring. "Deep breaths. Pulse against the ring. Easy, girl. Easy."

My hand trembling, I squeezed the ring. A pulse of energy

seared through me. My airways cleared and opened, and the bruises vanished.

Elias shooed the crew away, calling for my privacy. Kine returned with a large blanket. As soon as Arjax set me down, Kine flung it over my shoulders and hugged me close, turning me away from Brandt.

Brandt continued to rage. Lorna held him tight, his head well above the water though he remained immobilized. The waters frothed and surged around them as he kicked and bellowed.

Despite the healing, I kept gasping for breath. My lungs filled with the cold air, and I clutched the blanket close. Curse the Gola Resh. Curse her!

The image of Brandt's panicked eyes was burned into my mind. He had fought so hard against the curse for me, and I had been powerless to help him. Hadn't even been able to control myself enough to get away.

Kine tried to tug me toward the path that led back down to camp, but I refused. Water dripped down my body and pooled on the ground.

Shivering, I shook my head. "No." I wanted to go to him.

Arjax blocked my path, hands set on his waist as he towered over me. "We'll help him."

Lorna leaned back against the stones as she gripped Brandt. Her muscles strained, and her face was turned down with her chin tucked to protect her neck. "Not any kind of shifter disease," she called out. "This is something else." Lorna staggered back in the pool. She grunted, banding her arm tighter around Brandt. "He's going to wear out soon. Just go rest, Stella. We'll get him to sleep here, and it'll pass."

"How did he even get here?" Kine demanded, bewildered. He stood between Brandt and me, his manner almost helpless.

My muscles trembled. I didn't want to leave. "What are you going to do with him?"

Were they going to kuvaste him like Hord and Candy had done?

Brandt's bellows intensified as his frustration grew.

Lorna grimaced. "Quiet now," she said, adjusting her grip on him. He raged even harder.

Arjax scowled. "Do you need help, cousin?"

"No."

Brandt flung his head back, clipping her chin.

"Enough of this. He's going to hurt you and himself." Arjax strode over. He pressed his hand over Brandt's carotid arteries.

Brandt stiffened, then went limp as if he had been drugged. Arjax grunted.

Lorna lifted Brandt up easily and carried him out of the steaming waters. She then laid him down on the ground just beyond my sight. "Poor kid," she muttered.

Kine handed her the other heavy grey blanket he'd brought with him.

"Thanks, baby blue."

I still stood there, unable to move. I could see Brandt's feet sticking out from beyond the stones. Lorna wrapped the blanket around him, mumbling about how they likely had clothing that could fit him if they couldn't find his.

My eyes squeezed shut. That one had been early as well.

But we had saved time, so that meant this wasn't his last time before the insanity became permanent. I tried to run the calculations in my mind. There was one more, right? One more before his last.

How had it happened? What was causing it?

That horrible hazy sensation blurred everything. I staggered toward Brandt as Lorna searched for his clothes.

Arjax stepped in front of me. "Stella—" he started.

I tried to move around him.

He stood over me, sniffing the air. He lifted his hand, scowling. "Your smell changed."

"Wha—" I stared up at him, blinking. "What does that have to do with anything?" My voice shook a little at the end. I brushed my fingertips over my collarbone as if searching for the necklace.

"You no longer have that strange smell. It's changed." He strode back a few paces, muttering something to Lorna.

Lorna started searching as well.

Arjax crossed over and swept the necklace with the charm and moonstone up. His brow furrowed as he drew in a deep breath, inhaling the scent. He recoiled almost at once, his thumb pressing down over the smooth surface of the sephorite charm. "This is not from this place. Not from Terrea."

Brandt suddenly lurched up, his eyes blazing. The charm around his neck flared bright yellow *again*.

"No!" I screamed, my fingers digging into my scalp. "No!"

Lorna seized him by the throat and rendered him unconscious once more. He dropped to the ground like a sack of overboiled potatoes.

I didn't even have words any more.

Kine explained what I couldn't. His voice droned in my ears as everything faded away.

I knelt beside Brandt, collapsing over him. I didn't care.

The muscles in his face twitched. That vein along his neck and across his forehead was just as vivid. I tried to smooth the agony away. Dull fear clawed at me.

Trap.

Yes, it was probably a trap, but he was mine.

It wasn't over yet. We still had time.

I stroked his face, shaking. My fingertips pressed against his cheek, his jaw, his throat.

What the Gola Resh had done to him was unforgivable, but he wasn't gone yet.

I wouldn't let her take him from me.

Wouldn't let her destroy what he and I shared.

My head bowed low, my lips pressing to his brow. "It's not too late. It happened so fast, it couldn't possibly count. You're going to be fine. I know you are." My voice cracked.

His ragged breaths heated the shell of my ear, his chest rising and falling beneath me.

Arjax held the necklace up without touching it as he shouted something about where it was from. Lorna shouted about something else. Kine was asking to see the necklace.

A hand rested on my shoulder, light but firm.

I looked up into Elias's eyes, tears pouring down my cheeks as I sobbed.

"I'm sorry," he whispered, his dark-blue eyes filled with compassion. He placed his hand over mine, squeezing it tight and lifting it from Brandt's chest. "I am so sorry, Stella."

"It's not too late." Sobs racked my voice, shattering it. "He's still got his sanity. Maybe we can finish the ceremony and end the curse before it claims him again."

"We still have a day to get through the Keening Pass." He stroked my hand. "Even if he finds a way to fight it off for a few hours—even if you accomplish the impossible—the curse will take him again, and he will never awaken." He shook his head, his eyes shuttering. "I'm sorry."

"No! No." My voice choked. The screams became whimpers, pinched and desperate. "It might take less than a day to get through the Keening Pass and to the Ember Lord's Crest. As long as we don't hit trouble, we can do it. We just have to go fast!"

"How likely is that really?" He leaned even closer, his breath hot against my cheek. "All you can offer him now is mercy," he whispered. "The last thing Brandt would want is for you to see him descend into eternal madness."

"No." My whole body trembled, terror churning alongside rage.

"It is the kind thing to do. It is the loving thing to do. He would want you to. Brandt would tell you to do it himself, especially if it could save you. This is the only way you can both escape your fate in the lava."

His words snagged my attention. "What... What did you say?" The tears froze within me.

He dipped his head forward, his dark-red hair sliding over his shoulders as he gave me such a gentle, trustworthy look. His finger brushed the curve of my cheek. "The Gola Resh has shown a measure of mercy. Accept it. Take her deal. Slay Brandt so the Gola Resh will save you. Perhaps you can even negotiate for more from her."

Cold anger rippled within my chest. "Elias." My gaze snapped to his, my voice harsher than it had ever been. "How do you know about what the Gola Resh offered me?"

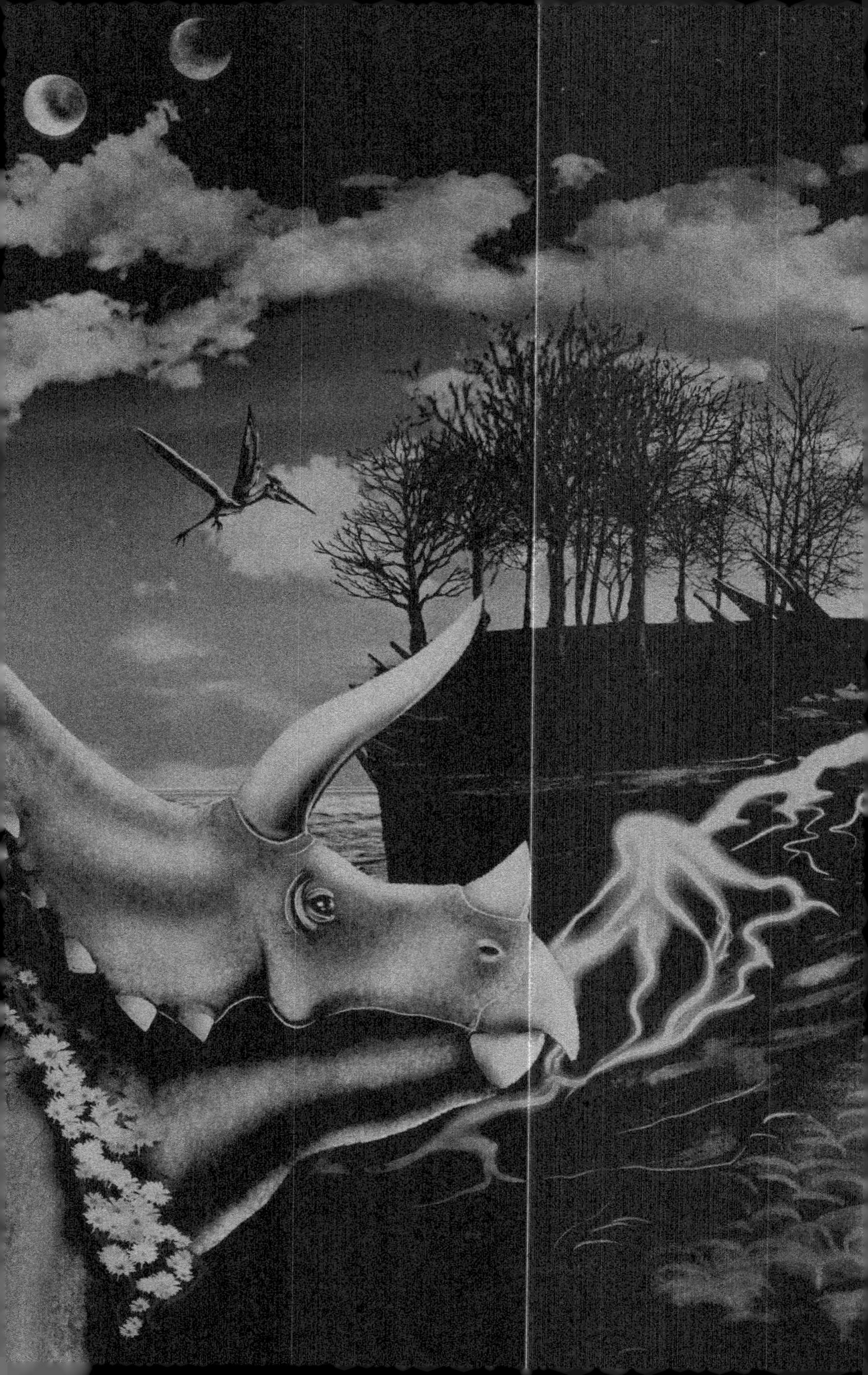

CHAPTER FORTY-FOUR: STELLA

My gaze remained fixed on Elias, horror deep within me. He shouldn't have known that. My tears were cold on my cheeks. Though I was still too close to him for my own comfort, I refused to move away from Brandt.

Arjax and Lorna's argument continued as they pressed Kine with questions. The moonlight shimmered on the hot spring, the steam rising and coiling into the night.

Elias hesitated. Then a glimmer sparked in his eyes. His upper lip curled as he tilted his head forward. "I'm a seer, Stella. I told you I've been seeing more. My gifts are changing."

"No." My fingers twitched.

Where were Elias's hands? Did he have a weapon? His right hand pressed at his chest, the other lingering near the waist of his robe.

"Get away from him," I growled as I lurched to my feet. "Get away from him now!"

"Why would I harm him?" Elias kept his gaze fixed on mine, but that hint of a smile danced in his eyes. "Stella, I wouldn't."

"There's something in the necklace charm. You're the one

who gave me the necklace. You're the reason the curse keeps moving forward."

"I'm just a seer, Stella." He spread his arms as he moved back. Though his tone was soft, almost meek, it had an edge to it. Coyness glinted in his eyes as if he could no longer contain it. "It's like I told you from the start. I have no shifting abilities. I'm nobody. I am defined by the vow I swore. All I want is for you to be safe. I could never harm you."

My muscles tightened. The mockery in his voice. The glint in his eye.

"Letting Brandt go is the best thing for both of you. He is becoming more beast than man. He will lose all that made him the Brandt you knew."

I knew this. I knew it! All that mattered was keeping him away from Brandt. Brandt might have tried to kill me because of the curse, but he had done everything in his power to stop.

"Hey, what's happening?" Kine suddenly stood beside me, his attention split between me and Elias. His hands rested on his sash.

"It's just a misunderstanding. Stella is getting paranoid." That same glint. That pull of his lips. The taunting in his eyes.

"What's not paranoid is this necklace charm and the moonstone. This is a psychic stone and an activator." Arjax held it up by the leather band. "Where did you get this? This is the forbidden arts and not of this world."

My fists balled up at my sides. Rage boiled deeper inside of me.

Elias ripped off the binding over his arm and gestured toward the vivid tattoo on his forearm. The dark swirls and patterns were like living darkness against his tanned flesh. "Must I prove myself again? How far must I go to prove my value and my resolution in this matter? I have dedicated my life to you, Your Majesty. I searched for you when no one else knew it was possible. I am the reason you are here! And you question me?" There was mockery in his tone, and yet why would he have bound himself in such a sacred manner when his plan was betrayal all along?

All I knew now was what my instincts warned. All his kind gestures, soothing words, and quiet presence meant nothing. He had been there for me, guiding me toward the path of Brandt's destruction. Undermining my marriage. Deceiving us all.

"I do question you. I question everything you have done!"

His brow furrowed, his eyes now hard as slate. "Then you question what it is to be Sepeazian. You question the basis of our honor, that a vow made from the ink of our heartstones, our most sacred and grounded form of magic—"

"It's a fake," Arjax said, still holding the leather band of the necklace. His black eyes burned, the edge of a cold smirk tugging at his mouth though his expression remained hard. "That ink. I can smell it. It isn't from a heartstone. It isn't sacred."

Kine looked as if someone had just struck him.

My fists clenched tighter.

Elias's eyes widened briefly. "You can't possibly—"

Arjax held his fist aloft. The necklace spun on the strand, the charm and moonstone sparkling. "I smell the taint of the forbidden arts on this necklace. I smell a world other than our own. Do *not* disgrace yourself further or dishonor me by offering such falsehoods." His mouth curled with disgust. "And you smell of cedar. Cedar obscures many other scents. It is no coincidence that it is what you have chosen, is it? What else are you hiding, traitor?"

If looks could have killed, I would have burned Elias to a briquette. I wrapped the blanket tighter around myself as I stood.

Elias's expression twisted. Disgust flared in his eyes. He fished a vial out of his outer robe and held it up. "Just this. Guess I'll be leaving now. Not going to worry about the spear. You have to bring it if you want to make your final attempt. We'll just take it when it arrives." He smirked, his expression hard, his gaze falling to me. "You haven't saved your beloved from anything except more suffering. See you soon, Stella. We'll see if you're in a more reasonable mood when you get to the Ember Lord's Crest."

Kine lunged as Elias smashed the vial on the ground. Orange and green smoke exploded out while purple light flashed. It pulsed in red at the edges. He sprang through it, vanishing. The edges of his robes flared with fire, and the air briefly smelled like burned cedar and charred vanilla.

"Crespa. The bastard had a blood portal," Arjax muttered.

Lorna swore under her breath. She took a cloth and thrust it into his hand.

Silence fell over us. The steaming water and strange sulfuric smell from the portal had obscured most of his scent, almost as much as the curse obliterated Brandt.

I dropped to my knees beside Brandt once more. He still slept fitfully, his lips parting and strange syllables whispering past. A muscle flinched in his jaw.

My love.

The Gola Resh and her vicious magic were stripping him from me piece by piece. He was slipping away from me like the sands in that wretched hourglass counting down our doom.

My fingers knotted in the blanket covering him. My throat was hoarse from emotion, my chest tight. It was going to be all right. Elias had been exposed.

"It really was clever." Arjax placed the charm and moonstone in the dark-grey cloth and indicated the mark and shapes on the back. "This is a type of psychic stone. You can impress into it different types of instructions that will then happen. Like a delayed spell. When it's cut like this, it shows the marks of the sigils. Look." He turned it over to reveal the part hidden by the metal backside. He grunted, his brow lined and his gaze sharp.

I barely managed to bring my gaze up. The sickness inside me intensified.

Arjax wrapped the stone up tight and bound it with a strip of cloth. "Most of that power went to forcing the curse to go faster. It pushes time forward. Destroying it won't destroy the curse, but it will keep it from advancing, but the other sigil here is, well, it's a calming. I'll bet you he wore his own charms and sigils but kept them hidden, ones similar to the cedar to mask those scents and hide that he had been to Earth as well."

Kine sank onto a boulder near me, his hands grasping at his head. "I don't know how I missed that."

Lorna gave him a sympathetic look as she finished fishing Brandt's clothing out of the hot spring. Arjax had disappeared through the thicket. "He came to you when you were grieving the loss of your sister and told you he, too, was in mourning. He offered you hope when you had none."

Kine scoffed, as if he could not accept that. "I was so...so desperate. I would have sacrificed myself to save you in a heartbeat, Bug." His tongue pressed at his lips. "I didn't take a life debt or a life bond, but I swore—I swore it, and I failed. Even worse, I let in someone who has been undermining everything from the start." He dragged his hand through his hair.

I could have blamed him. Could have snapped at him. Could have accused him. Instead, I shook my head, still kneeling beside Brandt. "Elias played us all for fools. He knew what he was doing."

"He played on your desperation and your fears. It was smart of him. You will see him again. He won't be alone, though." Lorna looked up as Arjax returned. He carried black iron shackles as well as a change of clothes, all of simple black cotton.

Kine rubbed the back of his neck, his words haltingly. "I didn't know. I didn't... I'm shocked you could smell ink that had been set for that long."

"He didn't. Arjax is a liar." Lorna tousled his braids as she held her hand out. "And he isn't even that good at bluffing."

Arjax shrugged, his massive shoulders lifting as he offered a smile without showing any teeth. Then he cast an amused and annoyed glance in her direction. "Who says I can't smell it?" He tossed her the clothing.

"I do." Lorna crouched beside me. Her gaze was hooded brown eyes soft. "Little cousin, listen now. Your veskare is resting, and we must prepare for the Keening Pass. Your heart is heavy, but summon up your strength. Arjax and I may know how to handle some of this. We need to think."

"And we will think of something," Arjax said. He tilted his head back, frowning a little. Then he gestured. "That's Hakon up there. Mages'll be coming for the venom soon."

Lorna nodded, but her gaze remained fixed on me, asking what I wanted to do.

I pressed my hand to his chest, my breaths shaking still. "The plan..." It might be too late for Brandt, but even if it was, I was the queen. I was fighting not just for us, but for Sepeazia.

My tongue moistened my lips as I spoke with effort, my fingertips curling along his high sculpted cheeks and the stubble of his chin. "We follow the original plan." I counted and recounted, measuring the days and calculating the time. And there was only one fact.

Kine stooped beside me, his hand on my shoulder. He knew. "I'm sorry, Bug."

Brandt could be seized by the curse one more time. After that, his madness would be permanent.

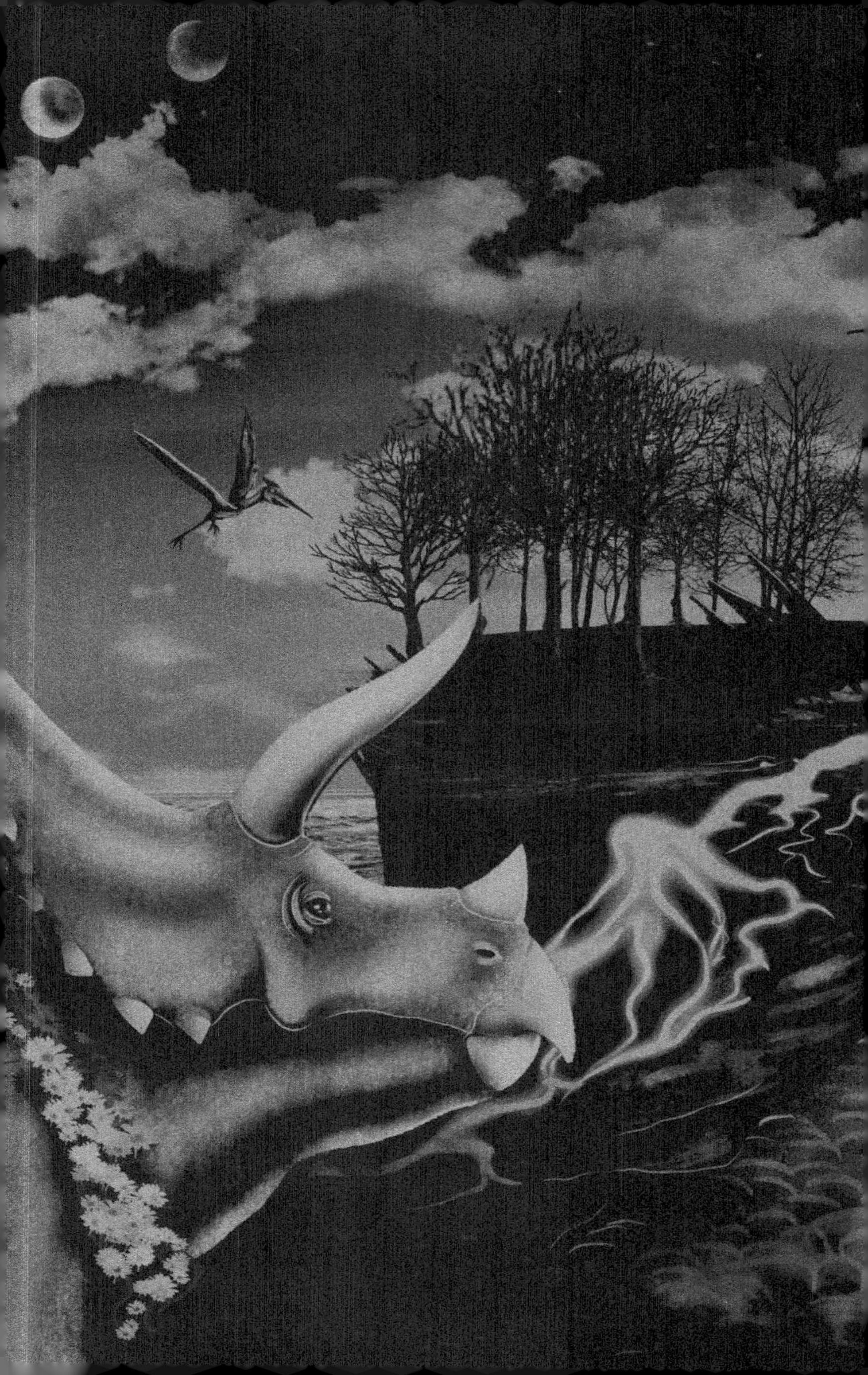

CHAPTER FORTY-FIVE: STELLA

*L*orna and Arjax dressed Brandt with care and then shackled his wrists and ankles.

"Just so we can make sure there's nothing else that will set him off," Lorna said.

I couldn't argue. Didn't have the strength to argue. Both Arjax and Lorna promised me that they weren't giving up. They might have something, but there were no specifics.

What was specific and what was real was that we were running out of time and fast and perhaps completely for Brandt.

Kine sent the crew back to the ship to make final preparations, including Elias's parasaur along with plenty of supplies and a promise that we would come soon. Arjax and Lorna carried Brandt back down to the fire in the main camp and placed him there.

Lorna fussed over pots and jars, moving items back and forth as she searched for something. The minutes ticked into hours. Numbly, I helped them pack what was needed and assisted in breaking down more of the meat so that nothing would be wasted.

Dawn was drawing near when Arjax drew me aside. He picked up a torch.

"Come on." Arjax gestured for me to follow him. "It'll do you good to walk a bit, and the mages are good folk. Bit quiet and secretive. Charming hawks. Kine and Lorna will finish tending the beasties. You should meet these folk."

I walked numbly beside him, not certain what to expect. There was little to say. At least, little from me.

Arjax made a few observations about the Wild Lands and all its wonders. I responded just enough, my words dull. He didn't seem offended, just walked with me and guided me down the path as the night seemed to darken even more.

The group of mages arrived soon after, silent on the darkened hill. There were five of them, two women and three men, all shrouded in hoods. They moved out from the thick-trunked trees, stepping into the torchlight.

A strongly built man strode forward, a hawk perched on his gloved forearm. He whispered something to it, then turned his focus up to Arjax. "Arjax?" He asked the question as if he already knew the answer.

Arjax grinned and dipped his head. "Cyland?" His voice boomed heartily as he stepped forward.

Cyland extended the arm without the hawk.

Arjax gripped it firmly, giving him a solid shake. "You are expected. Will you join us back at our camp? You must be hungry after the journey."

"We are short on time," said one of the dark-haired men. He was a little shorter than Cyland, powerfully built, with long hair and fierce yet contemplative features.

His voice cut deep. Great tragedy and struggle had brought them here. Perhaps tragedy like Sepeazia's.

I offered a small smile and inclined my head in greeting as well, my own heart almost too heavy for words.

Arjax glanced at me, then indicated the path with the thick brush. "This way."

Thorns glimmered in the torchlight like little shiny daggers. The mages glanced about with cautious gazes as if taking in the entirety of this place.

My eyes fell on the woman who held the dark-haired man's hand. There was something familiar about her. She had flame-red hair with golden highlights. Bold and elegant whorls and spirals curled across her hands in an inky design. She stared at me, eyes intense as we walked toward the camp.

I smiled a little, struggling to place the memory or the sensation. "I'm Stella. Apparently, I'm queen of Sepeazia."

The dark-haired man shot me an annoyed glare. "Apparently? You don't know?" A bit of stubble highlighted his squared jaw, intensifying the ruggedness of his appearance.

The flame-haired woman's eyes widened as she struck her hand over his muscular bicep. He grumbled something about her ripping flesh, but she kept her gaze fixed on me. "You're another sacrifice, aren't you?"

My pace broke. Yes! That was how I knew her. She was one of the women who had sacrificed herself in that pool, another who had returned after paying the ultimate price.

That flash of awareness blossomed into fuller and richer memories. All of us standing in that pool. The knives across our palms. The rising chant.

"You were one of the eight?" I asked.

She pressed a hand to her chest. "Adira. Were you in Las Vegas?"

"Ihlkit!" I gasped, smiling and somehow feeling a little lighter. "Yes. I'm still reeling a little, to be honest."

Adira shook her head. "I can't imagine what it's like to learn you can shift forms. I thought being told I'm basically a wizard was hard."

The third male released an irritated groan. "How long until

we rid that word from your mouth? There is nothing pathetically wizardly about us. Do we use wands? Of course not. Magic is in our blood, the way it ought to be."

Adira's pleasant mouth quirked as she snorted a laugh. "He's a little sensitive about titles. You really can shift, right?"

I chuckled, biting back my own sigh. Oh, that was complicated. "Yeah...it's...an experience. I'll say that."

"I'm still trying to recall everything and figure it out, but—" She sent an affectionate glance up at the dark-haired man and held his hand a little tighter. "It gets easier."

Seeing the quiet love and affection between them despite his gruffness comforted me.

We continued on our way until we reached the camp.

I glanced back at them and slowed so that I was closest to Adira. "Arjax and his cousin will want to feed you," I whispered. It was hard to imagine how they would get out without being blessed with the Vawtrian hospitality.

"He's incredibly tall," she whispered to me. "Are all the men like that?"

I smiled at this. "No. He's not even a water serpent. He's a Vawtrian, a general shapeshifter. Arjax and his cousin are a little like us. Both were brought here from another world. They seem to have acclimated well enough."

A bright smile flashed over Adira's face. "Then there's hope."

It was contagious, and I laughed as well. "Good news to hold on to."

We certainly needed all that we could get.

We continued to talk as we walked. Her companions had a few questions for me as well, though the man who held her hand—Kage—remained somber, the weight of whatever had brought them here obviously pressing hard on him.

I didn't ask why they needed the venom despite my curiosity. From a few murmurs between them, it sounded a bit like the mages had their own experience with terrifying curses. My knowledge of potion work was nearly nonexistent. Adira told me about another of the princesses, Ember, who had been kidnapped. Adira herself had been flung through a hell vortex.

As we reached the camp, I saw it had stilled so much from just an hour previously. The crew had already departed, taking with them the first of the supplies as they went to prepare the ship for our journey into the Keening Pass.

Brandt lay on the earth near the fire, still bound. My heart quailed, protectiveness surging through me. I didn't want anyone else to see him this way. My cheeks heated.

"Who is that?" Adira asked, edging closer to Kage.

"Oh." I bit the inside of my lip and released a tight breath. My smile wavered. "That's...that's my husband and the love of my life. The king of Sepeazia." My heart clenched as I said those words. Tears stung the backs of my eyes. Blinking them back, I fidgeted with my hair. "He would greet you and invite you to stay and eat, I'm sure." I paused, sighing. "Actually, he'd probably wish you well on your journey and bless your speedy return and progress. He doesn't like being delayed places either, but when the curse seizes him...measures have to be taken. It isn't him, though. Not really."

I quickly explained what happened with Brandt. My voice shook at the end as I resisted the urge to drop by his side and soothe him in his fitful sleep.

Kage's brow creased slightly, his expression tightening.

Adira glanced at him, and her fingers flexed slightly. Her smile pinched. "I am the curse breaker of Magiaria."

"Wildling, not all magics can impact others. The serpent king's curse comes from different power than ours," Kage whispered.

I offered a small nod, recalling what Brandt had said. Everyone had tried. So many over the years.

Regret stole over Adira's features as she straightened her shoulders. "Even still, should you need help, for what you're doing for us, we'll stand with you. We know what it is like to have others try to destroy that sort of love."

I started to assure her that it was appreciated but unnecessary when Cyland clicked his tongue. My gaze fell to him when I realized he was communicating with the hawk. With a twist of his head, the dusky-winged hawk spread his wings and leaped into the sky.

"He'll scan the return path back to the ship, but I do not think we should be out in the open on the Wildlands long."

"He's a gorgeous hawk," I offered.

Arjax strode alongside me, winking and then clapping his hand firmly on my shoulder before he looked at our guests. "What about food or drink? Either to eat here or carry with you on your way."

Lorna emerged from the brush on the other side of camp. She lifted her hand in greeting and grinned. "Yes, stay and eat, or take it with you. Either way, there's more than enough. Besides, we're traveling with them, and it's best this is eaten rather than wasted."

The mages at first refused, but then the second woman accepted some raw meat while Arjax finished tying down the stone lid to the basilisk venom.

"I guess you need that venom." I really was curious what it could be used for, but as Arjax had said, they valued their privacy.

Arjax picked up the large stone vessel, placing his hands on either side, framing the bold white sigils. Though he carried it easily, it looked heavy.

"We are indebted to you." Kage spoke through his teeth.

Arjax batted the words away. "So long as you use the basilisk venom wisely and do not waste it, then it is a gift. We've added more to the top. Basilisk venom is wretchedly toxic, so be certain to cover your hands."

"If it's so toxic, will it transport well?" one of the mages asked.

"It won't eat through this stone," Arjax said. His smile grew broader as he set it down on a boulder near them. "Use it with purpose, use it with care, and never use it on supper. At least if it's supper for people you care about."

Adira snorted another laugh, and I smiled. I liked her and the way she smiled even when she was fighting against her own heartache.

I set my hands on my waist as the mages secured the venom further.

Kage turned to face me, brow creased in a heavy line. "As Adira said, should you have need of our aid, we will stand with you."

"Are you sure there isn't another ingredient for your spell?" I could practically smell the bitter bite of the venom even though it was sealed.

Adira shook her head, her hair shining in the firelight. "We need the potency to truly kill the cruel magic in our soil. It's embedded so deeply only such a poison as this will do to lift it."

I managed a weak smile. So many dark and horrifying magics out there. So many cruel powers.

"Stella," Brandt mumbled thickly. "Run, please." It turned into a shout, the words slurring as if the nightmare had intensified.

His muscles tensed. Then his head dropped back against the packed earth.

My smile fell.

Adira's brow knit with concern. "Thank you," she said gently. "I wish you and your king luck."

My head bobbed in response as I steadied myself. "Be safe on your return, Adira."

She stepped forward and squeezed my hand. "I'm sure we will meet again one day. We're back where we belong, after all."

"Yes." I drew in a deep breath and forced myself to smile. "Yes, of course."

With that, we all bid one another farewell. Then, silently as they arrived, they slipped away.

I released a long sigh, my gaze falling back to Brandt. Adira's visit had reminded me of how we already had managed the impossible. Both she and I had died to save this world and been dragged back to memories of old lives with great challenges before us. Returning should have been impossible, but we had. Each of us. Brandt and I could do the impossible as well.

Arjax placed his hand on my shoulder. "Let's finish packing the camp and then get your beloved to the ship. We'll be ready for the Keening Pass in plenty of time."

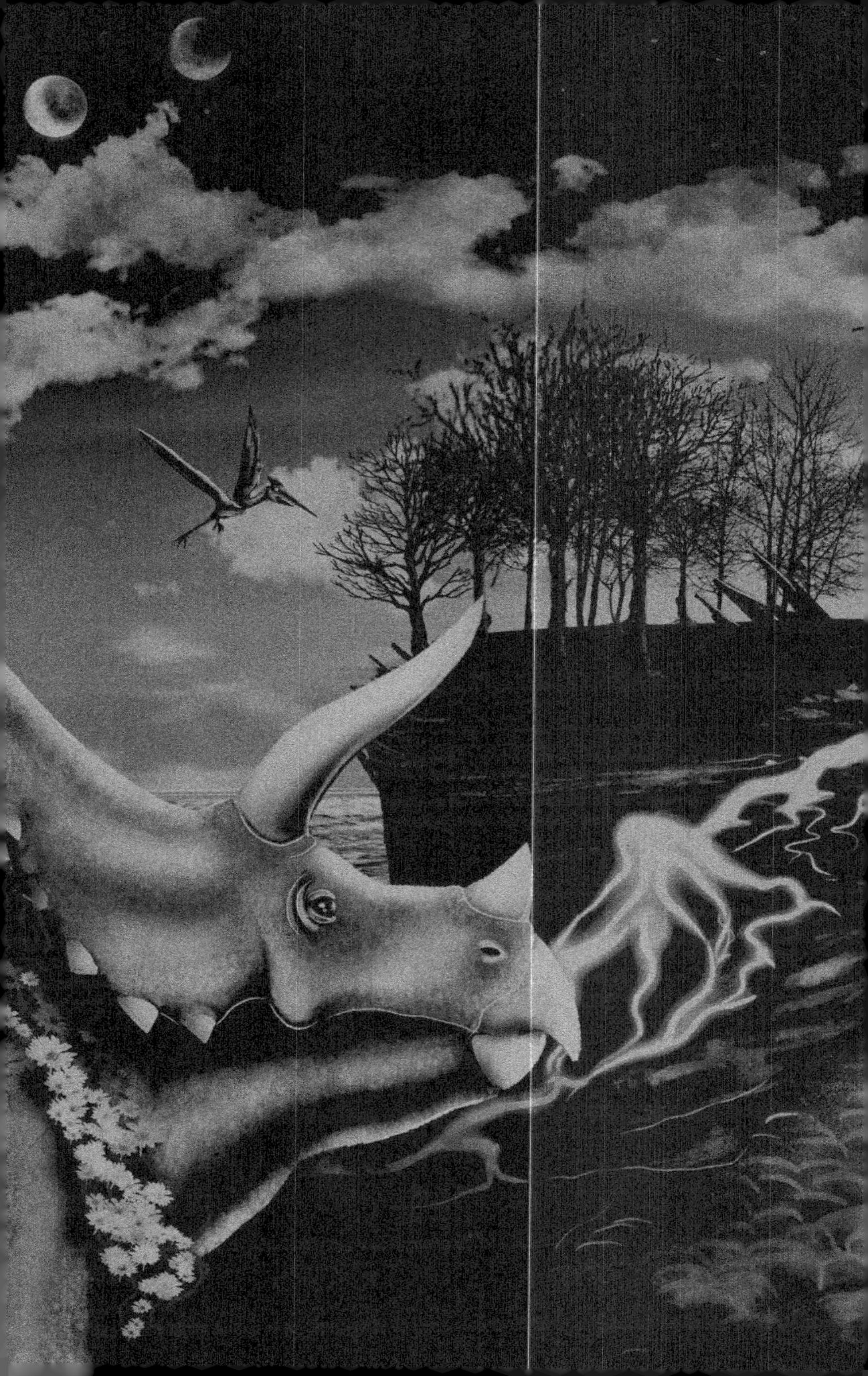

CHAPTER FORTY-SIX: STELLA

We packed and prepared for our departure, Arjax and Lorna indicating what needed to be tied down or secured so that their camp would be undisturbed during their absence. Most of the supplies and tools, including the ropes and dry racks, were placed in the cellar. Working over the fire at one of the small workstations, Lorna labored over some sort of concoction, the pungent scent of horseradish, lemon, and peppermint covering up almost every other scent except smoke.

Brandt groaned, his eyelids lifting. He rocked for a moment before realizing he was chained. Then his gaze met mine. He released a pained breath and dropped his head back, going limp. "You're all right."

I knelt beside him, smoothing the dust from his brow. Tears knotted my throat and burned the backs of my eyes. "I am. You?"

"A little...off." His voice cracked.

I fetched one of the waterskins and set it against his lips. He drank slowly, his gaze averted as if he couldn't bear to look at me.

"Did the Gola Resh bring you here?" I asked softly.

"Yes." He closed his eyes. "And—"

Lorna knelt behind him and started to unfasten the chains as Arjax sat beside me.

"No, don't unchain me!" Brandt bared his teeth, his voice dropping to a snarl. "I can't take this anymore. I don't know what is changing the timeline. If I lose—"

Lorna placed her hand on his shoulder, cutting him off. "Little cousin, listen. We can't free you from the curse, but this curse is similar to something else we have fought."

She and Arjax then explained to him what had happened with Elias and the charm and the curse. Brandt offered his own interjections and explanations, including that the Gola Resh had thrown him through with the intent to kill me.

Not that he was saying everything. He shifted uncomfortably and still did not look at me even as he massaged his wrists and ankles.

Kine remained silent through most of it, asking a couple questions.

"Well, all that to say, little cousin, I don't think you'll be sliding into the cursed state again without that necklace or something like it present." Arjax jerked his head in Lorna's direction as she removed the small silver pot from the fire.

"I don't want to risk it. You should keep me chained. The Gola Resh has proved too unpredictable." He kept his face turned from me, shame defining his posture. "She wants us to suffer, and she will make sure I am the reason Stella dies if she has her way. And I just… I cannot."

"Answer me this, Brandt." Lorna gestured over the pot as if to better smell it. "You're quite strong, aren't you?"

His eyebrow arched. "You might say that."

"And you know how to kill quickly, do you not?"

He nodded slowly.

I frowned at this question. Where was she going with this?

"In fact," Lorna continued, "I seem to recall one of the last times you visited before the curse fell upon you. You snapped a terror bird's neck with your bare hands. Not an easy feat." She tilted her head, her red-black eyes fierce but contemplative. "It's actually one of your skills. It took me a while to put this together, but I see it now." She gestured between us. "You tried to drown Stella and choke her with one hand. The other time, it was with both hands, but you didn't succeed. If I had to guess, I'd say that in each of the attempts to kill Stella, you have made critical errors in your responses."

It hadn't felt like they were errors at the time. At the time, they had been terrifying. I folded my arms.

Kine cleared his throat. "His strangulation stance was off the first time," he offered, holding up his hands to demonstrate the spacing.

My own hand went to my throat as I thought back. Strangulation wasn't one of my skills, and I wasn't sure...but there was something being implied here.

A little spark of hope burned inside me. "The second time, he flung me onto the ledge from the flooding river, and in the throne room, he could have attacked faster. He took things slower."

I hadn't really noticed it at the time beyond being shocked at how well I was doing.

Kine nodded in agreement. "We shouldn't have had a chance, but we got Stella out even after she dropped out of the form. He spent more time coiling than when I fought him."

Lorna exchanged glances with Arjax, then smiled. She tapped the spoon on the side of the pot. "Good."

"That confirms our theory then. Good news, Brandt. Lorna has something for you. It's helped other shifters," Arjax said.

"I don't struggle with shifting." Brandt's brow furrowed. "I don't even shift all the time, and I can't if I'm not wearing my ring. This curse goes beyond that."

"It does." Lorna brought the silver pot over, the strong scent intensifying.

I fanned my face to push the smell away. "Ihlkit. It's worse up close."

"So, obviously, you are capable of resisting the curse for a time," Lorna said, giving the pot a swift stir.

"There are moments of struggle," Brandt said, "but it's futile. Eventually it takes over."

"Yet you fight nonetheless, and some part of you continues to fight because that is the part that keeps you from being as deadly as you should be." Lorna smiled softly. "You are a warrior through and through, little cousin." She poured a spoonful of the foul-scented liquid into a small clay tumbler. "Horrifying as this is, the curse is fascinating. That charm was influencing both of you. Making the power of the curse far more...compelling in more ways than one."

I brushed my fingertips over Brandt's left hand. "It wasn't your fault. I know you've done your best."

And he had fought. I knew that now even more than before.

"My best doesn't matter when your life is at stake." He broke off as my fingertips grazed his knuckles. Then he caught my hand in his and gripped it close.

"That love is what the Gola Resh is trying to pervert and destroy, but it is also a strength." Lorna mixed up the liquid with hot water. "We have our veskares and veskaros, our most beloveds of all. The bond both of you share is uncommonly intense and the most like a Vawtrian bond I have ever seen between two non-Vawtrians. I don't know if it is from the magic our ancestors wove into your shifter rings or if it is simply because this is what you are and what you share. Take strength and comfort in the intensity of your connection. What the Gola Resh has done to you is obscene and blasphemous. It desecrates the sacred, yet your bond remains despite her efforts because, through all this, you have remained committed to one another. You have done your best to remain faithful and to put one another's needs before your own."

"That does little good if I am not in my right mind," Brandt said, his fingers still laced through mine. "If I cause harm, my intent does not matter."

"Perhaps in some respects, but it matters for the fight you must go through. For my people, shifting near one's mate is difficult, if not impossible, before a certain level of connection is established. But you, your whole race responds differently. You don't have that same struggle. It is instead a different sort of focus. The curse that the Gola Resh has put upon you is a torment. That is its whole purpose. It draws your conscious mind back into a pain-filled state in which you are tormented until you obey the command pressed upon you. It overwhelms and destroys everything but that command."

I bowed my head, remembering how swiftly it had come over me, how fast that pain had twisted my thoughts to a single conclusion.

Lorna placed the tumbler in his hand. "When you are being pulled down into the curse and it is taking over your senses, you must fight it, and you will fight it by remembering your love for Stella." She indicated the tumbler. "You need to drink this. It will help you with your focus."

He sniffed it and grimaced. "What is it?"

Her expression grew more serious. "One of the worst slurs you can speak against a Vawtrian is to call them a skin-changer. It's an insult that strikes to our core, but it's also a term for something that happens in...horrifying situations. Our minds break apart, and we are trapped in between forms, consumed by grief and rage. A Vawtrian enduring this will be consumed by a single focus, usually alleviating the source of the grief or the madness, and they will tear apart anyone who gets in their way. If there is enough time and we know that a Vawtrian is likely to encounter something that will result in this, we prepare this brew and have them drink it. It doesn't always stop it from happening, and many will fight it because they will want to deny the possibility of that loss ever occurring, but it does make it easier to resist the strain."

Brandt stared down at the liquid, scowling. "Do you think this will really work on me?"

"It's an educated guess," Arjax rumbled, his arm resting on his knee. "There's no way to know for certain, but it's a good guess. At the very least, it can't hurt anything but your taste buds. You probably won't enjoy any food for a while. That stuff tastes worse than it smells."

Lorna narrowed her eyes at him.

Arjax shrugged. "It does."

"Drink it fast. Finish with water." Lorna gestured toward the tumbler.

Brandt sighed, took a deep breath, and then drank it. With a sharp grimace, he shook his head. "Well...if foulness of flavor is any indication of efficacy, it'll work."

"Good." Lorna clapped him on the shoulder. "Now we're getting ready to move out. That charm on your neck will keep the countdown accurately unless the Gola Resh intervenes directly again. We'll be here if she does. Have more faith in yourself, little cousin. You've been fighting for your love all this time even when you felt like it was hopeless. I believe you'll make it to the end."

Brandt got to his feet, finally looking at me. The myriad of emotions that flashed through those gorgeous eyes of his mirrored what was in my heart—love, fear, hope, despair, and need. He brushed his fingers against my neck, his brow furrowed.

For the scarcest of heartbeats, I hesitated. Then I crossed the distance between us and wrapped my arms around his neck, hugging him tight.

There was no haze between us. This wasn't the curse trying to pull us toward one another. It couldn't be.

I just held him tight, savoring his heat and strength, even if his breath did smell like horseradish and lemons mixed with peppermint.

"Thank you for fighting," I whispered.

"I wish I were better at it," he murmured. "You're worth everything to me." Tentatively, he brought his arms around me and held me tight. His chin rested on my head.

This, I remembered. This, I craved. The closeness and the strength even amidst our grief. I just held on to him, savoring powerful arms around me.

All too soon, it was time to leave. We finalized everything. Kine carried the Great Spear. Buttercup greeted Brandt happily, wagging her thick tail and nudging him as she shifted her weight from one foot to another.

He smiled a little, some of the sadness and weight from his shoulders lifting as he stroked her front horn and snout. "Good to see you too, girl," he crooned.

"Kine said you looked after her while I was gone. I'd say you did a pretty fantastic job," I said as I walked to her other side. I scaled her swiftly and then settled behind her crest. With a coy smile, I glanced down at him. "Are you going my way?"

He offered me a faint smile. "You want me to ride with you? After everything? I could ride with Kine."

The way he looked at me now had some measure of shyness to it, as if he couldn't believe I'd really want to be near him.

Maybe he needed reminding.

I rested my elbow on Buttercup's crest and grinned down at him. More than anything, I wanted to make him smile, to remind him of what we had.

"You know...we should go out for coffee sometime because I definitely like you a latte."

His brow quirked, his expression almost pained. "A latte?"

I pursed my lips at him. "Never mind. Just get up here and put your arms around me."

He groused at me a little. "Were you trying to tell a joke, love?"

"I succeeded. It's not my fault you don't know what coffee is," I said.

"I know what coffee is. I don't know what a latte is."

"Right." I cut my eyes at him.

My stomach somersaulted as he settled in behind me. Oh, ihlkit, his arms around me...this position. Maybe it was because sex last night ended with him trying to kill me and thus it wasn't that satisfying, or maybe it was just that I really did adore him even if I couldn't remember everything. I loved his grumbling smile, his half smile, his crooked smile, and his annoyed scowl. I especially loved getting all of them at once.

"You definitely still like using your word games on me and teasing me and making me laugh," Brandt said, his arm banding around my waist. He hugged me back against his powerful torso and muscular thighs. "But before this, you were never so..."

"Witty?" I glanced up at him as I guided Buttercup to follow Arjax.

"Bizarrely sassy with all this strange wordplay." He dropped his mouth to my ear. "And where did all these bad word games come from?"

"Hmmm." I snuggled back against him. If all we had together were these last moments, I was going to make them count. "You know, I have a theory."

"Do tell."

"Someone stole all my oils lamps. You'd think I'd be upset..."

Brandt looked down at me, caution edging the concern. "That's horrible. When did this happen?"

I grinned. "I'm actually de-lighted."

He clicked his tongue, pulling back. "Are you testing the limits of this curse, woman?"

"What do you call an alligator in a vest?"

"I don't think I want to know," he grumbled as he nuzzled me.

"An in-vest-i-gator."

"If it weren't in such bad taste, I'd be tempted to seriously threaten you or push you off Buttercup into the river," he grumbled as he kissed my neck.

I tipped my head back and grinned at him. "You know where hamburgers go dancing, right? The meat ball."

The look he gave me made me cackle. I really didn't have much hope that we would make it out of this alive, but I did love to make him laugh and groan. The Gola Resh had taken quite a lot from us, but she would never take away this.

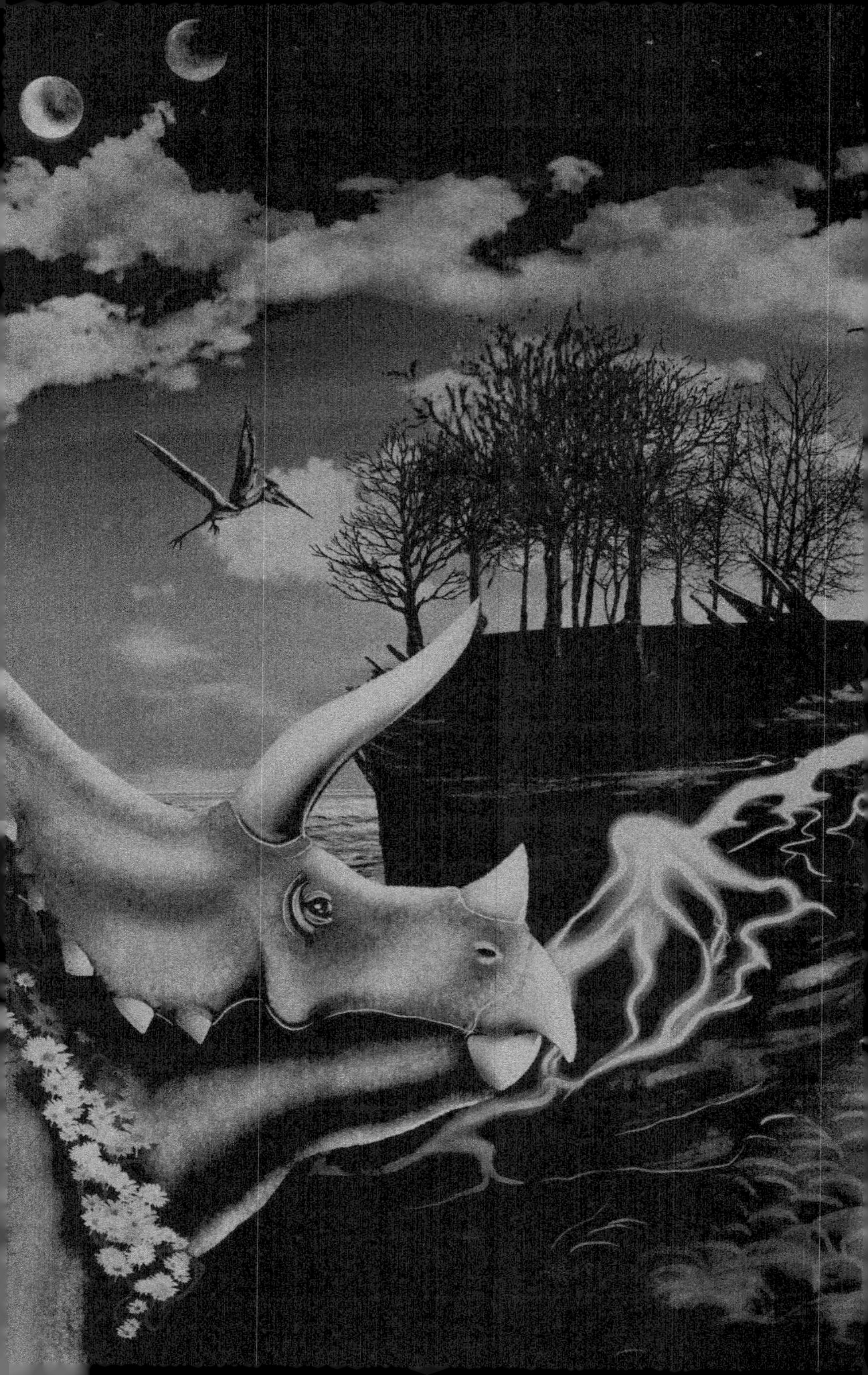

CHAPTER FORTY-SEVEN: STELLA

All too soon, we boarded the ship. Kine went ahead to speak with the captain to inform him Elias would not be returning. Some of the crew swore when they heard. Others muttered. All bowed when Brandt and I stepped on deck.

I kept my gaze fixed ahead of me, a little self-conscious. There was one thing I needed, though, and that was to speak with Auntie Runa before we reached the Ember Lord's Crest.

The captain had a water mirror in the map room. As they cast off, I entered the dimly lit room. The swinging metal lanterns cast flickering shadows all about as the windows were covered up. Oiled and framed maps lined every inch of the walls. In the center of the room, a slab oak table had been fastened to the floor. A simple white map with chalk markings indicated our current course. Everything here smelled of tobacco, chalk, and ink amidst all the salt water and kelp.

In the back of the room stood the stand with the water mirror in it. The silver basin glowed softly, the waters shimmering and reflecting off the wooden ceiling. I crossed to it at once, letting the door click shut behind me.

Now in silence, the gloom threatened to overwhelm me

again. That horrible vision that Elias had stolen filled my thoughts, a vision poured out in oils, one of the most vivid expressions of a vision possible.

Old memories guided me in drawing the connection through the water mirror. I desperately hoped that Auntie Runa had not cut off all magic as she had previously.

For a moment, the waters shimmered.

I held my breath.

Then her face appeared, wobbling within. "Stella!" Her murky eyes brightened, and she leaned closer, that wonderful smile lighting up her face. "What's happened? We don't have much time. The magic has become even more unstable. I don't think I can join the mirrors again after this."

As soon as I saw her, I found myself on the verge of tears. I told her everything.

"Auntie Runa," I whispered hoarsely. "I didn't know that was what he was going to show me. I swear I didn't, but then when he told me I could look away, I didn't. I wanted to know."

She did not look at me. Her mouth pinched. "There is nothing I can say regarding it now," she said tightly. "That vision was not meant for your eyes. Those who needed it have received it. You knowing it—" The tightness in her jaw intensified so much it seemed it might crack. "Stella." She pressed her hand to her temple. "You need to put that vision out of your mind. Put it out of your thoughts. You cannot rely on it to shape any decision that you make."

Even though she said that, we both knew I couldn't. How could I forget something so vividly depicted? Or the sight of the two forms disappearing into the lava as they embraced one another in their final act of doom?

"Do Brandt and I have to sacrifice ourselves? When I look at the future, all I see is darkness. Death."

"Stella, stop." Auntie Runa's mouth pinched again. She closed her eyes, then shook her head. Some of the herbs slid from her hair with the movement. "You don't understand just how bad this could be. Sweet girl, remember the kind of seer you are. You were never the one to receive grand visions of the future, and that is no slur against you. You would not see the images of how this ends. Your intuition has always been in sensing and impulses. What you see is general until the moment is at hand. It's why drawing them is so difficult for you and all you do is sensation and shapes."

Tears rolled down my cheeks.

"I could skin that fool. Damn Elias!" Auntie Runa said. The ripples in the water mirror intensified as if she had struck the table. Her voice distorted, becoming deeper. "Whatever you do, Stella, you must not share that vision with anyone else, especially not Brandt. Visions are dangerous when they are not treated with the proper care. Do you understand me?"

I nodded, but I had no more words left to speak. If there was anything good—any great force in all of these worlds—I prayed that this vision would not be so. My shoulders sagged. All I wanted to do was curl up beneath the blankets and hide.

"If this is the end, though, I want you to know how thankful I am to you."

Auntie Runa hissed, dragging her hand over her face. "Don't speak like that, child."

Even through the water mirror, I saw her pain. The uncertainty. The same uncertainty I'd seen when I was recovering in the channel.

"Just remember to use your mind, darling girl. Do you hear me? Remember what love is. Remember what it requires and what your purpose is. Remember what the Gola Resh wants above all else, her priorities, and her needs, and don't forget that you do have a choice in all this. Prophecies and visions do not tell the full story. On some rare occasions, perhaps they speak of a true final point or an immovable aspect, but that is not this. Your choices matter." Her hand pressed tight over her mouth. "Do not forget that, Stella. If it robs you of choice, it is wrong."

The floorboards creaked beneath my feet as the ship continued its steady progress. The silver basin was smooth beneath my fingertips.

"Is there anything else you can tell me?"

"Whatever else I have to say to you, I will say when I see you in person." The corners of her mouth shook. "Except...I'm proud of you, Stella, proud of you and Brandt. Oh!" Her reflection shuddered. She fell back. "Earthquake—"

The water mirror's connection broke.

I stood over it, my heart heavy. My fingers traced the edge of the basin again, trembling.

We were so close to the end. More than anything, I wanted some reassurance, some hope that Brandt and I would make it through, that Sepeazia would survive, that good would come out of this in some shape or form. Tears stung my eyes and rolled down my cheeks. A few dropped into the silver basin, but the magic did not stir.

What I craved was knowledge that was beyond me, a guarantee for something that might not exist.

But dwelling on that caused me to overlook what I had.

I wiped my eyes, combed my fingers through my hair, and then left. A heavy thudding drew my attention as soon as I reached the main deck.

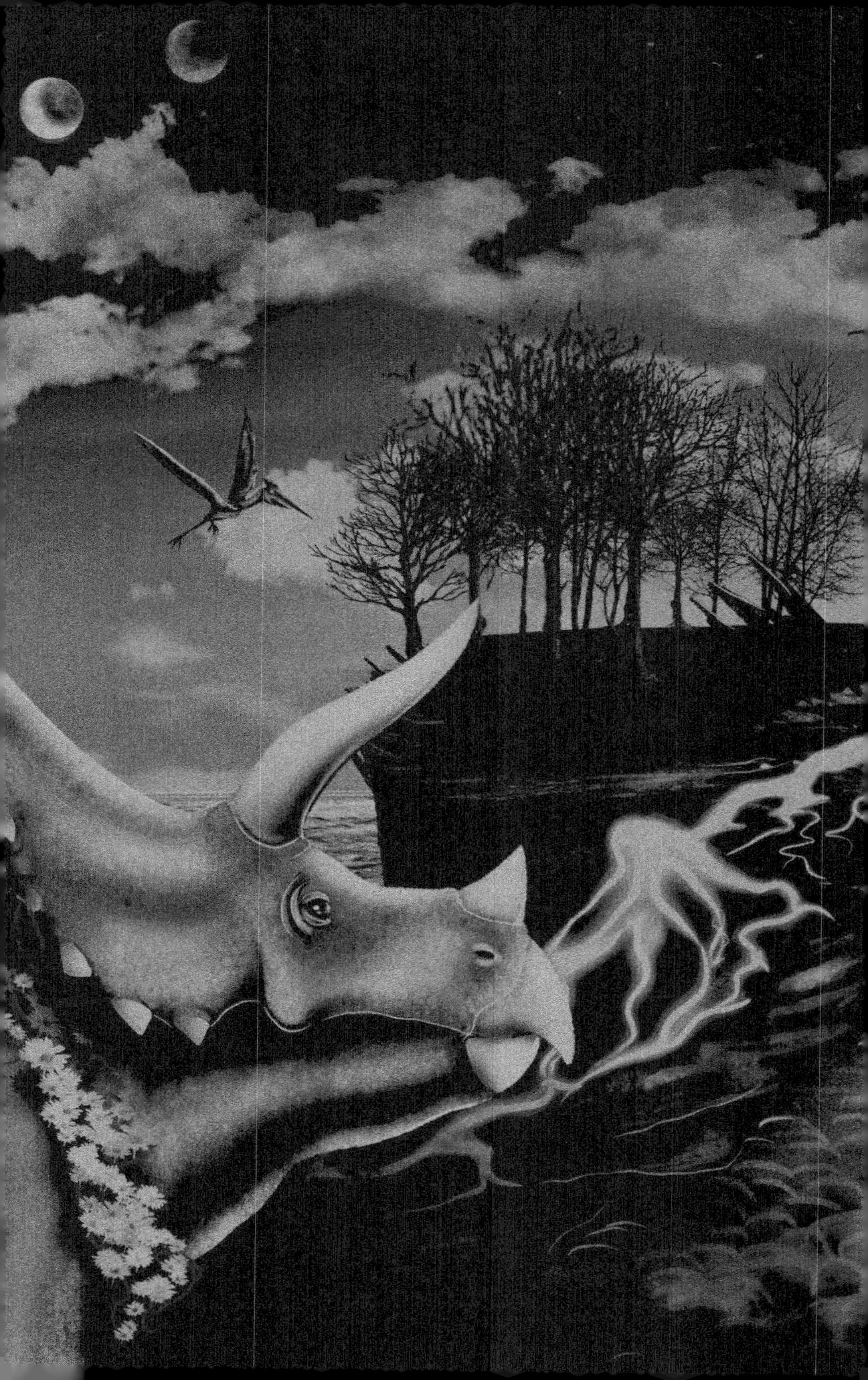

CHAPTER FORTY-EIGHT: STELLA

I sighed. I wasn't in the water drawing the ship along, but I hadn't given her attention.

Somehow, the ridiculousness of a tantrum-throwing triceratops comforted and amused me. I hurried down the narrow staircase, pressing my hand to the walls until I found my way to the left stable on the port hull.

The stable itself, like its match on the opposite side of the ship, smelled of hay and alfalfa. Three globe lamps provided added light even with the portholes open. Large and small leather straps hung from the walls, each one securely fastened into the wood. Someone had secured each of the dinosaurs to the wall with at least two bands each.

I had a vague recollection that the Keening Pass included fast currents which made sense, especially if it was going to take us less than a day to get through.

Buttercup bellowed and kicked at the walls until she saw me. Then she shook her head and lowed.

"Come on, baby. You just don't like the Keening Pass?" I tilted my head as I stroked her jaw. She lowed again.

"I can guarantee she doesn't." Brandt stepped out from

behind her. He no longer wore his tabard, just his black tunic tucked into his trousers and his belt. The scar on the left side of his face gave him an especially dramatic look in this light. His hand rested on Buttercup's rounded amber-yellow side. "You know, she missed you almost as much as I did."

Buttercup snorted, her nostrils flaring.

Brandt shrugged as he met her gaze. "You didn't miss her more than I did. I'll fight you on that one."

She swatted her tail against the wall once more.

"Okay, let's not fight." I crossed over and put my arms around her thick neck, though my gaze remained fixed on Brandt. Warmth and jitters mingled in my stomach. "Kine said you took her to meadows while I was gone. Basically you spoiled her."

"Yeah." Brandt crossed his arms over his broad chest. "She didn't like staying in the aviaries or stables or with anyone else really. Well, except for when the tiny pterosaurs are nesting and sing. Then she tolerates it, but no one else wants her in there because she knocks too much over."

That pose always made his muscles look especially cut and those serpents so exceptionally powerful. Then I remembered the ones that curled along his side, and more heat coiled within me. Spicy strawberry margarita man, indeed.

Brandt nudged her with his folded arm. "We'd go out at least once a week, sometimes three times if I was around, and nightly during the rose clover blooms. After Kine and Elias tried to bring you back the first time, she got really...anxious. That's why I had to have help when I took her out. She was always looking for you."

This brought a smile to my lips. "And so were you. Or, if not looking for me, pining for me and trying to find some way to bring me home."

His brow hitched. "Kine said Elias told you that I protested their seeking you out and imprisoned them for their defiance."

I nodded. "He did, and did he also tell you that I understand you had your reasons?"

"I imprisoned them so that they would not inadvertently make it worse. As for seeking you out, we didn't have answers. We weren't even a breath closer to ending the curse. I just couldn't risk you." He traced his thumb along my cheek, his gaze soft despite its intensity. "Even though I wanted to see you again, more than anything... Besides, the portal would have opened again in another fifty years."

"Another fifty years? Do you understand how old I'd have been by then?" I smirked even as my stomach twisted with butterflies. "I'd have come through almost eighty years old. I was aging at a normal rate for humans there."

He chuckled at this. "You think I wouldn't love you even if you came back wrinkled and old?"

"Would you?" My eyebrow arched.

He narrowed his eyes at me as he pressed his thumb to my chin and tilted my gaze up. "I would love you no matter how old and wrinkled you became. Especially if you had been able to carve out a life for yourself."

"My life on Earth..." I closed my eyes, tears brimming once more. "I was always missing something. Missing this. Kine. Buttercup." I hooked my fingers in his tunic and pulled him close. "Most of all you. Do you know how bland and colorless my world was without you?"

"If it was like mine without you, then..." He leaned closer, his breath whispering against my cheek. "I am truly sorry."

He must have taken something because he no longer smelled of horseradish and lemons. Instead, he just smelled like leather and smoke with only the faintest tinge of orange and bergamot coming from his black-and-red hair. Even if he had smelled like horseradish and lemon, though, I would have stayed close.

He nuzzled me, his nose tracing a line along my throat to the corner of my jaw. "Are you truly telling me that there was no one? No one caught your eye?"

"You know how much I have teased you and joked with you?"

He nodded, that crooked smile of his returning. "I do."

"I was never able to do that with anyone else. Ever."

"So I am the sole recipient of your dreadful wordplay?"

"My dreadful wordplay and all my love." I slid my hand up the planes of his chest. "I didn't belong there, and you were here...all this time. And you suffered."

He shook his head. His hand covered mine, stroking my fingers. He opened his mouth to speak, but no words came.

I stepped closer then, pressing my forehead to his shoulder. It felt so good to be back in his arms and against him. With my eyes closed, the world almost felt right.

"Every sixteen hours...for decades..."

He grunted. "It sounds worse than it is. There was no temptation to kill you while you were gone."

"But you were in pain. Pain with no possibility for relief."

"Let's not dwell on it." He stroked my back. "What matters is..." His mouth twisted, and his hand slid up along the back of my head. "When you were gone, I couldn't laugh, but you came back utterly..."

"You can call me ridiculous." I smirked at him.

"Yes." He hugged me tighter. "You were just so full of life and such infectious joy. I was so afraid and aroused and angry. And there you were, my brash seer. It was like you knew what I needed as soon as you saw me." He cradled me. "You were—You are ridiculous and wonderful. And I have loved every moment of it."

"Even the puns?"

He squinted at me as he grunted. "Don't push your luck, woman."

"You love them all." I burrowed closer.

"You. I love all of you." He rested his cheek on the top of my head.

The ship rocked a little harder. The flick of a silver tail on the outside indicated that the water serpent shifters were returning. No new splashes rose to show that the next wave had started.

I frowned. "What's changed?"

"We're probably ready for the Keening Pass." Brandt drew in a deep breath.

I peered out the window at the ocean. The morning sun remained pale yellow, almost watery despite its intensity, the waters themselves now grey and uncommonly still. But aside from that stillness and a large pillar of stone that had runes and sigils carved into it, there was nothing out of the ordinary about this place.

"What's wrong?" Brandt asked. He put out each of the lanterns, plunging us into dimness.

"I just...I expected the Pass to be more...pass-y," I said.

"All hands shelter. All hands shelter." The captain strode overhead, his steps swift and echoing. He struck his wooden baton on the walls as he went. From the echoing beats, it sounded as if someone else called out on the opposite side of the ship.

I frowned, glancing down at Brandt. "Who's steering the ship?"

He raised an eyebrow at me. "You don't actually remember what happens next."

I folded my arms over my breasts as I peered out the porthole. "What happens next?"

The ship seemed to be starting to turn as the currents took hold and guided us toward...nothing. The air crackled.

Buttercup moaned. The parasaurs and other triceratops also uttered bellows of complaint.

He gave me a dark smile as he looped his arm through one of

the straps and gestured for me to do the same. "You're going to hate it. Brace yourself, love, and hook yourself into that strap if you don't want to crack your head open."

"Could you be any more vague?" Hooking my arm through the leather strap, I looked back out the window when something dark jetted out beneath the ship. I opened my mouth to ask what it was when we plunged down. My legs shot out from under me as the entire ship screamed.

Walls of water rose around us, and the ship shot into the channel of living water. Light and water streaked around us. Enormous dark forms spiraled and spun among the waves. They towered above us, monstrous denizens with claws and teeth the size of our ship's mast.

Ihlkit!

This wasn't what I remembered. I'd remembered jagged rocks and rushing water. Something with stark, harsh sounds.

Not this fall.

Not these creatures. Beings with six eyes. Sinuous forms with black teeth as big as broadswords.

It was as if the fabric of the world had been torn open, exposing the blood and veins of a whole other realm. The shadowy creatures with their angular eyes and jagged mouths swept closer to us as we screamed down into the watery chasm.

Our double-hulled ship slid through, descending faster and faster. The shrieking wails surrounded us, throbbing inside me like a pulse. Then we were rising and spinning. A heavy rush of water surged against the prow.

My arm wrenched as I clung to the strap.

A yellow-eyed creature with four claws and a series of whip-like tentacles sliced through the water, swiping toward us. Dark waters slammed against us.

And all the while everything screeched and roared.

I seized tighter against another strap next to Brandt and pressed against him. Hay and alfalfa slid and piled against the back, filling the air with choking dust. He held me fast with one arm, bracing his feet against one of the beams. Buttercup curled closer, her tail sweeping around both of us.

I huddled closer to Brandt, pressing my head to his chest. Fear hollowed me out and chilled me. The wailing howls filled my ears, pushing out all sound, including his heartbeat. Yet I felt that heartbeat against my cheek.

Up and down, around, down.

The whole world twisted. My stomach lurched.

Time lost all meaning. There was nothing but howling and the strength of his arm tight around me.

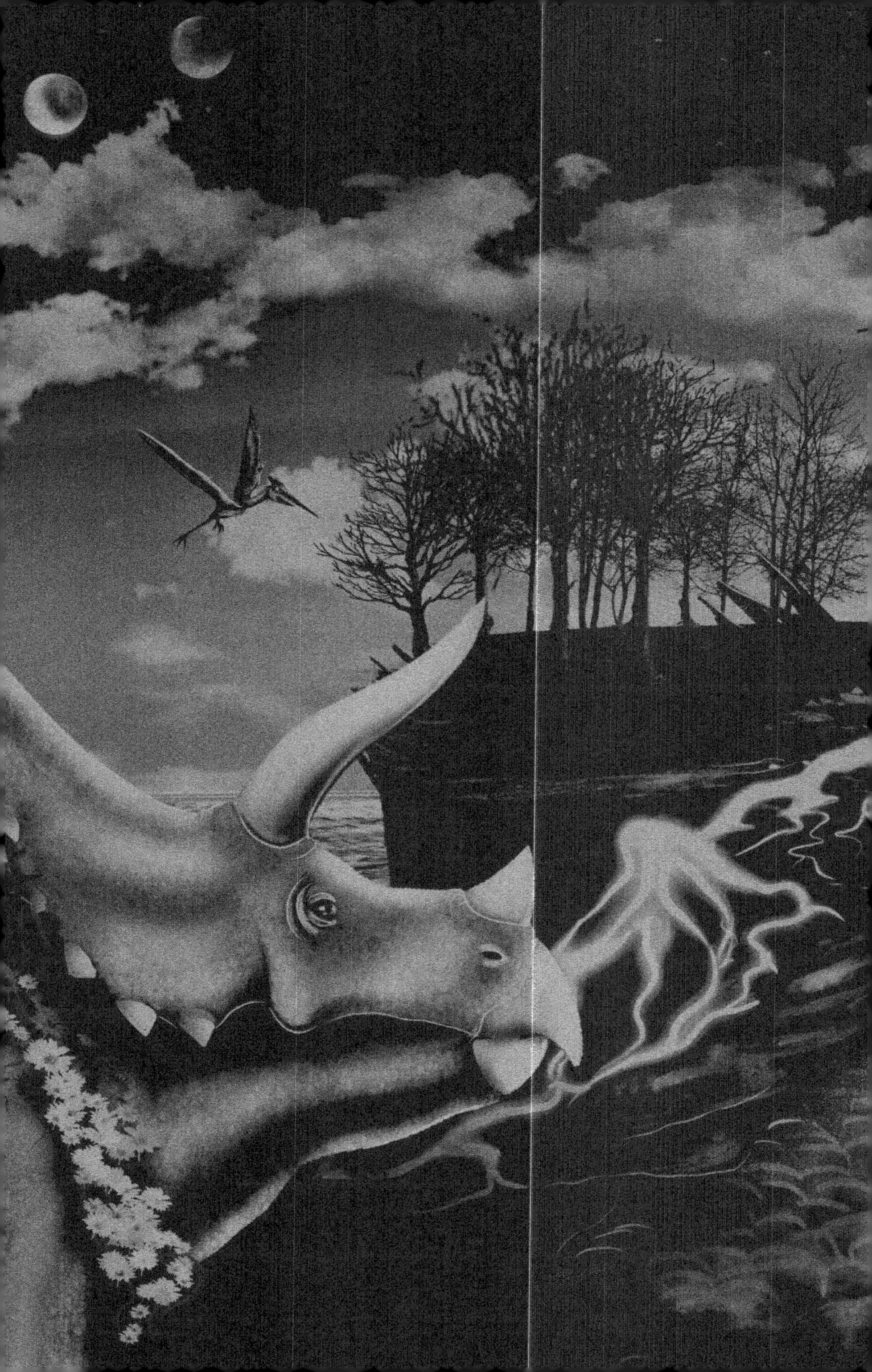

CHAPTER FORTY-NINE: STELLA

The Keening Pass seemed to stretch on and on, our ship twisting and dropping helplessly among the waters. Then, as fast as we entered, the Keening Pass ended.

Everything went still.

Slowly, my body relaxed. I rested against Brandt, breathless but alive.

The ship creaked as we righted. Heavy footsteps pounded on the deck as the captain called for everyone to return. The crew surged out. Water splashed up as six of the crew dove in, becoming water serpents once more. The ship creaked as they tugged against the ropes and swam forward.

Just like that, we had returned to ordinary sailing activities. Even the animals calmed.

I kissed Buttercup on the forehead, then let Brandt lead me up to the main deck slowly. My stomach continued to clench and flutter. For once, my sea legs weren't certain. I staggered.

"Easy there." Brandt steadied me, his arm curving around my waist as he pulled me to the railing. He chuckled, his voice low in his throat. "Probably should have given you more warning about the Keening Pass. It's not a particularly fun passage, and if you don't hit it at the right times, it's a lot more dangerous."

"Yeah. I figured that out." I accepted his help gratefully, my hands grasping the slick wood. If we never went through that passage again, it'd be too soon. I kept my head down, breathing in the salty air as I focused on settling my stomach and steadying my legs.

He kept his arm around me, watching me patiently and saying nothing until my breaths slowed. "Do you remember this?" He pointed toward a dark wall that loomed on the starboard side.

I looked up for the first time in what felt like minutes.

Oh.

A shudder tore through me as my grip on the railing tightened.

Cold memories clawed at my mind. That wall was sheer, made of a seamless purple-grey stone. Large black marks, similar to the ones I'd seen throughout Sepeazia, clawed over the wall's surface. These were far deeper and more jagged, but there were no spiderwebbed cracks or fissures to suggest it was near breaking.

"Taivren?" I whispered, my heart hammering.

He nodded. His fingers curled against my shoulder as he pulled me in tighter. "If not for you and the other seers, it would have been a bloodbath. The whole city was lost. The sages and arcanists barely erected the walls in time to prevent the toxins from entering the rest of the sea."

Maybe it was good that I couldn't remember. But his arms —oh...

"You saved my life there," I whispered. "There was a...sword. Everything was cold. It was...it was so cold." I brought my hands up against my torso, shivering. My body tightened as I remembered the slick, sucking sensation of dark energy and toxic tendrils wrapping around me. A current rushed up around me, too strong for me, but how had I been there? Fragments surfaced in my mind.

He stroked my cheek with the back of his thumb, leaning against me so that I was pinned between him and the railing. His weight comforted me. His heat reminded me those were only memories.

"Cahji," I whispered.

Images of a silver-eyed boy flashed into my mind. Panicked cries. I saw myself struggling in ever-surging waters. And there was Hord. Yes. I recognized him in the memory though his expression was near wild with grief, his eyes blazing and his arms outstretched. Tears pricked my eyes at once. There was a weight on my chest. I choked.

"Hmm?" Brandt tilted his head, then nodded. His chin scraped against my temple, bringing me back from the cold of the memory. "Yes, Cahji was there in the capital." His brow furrowed though his gaze remained soft. "Do you remember?"

"Not fully."

He grunted, hugging me close. "We were trying to get everyone out." His throat bobbed. "The Babadon and the Gola Resh had already stolen a fair bit of our magic. We'd been trying to stop them. They sent the hourglass as a warning, counting down our doom. The inner bulb held a representation of the city of Taivren. They both appeared to us and told us that because of our resistance, Taivren would be taken first. And if we did not sacrifice Taivren with all its bounty, they would take fifty of our children at random to drown in Taivren as it fell into the depths."

They truly were monstrous. I nestled tighter against him, my cheek firmly against his chest.

"You seers predicted nothing could be done to save the city. None of our allies could do anything to stop the corrosion that the Gola Resh and the Babadon had set upon the heartstones of Taivren. After all, the very foundation of Taivren was created through magic. Our people formed it when the peace accord was reached between Kropelki and Ognisko, and we became Sepeazia. It was directly between both continents, intended to join us and symbolize our united strength. The deep gouges in the earth and stone had spread throughout the entirety of the city. And it was clear they were going to take it." He pressed his forehead to the back of my head.

His breath stirred my hair. "Some on the council wanted a quiet evacuation of the important members of the city. Enough that it wouldn't draw the attention of the Gola Resh and the Babadon. All a select few of us had to do was not be there. But I refused to leave some of our people to die while I slipped away. Tensions were high that day. And you sprang to my side. You raged like blue fire. You said that even if foresight and visions did not confirm that we would be successful, it did not change what was right. And what was right was to evacuate the city and protect the children." He managed a low laugh. "Dromar asked you if you would stand by your words and stand guard in the city—if you would be willing to die to keep the children from being dragged down with Taivren. You told him you would, and you invited him to stand next to you."

I smiled slightly. The old Stella really had been ferocious. I could imagine the scene. Fragments of it stirred, like the remnants of taste from a day-old meal.

"So, we masked our efforts. None of the magical items were removed from the city until the end. And in those final hours, once we were certain the children were safe and far away, we moved in. Whether we actually surprised the Gola Resh and the Babadon or whether they let us think we had gotten away with it...I don't know." He shuddered. "Our friends from the other nations came to assist, including the elves on their winged jaguars and the fae with their gift of flight. Arjax and Lorna along with a few others too. They brought hot air balloons and gliders so that if the city started to collapse, they could help snatch us out of the waters. Most of the city had been emptied. All but a few. And—" He set his jaw. "We were just preparing to leave when suddenly we heard children screaming and crying in the city."

I stiffened. Those cries echoed in my mind. My skin prickled.

"The Gola Resh and the Babadon used blood portals to throw the children back into the city. Fifty of them. Which means they also murdered fifty people to create the portals and transport them." His fist knotted on the railing. He fell silent, his jaw working. "What followed was madness. Almost everyone scrambled to reach the children. Some of us were in places where we didn't know what was happening. So for this, I had to rely on what others told me. Including you." He stroked the column of my throat. "Most of the children were snatched up within seconds even as the city fell and the sea surged, which was good. Because it wasn't just sea water. The Gola Resh and the Babadon had cursed the waters as well, creating these toxic tendrils and vortexes that devoured like acid. Cahji though—he got stuck. He was looking for his mama. She barely heard him in time, and she tried to save him. But then she got pinned. And she passed him off to you."

I covered my mouth. Tears wet my eyes as a knot formed in my throat. Those memories I pushed back.

Or tried to.

They pushed up harder. That desperate look in her honey-brown eyes. The sternness in her voice as she screamed for me to get Cahji out. Knowing I couldn't help her. I bowed my head. I could practically feel Cahji's weight in my arms. Felt the gripping tear of the water around me as the filthy waves churned up and the toxic tendrils started to form in a vortex. Phantom pain coiled around my ankle, up my thigh, up my stomach, and around my lungs. I glanced down at it. There was nothing wrong. It just...felt real. Like the dream of the grotto.

Brandt kept speaking, his voice soft and even but heavy with sadness. "Truly, I don't know how you did it. You were on the top level of the library, but you still had to get out through the window with everything sinking and falling apart and turning toxic. All with a child who was terrified and struggling. Neither Hord nor I knew what was happening. We were with a few others retrieving some of the sacred and enchanted items, including the Sword of Kairos. We had to fight our way through the chaos and wreckage and sinking mass as well, and when we emerged—first thing I heard distinctly was Cahji screaming. You were trying to get him up onto one of the walkways to our allies, but everything kept slipping.

"Soon as he heard it though, Hord was gone. He was up on that crumbling stone and shooting out toward you. He tore himself up bad, but I've never seen him move that fast in his life. As he was getting there, you got yourself and Cahji onto a beam. Then it started to crack too. You had a choice to make. Stay there with Cahji and hope Hord got there in time. Or push Cahji forward even though it was going to crack off part of the beam and knock you right into that vortex. And you—you barely hesitated at all. You shoved that kid right at his dad hard enough Hord could catch him, and then you fell back into those waters." He dipped his head, pressing his forehead against the back of my neck.

I'd been afraid. That was why I'd hesitated. The cold sensation plucked at me, tight in my chest. "I didn't think anyone was coming for me," I whispered.

"That was when I knew I loved you," he said, his voice hoarse with emotion. "I had that sword—the Sword of Kairos. And I dropped it to go after you."

I twisted my head enough to peer up at him. "You chose

me..." Those fragments of memory said the Sword of Kairos was precious. "That sword...it wasn't just a token with a minor enchantment. It was important to our people."

He nodded, his expression almost stern as if he dared me to tell him he had chosen wrong. Those ruby-red eyes glittered fiercely. "One of our most sacred items. One of our greatest treasures." And later when deciding what to do with the heart of the Babadon and its magical properties, we had decided to use it to form other items, including the Goblet. A symbol of our unification. That had not gone over well with most of the factions.

"You paid for it, didn't you?" I searched his expression, trying to piece together the memories.

His arms closed around me as he cradled me closer, his chin pressing against the top of my head. "It is amusing how swiftly matters can become so clear. I'll never forget the expression on your face after you pushed Cahji toward Hord and the vortex's current seized you. The way it pulled you down. Letting go of that sword was the easiest thing I've ever done. That vortex sucked you so far down—you couldn't shift any more. It took the last of my strength to drag you up."

My eyes shuttered. That scene played out in harsh detail. The cold. Such deep cold. And then his heat. The way he had wrapped around me.

I paused. When the dark waters had engulfed me, I had been convinced that that was my end. It had certainly felt like it. The toxic tendrils wrapped around my leg. The crushing ice of the waters. The burning pressure in my lungs.

And all I had seen then was death as well.

I was always looking for the fulfillment of visions and foresight. Sometimes even trying to force it. And it was easy to spot patterns when I was looking for them. My sight—my intuition could provide aid, but it did not give the full picture. It never gave the full picture. I was not omniscient.

"You could have died too," I murmured. The steady rhythm of his heart beat against my ear.

"It was worth the risk if I could have saved you," he whispered. "And I would have if not for our friends. I had nearly spent all my strength by the time I broke free of the vortex and dragged us to the surface. But they helped us from there. And during that time, our sages and arcanists managed to erect walls at each end of the chasm to trap the toxic waters inside. That's what you see here." Brandt gestured toward the marbled wall.

"I didn't realize our magic was that powerful." I stared at it, awed to think that it had been created by our people.

"Sepeazia boasts many strengths. We were once warring nations who then became closer than blood and stronger than steel. But we're a long cry from that strength now. The Gola Resh has siphoned so much of our magic that even a dozen sages and arcanists would struggle to create a hundred-foot barrier, and it certainly would not endure as this one has. We are but a shadow of what we once were. I suppose we should count ourselves fortunate that the draining of our magic has not resulted in famine and disease, but we have been lessened all the same."

Something else troubled him.

"What is it?" I nudged him with my head.

He shifted his weight. When he spoke, his voice took on a lower and more dangerous tone. "I already spoke with Kine about this, but Elias may not be the only traitor close to us. In fact, I am all but certain of it."

"What do you mean?"

"The Gola Resh said—well—to be clearer, she suggested that Hord was involved. That he would do it to save Cahji."

"Hord?" I stiffened. "No!" I shook my head fiercely. "My memory may still be funny in some parts, but I will never believe Hord—"

"Would you have believed it of Elias?" His gaze cut into me.

I flinched. "Not easily," I admitted reluctantly. "Maybe. I don't know. But that was because of the life bond. I didn't think someone would fake it. I didn't know someone could. But when I looked at Elias, I didn't feel anything. I didn't know him. Hord? I felt like I knew him, and you have years of history with him."

Brandt's upper lip curled. "He loved Tanusa. Nothing can ever bring her back, and her death was wrong. It was tragic and senseless. Just because the Gola Resh and the Babadon chose to be cruel. And if the Gola Resh offered to spare Cahji, how could Hord refuse? He loves his son more than anyone."

I shook my head, pinching my lips. "No. Hord is a good man. He wouldn't betray his people for that. Let's wait until we know more." Turning, I placed my hand on his chest, peering up into his eyes. He returned my gaze, his expression pained and solemn. If Hord had betrayed us, it would be a far more grievous blow to him than Elias had been to me. "I can't imagine that Hord is a traitor. It just—it doesn't sit right with me. I admit I missed the truth about Elias. I could have missed it with Hord too. But Hord...he feels different."

His jaw worked. His gaze shifted back to the sparkling blue waters. A shark's fin skimmed the surface a short distance away before disappearing into the dark depths. "I can't imagine that it is true. But...if he is a traitor, then we have another problem. He is getting the Great Axe. He is to meet us at the Ember Lord's Crest. Candy is bringing the Peace Goblet. The Gola Resh needs the same items we require. And if she gets to the axe first, then—"

I placed my fingers against his lips. "Then we'll just get it back from her." Listening to the powerful and incredible fire of old Stella did not have me feeling especially confident about myself. I was nothing like who I used to be. A woman who could hear a lost child and seize the child to rescue them from the flood waters and sacrifice herself? Sure...I could sacrifice myself. But could I actually do something worthwhile to help on the way?

Even if I had shown significant progress in my shifting, I was lacking. I struggled to grip and aim. With Lorna's help, I might be able to keep my clothes on the next time I shifted, but that wasn't nearly as helpful as being powerful. Even worse, we were out of time. Him, on the other hand? "You are brilliant and clever and magnificent," I said, keeping my fingers against his lips.

He grunted in response, his eyes narrowing at me.

I lifted my eyebrows at him. "I mean it, Brandt. Look at all you have endured. All you have come through. Just because the Gola Resh has gotten a few over on us doesn't mean she's going to win. She's going to lose."

His expression softened as he nodded. "I would give my last breath to make it so."

Though I nodded, I prayed it wouldn't cost that. Even as I feared that it would.

We stood there in silence as the crew drew the ship farther away from the ruins of our capital. More memories seeped into my consciousness, some good, some bad. That was where Brandt and I had first met. I'd strode into that throne room full of confidence, eager to confront him. A brash seer—that's what he'd called me. And I'd called him an arrogant king.

But he wasn't.

Not in the end.

He'd listened. In more ways than one. Then he'd saved me.

I couldn't remember all the details. But I remembered those eyes of his. Boring into mine. Slicing deep. Spreading into my soul.

My mate.

My love.

My heart.

The waves lapped against the side of the ship. The purple-blue of the sky had deepened, much more vivid now than it had been when I'd first returned.

The heaviness pressed down on me as we continued toward the Ember Lord's Crest. Hord couldn't be a traitor. To fight against him and Elias and whoever else Elias brought with him —was I really ready for battle?

My thoughts spiraled, repeating without solution. Old Stella had been a fighter, a seer, and a water serpent shifter. I almost hated her for all she had been capable of doing. I had fought at Brandt's side before this. Fought for him. And recently I'd fought against him and only survived because he was holding back as best he could. But the Gola Resh would not hold back. My stomach heaved.

"I told you what troubles me," he said softly. "What troubles you?"

So much for being strong and firm. I was melting just thinking about everything. The words tumbled out as my stomach roiled. "We're getting ready for a fight against a supernatural entity that none of us understands or fully knows with a ritual that has never been done before and whose core components can be twisted to bring about another terrifying supernatural entity. And I am not the woman I once was. You even said I *used* to be a badass. I'm not one anymore. When we were with Arjax and Lorna and we were chasing the mirror foxes and fighting the terror birds, I barely got one. And I didn't kill anything. I'm brash, but I'm not the same water serpent and seer I once was."

His brow tweaked, his smile curling a little more to the left. "No. I suppose you aren't. But that does not make who you are now any less. You have changed in many ways, but in every matter that counts, you are who you were."

Scoffing, I shrugged and tipped my gaze back into the sky, noting just how much deeper that purple blue was now and how little time we had left. "I'm not a badass warrior. I'm a pretty blue-and-gold serpent who gets her horns crooked and tells goofball jokes. And the badass warrior is the one we need more right now."

He leaned against me, his arms and chest caging me against the railing. "You know...I can't really comment on your fighting since you came back. All I know is what Kine described. Sadly, I can't remember what happened in the throne room when the curse seized me. But, Stella...you brought me laughter again. Even if it was confusing. And sometimes a little painful."

"I don't see how that helps anything." My insides squirmed. I hadn't told him about the vision Elias had stolen from Auntie Runa, and I wouldn't. I struggled to put it aside, reminding myself that I couldn't control this. There were other things I could control.

"Because after years without laughter, it's a balm and a release. And it makes it easier now for me to focus. So I am glad for your terrible jokes and ridiculous wordplay. I am also grateful to Arjax and Lorna for allowing me these moments with you through that vile concoction. And you still have the same strength of spirit and will that you have always had. You have always been exactly what I need. Even when it's strange. And you are unquestionably a badass now." He pressed his forehead to my temple. "So...anything to make me laugh now?"

I nuzzled him back, comforted by his confidence in me and amused that a man who didn't know what latte meant knew what a badass was. "You want me to make you laugh?"

"Can you?" He kissed my neck, teeth grazing my skin.

Infernal man, trying to get under my skin and get me all distracted. A delicious shudder raced through me.

I shot him a mock side glare. "All right. Answer me this. What do you call a magician who has lost his magic?"

"I have no idea. Lost? Pointless? Scared?"

"Ian."

Brandt's mouth trembled slightly, and then he dropped his head against the back of my neck. He groaned loudly. "Stella…"

"You asked for it, husband of mine." I wrinkled my nose at him.

His head remained against my shoulder. "I did." He scoffed, his breath huffing over my neck and back. "I love you, Stella."

"I love you too, Brandt."

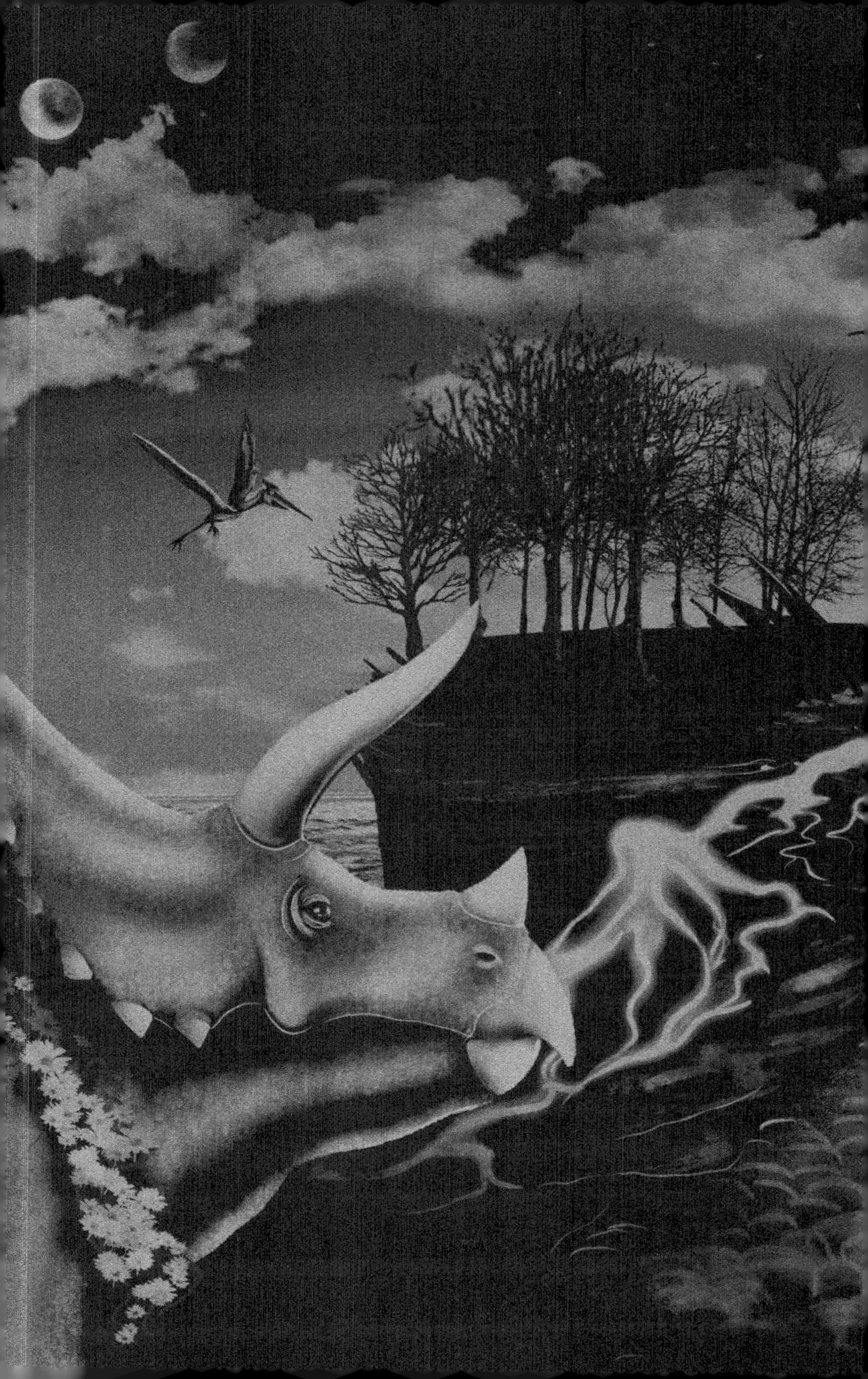

CHAPTER FIFTY: STELLA

*I*n good time, we reached the simple dock that led to the Ember Lord's Crest. Lorna had Brandt drink more of the vile potion. Though he gagged, he drank it and then chewed peppermint. The charm on his neck had turned orangish yellow. We had only hours before the curse seized him.

Kine brought the Great Spear up from the hold, his manner still subdued. When I tried to ask him what was wrong, he refused to answer, simply stating that he needed to focus on defeating the Gola Resh.

No clouds hung in the sky, but it was even darker now. The wind tugged at my hair, smelling of salt and sulfur. My eyes watered.

The broad, jagged mountain rose like a multi-tiered crown, the top smoking thanks to multiple ventilation shafts. The rocks were bladed and porous. Dark earth and black sands formed this shoreline.

Even here, those deep gouges from the Gola Resh existed. They were harder to see, but they sliced nonetheless, curling over the land like tendrils, deeper than when we had left. No vegetation grew here, though once it had. All was barren rock.

Large boulders and outcroppings jutted from the sand and stone, harsh and uneven.

Up ahead lay our meeting point.

My stomach tightened. That sense of foreboding worsened with every step, the short sword and dagger heavy at my side.

A small camp had been set up, a low fire burning in the center with pale smoke circling above. Figures circled the fire, some disappearing, hidden by the rough-surfaced pillars of rock. Candy, in her dark-pink attire, stood out even from here. The side of her face was badly bruised, but her arm was bloodied rather than broken. Could those be just from her encounter with Brandt? It was hard to tell from this distance, but they seemed different.

Tile sat beside the fire, hands folded before himself in quiet contemplation, dark red streaks in his fire-red hair like dried blood. Cahji struggled to fix what looked like a splintered spear. A bandage wound around his shoulder. A few others who I didn't recognize were also present, all in various states of contemplation or circling. No laughter or jokes or conversation reached us.

Something was wrong.

The wind shifted.

Blood. Fresh blood, old blood, burned blood.

Death.

My skin prickled with goose bumps. Brandt's jaw clenched as his nostrils flared. He glanced back at me, putting his arm out to indicate he wanted me to stay half a step back. Kine moved to my other side, still gripping the spear but ready to fight if need be. Arjax and Lorna flanked us.

"It wasn't just one fight," Lorna murmured. "Many have died here recently."

Something terrible had happened. The tension and malaise intensified, nauseating me. The wind masked our approach as we neared the first of the stone pillars outside the camp. I brushed my fingertips against Brandt's elbow. "Not even a lookout facing the ocean?" I whispered.

Brandt indicated the first of the stone pillars outside the camp. A sliver of shadow cut along the sand. Someone was waiting.

My stomach twisted.

No, please. Please no. Don't be Hord.

I closed my eyes, drawing in a deep breath as we continued forward. If he was waiting for us, it didn't mean he was a traitor. He was a good man. I knew it.

Brandt motioned for us to stop. He set his hands on his black belt, squaring his shoulders. "Whatever you have to say to us, come and say it," he said, his voice a low growl.

The sand shifted. Some of it kicked into a fine dust, carried away by the wind as Hord stepped out.

Blood streaked his face. Cuts and bruises marred his knuckles, and a dirty bandage had been affixed to his neck. His hunting knife was sheathed at his side, and he did not carry his spear. Pain haunted his burgundy eyes, and his face was hard. "Forgive me," he said, his voice strained. "The Gola Resh has the Great Axe."

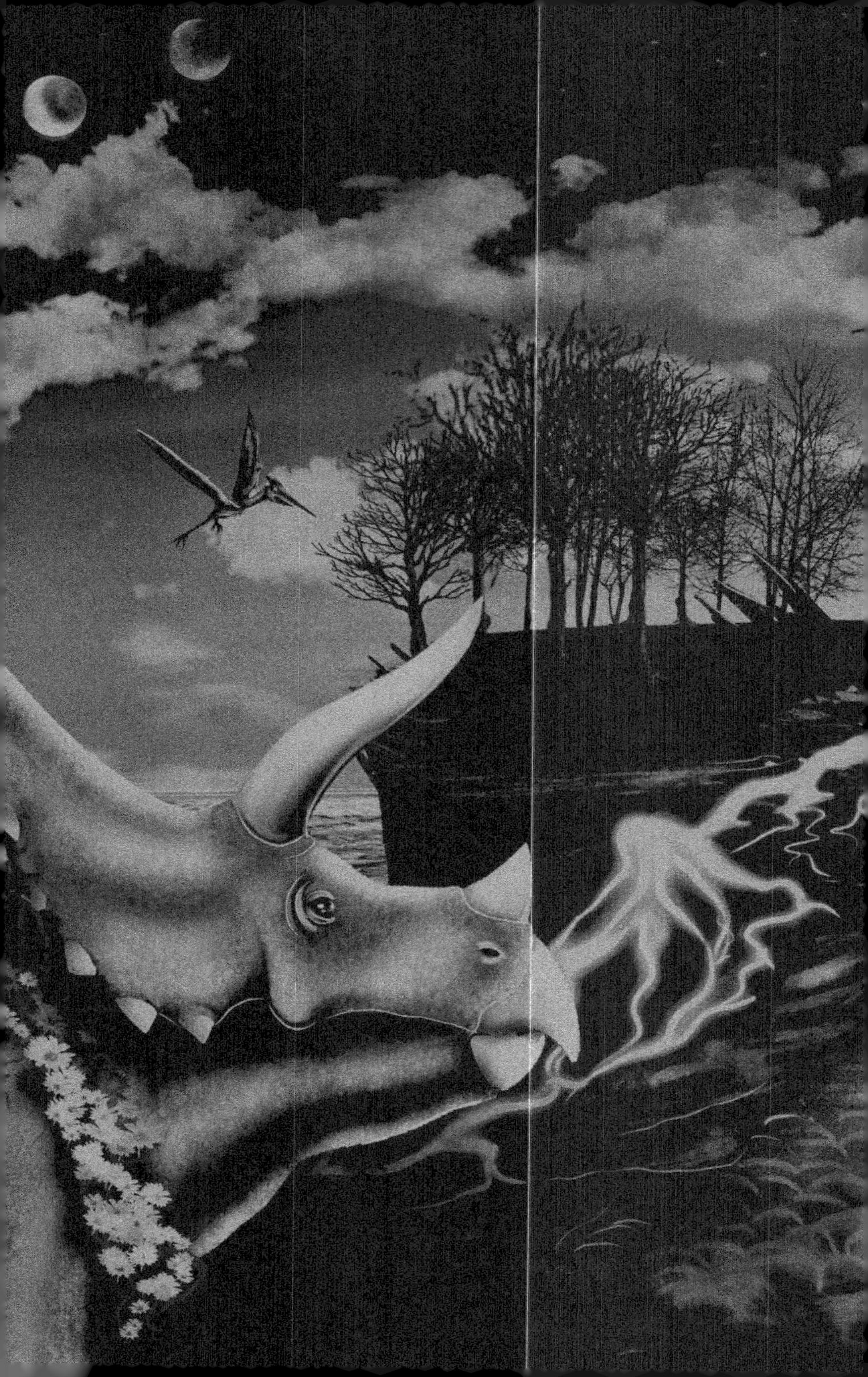

CHAPTER FIFTY-ONE: STELLA

My stomach sank.

No.

"I'm sorry," Hord said again, his voice shaking. "We did all we could."

Brandt's mouth turned in a snarl, his right arm twisting as if to strike. He stepped beneath the shadow of the stone outcropping, his gaze darting about with sharp-eyed scrutiny. "What happened?" The words ground out of him.

Hord remained stock still, arms at his side. "Elias came last night, but...it wasn't him exactly. We thought he returned with you. There were others with him. Hooded." His breaths hissed through his teeth. "He betrayed us. They took the Axe and the Goblet."

"It's you! Hord, why didn't you tell us they were here!" Candy bounded forward, her sandaled feet sliding over the coarse sand as she almost skidded into us. She flung her good arm around Brandt, breaking his focus. He staggered before he caught her, grunting with surprise. A spasm of pain twisted over her face as she straightened. "You're here! We were worried sick about you.

Elias is a traitor!" She kissed Brandt on the cheek, then looked back over her shoulder. "They're here! They're here, and they've got the spear." She then sprang toward me and snatched me up in a tight hug with only one arm as she kept talking. "He betrayed us. Can you believe him? He was working with one of the factions. He leads it! After all that time!" She crushed me so tight it hurt before she kissed me on the cheek and jumped to Kine. "We were so afraid he'd already gotten the spear from you or killed you or worse!"

"No, we're quite alive," Kine said, his voice cracking as Candy seized him. "Careful of your arm there, Candy. What happened? Your ring still isn't working?"

"No. None of our rings are working any more. We can't shift," Hord said. "And most of our weapons and armor and supplies are gone as well. They have been attacking regularly, trying to get the reagents now."

A reedy voice called out, "It's all right though." Tile made a far slower approach, coming around the stone pillar as the other members of the camp called out and drew closer. He limped along, favoring his right leg. "I still have enough of the reagents," he said, his hand over his chest. His breaths shuddered. "So long as all of them are cast into the heart of the Ember Lord's Crest along with the talismans fashioned from the Babadon's heart, this can still work. This is an undoing. And it is always easier to destroy than it is to create. So that is to our advantage. There's still hope."

Candy had already moved on to greet the rest, her arm now wrapped around Lorna's neck as the tall Vawtrian woman stooped down to greet her. "Yes!" Candy called out. "Yes, we have hope, and we are going to crush them."

Brandt looked about, his brow furrowed and his expression dark. "So none of you are in league with Elias?" he demanded, his voice rough.

I cringed. That was a little harsh and obvious but to the point. Not that I really blamed him. He was trying to make sense of the Gola Resh's words.

Those words were like a blow though.

Everyone's eyes widened, and the denials flooded in. Shock filled all their faces. Hurt as well.

Brandt's gaze rested too long on Hord as he scanned the group. "The Gola Resh said there was another traitor."

"You suspect me?" Hord's voice deepened as he crossed his arms. "You doubt me?"

Brandt maintained his intense gaze. "She implied that it was you. That she offered to spare you and Cahji."

"So you doubt me?" Hord's expression darkened.

"I could think of little more heartbreaking than to believe you capable of such betrayal, but I know you are a good man and a good father. You already lost Tanusa. How could you be asked to lose any more?" Brandt said, his voice tight. His attention remained fixed on Hord.

Hord lifted his square chin. His eyes flashed as he interrupted him. "If I had turned on you, I would not have brought him here with me. I would not have honored his request to fight for the salvation of Sepeazia. With all respect, do not dishonor me or the memory of my beloved by suggesting that I would tarnish everything I hold dear to save my own skin and my son. My sweet Tanusa laid down her life to save our future. The future of a Sepeazia vibrant and free. No such future exists under the Gola Resh. And...true though this may be, I have no way to prove it."

Brandt glanced back at me then, his jaw like marble. "Seer?"

My mouth went dry, but I lifted my chin. My own instincts flared clear. I didn't examine them. I knew. And I spoke. "I trust him. I don't think there are any more traitors among us. But there is torment that comes from doubting. The one strength we still have is one another." But something else bothered me in this. Something I couldn't quite put my finger on yet. It reminded me of the jealousy that had started to grow within me about Candy. Elias had tended those seeds well, but it had had the potential to sow dissension among us. And Hord, like Candy, was innocent. I was sure of it.

Brandt nodded slowly. His expression suggested he was still concerned. In fairness, there was little damage that Hord could do at the moment if he was a traitor, since Kine was not letting that spear out of his hands and Tile held the reagents.

"I apologize, Hord—" Brandt started.

Hord shook his head. Though his lips were pressed in a tight line and his brow furrowed, he spoke firmly. "The Gola Resh is the cause of this heartache and grief. It would be foolish of you to not at least question after she spoke. Had she offered to spare Cahji and me, I would have spit in her face." He gestured toward the now yellow-orange charm at Brandt's throat. "By the look of it, we don't have much time left to debate this matter."

Some of the tension and unease faded then. It still didn't feel quite right, but there was no longer a heaviness. We'd narrowly avoided another one of her traps, but what else awaited us? What else could she do in the little time that remained?

Brandt dipped his head forward in acknowledgment and gestured toward the camp. "Let's prepare to enter the Ember Lord's Crest. You said Elias attacked. Tell me everything."

"Elias has at least fifty in his faction," Hord said. "I suspect there are more inside. We keep trying to send out messages for reinforcements, but we've exhausted our eagles, pterosaurs, and every other option. Every time we've tried to send one up, it's been shot down. Whatever the Gola Resh has done, our magic is muted here. We can't even swim out. There's a barrier. You can get in, but you can't get out."

Even with the crew of our ship and the dinosaurs, we were badly outnumbered. My heart sank.

"What else?" Brandt demanded gruffly.

Hord explained swiftly, with interjections from the others. This wasn't just going to be a battle against a supernatural entity that was amorphous and couldn't be stabbed until the end of the ritual when she became corporeal. It would be a bloody battle against our own flesh and blood as well.

I brought my hand up and pushed my hair back from my face as the reality settled in. We were going to have to fight Sepeazians too. My guts clenched again. I hated the Gola Resh. It wasn't enough that she was draining our life away. She was going to make us kill our own people. She and the Babadon were twisted. She must have promised to spare those who fought with Elias. Was it a lie though? We were all tied to Sepeazia's life force. Her magic and the Babadon's was so far beyond us that perhaps there was a way. But something was off about it.

As I mulled this over and the others prepared our strategy, Cahji ran over and hugged me, mended spear in hand. He was so much taller than I remembered, all gangly limbs, with big silver eyes and thick silver hair. His mother's coloring with his father's features.

He looked down at me, an expression of shy awe on his face. "You didn't really change," he said. He held his hand up though as if measuring my height, then laughed.

That stirring of familiarity swept over me. The tears that rose up almost choked me. "You did though. Look at you. You're so tall!"

He ducked his head, his smile crooked. That smile was his mother's and almost too big for his face. "I'm glad I get to fight with you for Sepeazia," he said. His gaze darted to his father.

Hord nodded, his posture still tight. But there was pride in his gaze.

Pride swelled in my own heart as well. These were my people. And they were good.

In the moments that followed, we made our plans. Tile and

Candy had brought forces with them, though only three arcanists and five warriors had survived Elias's onslaught. Of the six that Hord and Cahji brought, only two had survived. We had twelve crewmen who were capable of fighting. Most of the weapons had survived Elias's attack.

Arjax and Lorna moved among our little—were we enough to count as an army?—and anyone who had a shifting ring, they took and remedied. Both shook out their arms as they finished, the energy sparking along their hands a little more muted than before. The wounded were able to use the shifting energy from the rings then to heal themselves.

As we finalized everything and the arcanists prepared the shields to protect us from the volcano's heat and strength, I broke free and slipped over to Kine. He had been avoiding me, and I had not made nearly as much of an effort to reach him because I had been focusing on Brandt. Now I realized, as dear as Brandt was to me, I shouldn't have left him by the wayside.

"Kine." I bit the inside of my lip. "I don't know what's going to happen in here, but—"

"I have failed you, Bug." He cupped my cheek, his gaze soft. The wind ruffled his azure curls. "I didn't question Elias as I should have. I gave in to my own desires to see you, and I broke my vow to protect you. He used me to gain access, and I failed you."

"No." I shook my head and hugged him tight. His heartbeat thudded dully against my ear, steady and slow. "No. No, what Elias did was not your fault. You made a mistake. That's all. We all make mistakes. I trusted Elias too, and I'm a seer. So did Auntie Runa."

He shook his head, his posture rigid and his expression hard. "It doesn't make it right. I should have known better. But somehow, I will find a way to fix this." He gripped the spear tighter, his knuckles yellowing.

He then pushed past me, striding after the rest.

There was nothing to do but follow and end this.
How were we going to survive?
Would we?
Probably not.
But maybe Sepeazia would.

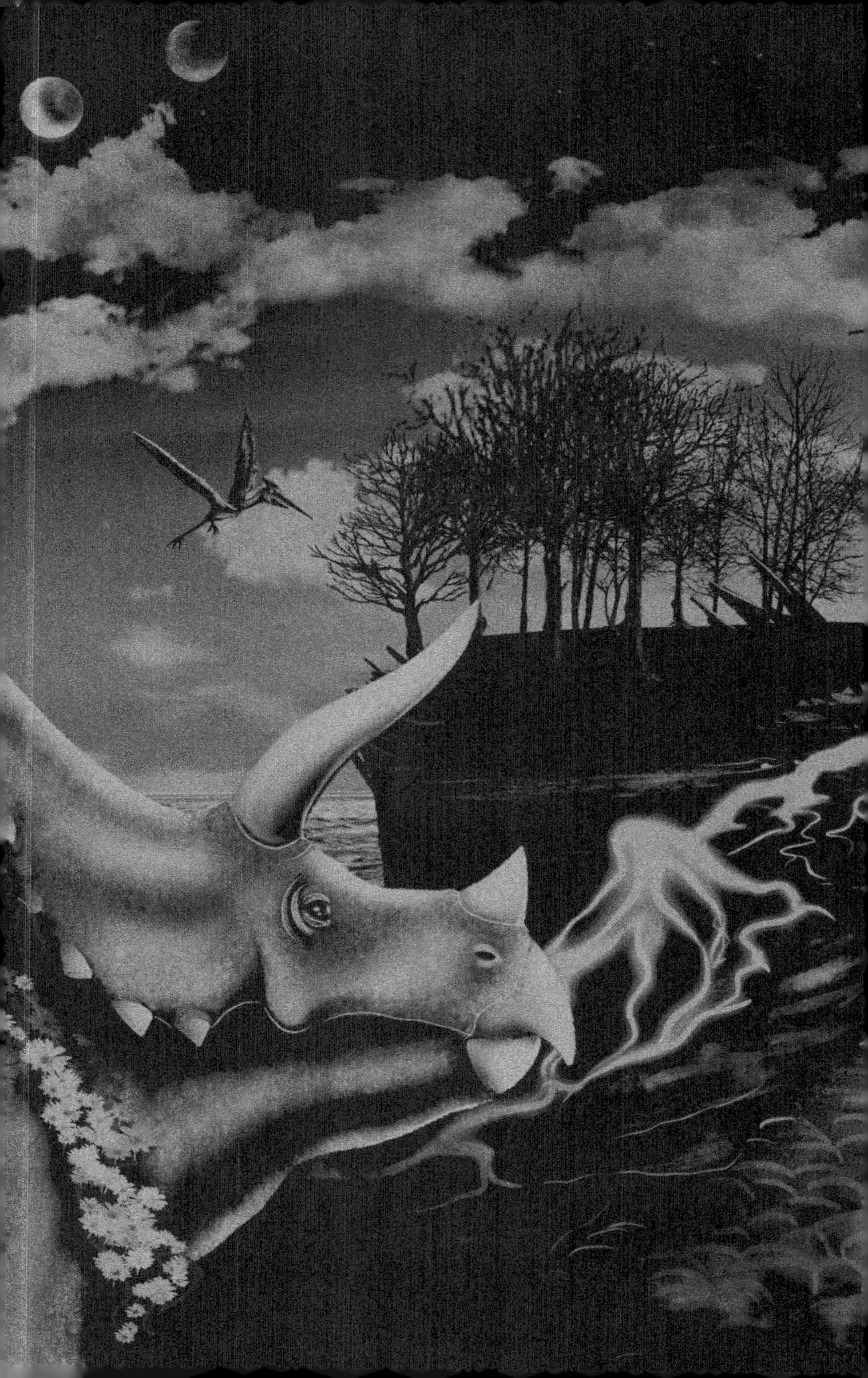

CHAPTER FIFTY-TWO: STELLA

Our plan was simple. Get in. Find the other talismans and throw them and the reagents into the heart of the Ember Lord's Crest. Easy enough. It was even outlined in blue lava.

Tile insisted that so long as the talismans went in first, the reagents could be cast into the heart in any order.

And there was only one safe way into the Ember Lord's Crest. A single opening led into the heart of the volcano where this ritual had to be completed. While it was possible that there were other ways, we didn't have enough time to seek them out. This way was the one that had been enchanted in heartstones. Carved deep into the rock itself.

It was simple. Terrifyingly simple.

The Gola Resh and Elias almost certainly knew about it if they had half a brain between them. She'd probably make it hard for us to find the Goblet and Axe. So we would have to begin our search once we reached the primary chamber.

Elias with his faction or the Gola Resh—perhaps both—would ambush us. Really it was just a question of when and where.

I choked down my fears and reminded myself I was a queen, a seer, and a water serpent. And I was in the best company a woman could ask for.

Brandt led the way, followed or flanked by Hord, depending on the pace. I followed behind, almost within arm's reach. Kine strode beside me, gripping the spear, eyes set straight ahead and jaw uncharacteristically fixed. Buttercup followed, nudging and lowing her complaints. Candy and Cahji were farther back with the crewmen and the few remaining arcanists who had survived, interspersed with a couple parasaurs and triceratopses and a handful of warriors. Arjax and Lorna brought up the rear, but they had already warned us in the case of an attack, they would shift into flying creatures and soar to the front for the element of surprise.

The path leading up to the volcano was rocky and uneven, surrounded by craggy cliffs and the ominous shadow of the looming mountain. Ugh. Even worse, the atmosphere intensified, humid and unpleasant. It tasted like bitter ash and metallic sulfur. The ground beneath our feet rumbled.

Ihlkit.

My hands worked at my sides, brushing against the dagger in my belt occasionally and working against my shifter ring at others. The sharp tang of the ring's energy reminded me of the power I could tap into.

Buttercup nudged me, lowing softly. I tried to comfort her, but I wasn't sure what to say. "Not your first time in battle, girl," I whispered. "But it's my first time in this body." And I had never felt less prepared for anything in my life.

Another gurgling growl from the volcano warned that something had disturbed it. The Gola Resh, almost assuredly. And she hadn't made it any more forgiving. Even with spells to provide protection, the heat of the volcano bled through my sandals.

It grew hotter and more treacherous as we reached the overhang and passed into the black stone chasm. My simple blue and white dress was already damp, and a sheen of sweat shone on everyone's faces.

Buttercup nudged me again when I hesitated. I stroked her snout. Her eyes were bright, her stance strong. If I had to guess, she was more worried about me than she was scared about entering the volcano.

A sudden bit of cold chattered down my spine as a rock clattered off the edge and plunged down into the river of lava below.

Auntie Runa's wretched vision played through my mind once more.

Death.

A couple embracing one another as they burned in lava like loose rocks.

This ended in death.

What other interpretation could there be?

It wasn't as if that was just metaphorical. That vision had even held the sulfuric blue ring of lava at the Crest's heart. Our choices were taking us deeper to the place where we would die. Didn't all choices simply bring us closer to death?

I glanced at Brandt as we continued, quickening my pace just enough to be near him. His charm had lightened a little more now. It had such an ominous glow. The urge to slip forward and tuck my hand in his thrust itself forward, but I stilled it. We both had to focus. I couldn't distract him.

He glanced back at me, his arm reaching back.

In that breath, his thumb brushed down the back of my hand. A small smile curled at his lips when my gaze caught his. A sad smile. A smile that said so much. I wanted to tell him another joke, but I couldn't think of one. All my humor had evaporated.

Lava bubbled menacingly below, threatening to pop and

bubble up at any moment, sometimes less than ten feet away. The ceiling above groaned as the ground rumbled. Over on the far side, a stalactite broke free and plunged into the molten rock. A fine arc of lava sprayed into the air, striking the walls.

I cringed inwardly.

Kine gave my arm a light squeeze. "It's all right, Bug," he whispered. "It'll all work out. You're gonna make it."

I glanced at him gratefully. "You will too."

His brow pinched as if he intended to contradict me. Then he shook his head and motioned for me to keep pace, indicating the narrowing of the path ahead.

Everything in me tightened. Fear sliced through my mind. This was it. That archway was barely big enough for a parasaur to slip through, and on the other side lay the heart. Despite the sweat rolling down my neck, my blood went cold. I reached back to place my hand on Buttercup's snout.

Another deep breath and we passed beneath the arch.

The air became electric.

As ominous and uneasy as the air of the beach had been, this was a thousand times worse.

My skin prickled as I took in everything I could.

This chamber was easily the size of the great hall in the palace, the ceiling arching so high above it disappeared in the darkness. The black walls gleamed and glowed with the pulsing red-yellow of the lava below. The stone smoothed out here, straight and even, like a platform. The rock floor fell away at intervals, with islands of rock on narrow columns of stone scattered throughout. Stalactites stabbed down at intervals, some easily twenty and thirty feet long. Perhaps longer.

An almost oppressive silence crushed down on us, stirred only by the hissing, bubbling pops of the lava in the chasm below.

And there it was.

A trap.

At the edge, before the tone cut off into a sheer drop of perhaps twenty-five feet or more, stood a stone table. Simple cut. Grey. Pitted and streaked with other minerals. A Goblet that was easily longer than my forearm rested next to an axe that was almost the proper size for Arjax. The other two talismans.

As if we would just run up there, grab them, and attempt to start our own ritual.

We all halted.

Not one word had to be said. It was so obvious it was insulting.

Brandt set his arms akimbo, then glanced about. His gaze narrowed. He strode forward, steps heavy, boots crunching over the heated stone. "Enough of these games, Gola Resh," he thundered.

A harsh but playful voice grated out of the air. "I have to admit, I'm a little disappointed you didn't just kill the arch general on the beach. It would have been amusing, and then we could have seen you suffer even more. I was really hoping they'd turn on you."

Like a shadow falling away, the Gola Resh appeared before the stone table. Her form was easily more than twelve feet now. Her eyes blazed orange and green, the colors swirling and melding together at points and yet at their most extreme, always maintaining their distinctness. Those same flickers of color danced along the edges of her dripping form. Long claws hooked from her arms. Power pulsed from her, like a chest-vibrating bass. Her features remained distorted unless she turned in profile. A dark-grey veil seemed to hang over her. It stirred in all the wrong directions, as if displaced by winds we could not feel.

"Still," the Gola Resh said with a dark chuckle. "There's

plenty of suffering to go around." Her gaze dropped to one of the stone columns.

"Your inner court was difficult to infiltrate. But it doesn't matter now." Elias strode out from behind a pillar, confident. He wore black-and-red robes as if he were still representing his people. He walked like a commander of nations, his shoulders thrown back, chin tilted up. His cold, dark-blue eyes took us in. "All draws to a close," he said as calmly as if observing the weather, "and the Gola Resh has still allowed her mercy to be obtained."

My hands balled into fists instinctively. How dare he stand there and lecture us! Angry words sprang to my mouth but died as the air shimmered.

Dark forms appeared behind him, magic unveiling them. Ten...twenty...thirty...forty...sixty... Who knew how many? All in heavy black hoods, silent and waiting. Some held towering spears or spike-toothed clubs. Some wore blades at their sides while holding bows and crossbows.

Damn. That weaponry alone... Elias had to be from one of the weapon-making factions. Those blades and shafts looked like some of our finest.

Brandt's gaze narrowed on Elias. He hadn't even flinched. "I won't pretend to understand why you betrayed us. If you had wanted to be king, you could have challenged me. You didn't need to pretend to care about Stella."

Elias scoffed. He sliced across the air with his right hand. "Sepeazia would have plunged into civil war had you been killed while Stella remained absent. We did not need that. You belittled enough of our institutions. You mocked our traditions and methods of peace. You let the very emblem of our union be destroyed and thought that the talismans could replace them?"

Brandt tilted his head, eyes hooded with confusion. "What are you talking about?"

Elias cut a glare at Brandt. "My family—my kin—my blood!"

He struck his fist to his chest, his teeth bared. "We are the ones who fashioned the Sword of Kairos. We are the ones who tended its fire and smithed it with runes. We are the ones who sought where the blessings might be obtained. We are the ones who conceived of the idea. In the great wars, my people died to protect it. My grandfather died for it as did others. Do you even know how many?"

Brandt scowled at him. "The sword was a symbol. And it did not protect us from the Gola Resh or the Babadon then. Why would that have changed? Symbols are not more important than people."

"They can be. Especially in times of need. You sacrificed one of our most sacred and powerful items for a woman." His gaze fell to me, his manner stiffening. His head cocked slightly as his voice cracked at the end. "An exceptional woman, I grant you, but a woman nonetheless."

My upper lip curled. Disgust rose within me. "So this was all just a long path to getting even because of a lost sword? It wouldn't have been destroyed in the first place if it wasn't for the Gola Resh and the Babadon?"

Elias's expression hardened. Something flickered in those dark-blue eyes. "It was a way to reclaim the power that he cast aside. In his decision, he proclaimed you more worthy than a sword which was—"

"Pointless," Brandt said flatly. "Weapons can be reforged. Things can be recreated. People cannot." He kept his hands braced against his broad belt. "I'm not fully certain I understand your plan. You brought Stella back. Members of your faction tried to kill me multiple times and failed. Surely that wasn't part of your plan. I'm sure it wasn't. After all, my actual inner court is exceptional. Between Hord and Candy, half never even made it to the throne room for kuvaste. You chose the coward's path and targeted our family's grief, manipulating her brother."

Kine lifted his chin, his muscles so tight they were almost

ready to snap. Rage burns in his golden eyes, dancing like flames. "You lied about everything."

Elias snarled. "I never lied about the importance or the sincerity of my desire to bring Stella back. You, Kine, were at least honest in your pursuit and your priorities. You, Brandt, are the true menace. You and all those who stand by you without question or thought."

Candy kissed the air at him. "Love you as well, traitor." She then spat on the stone. It hissed in response.

Hord scoffed. The darkness in his expression remained as he shifted his weight, his hands tensed at his sides.

Kine's gaze hardened. "You lied about enough. And for what?"

Elias glanced at the Gola Resh.

She wasn't even looking in his direction. She remained fixated on Brandt and me. Alarmingly so. Hatred simmered in those eyes. The coils of smoke and wisps that pulled about her intensified. What was she waiting for? It was as if she were weighing us.

"My bargain with the Gola Resh for my faction required providing the right kind of vengeance to the Gola Resh. Other factions have been moving, you know. Mine wasn't the only one trying to find a solution. Even if you were to find a way out of this, how will you mend Sepeazia, Brandt?" He spoke my beloved's name like a curse. "Do you even understand how broken we are? How much division there exists within the cities and towns? You thought you could protect the people by hiding the fact that the curse had resumed and the queen had truly returned, but—"

"This is boring me," the Gola Resh announced, lifting her hand. "Your petty squabbles mean nothing. Let's just make this simple, shall we? Not everything was a lie." She chuckled darkly. "And sometimes lies become truths, don't they, Elias?"

Elias's mouth twisted. His muscles tensed.

"And that makes all this so much more delicious," the Gola Resh continued. Her burning eyes narrowed as she held up one long-clawed finger. "I'll give you what you want. Brandt or Stella, I don't care which, one of you will push or cast the other into the lava below. Do it in the next five minutes, and I will consider freeing half the people of Sepeazia from the curse."

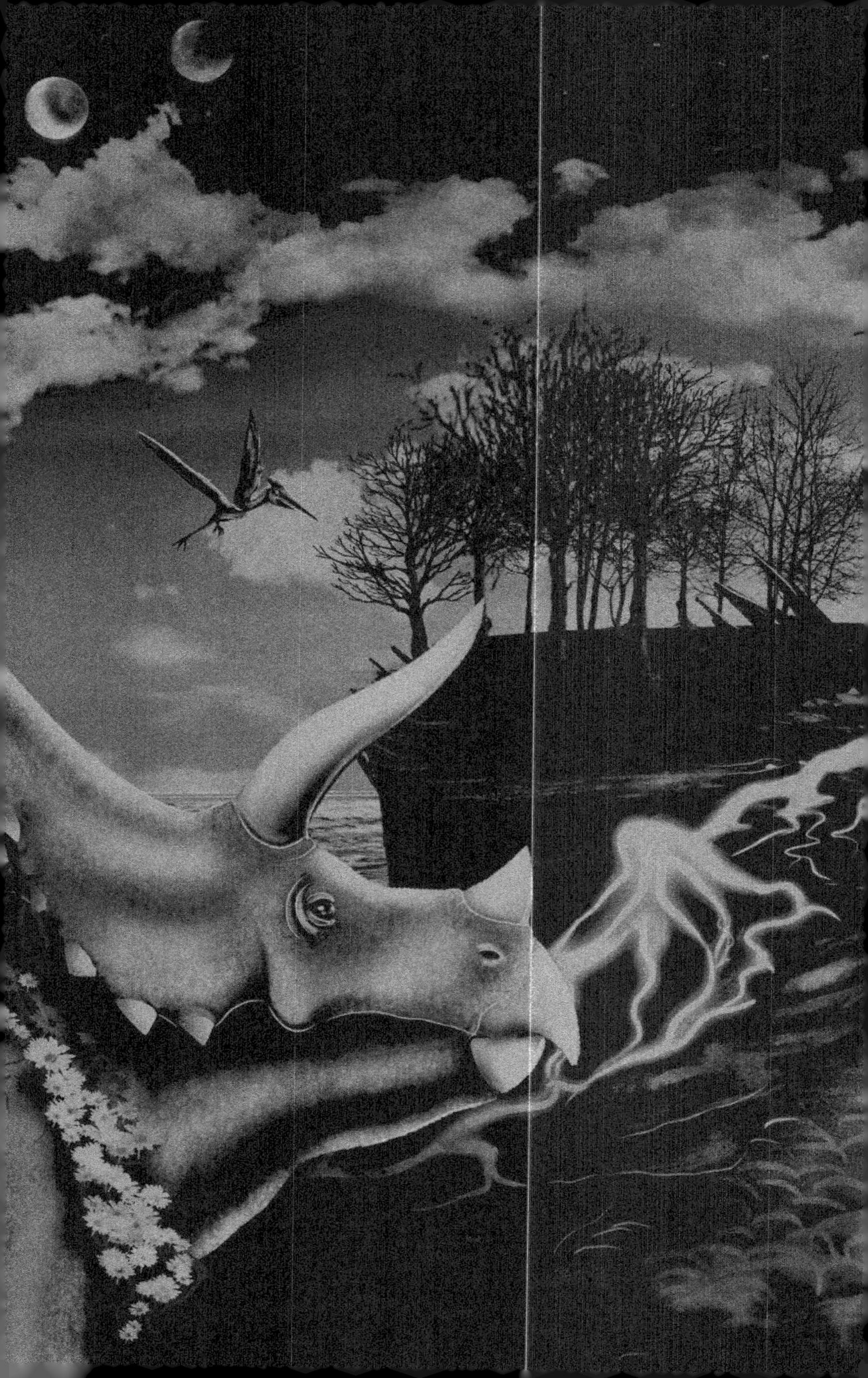

CHAPTER FIFTY-THREE: STELLA

Silence spread across the cavern, broken only by the hissing splats of bursting bubbles in the lava below. Brandt's jaw clenched so tight it looked like it might snap.

Elias's brow furrowed as his attention returned to the Gola Resh. "That was not part of the arrangement."

The Gola Resh scoffed as she at last dropped her gaze back to him. "The arrangement is what I say it is." With a roll of her eyes, she returned her focus to us. She drifted back toward the table with the weapons on it as if daring us to attempt to seize them. "All Brandt has to do is throw Stella into this pit and watch her die." She gestured toward the river of lava twenty feet below. "Or she can do the honors."

My heart clenched. Emotion clogged my throat. Memories of the dagger and my death at the sacred pool flashed back into my mind. If I had to die again, I would. But—it wasn't just going to be me, was it? Was Brandt going to cast himself in as well?

"There is no reason we should believe you," Brandt said slowly. The muscles in his sweat-sheened arms jumped. "And you only say you are willing to consider. Not guarantee."

Kine swore under his breath as Candy muttered something about not trusting the Gola Resh as far as she could float.

The Gola Resh just laughed. "Oh, consider is the best I can do. I want to see you suffer. And you can't follow her in, Brandt. I want you to watch her burn and know she is in agony because you could not protect her. In fact, I changed my mind. You are the one who must do it. Kill her, Brandt. Kill her, and I'll consider freeing half your people. That's what you wanted all along, wasn't it?"

"You have proved yourself untrustworthy." Brandt's voice shook as he glared at her. He shook his head. Sweat rolled along the sides of his face, highlighted the long scar that cut down the left side of his face. They might as well have been tears. "Why should we believe you?"

"Stella dies," the Gola Resh chortled. "She dies again, and there's nothing you can do to stop it."

Elias's teeth clenched as he glared up at her. "I have been nothing but faithful to your demands, Gola Resh. I brought you what you needed time and again. Yet you would break your word so easily? Stella was to be spared!"

The Gola Resh sneered. She flung her hands up in the air. "Fine. I don't care. One of you will push or cast the other into the lava below. And I'll guarantee that I'll spare all of the people of Sepeazia. As long as one of you dies and the other watches. Just do it!"

"If my death will satisfy you and you can give proof that you will spare Sepeazia—" Brandt started.

I sprang forward and grabbed his hand, eyes blazing. She'd overplayed. "No! This—it makes no sense. She wants vengeance, but..." I spun to face her once more, my mouth as dry as paper. A thought had been forming in my mind since the beach. Now it wriggled into clarity. "Your illness—the whole reason you came here and began to devour Sepeazia's life force was because you were dying. Neither you nor the Babadon wished to be separated."

"Yes. All we came for was my healing." She said it so simply, almost mockingly. As if we were being the unreasonable ones.

"And eternity together," Kine pointed out, still holding the spear tight.

Her breath hissed through her knife-like teeth. "There has never been any dispute about this. What is the purpose of your questions now?"

I glanced back at Tile, hoping he knew that I was asking him as much as confronting the Gola Resh. "Magic is not precise. It is not something that can be measured like water or stone. It is a type of energy. How do you store it? You don't use heartstones to embed your deepest incantations, Gola Resh. And you didn't stop once you were healed, even though you could have escaped without being seen. No, you decided to take everything. To destroy all of us and become true immortals."

Tile gave a nod of assent. His frown deepened.

"I have no need of heartstones or to store power," the Gola Resh said with dry amusement. She stalked closer. Her eyes narrowed, and the air around her grew more oppressive as she loomed over Brandt and me.

"The Babadon—once you bring him back—he is going to be weakened. What will replenish him? Not Sepeazia's life force. If it was enough for when you needed healing and for both of you to gain eternal life together, how can there be enough now that he must be restored in full? Or do you intend to go back to being ill so that he can be alive long enough for you to share a few years before you're separated once more?"

She paused then. Her jaws snicked together with such a sharp click I almost thought she broke her teeth. "There are other worlds, little girl. Other realms. Your little kingdom isn't that special."

I pressed my advantage, hands balled into fists. "Except

something about us is. Because you stayed even when we fought back. Maybe you were just so arrogant you didn't think it would make a difference. But I think it's something else. It's like your curses. Until they are completed, the line of energy remains open. And if that is the case, you cannot actually spare anyone from the destruction you will bring. Not all. Not fifty. Not ten. Not two. Not even one. You're drinking from a fire hydrant and pretending you can fill a teacup without spilling it. You have to take all of the life away from us or else you will lose everything you have taken." I cast my gaze to Elias, my voice hardening. "The Gola Resh would have perished along with the Babadon the night you attacked. The mortal wound she inflicted upon herself...were you there before she inflicted that or after?"

Elias's jaw set. "She was transferring her life force into a new form, trying to change things with those shifter rings. It was a new form that transcended what we knew. She swore so much torment and destruction upon our people. She offered freedom, life, and salvation for the Kairos Faction and all who would join with us up to a third of the population. A guarantee that none of us would die. We could have saved a third of our people."

I refused to look away. The words burned in me. "You gave her more shifter rings. You allowed her to start siphoning off their strength and energy as well."

"The Gola Resh turned our ancestors' gift into a curse," Lorna growled, her dark eyes hard as obsidian.

"Gifts into curses are my specialty," the Gola Resh preened. "But now I am offering you your precious people back. I'll take what we need from the animals and the plants. You won't get a better offer than that."

Buttercup huffed.

I placed my hand on her snout, glaring at the Gola Resh. "Really? You haven't really responded to my assertion. Was I wrong before? Maybe. It's remarkable how abundant and plentiful the life force of Sepeazia is. A life force that you desperately need. So let's go back. You needed all of it to start. Everything from our plants to our beasts, to our lives, to our land and sea. But then, suddenly, you don't need everything. Were you just greedy before, or are you only now realizing how much you need? It doesn't seem like this follows how your magic works."

Tile's brow lifted. He gave a determined nod. Lines of strain still bracketed his narrow mouth, but there was a fierceness in his gaze. Yes. I was right. This wasn't how her magic worked.

Brandt cast a look back at me. A hard one. But one with a faint smirk. One that said "brash seer." I lifted my chin, steeling my expression but sent him back my own glance to say, "brilliant king."

Pressing my advantage, small as it was, I continued, "You have made multiple offers time and time again. You'll spare one. No, two. No, ten. No, half. No, all! But what I have seen of your magic at every stage is that it is forceful and full of movement. It has its own momentum, like a tidal wave or a volcanic explosion, and you act as if you can just slow it or change its course at any time you choose. But you can't—can you? Even if you could, you think we are nothing. You despise us. You simply want our pain."

The Gola Resh hissed at me. "You said you wanted a guarantee for your pathetic little nation. I give it to you, and now you argue with me?" She slashed her hand through the air. The shadows that formed her body darkened, the skeletal frame intensifying in boldness. "All you have is my word. That is all that will be granted. I give you a chance for all to live. And you spit in my face?"

"Your word means nothing," Brandt growled. "You have proven yourself treacherous from the start. "Why should anyone believe you?"

"Elias," I called out, stepping forward and searching for his gaze. Brandt's eyebrow arched. Kine scowled. Neither made any move to stop me, though I suddenly felt the weight of their gazes upon me.

Elias's attention snapped to me. Anger filled his eyes—anger and something like regret.

My fingernails cut into my palms as I forced myself to look at him and not turn away in disgust. "Elias, you and your faction must know now that this is all a lie. The Gola Resh desires only vengeance against us. She wants us to suffer. But she will not spare anyone. She will drain us all till we are husks and cast us aside. Auntie Runa saw death. You were there with me when she told us. Whenever I have tried to see the end to this, that is all that I have seen. All any seer has seen. The Gola Resh and the Babadon bring death. The only choices they have offered us have been those that torment us and bring us suffering. They treat us like pawns and toys for their amusement, and they will throw us away after they have stripped away every choice from us they can."

Tile called out, his voice reedier in this cavern. "That has been the problem since the start. It may not even be the Gola Resh entirely. If it were not for our people being bound to this land and the sea itself, we could have fled. But we are as tied to its life as it is tied to ours. No magic of any of the other nations or realms has been able to sever this bond."

I scanned the faction before returning to Elias, my voice strengthening as I saw the fear and sorrow in their eyes. "Elias, you showed me what was in your book as well. The visions you were having. There was death in there as well. The Gola Resh offers only lies. Deep down, you know this." I started to step closer.

Brandt grunted, putting his arm out to stop me from getting any closer. A muscle in his jaw twitched before he looked back to the traitors. "Fight with us, not against us, Elias. You are still Sepeazian."

Elias's mouth twisted. Sweat glistened over his face, and his expression darkened. "Kairos Faction," he snarled. "Attack the Gola Resh."

The Gola Resh chuckled darkly as the hooded warriors spun around, their weapons pointed at her. "Do any of you think I would actually permit you to speak if this—" she gestured toward them as she floated backward over the lava, leaving the talismans unguarded, "—was in any way a threat to me?" She smirked, her voice dripping with derision. "But if you want to fight, far be it from me to deny you your last request." She then clenched her hands into fists, her claws curling up against her arms.

The ground shook, and the lava in the chasm below started to bubble and churn with a terrifying violence. With guttural roars, creatures formed from the lava and crawled up out of the fiery pool. Their hulking, misshapen bodies moved up the sides, deformed claws gouging into the stone.

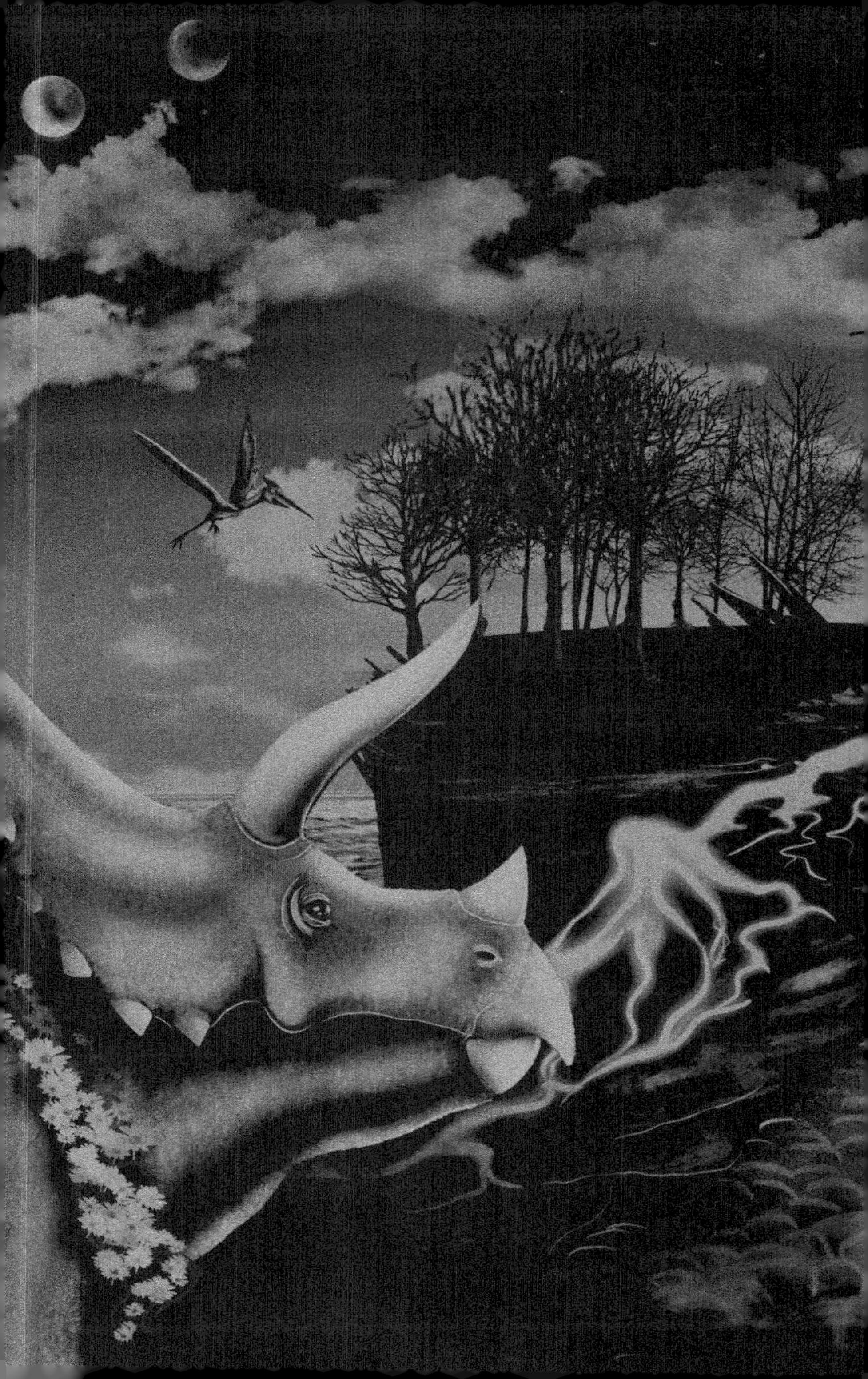

CHAPTER FIFTY-FOUR: STELLA

So much for turning the tide.
My pulse skipped. Time slowed.
Brandt's snarl shook the earth. "Shoot frost and water upon them. Don't let them reach the top."

Tile turned back to the arcanists, striking the air with his arms. He gestured for them to come to the center, uttering incomprehensible words.

Half of Elias's Kairos Faction strode to the edges, bringing out bows and white-tipped or black-tipped arrows and feathered bolts from within their cloaks. The arcanists swept up their hands and chanted their incantations. The bolt and arrow tips glowed bright and frosted, turning blue. Steam rose from the weapons. They at once rained down their arrows on the advancing creatures.

The melee warriors circled around the arcanists, Kairos Faction members mixing with those loyal to us from the start. They formed an armored circle with the dinosaurs there to help defend us as the arcanists chanted.

Several of the water serpent shifters without ranged

weapons transformed. They attacked the stalactites and boulders, pushing them off the edge to strike the creatures.

"Spear wielders," Brandt bellowed. "Strike at the cold." He turned toward me, jaw set. "Stella."

That was all he said, but I understood and tipped my head forward. He would handle fighting off the monsters. I would make sure the ritual was completed.

His body spasmed as he became the red and black serpent again, horns gleaming and scales shining. He coiled his body around a cluster of stone, snapped it off, and then chucked it off the side at one of the advancing monsters.

A spray of lava exploded up, striking the ceiling and hissing.

The spear wielders, with weapons easily fifteen to twenty feet long, sprang to the edges, adjusting their grip and jabbing downward. They struck at the advancing monsters, aiming at the dark patches where the cold and water had created vulnerabilities for the lava monsters.

The arcanists continued to chant. The ice-blue magic curled around the weapon blades and tips. Some wavered in coloration, a few didn't change, a few dropped what they had.

We didn't have much time. Our magic was failing too, probably drained by the Gola Resh. But it would be enough. The table was right there. We'd subverted the ambush.

Except—we were missing something. My heartbeat thundered in my ears.

Kine prepared to charge toward the table. I seized the sleeve of his robe. He spun back to face me. "Bug, you all right?"

I held up my finger. Why was the Gola Resh being so passive? She was just watching us, hovering over the lava, well out of reach of the weapons. Not even looking at the weapons. It was true that she had to cast them in so that the Babadon could be resurrected, and the two rituals were similar. We had to do the same.

Tile had our reagents. He stood in the center of the circle of arcanists, weaving and chanting and guiding. When it was time, he'd be ready.

But what else did the Gola Resh require to bring the Babadon back?

Was there any way to create life without taking it in a situation like this?

Was there another trap besides the ambush?

There had to be, because here was precisely what we needed all laid out like gifts.

Gifts she'd turned into curses.

Stretching out my hand, I approached the table. Kine followed, concern etched in his features, spear still gripped tight. The air started to change once I was within a foot. Not a heat. But an energy of sorts. It shimmered and danced like heat waves, only sharper and more electric. "No one touch the talismans!"

The Gola Resh cackled. She looped over the lava and spread her arms again. "Oh-oh, what did you find, children?" Her eyes rolled up, and she chanted.

"Tile!" I shouted, gesturing for him to come close.

The flame-haired council member slid out from the center of the circle and ran to me. His brow furrowed once he was within a foot of the table. "Something is wrong with this..." His palms turned up, his left hand shook once he was almost within touching distance of the axe.

Kine drew nearer as well, hovering his hand over the Goblet. He had almost grazed his palm over it when he jerked back. Blood streamed from his fingernails. He shook his head, falling back. His pupils enlarged, then shrunk. "Ihlkit!"

Tile gripped his own trembling hand. "Whoever picks these up will be drained of their life. Immediately. This won't just require two though. If anyone actually touches these weapons, it will start leaping from person to person, draining their life."

"How many?" I demanded. My gaze snapped back to the

Gola Resh. She was snarling and chanting, her eyes rolled back. The cavern trembled. Silt fell from the ceiling. "Is there any way to counter it?"

"A moment," Tile murmured, hand thrust in his thick hair. "Give me a moment."

The Gola Resh's voice echoed through the cavern, sending chills down my spine. Her body continued twisting and contorting. The air around us pulsed and vibrated, making my skin prickle as it washed over me.

Brandt dropped back into his human form, picked up a fallen enchanted spear, and slashed it downward. The other spear warriors stabbed and slashed downward as the archers rained down their arrows and bolts.

Tile's eyes remained closed in concentration as he held his hands over the weapons, assessing the spell. The blood welled along his fingernails.

Small hills formed across the rock floor. Spiderwebbing cracks fractured out as small puffs of dust and air shot up. Brandt commanded everyone to prepare. The warriors surrounding the arcanists swung their weapons into the ready position.

The Gola Resh continued to chant and sweep her arms through the air. The shadows that surrounded her intensified and twisted.

The small hills erupted. Bony claws and fragmented skeletons emerged.

I startled, my hand flying to the short sword.

Ragged skeletons thrust their way out of the ground. They dragged themselves up and out.

We were surrounded on all sides—lava monsters crawling up from below, undead rising around us, and the Gola Resh's magic pressing down. It was relentless. They just kept coming and coming.

The dinosaurs shrieked in fury, stomping the skeletons into

the stone and crushing them into dust. Buttercup pounced on them, jumping on one as it came up like a fox on a mouse. Cracks split through the ground as more pressed up, grasping and clawing. The melee warriors hacked away at them while the archers focused their barrage on the lava creatures. If it wasn't hopeless, it soon would be. We couldn't waste any more time!

I turned back to him. "Tile, I'm sorry to rush you, but we're running out of time here!"

The Gola Resh continued her demonic chanting, her body snaking in inhuman contortions.

"It's going to take at least fifty lives," Tile said hoarsely. "She's using the life energy to bring back the Babadon. They're tied to the talismans now. Once the talismans are in the lava and she has the fifty lives, the Babadon can come back. He won't be at full strength until the items are fully melted, which might take a little bit based on the metals that were used here. But this isn't the only way she can get the lives she needs to bring the Babadon back. She can just start throwing people into the heart or some other equivalent."

"Can't we just throw the reagents in after we get the weapons in and kill her before she does that?" Kine demanded. "We'll just find a way to launch the table into the heart without touching the weapons. Then we get the reagents in before she can take fifty lives."

"Is there any way we can cut this off so she won't claim fifty lives?" I demanded. She was fast. Any second now she might start swooping in, grabbing our people, and tossing them into the heart.

Tile shook his head. "Assuming any of us can leverage, launch, and aim a stone table with those talismans on it, we can try, but if she gets those fifty lives in before we kill her, then she'll have the Babadon back at full strength. Our ritual could only ever make them vulnerable to our attacks. It won't kill them. We have to do that on our own." His voice grew even more sober. "If we play this wrong, we will destroy our forces here, strengthen her, restore the Babadon, and hand her the victory in a gold cup."

A fiend got past the melee warriors and charged us. Kine spun around, swung the spear, and knocked it off the edge in a clean swipe. Buttercup had moved away from me, leaping on another fiend. She thrashed and trampled with zeal, then butted three right off the edge. Baby girl hated those skeletons. They arced through the air until they disappeared in a fiery splash.

All the while the Gola Resh kept chanting. More and more fiends jolted up from the ground just as more lava creatures attacked the sides of the cliff. We were running out of time. Keeping up at this pace was barely enough to contain them as it was.

I circled the table, searching for some hole in the energy, some weakness we could exploit without triggering the deaths.

Kine grabbed Tile's arm. "She poisoned the shifter rings to change the energy so she could absorb it. The Vawtrian energy in its original form was toxic to her. What if the reason she slowly siphoned it and changed the rings over time was because she was also changing it? She isn't a shifter. Their magic isn't natural to her. She would have to adapt it."

Tile's eyes widened. "All our people who were lost in Taivren...those rings vanished. If she took that power...if she changed it in the same way...that means changing the talismans with the energy again might be enough to keep the Babadon from coming back."

The dread intensified within me as I fought against the despair of the visions. It was easier to destroy than create, but the Gola Resh was still so far beyond us. There had to be a way. A choice. Something we could change.

An idea popped into my mind.

"Arjax and Lorna fixed our rings," I said, "but they can't touch the items on the table. Not without dying. What if they just changed the spear?"

Tile hesitated. "It could work. Eliminate the talismans without setting off the chain of sacrifices. Change the spear with the Vawtrian energy so it is no longer the same. That might be enough to throw her restoration ritual for the Babadon off entirely."

Kine gave me a firm nod, his features resolution. "Good thing the cousins are here."

My pulse throbbed. I cast my gaze around the cavern. The battle raged on. Brandt had ripped out more stone from the ceiling to pelt the monsters below. When a skeletal fiend raced toward him, he swung about, snapped it in half, and flung it over the side. Elias fought on the opposite side, wielding his quarterstaff with the frozen tips alongside his parasaur. Lorna and Arjax both remained in their ice wyrm forms, jagged teeth and icy breath making short work of the lava monsters that drew too close. Their tails served as clubs against the fiends. They were in the center of the right and left sides. Dozens of skeletal fiends stood between us and them.

"Tile, be ready to throw the reagents in as soon as we get the talismans in. Kine, you get Lorna. I'll get Arjax." I whistled for Buttercup to come back.

My fierce horned girl charged toward me, crashing through the line, shattering enemies like pottery on stone. A large axe-wielding skeleton lunged for her. I shot at him, letting the water serpent form take hold. The thick curve of my horned skull struck the fiend and bowled him over.

Buttercup bellowed and dropped on another that raced toward us. A sword blade struck my back, the force bruising but not piercing my scales. Buttercup bowed her head to let me on her crest. Shooting up onto Buttercup, I clicked my tongue and flicked my tail in the direction we were to go.

Kine was already jetting toward Lorna, striking at any who attacked him.

"Come on, Buttercup," I shouted.

Buttercup blazed with rage. She flung her head back and forth and bellowed. My triceratops hated these fiends, and she swatted and crushed them with zeal. She crashed across the stone platform to Arjax.

I slammed my horns into another fiend, then skidded alongside him. "Arjax!"

He sent down another icy blast, then turned his fiery black eyes on me. "Having fun, little cousin?"

"So much fun. And it's about to get more fun." I gestured with my chin toward the table and then explained as fast as I could.

Arjax listened attentively, his horned eyebrows pinching down. Then, with a hefty grunt, he lunged forward. With practiced ease and magnificent power, he shot across the cracked stone floor, bowling over the skeletal fiends. His armored plating crushing them effortlessly.

I seized the ribs of one in my jaws and flung it into the head of another. Their bodies snapped like dry twigs. My mouth still felt odd, not quite hinging properly. But I didn't have to be delicate or precise here.

Together we cut a path across the center of the stone platform until we reached the glistening edge with the cursed stone slab. Arjax lunged for the end of the table, remaining in his ice wyrm form. He blasted it with ice, freezing the table in a block of ice. Even though it started to melt almost at once, it created a sufficient barrier. Growling, he dropped back into his human form and seized it. The stone cracked and popped beneath the ice.

The Gola Resh stopped her chanting. "What are you doing?" She darted forward. Actual rage and surprise filled her voice.

Before she could reach him, he picked up the whole slab

table and flung it into the center of the Ember Lord's Heart. The lines of glowing blue sulfur that created the circle pulsed with energy.

The Gola Resh screamed with rage. The shadows that formed her pulsed and writhed, eyes blazing.

Kine reached Lorna and held up the spear, speaking swiftly as monsters below advanced. Her dark eyes hardened. She dipped her head forward and dropped back into her massive human form. With a nod, she grabbed the spear. Energy arced and coiled over her hand into the spear. It spiraled like golden lightning.

Arjax spun around to face the Gola Resh as she screeched. Her claws scraped the air over his head. He flattened, then returned to the ice wyrm form.

Snarling, she struck again. One of her shadowed claws tore his arm and side open. Black wisps darted around him as he howled. The ice wyrm form shuddered around him, and he collapsed. His breath hissed through his teeth. Jamming his hand against the stone, he struggled to rise.

I struck at her. My jaws snapped air. Foul-tasting air that coated my tongue. Then I tried to headbutt her. She didn't pay me any attention as she lashed at Arjax again.

"Get away from him!" Lorna's voice boomed through the cavern, echoing off the walls.

She charged forward, back in her spinosaurus form. The Gola Resh barely wrenched around in time to move back. Lorna's jaws snapped at the edge of her form. Cackling, the Gola Resh darted backward, leading Lorna away.

"Lorna!" I screamed, realizing how close she was to the edge.

Lorna pulled up short just in time. Bits of pebbles rolled off. A few chunks of stone crumbled from the edge. She snarled in response. "You think you can lure me to my death?"

"You're thick enough," the Gola Resh sneered darkly. "Do you really think your plans against me will work? That I haven't considered every eventuality?"

I slid beside Arjax, dropping back into my human form as Lorna taunted the Gola Resh. This time, I kept my clothes.

I tugged his good shoulder as I tried to move him. "Come on!"

He nodded, gritting his teeth. Blood spurted as his flesh and muscle struggled to knit back together. The darkness pierced the wound like needles, seeming to prevent the healing. He almost crushed me as I helped him beneath one of the obsidian overhangs.

"What do you need?" I asked.

He grimaced, clutching at his arm. A new wound opened in his side. "Focus. Damn venom." He doubled over. The wound spread again. Another injury opened in his shoulder. He closed his eyes. "Crespa! Nothing you can do, little cousin. Just fight. And don't let her touch you." Another pained cry tore from him.

Buttercup crushed a fiend that lunged for me. I picked up a fallen spear and swatted another. More and more were still coming! Even without the Gola Resh chanting. And they were slowly growing in number.

Lorna laughed at the Gola Resh, but the sound had a desperate, biting edge to it. "You will fall eventually! Come close and feel my teeth."

"I will never fall," the Gola Resh chortled, malicious delight filling her voice.

Light flared and pulsed within the heart, the blue sulfur lines of the lava pulsing and flaring out as the table with the talismans slipped down into the molten rock. The stone glowed yellow-red.

Kine ran to the edge and flung the Great Spear into the heart as well. It landed in the center, point first. The broad triangular head sank evenly into the molten rock. As several of the bubbles rose from the lava, a fine spray coated the handle, singeing it. Smoke and steam spiraled up.

The Gola Resh's form warped and twisted as if a great wind rushed up around her from all sides. Her skull-like features distorted. "You think you're so clever?" She laughed, clapping her hands together. "Fine. No willing sacrifices. I have those who swore fealty."

She clutched her fists and spread her arms. A horrid wailing chant rose into the air.

Fifty of the Kairos Faction stopped. Their muscles went rigid, their faces frozen. The weapons clattered from their hands. Their shadows intensified and stretched across the floor and against the walls, drawing toward the Gola Resh.

Elias spun around, gripping his enchanted quarterstaff. "Release them!" he bellowed. "If they are to fall, let it be in honorable combat!"

"You were all going to die anyway." The Gola Resh cackled. "You were always going to see this, Ruler of the Kairos. What a fine leader you make, so boldly leading your people into life. The Babadon's life. How foolish they were to trust you."

Ihlkit! Despite my anger toward Elias, pity surged within me. The utter horror and sorrow on his face was heartbreaking. And the poor men and women who had followed this bargain had done so to save their families.

Once more, the world slowed. Blood thundered in my ears. All I could do was watch.

The seized faction members withered into corpses in seconds, lurching into the air. Red mist shot out from their bodies as their shadows snapped off like dead twigs from a rotted tree. It was over in less than a breath.

Elias's jaw tensed. "Keep fighting!" he shouted to the remaining faction members.

"Fight, all you who remain," Brandt bellowed. He shouted something else that I did not catch, then slammed up into the air and broke off a trio of stalactites with his mouth. He hurled them down like missiles. Shrieks of pain and alarm rose along with the fine spray of lava as more and more monsters advanced from the depths. He spat black venom down upon the advancing monsters. There were barely fifteen of us left fighting.

I spun to shout for Tile to throw the reagents, but he lay face down on the ground, blood streaming from a wound in his head. Feathers and roots and packets of dust lay scattered.

No!

He hadn't thrown them in.

The red mist twisted around as the Great Spear sank lower and lower. The table had tilted, all the ice gone. The Great Axe and the Goblet had sunk halfway as the molten rock bubbled and burst around them. Out of that red mist and stolen shadows, a darkness coalesced in the shape of a massive man.

The Babadon.

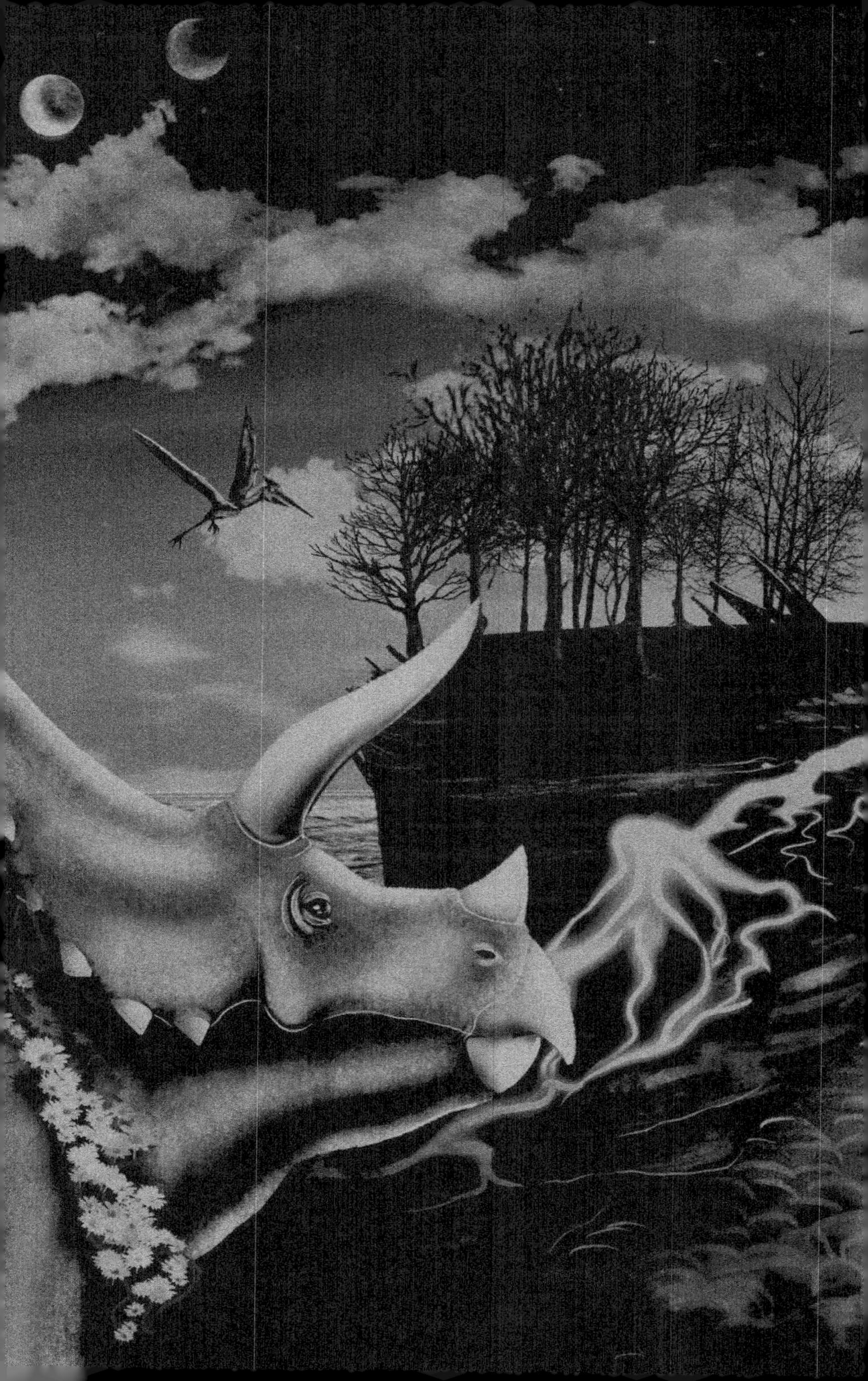

CHAPTER FIFTY-FIVE: STELLA

The Gola Resh laughed, reaching her hands up toward the arched ceiling. "My beloved," she cried out, swooping down to where he formed over the three talismans.

Memories of the Babadon staggered back into my mind. His coldness. His bladed shadows. His strength.

My spirit quailed. I wanted to run and hide, but I steeled myself. It wasn't over yet.

The Babadon's shadowy essence spun around as he stretched out his powerful arms. "Beautiful one," he murmured hoarsely, his voice rich and melodic. "I thought I would never look upon your face again."

She flew to him and circled, adoration shining in her eyes. Her wisps of shadow stretched out and spiraled about. Her features blurred, the skeletal structure becoming more apparent. He had not reformed enough for her to touch him.

Still delight filled her voice. "You, who are almost too wondrous for me to look upon, our vengeance is at hand."

His low, rumbling laugh followed.

My blood chilled, pounding in my ears. We had to hurry!

I turned back to Arjax. The wounds were still spreading over his form and tearing at his skin, though he healed as fast as he could.

Arjax lunged forward, striking a skeletal fiend before it reached me. "Just go. I'm fine," he said with a pained hiss. He gestured toward Tile, face twisted in agony.

Buttercup flung her head back and bellowed, her long ululating call shaking the cavern. She stomped on another fiend.

Good girl!

I staggered to my feet and ran to her, climbing up her side. There were still more fiends. Still more creatures. So little time!

The cavern tremored and pulsed and hissed as the lava monsters continued their assault.

Candy and Hord struggled to stay in their serpent forms, their shapes flickering, scales buckling and shining in unnatural ways. They seized stones and flung them over the edge. Cahji had abandoned his silver serpent form and simply rained down arrows. One of the fallen spears resting beside him, ready for him if needed.

Lorna had resumed her ice wyrm form, blasting ice in all directions. But her ice was not as potent. The blasts were farther apart, almost as if she choked.

"There's too many of them!" Candy shouted. "We'll be overrun in minutes."

"Don't let them up the side," Brandt commanded, his voice guttural and hoarse. Dropping back into his human form, he picked up a fallen bow. He struck one of the fiends in the skull with a black-tipped arrow and then shot it down into the chasm.

"Hold them back as long as you can. Give them time!" Brandt swung back, his gaze falling to me. His ruby-red eyes blazed, asking me if we could do this. Was there hope?

I nodded, my body tight.

We needed all the time he could give, and I didn't dare scream out what had happened with Tile. Not when it would take seconds for the Gola Resh to rip Tile off the edge of the cliff and to his death. Just because the Babadon was coming back didn't mean this was over.

We could do this.

We had to.

The Great Spear had only sunk a third of the way into the lava, its metal and surrounding enchantment more resistant to melting. The Goblet glowed bright red, its shape sagging. The Great Axe had nearly dissolved. Only the frame of the stone table remained.

Buttercup carried me forward, her footsteps thundering across the dark, cracked cavern floor. The few remaining arcanists continued with their chants, pouring all their wavering energy into the frost and ice magic to defend against the fiends and lava monsters.

Kine had already reached Tile and was collecting the reagents in between fighting. Buttercup and I skidded in alongside him just in time to take out a newly emerging fiend from the floor and another swinging dual swords from the left.

There was no way to know if we had gathered everything together. Pieces could be missing. I started sweeping them up in my hands as fast as I could, grabbing up feathers, roots, and herbs. The containers Tile had kept them in had shattered. Bits of glass sliced my forearms and the sides of my hands, stinging.

Another two fiends came for Tile. He rushed forward, returning once more to his water serpent form and striking both. One of the blows cut him across the scales. He coiled loosely around Tile.

Buttercup blocked on the other side. Her breaths were coming harder. Several scrapes had loosened the scales on her left, but her dark eyes burned with rage. She headbutted a towering skeletal warrior with two heads. Her front horn impaled it before she flung it off the edge.

Elias sprang forward to Kine's back. He brought the

knobbed end of his staff down on another fiend's skull, cracking it and sending it over the edge. "How much of each reagent do you need?"

"Just get it all in. We'll need weight. We need to tie it to something heavy, or it won't strike the heart," I said sharply.

Tile still bled, but his fingers twitched.

"Tile," Kine said. "Tile, can you wake up?"

Some of it could have been destroyed. Some had been lost.

Please let whatever we had be enough!

The items were still melting down. Maybe four minutes to go. Possibly five. I tore a strip from my dress and tied as many of the reagents onto a rock as I could. Blood stained the fabric, but it worked.

Standing, I chucked it into the heart. The rock heated at once, the feathers and herbs catching fire and flaring. Elias bashed a fiend as I stooped to grab another, and Kine swept around yet again.

My fingers shook as I prepared another chunk of rock with more of the reagents. I flung that rock in as well. It scraped the blue line of the heart's edge but tilted back in time.

We were almost through the reagents. Gently, I pressed Tile onto his back and searched the inside of his robe. There were a few more. A root and a few feathers and a silk bag of coarsely chopped plants. I bound them to a palm-sized rock, my hands shaking. Then I spotted another few feathers and herbs.

Elias seized the first one. "I've got this," he said. He dodged another attack, the bony knife scraping his side and cutting into his sleeve. He brought the quarterstaff down with a single hand, landing a solid blow.

I gathered up the last scraps, tore off another bit of my dress, and wrapped it around the hot rock. This had to be enough. Right?

More fiends crawled up over the edge. Arjax roared in pain as a blade bit into his side, dark blood splattering the stone before he forced a partial spinosaurus transformation and bit a fiend in half. Lorna's ice fire sputtered. She leaped up at the ceiling and shoved a stalactite down as if it were her own personal spear.

The Gola Resh and Babadon continued to coo over one another as if nothing else mattered. She spun and looked back at us on the stone platform before the lava river, sailing in front of the rock islands. Chuckling, she struck her hands together. The arcanists' incantations came to a strangled halt. Two dropped to their knees, gasping.

"That's quite enough," she said, glee filling her voice.

Light shimmered. Energy shields went up, separating Kine, Elias, Buttercup, Tile, and me from the rest. The monsters dropped, splashes of lava erupting.

She twisted about, her shadows flaring. "My love, my love, these are the ones responsible for all our woes and all our trials."

The Babadon turned his gaze on us, his blue-red eyes brilliant and sharp despite his face not being fully formed. A cold laugh escaped his jagged-toothed mouth. "I remember."

Kine dragged me behind him as Brandt lunged at the energy shield.

"Don't touch her!" Brandt bellowed. He struck at the barrier with his fist. "I will deal with you both."

The Gola Resh twined back around the Babadon, leering at us. "I just can't decide which of them I want to suffer more." Her orange-green eyes lit up with delight as she arched back to peer at the Babadon upside down. "Who do you want to see suffer?"

"Surprise me," the Babadon said. His form had become more corporeal, his voice stronger now. The wraith-like tatters at the end of his body resembled blades more than silk. "You always know how to make me happy."

"They're trying so hard with their little incantations and charms and rituals," the Gola Resh continued. "But the best they could do is one that makes us vulnerable. Not even one that makes us stop flying." Her gaze swept over us, hard and yet delighted.

She wanted us dead. The hatred in her eyes—it frightened me. Any move Brandt or I made, she'd probably notice. We needed a moment. Maybe we could use her focus on me?

As she glanced down to nuzzle the Babadon again, I slipped the stone with the reagents into Kine's hand and whispered to him. He gave a small nod. It was too dangerous with the Gola Resh's attention on our little group right now, even if she was gloating. But a chance would come.

Elias took advantage of her looking away and chucked his stone with the reagents forward. It sailed through the air, going longer than it should.

Horror sliced through me, ice cold.

The rock struck an overhang above the heart and landed on the edge.

My heart dropped.

No! I clapped my hands over my mouth. No, no, no!

Kine swore.

Elias clenched his jaw, his breath hissing through his teeth.

"It was so easy to deceive you," the Gola Resh said, her gaze returned to Elias. Either she didn't notice the trapped reagents or she didn't care. "You were so desperate to save the people you cared about. The legacy of your family. All of which meant nothing. All that work—all those traditions—all those weapons... They'll just dissolve. Just like your people." She snapped her clawed fingers.

The remaining Kairos Faction members went rigid. Their bodies pulsed in the air for a moment as their shadows pulled taut. Then they erupted in red mist and swirling shadows. They joined the lazy funnel circling the heart of the Ember Lord's Crest. The blue sulfur hissed as the red and yellow lava bubbled.

More laughter, harsher and biting. "If you had cooperated, I would not have tortured you in this way. Your reward would have been a peaceful death," the Gola Resh continued. "But instead, you chose *her* over me. Which is all the richer considering what led you to my doorstep. She doesn't love you. She'll never love you." The Gola Resh spat the words at him, mockery dripping from every syllable. "She pitied you. Like a pet. A guard dog to guide her back. And that was all. She used you when all the while her heart belonged to the king. You were too low for her to notice even before she was queen."

Elias scoffed. He lowered the staff. His gaze drifted back to me. Soot and blood streaked his tanned features, his dark-red hair slick and bloodied. But when he spoke, his voice did not tremble. "I was wrong. About everything. Except that you were worth saving, Stella. Not all love is meant to be returned. Especially not when it came from such a selfish place. For what it's worth—and I know it is not much—I am sorry."

I shook my head, not knowing what to say. Tears burned the backs of my eyes. I wanted to give him some comfort. Some hope. But the words wavered as the tears rolled down my cheeks. "I forgive you," I whispered hoarsely. "And—"

"Look at her false tears," the Gola Resh sneered. "She knows what comes next, doesn't she? She is a seer, after all. Well, let's not disappoint her." She drew closer, her shadows streaming around me. "I'll hold the brother back, and you kill the girl for me. How's that? Do it, and I'll spare you. Defy me, and I'll make sure you suffer. You took my bond, after all. I own you."

Elias looked down at his enchanted quarter staff and shrugged. "Never. I'll regret choosing to serve you for the rest of my life," Elias said. A grim smile stole over his features. "Lucky for me, that won't be too much longer, will it, you pedantic old hag?"

The Gola Resh's face contorted with rage. Shadows whipped violently around her. I tensed, preparing to make some sort of attack. Kine stayed in front of me, muscles poised to lunge.

Then Elias lunged forward at the edge of the cliff. He

jammed his quarterstaff against the stone and launched himself out over the lava. Then, just as smoothly, he swept the quarterstaff back around and flung it so that it knocked the stone with the reagents off into the heart.

The Gola Resh screeched with rage, darting forward fast as smoke. "Traitor!" Her claws sliced through the air in a shrieking rent, and Elias's body vanished.

A scream tore from me. "Elias!"

"Bastards!" Brandt bellowed.

Shouts of rage and horror rose from the few of us that remained.

Buttercup reared up, striking at the air with her forelegs as she wailed in response.

The Gola Resh's and Babadon's laughter echoed through the cavern, devouring all other sound.

But that penultimate bundle of rock and reagents started to burn and melt.

"You won't win." I glared at her. "You won't!"

Smirking, Gola Resh waved her hand again. All sound seemed to cut off except for her and the Babadon and what I could hear in this little bubble. Kine stayed in front of me, his arm taut and tense as if he could protect me.

Her malevolent orange-green eyes fixed on me once more as she leaned back against the Babadon. He was still so incorporeal that she passed through him with little resistance, but she swept back before him.

The Axe had fully melted now. The Goblet bubbled along its side, barely holding its shape. The Spear had slid a little farther down. The rocks with the reagents glowed brightly, half melted.

The Babadon chuckled darkly. "It saddens me to keep the love match separated," he said coolly. His form became stronger, more substantive, the more the weapons sank into the lava. He lifted one long, bladed hand, the movement heavy but graceful as he indicated Brandt. "Don't keep them apart on my account, dearest love."

Candy shook her head, screaming something that was likely a combination of obscenities and an offer to sacrifice herself.

Cahji looked on with horror while Hord readied the spear.

Brandt lifted his chin, the defiance vivid in his eyes.

The Gola Resh crooked her finger, gesturing for him to come forward without lowering the energy barrier. "You all thought you were so clever, completing the tasks early, breaking down the intervals. And I know there was some debate about how many cycles you had left," she purred. "But did you know, I can force the curse to move forward—to pinch time as your skinchanger said? But all that's left? It's gone, like the Kairos Faction."

She brought her fingers together, the light in her eyes brightening.

"No!" I screamed at her, balling my fists.

Brandt's body snapped arrow-straight. The light in his eyes flared. His fists clenched as he struck at his head, grunting and baring his teeth.

"Oh, he's fighting it!" The Gola Resh clapped her hands. "He's fighting it, my love. Look at him, trying so hard! As if he has a chance."

The Babadon chuckled at this, his sonorous voice booming over the molten rock and blackened stone.

My breaths raced, and my thoughts spun. It wasn't over. If Brandt could hold on until we made the Babadon and the Gola Resh and then killed them—

The Gola Resh swept her hand down as if peeling a layer away. Brandt lurched forward. Candy and Hord sprang after him, but the invisible barrier held them back. Arjax and Lorna shouted something, their mouths moving but the sound lost.

"Kill her," the Gola Resh murmured, her voice silky. "Kill the woman you love. And then I'll kill you and put everyone else out of their misery."

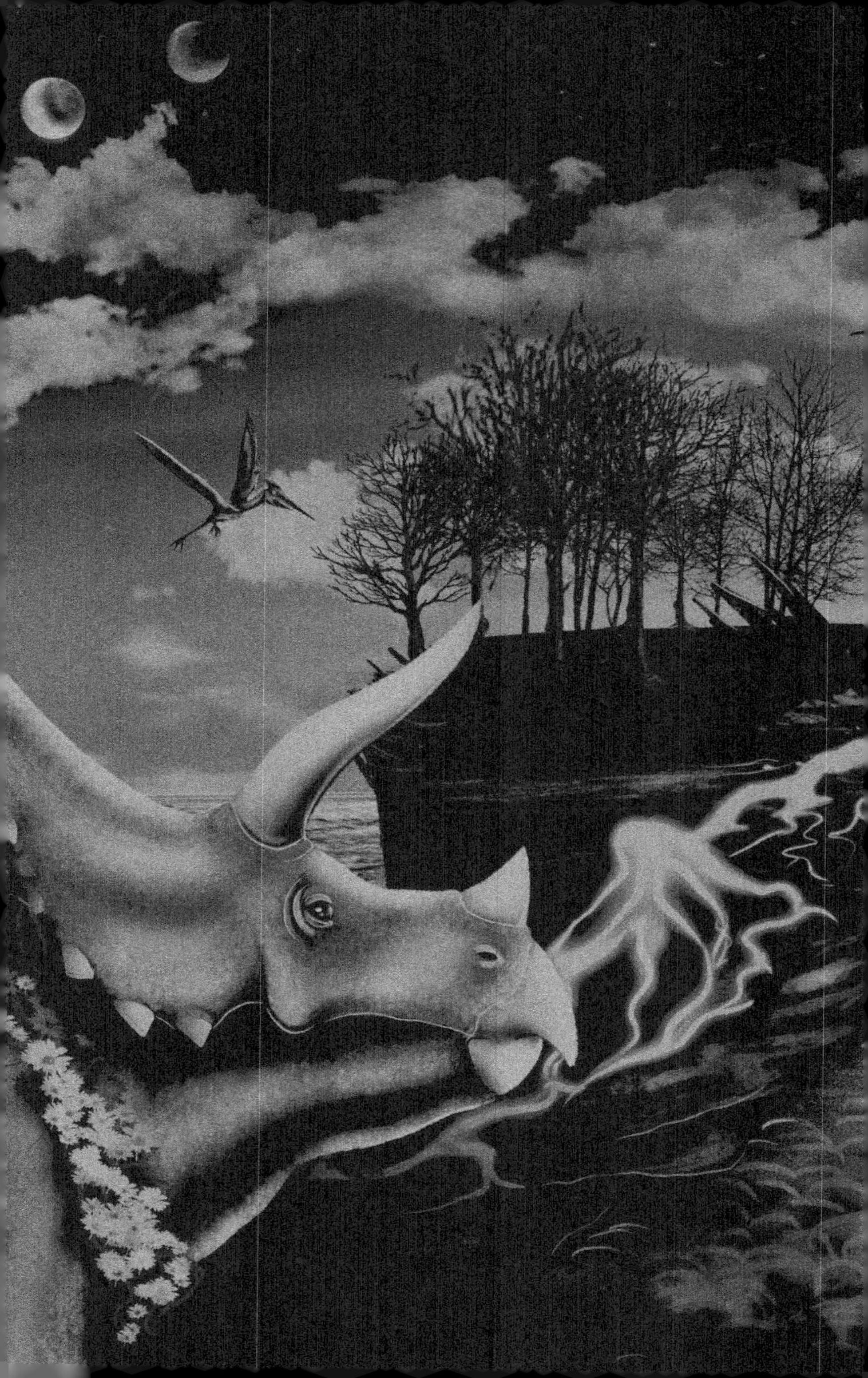

CHAPTER FIFTY-SIX: STELLA

Brandt staggered forward, shaking his head. Every muscle and sinew strained. His body trembled. The charm burned yellow. "I won't...let you...win..." he ground out through clenched teeth.

"Oh, it's already over, boy," the Gola Resh purred with a dark laugh. She glanced back at the Babadon.

His laughter merged with hers but hitched. He dragged his massive hand along his head. Though his face was still not fully returned, his eyes narrowed with what seemed like concern.

The Gola Resh's gaze darted between Brandt and me. That rolling laugh of hers grew. "Go on then, puppet. Throw her in the fire. Snap her pretty neck. Rip her throat out. I don't care. Just kill her."

"No," Brandt strained.

Veins bulged along his neck and arms. His breaths grew ragged, his body slick with sweat and stained with ash and blood. His fingers flexed and curled. Pain radiated through his features.

"You monster!" I screamed at her.

That only made her laugh harder.

The rooting terror tried to overtake me again. It clawed at my mind, but it was not so heavy this time. I fought to push it away and gulped in a breath. Minutes. Maybe seconds left.

Buttercup tossed her head and lowed, shaking her crest and horns with obvious distress.

Kine moved closer to the edge, his strides slow but steady as he avoided the Gola Resh's gaze. His hand slipped into the upper inner pocket of his stained, tattered robe.

"You don't want him to kill you? Then you kill him. Put the animal out of his misery," the Gola Resh chortled. "You insignificant little creatures sought to stand against us. Now you unravel and burn! Kill Brandt, little girl. Put him out of his misery. Even if you had somehow found a way to succeed, he's gone now!"

Brandt struggled, his face contorted in agony. More than any other time, he struggled. His jaw clenched. His eyes burned into me.

I couldn't look away. My breaths choked in my chest.

Tears streamed down my cheeks. The only comfort that flashed into my mind was that neither of us would have to suffer long without the other.

Then rage knifed inside me.

He was fighting in there. Even from this distance, that much was apparent. The panicked brightness. The bold defiance.

He was fighting, and so was I. So long as we both had breath, we would fight and not let this monstrosity turn us on one another.

"One of you, move," the Gola Resh shrieked.

The Babadon continued to stare down at his hands. He released a low, shuddering breath. The Goblet and Great Axe were gone now. All remnants of the table had vanished. The rocks with the reagents glowed red, the feathers, herbs, and roots all consumed—except for the one in Kine's robe. The spear had sunk even farther down, the metal shaft a brilliant yellow-red.

Something was happening. Once more, it slowed.

Kine drew closer to the edge.

I opened my mouth to speak and distract the Gola Resh, but Brandt lurched toward the cliff's edge. His gaze snapped to the molten lava nearly twenty feet below.

His mouth moved. "I'm sorry," he rasped.

"Brandt!" My eyes bugged. Wild energy surged through me yet held me in place, paralyzing me like a viper's bite. "Brandt, no!"

Brandt lunged off the edge of the cliff. Yellow-gold and blood-red lava twisted and bubbled below, the line of blue sulfur lava forming the perfect heart of the cavern.

No. Blue-hot terror pierced my heart.

Kine shifted into his water serpent form and sprang forward like silver liquid. His long, scaled body arched through the air, shining in the shimmering heat of the lava. He missed Brandt at first and then arched again in midair, barely striking him with his body. But it was just enough to knock both of them onto one of the tilted islands of stone that hung above the lava river below.

Brandt crashed backward. He cracked his head on the basalt. Kine collapsed, falling out of his serpent form. He shuddered for a moment, his body pulsing as he collapsed. His body angled toward the downward slope of the rock island.

It was too far for me to jump, even in water serpent form. But I had to get there. Every cell in me screamed that I had to be there at the wedge where the rock island split. That awareness spiked in my gut and flared up through my chest with an undeniable weight.

Spinning around, I forced myself back into the water serpent form. My body tightened and pulsed. The scales erupted. The horns dragged my head down.

"Buttercup, go!" I lunged onto her back. She charged forward, battering through the fiends. Their bones crunched beneath her feet. The hot air licked at my face. "Komul!" I screamed. She snapped her head down and halted so hard she sat on her hindquarters.

I soared off her back and over her crest, slicing through the air.

"Brandt!" I shouted. My heart stumbled as I struck the stone. It punched the air out of me.

The heat of the lava was too much. My form shrank, pulling back into my human shape as I struggled to focus. My dress reformed again, and within seconds, I was once more drenched with sweat. I jammed my foot into the spot that my instincts demanded, gasping.

The cavern shook again, the lava churning beneath us. The stone tilted. The jagged stone punched my knees, shredding them.

The lip beneath Kine broke.

His eyes widened.

I darted forward, despite the awful pain tearing through my legs. The ground struck me so hard. Somehow, I grabbed him. His weight dragged me down, his body yanking my arms so hard I thought they might wrench out of the sockets.

Words failed me. All I managed was a pained cry as I barely managed to hang on.

Brandt's attention snapped to me. He still fought, the muscles in his face twitching. Sweat poured down his brow.

Kine's weight was dragging me down. The stones dug into my thighs.

"Bug," Kine said hoarsely. "It's all right. Swing me out, and then let go of me. I've got the reagents. It'll be enough."

"No. No! I'm not losing either of you."

The cavern shook. I twisted around to Brandt. "Brandt, please!" I sobbed, trying to keep my grip on Kine's sweating hands. "Please!"

Every other time I had tried to cry out or scream when he

was under the curse's direct influence, my chest had been tight, my voice small. But this time—even with pain tearing through my body—all of me poured into my voice. The ragged screech was pure agony.

Brandt stiffened, the red in his eyes intensifying. It was as if he saw me again.

A sickening crack fractured the air.

Then the rock gave way. Kine and I both plunged down.

Brandt's expression twisted. Panic filled his eyes. With a strained yell, he flung himself forward and seized me. His right arm snagged around my waist, his fingers digging into my flesh as he slammed me back, my legs dangling in the air. His other arm locked around my shoulders, his fingers set against my throat. His breath rasped in my ear.

"Hold fast, Brandt," I said, my voice shaking. "I know you can do this."

"Stella." His voice shook.

I bit the inside of my lip.

Brandt held me tight, his foot hooked around one of the boulders. His mouth pressed against my throat. He grunted, struggling to support me as I held on to Kine.

"Hold fast, Brandt," I repeated, my voice cracking.

Fear spasmed within me. If he collapsed into the curse, he could bite my throat or rip it out while barely moving. His right hand already loosely pressed at my throat, his fingers curled as if he struggled even in that small act.

He shuddered against me. I could practically feel the curse sinking its talons into his mind. But he was fighting. Fighting as he never had before.

I tore my gaze from him to Kine, the pain in my arm twisting through me. "Don't you dare let go, Kine!"

The Gola Resh darted up. Her shadows coiled at my legs and Kine's torso, giving a sharp tug. I tried to kick her off, crying out in pain.

"Leave her alone," Kine snarled. He turned his face up to me. "Bug, you've got to let me go. You know why."

I whimpered. He wanted me to fling him toward the heart. The Gola Resh wouldn't try to stop him falling in. She'd delight in it. If she saw the reagents though, she'd intervene. This was one way to ensure we finished the task and finished making her and the Babadon vulnerable.

My stomach twisted. It was as if there were knives in my lungs and gut. "No."

The Gola Resh just chuckled. "Oh...oh, how has this gotten even better? What a joy for me. How have you two found a way to make this so much more delightful? So very, very delightful. Stella, darling, let your brother go. Let's watch him die next."

She circled us like a shark in the water. Her tendrils stretched out. Their cold contrasted with the searing heat of the lava all around us.

My mind spun. Kine's body hung, heavy against mine.

He stared up at me with those gold eyes, his brow furrowed. "Bug, do it. This ends in death. It's all right for it to be mine." He somehow smiled up at me, though the edges trembled.

I clung to him tighter. One of my fingers slipped. Kine started to swing. "No. No! No one else!" I screamed.

The Gola Resh circled back around, her eyes glowing in the darkness of her skull. She leered and cackled. "Yes, all!" She lunged at us.

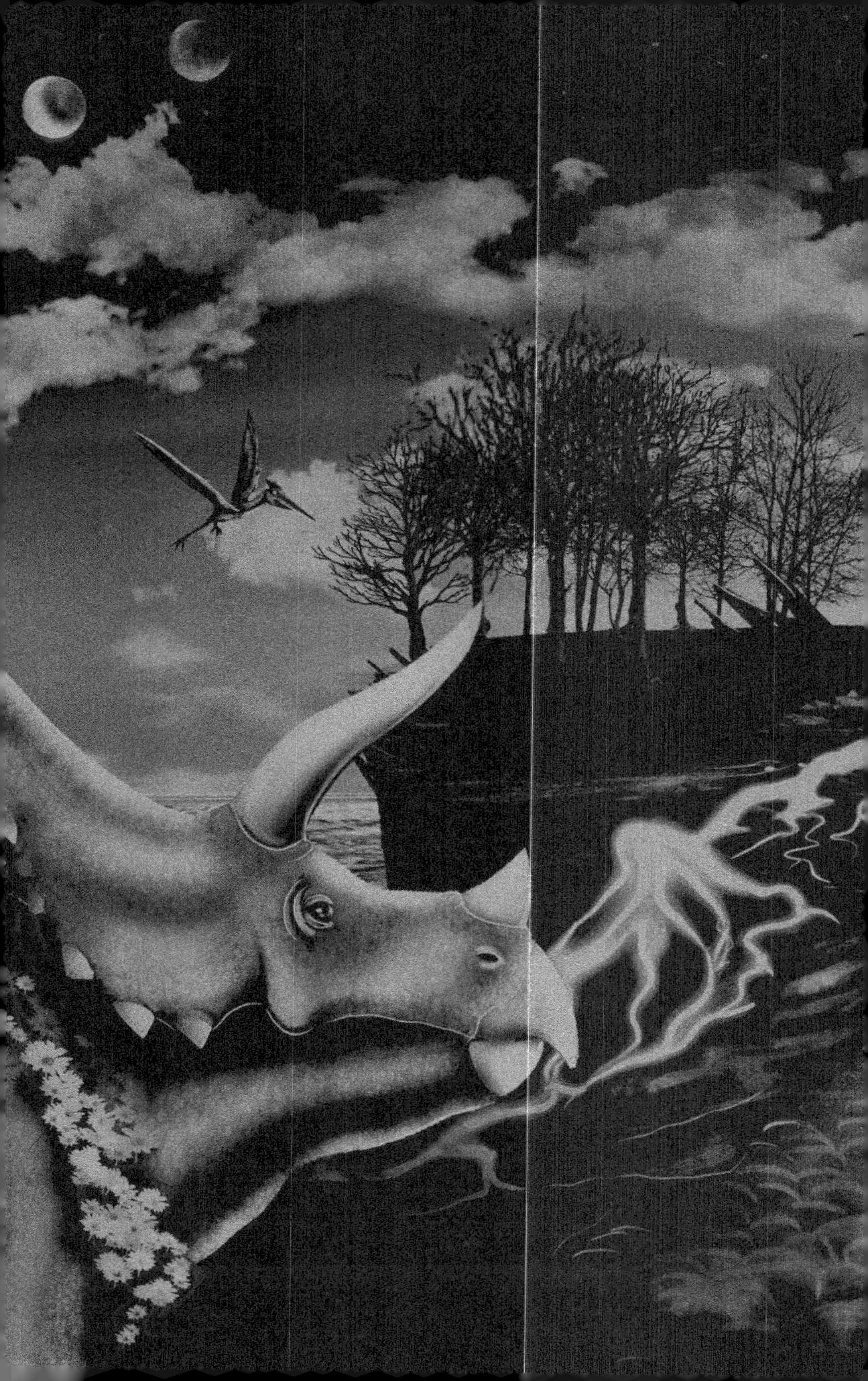

CHAPTER FIFTY-SEVEN: STELLA

I clutched Kine tighter, trying to hold on to him. My bloodied legs wrapped around his waist. Brandt clutched me harder, pulling my back against the jagged edges of the rock island. We all braced for the Gola Resh's attack.

The Great Spear sank down into the lava and vanished, sending out another pulse of blue light.

The Babadon uttered a strained moan.

The Gola Resh spun around. "What? You are in pain?" She was gone from us as swiftly as she had appeared. "What's wrong? Why haven't you finished reforming?" She pointed at the blue line where the spear had once been. "It's melted. The life force of fifty has sustained you. Fifty and more. What's wrong?"

He twitched. His blue-red eyes rose to hers, the colors softening. She was right; he still hadn't fully formed. "I'm not right. I'm…I'm not forming. Something happened."

A ragged breath dragged from my lips. I twisted my face back up to Brandt. "The spear. We did it," I whispered hoarsely.

We'd prevented his full transformation.

He stared down at me. The heat fought in his eyes. He struggled. His lips twitched, his breath hot against my skin.

"Stay with me," I begged. "Stay with me, Brandt. We're almost there." My body felt like it was being torn apart. "Kine..."

Kine peered up at me, then nodded. He understood.

"Don't you dare let go," I growled at him. Sweat dripped down my face. It burned my eyes. I tried to lift him higher, but my arm gave out.

"Just the one arm," he said.

I nodded tightly.

He hesitated. "You sure you have me, Bug? You could just swing me."

I nodded tightly. "I won't let go."

Every part of my frail human body hurt. My arms were being wrenched out of their sockets, and I couldn't get a full breath in.

Brandt struggled, his teeth gnashing. "Do it!" His boots scraped across the stone as he adjusted his grip. His fingers at my throat flexed and tightened as he fought the urge.

"What's wrong?" the Gola Resh demanded again. "How could it have gone wrong?" She darted around the Babadon, shooting down closer to the lava and then back up.

Kine pulled his left hand free.

Ah!

The pressure on my arm intensified, twisting me painfully against the stone. I stiffened, Brandt's fingers tightening against my throat.

Hurry, Kine. Hurry!

Kine reached into his robe. His hand shaking, he pulled the last of the reagents, an indigo root wrapped in grey feathers with a small grey bag tied to the palm-sized stone.

The Babadon groaned. "Something—something isn't right. I can't—" He tried to move away from the center of the heart, but his movements became heavier—sluggish. His body sunk lower. "I feel it."

"Feel what? Tell me what's wrong! Tell me what to do!" The Gola Resh tried to grab hold of his shoulders, but her clawed hands passed through him.

Kine flung the last of the reagents into the circle. The root and feathers skimmed past the blue sulfur lava and landed in the heart, reagents first. The rock turned red almost at once. Fire flared along the side for a breath, then vanished. He slapped his hand up once more to grab my arm. I gripped him tight, fighting for breath.

The Babadon held up his hands as if to clasp her face. "I missed you." Though he whispered, his voice echoed throughout the chamber. It filled my ears and clogged my mind.

I tightened my hold on Kine, feeling as if I were about to be torn in two. Brandt's hand at my throat and the stones in my back made it hard for me to breathe.

The Gola Resh twisted her head back and forth. "All of this—all of this was to gain eternity together. None of this matters without you." She screamed. The stalactites above trembled like melting icicles. "There has to be something. Something!"

"I am little more than shadow, my love. My essence is fading now." He leaned closer to her. Half his arm passed through her. Then his forehead rested near hers, as close as possible without touching. A low moan shuddered from him. "Don't leave me again, light of my soul."

"There has to be something." She clutched at him. Her fingers passed through the smoke and fog of his form. The panic in her voice intensified. "I am cured. I could live on. I could live on with endless power. Twice the power that I need. These wretches! These fools! Because of them, you are dying. I'll kill them all!" She turned on us, her eyes blazing.

"I am dead already, beautiful Gola," he whispered. "Centuries of wandering between the realms with you. Sliding between the chasms of the worlds. Drinking the life of the universe. And it ends here."

She turned back to him with a broken sob. Her entire body heaved, rising and falling in wrenching grief.

They both drifted lower and lower to the lava. The glow intensified the darkness of their shadows and highlighted the wisps of the Babadon's form. With each breath, less and less of him was solid.

He shuddered. "I can...I have just a little more strength to do one more thing," he murmured. A pulse of red-blue energy pulsed over him. His form grew heavier but more solid. He caught her into his arms then, clasping her close. "Now I can hold you again."

The Gola Resh continued to wail, her face buried in his shoulder. The cavern trembled. Rocks broke free from the ceiling and pelted down. "You can't die!"

The Babadon held her close, his hand against the back of her head. "Don't make me pass alone."

"Don't leave me," she sobbed. "You can't leave. Not again."

A great wind rushed through the cavern, pulling at Kine. My fingers tightened around his hand as I screamed, the pain in my arm and back almost unbearable. Brandt's arm around my waist trapped me, his mouth pressed hard against my neck.

The wind tore around us and spun about the Gola Resh and Babadon.

"Don't leave me," he murmured.

"Don't go," she sobbed.

And they sank, smoke-blackened forms pressed tight to one another. The molten rock bubbled and hissed. Piercing wails echoed off the walls as their shadowy forms melted together, charred, and vanished into the seething lava.

Orange-green and red-blue light shot out, melding and

twisting as it pulsed in waves. Like their eyes, the colors remained distinct at the farthest points and then melted together until they vanished in muddled hues.

The cavern shook, and the lava churned. Gases and steam erupted. The barriers the Gola Resh had formed fell away. Brandt's body went slack against mine as he gasped.

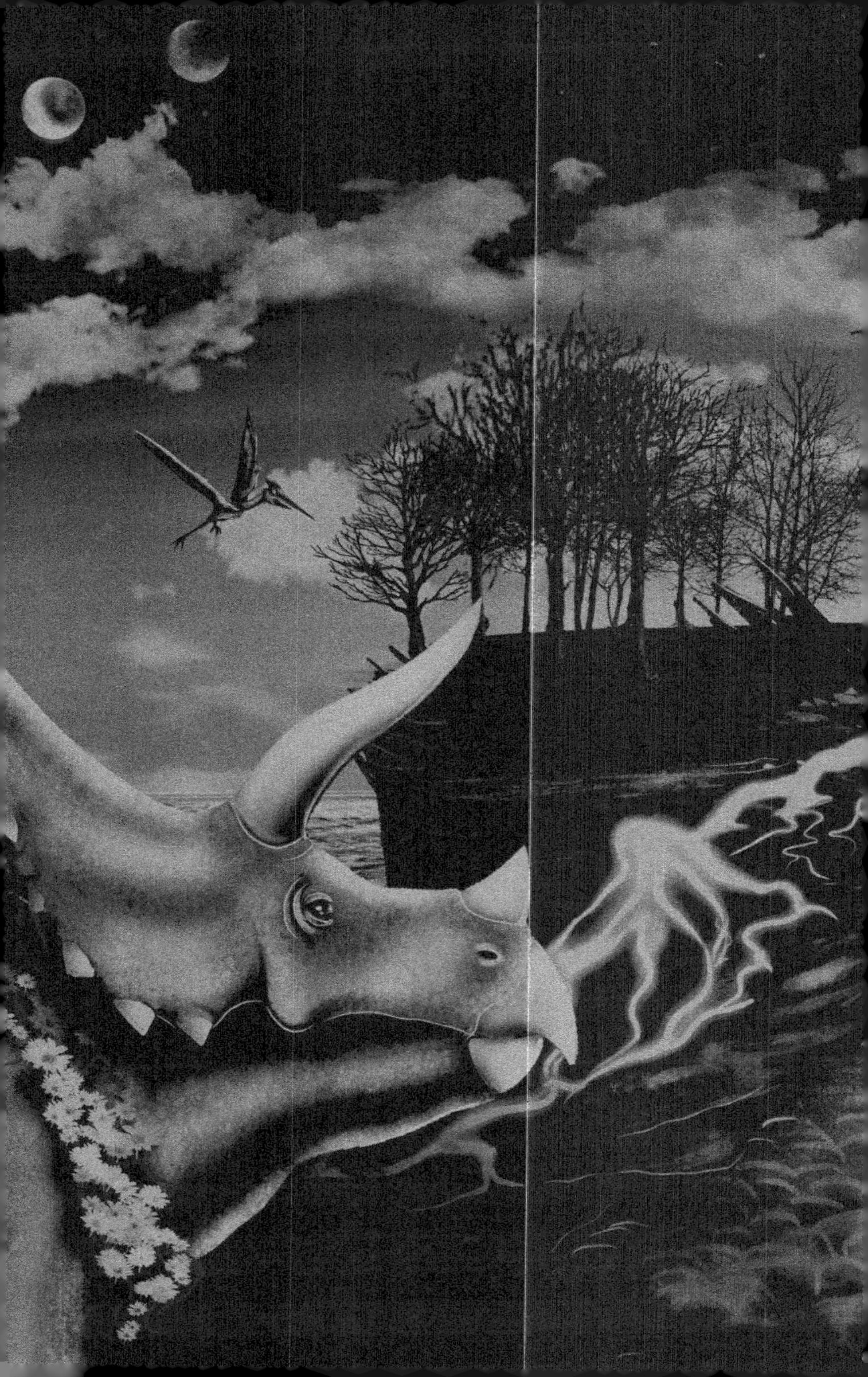

CHAPTER FIFTY-EIGHT: STELLA

I dangled there, barely able to breathe. Kine clung to my hand and arm. "They're dead. They're gone! We've won." He muttered the words shakily, almost as if he feared that speaking them might make something contradict them.

"Brandt?" I whispered weakly, unable to move against the piercing knots of stone against my back. "Brandt, are you still with me?"

His fingers weren't clutching at my throat. But his grip on my waist had remained steady.

"I'm here." His voice rasped low and dry. His left arm reached down around me as well, easing some of the strain on my body.

Heavy footsteps thudded on the rock island. The pressure against my back eased as something lifted Kine and me as easily as if we weighed nothing.

Arjax, with Lorna holding on to his waist to ground him, set us all on the stone. "Well done, little cousins." He looked me up and down, grunting. "Some of us will need to be fixed up."

"Your arm and side—" I indicated where the wounds had

been. There were dark scar marks there, like black lightning. But they were no longer open.

"All better," Arjax said with a grin that didn't quite reach his eyes. Weariness hung over him and Lorna. "Let's get back to the ship. We'll celebrate, heal, and rest. Not necessarily in that order."

Buttercup bellowed and snorted from the cliff's edge. I waved to her, my body sagging. Candy, Hord, and Cahji ran up beside her along with the other remaining survivors. Candy helped Tile to his feet. The older, flame-haired man leaned against her weakly.

"You scared me there, baby blue," Lorna said, striking Kine lightly on the shoulder. "Thought you were going to dive in." She gave him a fierce look.

He smiled weakly, raking his hand through his filthy azure curls. "It was a thought." Gaze soft, he looked at me. "Someone didn't know when to let go."

I smiled at him. Wanted to say that family never let go. But when I opened my mouth to speak, the words failed.

He winked at me as if he understood, much of his old pizazz back.

"I'm glad you're my brother." I managed to say around the knot of emotion. "Our parents would be so proud of you."

"And you, Bug."

I ducked my head, then turned to Brandt.

He was half kneeling on the cracked stone, his muscular forearm braced on his knee. Somehow, even in all the sweat and oils and ash of this place, his red-and-black hair retained much of its spike and body. The kohl around his eyes was smeared, making his eyes even more intense as he looked at me. He breathed heavily. But life sparked in his eyes.

His lips curved in that crooked smile, his gaze hungry but living. "You brash seer," he murmured.

I stepped in front of him, sliding my palms along his squared jaw and high cheekbones. His skin was warm under my touch. The hard planes of his face softened, his predatory gaze now tender as he stared up at me.

Those eyes of his—so beautiful. So expressive. They promised forever. They vowed his best. They swore love. They were everything I had ever searched for. And they were now focused entirely on me.

It would have been so easy to just believe that I had known how Auntie Runa's prophecy ended. It had been easy to believe. Yet here we now stood, the prophecy fulfilled. And it had ended in death. Not the deaths I anticipated. But death.

My eyelids slid shut as I leaned against him. The pain that coursed throughout my body sharpened my breath.

Brandt took my left hand in his and kissed each knuckle, his breaths whisper-light against my skin. Then he gently folded my fingers against my palm.

Yes—yes, I could heal. I clenched my fingers tight. The energy from the shifter ring pulsed through me. Itchy healing energy poured through me, the cuts and scrapes stitching together.

He did the same, the bloody wounds healing swiftly though they still left behind their angry streaks and ashy marks. Standing, he pulled me close.

A small moan escaped my lips as I collapsed in his arms.

"You're safe, Stella," he whispered, his hand cupping the back of my head. "You're safe."

Tears filled my eyes. Happy ones this time. "We both are."

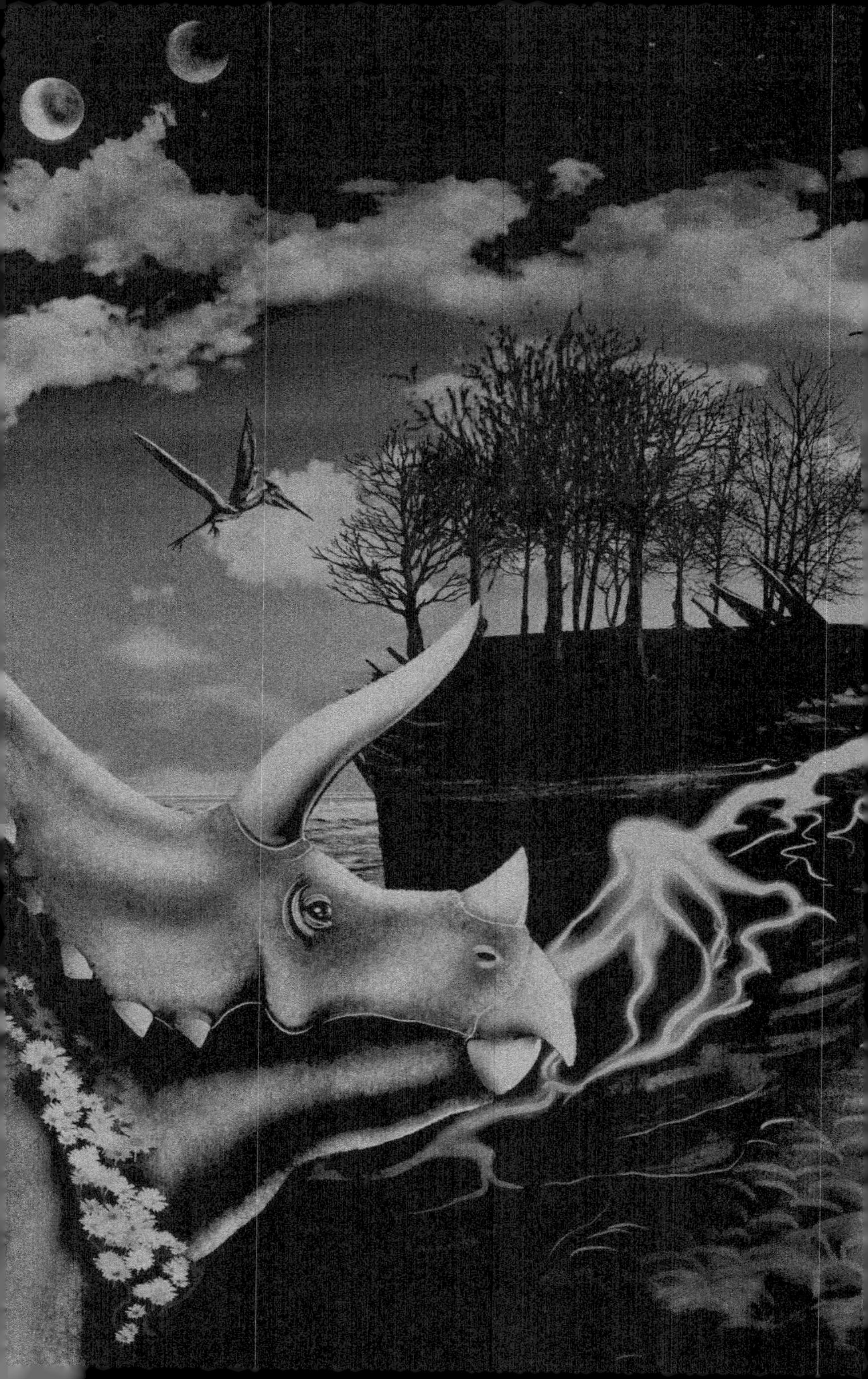

CHAPTER FIFTY-NINE: BRANDT

*I*t was remarkable how swiftly things could change in little more than a breath. The Gola Resh and Babadon had perished, their magic undone.

None of the Kairos Faction survived. That at least simplified things. Elias's betrayal—despite his efforts to resolve it in the end—would still send shockwaves throughout the kingdom. At least I didn't have to think of how to handle executing justice in this matter now.

The men and women who had come to our defense—the warriors, the arcanists, the crew—all those who fell would be honored and celebrated. Those who survived would be rewarded. We had a kingdom to rebuild.

Together we made our way down the long path out to the black sand beach. The remaining crew welcomed us aboard.

Already, the change was apparent. The purple cast had left the sky, leaving it as blue as the sea itself. The black cracks that burrowed their tendrils into the earth and stone had vanished without a trace. Even the air itself smelled better—crisper, cleaner.

And Stella—even bloodied and battered, there had never

been anyone like her. It was like seeing her with fresh eyes. Despite her weariness, she moved with such grace and confidence, her gaze constantly seeking mine and sparking with playful light.

My brash seer was probably plotting some dreadful pun to whisper in my ear when I least expected it.

And I couldn't wait.

Once on the ship, though, I knew I had to speak to a couple individuals. So I slipped back into the map room to use the water mirrors. They blazed to life, shining and shimmering like silver pearls. I traced my finger along the rim. Frost formed at the edges as a familiar voice blared out, unusually harsh compared to its usually measured tone.

"Fine?" he demanded, agitation edging his voice.

"Fine." I sighed. It really was fine. And it was going to get better. Somehow, we had made it.

"Fine." It sounded as if he sighed as well, relief in the voice.

The water within the mirror vibrated and pulsed as our connection ended. Of course we would have to speak together again soon. He didn't like to speak frankly over the water mirrors or through any other magical form if it could be helped. And there would be time enough to talk.

I then drew my finger along the rim once more and brought up the next. The waters rippled even faster, and the reflection turned dark, revealing a deep stone interior.

"Slumberous slow-speaking sidewinder."

I smirked. Some things never changed. "Impatient irritating impudence."

A grunt followed. Then a low chuckle.

We'd all meet again soon when it would be safe to talk. But at least my allies knew we were safe. Not being capable of aiding us had caused both of them great pain. Our next meeting would be one of grand celebration.

But for now, there were other more important matters.

Sen was already preparing what he called a great feast, though I wasn't sure that I'd be able to stomach any food for a while. Hord was standing with his arms folded, listening with amusement as Cahji told about their adventures in retrieving the Great Axe and how Cahji had gone on his own little adventure, rescuing the vampire king and queen from a shipwreck and getting them to safety all before his father noticed he was missing.

Lorna listened with rapt attention, her eyebrows lifting. Arjax sat on the railing, not holding on to anything but staring out over the edge and offering his own commentary and guess that Hord had, in fact, known what Cahji was doing but allowed him to complete the rescue.

Hord remained resolute, simply insisting he was proud of his son.

Candy agreed, sprawled on the deck, her arm flung over her face as she teased that Cahji might enjoy visiting the land of the vampires and demons and his rescuing their leadership all but guaranteed him a hearty welcome, so long as it wasn't politically expedient to deny his involvement in the rescue. The ship rocked and swayed in the sparkling waters, four of the crew swimming as water serpents and drawing us along.

Weariness clung to my body, but the cool, clean air filled my lungs. For the first time in years, I could breathe. And there was only one person I wanted to see.

Hord guessed it and told me which cabin was Stella's.

I knocked at the door and waited. She had never ceased to be my wife in my heart—and we had had sex twice. But that didn't mean she wanted someone walking in on her. "Stella, do you—"

The door flung open, and she appeared in the doorway, golden eyes wide and bright. "Get in here, spicy strawberry margarita man." She seized me by the collar and dragged me forward.

Ihlkit, she was magnificent.

I swept forward and caught hold of her, lifting her up and holding her tight. I buried my face in her neck, a low groan tearing free. Her fresh-washed hair covered my face, burying me in her fragrance: grapefruit, sea salt, strawberries, and trouble.

"Oh, make sounds like that, and I'm going to crawl out of my skin." She hugged me fiercely.

Her breath rushed against my neck, making my skin prickle. I squeezed her close, grateful for the Vawtrian magic that let us both heal so swiftly. There was so much that we needed to manage, and yet we could set it aside without the pain of bruises and cuts to distract us and ground us in the challenges that lay ahead. Here, in the sanctuary of this small room, we could just exist as a couple.

"You still fit so perfectly in my arms," I murmured against her skin.

"Seems like everything still fits perfectly." She pulled back and grinned up at me. Those eyes of hers sparked with life despite the bags and the lines of fatigue.

I lowered her to the ground, shaking my head at her. "You've gotten so bawdy."

I loved it.

I also loved how she looked. She'd cleaned up and put on a fresh dress, pale lavender with a violet belt. Her rich-blue hair hung down to her shoulders, loose and soft. Her smell was more natural now, only hints of the smoke, ash, and sulfur of the volcano with a bit of salt and the faintest whiff of soap and grapefruit. Her golden-tan skin with gold fern-like patterns was exactly as it had once been. If I hadn't had to live through the past horrific fifty years, I might have believed she never left at all.

She quirked her mouth at me. Her golden eyes, flecked with amber and chocolate, sparkled. "Well, yes. You know, you mocha me crazy."

"What's a mocha?" I cocked my eyebrow at her as I placed my hands on her waist. Now that I no longer had to fear murdering her, all I wanted to do was touch and hold her. My thumbs stroked circles along her sides.

"Something delicious that I'm going to make for you at some point. Once we trade with someone to get chocolate. Do we grow cacao beans? I think we do." Her expression pinched, her eyebrow arching playfully to mirror my own. She leaned against me, her soft breasts pressing to my torso. "Anyway, it's going to happen. Now that I know what chocolate is, we're going to be having it more often."

My mouth twisted into a crooked smile. How had she gotten more perfect in her time away? The softness in her gaze as she stared up at me, the gentleness in her manner, the sharpness of her wit. She was perfection. I had fallen in love with her over and over again in the time I courted and then married her. And I had the chance to fall in love with her over and over again now and for the rest of our days.

The burn of tears against the backs of my eyes intensified. "You are so beautiful."

Her breath sharpened. Her tongue flicked at her lips. "And you are incredibly, remarkably, wondrously handsome."

My arm tightened around her waist, pulling her closer. "Do you know what happens next?"

She nodded, biting her tongue as her eyebrows flicked upward. "Oh...do tell."

"I'm going to finish cleaning up from the battle. Then I'm going to make sweet love to you until you can't walk. Or we reach Castle Serpentfire. In which case, we'll retire to our bedchambers where I'll resume my attentions so you cannot walk." The excitement that surged through me was enough to counter the fatigue.

"Big talk." She grinned. "I'll assume you know where to go clean up. And I'll be waiting for you."

I kissed her once more, savoring her warmth and her sweetness. Then I went to clean up. My limbs grew heavier. The peacefulness of success merged with contentment as I scrubbed the ash and soot and blood away. And when I returned to the cabin, I beheld my beloved. She lay on her side, snoring with her arm thrown over her eyes to block the light from the curtains. Her rounded nose was pushed up, and a little bit of drool moistened the pillow.

She was perfect.

Gently, I climbed onto the bed beside her. Her heat reached me, seeping into my muscles as I pulled her close and brought her butt against my groin. She grunted, her snore gurgling a moment. Then she tucked her head down and pushed her butt harder against me. Oh. I was…I was so aroused and exhausted.

I wrapped my arms around her and held her close. She tucked her icy feet in between my legs. Abyssal damnation, that hadn't taken her long. How could her feet be this cold this fast? I grunted at her in protest but didn't even try to shift away.

It was so peaceful. I'd just give her a little time to rest. Then I'd wake her with a kiss. My eyelids slid shut. I held her close. Just a little rest and…

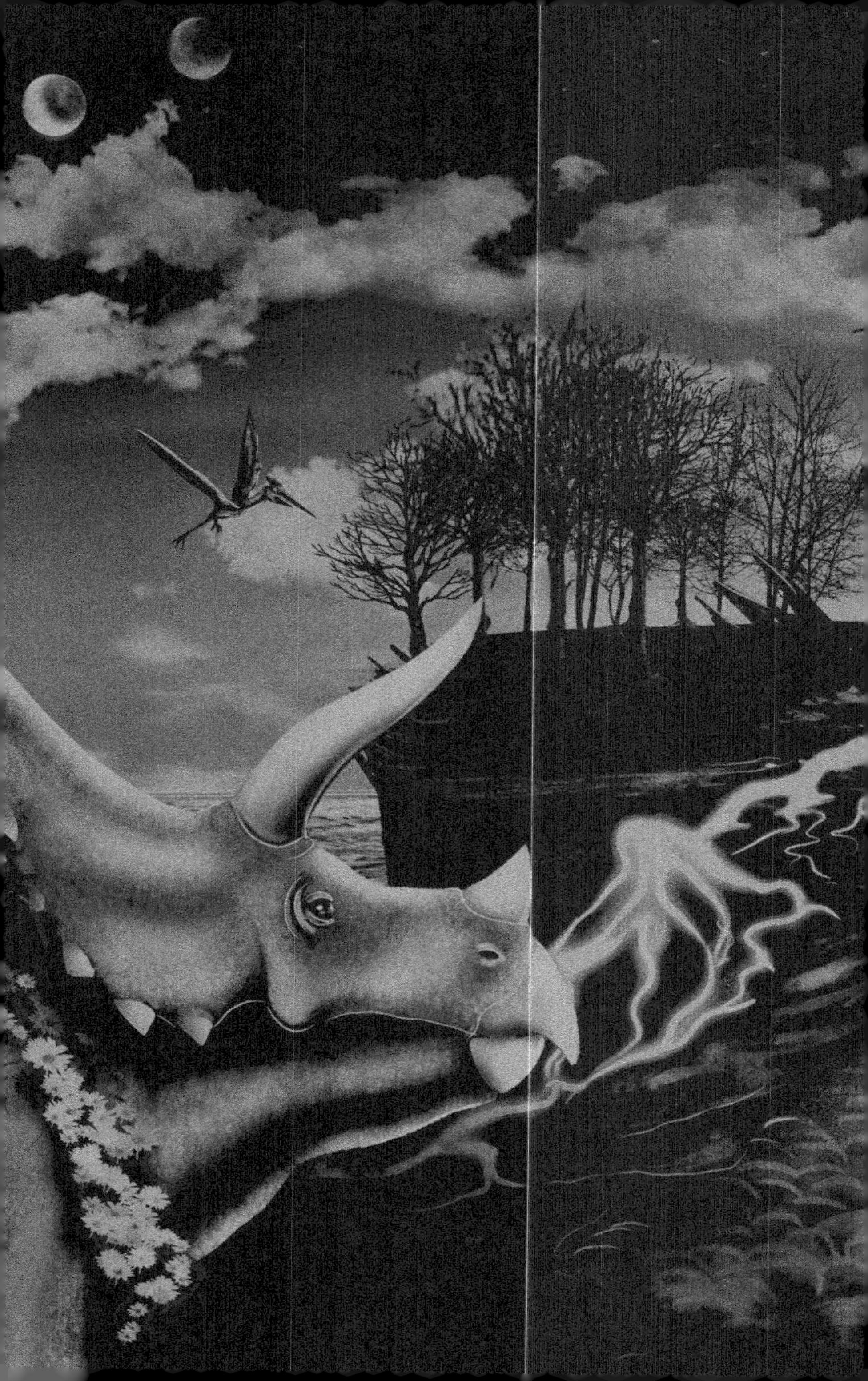

CHAPTER SIXTY: STELLA

A FEW WEEKS LATER

*D*rums beat a rapid rhythm to prepare for my entrance. I stood beneath an obsidian archway over a pressed white stone path that led to a dais on the edge of the jagged red cliffs. Brandt waited for me at the end, framed by the burnished bronze sunset.

Oh, yes. That was my Brandt. Stance broad, chin lifted high, a faint smile tugged at the corners of his mouth.

Behind him, poles affixed with black, red, and gold scarves stood, the wind tugging at the fabric. Two large pots—one black, red, and gold and another blue, white, and gold—sat on either side of the dais.

I leaned forward on Buttercup's crest to peer into the crowd from my hidden vantage point at the back of the path, recognizing so many friends and loved ones. People I had once forgotten. People who were as dear to me as life.

The past days had been full of meetings and reunions. My people welcomed me back with open arms, though some chafed at the fact I had not come to them or a Kropelkian household for aid. Some of the factions remained uncertain. Proof regarding my identity required performing multiple rituals and tremendous patience. And the memorials for those who had fallen for Sepeazia wearied and grieved me. But all of that was worth it, and far better than the alternative of not being here at all.

Now was the time to celebrate and mark the opening of a new chapter in our lives. Tomorrow the hard work began anew, including plans to restore Taivren from the depths. Soon we would also travel to meet with the other royals who had sacrificed themselves and returned from death. And Brandt had promised me we would go to meet his two friends, Hadeon of the Elves and Kieran of the Winter Fae.

Even more wonderful, I'd discovered that Evera, my dear, sweet, beautiful friend, was one of the eight sacrifices just like me. She too had returned, alive and was thrust into the middle of danger and struggle. But all was well now. In fact, she'd told me through the water mirror that she was expecting! Soon we'd get together and she'd tell me all about her harrowing adventures and wolfish love, and I'd tell her all I had been through as well.

We all had so much to look forward to.

"Stop shifting forward like that," Kine scolded lightly as he smoothed the long train down and kept it from getting tangled or caught on Buttercup's foreleg.

I glanced back at him and then sat sidesaddle on Buttercup's neck once more. "So bossy," I muttered. "Don't you know I'm about to be a queen?"

"You already are a queen," he chuckled. "And you look every inch of one."

I blushed a little. Though I could have had many servants to help me, I'd wanted to do it myself. Kine, however, insisted on being there, and he fussed over me more than I had expected.

"Kind of hard to believe," I murmured.

The silk was a mixture of blues and whites with gold fasteners and water serpents woven in gold on the center bodice. It had been hard to believe it was possible, but the material felt lighter and prettier than it looked. The cool evening air kissed my bare shoulders. Like Brandt's attire, my shoulders and arms were exposed except for the light silk that formed the off-shoulder twists. It was distinct from my first coronation gown. This time I had insisted on multiple water serpents being woven into the bodice to represent those who were so important to me. My hair was mostly down with a few sections wrapped and twisted to keep it from falling in my face and to provide a base for the black and white pearls woven throughout my hair like a decorative ivy.

"Not at all." Kine climbed halfway up Buttercup's side and squeezed my hand. "You look like a vision, Bug. One set in oil paints to indicate a fixed wonderful point."

My breaths tightened, and I clung to his hand tighter. "I couldn't have done any of this without you, Kine. You know, I don't remember if I told you all of this, but the whole time I was on Earth, things never felt right. And I always felt like I was supposed to have a big brother. Sometimes in the foster families, there was one or two. But they were never really my brothers. They didn't even want to be. You, though...you were my brother even when I was gone."

He climbed up onto Buttercup's neck and pressed his forehead to mine, careful not to muss my hair. "Easy answer for that one. You were always my sister. Even when you were gone."

"And you never actually gave up on me," I murmured.

He shrugged. "I guess I couldn't let go. Seems to run in the family." His lips brushed my cheek. "Don't go missing again, all right, Bug?" With a wink, he hopped back down. "Looks like it's almost time. I need to take my seat."

Attendants strode forward, whisking and spinning with scarves of blue, white, and gold. They danced the broad path, leading the way. I watched as they continued down, waiting for my mark.

The singers now chanted and sang about the joining of our two nations into a single kingdom: Sepeazia. A king from one side, a queen from another, peace for all.

Hord stood at attention in his military uniform, off to Brandt's left with the other remaining leaders. Kine had gotten to Auntie Runa, a great big grin on his face as she teased him about something. Despite the fact that he had probably had to run, his hair was perfectly styled, bright flowing, azure curls setting off sparkling gold eyes. Auntie Runa wore an elegant robe with shimmering trousers, and she applauded me with delicate grace as her dark-gold eyes sparkled. She still wore the herbs in her hair, but this time, she had added some flowers, including a vibrant gold orchid. Candy whistled and whooped. Her hair had been braided and coiled in an elaborate fashion with a silver and black serpent fastened into the center. Cahji stood behind her, glancing at her and mimicking her whistles.

Farther back stood Arjax and Lorna, at the very edge of the assembly. They towered over all the guests. Both wore far more luxurious clothing, robes that were layered and had both red and black as well as blue and white components with sleek sashes to signify their connection with all of Sepeazia. Both still wore the grey feathers in their bound braids. They looked so proud standing there, arms crossed over their chests, nudging one another and whispering.

And at the very end was Brandt. My Brandt.

He looked every inch a king. He wore a woven crown with opaque gems fashioned to resemble flames. His red-and-black hair had been styled even more than mine, each lock and segment curled or straightened to create its intimidating and magnificent effect. Striking as always. Then again, I expected nothing less. His dark-red eyes remained on me. As soon as my gaze met his, the world narrowed down to him. He was all I could see. All I could breathe. He stood with his arms at his sides, his manner easy and confident.

Buttercup continued her easy stride. Occasionally, she glanced up at me. For the event, she had been outfitted with numerous flower chains draped over her horns and crest. And she wore a large blue and white weaving on her back that she seemed indifferent about. The flowers she wanted to eat. Especially the pink ones.

Once the attendants reached the dais, they placed the scarves with the blue, white, and gold into stands. And then I was there. Buttercup was the perfect height, so I simply had to step off onto the second to last step leading up to the dais, turn so that my train remained perfectly aligned, and cross to Brandt.

Once I reached him, I knelt. The soft fabric swooshed around me, my train long.

One by one, each of the councilors walked forward onto the dais. They spoke of Sepeazia. Of her traditions. Of this custom. Of the need for rulers from both Kropelki and Ognisko. And of the joy in seeing the peace realized in a single union.

I glossed over the words, my gaze fixed on Brandt. The sea breeze tugged at my hair and my gown. More than anything, I was happy to be here with him. To know that I would share in this adventure with him. Learning, growing, teasing, being.

After the last of the councilors had spoken, Brandt removed a crown that matched his in shape but not color. It was delicate, infused with the palest shades of blue, like ice or the edges of the sulfur lava. He placed it on my head. The black and white pearls twined through my hair highlighted the crown's elegance and helped support it.

His hand slipped down to my chin and tilted my gaze to his. That delicious heat flared through me as I breathed in his exceptional scent. I cut my gaze up at him with a flirtatious smile. Was now an appropriate time to tease him?

Probably not.

He raised an eyebrow at me ever so slightly as if he guessed. Then that smile of his curled just a little higher at the corners, and his thumb briefly brushed my lower lip before he drew me to my feet. He took my hand in his. "Behold your queen, returned to us from the dead and restored to her true position at my right hand." His voice boomed out over the assembled crowd. "Honor and obey her."

Cheers and applause erupted as the drums resumed beating faster and faster and faster. The hint of a smile curved at his mouth as he helped me bind up my train, then drew me forward to the pots. One more formality before we could start the real celebration.

Together, we carried the pots with the representations of our particular nations down the path to the sea. Inside mine were dozens of small sea serpents, all blue and white. His were the same but red and black.

The waves crashed against the cliffs below as Brandt and I made our way to it. Our respective friends and family and court and members followed behind at a respectful distance as the wind tugged and pulled at our hair.

We reached the ocean and waded out up to our knees. Then both of us leaned forward as a wave rolled up, and we lowered the pots together.

It was quiet despite being dusk. Surprisingly, there were no predators, which was unusual and seen as a good omen. Gently, I knelt and released the little serpents into the waves. They darted forward and vanished, slipping beneath the waves. Would they face dangers within the sea? Of course they would. Who could say what waited for them in the dark waters? But they would carry on the fight. And the struggle didn't make their existence any less meaningful.

We watched the little serpents until they vanished completely into the waves. Then we turned, placing the pots in the wet sand.

Brandt then lifted my hand with his. "Rulers of Sepeazia. Union of nations."

The drums resumed their rapid beat as the chanting continued. Then it ended with gongs.

Brandt and I exchanged looks as Tile strode before the assembly and invited all to join us in the celebration. Throughout the kingdom, there were numerous other locations for all to join in feasting where they were without traveling. And it was all set to start as the sun went down.

Brandt swept me up into his arms as the surf crashed and foamed at our feet.

I gasped and giggled, wrapping my arms around his neck.

"Are you ticklish, Stella? I can't remember." He nuzzled my neck, making me giggle more until I snorted. "Once I get you back, I intend to make love to you until the dawn rises," he whispered in my ear. He waggled his eyebrows suggestively and then kissed my temple.

I laughed, tilting my head back. The moons had risen, bright and beautiful in the clear night sky.

"Ah, so you mean we'll collapse in each other's arms and sleep until morning."

It had been disconcerting, hilarious, and peaceful to awaken with one another like that on our return to Castle Serpentfire. We'd slept all the way back. It had been so comforting to be in his arms once more and feel his hardness against my butt and hip. Not to mention his heat. But I had no intention of ever letting him live that down.

He gave me a mock scowl as he carried me out of the surf. "Well, I wouldn't say no to sleeping until morning. I'm getting old, woman. And how can I resist it when your snores are my lullaby?"

I pressed my lips in a tight line. "So romantic."

He nudged me with his cheek. "Smart mouth."

"Just the way you like me."

He grunted and grinned. We both knew the truth and loved it.

All the formalities had ceased, and now the party began.

Farther up on the beach were tables and tables of food beneath serpent lanterns and flower sculptures. The scents made my stomach cramp in hunger. There were so many options I could barely see them all—purple taro rolls still steaming from the oven, roasted sweet potatoes with fresh herbs, browned pineapple glistening with sugar sauce, pellets of fast-fried white corn, mashed cassava with garlic and herbs, and roasted butter fish with crisp skin. Bowls of fruit—some fresh, some cut—brought brilliant color, the pomegranates, strawberries, citrus, and melons like gems. Whole barrels of tart autumn wine and melon beer along with dozens of juices filled one whole table.

The fountains with their delicate carved serpents and the columns of magically contained lava interspersed the dance floor. The little mini raptors, including Scarlett, wove in and out among the tables. They nipped a few guests if they were not given treats, but most were happy to pay the toll of food and scratches. The Little Empress demanded much tribute from all.

Our feasting went late into the night as did the dancing and the celebration. Flutes, rattles, drums, and chimes all brought us together. And unlike in the Wild Lands, this time I was with Brandt.

We danced with everyone.

Halfway through the night, Brandt whisked me away to our quarters in Castle Serpentfire.

That wonderful combination of scents—his and mine—rushed over me. He had barely gone into the bedchamber in my absence, instead choosing to sleep on the couch in the gathering area outside. Now we were both together once more, among the items we had acquired in the first half of our marriage.

As I walked inside, I took it all in. That wonderful comforting mixture of our perfume and cologne embraced me: strawberries, grapefruit, and salt water with hints of orange, smoke, leather, and bergamot. The massive four-poster bed with red silk sheets and a black coverlet had already been turned down, waiting for our arrival.

The heavy curtains had been flung back, letting the moonlight stream through. It really did feel right to be here. The air smelled right. The sky looked right. And the people—my breaths tightened in my chest. Just thinking about all that had happened—I pressed my lips into a tight line.

"Is everything all right, my love?" He caged me against the wall, leaning over me, muscles tensed, heat radiating from him. Somehow he'd already stripped half his clothes off and left them in a pile on the floor. Those gorgeous serpent tattoos coiled along his arms and sides.

"I was just thinking how glad I am to be back. How much I missed you. How, even not knowing you, no one ever measured up."

He grinned, his eyebrows lifting playfully. "I ruined you so much for other men that it lasted into a second life. I may decide to be proud of that."

"You should be." I stuck my tongue out at him.

"And you should be proud that I never moved on from you." He traced a line up my chin and over my nose up to my forehead with the tip of his nose.

"Hmmm...so unhealthy. So sexy."

He laughed. "I knew you were coming back, you ridiculous little minx. And don't act like you wouldn't have been jealous if I had moved on." He fiddled with the side clasps of my dress.

"Hmmm. I was ready to rip Candy's throat out."

"Candy?" He pulled back. His smile quirked crooked. "You thought Candy and I—"

"Well, Elias implied it. And she's gorgeous." I shrugged, drawing my finger in a circle over his shoulder along the line of one of the tattooed serpents.

He laughed at this, the sound rich and rolling. His body

vibrated against mine. "She is, but she isn't my type. I seem to be fond of a very particular blue."

"Cerulean. My hair is cerulean." I wrinkled my nose at him and winked.

"Cerulean." He kissed me, his lips lingering against my forehead. "Point being...you're the only one for me. But you probably know that by now."

"I am a little suspicious that that is the case. But I wouldn't mind some more convincing." I had smiled so much these past days that it hurt to smile now.

He leaned over me once more and kissed me again, his lips firm, warm, and soft against my forehead. "Then let me make this exceptionally clear," he whispered, his voice rumbling in that delicious way. His hands gripped my waist. "You are the only one for me. The one whom I vowed to protect with my blood, soul, spirit, marrow, bone, and sinew. To use a Vawtrian word, you are my veskaro, my most beloved of all, the love I hold above all others."

"So romantic," I murmured, smiling up at him. "And you are mine. The one whom I vowed to protect with my blood, soul, spirit, marrow, bone, and sinew. Now and always. My veskare."

He pressed his lips to mine, a whispered promise and a sweet sigh. His tongue traced my bottom lip, his teeth gently scraping. The air smelled so pleasant, his cologne embracing me and filling my lungs with his taste. His roughened palm caressed my side, moving up to my breast.

I moaned. My hips curled. He practically ripped the dress off me and pressed his knee between my thighs before he settled against me, pinning me between himself and the wall.

As I gasped in response, my hands roved the planes of his body, tracing the patterns of his tattooed serpents. I teased my foot along his back.

This—every time we made love, it was perfection. Even with flaws and weaknesses and falling asleep on top of each other and drooling on each other's shoulder. It was just exactly what we needed it to be.

I moved; he chased. I met; he demanded. All the dance steps from before we repeated now in a more intimate fashion. Kissing, nipping, biting, teasing, grinding. It built and built between us until he trapped me on the bed, his body against mine.

"I need you." He pressed his mouth against my ear, his voice rough with desire.

I nipped at his chin as I leaned back, exposing the column of my throat.

Hold me.

Kiss me.

Take me.

Make me yours forever.

"I need you too," I whispered, wrapping my legs around his waist.

With a groan, he entered me in one smooth stroke. I cried out, arching into him as he filled me completely. We began to move together, our bodies attuned from long familiarity. His powerful frame surrounded me, his muscles flexing as he drove into me again and again. I clung to him, nails digging into the shifting serpents on his back.

"You are mine," he growled against my neck as he held me tight.

"And you are mine!" I gasped out, my breaths hitching as he continued to thrust against me.

The pressure and tension between us built and built, coiling with heat through my core and belly. I writhed and bucked as his mouth found a sensitive point on my neck, then moved down and discovered my breast. My nails raked down his back as we found a new rhythm.

My body tightened and arched. Then a great rush of pleasure surged through me. I cried out, lifting myself against him. He too soon found his release and then collapsed against me.

As we basked in the delight of being with one another, I traced my finger over his cheeks and mouth. His lips were so perfectly firm and soft. I slid my finger down the column of his throat to the center of his chest, tracing the line of his pectorals.

He wriggled a little as I reached the tip of the first serpent coil. "You find something fascinating?"

"Mostly your body." I grinned at him, resting on my elbow. "Can you blame me?"

"Only for making me the happiest man to live," he said. His gaze softened as he pressed his thumb to my lips. "There will never be anyone else for me, Stella."

And there would never be anyone else for me.

I smiled and kissed his thumb. "Hey...do you want to know something?"

He gave me a mock scowl, as if he already felt the pun brewing. "What?"

"If you were a triangle, you'd be acute one." I stuck my tongue out at him.

He grimaced, then laughed and groaned. His hand pressed over his eyes. "Stella..."

"Wait." I held up my finger and tapped the tip of his nose. "If you were a fruit, what kind would you be?"

He frowned, his brow pinching. "A...banana? No. You said strawberry."

I giggled, shaking my head at him. "No. A fineapple!"

The way he looked at me—like he wanted to tackle me, shove me, devour me—maybe all three.

He bit the tip of his tongue as he cocked his head. "What should I do with you?"

I sat up beside him and grinned, walking my fingers up his broad chest. "If you were—"

Smirking, he captured my mouth with his and pushed me back onto the pillows. I laughed in response as he kissed me with irresistible finesse. I kissed him back and snuggled close.

"I'm so glad to be with you again, my spicy strawberry margarita man."

Everything felt right.

THE END

THANK you so much for reading. Want to read a true slow burn enemies to lovers of fated mates where he's the villain she's destined to kill (except she's cursed and they got married without her knowing it)? He's a Vawtrian, but a lot more vicious than Arjax and Lorna. He does however come with charismatic shapeshifting brothers who are determined to bring her into the family, even while she's trying to kill them.

Click here to read *Identity Revealed* and keep scrolling for a sneak peek, including a look at the new cover.

Want to learn what happened to Evera? Click here to order *Of Claws and Chaos* and scroll down to read a sneak peek of chapter one.

Of Serpents and Ruins
Pronunciation Guide

Brandt	**Brant**
Stella	**Stel-uh**
Kine	**Kine**
Elias	**Ee-lie-us**
Runa	**Roo-nuh**
Candy	**Can-dee**
Hord	**Hoard**
Cahji	**Caw-gee**
Arjax	**Arh-jacks**
Lorna	**Lohr-nuh**
Tanusa	**Tah-nu-sah**
Gola Resh	**Go-lah Resh**
Babadon	**Bah-bah-don**
Ihlfit	**Ill-fiht**
Vawtrian	**Vah-tree-in**
Veskaro	**Veh-ska-row**
Veskare	**Veh-ska-ray**
Kuvaste	**Koo-vah-stay**

Forgotten Kingdoms
Pronunciation Guide

TERREA (World Name) — TER-AY-YUH

HAVESTIA (Festival when the veil between worlds opens) — HAV-EST-EE-UH

AELVARIA — EL-VAHR-EE-UH
- EMBER — EM-BURR
- HADEON — HAY-DEE-ON

DRACONIA — DRAH-CONE-EE-UH
- SAPHIRA — SA-FEE-RUH
- RYKER — RYE-KURR

ISRAMAYA — IS-RUH-MY-UH
- RHODELIA — ROW-DEL-EE-UH
- VARAN — VAIR-EN

ISRAMORTA — IS-RUH-MOR-TUH
- MORGANA — MOR-GAHN-UH
- AVALON — AV-UH-LAHN

MAGIARIA — MAYJ-AIR-EE-UH
- ADIRA — AH-DEER-UH
- KAGE — KAYJ

SEPEAZIA — SEH-PEE-ZEE-UH
- STELLA — STEL-UH
- BRANDT — BRANT

TALAMH — TAL-AHV
- ALINA — AH-LEEN-UH
- KIERAN — KEER-AN

VARGR — VAR-GUR
- EVERA — EH-VEER-UH
- AXEL — AX-EL

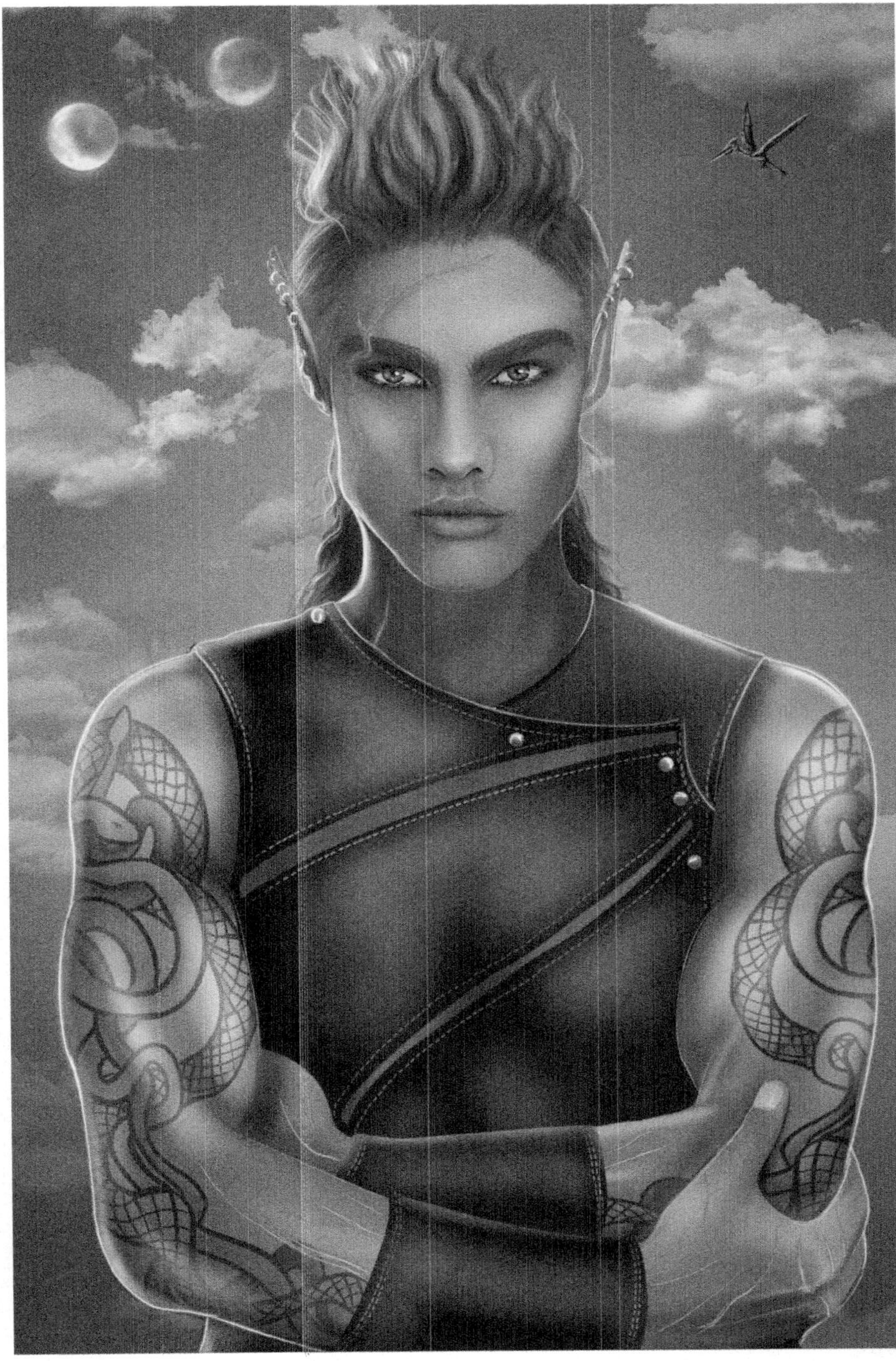

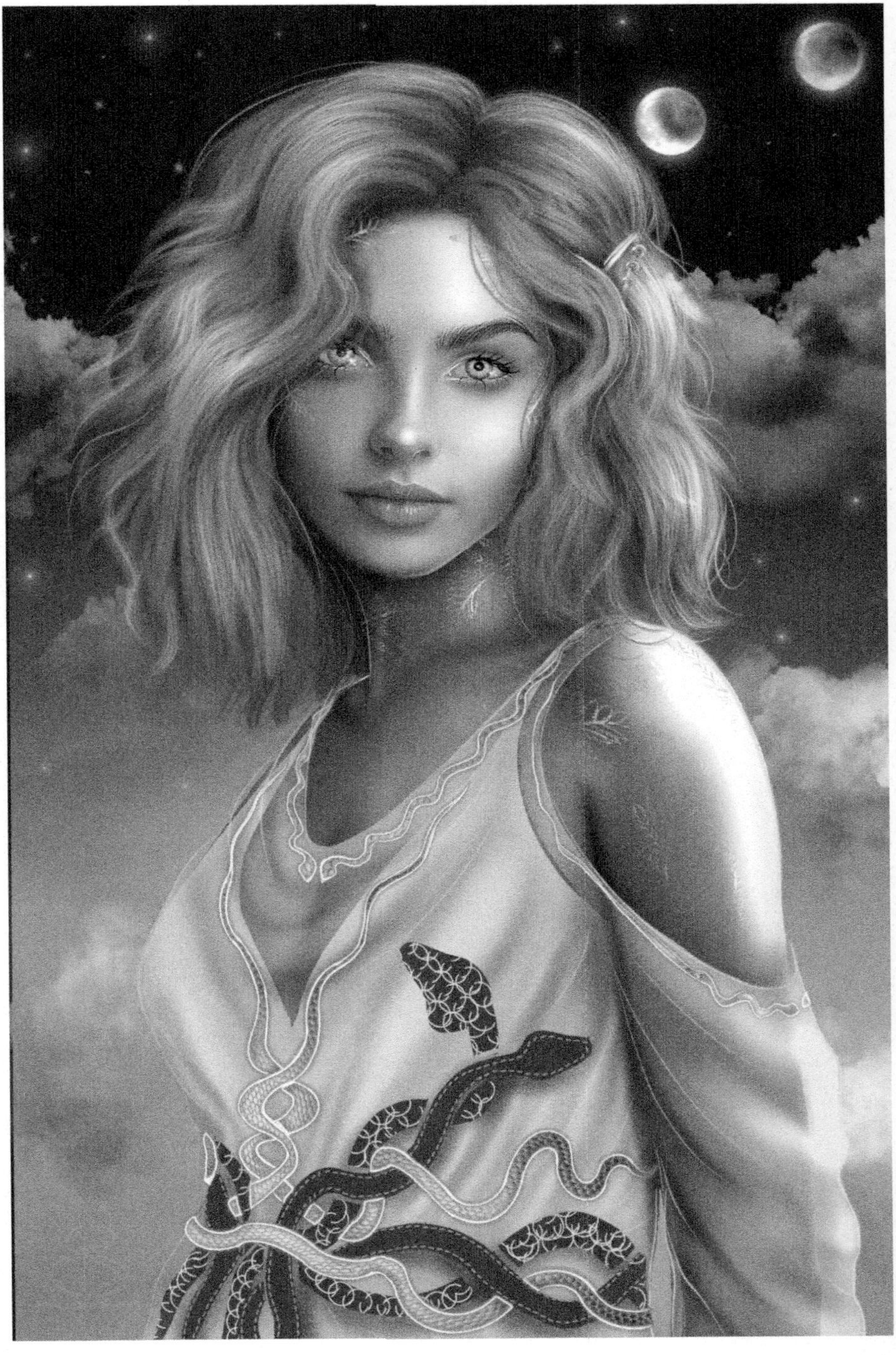

GLOSSARY

- **Caldride** - a chemical found in the lava that leads to lines of it being blue and remaining roughly in place in conjunction with the sulfur
- **Crespa** - an expression of surprise and exclamation among Vawtrians
- **Elonumato** - the Creator
- **Forbidden Arts** - various arcane and magical practices that rely on suffering and pain from one or multiple persons to accomplish the intended goal
- **Ihlkit** - an expression of surprise and exclamation among Sepeazians
- **Kropelki** - one of the two nations in Sepeazia located to the west
- **Kuvaste** - combat designed to address an issue or conflict; can be friendly or to surrender or to the death
- **Lithok** - a silver ear cuff that designates Vawtrian shifter abilities and skills
- **Ognisko** - one of the two nations in Sepeazia located to the east

GLOSSARY

- **Sepeazia** - the kingdom of water serpents that includes Kropelki and Ognisko
- **Vawtrians** - a shapeshifter race
- **Veskaro/Veskare** - a Vawtrian term which means, among other things, most beloved of all and over all others
- **Unatos** - a healer and poisoner race

OF CLAWS AND CHAOS CHAPTER ONE: EVERA

Everything about this place was an illusion.

I stood, tray against my hip, waiting for a set of drink orders as I eyed the casino floor, my chest squeezing uncomfortably with the knowledge that *I* was part of that illusion. It was early evening, but in this building it was permanently night, the twinkling stars replaced by glittering chandeliers. Wealthy, luxuriously dressed clientele weaved in and out of tables, placing bets and throwing around money I couldn't even conceive of. The lack of windows, pounding EDM music, and heavy smoke only added to the blanket of haze that coated the scene.

And here I was, watching all of it, feeling...feeling detached. I shouldn't have. In fact, after everything I'd been through today, I should have been fed up. Angry. Maybe it was the long work hours, or maybe it was that my toes were numb from the stilettos I was forced into, but I just couldn't find it in me to muster the energy.

"Evera." Christina appeared next to me, looking chipper and well rested before her shift. "You can go home. Doug wants to talk before you leave, but I'm taking over twenty minutes early. He said to not worry, that it won't affect pay."

"What pay?" I murmured. Her lips pressed up knowingly, and she took the tray I offered. Letting out a small sigh, I made my way across the expansive floor of the casino, to the hallway that led to the staff dressing room and Doug's office. To say our floor manager made me uncomfortable was the understatement of the century.

I really hoped the reason he wanted to talk to me had nothing to do with going out for dinner. I had used every excuse in the book so far, not wanting to outright reject him in fear of losing this damn job, but I was growing limited in options.

Deciding to get it over with, I approached the door of his office, pausing only momentarily to knock before stepping into the darkened space. His office was as eccentric and obnoxious as he was, filled with dark leather furniture and posters of naked women on the walls, as if flexing his ability to openly objectify whatever and whoever he wanted made his position enviable.

To be fair, it wasn't that far off base, considering his wealth and power.

Almost immediately upon entering I had to moderate my expression, my nose twitching in discomfort. Doug was more than occupied, it seemed, a woman with bright pink hair positioned on his lap, completely naked from the waist down. Her words were cut off as she let out a shocked sound and nearly fell off his lap, covering her chest and darting towards a bathroom nearby.

"Evera wouldn't have minded!" Doug called out, offering me an amused look. "Or maybe you would have."

"None of my business," I said quietly. His gaze narrowed on my expression before darting down my frame, openly staring at every curve of my body. Which considering my lack of groceries or any real meals outside of when I worked at the Daily Egg Diner each morning, weren't very obvious.

Even my uniform seemed to fit a bit looser now that my rent had increased. The once tight leather skirt and matching corset half-top now felt a bit more comfortable, despite showing the same amount of skin.

"It could be," Doug offered. "And it sounds like you need it."

"What do you mean?" I demanded, crossing my arms defensively. I may have noticed the differences in how I looked, but I hadn't thought others could.

"The chefs told me you've been taking leftovers home."

That would explain it.

Shame and embarrassment pressed heavily onto my chest and caused my cheeks to flush. It had to be Tony who'd opened his chauvinistic mouth. He was pissed because I'd rejected his offer to make sure I was always well fed with his—

I inhaled, not wanting to go down that particular memory lane as I tried to read Doug's expression. It was cocky and amused, not an ounce of sympathy to be seen. As if he liked that he was backing me into a corner.

Steadying myself, I shrugged. "If the food is just going to be tossed at the end of the night, I don't see an issue. It's damn good food; someone should eat it."

Doug's smile turned dark. "The food here is fucking awful. I think your situation is worse than you let on, Evera. It sounds like you need help."

Not from him. Never from Doug.

"I promise I'm good," I said, trying to infuse indifference into my voice, "but it won't happen again."

"Be sure it doesn't, or else we may have to do something about it." He nodded towards the door. "That's all."

My jaw tightened as I turned towards the door and slipped out. I hadn't wanted to be there in the first place, but being so summarily dismissed stung, and it wasn't long before tears of shame and frustration filled my eyes.

Mostly because Doug wasn't wrong.

Even with two shifts and a studio apartment in a converted motel twenty minutes away from the strip, I was barely making ends meet. Most nights—hell, most *days*—I barely ate, and sleeping was damn near impossible with the array of stuff happening outside my door. From a couple that liked to screw right against the railing of the balcony outside my front door to gunshots and police sirens that sang through the night in mockery of a lullaby, I rarely was able to relax enough to sleep. I spent most of the night tossing and turning, waking up exhausted around three a.m. to get ready for my eight-hour shift at the Daily Egg and then coming here to work six more.

It was little wonder I looked like crap.

Pushing into the dressing room, I went to my locker and stripped out of the dumb uniform, trading it for a pair of oversized jeans and a hoodie. I didn't pause to look in the mirror before pulling on my sneakers and my threadbare backpack—I didn't want to see the truth in my dull gaze, the thought that was plaguing me and making my soul so damn heavy I could barely breathe.

I couldn't do this forever. But I didn't have any other options.

Now that I was out of uniform, I wasn't allowed on the casino floor, so I made my way down back hallways to an exit. As I cut through the kitchen, which was mostly empty right now, I narrowed my eyes at Tony, who offered me a dark smirk from where he stood across the room talking to one of the servers. I was tempted to flip him off, but I knew it wasn't worth it—he had a bad temper, and one I didn't want to ignite.

I'd seen the girls he dated. I'd also noticed when they disappeared, just never coming into work one day.

Breaking out of the exit and into the warm evening air, I shielded my eyes from the hot sunlight bearing down on me, the dry heat oddly soothing against my skin.

Tightening one hand on my backpack, I slid on a pair of dollar sunglasses and made my way towards the bus stop. The traffic was heavier than normal today, and I had to dodge a lot of people dressed in costumes...what the heck was going on? Seeing people dressed up wasn't an uncommon occurrence in Las Vegas, but this many was odd.

When I reached the bus stop, it came to me—Halloween.

It was Halloween. Now I understood why so many of my coworkers had been talking about going to parties tonight. Swallowing down the bitter reminder of how many of them had completely normal lives, I made myself comfortable on the bench and began to list all of the things I was thankful for.

It was something I did when I felt desperate. When I felt hopeless.

Luckily, by the time I'd listed out what felt like a fairly small collection of blessings, the bus pulled up and I joined the ten others boarding. I threw myself into one of the worn plastic seats and let my eyes close, planning to take advantage of the twenty-plus minutes until we arrived at my stop.

Even in sleep though I couldn't avoid the truth—*something had to change and soon.*

⁓

A forsaken wolf princess.
A new king risen to power.
One opportunity to unite their broken lands and love.

Overcome by the exhaustion of her monotonous day-to-day life, all Evera wants is one fun night out. A chance to escape a rigorous work schedule that drains her of all semblance of happiness. When a mysterious portal consumes the air before her and an enigmatic, intense man pulls her through, she wonders if her wish is being granted.

As she's swept into a foreign, magical land she doesn't recognize, Evera finds herself separated from the man who pulled her there—a man who not only knew her name, but seemingly everything about her.

Completely alone, Evera treks through a mountainous landscape to reach the Kingdom of Nightfall. With each step, she encounters its foreboding and mysterious qualities, making it clear that she's not on Earth anymore.

Arriving in Nightfall brings more questions than answers, though, as she discovers that not only does she have royal blood, but there's a primal magic running through her veins that allows her the ability to shift into a wolf. What startles Evera the most to learn is that she had a life in this world before—with the very man who stole her through the portal: Axel, the King of Nightfall.

Memories begin to resurface, and she quickly recalls that Axel had been the only person she trusted—the only one standing between her and the darkness of her parents' rule. But has time changed the man who once swore to protect her?

A war is waged between two kingdoms upon news of her return, and Evera is the prize.

A single question wreaks havoc in Evera's heart: Does she want to belong to anyone at the end of this?

<u>Author note:</u> This book contains a sweet female lead, a growly alpha wolf that would burn the world down for her, and a love so deep it will mend the rifts of their kingdom. High spice. Content is intended for mature audiences and 18+ recommended.

Want to read Evera's story? Don't wait! Click here. https://geni.us/OfClawsAndChaos

And join her Facebook Group: https://www.facebook.com/groups/loveandmadness

IDENTITY REVEALED CHAPTER ONE: AMELIA

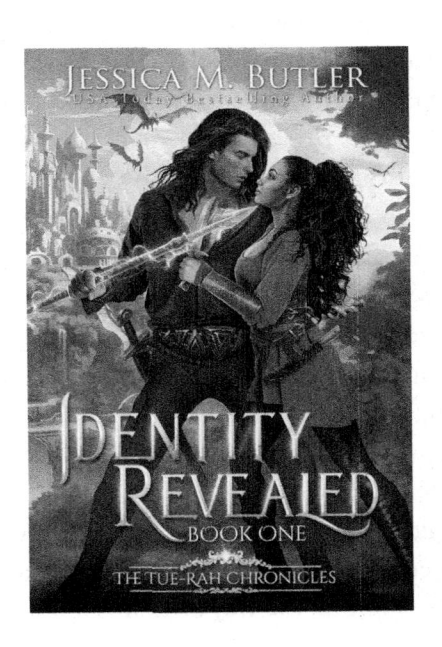

Amelia snapped the gun out of its holster and pointed it at Naatos's head.

Standing there on the top of the grassy hill in full daylight, he was every bit as terrifying as she remembered. Tall with an ice-blue stare that sliced through her soul. The same jagged hunting knife hung at his side, and he wore all-black with etchings in his leather doublet of chimeras and dragons as well as lions, serpents, and other creatures.

Yet despite all this, he appeared relaxed, his powerful shoulders squared and back, his arms folded over his broad chest. A gleam of amusement played in his eyes as he assessed her, a hint of a smile pulling at his lips. No sign of the fear he should be feeling. No awareness of who he was dealing with. And he wouldn't know until it was too late.

"Apparently you have no sense of self preservation. And you lied about more than your race." His gaze raked over her. "Though I do not understand your reasoning. Why pretend? I would have gladly spoken with you had you admitted to being a Neyeb. I deal with all matters involving the Neyeb."

She frowned. It was strange to see him. Despite the coolness of the wind, her elmis prickled, the small patches on her palms and wrists far more sensitive and ready to make her the killer she was cursed to be. An odd sensation rippled through her core. A familiarity. A knowledge of some sort. But at a far deeper level. More than his name and what he was—something —something else.

The aggression and blood lust would kick in at any moment. Here she stood, eyes fixed on the man she had sworn to kill. If ever there was a time, it was now. Wasn't it? Knives twisted in her stomach. Her first true kill.

Josiah struggled to his feet near her, pushing away the cut ropes. He looked even younger than his ten years, his eyes so wide the whites shone all the way around. He wasn't quite ready to run yet, and she couldn't risk triggering the blood curse until he and Mama were safely away from her. Naatos would be her first target, but who knew what she'd do afterward? Just a couple minutes more to give him time to regain his balance and feeling in his legs.

"Who says I'm a Neyeb?" she demanded, her hand working along the grip of her gun.

Naatos laughed. When he smiled, the family resemblance to WroOth appeared far stronger, though he was much colder than his brother. "I'll presume you were raised by Awdawms then."

What did that have to do with anything? She scowled.

Mama gave a panicked cry on the far side of the hill beyond the bushes that lined the eastern edge. "Josiah!"

Josiah started toward their mother with a strangled response, scraps of rope falling away. Amelia snagged him by the arm and hauled him back, keeping the gun trained on Naatos at all times. "You don't run in front of him. Go the long way."

Naatos's attention briefly returned to Josiah. "She's right, young prince. Cross me, and you won't be returning to your mother with all your limbs. Or maybe I'll return you to her in pieces." His gaze returned to Amelia, scanning her up and down, then up again as if curious about her true intentions. "As for you, woman, end this charade. There is nothing to be gained from denying what you are or who you are for that matter."

Oh but there was. She pointed the gun at his head. "Take one step toward either Josiah or Alita, and I will shoot you."

He smirked. "That weapon doesn't even contain lasers or energy beams. I've seen its like before. If you were going to attack me with a device from another world, I would think you would choose one with a little more strength than mere metal and powder. Besides." He chuckled as he shook his head. "There's only one who can stop me, and apparently you forgot to bring her."

"Something like this should at least sting, I'll bet." How did he even know what a gun was? That unsettled her more than the calm curiosity in his gaze. She pushed Josiah back and stepped in front of him. Her elmis weren't kicking in and bringing her rage at all. They weren't even stirring. The blades of energy in her stomach stabbed and burned. "Don't worry, Josiah. It's going to be fine. I'm going to save you and your mother."

"Are you now?" Naatos removed a cylinder from his side. It had been hanging from his thick belt directly opposite the hunting knife. Silver-white runes adorned the sides. He twisted it. It telescoped out into what appeared to be an ornately carved spear, at least eight feet in length. Silver-blue energy briefly arced along its length. "It is possible we may come to an agreement. But if you think you are going to keep Inale from me, then you are greatly mistaken. Where is she?"

"Alita," she called. "Get ready. Run to the forest when I say." She set her jaw as she gripped the gun with both hands now. "I know where Inale is, Naatos. They don't. You don't need to worry about them."

"Get ready?" Naatos's smirk broadened. "WroOth is right. You are brazen." He pressed his hand across the silver runes at the top of the spear. The spear head vanished, replaced by a triple-pointed blade with curved edges. "Surely not brazen enough to think you can escape me. Surrender any time you like. This doesn't have to be difficult."

"All right. Let Alita and Josiah go."

"Where is Inale?" he asked. "The longer you keep her from me, the more unpleasant this becomes for you."

"Inale is safe. Let Alita and Josiah go. Guarantee their safety and that you will give them no grief."

"No." He examined the spearhead and then struck it out as the silver-blue light arced along it once more. The sharp scent of heat and electricity sparked.

It was time. Her elmis hadn't changed her yet, and there was no suggestion whatsoever that any change was happening unless she had to draw blood for the curse to take effect. To delay further was to risk AaQar and WroOth and the mercenaries returning. Maybe drawing blood with her elmis exposed was the real way to activate the curse?

The amusement faded as he stared her down. "Don't try my patience, woman."

Bastard. She squeezed the trigger, released, and squeezed again. One, two, three times.

Josiah dropped to the ground, covering his ears. Mama pressed her hands over her mouth.

Naatos's expression changed from shock to anger. Each time the gun cracked, he lurched back. But he didn't fall.

He stabbed his spear into the ground and caught his balance as he staggered back another step. Blood trickled down his face and chest, disappearing into his clothing. He rubbed his hand over his face, his expression disoriented.

What? How! Her elmis hadn't taken over anything. No bloodlust or anger beyond what she already felt had swept over her. She tightened her grip on the gun, her hand shaking briefly. What else did she have to do? Bathe in his blood? How specific was this curse? And, by Elonumato—he was still moving. He was standing straight again, favoring his right leg, murderous rage twisting his features.

"Alita, run now!" Amelia shouted as she squeezed the trigger again. This time the bullet struck his supporting leg. With a groan, he collapsed to his knees.

She shoved Josiah toward the forest and his mother, but he reeled to a halt.

"Josiah!" Mama screamed from the mid-point of the hill, hands cupped around her mouth. She hadn't moved at all!

Why weren't they going? Was no one listening to her? Amelia seized Josiah by the arm and dragged him toward safety. "Come on!"

The sounds of the fake battle had disappeared. AaQar, WroOth, and their mercenaries would return in minutes, particularly after those gunshots. Dread and panic set into her as she rewrote her plan. No great force had taken over her to give her power and ferocity. Naatos wasn't dead. How badly was he wounded? How long would he stay down? Seconds? Minutes?

How had this gone so wrong?

Mama ran toward the forest as well now. Amelia raced with Josiah to the left, taking him into the forest by a different route. Fallen leaves kicked up around their feet, rustling, crackling, and crunching.

"Josiah!" Mama appeared at the crest of the second hill point. She ran toward them and swept Josiah into her arms. "Where's Inale?"

"We don't have time." She grabbed Mama's hands and pulled forward. "Straight down and to the left of the embankment. There's a bruin down there. Halig. Use him to get to Plaohi. Go now! I'll bring Inale when it's safe." She shoved Mama and Josiah ahead of her and then doubled back.

Naatos pushed to his feet as she emerged from the clearing. He held his wounded leg, blood running down his face, his neck, and his chest. The entry wounds had already vanished. Rage burned in his light-blue eyes, an icy fire as horrifying as her nightmares. "You pathetic—"

"Save it." She met his gaze as she pointed the gun at him again. Though fear swelled up over the anger, she wouldn't let him see it. "You will leave them alone, and let me tell you why. I know exactly where Inale is. I'm the only one who does, all right? And she'll only come when I call her. If I tell her to go, she'll go. If you want her to come, you go through me. So leave that family alone. And if you're so determined to terrify someone, terrify me!" She then pulled the trigger three more times, once in each leg and once in the heart.

The gun shook in her hand. Nausea snarled within her. This didn't feel as good as she expected. His exclamation of pain wasn't so pleasant either.

IDENTITY REVEALED CHAPTER ONE: AMELIA

She bolted down the hill away from the path she'd set Mama and Josiah on. They'd need ten minutes or so to find Halig and start their escape. Every added minute after that would help them. Naatos would surely follow her to get to Inale. She just had to get to the—

A dragon roar bellowed out as she reached the bottom of the third hill leading up to the peak. WroOth soared up behind her in the red dragon form, wings spread wide.

Why did these brothers have to be so efficient!

ABOUT THE AUTHOR

Jessica M. Butler is an adventurer, author, and attorney who never outgrew her love for telling stories and playing in imaginary worlds. She is the author of the epic fantasy romance series *Tue-Rah Chronicles* including *Identity Revealed, Enemy Known,* and *Princess Reviled, Wilderness Untamed, Shifter King* along with independent novellas *Locked, Cursed,* and *Alone,* set in the same world. She has also written numerous fantasy tales such as *Mermaid Bride, Little Scapegoat, Through the Paintings Dimly, Why Yes, Bluebeard, I'd Love To,* and more. For the most part, she writes speculative fiction with a heavy focus on multicultural high fantasy and suspenseful adventures and passionate romances. She lives with her husband and law partner, James Fry, in rural Indiana where they are quite happy with their five cats: Thor, Loptr, Fenrir, Hela, and Herne.

For more books or updates:
www.jmbutlerauthor.com

Read More from Jessica M. Butler

(jmbutlerauthor.com)

facebook.com/jmbutler1728
x.com/jessicabfry
instagram.com/jessicambutlerauthor

ALSO BY JESSICA M. BUTLER

The Tue-Rah Chronicles

Identity Revealed

Enemy Known

Princess Reviled

Wilderness Untamed

Shifter King

Empire Undone

Tue-Rah Tales

Locked

Alone

Cursed

Standalones

The Mermaid Bride

Bound By Blood

Through the Paintings Dimly

The Celebrity

Little Scapegoat

Vellas

Fae Rose Bride

Anthologies

Once Upon Now

Vices and Virtues

Fierce Hearts

Adamant Spirits

Printed in Great Britain
by Amazon

45152992R00374